William 1564-1616 Shakespeare, Henry Irving, Frank A. Marshall

The works of William Shakespeare

Volume 4

William 1564-1616 Shakespeare, Henry Irving, Frank A. Marshall

The works of William Shakespeare
Volume 4

ISBN/EAN: 9783337413804

Printed in Europe, USA, Canada, Australia, Japan

Cover: Foto ©Andreas Hilbeck / pixelio.de

More available books at **www.hansebooks.com**

THE WORKS

OF

SHAKESPEARE.

THE HENRY IRVING SHAKESPEARE.

THE WORKS

OF

WILLIAM SHAKESPEARE

EDITED BY

HENRY IRVING AND FRANK A. MARSHALL.

WITH

NOTES AND INTRODUCTIONS TO EACH PLAY BY F. A. MARSHALL
AND OTHER SHAKESPEARIAN SCHOLARS,

AND

NUMEROUS ILLUSTRATIONS BY GORDON BROWNE.

VOLUME IV.

LONDON:
BLACKIE & SON, 49 & 50 OLD BAILEY, E.C.;
GLASGOW, EDINBURGH, AND DUBLIN.
1888.

PREFATORY NOTE.

The present volume contains some of the most interesting of Shakespeare's plays. With Henry V. is completed the trilogy, if we may so call it, which has for its hero Henry of Monmouth. In the two first plays of the series Jack Falstaff shared the honours with the serious hero; but in the third and concluding one there is only room for his death: and we have in The Merry Wives of Windsor the promised continuation of his exploits. The three comedies which complete the volume are certainly amongst the best that Shakespeare wrote; if indeed they can be said to have any rivals in this branch of Dramatic Literature, either in our poet's own works or in those of his contemporaries. As in the case of the First Part of Henry IV., a considerable portion of the Notes on Henry V. are by myself. To such Notes I have, in nearly all cases, appended my initials, as many of them involve matters of opinion for which Mr. Adams cannot be held responsible. I have adopted the same means of distinguishing those very few Notes which I have added to other plays edited by any of our collaborators, and also those Stage Histories which I have supplied in some of the Introductions.

We have been fortunate in securing the aid of two such Shakespearean scholars as Mr. A. Wilson Verity and Mr. Arthur Symons, who will, I am glad to say, continue their connection with this edition until its completion,—a task which, without such loyal and able co-operation, could not be accomplished within any reasonable time. The supervision and carrying out of the special features of such a work as this involve an amount of care and labour which, even at the rate of publication announced, leave one little time for any other pursuit.

I wish that Mr. P. A. Daniel could have collaborated to a greater extent in this edition than unfortunately he has been able to do. Such work as he has done on The Merry Wives of Windsor cannot fail to add to the value of the book.

I ought to mention that Mr. Daniel is only responsible for the first part of the Introduction to that play—the Literary History, which is much the most valuable portion. The Stage History, and Critical Remarks, belonging to that play, as well as the Foot-notes to the Text, were added by me.

I have again to thank many correspondents who have kindly furnished me with valuable information, and others who have courteously pointed out some errors or omissions in the volumes already published. All such corrections, or suggested additions, whether made publicly or privately, shall receive most careful attention; but the Corrigenda and Addenda cannot be given till the concluding volume.

F. A. MARSHALL.

LONDON, *August*, 1888.

CONTENTS.

PASSAGES AND SCENES ILLUSTRATED.

KING HENRY V.

THE MERRY WIVES OF WINDSOR.

MUCH ADO ABOUT NOTHING.

AS YOU LIKE IT.

TWELFTH NIGHT; OR, WHAT YOU WILL.

KING HENRY V.

NOTES AND INTRODUCTION
BY
OSCAR FAY ADAMS AND F. A. MARSHALL.

DRAMATIS PERSONÆ.

KING HENRY THE FIFTH.
DUKE OF GLOUCESTER, } brothers to the King.
DUKE OF BEDFORD, }
DUKE OF EXETER, uncle to the King.
DUKE OF YORK, cousin to the King.
EARLS OF SALISBURY, WESTMORELAND, and WARWICK.
ARCHBISHOP OF CANTERBURY.
BISHOP OF ELY.
EARL OF CAMBRIDGE.
LORD SCROOP.
SIR THOMAS GREY.
SIR THOMAS ERPINGHAM, GOWER, FLUELLEN, MACMORRIS, JAMY, officers in King Henry's army.
BATES, COURT, WILLIAMS, soldiers in the same.
PISTOL, NYM, BARDOLPH.
Boy.
A Herald.
CHARLES THE SIXTH, King of France.
LEWIS, the Dauphin.
DUKES OF BURGUNDY, ORLEANS, and BOURBON.
The Constable of France.
RAMBURES and GRANDPRÉ, French Lords.
Governor of Harfleur.
MONTJOY, a French Herald.
Ambassadors to the King of England.

ISABEL, Queen of France.
KATHARINE, daughter to Charles and Isabel.
ALICE, a lady attending on her.
Hostess of a tavern in Eastcheap, formerly Mistress Quickly and now married to Pistol.

Lords, Ladies, Officers, Soldiers, Citizens, Messengers, and Attendants. Chorus.

SCENE—England; afterwards France.

HISTORIC PERIOD: from 1414, the second year of Henry's reign, to May 20th, 1420, the date of his betrothal to Katharine.

TIME OF ACTION.

The action, according to Daniel (who is clearly right in his analysis), covers nine days, with intervals, as follows:—

1st CHORUS. Prologue.
Day 1: Act I. Scenes 1, 2.
2nd CHORUS. Interval.
Day 2: Act II. Scene 1.—Interval; Falstaff's sickness and death, &c.
Day 3: Act II. Scenes 2, 3.—Interval: time for the arrival of the English army in France, and for the further journey of Exeter to the French court.
Day 4: Act II. Scene 4.
3rd Chorus. Interval.
Day 5: Act III. Scenes 1-3.—Interval; march of King Henry towards Calais.
[Act III. Scene 4.—Some time of the interval succeeding Day 4.]
Day 6: Act III. Scene 5.—Interval; a day or two.
Day 7: Act III. Scene 6 and first part of Scene 7.
Day 8: Act III. Scene 7, second part. 4th CHORUS, and Act IV. Scenes 1-8.
5th CHORUS. Interval.
[Act V. Scene 1.—Some time in the early part of the last Interval.]
Day 9: Act V. Scene 2.
6th CHORUS. Epilogue.

KING HENRY V.

INTRODUCTION.

LITERARY HISTORY.

King Henry the Fifth was first printed in quarto form in 1600, with the following title-page:—THE | CRONICLE | History of Henry the fift, | With his battell fought at *Agin Court* in | France. Togither with *Auntient* | *Pistoll.* | *As it hath bene sundry times playd by the Right honourable* | *the Lord Chamberlaine his seruants.* | LONDON | Printed by *Thomas Creede,* for Tho. Milling- | ton, and Iohn Busby. And are to be | sold at his house in Carter Lane, next | the Powle head. 1600. This edition, which is very imperfect, was evidently brought out in a hurried manner, and the text was probably prepared from shorthand notes taken in the theatre.

Fleay (Chronicle History of William Shakespeare, p. 206) expresses the opinion that the Quarto is "a shortened version of a play written in 1598 for the Curtain Theatre, and that the Folio (except such alterations as were made after James's accession) is a version enlarged and improved for the Globe Theatre later in the same year."

A second quarto edition, reprinted from the first, was issued in 1602, "by Thomas Creede, for Thomas Pauier," and "sold at his shop in Cornhill, at the signe of the Cat and Parrets, neare the Exchange." A third quarto, in similar style, "Printed for T. P" (the same Thomas Pavier) appeared in 1608.

No complete edition of the play was published until it was incorporated in the Folio of 1623, which must be regarded as the sole authority for the text. The quartos, however, are of use in a few instances for the correction of typographical errors in F. 1. It should be noticed that the play as it stands in the quarto of 1600 is shorter by more than one half than the version given by the folio; and this leads to an interesting but difficult question: was the Henry V. of the folio an expansion (by Shakespeare) of the Henry V. of the quarto; or does the former represent the original draft of the piece, which the author (or some one else) abridged for stage purposes, and which in this abridged version was published in the quarto?

The arguments on both sides are intricate and involved, and we may perhaps be content with Mr. Aldis Wright's summary of the disputed points; his conclusion is as follows: that the play was shortened for the stage; that the abridgment was not made by Shakespeare; and that of this abridged version the quarto gives an imperfect and surreptitiously-obtained representation.

The date of the play is sufficiently fixed by the following passage in the Chorus of act v.:

Were now the general of our gracious empress,
As in good time he may, from Ireland coming, &c.

The reference is to the expedition of Essex, who went to Ireland on the 15th of April, 1599, and returned on the 28th of the following September. As it is improbable that the passage was inserted after the play was written, the date of composition must be placed within the limits specified. The play is not mentioned by Meres in 1598, though Henry IV., its immediate predecessor, is included in his list.

Shakespeare drew the main incidents of his plot, as in the Henry IV., from Holinshed's Chronicles and the anonymous play entitled The Famous Victories of Henry the Fifth, which must have been written as early as 1588, since the famous Tarlton, who died in that year, is known to have taken the part of the Clown in the play. It was not entered on the Stationers' Registers until May 14, 1594, and the earliest edition now extant is dated 1598. It was printed by Thomas Creede, like Q. 1 of the present play.—O.F.A.

STAGE HISTORY.

Henry V. appears to have been a popular play on the stage from its very first production, which was, perhaps, at the Curtain Theatre not long before the building of the Globe in 1599. It was reproduced at the latter theatre in the course of the same year. It was probably also the play presented at court by the Lord Chamberlain's men during the Christmas festivities of 1599–1600. A later performance at court was on the 7th of January, 1605. The record of this and sundry other performances of Shakespeare's plays, in the accounts of the Master of the Revels, has been proved to be a forgery; but, as Halliwell-Phillipps (Outlines, 7th ed. vol. ii. pp. 161–167) conclusively shows, the information is genuine though the record is spurious.

In the next century, when nearly all of Shakespeare's plays were brought out in "improved" versions, more or less garbled and mixed with foreign matter, Henry V. did not escape such profanation. One of the worst of these mongrel dramas was that concocted by Aaron Hill, "poet, critic, amateur actor, playwright, and adapter from the French," which was brought out at Drury Lane in 1723; according to Genest, it was acted six times; he says that "it has considerable merit, but, after all, it is but a bad alteration of Shakespeare's play . . . his taste was too Frenchified to relish the humour of Fluellin" (*sic*) (vol. iii. p. 130). Certain portions of the original matter were retained, but a new underplot was introduced, in which Harriet, a niece of Lord Scrope, was a prominent figure. She was represented as having been formerly betrayed by Henry, and follows him to the wars in masculine apparel, watching over him faithfully notwithstanding his infidelity to her. Three independent adaptations of Henry V. were made by Kemble. The first was produced at Drury Lane in 1789, the second at the same theatre in 1801, and the third at Covent Garden in 1806.

On the first of these occasions (Oct. 1, 1789) the cast had Kemble as the King, Baddeley (Fluellen), Barrymore (Dauphin), and Mrs. Booth as Hostess (see Genest, vi. 575). In the 1803 revival Charles Kemble was Gloucester, and Blanchard, Fluellen. For the rest, Henry V. appears to have been popular with last-century audiences. From the restoration of the play to the stage in 1735 at the theatre in Goodman's Fields, down to 1801, Genest chronicles some ten separate and notable reproductions of what dramatically is scarcely a strong piece, and amongst the actors who took part in these revivals not a few great names occur—Macklin, Yates, Ryan, Woodward, Garrick, Elliston.

It was at Drury Lane on March 8, 1830, that Edmund Kean, in this play, made what proved to be his last attempt in a new part. The result was a melancholy failure. In vain he struggled against physical suffering, and against what was of more importance in such a part, the almost total decay of his memory. At the end of the fourth act he made a touching and apologetic appeal to the audience, pleading that this was the first time that he had ever presented himself before them in such a condition as to be unable to fulfil his duties. The appeal was not made in vain; for they stretched indulgence to its utmost limits. The one redeeming point, in this sad exhibition of his decaying powers, was the soliloquy in the camp after the scene with Williams. In such parts as Shylock, Hamlet, Othello, which he had known by heart long before the decay of both body and mind had set in, Kean could still recall the glory of his early triumphs; but to study such a part as Henry V. for the first time was a task far beyond his powers.

In 1839 the play was revived by Macready at Covent Garden, with brilliant scenic effects, for which the manager was largely indebted to Stanfield the painter. The cast included several well-known players: Phelps as Charles d'Albret (Constable of France); Howe (Duke of Orleans); Meadows (Fluellen); Paul Bedford (Bardolph); Harley (Pistol); Anderson (Gower); Vandenhoff (Chorus); Miss P. Horton the Boy; and Miss Vandenhoff as Katharine.[1] Macready's own account of the first

[1] Of these the only survivors are Mr. Howe (still acting at the Lyceum); Mr. Anderson, who has retired from the stage; and Miss P. Horton (Mrs. German Reed).

night is worth giving: "*June 10th.* Began the play of 'King Henry V.' in a very nervous state, but endeavouring to keep my mind clear. Acted sensibly at first, and very spiritually at last; was very greatly received, and when called on at last, the whole house stood up and cheered me in a most fervent manner. I gave out the repetition of the play for four nights a week till the close of the season. . . . It is the last of my attempts to present to the audience Shakespeare's own meaning" (Macready's Reminiscences, vol. ii. p. 145). A week later we find him playing with even greater success: "Acted King Henry V. better than I had yet done, and the house responded to the spirit in which I played. The curtain fell amidst the loudest applause . . . and I went before the curtain, and amidst shoutings and waving of hats and handkerchiefs by the whole audience standing up, the stage was literally covered with wreaths, bouquets, and bunches of laurel" (*ut supra*, p. 147). It was probably the success of this experiment which led Phelps to bring out the play at Sadler's Wells; and later Charles Kean followed the example by producing it at the Princess's Theatre. This was Kean's "last Shakespearian revival," and the play ran for eighty-four nights from March 28, 1859. Here also the scenic display was remarkable for the time. Cole, the biographer of Kean, declares that it "formed altogether the most marvellous realization of war, in its deadliest phase, that imitative art has ever attempted."

In 1872 there was another notable reproduction of the play, by Calvert at Manchester, the spectacular effects being of a striking character. In 1875 this arrangement of the play was produced at Booth's Theatre in New York, under the supervision of Mr. Calvert. The next year the play was performed at the Queen's Theatre, Long Acre (see Introd. to II. Henry IV.), John Coleman taking the title *rôle*, and was moderately successful. In 1879 Calvert's version was again revived, with George Rignold as Henry, and had a good run on both sides of the Atlantic. The mounting was in most magnificent style, though the appearance of the King on horseback in the scene before Harfleur was in questionable taste.—F.A.M.

CRITICAL REMARKS.

As has been said in the introduction to I. Henry IV., the character of Henry V. had made a remarkable impression upon the mind of Shakespeare. He desired to set him forth as "the mirror of all Christian kings;" and the two plays in which his youthful follies, and his throwing off that "loose behaviour" on the death of his father, are shown, might almost be regarded as written mainly to prepare the way for the present drama, in which we see him as monarch, in nature no less than in name.

But, as the poet approached his task in this final portion of the trilogy, he must have felt the peculiar difficulties it involved. The title-page of the first edition of the play terms it a "chronicle history," and, though it is not probable that the form of the title is due to the author, it nevertheless aptly expresses the character of the production. It is an epical treatment of his subject, though cast in a dramatic mould. Like Homer, he begins by invoking the Muse, and, like the ancient poet, he dwells at times on details prosaic in themselves—such as the grounds of Henry's title to the crown—which, though unpoetical, were an important part of the history, and therefore interesting to his countrymen. The choruses, which, though they answer a purpose in bridging over the long intervals in the action, are not absolutely necessary, appear to have been due in part to this merely semi-dramatic method of composition. As has been well said, they are "a series of brief lyrical poems; for, though not lyrical in metre, they are strictly so in spirit, crowded with a quick succession of rapidly-passing brilliant scenes, majestic images, glowing thoughts, and kindling words."

The result of this peculiar treatment of the poet's materials is naturally unlike all his other dramas. It is the least dramatic of the series. The king is really all the play; it is a "magnificent monologue," and he the speaker of it. The other characters serve little purpose except to afford him breathing-spaces, and to set off his glory by contrast. In the preceding plays, we got "under the veil of wildness" glimpses of his nobler nature. He was "the true prince" even when he played the fool for lack of anything better to do. Weary with the formality of court life, he sought relief and diversion in scenes of low life—low, but with no shame about it—filled with characters worthless enough, but interesting as studies of human nature. The prince mingled with them, but was never really one of them. He never forgot his royal destiny, never lost his true self, but let it lie latent, ready to awake when the call should come for action worthy of it.

And now the prince, to whose advent to the throne his father and all who were thoughtful for the weal of England looked forward with fear and anxiety, has become the king—and what a change!

> The breath no sooner left his father's body,
> But that his wildness, mortifi'd in him,
> Seem'd to die too.

His prodigal habits drop from him like a jester's robe that he had assumed as a disguise, and the real man who had been masquerading in them stands forth "every inch a king." He is the poet's ideal king—one to whom the sturdiest republican might concede the divine right to rule, so completely do all royal gifts and graces unite in his character. He is profoundly conscious of his responsibilities and duties as a sovereign, yet not weakly sinking under them, but accepting the trust as from God and doing the work as for God, relying on Him in battle and rendering to Him the praise of the victory. This was indeed not the Henry of history; but as an ideal hero, the perfect flower of chivalry and piety, the character is unmatched in its way in Shakespeare's long gallery of manly portraiture.

On the other characters in the play it is not necessary to dwell. It has been said that Shakespeare does not appear to be much interested in any of them except Fluellen, but perhaps that is too strong a statement. The brave Welshman, whom we admire and honour while we laugh at him, is, indeed, the finest piece of characterization in the play, next to the king. As Henry himself says:

> Though it appear a little out of fashion,
> There is much care and valour in this Welshman.

But the other comic characters are by no means to be despised. Pistol is almost as perfect in his way as Fluellen. His fustian and brag are inimitable. How like a turkey-cock he swells in the scene with his French captive, and how thoroughly is the conceit taken out of him by Fluellen! How is the mighty fallen, when this "most brave, valorous, and thrice-worthy seignior of England," as the poor Frenchman thought him, is cudgelled by the Welsh captain and forced to eat the leek he had sneered at the day before! Even here, though his cowardice is as completely as it is comically shown up, he cannot refrain from his blatant threatenings. He will "most horribly revenge" this ignominy to which he tamely submits; he takes the groat "in earnest of revenge;" and his last words when the whipping is finished are "All hell shall stir for this." He disappears from the scene, the last straggler of that incomparable group of comic characters that had gathered around Falstaff, held by the attraction of his giant bulk as planets by the sun; but we cannot doubt that he regained his native impudence when he returned to England, and boasted in the old grandiloquent style of the scars he had got "in the Gallia wars."

The only part of the play the authorship of which has been seriously questioned is the scene in which Katharine takes a lesson in English. Warburton pronounced it "ridiculous," and Hanmer rejected it from the text as not Shakespeare's. Fleay has more recently expressed the opinion that Thomas Lodge wrote it. Johnson defended it as in keeping with French character, and as diverting on the stage. Shakespeare probably wrote it, slight as it is. The epilogue to II. Henry IV. had promised that the audience should be made merry with "fair Katharine of France," and this scene fulfils that promise. It was only in some such harmless way that the poet would wish to make sport of the princess who was to be the bride of his favourite hero. To have made her seriously ridiculous would have been an indirect reflection upon him for falling in love with her.

But the same epilogue had promised that Falstaff should also be brought upon the stage again, and it may be asked why this was not likewise done. Perhaps it had been already done in the Merry Wives of Windsor, which may have been written before Henry V. The introduction of the death of Falstaff in the latter play perhaps supports the view that this was written after the Merry Wives. However that may be, Falstaff would have been an unmanageable character in Henry V. If the poet at first intended to bring him into the play, his sober second thought must have led him to give up the idea. After the king had banished him from his presence, Falstaff's occupation was gone. To be sure, he could have regained the royal favour by reforming, but it is not easy to conceive of Falstaff reformed. It would have required a re-forming indeed, a radical renovation that would have left him scarcely recognizable, unless by his mere corporal bulk—and could even that have been maintained without his unlimited potations of sack? The delightful old reprobate would, I fear, have been rather dull in a more virtuous and responsible *rôle*. The better course was to get him out of the way as gently as possible, and Dame Quickly's account of his death—foolish though the woman be—is as pathetic as it is natural.—O.F.A.

Cant. It must be thought on. If it pass against us,
We lose the better half of our possession.—(Act I. 1. 7, 8.)

KING HENRY V.

PROLOGUE.

SCENE: *England; afterwards France.*

Enter Chorus.

Chor. O for a Muse of fire, that would ascend
The brightest heaven of invention,[1]
A kingdom for a stage, princes to act
And monarchs to behold the swelling scene!
Then should the warlike Harry, like himself,
Assume the port of Mars; and at his heels,
Leash'd in like hounds, should famine, sword and fire
Crouch for employment. But pardon, gentles all,
The flat unraised spirits that have dar'd
On this unworthy scaffold[2] to bring forth
So great an object: can this cockpit hold
The vasty fields of France? or may we cram
Within this wooden O the very casques
That did affright the air at Agincourt?
O, pardon! since a crooked figure may
Attest[3] in little place a million;
And let us, ciphers to this great accompt,
On your imaginary[4] forces work.
Suppose within the girdle of these walls
Are now confin'd two mighty monarchies,
Whose high upreared and abutting fronts
The perilous narrow ocean parts asunder:
Piece out our imperfections with your thoughts;
Into a thousand parts divide one man,
And make imaginary puissance;[5]
Think, when we talk of horses, that you see them
Printing their proud hoofs i' the receiving earth;
For 't is your thoughts that now must deck our kings,
Carry them here and there; jumping o'er times,
Turning th' accomplishment of many years
Into an hour-glass: for the which supply
Admit me Chorus to this history;
Who prologue-like your humble patience pray,
Gently to hear, kindly to judge, our play.
[*Exit.*

[1] *Invention*, imagination; metrically a quadrisyllable.
[2] *Scaffold*, stage.
[3] *Attest*, stand for.
[4] *Imaginary*, imaginative.
[5] *Puissance*, army; a trisyllable here.

ACT I.

[SCENE I. *London. An ante-chamber in the King's palace.*

Enter the ARCHBISHOP OF CANTERBURY, *and the* BISHOP OF ELY.

Cant. My lord, I'll tell you; that self[1] bill is urg'd,
Which in th' eleventh year of the last king's reign
Was like,[2] and had indeed against us pass'd,
But that the scambling[3] and unquiet time
Did push it out of farther question.

Ely. But how, my lord, shall we resist it now?

Cant. It must be thought on. If it pass against us,
We lose the better half of our possession:
For all the temporal lands which men devout
By testament have given to the church
Would they strip from us; being valu'd thus:
As much as would maintain, to the king's honour,
Full fifteen earls and fifteen hundred knights,
Six thousand and two hundred good esquires;
And, to relief of lazars[4] and weak age,
Of indigent faint souls past corporal toil,
A hundred almshouses right well suppli'd;
And to the coffers of the king beside,
A thousand pounds by th' year: thus runs the bill.

Ely. This would drink deep.

Cant. 'T would drink the cup and all.

Ely. But what prevention?

Cant. The king is full of grace and fair regard.

Ely. And a true lover of the holy church.

Cant. The courses of his youth promis'd it not.
The breath no sooner left his father's body,
But that his wildness, mortifi'd[5] in him,
Seem'd to die too; yea, at that very moment
Consideration, like an angel, came
And whipp'd th' offending Adam out of him,
Leaving his body as a paradise,
T' envelope and contain celestial spirits.
Never was such a sudden scholar made;
Never came reformation in a flood,
With such a heady currance,[6] scouring faults;
Nor never Hydra-headed wilfulness
So soon did lose his seat and all at once
As in this king.

Ely. We are blessed in the change.

Cant. Hear him but reason in divinity,
And all-admiring with an inward wish
You would desire the king were made a prelate:
Hear him debate of commonwealth affairs,
You'd say it hath been all in all his study:
List his discourse of war, and you shall hear
A fearful battle render'd you in music:
Turn him to any cause of policy,
The Gordian knot of it he will unloose,
Familiar as his garter: that, when he speaks,
The air, a charter'd libertine, is still,
And the mute wonder lurketh in men's ears,
To steal his sweet and honey'd sentences;
So that the art and practic[7] part of life
Must be the mistress to this theoric:
Which is a wonder how his grace should glean it,
Since his addiction[8] was to courses vain,
His companies[9] unletter'd, rude and shallow,
His hours fill'd up with riots, banquets, sports,
And never noted in him any study,
Any retirement, any sequestration
From open haunts and popularity.[10]

Ely. The strawberry grows underneath the nettle,
And wholesome berries thrive and ripen best
Neighbour'd by fruit of baser quality:
And so the prince obscur'd his contemplation[11]
Under the veil of wildness; which, no doubt,
Grew like the summer grass, fastest by night,
Unseen, yet crescive[12] in his faculty.

Cant. It must be so; for miracles are ceas'd;
And therefore we must needs admit the means
How things are perfected.

Ely. But, my good lord,
How now for mitigation of this bill
Urg'd by the commons? Doth his majesty
Incline to it, or no?

---

[1] *Self*, same. [2] *Was like*, was likely to pass
[3] *Scambling*, scrambling, turbulent.
[4] *Lazars*, diseased beggars or lepers.
[5] *Mortifi'd*, destroyed, killed.

[6] *Currance*, current. [7] *Practic*, practical.
[8] *Addiction*, inclination. [9] *Companies*, companions.
[10] *Popularity*, publicity.
[11] *Contemplation*, seriousness. [12] *Crescive*, increasing.

Cant. He seems indifferent,
Or rather swaying more upon our part
Than cherishing th' exhibiters against us;
For I have made an offer to his majesty,
Upon our spiritual convocation
And in regard of causes now in hand,
Which I have open'd to his grace at large,
As touching France, to give a greater sum
Than ever at one time the clergy yet
Did to his predecessors part withal.

Ely. How did this offer seem receiv'd, my lord?

Cant. With good acceptance of his majesty;
Save that there was not time enough to hear,
As I perceiv'd his grace would fain have done,
The severals[1] and unhidden passages
Of his true title to some certain dukedoms
And generally to the crown and seat of France
Deriv'd from Edward, his great-grandfather.

Ely. What was th' impediment that broke this off?

Cant. The French ambassador upon that instant
Crav'd audience; and the hour, I think, is come
To give him hearing: it is four o'clock?

Ely. It is.

Cant. Then go we in, to know his embassy;
Which I could with a ready guess declare,
Before the Frenchman speak a word of it.

Ely. I'll wait upon you, and I long to hear it.
[*Exeunt.*]

SCENE II. *The same. A room of state in the King's palace.*

Trumpets.—KING HENRY *on throne*, GLOUCESTER, BEDFORD, EXETER, WARWICK, WESTMORELAND, *Lords, Officers, and Attendants discovered.*

King. Where is my gracious Lord of Canterbury?

Exe. Not here in presence.

King. Send for him, good uncle.

West. Shall we call in th' ambassador, my liege?

King. Not yet, my cousin: we would be resolv'd,[2]
Before we hear him, of some things of weight
That task our thoughts, concerning us and France.

Enter the ARCHBISHOP OF CANTERBURY, *and the* BISHOP OF ELY.

Cant. God and his angels guard your sacred throne
And make you long become it!

King. Sure, we thank you.
My learned lord, we pray you to proceed
[And justly and religiously unfold
Why the law Salique that they have in France
Or should, or should not, bar us in our claim:]
And God forbid, my dear and faithful lord,
That you should [fashion, wrest, or bow your reading,
Or nicely] charge your understanding soul
With opening titles miscreate, whose right
Suits not in native colours with the truth;
For God doth know how many now in health
Shall drop their blood in approbation[3]
Of what your reverence shall incite us to.
Therefore take heed how you impawn[4] our person,
How you awake our sleeping sword of war:
We charge you, in the name of God, take heed;
For never two such kingdoms did contend
Without much fall of blood; whose guiltless drops
Are every one a woe, a sore complaint
'Gainst him whose wrong gives edge unto the swords
That make such waste in brief mortality.
Under this conjuration speak, my lord;
[For we will hear, note and believe in heart
That what you speak is in your conscience wash'd
As pure as sin with baptism.

Cant. Then hear me, gracious sovereign, and you peers,
That owe yourselves, your lives and services
To this imperial throne. There is no bar
To make against your highness' claim to France
But this, which they produce from Pharamond,
"In terram Salicam mulieres ne succedant;"
"No woman shall succeed in Salique land:"
Which Salique land the French unjustly gloze[5]
To be the realm of France, and Pharamond

[1] *Severals*, details. [2] *Resolv'd*, satisfied.

[3] *Approbation*, proving. [4] *Impawn*, pledge. [5] *Gloze*, explain sophistically.

The founder of this law and female bar.
Yet their own authors faithfully affirm
That the land Salique is in Germany,
Between the floods of Sala and of Elbe;
Where Charles the Great,[1] having subdu'd the Saxons,
There left behind and settl'd certain French;
Who, holding in disdain the German women
For some dishonest manners[2] of their life,
Establish'd then this law; to wit, no female
Should be inheritrix in Salique land:
Which Salique, as I said, 'twixt Elbe and Sala,
Is at this day in Germany call'd Meisen.
Then doth it well appear the Salique law
Was not devised for the realm of France;
Nor did the French possess the Salique land
Until four hundred one and twenty years
After defunction[3] of King Pharamond,
Idly suppos'd the founder of this law;
Who died within the year of our redemption
Four hundred and twenty-six; and Charles the Great
Subdu'd the Saxons, and did seat the French
Beyond the river Sala, in the year
Eight hundred five. Besides, their writers say,
King Pepin, which deposed Childeric,
Did, as heir general, being descended
Of Blithild, which was daughter to King Clothair,
Make claim and title to the crown of France.
Hugh Capet also, who usurp'd the crown
Of Charles the duke of Lorraine, sole heir male
Of the true line and stock of Charles the Great,
To find his title with some shows of truth,
Though, in pure truth, it was corrupt and naught,
Convey'd himself as heir to the Lady Lingare,
Daughter to Charlemain, who was the son
To Lewis the emperor, and Lewis the son
Of Charles the Great. Also King Lewis the Tenth,
Who was sole heir to the usurper Capet,
Could not keep quiet in his conscience,[4]
Wearing the crown of France, till satisfi'd
That fair Queen Isabel, his grandmother,
Was lineal of[5] the Lady Ermengare,
Daughter to Charles the foresaid duke of Lorraine:
By the which marriage the line of Charles the Great
Was re-united to the crown of France.
So that, as clear as is the summer's sun,
King Pepin's title and Hugh Capet's claim,
King Lewis his satisfaction, all appear
To hold in right and title of the female:
So do the kings of France unto this day;
Howbeit they would hold up this Salique law
To bar your highness claiming from the female,
And rather choose to hide them in a net
Than amply to imbar their crooked titles
Usurp'd from you and your progenitors.

King.] May I with right and conscience make this claim?

Cant. The sin upon my head, dread sovereign!
For in the book of Numbers is it writ,
When the man dies, let the inheritance
Descend unto the daughter. Gracious lord,
Stand for your own; unwind your bloody flag;[6]
Look back into your mighty ancestors:
Go, my dread lord, to your great-grandsire's[7] tomb,
From whom you claim; invoke his warlike spirit,
And your great-uncle's, Edward the Black Prince,
[Who on the French ground play'd a tragedy,
Making defeat on the full power of France,
Whiles his most mighty father on a hill
Stood smiling to behold his lion's whelp
Forage in blood of French nobility.
O noble English, that could entertain
With half their forces the full pride of France
And let another half stand laughing by,
All out of work and cold for action!]

Ely. Awake remembrance of these valiant dead
[And with your puissant arm renew their feats.
You are their heir; you sit upon their throne;]
The blood and courage that renowned them

[1] *Charles the Great*, Charlemagne.
[2] *Dishonest manners*, immoral practices.
[3] *Defunction*, demise, death.
[4] *Conscience*, metrically a trisyllable.
[5] *Lineal of*, in direct descent from.
[6] *Unwind your bloody flag*, unfurl your battle pennon or banner.
[7] *Great grandsire*, i.e. Edward III.

Runs in your veins; and my thrice-puissant liege
Is in the very May-morn of his youth,
Ripe for exploits and mighty enterprises.

Exe. Your brother kings and monarchs of the earth
Do all expect that you should rouse yourself,
As did the former lions of your blood.

West. They know your grace hath cause and means and might;
So hath your highness; never king of England
Had nobles richer and more loyal subjects,
Whose hearts have left their bodies here in England
And lie pavilion'd in the fields of France.

Cant. O, let their bodies follow, my dear liege,
With blood and sword and fire to win your right;
In aid whereof we of the spirituality[1]
Will raise your highness such a mighty sum
As never did the clergy at one time
Bring in to any of your ancestors.

[*King.* We must not only arm t' invade the French,
But lay down our proportions[2] to defend
Against the Scot, who will make road[3] upon us
With all advantages.[4]

Cant. They of those marches,[5] gracious sovereign,
Shall be a wall sufficient to defend
Our inland from the pilfering borderers.

King. We do not mean the coursing snatchers[6] only,
But fear the main intendment[7] of the Scot,
Who hath been still a giddy[8] neighbour to us;
For you shall read that my great-grandfather
Never went with his forces into France
But that the Scot on his unfurnish'd kingdom
Came pouring, like the tide into a breach,
With ample and brim fulness[9] of his force,
Galling the gleaned[10] land with hot assays,[11]
Girding with grievous siege castle and towns;
That England, being empty of defence,
Hath shook and trembled at th' ill neighbourhood.

Cant. She hath been then more fear'd[12] than harm'd, my liege;
For hear her but exampl'd by herself:
When all her chivalry hath been in France
And she a mourning widow of her nobles,
She hath herself not only well defended
But taken and impounded as a stray
The King of Scots; whom she did send to France,
To fill King Edward's fame with prisoner kings
And make her chronicle as rich with praise
As is the ooze and bottom of the sea
With sunken wreck and sumless treasuries.

West. But there 's a saying very old and true,
"If that you will France win,
Then with Scotland first begin:"
For once the eagle England being in prey,[13]
To her unguarded nest the weasel Scot
Comes sneaking and so sucks her princely eggs,
Playing the mouse in absence of the cat,
To tear and havoc[14] more than she can eat.

Exe. It follows then the cat must stay at home:
Yet that is but a crush'd necessity,
Since we have locks to safeguard necessaries,
And pretty traps to catch the petty thieves.
While that the armed hand doth fight abroad,
Th' advised[15] head defends itself at home;
For government, though high and low and lower,
Put into parts, doth keep in one consent,
Congreeing[16] in a full and natural close,[17]
Like music.

Cant. Therefore doth heaven divide
The state of man in divers functions,
Setting endeavour in continual motion;
To which is fixed, as an aim or butt,
Obedience: for so work the honey-bees,
Creatures that by a rule in nature teach
The act of order to a peopled kingdom.
They have a king and officers of sorts;
Where some, like magistrates, correct at home,
Others, like merchants, venture trade abroad,
Others, like soldiers, armed in their stings,

---

1 *The spirituality*, the clergy.
2 *Lay down our proportions*, apportion our troops.
3 *Make road*, advance.
4 *Advantages*, favourable conditions.
5 *Marches*, borders. 6 *Coursing snatchers*, freebooters.
7 *Main intendment*=chief attack.
8 *Giddy*, fickle, untrustworthy, excitable.
9 *Brim fulness*, overpowering numbers.
10 *Gleaned*, exhausted. 11 *Assays*, attacks, incursions.
12 *Fear'd*, frightened, terrified.
13 *In prey*, in quest of prey.
14 *Havoc*, destroy or make worthless.
15 *Advised*, wary. 16 *Congreeing*, agreeing.
17 *Close*, cadence.

Make boot upon[1] the summer's velvet buds,
Which pillage they with merry march bring home
To the tent royal of their emperor:
Who, busied in his majesty, surveys
The singing masons building roofs of gold,
The civil citizens kneading up the honey,
The poor mechanic porters crowding in
Their heavy burdens at his narrow gate,
The sad-ey'd[2] justice, with his surly hum,
Delivering o'er to executors[3] pale
The lazy yawning drone. I this infer,
That many things, having full reference
To one consent, may work contrariously:

King. But, tell the Dauphin, I will keep my state,
Be like a king and show my sail of greatness
When I do rouse me in my throne of France.—(Act i. 2. 273-275.)

As many arrows, loosed several ways,
Come to one mark; as many ways meet in one town;
As many fresh streams meet in one salt sea;
As many lines close in the dial's centre;
So many a thousand actions, once afoot,
End in one purpose, and be well borne
Without defeat. Therefore to France, my liege.
Divide your happy England into four;
Whereof take you one quarter into France,
And you withal shall make all Gallia shake.
If we, with thrice such powers left at home,
Cannot defend our own doors from the dog,
Let us be worried and our nation lose
The name of hardiness and policy.]

King. Call in the messengers sent from the Dauphin.

[*Exeunt some Lords and Attendants.*

Now are we well resolv'd; and, by God's help,
And yours, the noble sinews of our power,
France being ours, we'll bend it to our awe,
Or break it all to pieces: [or there we'll sit,
Ruling in large and ample empery[4]
O'er France and all her almost kingly dukedoms,
Or lay these bones in an unworthy urn,
Tombless, with no remembrance over them:

[1] *Make boot upon*, plunder.
[2] *Sad-ey'd*, serious-eyed.
[3] *Executors*, executioners.
[4] *Empery*, dominion.

Either our history shall with full mouth
Speak freely of our acts, or else our grave,
Like Turkish mute, shall have a tongueless mouth,
Not worshipp'd with a waxen epitaph.]

Enter Ambassadors of France, two Lords carrying a chest, and Attendants.

Now are we well prepar'd to know the pleasure
Of our fair cousin Dauphin; for we hear
Your greeting is from him, not from the king.
First Amb. May't please your majesty to give us leave
Freely to render what we have in charge;
Or shall we sparingly show you far off
The Dauphin's meaning and our embassy?
King. We are no tyrant, but a Christian king;
Unto whose grace our passion is as subject
As are our wretches fetter'd in our prisons:
Therefore with frank and with uncurbed plainness
Tell us the Dauphin's mind.
First Amb. Thus, then, in few.
Your highness, lately sending into France,
Did claim some certain dukedoms, in the right
Of your great predecessor, King Edward the Third.
In answer of which claim, the prince our master
Says that you savour too much of your youth,
And bids you be advis'd there's nought in France
That can be with a nimble galliard[1] won;
You cannot revel into dukedoms there.
He therefore sends you, meeter for your spirit,
This tun of treasure; and, in lieu of this,
Desires you let the dukedoms that you claim
Hear no more of you. This the Dauphin speaks.
King. What treasure, uncle?
Exe. [*Who has examined the chest*] Tennis-balls, my liege.
King. We're glad the Dauphin is so pleasant with us;
His present and your pains we thank you for:
When we have match'd our rackets to these balls,
We will, in France, by God's grace, play a set[2]
Shall strike his father's crown into the hazard.[3]
Tell him [he hath made a match with such a wrangler
That all the courts of France will be disturb'd
With chases.[4] And] we understand him well,
How he comes o'er us with our wilder days,
Not measuring what use we made of them.
[We never valu'd this poor seat of England;
And therefore, living hence, did give ourself
To barbarous license; as 't is ever common
That men are merriest when they are from home.]
But, tell the Dauphin, I will keep my state,
Be like a king and show my sail of greatness[5]
When I do rouse me[6] in my throne of France:
For [that I have laid by my majesty
And plodded like a man for working-days,
But] I will rise there with so full a glory
That I will dazzle all the eyes of France,
Yea, strike the Dauphin blind to look on us.
And tell the pleasant prince this mock of his
Hath turned his balls to gun-stones; and his soul
Shall stand sore charged for the wasteful vengeance
That shall fly with them: for many a thousand widows
Shall this his mock mock out of their dear husbands;
[Mock mothers from their sons, mock castles down;]
And some are yet ungotten and unborn
That shall have cause to curse the Dauphin's scorn.
But this lies all within the will of God,
To whom I do appeal; and in whose name
Tell you the Dauphin I am coming on,
To venge me as I may and to put forth
My rightful hand in a well-hallow'd cause.
So get you hence in peace; and tell the Dauphin
His jest will savour but of shallow wit,
When thousands weep more than did laugh at it.
Convey them with safe conduct. Fare you well.
[*Exeunt Ambassadors.*
Exe. This was a merry message.
King. We hope to make the sender blush at it.
[*Descends from the throne.*
Therefore, my lords, omit no happy[7] hour
That may give furtherance to our expedition;
For we have now no thought in us but France,

[1] *Galliard*, a spirited French dance. [2] *Set*, game.
[3] *Hazard*, a term in tennis. See note 74.

[4] *Chases*, a term in tennis. See note 75.
[5] *Sail of greatness*, full majesty.
[6] *Rouse me*, raise myself to my full height.
[7] *Happy*, favourable.

Save those to God, that run before our business.
Therefore let our proportions[1] for these wars
Be soon collected and all things thought upon
That may with reasonable swiftness add
More feathers to our wings; for, God before,
We 'll chide this Dauphin at his father's door.
[Therefore let every man now task his thought,[2]
That this fair action may on foot be brought.]

[*Flourish. Exeunt.*

ACT II.

PROLOGUE.

Enter Chorus.

Chor. Now all the youth of England are on fire,
And silken dalliance in the wardrobe lies:
Now thrive the armourers, and honour's thought
Reigns solely in the breast of every man:
They sell the pasture now to buy the horse,
Following the mirror of all Christian kings,
With winged heels, as English Mercuries.
For now sits Expectation in the air,
And hides a sword from hilts unto the point
With crowns imperial, crowns and coronets,
Promis'd to Harry and his followers.
The French, advis'd by good intelligence
Of this most dreadful preparation,
Shake in their fear and with pale policy
Seek to divert the English purposes.
O England! model to thy inward greatness,
Like little body with a mighty heart,
What mightst thou do, that honour would thee do,
Were all thy children kind and natural!
But see thy fault! France hath in thee found out
A nest of hollow bosoms,[3] which he fills
With treacherous crowns; and three corrupted men,
One, Richard Earl of Cambridge, and the second,
Henry Lord Scroop of Masham, and the third,
Sir Thomas Grey, knight, of Northumberland,
Have, for the gilt of France,[4]—O guilt indeed!—
Confirm'd conspiracy with fearful France;
And by their hands this grace of kings must die,
If hell and treason hold their promises,
Ere he take ship for France, and in Southampton.
Linger your patience on; and we 'll digest
The abuse of distance; force a play:
The sum is paid; the traitors are agreed;
The king is set from London; and the scene
Is now transported, gentles,[5] to Southampton;
There is the playhouse now, there must you sit:
And thence to France shall we convey you safe,
And bring you back, charming the narrow seas
To give you gentle pass; for, if we may,
We 'll not offend one stomach with our play.
But, till the king come forth, and not till then,
Unto Southampton do we shift our scene.

[*Exit.*

SCENE I. *London. Before the Boar's Head Tavern in Eastcheap.*

Enter CORPORAL NYM *and* LIEUTENANT BARDOLPH.

Bard. Well met, Corporal Nym.

Nym. Good morrow, Lieutenant Bardolph.

Bard. What, are Ancient[6] Pistol and you friends yet?

Nym. For my part, I care not; I say little; but when time shall serve, there shall be smiles; but that shall be as it may. I dare not fight; but I will wink and hold out mine iron: it is a simple one; but what though? it will toast cheese, and it will endure cold as another man's sword will: and there's an end.

Bard. I will bestow a breakfast to make you friends; and we'll be all three sworn brothers to France: let it be so, good Corporal Nym.

---

[1] *Proportions*, fixed number of troops.
[2] *Task his thought*, dispose his thought.
[3] *Hollow bosoms*, treacherous hearts.
[4] *The gilt of France*, French gold.

[5] *Gentles*, gentlefolk.
[6] *Ancient*, a corruption of *ensign*.

Nym. Faith, I will live so long as I may, that's the certain of it; and when I cannot live any longer, I will do as I may: that is my rest, that is the rendezvous of it.

Bard. It is certain, corporal, that he is married to Nell Quickly: and certainly she did you wrong; for you were troth-plight to her.

Nym. I cannot tell: things must be as they may: men may sleep, and they may have their throats about them at that time; and some say knives have edges. It must be as it may:

Chor. They sell the pasture now to buy the horse,
Following the mirror of all Christian kings.—(Act ii. Prol. 5, 6.)

though patience be a tir'd mare, yet she will plod. There must be conclusions. Well, I cannot tell.

Enter Pistol *and Hostess from the Tavern.*

Bard. Here comes Ancient Pistol and his wife: good corporal, be patient here. How now, mine host Pistol!

Pist. Base tike,[1] call'st thou me host?
Now, by this hand, I swear, I scorn the term;
Nor shall my Nell keep lodgers.

Host. [No, by my troth, not long; for we cannot lodge and board a dozen or fourteen gentlewomen that live honestly by the prick of their needles, but it will be thought we keep a bawdy house straight.] [*Nym draws his sword.*] O well a day, Lady, if he be not drawn now! we shall see wilful adultery and murder committed.

Bard. Good lieutenant! good corporal! offer nothing here.

Nym. Pish!

Pist. Pish for thee, Iceland dog! thou prick-ear'd cur of Iceland!

Host. Good Corporal Nym, show thy valour, and put up your sword.

Nym. Will you shog[2] off? I would have you *solus*. [*Sheathing his sword.*

Pist. '*Solus*,' egregious dog? O viper vile!
The *solus* in thy most mervailous[3] face;
The *solus* in thy teeth, and in thy throat,
And in thy hateful lungs, yea, in thy maw, perdy,[4]

[1] *Tike*, cur.

[2] *Shog*, a word which Nym blunderingly uses for *jog*.

[3] *Mervailous*, probably marvellous.

[4] *Perdy*, par Dieu (by God).

And, which is worse, within thy nasty mouth!
I do retort the *solus* in thy bowels;
[For I can take, and Pistol's cock is up,
And flashing fire will follow.]

Nym. I am not Barbason;[1] you cannot conjure me. I have an humour to knock you indifferently well. If you grow foul with me, Pistol, I will scour you with my rapier, as I may, in fair terms: [if you would walk off, I would prick your guts a little, in good terms, as I may:] and that's the humour of it.

Pist. O braggart vile and damned furious wight!
The grave doth gape, and doting death is near;
Therefore exhale. [*Draws his sword.*

Bard. Hear me, hear me what I say: he that strikes the first stroke, I'll run him up to the hilts, as I am a soldier. [*Draws his sword*

Pist. An oath of mickle might; and fury shall abate.
Give me thy fist, thy fore-foot to me give:
Thy spirits are most tall.
[*They sheathe their swords.*

Nym. I will cut thy throat, one time or other, in fair terms: that is the humour of it.

Pist. *Coupe la gorge!*[2]
That is the word. I thee defy again.
O hound of Crete, think'st thou my spouse to get?
No; to the spital[3] go,
[And from the powdering tub of infamy]
Fetch forth the lazar kite of Cressid's kind,
Doll Tearsheet she by name, and her espouse:
I have, and I will hold, the *quondam* Quickly
For the only she; and—*Pauca*,[4] there's enough.
Go to.

Enter the Boy from the Tavern.

Boy. Mine host Pistol, you must come to my master, and you, hostess: he is very sick, and would to bed. Good Bardolph, put thy face between his sheets, and do the office of a warming-pan. Faith, he's very ill.

Bard. Away, you rogue!

Host. By my troth, he'll yield the crow a pudding one of these days. The king has kill'd his heart.—Good husband, come home presently.[5]

[*Exeunt Hostess and Boy into the Tavern.*

Bard. Come, shall I make you two friends? We must to France together: why the devil should we keep knives to cut one another's throats?

Pist. Let floods o'erswell, and fiends for food howl on!

Nym. You'll pay me the eight shillings I won of you at betting?

Pist. Base is the slave that pays.

Nym. That now I will have: that's the humour of it.

Pist. As manhood shall compound:[6] push home. [*Pistol and Nym draw their swords.*

Bard. By this sword, he that makes the first thrust, I'll kill him; by this sword, I will. [*Draws his sword.*

Pist. Sword is an oath, and oaths must have their course.

Bard. Corporal Nym, an thou wilt be friends, be friends: an thou wilt not, why, then, be enemies with me too. Prithee, put up.

Nym. I shall have my eight shillings I won of you at betting?

Pist. A noble shalt thou have, and present pay;
And liquor likewise will I give to thee,
And friendship shall combine, and brotherhood:
I'll live by Nym, and Nym shall live by me;
Is not this just? for I shall sutler be
Unto the camp, and profits will accrue.
Give me thy hand. [*They sheathe their swords.*

Nym. I shall have my noble?

Pist. In cash most justly paid.

Nym. Well, then, that's the humour of it. [*Shakes Pistol's hand.*

Re-enter Hostess from the Tavern.

Host. As ever you came of women, come in quickly to Sir John. Ah, poor heart! he is so shak'd of a burning quotidian tertian, that it is most lamentable to behold. Sweet men come to him.

Nym. The king hath run bad humours on the knight; that's the even of it.

---

[1] *Barbason*, the name of a devil.
[2] *Coupe la gorge*, cut the throat.
[3] *Spital*, hospital.
[4] *Pauca*, briefly; literally, few [words].
[5] *Presently*, immediately.
[6] *Compound*, arrange, come to terms.

Pist. Nym, thou hast spoke the right;
His heart is fracted[1] and corroborate.

Nym. The king is a good king: but it must be as it may; he passes some humours and careers.

Pist. Let us condole the knight; for, lambkins, we will live. [*Exeunt into Tavern.*

SCENE II. *Southampton. A council chamber.*

Enter EXETER, BEDFORD, *and* WESTMORELAND.

Bed. 'Fore God, his grace is bold, to trust these traitors.
Exe. They shall be apprehended by and by.
West. How smooth and even they do bear themselves!
As if allegiance in their bosoms sat,
Crowned with faith and constant loyalty.
Bed. The king hath note of all that they intend,
By interception which they dream not of.
Exe. Nay, but the man that was his bed-fellow,
Whom he hath dull'd and cloy'd with gracious favours,
That he should, for a foreign purse, so sell
His sovereign's life to death and treachery.

Trumpets sound. Enter KING HENRY, SCROOP, CAMBRIDGE, GREY, *Lords, Guards, and Attendants.*

King. Now sits the wind fair, and we will aboard.
My Lord of Cambridge, and my kind Lord of Masham,
And you, my gentle knight, give me your thoughts:
Think you not that the powers[2] we bear with us
Will cut their passage through the force of France,
Doing the execution and the act
For which we have in head[3] assembled them?
Scroop. No doubt, my liege, if each man do his best.
King. I doubt not that; since we are well persuaded
We carry not a heart with us from hence
That grows not in a fair consent with ours,
Nor leave not one behind that doth not wish
Success and conquest to attend on us.
Cam. Never was monarch better fear'd and lov'd
Than is your majesty: there's not, I think, a subject
That sits in heart-grief and uneasiness
Under the sweet shade of your government.
Grey. True: those that were your father's enemies
Have steep'd their galls in honey and do serve you
With hearts create of duty and of zeal.
King. We therefore have great cause of thankfulness;
And shall forget the office[4] of our hand,
Sooner than quittance of desert and merit
According to the weight and worthiness.
Scroop. So service shall with steeled sinews toil,
And labour shall refresh itself with hope,
To do your grace incessant services.
King. We judge no less. Uncle of Exeter,
Enlarge the man committed yesterday,
That rail'd against our person: we consider
It was excess of wine that set him on:
And on his more advice[5] we pardon him.
Scroop. That's mercy, but too much security:[6]
Let him be punish'd, sovereign, lest example
Breed, by his sufferance,[7] more of such a kind.
King. O, let us yet be merciful.
Cam. So may your highness, and yet punish too.
Grey. Sir,
You show great mercy, if you give him life,
After the taste of much correction.
King. Alas, your too much love and care of me
Are heavy orisons[8] 'gainst this poor wretch!
If little faults, proceeding on distemper,[9]
Shall not be wink'd at, how shall we stretch our eye[10]

1 *Fracted*, broken. 2 *Powers*, soldiers, forces.
3 *In head*, in force.

4 *Office*, function, use.
5 *On his more advice*, i.e. on his becoming more sensible. 6 *Security*, easy confidence.
7 *By his sufferance*, i.e. by his being suffered to go unpunished. 8 *Heavy orisons*, weighty prayers.
9 *Proceeding on distemper*, resulting from intoxication.
10 *Stretch our eye*, i.e. open it wide.

When capital crimes, chew'd, swallow'd, and digested,
Appear before us? We 'll yet enlarge[1] that man,
Though Cambridge, Scroop and Grey, in their dear care
And tender preservation of our person,
Would have him punish'd. And now to our French causes:
Who are the late[2] commissioners?

Cam. I one, my lord:
Your highness bade me ask for it to-day.

Scroop. So did you me, my liege.

Grey. And I, my royal sovereign.

King. Then, Richard Earl of Cambridge, there is yours; [*Giving each a scroll.*
There yours, Lord Scroop of Masham; and, sir knight,
Grey of Northumberland, this same is yours:
Read them; and know, I know your worthiness. [*They unfold the scrolls, and, on reading them, are much agitated.*
My Lord of Westmoreland, and uncle Exeter,
We will aboard to-night. Why, how now, gentlemen!
What see you in those papers that you lose
So much complexion? Look ye, how they change!
Their cheeks are paper.[3] Why, what read you there,
That hath so cowarded and chas'd your blood
Out of appearance?

Cam. I do confess my fault;
And do submit me to your highness' mercy.

Grey.
Scroop. } To which we all appeal.
[*All three kneel: the other Lords shrink away from them.*

King. The mercy that was quick[4] in us but late,
By your own counsel is suppress'd and kill'd:
You must not dare, for shame, to talk of mercy;
[For your own reasons turn into your bosoms,
As dogs upon their masters, worrying you.]
See you, my princes and my noble peers,
These English monsters! My Lord of Cambridge here,
You know how apt our love was to accord
To furnish him with all appertinents[5]
Belonging to his honour; and this man
Hath, for a few light crowns, lightly conspir'd,
And sworn unto the practices of France,
To kill us here in Hampton: to the which
This knight, no less for bounty bound to us
Than Cambridge is, hath likewise sworn. But, O,
What shall I say to thee, Lord Scroop? thou cruel,
Ingrateful, savage and inhuman creature!
Thou that didst bear the key of all my counsels,
That knew'st the very bottom of my soul,
That almost mightst have coin'd me into gold,
Wouldst thou have practis'd on me for thy use,
May it be possible, that foreign hire
Could out of thee extract one spark of evil
That might annoy my finger? 't is so strange,
That, though the truth of it stands off as gross[6]
As black and white, my eye will scarcely see it.
[Treason and murder ever kept together,
As two yoke-devils sworn to either's purpose,
Working so grossly[7] in a natural cause,
That admiration did not hoop[8] at them.
But thou, 'gainst all proportion,[9] didst bring in
Wonder to wait on treason and on murder:]
And whatsoever cunning fiend it was
That wrought upon thee so preposterously[10]
Hath got the voice[11] in hell for excellence:
[All other devils that suggest by treasons
Do botch and bungle up damnation
With patches, colours, and with forms being fetch'd
From glistering semblances of piety;
But he that temper'd thee bade thee stand up,
Gave thee no instance[12] why thou shouldst do treason,
Unless to dub thee with the name of traitor.]
If that same demon that hath gull'd thee thus
Should with his lion gait walk the whole world,
He might return to vasty Tartar[13] back,
And tell the legions "I can never win
A soul so easy as that Englishman's."
O, how hast thou with jealousy infected
The sweetness of affiance![14] Show men dutiful?

[1] *Enlarge*, set at liberty. [2] *Late*, i.e. lately appointed.
[3] *Paper*, as colourless as paper. [4] *Quick*, living.
[5] *Appertinents*, appointments.

[6] *Gross*, plain. [7] *Grossly*, palpably.
[8] *Hoop*, old spelling of whoop = "shout in wonder."
[9] *'Gainst all proportion*, against all precedent.
[10] *Preposterously*, strangely. [11] *Voice*, verdict.
[12] *Instance*, excuse, warrant. [13] *Tartar*, Tartarus.
[14] *Affiance*, confidence.

Why, so didst thou: seem they grave and learned?
Why, so didst thou: come they of noble family?
Why, so didst thou: seem they religious?
Why, so didst thou: [or are they spare in diet,
Free from gross passion or of mirth or anger,
Constant in spirit, not swerving with the blood,
Garnish'd and deck'd in modest complement,
Not working with the eye without the ear,
And but in purged judgment trusting neither?
Such and so finely bolted[1] didst thou seem:]
And thus thy fall hath left a kind of blot,
To mark the full-fraught man and best indu'd
With some suspicion. I will weep for thee:
For this revolt of thine, methinks, is like

King. Why, how now, gentlemen!
What see you in those papers that you lose
So much complexion?—(Act ii. 2. 71-73.)

Another fall of man. Their faults are open:
Arrest them to the answer of the law;
And God acquit them of their practices!

[*The Guard disarm all three, as Exeter arrests them.*

Exe. I arrest thee of high treason, by the name of Richard Earl of Cambridge.

I arrest thee of high treason, by the name of Henry Lord Scroop of Masham.

I arrest thee of high treason, by the name of Thomas Grey, knight, of Northumberland.

Scroop. [*Kneeling*] Our purposes God justly hath discover'd;[2]
And I repent my fault more than my death;
Which I beseech your highness to forgive,
Although my body pay the price of it.

Cam. [*Kneeling*] For me, the gold of France did not seduce;
Although I did admit it as a motive
The sooner to effect what I intended:
But God be thanked for prevention;
Which I in sufferance heartily will rejoice,
Beseeching God and you to pardon me.

Grey. [*Kneeling*] Never did faithful subject more rejoice
At the discovery of most dangerous treason
Than I do at this hour joy o'er myself,

[1] *Bolted*, sifted, tested.

[2] *Discover'd*, disclosed.

Prevented from a damned enterprise:
My fault, but not my body, pardon, sovereign.

King. God quit you in his mercy! Hear your sentence.
You have conspir'd against our royal person,
Join'd with an enemy proclaim'd and from his coffers
Receiv'd the golden earnest[1] of our death;
Wherein you would have sold your king to slaughter,
His princes and his peers to servitude,
His subjects to oppression and contempt
And his whole kingdom into desolation.
Touching our person seek we no revenge;
But we our kingdom's safety must so tender,[2]
Whose ruin you have sought, that to her laws
We do deliver you. Get you therefore hence,
Poor miserable wretches, to your death:
The taste whereof, God of his mercy give
You patience to endure, and true repentance
Of all your dear[3] offences! Bear them hence.

[*Exeunt Cambridge, Scroop and Grey, guarded.*

Now, lords, for France; the enterprise whereof
Shall be to you, as us, like glorious.
We doubt not of a fair and lucky war,
Since God so graciously hath brought to light
This dangerous treason lurking in our way
To hinder our beginnings. We doubt not now
But every rub[4] is smoothed on our way.
Then forth, dear countrymen: let us deliver
Our puissance into the hand of God,
Putting it straight in expedition.[5]
Cheerly to sea; the signs of war[6] advance:
No king of England, if not king of France.

[*Exeunt.*

Scene III. *London. Before "The Boar's Head" Tavern in Eastcheap.*

Enter Pistol, Nym, *and* Bardolph, *with arms, wallets, &c., as going to join the army; Hostess, and Boy.*

Host. Prithee, honey-sweet husband, let me bring thee[7] to Staines.

Pist. No; for my manly heart doth yearn.[8]
Bardolph, be blithe: Nym, rouse thy vaunting veins:
Boy, bristle thy courage up; for Falstaff he is dead,
And we must yearn therefore.

Bard. Would I were with him, wheresome'er he is, either in heaven or in hell!

Host. Nay, sure, he's not in hell: he's in Arthur's bosom,[9] if ever man went to Arthur's bosom.[9] A' made a finer end and went away an it had been any christom child; a' parted even just between twelve and one, even at the turning o' the tide: for after I saw him fumble with the sheets and play with flowers and smile upon his fingers' ends, I knew there was but one way; for his nose was as sharp as a pen, and a' babbled of green fields. "How now, Sir John!" quoth I: "what, man! be o' good cheer." So a' cried out "God, God, God!" three or four times. Now I, to comfort him, bid him a' should not think of God; I hop'd there was no need to trouble himself with any such thoughts yet. So a' bade me lay more clothes on his feet: I put my hand into the bed and felt them, and they were as cold as any stone; [then I felt to his knees, and they were as cold as any stone, and so upward and upward, and all was as cold as any stone.]

Nym. They say he cried out of sack.

Host. Ay, that a' did.

Bard. And of women.

Host. Nay, that a' did not.

Boy. Yes, that a' did; and said they were devils incarnate.

Host. A' could never abide carnation; 't was a colour he never liked.

Boy. A' said once, the devil would have him about women.

Host. A' did in some sort, indeed, handle women; but then he was rheumatic,[10] and talked of the whore of Babylon.

Boy. Do you not remember, a' saw a flea stick upon Bardolph's nose, and a' said it was a black soul burning in hell-fire?

Bard. Well, the fuel is gone that maintained that fire: that's all the riches I got in his service.

---

[1] *Earnest* = earnest money.
[2] *Tender*, cherish.
[3] *Dear*, grievous.
[4] *Rub*, impediment.
[5] *Expedition*, march.
[6] *Signs of war*, banners.
[7] *Bring thee*, go with thee.
[8] *Yearn*, grieve, mourn.

[9] *Arthur's bosom*, a blunder for *Abraham's bosom*.
[10] *Rheumatic*, a blunder for *fanatic*.

Nym. Shall we shog? the king will be gone from Southampton.

Pist. Come, let's away. My love, give me thy lips.
Look to my chattels and my movables:
Let senses rule; the word is "Pitch and Pay;"
Trust none;
For oaths are straws, men's faiths are wafer-cakes,
And hold-fast is the only dog, my duck:
Therefore, *caveto* be[1] thy counsellor.
Go, clear thy crystals.[2] Yoke-fellows in arms,
Let us to France; like horse-leeches, my boys,
To suck, to suck, the very blood to suck!

Boy. And that's but unwholesome food, they say.

Pist. Touch her soft mouth, and march.

Bard. Farewell, hostess. [*Kissing her. Exit.*

Nym. I cannot kiss, that is the humour of it; but, adieu. [*Exit.*

Pist. Let housewifery appear: keep close, I thee command. [*Exit.*

Host. Farewell; adieu. [*Exit into Tavern.*

Scene IV. *France. The King's palace.*

Flourish. Enter the French King *attended; the* Dauphin, *the* Duke of Burgundy, *the* Constable, *and others.*

Fr. King. Thus comes the English with full power upon us;
And more than carefully it us concerns
To answer royally in our defences.
Therefore the Dukes of Berri and of Bretagne,
Of Brabant and of Orleans, shall make forth,[3]
And you, Prince Dauphin, with all swift dispatch,
To line[4] and new repair our towns of war
With men of courage and with means defendant;
For England[5] his approaches makes as fierce
As waters to the sucking of a gulf.
[It fits us then to be as provident
As fear may teach us out of late examples
Left by the fatal and neglected English
Upon our fields.]

Dau. My most redoubted father,
It is most meet we arm us 'gainst the foe;
For peace itself should not so dull[6] a kingdom,
Though war nor no known quarrel were in question,
But that defences, musters,[7] preparations,
Should be maintain'd, assembled and collected,
As were a war in expectation.
Therefore, I say 't is meet we all go forth
To view the sick and feeble parts of France:
And let us do it with no show of fear;
No, with no more than if we heard that England
Were busied with a Whitsun morris-dance:
For, my good liege, she is so idly king'd,
Her sceptre so fantastically borne
By a vain, giddy, shallow, humorous[8] youth,
That fear attends her not.

Con. O peace, Prince Dauphin!
You are too much mistaken in this king:
Question your grace the late ambassadors,
With what great state he heard their embassy,
How well supplied with noble counsellors,
How modest in exception,[9] and withal
How terrible in constant[10] resolution,
And you shall find his vanities forespent[11]
Were but the outside of the Roman Brutus,
Covering discretion with a coat of folly;
[As gardeners do with ordure hide those roots
That shall first spring and be most delicate.]

Dau. Well, 't is not so, my lord high constable;
But though we think it so, it is no matter:
In cases of defence 't is best to weigh
The enemy more mighty than he seems:
[So the proportions of defence are fill'd;
Which of a weak and niggardly projection
Doth, like a miser, spoil his coat with scanting
A little cloth.]

Fr. King. Think we King Harry strong;
And, princes, look you strongly arm to meet him.
[The kindred of him hath been flesh'd upon us;
And he is bred out of that bloody strain
That haunted us in our familiar paths:
Witness our too much memorable shame
When Cressy battle fatally was struck,
And all our princes captiv'd by the hand
Of that black name, Edward, Black Prince of Wales;

1 *Caveto be*, i.e. Let "take care" be.
2 *Crystals*, eyes.
3 *Make forth*, go forth.
4 *Line*, fortify.
5 *England*, the king of England.
6 *Dull*, make careless.
7 *Musters*, levies of troops.
8 *Humorous*, changeful, capricious.
9 *In exception*, in objection.
10 *Constant*, firm.
11 *Forespent*, past.

[Whiles that his mountain sire, on mountain standing,
Up in the air, crown'd with the golden sun,
Saw his heroical seed, and smil'd to see him,
Mangle the work of nature and deface
The patterns that by God and by French fathers
Had twenty years been made. This is a stem
Of that victorious stock; and let us fear
The native mightiness and fate of him.]

Enter a Messenger.

Mess. Ambassadors from Harry King of England

Chor. Follow, follow:
Grapple your minds to sternage of this navy,
And leave your England, as dead midnight still,
Guarded with grandsires, babies and old women,
Either past or not arriv'd to pith and puissance.
—(Act iii. Prol. 17-21.)

Do crave admittance to your majesty.

Fr. King. We'll give them present[1] audience. Go, and bring them.

[*Exeunt Messenger and certain Lords.*

You see this chase is hotly follow'd, friends.

Dau. Turn head, and stop pursuit; for coward dogs
Most spend their mouths[2] when what they seem to threaten
Runs far before them. Good my sovereign,
Take up the English short, and let them know
Of what a monarchy you are the head:
Self-love, my liege, is not so vile a sin
As self-neglecting.

Re-enter Lords, with EXETER *and train.*

Fr. King. From our brother England?

Exe. From him; and thus he greets your majesty.
He wills you, in the name of God Almighty,
That you divest yourself, and lay apart
The borrow'd glories that by gift of heaven,
By law of nature and of nations, 'long
To him and to his heirs; namely, the crown
And all wide-stretched honours that pertain
By custom and the ordinance of times
Unto the crown of France. That you may know

[1] *Present*, immediate.
[2] *Spend their mouths*, bark.

'T is no sinister[1] nor no awkward claim,
[Pick'd from the worm-holes of long-vanish'd days,
Nor from the dust of old oblivion rak'd,]
He sends you this most memorable line,[2]
[In every branch truly demonstrative;
Willing you overlook[3] this pedigree:]
And when you find him evenly[4] deriv'd
From his most fam'd of famous ancestors,
Edward the Third, he bids you then resign
Your crown and kingdom, indirectly held
From him the native and true challenger.

Fr. King. Or else what follows?

Exe. Bloody constraint; for if you hide the crown
Even in your hearts, there will he rake for it:
Therefore in fiery tempest is he coming,
In thunder and in earthquake, like a Jove,
That, if requiring[5] fail, he will compel;
[And bids you, in the bowels of the Lord,
Deliver up the crown, and to take mercy
On the poor souls for whom this hungry war
Opens his vasty jaws; and on your head
Turning the widows' tears, the orphans' cries,
The dead men's blood, the pining maidens' groans,
For husbands, fathers and betrothed lovers,
That shall be swallow'd in this controversy.]
This is his claim, his threatening and my message;
Unless the Dauphin be in presence here,
To whom expressly I bring greeting too.

Fr. King. For us, we will consider of this further:
To-morrow shall you bear our full intent
Back to our brother England.

Dau. For the Dauphin,
I stand here for him: what to him from England?

Exe. Scorn and defiance; slight regard, contempt,
And anything that may not misbecome
The mighty sender, doth he prize you at.
Thus says my king; an if your father's highness
Do not, in grant of all demands at large,
Sweeten the bitter mock you sent his majesty,
He 'll call you to so hot an answer of it,
That caves and womby vaultages of France
Shall chide your trespass[6] and return your mock
In second accent of his ordinance.[7]

Dau. Say, if my father render fair return,
It is against my will; for I desire
Nothing but odds with England: to that end,
As matching to his youth and vanity,
I did present him with the Paris balls.

Exe. He 'll make your Paris Louvre shake for it,
Were it the mistress-court of mighty Europe:
And, be assur'd, you 'll find a difference,
As we his subjects have in wonder found,
Between the promise of his greener days
And these he masters[8] now: now he weighs time
Even to the utmost grain: that you shall read
In your own losses, if he stay in France.

Fr. King. To-morrow shall you know our mind at full.

Exe. Dispatch us with all speed, lest that our king
Come here himself to question our delay;
For he is footed[9] in this land already.

Fr. King. You shall be soon dispatch'd with fair conditions:
A night is but small breath and little pause
To answer matters of this consequence.
[*Flourish. Exeunt.*

ACT III.

PROLOGUE.

Enter Chorus.

Chor. Thus with imagin'd wing our swift scene flies
In motion of no less celerity
Than that of thought. Suppose that you have seen
The well-appointed[10] king at Hampton pier

1 *Sinister*, accent on second syllable.
2 *Line*, pedigree.
3 *Overlook*, examine.
4 *Evenly*, directly.
5 *Requiring*, requesting.
6 *Chide your trespass*, proclaim your offence.
7 *Ordinance*, ordnance.
8 *Masters*, possesses.
9 *Footed*, landed.
10 *Well-appointed*, well-equipped.

Embark his royalty,[1] and his brave fleet
With silken streamers the young Phœbus fanning:
Play with your fancies, and in them behold
Upon the hempen tackle ship-boys climbing;
Hear the shrill whistle which doth order give
To sounds confus'd; behold the threaden sails,
Borne with th' invisible and creeping wind,
Draw the huge bottoms through the furrow'd sea,
Breasting the lofty surge: O, do but think
You stand upon the rivage[2] and behold
A city on th' inconstant billows dancing;
For so appears this fleet majestical,
Holding due course to Harfleur. Follow, follow:
Grapple your minds to sternage[3] of this navy,
And leave your England, as dead midnight still,
[Guarded with grandsires, babies and old women,
Either past or not arriv'd to pith[4] and puissance;[5]
For who is he, whose chin is but enrich'd
With one appearing hair, that will not follow
These cull'd and choice-drawn cavaliers to France?]
Work, work your thoughts, and therein see a siege;
Behold the ordnance on their carriages,
With fatal mouths gaping on girded Harfleur.
Suppose th' ambassador from the French comes back;
Tells Harry that the king doth offer him
Katharine his daughter, and with her, to dowry,
Some petty and unprofitable dukedoms.
The offer likes not: and the nimble gunner
With linstock now the devilish cannon touches,
[Alarum, and distant cannon heard.
And down goes all before them. Still be kind,
And eke out our performance with your mind.
[Exit.

Scene I. *France. Before the gates of Harfleur.*

A breach in the walls defended by the French. Alarums. Enter King Henry, Exeter, Bedford, Gloucester, *and Soldiers with scaling-ladders.*

King. Once more unto the breach, dear friends, once more;
Or close the wall up with our English dead.
In peace there's nothing so becomes a man
As modest stillness and humility:
But when the blast of war blows in our ears,
Then imitate the action of the tiger;
Stiffen the sinews, summon up the blood,
Disguise fair nature with hard-favour'd rage;
Then lend the eye a terrible aspéct;
[Let it pry through the portage[6] of the head
Like the brass cannon; let the brow o'erwhelm it
As fearfully as doth a galled rock
O'erhang and jutty[7] his confounded[8] base,
Swill'd with the wild and wasteful ocean.[9]
Now set the teeth and stretch the nostril wide,]
Hold hard the breath and bend up every spirit
To his full height. On, on, you noblest English,
Whose blood is fet[10] from fathers of war-proof!
[Fathers that, like so many Alexanders,
Have in these parts from morn till even fought
And sheath'd their swords for lack of argument:[11]]
Dishonour not your mothers; now attest
That those whom you call'd fathers did beget you.
Be copy now to men of grosser blood,
And teach them how to war. And you, good yeomen,
Whose limbs were made in England, show us here
The mettle of your pasture; let us swear
That you are worth your breeding; which I doubt not;
For there is none of you so mean and base,
That hath not noble lustre in your eyes.
I see you stand like greyhounds in the slips,
Straining upon the start. The game's afoot:
Follow your spirit; and upon this charge
Cry "God for Harry, England, and Saint George!"
[Exeunt. Alarum, and cannons heard: the English attack the walls.

[1] *His royalty*, his majesty.
[2] *Rivage*, shore.
[3] *Sternage*, steerage.
[4] *Pith*, strength.
[5] *Puissance*, a dissyllable here.
[6] *Portage*, port-hole.
[7] *Jutty*, extend beyond.
[8] *Confounded*, eaten by the waves.
[9] *Ocean*, here a trisyllable.
[10] *Fet*, fetched.
[11] *Argument*, business.

SCENE II. *The same. Before another part of the walls.*

Enter NYM, BARDOLPH, PISTOL, *and Boy.*

Bard. On, on, on, on, on! to the breach, to the breach!

Nym. Pray thee, corporal, stay: the knocks are too hot; and, for mine own part, I have not a case of lives: [*Alarums*] the humour of it is too hot, that is the very plain-song of it.

Pist. The plain-song is most just; for humours do abound:

Knocks go and come; God's vassals drop and die;
And sword and shield,
In bloody field,
Doth win immortal fame. [*Alarums.*

King. On, on, you noblest English.—(Act iii. 1. 17.)

Boy. Would I were in an alehouse in London! I would give all my fame for a pot of ale and safety. [*Alarums.*

Pist. And I:

If wishes would prevail with me,
My purpose should not fail with me,
But thither would I hie.

Boy. As duly, but not as truly,
As bird doth sing on bough. [*Alarums.*

Enter FLUELLEN.[1]

Flu. Got's plood!—Up to the breach, you dogs! avaunt, you cullions! [*Driving them forward.*

Pist. Be merciful, great duke, to men of mould.

Abate thy rage, abate thy manly rage,
Abate thy rage, great duke!
Good bawcock,[2] bate thy rage; use lenity, sweet chuck!

Nym. These be good humours! your honour wins bad humours.

[*Exeunt Nym, Pistol, Bardolph, and Fluellen, driving them off.*

Boy. As young as I am, I have observ'd these three swashers.[3] I am boy to them all three: but all they three, though they would serve me, could not be man to me; for indeed three such antics do not amount to a man. For Bardolph, he is white-liver'd[4] and red-fac'd; by the means whereof a' faces it out, but fights not. For Pistol, he hath a killing tongue and a quiet sword; by the means whereof a' breaks words, and keeps whole weapons. For Nym, he hath heard that men of few words are the best men; and therefore he scorns to say his prayers, lest a' should be thought a coward: but his few bad words are match'd with as few good deeds; for a' never broke any man's head but his own, and that was against a post when he was drunk. They will steal any thing, and call it purchase. Bardolph stole a lute-case,

[1] *Fluellen*, an approach to the Welsh pronunciation of *Llewellyn.*

[2] *Bawcock*, an endearing epithet—*beau coq.*

[3] *Swashers*, bullies.

[4] *White-liver'd*, cowardly.

bore it twelve leagues, and sold it for three half-pence. Nym and Bardolph are sworn brothers in filching, and in Calais they stole a fire-shovel. I knew by that piece of service the men would carry coals.[1] They would have me as familiar with men's pockets as their gloves or their handkerchers: which makes much against my manhood, if I should take from another's pocket to put into mine; for it is plain pocketing up of wrongs. I must leave them, and seek some better service: their villany goes against my weak stomach, and therefore I must cast it up. [*Exit.*

Re-enter FLUELLEN, GOWER *following.*

Gow. Captain Fluellen, you must come presently to the mines: the Duke of Gloucester would speak with you.

Flu. To the mines! tell you the duke, it is not so good to come to the mines; for, look you, the mines is not according to the disciplines of the war: the concavities of it is not sufficient; for, look you, th' athversary, you may discuss unto the duke, look you, is digt himself four yard under the countermines: by Cheshu, I think a' will plow up[2] all, if there is not better directions.

Gow. The Duke of Gloucester, to whom the order of the siege is given, is altogether directed by an Irishman, a very valiant gentleman, i' faith.

Flu. It is Captain Macmorris, is it not?

Gow. I think it be.

Flu. By Cheshu, he is an ass, as in the world: I will verify as much in his beard: he has no more directions in the true disciplines of the wars, look you, of the Roman disciplines, than is a puppy-dog.

Enter MACMORRIS *and Captain* JAMY.

Gow. Here a' comes; and the Scots captain, Captain Jamy, with him.

Flu. Captain Jamy is a marvellous falorous gentlemen, that is certain; and of great expedition and knowledge in th' aunchient wars, upon my particular knowledge of his directions: by Cheshu, he will maintain his argument as well as any military man in the world, in the disciplines of the pristine wars of the Romans.

Jamy. I say gud-day, Captain Fluellen.

Flu. God-den[3] to your worship, good Captain James.

Gow. How now, Captain Macmorris! have you quit the mines? have the pioners given o'er?

Mac. By Chrish, la! tish ill done: the work ish give over, the trompet sound the retreat. By my hand, I swear, and my father's soul, the work ish ill done; it ish give over: I would have blow'd up the town, so Chrish save me, la! in an hour: O, tish ill done, tish ill done; by my hand, tish ill done!

Flu. Captain Macmorris, I beseech you now, will you voutsafe me, look you, a few disputations with you, as partly touching or concerning the disciplines of the war, the Roman wars, in the way of argument, look you, and friendly communication; partly to satisfy my opinion, and partly for the satisfaction, look you, of my mind, as touching the direction of the military discipline; that is the point.

Jamy. It sall be vary gud, gud feith, gud captains bath: and I sall quit you[4] with gud leve, as I may pick occasion; that sall I, marry.

Mac. It is no time to discourse, so Chrish save me: the day is hot, and the weather, and the wars, and the king, and the dukes: it is no time to discourse. The town is beseech'd, and the trumpet calls us to the breach; and we talk, and, be Chrish, do nothing: 't is shame for us all: so God sa' me, 't is shame to stand still; it is shame, by my hand: and there is throats to be cut, and works to be done; and there ish nothing done, so Chrish sa' me, la!

Jamy. By the mess,[5] ere theise eyes of mine take themselves to slomber, ay'll do gud service, or ay'll lig i' the grund for it; ay, or go to death; and ay'll pay 't as valorously as I may, that sall I suerly do, that is the breff and the long.[6] Marry, I wad full fain hear some question 'tween you tway.

Flu. Captain Macmorris, I think, look you, under your correction, there is not many of your nation—

Mac. Of my nation! What ish my nation?

[1] *Carry coals*, put up with insults.
[2] *Plow up*, blow up.

[3] *God-den*, good evening.
[4] *Quit you*, answer you, requite you.
[5] *Mess*, mass.
[6] *The breff and the long*, i.e. the long and the short of it.

Ish a villain, and a bastard, and a knave, and a rascal. What ish my nation? Who talks of my nation?

Flu. Look you, if you take the matter otherwise than is meant, Captain Macmorris, peradventure I shall think you do not use me with that affability as in discretion you ought to use me, look you; being as good a man as yourself, both in the disciplines of war, and in the derivation of my birth, and in other particularities.

Mac. I do not know you so good a man as myself: so Chrish save me, I will cut off your head.

Gow. Gentlemen both, you will mistake each other.

Jamy. A! that's a foul fault.]

[*A parley sounded.*

Gow. The town sounds a parley.

[*Flu.* Captain Macmorris, when there is more better opportunity to be required, look you, I will be so bold as to tell you I know the disciplines of war; and there is an end.]

[*Exeunt.*

SCENE III. *The same. Before the gates.*

The Governor and some Citizens on the walls with a flag of truce; the English forces below. Enter KING HENRY *and his train.*

King. How yet resolves the governor of the town?
This is the latest parle[1] we will admit:
Therefore to our best mercy give yourselves;
Or like to men proud of destruction[2]
Defy us to our worst: for, as I am a soldier,
A name that in my thoughts becomes me best,
If I begin the battery once again,
I will not leave the half-achieved Harfleur
Till in her ashes she lie buried.
[The gates of mercy shall be all shut up,
And the flesh'd[3] soldier, rough and hard of heart,
In liberty of bloody hand shall range
With conscience wide as hell, mowing like grass
Your fresh-fair virgins and your flowering infants.
What is it then to me, if impious war,
Array'd in flames like to the prince of fiends,
Do, with his smirch'd complexion, all fell feats[4]
Enlink'd to waste and desolation?
What is't to me, when you yourselves are cause,
If your pure maidens fall into the hand
Of hot and forcing violation?
What rein can hold licentious wickedness
When down the hill he holds his fierce career?
We may as bootless spend our vain command
Upon th' enraged soldiers in their spoil
As send precepts[5] to the leviathan
To come ashore.] Therefore, you men of Harfleur,
Take pity of your town and of your people,
Whiles yet my soldiers are in my command;
[Whiles yet the cool and temperate wind of grace
O'erblows the filthy and contagious clouds
Of heady[6] murder, spoil and villany.
If not, why, in a moment look to see
The blind and bloody soldier with foul hand
Defile the locks of your shrill-shrieking daughters;
Your fathers taken by the silver beards,
And their most reverend heads dash'd to the walls,
Your naked infants spitted upon pikes,
Whiles the mad mothers with their howls confused
Do break the clouds, as did the wives of Jewry[7]
At Herod's bloody-hunting slaughtermen.]
What say you? will you yield, and this avoid,
Or, guilty in defence,[8] be thus destroy'd?

Gov. Our expectation hath this day an end:
The Dauphin, whom of succours we entreated,
Returns us[9] that his powers are yet not ready
To raise so great a siege. Therefore, great king,
We yield our town and lives to thy soft mercy.
Enter our gates; dispose of us and ours;
For we no longer are defensible.

King. Open your gates. [*The Governor and his train descend from walls.*] Come, uncle Exeter,

1 *Parle*, parley.
2 *Destruction*, metrically a quadrisyllable.
3 *Flesh'd*, fierce.
4 *Fell feats*, savage customs.
5 *Precepts*, accented on the second syllable.
6 *Heady*, impetuous, reckless.
7 *Jewry*, Judea.
8 *In defence*, in thus resisting.
9 *Returns us*, sends us back word.

Go you and enter Harfleur; there remain,
And fortify it strongly 'gainst the French:
Use mercy to them all. For us, dear uncle,
The winter coming on and sickness growing
Upon our soldiers, we 'll retire to Calais.
To-night in Harfleur we will be your guest;
To-morrow for the march are we addrest.[1]

[*Flourish. The King and his train enter the town.*

[SCENE IV. *Rouen. A room in the palace.*[2]

Enter KATHARINE *and* ALICE.

Kath. Alice, tu as été en Angleterre, et tu parles bien le langage.

Alice. Un peu, madame.

Kath. Je te prie, m'enseignez; il faut que j'apprenne à parler. Comment appelez-vous la main en Anglois?

Alice. La main? elle est appelée de hand.

Kath. De hand. *Et les doigts?*

Alice. Les doigts? ma foi, j'oublie les doigts; mais je me souviendrai. Les doigts? je pense qu'ils sont appelés de fingres; *oui,* de fingres.

Kath. La main, de hand; *les doigts,* de fingres. *Je pense que je suis le bon écolier; j'ai gagné deux mots d'Anglois vitement. Comment appelez-vous les ongles?*

Alice. Les ongles? nous les appelons de nails.

Kath. De nails. *Ecoutez; dites-moi, si je parle bien:* de hand, de fingres, *et* de nails.

Alice. C'est bien dit, madame; il est fort bon Anglois.

Kath. Dites-moi l'Anglois pour le bras.

Alice. De arm, *madame.*

Kath. Et le coude?

Alice. De elbow.

Kath. De elbow. *Je m'en fais la répétition de tous les mots que vous m'avez appris dès à présent.*

Alice. Il est trop difficile, madame, comme je pense.

Kath. Excusez-moi, Alice; écoutez: de hand, de fingres, de nails, de arm, de bilbow.

Alice. De elbow, *madame.*

Kath. O Seigneur Dieu, je m'en oublie! de elbow. *Comment appelez-vous le col?*

Alice. De neck, *madame.*

Kath. De nick. *Et le menton?*

Alice. De chin.

Kath. De sin. *Le col,* de nick; *de menton,* de sin.

Alice. Oui. Sauf votre honneur, en vérité, vous prononcez les mots aussi droit que les natifs d'Angleterre.

Kath. Je ne doute point d'apprendre, par la grace de Dieu, et en peu de temps.

Alice. N'avez-vous pas déjà oublié ce que je vous ai enseigné?

Kath. Non, je reciterai à vous promptement: de hand, de fingres, de mails,—

Alice. De nails, *madame.*

Kath. De nails, de arm, de ilbow.

Alice. Sauf votre honneur, de elbow.

Kath. Ainsi dis-je; de elbow, de nick, *et* de sin. *Comment appelez-vous le pied et la robe?*

Alice. De foot, madame; et de coun.

Kath. De foot *et* de coun! *O Seigneur Dieu! ce sont mots de son mauvais, corruptible, gros, et impudique, et non pour les dames d'honneur d'user: je ne voudrais prononcer ces mots devant les seigneurs de France pour tout le monde. Foh!* de foot *et* de coun! *Néanmoins, je reciterai une autre fois ma leçon ensemble:* de hand, de fingres, de nails, de arm, de elbow, de nick, de sin, de foot, de coun.

Alice. Excellent, madame!

Kath. C'est assez pour une fois: allons-nous à diner. [*Exeunt.*]

SCENE V. *The same. Another room in the palace.*

Enter the KING OF FRANCE, *the* DAUPHIN, *the* DUKE OF BOURBON, *the* CONSTABLE OF FRANCE, *and others.*

Fr. King. 'T is certain he hath pass'd the river Somme.
Con. And if he be not fought withal, my lord,
Let us not live in France; let us quit all
And give our vineyards to a barbarous people.
[*Dau. O Dieu vivant!* shall a few sprays of us,
The emptying of our father's luxury,[3]

[1] *Addrest*, prepared.
[2] The scene is translated in the notes, as the translation would be rather too long for insertion here.
[3] *Luxury*, lust.

Our scions, put in wild and savage[1] stock,
Spirt up so suddenly into the clouds,
And overlook their grafters?
Bour. Normans, but bastard Normans, Norman bastards!
Mort de ma vie! if they march along
Unfought withal, but I will sell my dukedom,
To buy a slobbery[2] and a dirty farm
In that nook-shotten isle of Albion.
Con. Dieu de batailles! where have they this mettle?
Is not their climate foggy, raw and dull,
On whom, as in despite, the sun looks pale,
Killing their fruit with frowns? Can sodden water,
A drench for sur-rein'd[3] jades, their barley-broth,[4]
Decoct their cold blood to such valiant heat?

Kath. Excusez-moi, Alice; écoutez: de hand, de fingres, de nails, de arm, de billow.—(Act iii. 4. 30, 31.)

And shall our quick blood, spirited with wine,
Seem frosty? O, for honour of our land,
Let us not hang like roping icicles
Upon our houses' thatch, whiles a more frosty people
Sweat drops of gallant youth in our rich fields!
Poor we may call them in their native lords.]
Dau. By faith and honour,
Our madams mock at us, and plainly say
Our mettle is bred out [and they will give
Their bodies to the lust of English youth
To new-store France with bastard warriors.]
Bour. They bid us to the English dancing-schools,
And teach lavoltas[5] high and swift corantos;[5]
Saying our grace is only in our heels,
And that we are most lofty runaways.
Fr. King. Where is Montjoy the herald? speed him hence:
Let him greet England with our sharp defiance.
Up, princes! and, with spirit of honour edg'd
[More sharper than your swords, hie to the field:
Charles Delabreth, high constable of France;

[1] *Savage*, uncultivated. [2] *Slobbery*, wet.
[3] *Sur-rein'd*, exhausted, overridden.
[4] *Barley-broth*, beer.

[5] *Lavoltas* and *corantos*, the names of certain lively dances.

You Dukes of Orleans, Bourbon, and of Berri,
Alençon, Brabant, Bar, and Burgundy;
Jaques Chatillon, Rambures, Vaudemont,
Beaumont, Grandpré, Roussi, and Fauconberg,
Foix, Lestrale, Bouciqualt, and Charolois;
High dukes, great princes, barons, lords, and knights,
For your great seats now quit you[1] of great shames.]
Bar Harry England,[2] that sweeps through our land
With pennons painted in the blood of Harfleur;
Rush on his host, as doth the melted snow
Upon the valleys, whose low vassal seat
The Alps doth spit and void his rheum upon:
Go down upon him, you have power enough,
And in a captive chariot into Rouen
Bring him our prisoner.

Con. This becomes the great.
Sorry am I his numbers are so few,
His soldiers sick and famish'd in their march,
For I am sure, when he shall see our army,
He'll drop his heart into the sink of fear
And for achievement offer us his ransom.

Fr. King. Therefore, lord constable, haste on Montjoy,
And let him say to England that we send
To know what willing ransom he will give.
Prince Dauphin, you shall stay with us in Rouen.

Dau. Not so, I do beseech your majesty.

Fr. King. Be patient, for you shall remain with us.
Now forth, lord constable and princes all,
And quickly bring us word of England's fall.
[*Exeunt.*

Scene VI. *The English camp in Picardy.*

Enter Gower *and* Fluellen, *meeting.*

Gow. How now, Captain Fluellen! come you from the bridge?

Flu. I assure you, there is very excellent services committed at the bridge.

Gow. Is the Duke of Exeter safe?

Flu. The Duke of Exeter is as magnanimous as Agamemnon; and a man that I love and honour with my soul, and my heart, and my duty, and my life, and my living, and my uttermost power: he is not—God be praised and blessed!—any hurt in the world; but keeps the bridge most valiantly, with excellent discipline. There is an aunchient there at the pridge, I think in my very conscience he is as valiant a man as Mark Antony; and he is a man of no estimation in the world; but I did see him do as gallant service.

Gow. What do you call him?

Flu. He is called Aunchient Pistol.

Gow. I know him not.

Enter Pistol.

Flu. Here is the man.

Pist. Captain, I thee beseech to do me favours:
The Duke of Exeter doth love thee well.

Flu. Ay, I praise God; and I have merited some love at his hands.

Pist. Bardolph, a soldier, firm and sound of heart,
Of buxom[3] valour, hath, by cruel fate,
And giddy fortune's furious fickle wheel,
That goddess blind,
That stands upon the rolling restless stone—

Flu. By your patience, Aunchient Pistol. Fortune is painted blind, with a muffler[4] afore her eyes, to signify to you, that Fortune is blind; and she is painted also with a wheel, to signify to you, which is the moral of it, that she is turning, and inconstant, and mutability, and variation: and her foot, look you, is fixed upon a spherical stone, which rolls, and rolls, and rolls: in good truth, the poet makes a most excellent description of it: Fortune is an excellent moral.

Pist. Fortune is Bardolph's foe, and frowns on him:
For he hath stolen a pax,[5] and hanged must a' be:
A damned death!
Let gallows gape for dog; let man go free
And let not hemp his wind-pipe suffocate:
But Exeter hath given the doom of death
For pax[5] of little price.

[1] *Quit you*, free yourselves.
[2] *Harry England*, i.e. Harry King of England.
[3] *Buxom*, lively.
[4] *Muffler*, bandage.
[5] *Pax*, a metal plate, with sacred figures on it, used in the Roman mass. See note 181.

Therefore, go speak: the duke will hear thy voice;
And let not Bardolph's vital thread be cut
With edge of penny cord and vile reproach:
Speak, captain, for his life, and I will thee requite.

Flu. Aunchient Pistol, I do partly understand your meaning.

Pist. Why then, rejoice therefóre.

Flu. Certainly, aunchient, it is not a thing to rejoice at: for if, look you, he were my brother, I would desire the duke to use his good pleasure, and put him to execution; for discipline ought to be used.

Pist. Die and be damn'd! and figo for thy friendship!

Pist. Die and be damn'd! and figo for thy friendship!
Flu. It is well.
Pist. The fig of Spain!
Flu. Very good.—(Act iii. 6. 59-63.)

Flu. It is well.

Pist. The fig of Spain! [*Exit.*

Flu. Very good.

Gow. Why, this is an arrant counterfeit rascal; I remember him now; a bawd, a cutpurse.

Flu. I'll assure you, a' utt'red as brave words at the bridge as you shall see in a summer's day. But it is very well; what he has spoke to me, that is well, I warrant you, when time is serve.

Gow. Why, 't is a gull, a fool, a rogue, that now and then goes to the wars, to grace himself at his return into London under the form of a soldier. And such fellows are perfect in the great commanders' names: and they will learn you by rote where services were done; at such and such a sconce,[1] at such a breach, at such a convoy; who came off bravely, who was shot, who disgrac'd, what terms the enemy stood on; and this they con perfectly in the phrase of war, which they trick up with new-tuned oaths: and what a beard of the general's cut and a horrid suit of the camp will do among foaming bottles and ale-wash'd wits, is wonderful to be thought on. But you must learn to know such slanders of the age, or else you may be marvellously mistook.

Flu. I tell you what, Captain Gower; I do perceive he is not the man that he would

[1] *Sconce*, bulwark

gladly make show to the world he is: if I find a hole in his coat, I will tell him my mind. [*Drum heard.*] Hark you, the king is coming, and I must speak with him from the pridge.

Enter KING HENRY, GLOUCESTER, *and Soldiers.*

God pless your majesty!

King. How now, Fluellen, cam'st thou from the bridge?

Flu. Ay, so please your majesty. The Duke of Exeter has very gallantly maintained the pridge: the French is gone off, look you; and there is gallant and most prave passages;[1] marry, th' athversary was have possession of the pridge; but he is enforced to retire, and the Duke of Exeter is master of the pridge: I can tell your majesty, the duke is a prave man.

King. What men have you lost, Fluellen?

Flu. The perdition of th' athversary hath been very great, reasonable great: marry, for my part, I think the duke hath lost never a man, but one that is like to be executed for robbing a church, one Bardolph, if your majesty know the man: his face is all bubukles,[2] and whelks,[3] and knobs, and flames o' fire: and his lips blows at his nose, and it is like a coal of fire, sometimes plue and sometimes red; but his nose is executed, and his fire's out.

King. We would have all such offenders so cut off: and we give express charge, that in our marches through the country, there be nothing compell'd[4] from the villages, nothing taken but paid for, none of the French upbraided or abused in disdainful language; for when lenity and cruelty play for a kingdom, the gentler gamester is the soonest winner.

Tucket. *Enter* MONTJOY.

Mont. You know me by my habit.[5]

King. Well then I know thee: what shall I know of thee?[6]

Mont. My master's mind.

King. Unfold it.

Mont. Thus says my king: Say thou to Harry of England: Though we seem'd dead, we did but sleep: advantage[7] is a better soldier than rashness. Tell him we could have rebuk'd him at Harfleur, but that we thought not good to bruise an injury till it were full ripe: now we speak upon our cue,[8] and our voice is imperial: England shall repent his folly, see his weakness, and admire our sufferance. Bid him therefore consider of his ransom; which must proportion[9] the losses we have borne, the subjects we have lost, the disgrace we have digested,[10] which in weight to re-answer,[11] his pettiness would bow under. For our losses, his exchequer is too poor; for the effusion of our blood, the muster of his kingdom too faint a number; and for our disgrace, his own person, kneeling at our feet, but a weak and worthless satisfaction. To this add defiance: and tell him, for conclusion, he hath betrayed his followers, whose condemnation is pronounc'd. So far my king and master; so much my office.

King. What is thy name? I know thy quality.[12]

Mont. Montjoy.

King. Thou dost thy office fairly. Turn thee back,
And tell thy king I do not seek him now;
But could be willing to march on to Calais
Without impeachment:[13] for, to say the sooth,
Though 't is no wisdom to confess so much
Unto an enemy of craft and vantage,[14]
My people are with sickness much enfeebl'd,
My numbers lessen'd, and those few I have
Almost no better than so many French;
Who when they were in health, I tell thee, herald,
I thought upon one pair of English legs
Did march three Frenchmen. Yet, forgive me, God,
That I do brag thus! This your air of France
Hath blown that vice in me; I must repent.
Go therefore, tell thy master here I am;
My ransom is this frail and worthless trunk,

[1] *Passages*, acts, occurrences.
[2] *Bubukles*=carbuncles. [3] *Whelks*, pimples.
[4] *Compell'd*, taken by force.
[5] *Habit*, i.e. his herald's dress.
[6] *Of thee*, from thee.

[7] *Advantage*, opportunity. [8] *Upon our cue*, in our turn.
[9] *Proportion*, correspond to. [10] *Digested*, put up with.
[11] *In weight to re-answer*, fully to make up for.
[12] *Quality*, profession.
[13] *Impeachment*, hinderance (Fr. *empêchement*).
[14] *Of craft and vantage*, wily and favoured by circumstances.

My army but a weak and sickly guard;
Yet, God before, tell him we will come on,
Though France himself and such another neighbour
Stand in our way. There's for thy labour, Montjoy.
Go, bid thy master well advise himself:
If we may pass, we will; if we be hinder'd,
We shall your tawny ground with your red blood
Discolour: and so, Montjoy, fare you well.
The sum of all our answer is but this:
We would not seek a battle, as we are;
Nor, as we are, we say we will not shun it:
So tell your master.

Mont. I shall deliver so.[1] Thanks to your highness. [*Exit.*

Glo. I hope they will not come upon us now.

King. We are in God's hand, brother, not in theirs.
March to the bridge; it now draws towards night:
Beyond the river we'll encamp ourselves,
And on to-morrow bid them march away. [*Exeunt.*

SCENE VII. *The French camp, near Agincourt.*

Enter the CONSTABLE OF FRANCE, *the* LORD RAMBURES, DUKE OF ORLEANS, DAUPHIN, *with others.*

Con. Tut! I have the best armour of the world. Would it were day!

Orl. You have an excellent armour; but let my horse have his due.

Con. It is the best horse of Europe.

Orl. Will it never be morning?

[*Dau.* My lord of Orleans, and my lord high constable, you talk of horse and armour?

Orl. You are as well provided of both as any prince in the world.

Dau. What a long night this is! I will not change my horse with any that treads but on four pasterns. *Ça, ha!* he bounds from the earth, as if his entrails were hairs; *le cheval volant,*[2] the Pegasus, *qui a les narines de feu!*[3] When I bestride him, I soar, I am a hawk: he trots the air; the earth sings when he touches it; the basest horn of his hoof is more musical than the pipe of Hermes.[4]

Orl. He's of the colour of the nutmeg.

Dau. And of the heat of the ginger. It is a beast for Perseus: he is pure air and fire; and the dull elements of earth and water never appear in him, but only in patient stillness while his rider mounts him: he is indeed a horse; and all other jades you may call beasts.

Con. Indeed, my lord, it is a most absolute[5] and excellent horse.

Dau. It is the prince of palfreys; his neigh is like the bidding of a monarch and his countenance enforces homage.

Orl. No more, cousin.

Dau. Nay, the man hath no wit that cannot, from the rising of the lark to the lodging of the lamb, vary deserved praise on my palfrey; it is a theme as fluent as the sea; turn the sands into eloquent tongues, and my horse is argument[6] for them all: 't is a subject for a sovereign to reason on, and for a sovereign's sovereign to ride on; and for the world, familiar to us and unknown, to lay apart their particular functions and wonder at him. I once writ a sonnet in his praise and began thus: "Wonder of nature,"—

Orl. I have heard a sonnet begin so to one's mistress.

Dau. Then did they imitate that which I composed to my courser, for my horse is my mistress.

Orl. Your mistress bears well.

Dau. Me well; which is the prescript[7] praise and perfection of a good and particular mistress.

Con. Nay, for methought yesterday your mistress shrewdly[8] shook your back.

Dau. So perhaps did yours.

Con. Mine was not bridled.

Dau. O then belike she was old and gentle; and you rode, like a kern of Ireland, your French hose off, and in your strait strossers.[9]

Con. You have good judgment in horsemanship.

[1] *Deliver so*, say so.
[2] "The flying horse."
[3] "Which has nostrils of fire," *i.e.* fiery nostrils.
[4] *Hermes*, Mercury (his Greek name).
[5] *Absolute*, without a fault.
[6] *Argument*, subject.
[7] *Prescript*, usual.
[8] *Shrewdly*, unquestionably.
[9] *Strossers*, tight dresses or breeches.

Dau. Be warned by me, then: they that ride so and ride not warily, fall into foul bogs. I had rather have my horse to my mistress.

Con. I had as lief have my mistress a jade.

Dau. I tell thee, constable, my mistress wears his own hair.

Con. I could make as true a boast as that, if I had a sow to my mistress.

Dau. *Le chien est retourné à son propre vomissement, et la truie lavée au bourbier:*[1] thou makest use of any thing.

Con. Yet do I not use my horse for my mistress, or any such proverb so little kin to the purpose.

Ram. My lord constable, the armour that I saw in your tent to-night, are those stars or suns upon it?

Con. Stars, my lord.

Dau. Some of them will fall to-morrow, I hope.

Con. And yet my sky shall not want.

Dau. That may be, for you bear a many superfluously, and 't were more honour some were away.

Con. Even as your horse bears your praises: who would trot as well, were some of your brags dismounted.

Dau. Would I were able to load him with his desert! Will it never be day? I will trot to-morrow a mile, and my way shall be paved with English faces.

Con. I will not say so, for fear I should be faced out of my way: but I would it were morning; for I would fain be about the ears of the English.]

Ram. Who will go to hazard with me for twenty prisoners?

Con. You must first go yourself to hazard, ere you have them.

Dau. 'T is midnight; I 'll go arm myself. [*Exit.*

Orl. The Dauphin longs for morning.

Ram. He longs to eat the English.

Con. I think he will eat all he kills.

Orl. By the white hand of my lady, he 's a gallant prince.

[*Con.* Swear by her foot, that she may tread out the oath.

Orl. He is simply the most active gentleman of France.

Con. Doing is activity; and he will still be doing.

Orl. He never did harm, that I heard of.

Con. Nor will do none to-morrow: he will keep that good name still.

Orl.] I know him to be valiant.

Con. I was told that by one who knows him better than you.

Orl. What 's he?

Con. Marry, he told me so himself; and he said he cared not who knew it.

Orl. He needs not; it is no hidden virtue in him.

Con. By my faith, sir, but it is; never any body saw it but his lackey:[2] 't is a hooded valour; and when it appears, it will bate.[3]

[*Orl.* Ill will never said well.

Con. I will cap that proverb with—There is flattery in friendship.

Orl. And I will take up that with—Give the devil his due.

Con. Well placed: there stands your friend for the devil: have at the very eye of that proverb, with—A pox of the devil.

Orl. You are the better at proverbs, by how much—A fool's bolt[4] is soon shot.

Con. You have shot over.

Orl. 'T is not the first time you were overshot.]

Enter a Messenger.

Mess. My lord high constable, the English lie within fifteen hundred paces of your tents.

Con. Who hath measured the ground?

Mess. The Lord Grandpré.

Con. A valiant and most expert gentleman. Would it were day! Alas, poor Harry of England! he longs not for the dawning as we do.

Orl. What a wretched and peevish[5] fellow is this king of England, to mope with his fat-brain'd[6] followers so far out of his knowledge!

Con. If the English had any apprehension,[7] they would run away.

[1] *i.e.* "the dog is returned to his own vomit, and the washed sow to the mire."

[2] *But his lackey*, *i.e.* the only person he has had courage to beat is his lackey. [3] *Bate*, *i.e.* flutter, like a hawk.

[4] *Bolt*, a blunt-headed arrow.

[5] *Peevish*, foolish. [6] *Fat-brain'd*, stupid.

[7] *Apprehension*, intelligence.

Orl. That they lack; for if their heads had any intellectual armour, they could never wear such heavy head-pieces.

Ram. That island of England breeds very valiant creatures; their mastiffs are of unmatchable courage.

Orl. Foolish curs, that run winking into the mouth of a Russian bear, and have their heads crushed like rotten apples! You may as well say, that 's a valiant flea that dare eat his breakfast on the lip of a lion.

Con. Just, just; and the men do sympathize with the mastiffs in robustious[1] and rough coming on, leaving their wits with their wives: and then give them great meals of beef and iron and steel, they will eat like wolves and fight like devils.

Orl. Ay, but these English are shrewdly[2] out of beef.

Con. Then shall we find to-morrow they have only stomachs to eat and none to fight. Now it is time to arm: come, shall we about it?

Orl. It is now two o'clock: but, let me see, —by ten
We shall have each a hundred Englishmen.
[*Exeunt.*

ACT IV.

PROLOGUE.

Enter Chorus.

Chor. Now entertain conjecture of a time
When creeping murmur and the poring[3] dark
Fills the wide vessel of the universe.
From camp to camp through the foul womb of night
The hum of either army stilly[4] sounds,
That the fix'd sentinels almost receive
The secret whispers of each other's watch:
Fire answers fire, and through their paly flames
Each battle sees the other's umber'd face;
Steed threatens steed, in high and boastful neighs
Piercing the night's dull ear, and from the tents
The armourers, accomplishing[5] the knights,
With busy hammers closing rivets up,
Give dreadful note of preparation:
The country cocks do crow, the clocks do toll,
And the third hour of drowsy morning name.
Proud of their numbers, and secure in soul,
The confident and over-lusty[6] French
Do the low-rated English play at dice;
And chide the cripple tardy-gaited night
Who, like a foul and ugly witch, doth limp
So tediously away. The poor condemned English,
Like sacrifices, by their watchful fires
Sit patiently, and inly ruminate
The morning's danger, and their gesture sad
Investing lank-lean cheeks and war-worn coats
Presenteth them unto the gazing moon
So many horrid ghosts. O now, who will behold
The royal captain of this ruin'd band
Walking from watch to watch, from tent to tent,
Let him cry "Praise and glory on his head!"
For forth he goes and visits all his host,
Bids them good morrow with a modest smile
And calls them brothers, friends and countrymen.
Upon his royal face there is no note[7]
How dread an army hath enrounded[8] him,
Nor doth he dedicate one jot of colour
Unto the weary and all-watched[9] night,
But freshly looks and over-bears attaint[10]
With cheerful semblance and sweet majesty;
That every wretch, pining and pale before,
Beholding him, plucks comfort from his looks:
A largess universal like the sun
His liberal eye doth give to every one,
Thawing cold fear, that mean and gentle all,
Behold, as may unworthiness define,
A little touch of Harry in the night.
And so our scene must to the battle fly;

---

1 *Robustious*, sturdy.
2 *Shrewdly*, assuredly.
3 *Poring*, purblind.
4 *Stilly*, softly.
5 *Accomplishing*, furnishing.
6 *Over-lusty*, over merry.
7 *No note*, nothing to show.
8 *Enrounded*, surrounded.
9 *All-watched*, spent in watching.
10 *Over-bears attaint*, conceals his anxiety.

Where—O for pity!—we shall much disgrace
[With four or five most vile and ragged foils,[1]
Right ill-dispos'd in brawl ridiculous,]
The name of Agincourt. Yet sit and see,
Minding[2] true things by what their mockeries be. [*Exit.*

SCENE I. *The English camp at Agincourt. Night.*

Enter KING HENRY *and* GLOUCESTER.

King. Gloucester, 't is true that we are in great danger;
The greater therefore should our courage be.

Chor. Proud of their numbers, and secure in soul,
The confident and over-lusty French
Do the low-rated English play at dice.—(Act iv. Prol. 17-19.)

Enter BEDFORD.

Good morrow, brother Bedford.—[God Almighty!]
There is some soul of goodness in things evil,
Would men observingly distil it out.
For our bad neighbour makes us early stirrers,
Which is both healthful and good husbandry:
[Besides, they are our outward consciences,
And preachers to us all, admonishing
That we should dress us[3] fairly for our end.
Thus may we gather honey from the weed,
And make a moral of the devil himself.]

Enter ERPINGHAM.

Good morrow, old Sir Thomas Erpingham:
A good soft pillow for that good white head
Were better than a churlish turf of France.

Erp. Not so, my liege: this lodging likes me better,
Since I may say, "Now lie I like a king."

King. 'T is good for men to love their present pains
Upon example; so the spirit is eas'd;
[And when the mind is quicken'd, out of doubt,
The organs, though defunct and dead before,

[1] *Foils*, swordsmen.
[2] *Minding*, thinking of.
[3] *Dress us*, prepare ourselves.

Break up their drowsy grave and newly move,
With casted slough and fresh legerity.[1]]
Lend me thy cloak, Sir Thomas. Brothers both,
Commend me to the princes in our camp;
Do my good morrow to them, and anon
Desire[2] them all to my pavilion.

Glo. We shall, my liege.

[*Exeunt Gloucester and Bedford.*

Erp. Shall I attend your grace?

King. No, my good knight;
Go with my brothers to my lords of England:
I and my bosom must debate a while,
And then I would no other company.

Erp. The Lord in heaven bless thee, noble Harry! [*Exit Erpingham.*

King. God-a-mercy,[3] old heart! thou speak'st cheerfully.

Enter PISTOL.

Pist. *Qui va là?*[4]

King. A friend.

Pist. Discuss unto me; art thou officer?
Or art thou base, common, and popular?[5]

King. I am a gentleman of a company.

Pist. Trail'st thou the puissant pike?

King. Even so. What are you?

Pist. As good a gentleman as the emperor.

King. Then you are a better than the king.

Pist. The king 's a bawcock,[6] and a heart of gold,
A lad of life, an imp[7] of fame;
Of parents good, of fist most valiant,
I kiss his dirty shoe, and from heart-string
I love the lovely bully.—What is thy name?

King. Harry *le Roi.*

Pist. Le Roy! a Cornish name: art thou of
Cornish crew?

King. No, I am a Welshman.

Pist. Know'st thou Fluellen?

King. Yes.

Pist. Tell him, I'll knock his leek about his pate
Upon Saint Davy's day.

King. Do not wear your dagger in your cap that day, lest he knock that about yours.

Pist. Art thou his friend?

King. And his kinsman too.

Pist. The *figo*[8] for thee, then!

King. I thank you: God be with you!

Pist. My name is Pistol call'd. [*Exit.*

King. It sorts[9] well with your fierceness.

Enter FLUELLEN *and* GOWER.

Gow. Captain Fluellen!

Flu. So! in the name of Cheshu Christ, speak lower. It is the greatest admiration in the universal 'orld, when the true and auncient prerogatifs and laws of the wars is not kept: if you would take the pains but to examine the wars of Pompey the Great, you shall find, I warrant you, that there is no tiddle-taddle[10] nor pibble-pabble[11] in Pompey's camp; I warrant you, you shall find the ceremonies of the wars, and the cares of it, and the forms of it, and the sobriety of it, and the modesty of it, to be otherwise.

Gow. Why, the enemy is loud; you hear him all night.

Flu. If the enemy is an ass and a fool and a prating coxcomb, is it meet, think you, that we should also, look you, be an ass and a fool and a prating coxcomb? in your own conscience, now?

Gow. I will speak lower.

Flu. I pray you and peseech you that you will. [*Exeunt Gower and Fluellen.*

King. Though it appear a little out of fashion,
There is much care and valour in this Welshman.

Enter three Soldiers, JOHN BATES, ALEXANDER COURT, *and* MICHAEL WILLIAMS.

Court. Brother John Bates, is not that the morning which breaks yonder?

Bates. I think it be: but we have no great cause to desire the approach of day.

Will. We see yonder the beginning of the day, but I think we shall never see the end of it. Who goes there?

[1] *Legerity*, alacrity (Fr. *légèreté*).
[2] *Desire*, invite.
[3] *God a-mercy*, God have mercy.
[4] *Qui va là?* "who goes there?"
[5] *Popular*, plebeian.
[6] *Bawcock*, from Fr. *beau coq.* = fine cock.
[7] *Imp*, youngster.

[8] *Figo*, a gesture of contempt.
[9] *Sorts*, agrees.
[10] *Tiddle-taddle* = tittle-tattle.
[11] *Pibble-pabble*, a coined word = idle prattle.

King. A friend.

Will. Under what captain serve you?

King. Under Sir Thomas Erpingham.

Will. A good old commander and a most kind gentleman: I pray you, what thinks he of our estate?

King. What are you?
Pist. As good a gentleman as the emperor.—(Act iv. 1. 41, 42.)

King. Even as men wreck'd upon a sand, that look to be wash'd off the next tide.

Bates. He hath not told his thought to the king?

King. No; nor it is not meet he should. For, though I speak it to you, I think the king is but a man, as I am: the violet smells to him as it doth to me; the element[1] shows to him as it doth to me; all his senses have but human conditions:[2] his ceremonies laid by, in his nakedness he appears but a man; and though his affections are higher mounted than ours, yet, when they stoop, they stoop with the like wing. Therefore when he sees reason of fears, as we do, his fears, out of doubt, be of the same relish as ours are: yet, in reason, no man should possess him with any appearance of fear, lest he, by showing it, should dishearten his army.

Bates. He may show what outward courage he will; but I believe, as cold a night as 't is, he could wish himself in Thames up to the neck;—and so I would he were, and I by him, at all adventures, so we were quit here.

King. By my troth, I will speak my conscience[3] of the king: I think he would not wish himself any where but where he is.

Bates. Then I would he were here alone; so should he be sure to be ransomed, and a many poor men's lives saved.

King. I dare say you love him not so ill, to wish[4] him here alone, howsoever you speak this to feel other men's minds: methinks I could not die any where so contented as in the king's company; his cause being just, and his quarrel honourable.

Will. That's more than we know.

Bates. Ay, or more than we should seek after; for we know enough, if we know we are the king's subjects: if his cause be wrong, our obedience to the king wipes the crime of it out of us.

Will. But if the cause be not good, the king himself hath a heavy reckoning to make, when all those legs and arms and heads, chopp'd off in a battle, shall join together at the latter[5] day and cry all "We died at such a place;" some swearing, some crying for a surgeon, some upon their wives left poor behind them, some upon the debts they owe, some upon their children rawly left.[6] I am afeard[7] there are few die well that die in a battle; for how can they charitably dispose of any thing, when blood is their argument? Now, if these men

[1] *Element*, the sky.

[2] *Conditions*, qualities.

[3] *My conscience*, my opinion.

[4] *To wish*, as to wish.

[5] *Latter*, last.

[6] *Rawly left*, i.e. prematurely left alone, or, perhaps, left unprovided for.

[7] *Afeard*, afraid.

do not die well, it will be a black matter for the king that led them to it; whom to disobey were against all proportion of subjection.[1]

King. So, if a son that is by his father sent about merchandise do sinfully miscarry upon the sea,[2] the imputation of his wickedness, by your rule, should be imposed upon his father that sent him: [or if a servant, under his master's command transporting a sum of money, be assailed by robbers and die in many irreconcil'd iniquities, you may call the business of the master the author of the servant's damnation:] but this is not so: the king is not bound to answer the particular endings of his soldiers, the father of his son, nor the master of his servant; for they purpose not their death, when they purpose their services. [Besides, there is no king, be his cause never so spotless, if it come to the arbitrement of swords, can try it out with all unspotted soldiers: some peradventure have on them the guilt of premeditated and contrived[3] murder; some, of beguiling virgins with the broken seals of perjury; some, making the wars their bulwark, that have before gored the gentle bosom of peace with pillage and robbery. Now, if these men have defeated the law and outrun native[4] punishment, though they can outstrip men, they have no wings to fly from God: war is his beadle, war is his vengeance; so that here men are punish'd for before-breach of the king's laws in now the king's quarrel: where they feared the death, they have borne life away; and where they would be safe, they perish: then if they die unprovided, no more is the king guilty of their damnation than he was before guilty of those impieties for the which they are now visited.] Every subject's duty is the king's; but every subject's soul is his own. Therefore should every soldier in the wars do as every sick man in his bed, wash every mote out of his conscience: and dying so, death is to him advantage; or not dying, the time was blessedly lost wherein such preparation was gained: and in him that escapes, it were not sin to think that, making God so free an offer, He let him outlive that day to see his greatness and to teach others how they should prepare.

Will. 'T is certain, every man that dies ill, the ill upon his own head, the king is not to answer it.

Bates. I do not desire he should answer for me; and yet I determine to fight lustily for him.

King. I myself heard the king say he would not be ransom'd.

Will. Ay, he said so, to make us fight cheerfully: but when our throats are cut, he may be ransom'd, and we ne'er the wiser.

King. If I live to see it, I will never trust his word after.

Will. You pay him then. That 's a perilous shot out of an elder-gun[5] that a poor and a private displeasure can do against a monarch! you may as well go about[6] to turn the sun to ice with fanning in his face with a peacock's feather. You'll never trust his word after! come, 't is a foolish saying.

King. Your reproof is something too round:[7] I should be angry with you, if the time were convenient.

Will. Let it be a quarrel between us, if you live.

King. I embrace it.

Will. How shall I know thee again?

King. Give me any gage of thine, and I will wear it in my bonnet: then, if ever thou dar'st acknowledge it, I will make it my quarrel.

Will. Here 's my glove: give me another of thine.

King. There.

Will. This will I also wear in my cap: if ever thou come to me and say, after to-morrow, "This is my glove," by this hand, I will take thee[8] a box on the ear.

King. If ever I live to see it, I will challenge it.

Will. Thou dar'st as well be hanged.

King. Well, I will do it, though I take[9] thee in the king's company.

Will. Keep thy word: fare thee well.

---

[1] *Proportion of subjection*, reasonable service.
[2] *Miscarry upon the sea*, be lost at sea.
[3] *Contrived*, preconcerted.
[4] *Native*, in their own country.
[5] *Elder-gun*, pop-gun.
[6] *Go about*, undertake.
[7] *Too round*, too blunt, too plain-spoken.
[8] *I will take thee, i.e.* as we say, I will take and give thee.
[9] *Take*, catch, find.

Bates. Be friends, you English fools, be friends: we have French quarrels enow,[1] if you could tell how to reckon.

[*King.* Indeed, the French may lay twenty French crowns to one, they will beat us; for

King. O hard condition,
Twin-born with greatness, subject to the breath
Of every fool, whose sense no more can feel
But his own wringing!—(Act iv. 1. 250-253.)

they bear them on their shoulders: but it is no English treason to cut French crowns, and to-morrow the king himself will be a clipper.]

[*Exeunt the three Soldiers.*

Upon the king! let us our lives, our souls,
Our debts, our careful[2] wives,
Our children and our sins lay on the king!
We must bear all. O hard condition,[3]
Twin-born with greatness, subject to the breath
Of every fool, whose sense no more can feel
But his own wringing![4] What infinite heart's-ease
Must kings neglect, that private men enjoy!
And what have kings, that privates have not too,
Save ceremony, save general ceremony?
And what art thou, thou idol ceremony?
[What kind of God art thou, that suffer'st more
Of mortal griefs than do thy worshippers?
What are thy rents? what are thy comings in?
O ceremony, show me but thy worth!
What is thy soul of adoration?]
Art thou aught else but place, degree and form,
Creating awe and fear in other men?
Wherein thou art less happy being fear'd
Than they in fearing.
[What drink'st thou oft, instead of homage sweet,
But poison'd flattery? O, be sick, great greatness,]
And bid thy ceremony give thee cure!
[Think'st thou the fiery fever will go out
With titles blown from adulation?
Will it give place to flexure and low bending?]
Canst thou, when thou command'st the beggar's knee,
Command the health of it? No, thou proud dream,
That play'st so subtly with a king's repose;
I am a king that find thee, and I know
'T is not the balm,[5] the sceptre and the ball,
The sword, the mace, the crown imperial,
[The intertissu'd robe of gold and pearl,
The farced title running 'fore the king,]
The throne he sits on, nor the tide of pomp
That beats upon the high shore of this world.
No, not all these, thrice-gorgeous ceremony,
Not all these, laid in bed majestical,
Can sleep so soundly as the wretched slave,
Who with a body fill'd and vacant mind
Gets him to rest, cramm'd with distressful[6] bread;
[Never sees horrid night, the child of hell,

---

[1] *Enow*, enough (used with plural nouns).
[2] *Careful*, anxious.
[3] *Condition*, metrically a quadrisyllable.
[4] *Wringing*, suffering.
[5] *Balm*, the anointing oil used at coronations.
[6] *Distressful*, laboriously earned.

But, like a lackey, from the rise to set
Sweats in the eye of Phœbus and all night
Sleeps in Elysium; next day after dawn,
Doth rise and help Hyperion to his horse,[1]
And follows so the ever-running year,
With profitable labour, to his grave:]
And, but for ceremony, such a wretch,
Winding up days with toil and nights with sleep,
Had the fore-hand and vantage of a king.
[The slave, a member of the country's peace,
Enjoys it; but in gross brain little wots[2]
What watch the king keeps to maintain the peace,
Whose hours the peasant best advantages.[3]]

Enter ERPINGHAM.

Erp. My lord, your nobles, jealous of your absence,
Seek through your camp to find you.
King. Good old knight,
Collect them all together at my tent:
I'll be before thee.
Erp. I shall do't, my lord. [*Exit.*
King. [*Kneeling*] O God of battles! steel my soldiers' hearts;
Possess them not with fear; take from them now
The sense of reckoning, if th' opposed numbers
Pluck their hearts from them. Not to-day, O Lord,
O, not to-day, think not upon the fault
My father made in compassing the crown!
I Richard's body have interred new;
And on it have bestow'd more contrite tears
Than from it issu'd forced drops of blood:
Five hundred poor I have in yearly pay,
Who twice a-day their wither'd hands hold up
Towards heaven, to pardon blood; and I have built
Two chantries, where the sad[4] and solemn priests
Sing still[5] for Richard's soul. More will I do;
Though all that I can do is nothing worth,
Since that my penitence comes after all,
Imploring pardon.

Enter GLOUCESTER.

Glo. My liege! [*The King rises.*]
King. My brother Gloucester's voice? Ay;
I know thy errand, I will go with thee:
The day, my friends and all things stay for me. [*Exeunt.*

SCENE II. *The French camp. Sunrise.*

Enter the DAUPHIN, ORLEANS, RAMBURES, *and others.*

Orl. The sun doth gild our armour; up, my lords!
Dau. *Montez à cheval!* My horse! *varlet!*[6] *laquais!* ha!
Orl. O brave spirit!
Dau. *Via! les eaux et la terre,—*
Orl. *Rien puis? l'air et le feu,—*
Dau. *Ciel!* cousin Orleans.

Enter CONSTABLE.

Now, my lord constable!
Con. Hark, how our steeds for present service neigh!
Dau. Mount them, and make incision in their hides,
That their hot blood may spin in English eyes,
And dout[7] them with superfluous courage, ha!
Ram. What, will you have them weep our horses' blood?
How shall we, then, behold their natural tears?

Enter Messenger.

Mess. The English are embattled,[8] you French peers.
Con. To horse, you gallant princes! straight to horse!
Do but behold yon poor and starved band,
[And your fair show shall suck away their souls,
Leaving them but the shales[9] and husks of men.]
There is not work enough for all our hands;
Scarce blood enough in all their sickly veins
To give each naked curtle-axe[10] a stain,
[That our French gallants shall to-day draw out,

[1] *Help Hyperion to his horse*, is up before sunrise.
[2] *Wots*, knows.
[3] *The peasant best advantages*, i.e. benefit the peasant most.
[4] *Sad*, serious, grave.
[5] *Still*, constantly.

[6] *Varlet* (Old French) = page.
[7] *Dout*, do out, i.e. extinguish.
[8] *Embattled*, i.e. in battle array.
[9] *Shales*, shells.
[10] *Curtle-axe*, cutlass.

And sheath for lack of sport: let us but blow on them,
The vapour of our valour will o'erturn them.]
'T is positive 'gainst all exceptions, lords,
That our superfluous lackeys [and our peasants,
Who in unnecessary action swarm
About our squares[1] of battle,] were enow
To purge this field of such a hilding[2] foe,
Though we upon this mountain's basis by
Took stand for idle speculation:
But that our honours must not. What 's to say?
A very little little let us do,
And all is done. Then let the trumpets sound
The tucket sonance[3] and the note to mount;
For our approach shall so much dare the field
That England shall couch down in fear and yield.

Enter GRANDPRÉ.

Grand. Why do you stay so long, my lords of France?
Yon island carrions, desperate of their bones,[4]
Ill-favour'dly become the morning field:
Their ragged curtains[5] poorly are let loose,
And our air shakes them passing scornfully:
Big Mars seems bankrupt in their beggar'd host
And faintly through a rusty beaver[6] peeps:
[The horsemen sit like fixed candlesticks,
With torch-staves in their hand; and their poor jades
Lob[7] down their heads, dropping the hides and hips,
The gum down-roping[8] from their pale-dead eyes,
And in their pale dull mouths the gimmal bit[9]
Lies foul with chew'd grass, still and motionless;]
And their executors, the knavish crows,
Fly o'er them, all impatient for their hour.
[Description cannot suit itself in words
To demonstrate the life of such a battle
In life so lifeless as it shows itself.]

Con. They 've said their prayers, and they stay for death.

Dau. Shall we go send them dinners and fresh suits
And give their fasting horses provender,
And after fight with them?

Con. I stay but for my guidon:[10] to the field!
I will the banner from a trumpet take,
And use it for my haste. Come, come, away!
The sun is high, and we outwear[11] the day.
[*Exeunt.*

SCENE III. *The English camp.*

Enter the English host; GLOUCESTER, BEDFORD, EXETER, SALISBURY *and* WESTMORELAND.

Glo. Where is the king?

Bed. The king himself is rode to view their battle.

West. Of fighting men they have full three score thousand.

Exe. There 's five to one; besides, they all are fresh.

Sal. God's arm strike with us! 't is a fearful odds.
God be wi' you, princes all; I 'll to my charge:
If we no more meet till we meet in heaven,
Then, joyfully, my noble Lord of Bedford,
My dear Lord Gloucester, and my good Lord Exeter,
And my kind kinsman, warriors all, adieu!

Bed. Farewell, good Salisbury; and good luck go with thee!

[*Exe.* Farewell, kind lord; fight valiantly to-day:
And yet I do thee wrong to mind[12] thee of it,
For thou art fram'd of the firm truth of valour.]
[*Exit Salisbury.*

Bed. He is as full of valour as of kindness;
Princely in both.

Enter the KING.

West. O that we now had here
But one ten thousand of those men in England
That do no work to-day!

King. What 's he that wishes so?
My cousin Westmoreland? No, my fair cousin:
If we are mark'd to die, we are enow[13]
To do our country loss; and if to live,

1 *Squares*, squadrons. 2 *Hilding*, base, cowardly.
3 *The tucket sonance*, a flourish on a trumpet.
4 *Desperate of their bones*, reckless of their fate.
5 *Ragged curtains*, torn banners.
6 *Beaver*, the visor of a helmet. 7 *Lob*, hang heavily.
8 *Down-roping*, i.e. dripping down (Fr. *roupie*).
9 *Gimmal bit*, a bit with double rings.

10 *Guidon*, ensign, standard.
11 *We outwear*, we are wasting.
12 *Mind*, remind. 13 *Enow*, enough.

The fewer men, the greater share of honour.
God's will! I pray thee, wish not one man more.
By Jove, I am not covetous for gold,
Nor care I who doth feed upon my cost;
It yearns[1] me not if men my garments wear;
Such outward things dwell not in my desires:
But if it be a sin to covet honour,
I am the most offending soul alive.
No, faith, my coz, wish not a man from England:
God's peace! I would not lose so great an honour
As one man more, methinks, would share from me
For the best hope I have. O, do not wish one more!
Rather proclaim it, Westmoreland, through my host,

King. I pray thee, bear my former answer back:
Bid them achieve me and then sell my bones.—(Act iv. 3. 90, 91.)

That he which hath no stomach to this fight,
Let him depart; his passport shall be made
And crowns for convoy[2] put into his purse:
We would not die in that man's company
That fears his fellowship to die with us.
This day is called the feast of Crispian:
He that outlives this day, and comes safe home,
Will stand a tip-toe when this day is nam'd,
And rouse him at the name of Crispian.
He that shall live this day, and see old age,
Will yearly on the vigil[3] feast his neighbours,
And say "To-morrow is Saint Crispian:"
Then will he strip his sleeve and show his scars,
And say "These wounds I had on Crispin's day."
Old men forget; yet all shall be forgot,
But he 'll remember with advantages[4]
What feats he did that day: then shall our names,
Familiar in his mouth as household words,
Harry the king, Bedford and Exeter,
Warwick and Talbot, Salisbury and Gloucester,
Be in their flowing cups freshly remember'd.
This story shall the good man teach his son;
And Crispin Crispian shall ne'er go by,
From this day to the ending of the world,
But we in it shall be remembered;
We few, we happy few, we band of brothers;
For he to-day that sheds his blood with me

[1] *Yearns*, grieves.
[2] *Convoy*, conveyance, travelling expenses.
[3] *Vigil*, the day preceding a holy day.
[4] *With advantages*, with profit.

Shall be my brother; be he ne'er so vile,
This day shall gentle his condition:[1]
And gentlemen in England, now a-bed,
Shall think themselves accurs'd they were not here;
And hold their manhoods cheap whiles any speaks
That fought with us upon Saint Crispin's day.

Re-enter SALISBURY.

Sal. My sovereign lord, bestow yourself[2] with speed:
The French are bravely[3] in their battles[4] set,
And will with all expedience[5] charge on us.
King. All things are ready, if our minds be so.
West. Perish the man whose mind is backward now!
King. Thou dost not wish more help from England, coz?
West. God's will! my liege, would you and I alone,
Without more help, could fight this royal battle!
King. Why, now thou hast unwish'd five thousand men:
Which likes me better than to wish us one.
You know your places: God be with you all!

Tucket. Enter MONTJOY *and Attendants.*

Mont. Once more I come to know of thee, King Harry,
If for thy ransom thou wilt now compound,
Before thy most assured overthrow:
[For certainly thou art so near the gulf,
Thou needs must be englutted.[6] Besides, in mercy,
The constable desires thee thou wilt mind
Thy followers of repentance; that their souls
May make a peaceful and a sweet retire
From off these fields, where, wretches, their poor bodies
Must lie and fester.]
King. Who hath sent thee now?
Mont. The Constable of France.
King. I pray thee, bear my former answer back:
Bid them achieve[7] me and then sell my bones.
Good God! why should they mock poor fellows thus?
The man that once did sell the lion's skin
While the beast liv'd, was kill'd with hunting him.
A many of our bodies shall no doubt
Find native graves; upon the which, I trust,
Shall witness live in brass of this day's work:
And those that leave their valiant bones in France,
Dying like men, though buried in your dunghills,
They shall be fam'd; [for there the sun shall greet them,
And draw their honours reeking up to heaven;
Leaving their earthly parts to choke your clime,
The smell whereof shall breed a plague in France.
Mark then abounding valour in our English,
That being dead, like to the bullet's grazing,
Break out into a second course of mischief,
Killing in relapse of mortality.
Let me speak proudly: tell the constable
We are but warriors for the working day;
Our gayness and our gilt[8] are all besmirch'd
With rainy marching in the painful field;
There's not a piece of feather in our host—
Good argument, I hope, we will not fly—
And time hath worn us into slovenry:[9]
But, by the mass, our hearts are in the trim;
And my poor soldiers tell me, yet ere night
They'll be in fresher robes, or they will pluck
The gay new coats o'er the French soldiers' heads
And turn them out of service. If they do this,—
As, if God please, they shall,—my ransom then
Will soon be levied.] Herald, save thou thy labour;
Come thou no more for ransom, gentle herald:
They shall have none, I swear, but these my joints;
Which if they have as I will leave 'em them,
Shall yield them little, tell the constable.
Mont. I shall, King Harry. And so fare thee well:
Thou never shalt hear herald any more.
[*Exeunt Montjoy and Attendants.*

1 *Gentle his condition*, make him a gentleman.
2 *Bestow yourself*, return to your post.
3 *Bravely*, with much display.
4 *Battles*, battalions.
5 *Expedience*, haste.
6 *Englutted*, swallowed up, absorbed.
7 *Achieve*, capture.
8 *Gilt*, fine trappings.
9 *Slovenry*, slovenliness.

King. I fear thou 'lt once more come again for ransom.

Enter YORK.

York. My lord, most humbly on my knee I beg
The leading of the vaward.[1]

King. Take it, brave York. Now, soldiers, march away:
And how[2] thou pleasest, God, dispose the day!
[*Exeunt.*

[SCENE IV. *The field of battle.*

Alarum. Excursions. Enter PISTOL, *French Soldier, and Boy.*

Pist. Yield, cur!

Fr. Sol. Je pense que vous êtes gentilhomme de bonne qualité.[3]

Pist. Qualitie calmie custure me![4] Art thou a gentleman? what is thy name? discuss.

Fr. Sol. O Seigneur Dieu!

Pist. O, Signieur Dew should be a gentleman:
Perpend my words, O Signieur Dew, and mark;
O Signieur Dew, thou diest on point of fox,[5]
Except, O signieur, thou do give to me
Egregious ransom.

Fr. Sol. O, prenez miséricorde! ayez pitié de moi![6]

Pist. Moy[7] shall not serve; I will have forty moys;
Or I will fetch thy rim[8] out at thy throat
In drops of crimson blood.

Fr. Sol. Est-il impossible d'échapper la force de ton bras?[9]

Pist. Brass, cur!
Thou damned and luxurious[10] mountain goat,
Offer'st me brass?

Fr. Sol. O pardonnez moi!

Pist. Say'st thou me so? is that a ton of moys?
Come hither, boy: ask me this slave in French
What is his name.

Boy. Ecoutez: comment êtes-vous appelé?[11]

Fr. Sol. Monsieur le Fer.

Boy. He says his name is Master Fer.

Pist. Master Fer! I'll *fer* him, and firk[12] him, and ferret[13] him: discuss the same in French unto him.

Boy. I do not know the French for fer, and ferret, and firk.

Pist. Bid him prepare; for I will cut his throat.

Fr. Sol. Que dit-il, monsieur?

Boy. Il me commande de vous dire que vous faites vous prêt; car ce soldat ici est disposé tout à cette heure de couper votre gorge.[14]

Pist. Owy, cuppele gorge, permafoy,[15]
Peasant, unless thou give me crowns, brave crowns;
Or mangled shalt thou be by this my sword.

Fr. Sol. O, je vous supplie, pour l'amour de Dieu, me pardonner! Je suis gentilhomme de bonne maison: gardez ma vie, et je vous donnerai deux cents écus.[16]

Pist. What are his words?

Boy. He prays you to save his life: he is a gentleman of a good house; and for his ransom he will give you two hundred crowns.

Pist. Tell him my fury shall abate, and I
The crowns will take.

Fr. Sol. Petit monsieur, que dit-il?

Boy. Encore qu'il est contre son jurement de pardonner aucun prisonnier, néanmoins, pour les écus que vous l'avez promis, il est content de vous donner la liberté, le franchisement.[17]

Fr. Sol. Sur mes genoux je vous donne mille remercimens; et je m'estime heureux que je suis tombé entre les mains d'un chevalier, je pense, le

---

1 *Vaward*, vanguard. 2 *How*, as.
3 "I think that you are a gentleman of good quality."
4 See note 233. 5 *Point of fox*, point of sword.
6 "O, take compassion! have pity on me!"
7 *Moy*. See note 237.
8 *Rim*, the peritoneum; or, perhaps, the diaphragm.
9 "Is it impossible to escape the force of thy arm!"
10 *Luxurious*, lustful.

11 "Listen; how are you called?" ("what's your name?")
12 *Firk*, beat. 13 *Ferret*, worry.
14 "He orders me to tell you to make yourself ready; for this soldier here is disposed this very hour to cut your throat."
15 This is Pistol's idea of French. He means, "O yes, cut his throat, by my faith."
16 "O, I entreat you for the love of God to pardon me! I am a gentleman of good family: preserve my life, and I will give you two hundred crowns."
17 "Although it is against his oath to pardon any prisoner, nevertheless (in return) for the crowns you have promised him, he is content to give (you) your liberty, your release."

plus brave, vaillant, et tres distingué seigneur d'Angleterre.[1] 61

Pist. Expound unto me, boy.

Boy. He gives you, upon his knees, a thousand thanks; and he esteems himself happy that he hath fallen into the hands of one, as he thinks, the most brave, valorous, and thrice-worthy signior of England.

Pist. As I suck blood, I will some mercy show. Follow me! 69

Boy. Suivez-vous le grand capitaine.[2] [*Exeunt Pistol, and French Soldier.*] I did never know so full a voice issue from so empty a heart: but the saying is true,—The empty vessel makes the greatest sound. Bardolph and Nym had ten times more valour than this roaring devil i' the old play, that every one may pare his nails with a wooden dagger; and they are both hanged; and so would this be, if he durst steal any thing adventurously.[3]

Boy. He prays you to save his life: he is a gentleman of a good house.—(Act iv. 4. 47, 48.)

I must stay with the lackeys, with the luggage of our camp: the French might have a good prey of us, if he knew of it; for there is none to guard it but boys. [*Exit.*]

SCENE V. *Another part of the field.*

Enter CONSTABLE, ORLEANS, BOURBON, DAUPHIN, RAMBURES, *and others in confusion.*

Con. O diable!

Orl. O seigneur! le jour est perdu, tout est perdu![4]

Dau. Mort de ma vie! all is confounded, all!
Reproach and everlasting shame
Sits mocking in our plumes. *O méchante fortune!*[5]
Do not run away. [*A short alarum.*

Con. Why, all our ranks are broke.

Dau. O perdurable[6] shame! let 's stab ourselves.
Be these the wretches that we play'd at dice for?

1 "Upon my knees I give you a thousand thanks; and I esteem myself happy to have fallen into the hands of a knight, I think, the most brave, valiant, and highly distinguished lord in England."

2 "Follow the great captain." 3 *Adventurously*, boldly.

4 "O my lord, the day is lost, all is lost!"

5 "O wicked fortune!"

6 *Perdurable*, enduring, lasting.

Orl. Is this the king we sent to for his ransom?

Bour. Shame and eternal shame, nothing but shame!
Let 's die in honour: once more back again;
[And he that will not follow Bourbon now,
Let him go hence, and with his cap in hand,
Like a base pander, hold the chamber-door
Whilst by a slave, no gentler than my dog,
His fairest daughter is contaminated.]

Con. Disorder, that hath spoil'd us, friend[1] us now!
Let us on heaps go offer up our lives.

Orl. We are enow[2] yet living in the field
To smother up the English in our throngs,
If any order might be thought upon.

Bour. The devil take order now! I 'll to the throng:
Let life be short; else shame will be too long.
[*Exeunt.*

[SCENE VI. *Another part of the field.*

Alarums. Enter KING HENRY *and Forces,* EXETER, *and others.*

King. Well have we done, thrice valiant countrymen:
But all 's not done; yet keep the French the field.

Exe. The Duke of York commends him to your majesty.

King. Lives he, good uncle? thrice within this hour
I saw him down; thrice up again, and fighting;
From helmet to the spur all blood he was.

Exe. In which array, brave soldier, doth he lie,
Larding[3] the plain; and by his bloody side,
Yoke-fellow to his honour-owing[4] wounds,
The noble Earl of Suffolk also lies.
Suffolk first di'd: and York, all haggled[5] over,
Comes to him, where in gore he lay insteep'd,
And takes him by the beard; kisses the gashes
That bloodily did yawn upon his face;
And cries aloud "Tarry, dear cousin Suffolk!
My soul shall thine keep company to heaven;
Tarry, sweet soul, for mine, then fly abreast,
As in this glorious and well-foughten field
We kept together in our chivalry!"
Upon these words I came and cheer'd him up:
He smil'd me in the face, raught[6] me his hand,
And, with a feeble gripe, says "Dear my lord,
Commend my service to my sovereign."
So[7] did he turn and over Suffolk's neck
He threw his wounded arm and kiss'd his lips;
And so espous'd to death, with blood he seal'd
A testament of noble-ending love.
The pretty and sweet manner of it forc'd
Those waters from me which I would have stopp'd;
But I had not so much of man in me,
And all my mother came into mine eyes
And gave me up to tears.

King. I blame you not;
For, hearing this, I must perforce[8] compound
With mistful eyes, or they will issue too.
[*Alarum.*
But, hark! what new alarum is this same?
The French have reinforc'd their scatter'd men:
Then every soldier kill his prisoners:
Give the word through [*Exeunt.*]

SCENE VII. *Another part of the field.*

Enter FLUELLEN *and* GOWER.

Flu. Kill the poys and the luggage! 't is expressly against the laws of arms: 't is as arrant a piece of knavery, mark you now, as can be offer't; in your conscience, now, is it not?

Gow. 'T is certain there 's not a boy left alive; and the cowardly rascals that ran from the battle ha' done this slaughter: besides, they have burn'd and carried away all that was in the king's tent; wherefore the king, most worthily, hath caus'd every soldier to cut his prisoner's throat. O, 't is a gallant king!

Flu. Ay, he was porn at Monmouth, Captain Gower. What call you the town's name where Alexander the Pig was porn!

Gow. Alexander the Great.

---

[1] *Friend*, befriend. [2] *Enow*, enough.
[3] *Larding*, enriching.
[4] *Honour-owing*, honour-owning, honourable.
[5] *Haggled*, mangled.

[6] *Raught*, reached. [7] *So*, then. [8] *Perforce*, necessarily.

Flu. Why, I pray you, is not pig great? the pig, or the great, or the mighty, or the huge, or the magnanimous, are all one reckonings, save the phrase is a little variations.

Gow. I think Alexander the Great was born in Macedon: his father was called Philip of Macedon, as I take it?

Flu. I think it is in Macedon where Alexander is porn. I tell you, captain, if you look in the maps of the 'orld, I warrant you sall find, in the comparisons between Macedon and Monmouth, that the situations, look you, is both alike. There is a river in Macedon; and there is also moreover a river at Monmouth: it is called Wye at Monmouth; but it is out of my prains what is the name of the other river; but 't is all one, 't is alike as my fingers is to my fingers, and there is salmons in both. If you mark Alexander's life well, Harry of Monmouth's life is come after it indifferent well; for there is figures in all things. Alexander,—Got knows, and you know,—in his rages, and his furies, and his wraths, and his cholers, and his moods, and his displeasures, and his indignations, and also being a little intoxicates in his prains, did, in his ales and his angers, look you, kill his pest friend, Cleitus.

Gow. Our king is not like him in that: he never kill'd any of his friends.

Flu. It is not well done, mark you now, to take the tales out of my mouth, ere it is made and finish'd. I speak but in the figures and comparisons of it: as Alexander killed his friend Cleitus, being in his ales and his cups; so also Harry Monmouth, being in his right wits and good judgements, turn'd away the fat knight with the great-belly doublet: he was full of jests, and gipes, and knaveries, and mocks; I have forgot his name.

Gow. Sir John Falstaff.

Flu. That is he: I'll tell you there is good men porn at Monmouth.

Gow. Here comes his majesty.

Alarum. Enter KING HENRY, *and forces;* WARWICK, GLOUCESTER, EXETER, *and others.*

King. I was not angry since I came to France
Until this instant. Take a trumpet,[1] herald;
Ride thou unto the horsemen on yon hill:
If they will fight with us, bid them come down,
Or void[2] the field; they do offend our sight:
If they'll do neither, we will come to them,
And make them skirr[3] away, as swift as stones
Enforced[4] from the old Assyrian slings:
Besides, we'll cut the throats of those we have,
And not a man of them that we shall take
Shall taste our mercy. Go and tell them so.

Enter MONTJOY *and Attendants.*

Exe. Here comes the herald of the French, my liege.

Glo. His eyes are humbler than they us'd to be.

King. How now! what means this, herald? know'st thou not
That I have fin'd these bones of mine for ransom?
Com'st thou again for ransom?

Mont. [*Kneeling*] No, great king:
I come to thee for charitable license,[5]
That we may wander o'er this bloody field
To book[6] our dead, and then to bury them;
To sort our nobles from our common men.
For many of our princes—woe the while!—
Lie drown'd and soak'd in mercenary blood;[7]
[So do our vulgar[8] drench their peasant limbs
In blood of princes; and their wounded steeds
Fret fetlock deep in gore and with wild rage
Yerk[9] out their armed heels at their dead masters,
Killing them twice. O, give us leave, great king,
To view the field in safety and dispose
Of their dead bodies!]

King. I tell thee truly, herald,
I know not if the day be ours or no;
For yet a many of your horsemen peer
And gallop o'er the field.

Mont. [*Rising*] The day is yours.

---

1 *Trumpet*, i.e. trumpeter. 2 *Void*, leave.
3 *Skirr*, hurry. 4 *Enforced*, hurled.
5 *License*, permission. 6 *To book*, i.e. to register.
7 *Mercenary blood*, i.e. the blood of mercenaries.
8 *Our vulgar*, i.e. our common soldiers.
9 *Yerk*, thrust.

King. Praised be God, and not our strength, for it!
What is this castle call'd that stands hard by?

Mont. They call it Agincourt.

King. Then call we this the field of Agincourt,
Fought on the day of Crispin Crispianus.
[*Flourish of trumpets.*

[*Flu.* Your grandfather of famous memory, an't please your majesty, and your great-uncle Edward the Plack Prince of Wales, as I have read in the chronicles, fought a most prave pattle here in France.

King. They did, Fluellen.

Flu. Your majesty says very true: if your majesties is remembered of it, the Welshmen did good service in a garden where leeks did grow, wearing leeks in their Monmouth caps; which, your majesty know, to this hour is an honourable badge of the service; and I do believe your majesty takes no scorn to wear the leek upon Saint Tavy's day.

King. I wear it for a memorable honour;
For I am Welsh, you know, good countryman.

Flu. All the water in Wye cannot wash your majesty's Welsh plood out of your pody, I can tell you that: God pless it and preserve it, as long as it pleases his grace, and his majesty too!

King. Thanks, good my countryman.

Flu. By Jeshu, I am your majesty's countryman, I care not who know it; I will confess it to all the 'orld: I need not to be ashamed of your majesty, praised be God, so long as your majesty is an honest man.

King. God keep me so!] Our heralds go with him:
Bring me just notice[1] of the numbers dead
On both our parts. [*Exeunt Heralds with Montjoy.*] Call yonder fellow hither.
[*Points to Williams.*

Exe. [*To Williams*] Soldier, you must come to the king. [*Williams advances, having the King's glove in his cap.*

King. Soldier, why wearest thou that glove in thy cap?

Will. An't please your majesty, 'tis the gage of one that I should fight withal, if he be alive.

King. An Englishman?

Will. An't please your majesty, a rascal that swagger'd with me[2] last night; who, if alive and ever dare to challenge this glove, I have sworn to take him a box o' th' ear: or if I can see my glove in his cap, which he swore, as he was a soldier, he would wear if alive, I will strike it out soundly.

King. What think you, Captain Fluellen? is it fit this soldier keep his oath?

Flu. He is a craven and a villain else, an't please your majesty, in my conscience.

King. It may be his enemy is a gentleman of great sort,[3] quite from the answer of his degree.

Flu. Though he be as good a gentleman as the tevil is, as Lucifer and Belzebub himself, it is necessary, look your grace, that he keep his vow and his oath: [if he be perjured, see you now, his reputation is as arrant a villain and a Jacksauce,[4] as ever his black shoe trod upon God's ground and his earth, in my conscience, la!]

King. Then keep thy vow, sirrah, when thou meet'st the fellow.

Will. So I will, my liege, as I live.

King. Who serv'st thou under?

Will. Under Captain Gower, my liege.

Flu. Gower is a good captain, and is good knowledge and literatured in the wars.

King. Call him hither to me, soldier.

Will. I will, my liege. [*Exit.*

King. Here, Fluellen; wear thou this favour for me and stick it in thy cap; when Alençon and myself were down together, I pluck'd this glove from his helm: if any man challenge this, he is a friend to Alençon, and an enemy to our person; if thou encounter any such, apprehend him, an thou dost me love.

Flu. Your grace does me as great honours as can be desir'd in the hearts of his subjects: I would fain see the man, that has but two legs, that shall find himself aggrief'd at this glove; that is all; but I would fain see it once, and please God of his grace that I might see.

[1] *Just notice*, true information.

[2] *Swagger'd with me*, bullied me.

[3] *Great sort*, high rank.

[4] *Jacksauce*, Fluellen's blunder for *Saucy Jack*.

King. Knowest thou Gower?

Flu. He is my dear friend, an please you.

King. Pray thee, go seek him, and bring him to my tent.

Flu. I will fetch him. [*Exit.*

King. My Lord of Warwick, and my brother Gloucester,
Follow Fluellen closely at the heels:
The glove which I have given him for a favour
May haply purchase him a box o' th' ear;
It is the soldier's; I by bargain should
Wear it myself. Follow, good cousin Warwick:
If that the soldier strike him, as I judge
By his blunt bearing he will keep his word,
Some sudden mischief may arise of it;
For I do know Fluellen valiant[1]
And, touch'd with choler, hot as gunpowder,
And quickly will return an injury:
Follow, and see there be no harm between them.
Go you with me, uncle of Exeter. [*Exeunt.*

SCENE VIII. *Before King Henry's pavilion.*

Enter GOWER *and* WILLIAMS.

Will. I warrant it is to knight you, captain.

Enter FLUELLEN.

Flu. God's will and his pleasure, captain, I beseech you now, come apace to the king: there is more good toward you peradventure than is in your knowledge to dream of.

Will. Sir, know you this glove?

Flu. Know the glove! I know the glove is a glove.

Will. I know this; and thus I challenge it. [*Strikes him.*

Flu. 'S blood! an arrant traitor as any is in the universal world, or in France, or in England!

Gow. How now, sir! you villain!

Will. Do you think I 'll be forsworn?

Flu. Stand away, Captain Gower; I will give treason his payment into plows, I warrant you.

Will. I am no traitor.

Flu. That 's a lie in thy throat. I charge you in his majesty's name, apprehend him: he 's a friend of the Duke Alençon's.

Enter WARWICK *and* GLOUCESTER.

War. How now, how now! what's the matter?

Flu. My Lord of Warwick, here is—praised be Got for it!—a most contagious treason come to light, look you, as you shall desire in a summer's day. Here is his majesty.

Enter KING HENRY *and* EXETER.

King. How now! what 's the matter?

Flu. My liege, here is a villain and a traitor, that, look your grace, has struck the glove which your majesty is take out of the helmet of Alençon.

Will. My liege, this was my glove; here is the fellow of it; and he that I gave it to in change promis'd to wear it in his cap: I promised to strike him, if he did: I met this man with my glove in his cap, and I have been as good as my word.

Flu. Your majesty hear now, saving your majesty's manhood, what an arrant, rascally, beggarly, lousy knave it is: I hope your majesty is pear me testimony and witness, and will avouchment, that this is the glove of Alençon, that your majesty is give me; in your conscience, now?

King. Give me thy glove, soldier; look, here is the fellow of it.
'T was I, indeed, thou promised'st to strike;
And thou hast given me most bitter terms.[2]

Flu. An please your majesty, let his neck answer for it, if there is any martial law in the world.

King. How canst thou make me satisfaction?

Will. All offences, my lord, come from the heart: never came any from mine that might offend your majesty.

King. It was ourself thou didst abuse.

Will. Your majesty came not like yourself: you appear'd to me but as a common man; witness the night, your garments, your lowliness,[3] and what your highness suffer'd under that shape, I beseech you take it for your own fault and not mine: for had you been as I took you for, I made no offence; therefore, I beseech your highness, pardon me.

[1] *Valiant*, metrically a trisyllable.

[2] *Bitter terms*, bitter words.

[3] *Lowliness*, humble appearance.

King. Here, uncle Exeter, fill this glove with crowns,
And give it to this fellow. Keep it, fellow;
And wear it for an honour in thy cap
Till I do challenge it. Give him the crowns:
And, captain, you must needs[1] be friends with him.

Flu. By this day and this light, the fellow has mettle enough in his belly. Hold, there is twelve pence for you; and I pray you to serve Got, and keep you out of prawls, and prabbles,[2] and quarrels, and dissensions, and, I warrant you, it is the better for you.

Will. I will none of your money.

Flu. It is with a good will; I can tell you, it will serve you to mend your shoes: come, wherefore should you be so pashful? your shoes is not so good: 't is a good silling, I warrant you, or I will change it.

Enter an English Herald.

King. Now, herald, are the dead number'd?

Her. Here is the number of the slaughter'd French.

King What prisoners of good sort[3] are taken, uncle?

Exe. Charles Duke of Orleans, nephew to the king;
John Duke of Bourbon, and Lord Bouciqualt:
Of other lords and barons, knights and squires,
Full fifteen hundred, besides common men.

King. This note doth tell me of ten thousand French
That in the field lie slain; of princes, in this number,
And nobles bearing banners, there lie dead
One hundred twenty six: added to these,
Of knights, esquires, and gallant gentlemen,
Eight thousand and four hundred; [of the which,
Five hundred were but yesterday dubb'd knights:
So that, in these ten thousand they have lost,
There are but sixteen hundred mercenaries,[4]
The rest are princes, barons, lords, knights, squires,
And gentlemen of blood and quality.
The names of those their nobles that lie dead:
Charles Delabreth, high constable of France;
Jacques of Chatillon, admiral of France;
The master of the cross-bows, Lord Rambures;
Great Master of France, the brave Sir Guichard Dolphin,
John Duke of Alençon, Anthony Duke of Brabant,
The brother to the Duke of Burgundy,
And Edward Duke of Bar: of lusty earls,
Grandpré and Roussi, Fauconberg and Foix,
Beaumont and Marle, Vaudemont and Lestrale.]
Here was a royal fellowship of death!
Where is the number of our English dead?

[*Herald shows him another paper.*

Edward the Duke of York, the Earl of Suffolk,
Sir Richard Ketly, Davy Gam, esquire:
None else of name;[5] and of all other men
But five and twenty. O God, thy arm was here;
And not to us, but to thy arm alone,
Ascribe we all! When, without stratagem,
But in plain shock and even play of battle,
Was ever known so great and little loss
On one part and on th' other? Take it, God,
For it is none but thine!

Exe. 'T is wonderful!

King. Come, go we in procession to the village:
And be it death proclaimed through our host
To boast of this or take that praise from God
Which is his only.

Flu. Is it not lawful, an please your majesty, to tell how many is killed?

King. Yes, captain; but with this acknowledgment,
That God fought for us.

Flu. Yes, my conscience, he did us great goot.

King. Do we all holy rites;
Let there be sung "Non nobis" and "Te Deum;"
The dead with charity enclos'd in clay:
And then to Calais; and to England then;
Where ne'er from France arriv'd more happy men. [*Exeunt.*

[1] *Needs*, of necessity. [2] *Prabbles*, petty disputes.
[3] *Sort*, rank. [4] *Mercenaries*, hired soldiers.
[5] *Of name*, of note or rank.

ACT V.

PROLOGUE.

Enter Chorus.

Chor. Vouchsafe to those that have not read the story,
That I may prompt them: [and of such as have,
I humbly pray them to admit th' excuse
Of time, of numbers and due course of things,
Which cannot in their huge and proper life
Be here presented.] Now we bear the king
Toward Calais: grant him there; there seen,
Heave him away upon your winged thoughts
Athwart[1] the sea. Behold, the English beach
Pales in[2] the flood with men, with wives, and boys,
Whose shouts and claps out-voice the deep-mouth'd sea,
Which, like a mighty whiffler[3] 'fore the king,
Seems to prepare his way: so let him land,
And solemnly see him set on to London.
So swift a pace hath thought, that even now
You may imagine him upon Blackheath;
[Where that his lords desire him to have borne
His bruised helmet and his bended sword
Before him through the city: he forbids it,
Being free from vainness and self-glorious pride;
Giving full trophy, signal and ostent
Quite from himself to God. But now behold,
In the quick forge and working-house of thought,]
How London doth pour out her citizens!
The mayor and all his brethren in best sort,[4]—
Like to the senators of th' antique Rome,
With the plebeians swarming at their heels,—
Go forth and fetch their conquering Cæsar in:
[As, by a lower but loving likelihood,[5]
Were now the general of our gracious empress,
As in good time he may, from Ireland coming,
Bringing rebellion broached[6] on his sword,
How many would the peaceful city quit,
To welcome him! much more, and much more cause,
Did they this Harry.] Now in London place him;
As yet the lamentation of the French
Invites the King of England's stay at home;
The emperor's coming in behalf of France,
To order peace between them; and omit
All the occurrences, whatever chanced,
Till Harry's back-return again to France:
There must we bring him: and myself have play'd
The interim, by remembering you[7] 't is past.
Then brook abridgment, and your eyes advance,
After your thoughts, straight back again to France. [*Exit.*

[1] *Athwart*, across.
[2] *Pales in*, encircles.
[3] *Whiffler*, a person who goes before a procession to clear the way.
[4] *Sort*, style or manner.
[5] *Likelihood*, similitude.
[6] *Broached*, transfixed.

SCENE I. *France. The English camp.*

Enter FLUELLEN *and* GOWER.

Gow. Now, that 's right; but why wear you your leek to-day? Saint Davy's day is past.

Flu. There is occasions and causes why and wherefore in all things: I will tell you, asse my friend, Captain Gower: the rascally, scald,[8] peggarly, lousy, pragging knave, Pistol, which you and yourself and all the world know to be no petter than a fellow, look you now, of no merits, he is come to me and prings me pread and salt yesterday, look you, and bid me eat my leek: it was in a place where I could not preed no contention with him; but I will be so pold as to wear it in my cap till I see him once again, and then I will tell him a little piece of my desires.

Enter PISTOL.

Gow. Why, here he comes, swelling like a turkey-cock.

Flu. 'T is no matter for his swellings nor his turkey-cocks. Got pless you, Aunchient

[7] *Remembering you*, reminding you.
[8] *Scald*, scurvy.

Pistol! you scurvy, lousy knave, Got pless you!

Pist. Ha! art thou bedlam? dost thou thirst, base Trojan,
To have me fold up Parca's fatal web?
Hence! I am qualmish at the smell of leek.

Flu. I peseech you heartily, scurvy, lousy knave, at my desires, and my requests, and my petitions, to eat, look you, this leek: because, look you, you do not love it, nor your affections and your appetites and your digestions doo's not agree with it, I would desire you to eat it.

Pist. Not for Cadwallader[1] and all his goats.

Flu. There is one goat for you. [*Strikes him.*] Will you be so good, scald[2] knave, as eat it?

Pist. By this leek, I will most horribly revenge:
I eat and eat, I swear.—(Act v. 1. 49, 50.)

Pist. Base Trojan, thou shalt die.

Flu. You say very true, scald knave, when God's will is: I will desire you to live in the mean time, and eat your victuals: come, there is sauce for it. [*Strikes him.*] You called me yesterday mountain-squire; but I will make you to-day a squire of low degree. I pray you, fall to: if you can mock a leek, you can eat a leek.

Gow. Enough, captain: you have astonished[3] him.

Flu. I say, I will make him eat some part of my leek, or I will peat his pate four days.—Pite, I pray you: it is good for your green wound and your ploody coxcomb.

Pist. Must I bite?

Flu. Yes, certainly, and out of doubt and out of question too, and ambiguities.

Pist. By this leek, I will most horribly revenge:
I eat and eat, I swear—

Flu. Eat, I pray you; will you have some more sauce to your leek? there is not enough leek to swear by.

Pist. Quiet thy cudgel; thou dost see I eat.

Flu. Much good to you, scald knave, heartily. Nay, pray you, throw none away; the skin is good for your proken coxcomb.

[1] *Cadwallader*, the last of the Welsh kings.
[2] *Scald*, scurvy.
[3] *Astonished*, stunned.

When you take occasions to see leeks hereafter, I pray you, mock at 'em; that is all.

Pist. Good.

Flu. Ay, leeks is good: hold you, there is a groat to heal your pate.

Pist. Me a groat!

Flu. Yes, verily and in truth, you shall take it; or I have another leek in my pocket, which you shall eat.

Pist. I take thy groat in earnest of revenge.

Flu. If I owe you any thing, I will pay you in cudgels: you shall be a woodmonger, and buy nothing of me but cudgels. God b' wi' you, and keep you, and heal your pate. [*Exit.*

Pist. All hell shall stir for this.

Gow. Go, go; you are a counterfeit cowardly knave. Will you mock at an ancient tradition, begun upon an honourable respect, and worn as a memorable trophy of predeceased valour and dare not avouch in your deeds any of your words? I have seen you gleeking[1] and galling[2] at this gentleman twice or thrice. You thought, because he could not speak English in the native garb, he could not therefore handle an English cudgel: you find it otherwise; and henceforth let a Welsh correction teach you a good English condition.[3] Fare ye well. [*Exit.*

Pist. Doth Fortune play the huswife[4] with me now?
[News have I, that my Nell is dead i' the spital[5]
Of malady of France;
And there my rendezvous is quite cut off.]
Old I do wax; and from my weary limbs
Honour is cudgell'd. [Well, bawd I'll turn,
And something lean to cutpurse of quick hand.]
To England will I steal, and there I'll steal:
And patches will I get unto these cudgell'd scars,
And swear I got them in the Gallia wars. [*Exit.*

SCENE II. *Troyes in Champagne. An apartment in the King's palace.*

Enter, at one door, KING HENRY, EXETER, BEDFORD, GLOUCESTER, WARWICK, WESTMORELAND, *and other Lords; at another, the* FRENCH KING, QUEEN ISABEL, *the* PRINCESS KATHARINE, ALICE, *and other Ladies; the* DUKE OF BURGUNDY, *and his train.*

King. Peace to this meeting, wherefore[6] we are met!
Unto our brother France, and to our sister,
Health and fair time of day; joy and good wishes
To our most fair and princely cousin Katharine;
And, as a branch and member of this royalty,
By whom this great assembly is contriv'd,
We do salute you, Duke of Burgundy;
And princes French, and peers, health to you all!

Fr. King. Right joyous are we to behold your face,
Most worthy brother England; fairly met:—
So are you, princes English, every one.

Queen. So happy be the issue, brother England,
Of this good day and of this gracious meeting,
As we are now glad to behold your eyes;
Your eyes, which hitherto have borne in them
Against the French, that met them in their bent,
The fatal balls[7] of murdering basilisks:[8]
The venom of such looks, we fairly hope,
Have lost their quality, and that this day
Shall change all griefs and quarrels into love.

King. To cry amen to that, thus we appear.

Queen. You English princes all, I do salute you.

Bur. My duty to you both, on equal love,
Great Kings of France and England! That I have labour'd,
With all my wits, my pains and strong endeavours,
To bring your most imperial majesties
Unto this bar and royal interview,

[1] *Gleeking*, sneering.
[2] *Galling*, scoffing.
[3] *Condition*, temper.
[4] *Huswife*, hussy.
[5] *Spital*, hospital.
[6] *Wherefore*, for which.
[7] *Balls*, eyeballs.
[8] *Basilisks*; a pun on *basilisks*=snakes and *basilisks*, large cannon.

Your mightiness on both parts best can witness.
Since then my office hath so far prevail'd
That, face to face and royal eye to eye,
You have congreeted,[1] let it not disgrace me,
If I demand, before this royal view,
What rub[2] or what impediment there is,
Why that the naked, poor and mangled Peace,
Dear nurse of arts, plenties and joyful births,
Should not in this best garden of the world
Our fertile France, put up her lovely visage?
[Alas, she hath from France too long been chas'd,
And all her husbandry doth lie on heaps,
Corrupting in its own fertility.
Her vine, the merry cheerer of the heart,
Unpruned dies; her hedges even-pleach'd,[3]
Like prisoners wildly overgrown with hair,
Put forth disorder'd twigs; her fallow leas
The darnel, hemlock and rank fumitory
Doth root upon, while that the coulter rusts
That should deracinate[4] such savagery;[5]
The even mead, that erst brought sweetly forth
The freckl'd cowslip, burnet and green clover,
Wanting the scythe, all uncorrected, rank,
Conceives by idleness and nothing teems
But hateful docks, rough thistles, kecksies,[6] burs,
Losing both beauty and utility.
And as our vineyards, fallows, meads and hedges,
Defective in their natures, grow to wildness,
Even so our houses and ourselves and children
Have lost, or do not learn for want of time,
The sciences that should become our country;
But grow like savages,—as soldiers will
That nothing do but meditate on blood,—
To swearing and stern looks, diffus'd attire
And every thing that seems unnatural.
Which to reduce into our former favour[7]
You are assembl'd: and my speech entreats
That I may know the let,[8] why gentle Peace
Should not expel these inconveniences
And bless us with her former qualities.

[1] *Congreeted*, met with friendliness.
[2] *Rub*, obstacle.
[3] *Even-pleach'd*, smoothly interwoven.
[4] *Deracinate*, uproot.
[5] *Savagery*, wild growth
[6] *Kecksies*, dry hemlock stems.
[7] *Favour*, appearance.
[8] *Let*, hinderance.

King. If, Duke of Burgundy, you would[9] the peace
Whose want gives growth to th' imperfections
Which you have cited, you must buy that peace
With full accord to all our just demands;

King. Fair Katharine, and most fair,
Will you vouchsafe to teach a soldier terms
Such as will enter at a lady's ear
And plead his love-suit to her gentle heart?—(Act v. 2. 98-101.)

Whose tenours and particular effects
You have enschedul'd briefly in your hands.
Bur. The king hath heard them; to the which as yet
There is no answer made.
King. Well then the peace,
Which you before so urg'd, lies in his answer.]
[*Burgundy gives the French King a scroll.*
Fr. King. I have but with a cursorary eye

[9] *Would*, wish.

O'erglanced the articles: pleaseth your grace
T' appoint some of your council presently
To sit with us once more, with better heed
To re-survey them, we will suddenly
Pass our accept[1] and peremptory answer.

King. Brother, we shall. Go, uncle Exeter,
And brother Clarence, and you, brother Gloucester,
Warwick and Huntingdon, go with the king;
And take with you free power to ratify,
Augment, or alter, as your wisdoms best
Shall see advantageable[2] for our dignity,
Any thing in or out of our demands,
And we'll consign[3] thereto. Will you, fair sister,
Go with the princes, or stay here with us?

Queen. Our gracious brother, I will go with them:
Haply a woman's voice may do some good,
When articles too nicely[4] urg'd be stood on.

King. Yet leave our cousin Katharine here with us:
She is our capital demand, compris'd
Within the fore-rank of our articles.

Queen. She hath good leave.

[*Exeunt all except Henry, Katharine, and Alice.*

King. Fair Katharine, and most fair,
Will you vouchsafe to teach a soldier terms
Such as will enter at a lady's ear
And plead his love-suit to her gentle heart?

Kath. Your majesty shall mock at me; I cannot speak your England.

King. O fair Katharine, if you will love me soundly with your French heart, I will be glad to hear you confess it brokenly with your English tongue. Do you like me, Kate?

Kath. *Pardonnez-moi,* I cannot tell vat is "like me."

King. An angel is like you, Kate, and you are like an angel.

Kath. Que dit-il? que je suis semblable à les anges?[5]

Alice. Oui, vraiment, sauf votre grace, ainsi dit-il.[6]

King. I said so, dear Katharine; and I must not blush to affirm it.

Kath. O bon Dieu! les langues des hommes sont pleines de tromperies.[7]

King. What says she, fair one? that the tongues of men are full of deceits?

Alice. Oui, dat de tongues of de mans is be full of deceits: dat is de princess.[8]

King. The princess is the better Englishwoman. I' faith, Kate, my wooing is fit for thy understanding: I am glad thou canst speak no better English: for, if thou couldst, thou wouldst find me such a plain king that thou wouldst think I had sold my farm to buy my crown. I know no ways to mince it in love, but directly to say "I love you:" then if you urge me farther than to say "do you in faith?" I wear out my suit. Give me your answer; i' faith do: and so clap hands and a bargain: how say you, lady?

Kath. Sauf votre honneur, me understand vell.

King. Marry, if you would put me to verses or to dance for your sake, Kate, why you undid me:[9] for the one, I have neither words nor measure, and for the other, I have no strength in measure,[10] yet a reasonable measure in strength. If I could win a lady at leap-frog, or by vaulting into my saddle with my armour on my back, under the correction of bragging be it spoken, I should quickly leap into a wife. Or if I might buffet[11] for my love, or bound my horse for her favours, I could lay on like a butcher and sit like a jack-an-apes,[12] never off. But before God, Kate, I cannot look greenly[13] nor gasp out my eloquence, nor I have no cunning in protestation: only downright oaths, which I never use till urged, nor never break for urging. If thou canst love a fellow of this temper, Kate, whose face is not worth sunburning, that never looks in his glass for love of any thing he sees there, let thine eye be thy cook. I speak to thee plain soldier: if thou canst love me for this, take me; if not,

---

1 *Pass our accept*, declare our acceptance.
2 *Advantageable*, profitable.
3 *Consign*, agree.
4 *Nicely*, sophistically.
5 "What says he? that I am like the angels?"
6 "Yes, truly, save your grace, so he says."

7 "O good God! the tongues of men are full of deceits."
8 *Dat is de princess*, i.e. that is what the princess says.
9 *You undid me*, i.e. you would undo me.
10 *In measure*, in dancing.
11 *Buffet*, box.
12 *Jack-an-apes*, a monkey.
13 *Greenly*, foolishly.

to say to thee that I shall die, is true; but for thy love, by the Lord, no; yet I love thee too. And while thou livest, dear Kate, take a fellow of plain and uncoined constancy; for he perforce must do thee right, because he hath not the gift to woo in other places: for these fellows of infinite tongue, that can rhyme themselves into ladies' favours, they do always reason themselves out again. What! a speaker is but a prater; a rhyme is but a ballad. A good leg will fall:[1] a straight back will stoop; a black beard will turn white; a curled pate will grow bald; a fair face will wither; a full eye will wax hollow: but a good heart, Kate, is the sun and the moon; or rather the sun and not the moon; for it shines bright and never changes, but keeps his course truly. If thou would have such a one, take me; and take me, take a soldier; take a soldier, take a king. And what sayest thou then to my love? speak, my fair, and fairly, I pray thee.

Kath. Is it possible dat I sould love de enemy of France?

King. No; it is not possible you should love the enemy of France, Kate; but, in loving me, you should love the friend of France; for I love France so well that I will not part with a village of it; I will have it all mine: and, Kate, when France is mine and I am yours, then yours is France and you are mine.

Kath. I cannot tell vat is dat.

King. No, Kate? [I will tell thee in French; which I am sure will hang upon my tongue like a new-married wife about her husband's neck, hardly to be shook off. *Quand j'ai le possession de France, et quand vous avez le possession de moi,*—let me see, what then? Saint Denis be my speed!—*donc votre est France et vous êtes mienne.*[2] It is as easy for me, Kate, to conquer the kingdom as to speak so much more French: I shall never move thee in French, unless it be to laugh at me.

Kath. Sauf votre honneur, le François que vous parlez, il est meilleur que l'Anglois lequel je parle.[3]

King. No, faith, is't not, Kate: but thy speaking of my tongue, and I thine, most truly-falsely, must needs be granted to be much at one.] But, Kate, dost thou understand thus much English, canst thou love me?

Kath. I cannot tell.

King. Can any of your neighbours tell, Kate? I'll ask them. Come, I know thou lovest me: and at night, when you come into your closet, you'll question this gentlewoman about me; and I know, Kate, you will to her dispraise those parts in me that you love with your heart; but, good Kate, mock me mercifully; the rather, gentle princess, because I love thee cruelly. If ever thou beest mine, Kate, as I have a saving faith within me tells me thou shalt, [I get thee with scambling,[4] and thou must therefore needs prove a good soldier-breeder:] shall not thou and I, between Saint Denis[5] and Saint George, compound a boy, half French, half English, that shall go to Constantinople and take the Turk by the beard? shall we not? what sayest thou, my fair flower-de-luce?

[*Kath.* I do not know dat.

King. No; 't is hereafter to know, but now to promise: do but now promise, Kate, you will endeavour for your French part of such a boy; and for my English moiety take the word of a king and a bachelor.] How answer you, *la plus belle Katharine du monde, mon très cher et devin déesse?*[6]

Kath. Your *majesté* ave *fausse* French enough to deceive de most *sage demoiselle* dat is *en France.*

King. Now, fie upon my false French! By mine honour, in true English, I love thee, Kate: by which honour I dare not swear thou lovest me; yet my blood begins to flatter me that thou dost, notwithstanding the poor and untempering effect of my visage. [Now, beshrew my father's ambition! he was thinking of civil wars when he got me: therefore was I created with a stubborn outside, with an aspect of iron, that, when I come to woo ladies, I fright them.] But, in faith, Kate,

[1] *Fall*, shrink.

[2] "When I have possession of France and you have the possession of me—then France is yours and you are mine."

[3] "Saving your honour, the French that you speak, it is better than the English which I speak."

[4] *Scambling*, struggling.

[5] *Saint Denis*, the French patron saint.

[6] "The most beautiful Katharine in the world, my very dear and divine goddess."

the elder I wax, the better I shall appear: my comfort is, that old age, that ill layer up of beauty, can do no more spoil upon my face: thou hast me, if thou hast me, at the worst; and thou shalt wear me, if thou wear me, better and better: and therefore tell me, most fair Katharine, will you have me? Put off your maiden blushes; avouch the thoughts of your heart with the looks of an empress; take me by the hand, and say "Harry of England, I am thine:" which word thou shalt no sooner bless mine ear withal, but I will tell thee aloud "England is thine, Ireland is thine, France is thine, and Henry Plantagenet is thine:" who, though I speak it before his face, if he be not fellow with the best king, thou shalt find the best king of good fellows. Come, your answer in broken music; for thy voice is music and thy English broken; therefore, queen of all, Katharine, break thy mind to me in broken English; wilt thou have me?

Kath. Dat is as it sall please de *roi mon père.*

King. Nay, it will please him well, Kate; it shall please him, Kate.

Kath. Den it sall also content me.

King. Upon that I kiss your hand, and I call you my queen.

Kath. *Laissez, mon seigneur, laissez, laissez: ma foi, je ne veux point que vous abaissiez votre grandeur en baisant la main d'une de votre seigneurie indigne serviteur; excusez-moi, je vous supplie, mon très-puissant seigneur.*[1]

King. Then I will kiss your lips, Kate.

Kath. *Les dames et demoiselles pour être baisées devant leur noces, il n'est pas la coutume de France.*[2]

King. Madam my interpreter, what says she?

Alice. Dat it is not be de fashion *pour les* ladies of France,—I cannot tell vat is *baiser en* Anglish.

King. To kiss.

Alice. Your majesty *entendre* bettre *que moi.*

King. It is not a fashion for the maids in France to kiss before they are married, would she say?

Alice. *Oui, vraiment.*

King. O Kate, nice customs curtsy to great kings. Dear Kate, you and I cannot be confined within the weak list[3] of a country's fashion: we are the makers of manners, Kate; and the liberty that follows our places stops the mouth of all find-faults;[4] as I will do yours, for upholding the nice fashion of your country in denying me a kiss: therefore, patiently and yielding. [*Kissing her.*] You have witchcraft in your lips, Kate: there is more eloquence in a sugar touch of them than in the tongues of the French council; and they should sooner persuade Harry of England than a general petition of monarchs. Here comes your father.

Re-enter the FRENCH KING *and his* QUEEN, BURGUNDY, *and other Lords.*

Bur. God save your majesty! my royal cousin, teach you our princess English?

King. I would have her learn, my fair cousin, how perfectly I love her; and that is good English.

Bur. Is she not apt?

King. Our tongue is rough, coz, and my condition[5] is not smooth; so that, having neither the voice nor the heart of flattery about me, I cannot so conjure up the spirit of love in her, that he will appear in his true likeness.

[*Bur.* Pardon the frankness of my mirth, if I answer you for that. If you would conjure in her, you must make a circle; if conjure up love in her in his true likness, he must appear naked and blind. Can you blame her then, being a maid yet rosed over with the virgin crimson of modesty, if she deny the appearance of a naked blind boy in her naked seeing self? It were, my lord, a hard condition for a maid to consign[6] to.

King. Yet they do wink and yield, as love is blind and enforces.

---

[1] "Let be, my lord, let be, let be: my faith, I do not wish that you should abase your greatness in kissing the hand of one of your lordship's unworthy servants; excuse me, I entreat you, my very powerful lord."

[2] "For ladies and girls to be kissed before their marriage, it is not the custom in France."

[3] *List*, compass, confine.

[4] *Find-faults*, fault-finders.

[5] *Condition*, temper.

[6] *Consign*, agree.

Bur. They are then excused, my lord, when they see not what they do.

King. Then, good my lord, teach your cousin to consent winking.

Bur. I will wink on her to consent, my lord, if you will teach her to know my meaning: for maids, well summered and warm kept, are like flies at Bartholomew-tide,[1] blind, though they have their eyes; and then they will endure handling, which before would not abide looking on.

King. This moral ties me over to time and a hot summer; and so I shall catch the fly, your cousin, in the latter end and she must be blind too.

Bur. As love is, my lord, before it loves.

King. It is so: and you may, some of you, thank love for my blindness, who cannot see many a fair French city for one fair French maid that stands in my way.

Fr. King. Yes, my lord, you see them perspectively, the cities turned into a maid; for they are all girdled with maiden walls that war hath never entered.]

King. Shall Kate be my wife?

Fr. King. So please you.

King. I am content; [so the maiden cities you talk of may wait on her: so the maid that stood in the way for my wish shall show me the way to my will.

Fr. King. We have consented to all terms of reason.

King. Is't so, my lords of England?]

West. The king hath granted every article:
His daughter first, and then in sequel all,
According to their firm proposed natures.

[*Exe.* Only he hath not yet subscribed this:
Where your majesty demands, that the King of France, having any occasion to write for matter of grant, shall name your highness in this form and with this addition, in French, *Notre très-cher fils Henri, Roi d'Angleterre, Héritier de France;*[2] and thus in Latin, *Præclarissimus filius noster Henricus, Rex Angliæ, et Hæres Franciæ.*[3]

Fr. King. Nor this I have not, brother, so denied,
But your request shall make me let it pass.

King. I pray you then, in love and dear alliance,
Let that one article rank with the rest;
And thereupon give me your daughter.]

Fr. King. Take her, fair son, and from her blood raise up
Issue to me; that the contending kingdoms
Of France and England, whose very shores look pale
With envy of each other's happiness,
May cease their hatred, and this dear conjunction
Plant neighbourhood and Christian-like accord
In their sweet bosoms, that never war advance
His bleeding sword 'twixt England and fair France.

All. Amen!

King. Now, welcome, Kate: and bear me witness all,
That here I kiss her as my sovereign queen.
[*Flourish.*

[*Queen.* God, the best maker of all marriages,
Combine your hearts in one, your realms in one!
As man and wife, being two, are one in love,
So be there 'twixt your kingdom such a spousal,
That never may ill office, or fell jealousy,
Which troubles oft the bed of blessed marriage,
Thrust in between the paction[4] of these kingdoms,
To make divorce of their incorporate league;
That English may as French, French Englishmen,
Receive each other. God speak this Amen!

All. Amen!

King.] Prepare we for our marriage: on which day,
My lord of Burgundy, we'll take our oath,
And all the peers', for surety of our league.
Then shall I swear to Kate, and you to me;
And may our oaths well kept and prosperous be!
[*Sennet. Exeunt.*

[1] *Bartholomew-tide*, the 24th of August.

[2] "Our very dear son Henry, King of England, heir (apparent) of France."

[3] "Our most illustrious son Henry, King of England, and heir (apparent) of France."

[4] *Paction*, alliance.

[EPILOGUE.

Enter Chorus.

Chor. Thus far, with rough and all-unable[1] pen,
Our bending author hath pursu'd the story,
In little room confining mighty men,
Mangling by starts[2] the full course of their glory.
Small time, but in that small most greatly liv'd
This star of England: Fortune made his sword;
By which the world's best garden he achiev'd,
And of it left his son imperial lord.
Henry the Sixth, in infant bands crown'd King
Of France and England, did this king succeed;
Whose state so many had the managing,
That they lost France and made his England bleed:
Which oft our stage hath shown; and, for their sake,
In your fair minds let this acceptance take.[3]
[*Exit.*]

[1] *All-unable*, weak.

[2] *By starts*, by fragmentary and imperfect representation.

[3] *Let this*, &c., let this play find favour.

MAP TO ILLUSTRATE KING HENRY V.

NOTES TO KING HENRY V.

DRAMATIS PERSONÆ.

1. King Henry the Fifth. For some account of Henry's earlier years see note 2, I. Henry IV. and note 3, II. Henry IV. With reference to his marriage it may be noted that the king had been a suitor for the hand of Isabel of France, the young widow of Richard II., and subsequently for that of her next sister Marie, who went into a convent. He then sought to win their youngest sister, Katharine, but it was not till some years later that his wooing proved successful. They were married at Troyes on the 3rd of June, 1420. Their only issue was Henry of Windsor, born in that town on the 6th of December, 1421. The king, while engaged in preparations for

fresh wars, was taken sick with pleurisy, and died August 31st, 1422, of the fever that followed this attack. His body was brought to England with great pomp and ceremony, and finally entombed in Westminster Abbey on the 11th of November in the same year.

2. DUKE OF GLOUCESTER. This was Prince Humphrey Plantagenet, the only one of Henry's brothers who was actually present at Agincourt, where he fought bravely and was wounded, his royal brother coming to his rescue and defending him until he could be borne from the field. He was also at the meeting of the French and English princes at Troyes. See note 3, I. Henry VI.

3. DUKE OF BEDFORD. This is the person who figured as Prince John of Lancaster in I. and II. Henry IV. (See note 3, I. Henry IV.) Henry created him Earl of Kendal and Duke of Bedford on the 6th of May, 1414. He also appointed him to be "Lieutenant of the whole realm of England" during his own absence in France. The dramatist is therefore at fault in representing the duke as present before Harfleur and at Agincourt. For a fuller account of this character see note 2, I. Henry VI.

4. DUKE OF EXETER. This was Thomas Beaufort, for an account of whom see note 4, I. Henry VI.[1] At the time of the battle of Agincourt he was only Earl of Dorset and not Duke of Exeter, as Shakespeare calls him. As French remarks, he was *not present* at Agincourt, although nearly all writers agree with Shakespeare in putting him in command of the rear-guard there. It is remarkable that the poet has given a sufficient reason for his absence in iii. 3. 51-53:

> Come, uncle Exeter,
> Go you and enter Harfleur; there remain,
> And fortify it strongly 'gainst the French.

This is true to history, Dorset having remained in charge of Harfleur after its capture. The town was twice attacked by the Count of Armagnac, who was in both instances repulsed by the garrison under the command of Dorset.

5. DUKE OF YORK. This is the Edward Plantagenet, Earl of Rutland and Duke of Aumerle, who appears in Richard II. (See note 5 of that play.) He was restored to his father's former title by Henry IV. in 1406. He fell at Agincourt, fighting bravely in command of the van. "He was very corpulent, and having been struck down by the Duke of Alençon, it was in stooping to assist his cousin that the king himself was assailed by that French prince, who struck off Henry's jewelled coronet" (French).

6. EARL OF SALISBURY. This was Thomas Montacute, eldest son of the Earl of Salisbury who appears in the play of Richard II. (See note 8 of that play.) Henry IV. restored him to the title his father had forfeited. For an account of him see note 9, I. Henry VI.

7. EARL OF WESTMORELAND. The Ralph Neville of the preceding plays. (See note 4, I. Henry IV., and note 8, II. Henry IV.) He could not have been at Agincourt, since his duties as one of the council to the Regent Bedford, and also as warden of the West Marches towards Scotland, would require his presence in England. Compare what Henry says in i. 2. 136-139:

> We must not only arm t' invade the French,
> But lay down our proportions to defend
> Against the Scot, who will make road upon us
> With all advantages.

8. EARL OF WARWICK. This was Richard Beauchamp, some account of whom will be found in note 7, II. Henry IV., and note 8, I. Henry VI. He was at Harfleur, but not at Agincourt, having returned to England after the capture of the former city. He subsequently returned to France, and was made governor of Caen after it was taken by Henry. He was one of the ambassadors sent to treat of the king's marriage, and was present at Troyes, as represented in the play (act v. scene 2). Henry, on his death-bed, appointed him tutor to his infant son, on the ground that "no fitter person could be provided to teach him all things becoming his rank."

9. ARCHBISHOP OF CANTERBURY. Henry Chicheley, who was born about 1362, at Higham Ferrars, where in 1415 he founded and endowed a college for secular priests. He had been archdeacon of Salisbury and bishop of St. David's before his appointment to the see of Canterbury in 1414. He founded All Souls' College at Oxford, and enlarged and adorned Lambeth Palace. He died April 12, 1443.

10. BISHOP OF ELY. John Fordham, who, after being Dean of Wells, was promoted to the see of Durham, and subsequently transferred to Ely. He died in 1425.

11. EARL OF CAMBRIDGE. Richard Plantagenet, brother of the Duke of York in this play, and second son of the Duke of York in Richard II. He married Anne, daughter of Roger Mortimer, fourth earl of March; and their son, Richard Plantagenet, became the head of the Yorkists, or party of the White Rose in the subsequent reign. (See note 7 of I. Henry VI. and note 4 of II. Henry VI.) Having been engaged in the conspiracy against Henry V., he was beheaded at Southampton on the 5th of August, 1415. The plan of the conspirators was to put his brother-in-law, Edmund Mortimer, on the throne; but the latter disclosed the plot to the king, who was his intimate friend.

12. LORD SCROOP. Henry Scroop was the eldest son of Sir Stephen Scroop or Scrope. (See note 21, Richard II.) He was employed by Henry V. on certain embassies to Denmark and France; but, under the influence of French bribes, he plotted the destruction of his sovereign, and drew the Earl of Cambridge and Sir Thomas Grey into the conspiracy. He was tried, attainted, and beheaded on the same day with his confederate Cambridge.

13. SIR THOMAS GREY. He was the son of Sir Thomas Grey of Berwick, Constable of Norham Castle. He was executed at Southampton on the 2nd of August, 1415. His eldest brother, Sir John Grey, distinguished himself in the wars of Henry V., from whom he received the earldom of Tancarville.

14. GOWER, FLUELLEN, MACMORRIS, AND JAMY. As French remarks: "Shakespeare probably selected these names to represent the four nations which sent contingents to Henry's army in France." He calls attention also

[1] In that note, by an accidental error, he is twice called Duke of *Gloucester* (lines 19 and 21 of note 4, vol. i. p. 315).

to the fact that Fluellen (as the Welsh *Llewellyn* is pronounced) was the name of a townsman of the dramatist at Stratford.

15. NYM, BARDOLPH, AND PISTOL. Bardolph was also a Stratford name in the time of Shakespeare. Pistol appears to have been a favourite character, as his name is given in the titles of some editions of II. Henry IV. (see the Introduction to that play); and "Ancient Pistol" is also mentioned in the title-pages of the quartos of the present play.

16. CHARLES THE SIXTH, KING OF FRANCE. The monarch was not at Agincourt, having been urged to keep away by his uncle, the Duc de Berri, who had served at Poitiers, and who told Charles that it was better to lose a battle than a battle and a king also. Neither was he at Troyes at the time of the betrothal of his daughter, being then the victim of one of the fits of insanity to which he had long been subject. Charles had come to the throne in 1380 as successor to his father, Charles V. He married Isabel, daughter of Stephen II. of Bavaria, by whom he had three sons and five daughters. Of the latter the eldest was Isabel, who became the second queen of Richard II. (see note 23, Richard II.); and the fifth was Katharine the Fair, who figures in this play. Charles died on the 21st of October, 1422, a few weeks after Henry V.

17. LEWIS, THE DAUPHIN. He is called simply "the Dolphin" by Shakespeare. At the beginning of the play, Louis, the eldest son of Charles, was Dauphin, but he died soon after the battle of Agincourt. He was succeeded by his next brother, John, who died in 1417, and was in turn succeeded by his brother Charles, afterwards King Charles VII., who is a character in I. Henry VI. See note 22 of that play.

18. DUKE OF BURGUNDY. During the time of act i. this would be John Sans-Peur, or the Fearless, who was assassinated September 10th, 1418. His son, Philip, Count of Charolois, is the Duke of Burgundy in act v. of the play. He was not at Agincourt, though he visited the field soon after the battle, in which his uncles, the Duke of Brabant (mentioned in iv. 8. 101) and the Duke of Nevers, had been killed. He was present at Troyes during the negotiations for peace (act v. scene 2).

19. DUKE OF ORLEANS. Son of Louis, Duke of Orleans, brother to Charles VI. In 1408 he married his cousin Isabel, widow of Richard II. After the battle of Agincourt he "was discovered by an English esquire, Richard Waller, under a heap of slain, showing but faint signs of life, and after a captivity of twenty-five years in England he was released on payment of 80,000 crowns, in part of the sum fixed for his ransom, April, 1440" (French, p. 113). While imprisoned in the Tower of London he wrote several poems of no mean character. He died in 1465, and his son became King Louis XII. of France.

20. DUKE OF BOURBON. John, Duke of Bourbon, who served at Agincourt, was taken prisoner, and carried to England, where he died in 1433. He was buried at Christ Church, Newgate, London.

21. THE CONSTABLE OF FRANCE. Charles d'Albret, a natural son of Charles le Mauvais, King of Navarre, and half-brother to Queen Joan, stepmother of Henry V. He led the van at Agincourt, was wounded, and died the next day.

22. RAMBURES and GRANDPRÉ. The former French lord was "Master of the Crossbows," and had a high command in the van at Agincourt; the latter was a leader in the main body with the Dukes of Alençon and Bar. Both fell in the battle.

23. GOVERNOR OF HARFLEUR. This was Jean, Lord d'Estouteville, at the time when the siege began; but on the arrival of reinforcements under Raoul, Sieur de Gaucourt, that general appears to have taken charge of the defence. Both these lords were sent as prisoners to England, and Gaucourt wrote a narrative of the siege.

24. MONTJOY, A FRENCH HERALD. "The principal king at arms was taken prisoner at Agincourt, and it was from him that Henry V. learned that he had gained the field, and the name of the place, as stated in the play" (French, p. 117).

25. AMBASSADORS TO THE KING OF ENGLAND. According to Rymer the ambassadors on the present occasion were "Louis, Earl of Vendôme; Monsieur William Bouratin, the archbishop of Bourges; the bishop of Lisieux; the lords of Ivry and Braquemont, with Jean Andrée and Master Gualtier Cole, the king's secretaries."

26. ISABEL, QUEEN OF FRANCE. See note 16 above. She died September 24, 1435, three days after the ratification of the second treaty of Troyes, in bringing about which she had been largely instrumental.

27. THE PRINCESS KATHARINE. She was born at Paris, October 27th, 1401. After the betrothal at Troyes she was committed by Henry V. to the care of Sir Louis Robsert, who was likewise her escort to England after her husband's death. She subsequently married Owen Tudor, a Welsh gentleman of excellent family but small estates. He is said to have saved the life of Henry V. at Agincourt, and the king made him one of his "esquires of the body." The marriage with the widow of Henry, nevertheless, gave offence to her high-born kindred in both countries, and she passed the remainder of her life in obscurity. (See Introduction to II. Henry VI. vol. ii. p. 11.) Her death occurred at Bermondsey Abbey, January 3rd, 1437. Edmund, the eldest son of Owen Tudor and Katharine, was made Earl of Richmond in 1452 by his half-brother, Henry VI., and subsequently married Margaret Beaufort, heiress of the Dukes of Somerset. Their only child came to the throne of England as Henry VII.

PROLOGUE.

28. In the Folios the play is divided into acts but not into scenes, although to the first is prefixed *Actus Primus, Scena Prima.* The division into scenes was first made by Pope.

29. Lines 1, 2.—Warburton sees here an allusion to the Peripatetic system with its several heavens, "the highest

of which was one of fire;" but, as Douce remarks, the poet "simply wishes for poetic fire and a due proportion of inventive genius" (Illustrations of Shakespeare, p. 295).

30. Line 7: *Leash'd in like hounds*, &c.—Holinshed tells us that Henry V. announced to the people of Rouen "that the goddesse of battell, called Bellona, had three handmaidens, euer of necessitie attending vpon hir, as blood, fire, and famine" (vol. iii. p. 104).

31. Line 13: *this wooden O.*—The reference is to the Globe Theatre, which was of wood and circular in shape. Built in 1599 (or 1596), it was burnt down on the 29th June, 1613. In the Prolegomena to the Var. Ed. (vol. iii. p. 64) there is a woodcut of the Globe Theatre, and in Dancker's large map of London, published at Antwerp in 1647, there is also a tolerably good representation of this theatre as it then appeared. Malone says that he believes the house was called the Globe, not from its circular shape, but from its sign, "which was a figure of Hercules supporting the Globe, under which was written *Totus mundus agit histrionem*" (*ut supra*, p. 67). Compare note on As You Like It, ii. 7. 139-143. For *wooden O*, cf. Antony and Cleopatra, v. 2. 80, 81:

> And lighted
> The little *O*, the earth.

32. Line 22: *The* PERILOUS *narrow ocean.*—Steevens would make *perilous* an adverb = very, as in Beaumont and Fletcher, Humorous Lieutenant: "She is *perilous* crafty," &c.; but it is clearly an adjective. M. Mason cites Merchant of Venice, iii. 1. 4: "wrecked on the *narrow seas*; the Goodwins, I think they call the place; a very *dangerous* flat," &c. See Merchant of Venice, note 203.

33. Line 30: *Turning th' accomplishment*, &c.; *i.e.* "representing the work of many years within the time of an hour-glass."

34. Line 33: *prologue-like.*—Like one who delivers a *prologue*. The prologue was formerly ushered in by trumpets. (See Midsummer Night's Dream, note 262.) The Folio heads this division of the play with "Enter Prologue;" but compare line 32: "Admit me *Chorus*."

ACT I. Scene 1.

35.—The events narrated in this scene took place in Leicester, where the king held a parliament in 1414, but Shakespeare has chosen to make London the scene of the first act.

36. Line 1: *that* SELF *bill.*—The bill here referred to was one brought before parliament in the reign of Henry IV., providing that the temporal lands bequeathed to the church should revert to the crown, as is explained in lines 9-19. This measure naturally excited much commotion among the religious orders, whom, as Holinshed says, "suerlie it touched verie neere, and therefore to find remedie against it, they determined to assaie all waies to put by and ouerthrow this bill" (vol. iii. p. 65). It is in pursuance of this determination that the Archbishop in scene 2 opposes the Salic law. *Self* is here used in the sense of selfsame, and the literal rendering of the passage is that "the bill now urged is one and the same with that brought forward in the eleventh year," &c.

37. Line 4: *the* SCAMBLING *and unquiet time.*—For *scambling* see King John, note 252.

38. Line 8: *of our* POSSESSION.—Hanmer and Dyce read *possessions*.

39. Line 24: *The courses of his youth*, &c.—The habits of his youth gave no evidence of what was in him. The change in the character of Henry, great as it is, is not in itself an unusual one. Many a careless, free-living young man, who has beneath all his frivolities "a solid base of temperament," has made just such a radical change in his practices when suddenly brought face to face with the responsibilities of life. The archbishop, however, speaking in the true courtier spirit, persists in thinking that so remarkable a conversion was never known before.

40. Line 28: *Consideration*, &c.—"As paradise, when sin and Adam were driven out by the angel, became the habitation of celestial spirits, so the king's heart, since *consideration* has driven out his follies, is now the receptacle of wisdom and of virtue" (Johnson).

41. Line 33: *in a flood.*—Probably an allusion to the cleansing of the Augean stables by Hercules, who turned a river through them.

42. Line 34: *a heady* CURRANCE.—This is the reading of F. 1, and may well stand, as *currance* (= flux, flow) is found in writers of the time. F. 2 has *current*, which many editors prefer.

43. Line 36: *all at once.*—"And all the rest, and everything else" (Schmidt). Compare As You Like It, iii. 5. 35-37:

> Who might be your mother,
> That you insult, exult, and *all at once*,
> Over the wretched?

Staunton says it was a trite phrase in the time of Shakespeare, and quotes F. Sabie, Fisherman's Tale, 1594: "She wept, she cride, she sob'd, and *all at once*;" and Middleton, Changeling, iv. 3:

> Does love turn fool, run mad, and *all at once*?
> —Works (Dyce's edn.), vol. iv. p. 275.

44. Line 51: *practic.*—Used by Shakespeare nowhere else. The passage 51-59 is thus explained by Johnson: "His theory must have been taught by art and practice; which, says he, is strange, since he could see little of the true art or practice among his loose companions, nor ever retired to digest his practice into theory."

45. Line 52: *theoric.*—Theory. This word occurs in All's Well That Ends Well, iv. 3. 162, 163: "that had the whole *theoric* of war in the knot of his scarf;" and in Othello, i. 1. 24: "the bookish *theoric*." Some editors adopt *his theoric*, the reading of F. 3.

46. Line 60: *The strawberry grows*, &c.—"It was a common opinion in the time of Shakespeare that plants growing together imbibed each other's qualities. Sweet flowers were planted near fruit-trees with the idea of improving the flavour of the fruit, while ill-smelling plants were carefully cleared away lest the fruit should be tainted by them. But the strawberry was supposed to be an exception to the rule, and not to be corrupted by the 'evil communications' of its neighbours" (Rolfe).

47. Line 74: *Than cherishing th'* EXHIBITERS.—*Exhibiter* was used technically of those who introduced a bill. The verb *exhibit* occurs in this sense in Merry Wives, ii. 1. 29: "Why, I'll *exhibit a bill in the parliament* for the putting-down of fat men." So Measure for Measure, iv. 4. 11. The archbishop in effect says that the king, if not wholly indifferent, is at least more inclined to listen to the clergy than to those who would strip the church of its possessions.

ACT I. Scene 2.

48. Line 3: *Shall we, &c.*—The Qq. make the play begin here.

49. Line 11: *the law Salique.*—See the archbishop's own explanation below, lines 38–50.

50. Line 15: *Or nicely charge, &c.*—The king warns the archbishop against knowingly burdening his conscience with the guilt of proclaiming, by fallacious reasoning, a title which may possibly be false.

51. Line 27: *gives edge unto the* SWORDS.—Dyce and some others read *sword.*

52. Line 37: *Pharamond.*—A king of the Franks who instituted the Salic law in 424, which was afterwards ratified by Clovis I. in a council of state.

53. Line 57: *four hundred one and twenty years.*—Rolfe remarks, "No commentator has called attention to the error in subtracting 426 from 805, which leaves 379, not 421. Shakespeare follows Holinshed, who appears to have taken 405 from 826."

54. Line 72: *To* FIND *his title.*—So Ff.; the Qq. have *fine*, which Dyce adopts. Johnson proposed *line* (that is, strengthen, fortify). Retaining *find* we may explain it, either = "find out,' or—which is more probable, = "furnish with." In the latter sense *find*, though now it is rather a colloquialism, was very regularly used.

55. Line 74: *the Lady Lingare.*—No such person appears in French history. Holinshed has *Lingard.*

56. Line 94: *imbar.*—The reading of F. 3, F. 4; F. 1, F. 2 read *imbarre;* Q. 1, Q. 2, *imbace;* and Q. 3, *embrace. Imbare*, the suggestion of Warburton, was adopted by Theobald and has been followed by Halliwell and others. *Imbar* means "to bar in," "to secure."

57. Lines 99, 100:

> *When the man dies, let the inheritance*
> *Descend unto the daughter.*

The meaning obviously is, when he dies *without a son.* The Qq. have *sonne* for *man;* but the wording of Numbers xxvii. 8, "And thou shalt speak unto the children of Israel, saying, If a man die, and have no son, then ye shall cause his inheritance to pass unto his daughter," favours the Folio reading.

58. Line 108: *Whiles his most mighty father on a hill, &c.*—Allusion is here made to an incident at the battle of Cressy, thus described by Holinshed: "The earle of Northampton and others sent to the king, where he stood aloft on a windmill hill, requiring him to advance forward, and come to their aid, they being as then sore laid to of their enimies. The king demanded if his sonne were slaine, hurt, or felled to the earth. "No," said the knight that brought the message, "but he is sore matched." "Well," (said the king,) "returne to him and them that sent you, and saie to them that they send no more to me for any adventure that falleth, so long as my son is alive, for I will that this iournie be his, with the honour thereof" (Holinshed, vol. ii. p. 639).

59. Line 114: *cold for action.*—"The unemployed forces seeing the work done to their hands, stood laughing by and indifferent for action—*unmoved to action*" (Knight).

60. Line 125: *They know your grace hath cause and means and might.*—Dyce, adopting Walker's suggestion, transfers this line to the preceding speech; but *hath* in the next line is to be emphasized, as Malone suggested: "your highness *hath* indeed what they think and know you have."

61. Line 129: *pavilion'd.*—Tented. The eagerness of the English to engage in conflict with the French is well brought out in the imaginative words of Westmoreland. Although their bodies yet remain here, he seems to say, their hearts are already in the tents on the French fields ready for battle on the morrow.

62. Line 161: *The King of Scots.*—David II., who was taken prisoner by Queen Phillippa at the battle of Neville's Cross, Oct. 1346, and held in captivity for eleven years.

63. Line 163: HER *chronicle.*—The Qq. have *your*, and the Ff. *their.*

64. Lines 166–173.—The Folio assigns this speech to the Bishop of Ely; but on examination of Holinshed it will be readily seen that it belongs to the Earl of Westmoreland. For *tear* in 173 the Qq. have *spoile*, and the Ff. *tame.* Rowe made the correction.

65. Line 175: *crush'd.*—The Folio reading, followed by Cambridge editors, and explained by Schmidt to mean "forced" or "strained." The Quarto reading is *curst*, which some editors retain and explain variously as "perverse," "froward," or "sharp," "bitter."

66. Line 187.—Malone pointed out that, in the description which follows, Shakespeare may have had in his mind's eye a similar picture drawn by Lyly, in his Euphues (pp. 262–264, Arber's ed.).

67. Line 189: *The* ACT *of order.*—That is, "orderly action." Pope substitutes *art*, which Dyce adopts.

68. Line 208: *as many* WAYS *meet in one town.*—Both the Qq. and Ff. have *wayes* (with some variations in the context), but Dyce adopts Lettsom's conjecture of *streets.*

69. Line 224: *bend it to our awe; i.e.* "force it to acknowledge our supremacy."

70. Line 233: *worshipp'd with a waxen epitaph.*—The reading of the Folio; the Quarto has "paper," the meaning in either case being "easily effaced," as Schmidt explains it. As Hunter remarks, *worshipp'd* is used in the sense of *honoured*, and the passage perhaps means "a grave without any inscription, not even one of the meanest and most fugitive." More probably, however, Shake-

speare is referring to the now obsolete custom of fastening laudatory stanzas, epitaphs, &c., to the hearse, or grave, of a distinguished man. For a full and interesting note on the practice, the student must turn to Gifford's Ben Jonson, ix. 58, where the editor goes out of his way to explain the present passage. Compare also Bullen's Middleton, v. 100, and see Much Ado About Nothing, note 303.

71. Line 252: *galliard*.—Compare Twelfth Night, i. 3. 127: "What is thy excellence in a *galliard*, knight?" Sir John Davies, in his Orchestra (stanzas 67 and 68, Grosart's edition, 1869), describes the dance thus:

> But, for more divers and more pleasing show
>   A swift and wandring daunce she did invent,
> With passages uncertaine, to and fro,
>   Yet with a certaine answer and consent
>   To the quicke musicke of the instrument.
> Five was the number of the Musick's feet,
> Which still the daunce did with five paces meet.
> A gallant daunce, that lively doth bewray
>   A spirit, and a vertue masculine,
> Impatient that her house on earth should stay,
>   Since she herselfe is fiery and divine:
>   Oft doth she make her body upward fline;
> With lofty turnes and capriols in the ayre,
> Which with the lusty tunes accordeth faire.

Halliwell quotes Lanquettes Chronicle: "About this time [1541] a new trade of dauncyng *gallardes* upon five paces, and vaunting of horses, was brought into the realme by Italians, which shortly was exercised commonly of all yonge men, and the old facion lefte."

72. Line 258: *Tennis-balls*.—In the old play of The Famous Victories of Henry the Fifth the Dauphin's present is a gilded ton of *tennis-balls*.

73. Line 259: *So pleasant with us*.—The fine irony of this speech of the king's can best be appreciated when one contrasts the natures of the two men, Henry V. and the Dauphin. Up to a certain period, the death of Henry IV., their lives appear to have run in similar channels But the occasion for independent action has arrived, and Henry has successfully summoned up all his powers to meet it, while the Dauphin is still held captive by the "pleasant vices" of his youth. It is easy to call up the picture of the French ambassadors shrinking back from the king's presence, as they listen to the scorching words they are commissioned to deliver to their master, their "pleasant prince," who had so imperfectly comprehended the nature of the man with whom he had to deal. "This *mock* of his" is to recoil with terrible emphasis upon his own head.

74. Line 263: *strike his father's crown into the hazard*. —This expression, like many of those in the first part of this speech, is taken from the game of *Tennis*, a game, as is well known, of great antiquity, though it was originally played, as its French name *jeu de paume* indicates, with the hand only, like our modern game of *Fives*. Afterwards a kind of glove was introduced, and later still a *racket;* though the introduction of this instrument took place very early, for Chaucer, in his Troilus and Creseide, bk. iv., mentions it:

> But thou canst plaien *raket* to and fro.
> —Minor Poems, vol. ii. p. 164.

The exact date when the game was introduced into England is not known; but it was among the games against which an act was passed in the reign of Edward III. 1365. The object of this and other similar restrictive measures was to encourage archery at the expense of all other pastimes. As to the exact meaning of *hazard* in this passage there is some uncertainty. In the *Tennis Court* of the present day the *hazard* side is that side opposite the *dedans*, or the opposite side of the court to the server; and it is on this side of the court that there are two openings called respectively the *grille* and "the last gallery," into either of which, if the ball be struck by the player on the opposite side, it counts as a stroke. But in Howell's Dictionary, 1660 (known as the Lexicon Tetraglotton), we find under *hazard*: "The *Lower Hazard* of a Tennis Court; *Pelouse*." *Pelouse* in Cotgrave, among other synonyms, is explained as in Howell; and the synonyms given by the latter, in Italian and Spanish, leave no doubt that *hazard* meant a little hole in the wall, and that it is the same as what was called *le petit trou*, which was a little hole close to the floor in the service or *dedans* side of the court. In Mr. Julian Marshall's Annals of Tennis, plate 10, is seen a *hazard;* it is lettered *l;* and at page 82 of the same work there is a copy of the print of James Duke of York, son of Charles I. (in a *Tennis court*), which is taken from a rare quarto pamphlet published in 1641. In this plate the young prince is represented as standing with his back to the *dedans*, and in the wall there are two holes, one high up on his left-hand side, and the other on the ground on his right-hand side. This latter was the *petit trou* or *lower hazard;* and there is very little doubt that the meaning of the phrase in our text is that Henry would strike the king's crown into the *lower hazard*, there being no doubt also a play upon the word *hazard* = danger. A stroke into the *lower hazard* would be a winning stroke, so the meaning of the passage is quite clear, namely, that he would "win the crown of France." The word *hazard* is now used for a pocket in a billiard-table, and is commonly applied to a stroke which puts one of the balls into a pocket, a stroke which is described by billiard players as a losing or a winning *hazard*, accordingly as it is your own ball or one of the other balls that is put into the pocket. At what time, exactly, *hazard* came to be used in this sense is uncertain; but we find in Phillips's World of Words (1706) "*Hazard* (Fr.) . . . at Billiards, Hazards, are the Holes in the sides and Corners of the Table, into which the Gamesters endeavour to strike their Adversaries Ball."—F. A. M.

75. Line 266: *chases*.—[Scaino in his Trattato della Palla, Venice, 1555, thus explains the word *caccia* "as being equivalent to *the mark*, or *marking, of a ball that is sent*, or *pursued* (*cacciata*); and he defines it as the point at which the ball terminates its flight, when struck, neither out-of-court nor in a manner contrary to any other rules (*senza commissione di fallo*)" (Annals of Tennis, p. 133). He uses the word *caccie* indifferently for both "strokes" and *chases* as we understand the latter word nowadays. Anyone who has been in a Tennis Court will have noticed upon the floor a number of lines on the server's side or side of the *dedans*. There are six a yard apart beginning from the end wall, with intermediate lines beginning at

every half-yard. Besides these there are other lines not numbered which are called respectively Last Gallery, Second Gallery, Door and First Gallery, the latter being nearest to the net which divides the court into two parts. On the *hazard* side there are only seven lines, the first commencing four yards from the end wall. A full explanation of them will be found in the Annals of Tennis, p 118.—F. A. M.] Compare Sidney's Arcadia (book iii. p. 443, London, 1774): "Then Fortune (as if she had made *chases* (now on the one side of the bloody Tenis-court) went of the other side of the line," &c. Halliwell quotes a dialogue from the Marow of the French Tongue, 1625: "I have thirty, and a *chase*. . . . And I, I have two *chases*. —Sir, the last is no *chase*, but a losse."

76. Line 276: *For* THAT *I have laid by my majesty.*—The Folio reading. The Qq. have *For this*, and Collier's MS. corrector has *For here*.

77. Line 282: *gun-stones.*—Cannon-balls were originally made of stone. Steevens quotes Holinshed: "About seaven of the clocke marched forward the light pieces of ordinance, with stone and powder." In the Brut of England, it is said that Henry "anone lette make tenes balles for the Dolfin in all the haste that they myght, and they were great gonnestones for the Dolfin to playe with alle. But this game at tenes was too rough for the besieged, when Henry playede at the tenes with his hard gonnestones," &c.

78. Line 306: *with* REASONABLE *swiftness.*—Both Collier's and Singer's MS. correctors have *seasonable*.

ACT II. Prologue.

79. Line 2: *silken dalliance*, &c.; *i.e.* that with the prospect of war all effeminacy is put aside with the *silken* suits of peaceful times.

80. Line 26: *for the* GILT *of France,—O* GUILT *indeed!* —We are reminded at once of Lady Macbeth's (ii. 2. 55-57) ghastly jest:

> If he do bleed,
> I'll *gild* the faces of the grooms withal;
> For it must seem their *guilt*.

81. Lines 31, 32:

> *Linger your patience on; and we'll digest*
> *The abuse of distance; force a play.*

A corrupt passage, which is variously rendered by commentators. Steevens explains *force a play* as "to produce a play by compelling many circumstances into a narrow compass." Pope and Dyce read *well digest*. The lines seem out of place, and Knight believes that the author intended to erase them.

[In Charles Kean's revival of the play at the Princess's Theatre (in March, 1859), immediately before these two lines were spoken, the scene opened and discovered "a tableau, representing the three conspirators receiving the bribe from the emissaries of France." The chorus in this revival was represented by Mrs. Charles Kean, who appeared as Clio, the Muse of History. Shakespeare has assigned no personality to the chorus of this play, and it was generally represented under the figure of Time; but Charles Kean's alteration was a very sensible one, especially as it enabled Mrs. Charles Kean to take part in the revival.—F. A. M.]

82. Line 40: *We'll not offend*, &c.; *i.e.* "You shall cross the sea without being sea-sick."

83. Line 41: *till the king come*, &c.; *i.e.* "until the appearance of the king the scene will not be shifted to Southampton." Hanmer reads, *But when the king comes*, &c.; and Malone suggests:

> Not till the king come forth, and but till then.

ACT II. Scene 1.

84. Line 2: *Lieutenant Bardolph.*—It appears from an old MS. in the British Museum, that Wm. Pistail and R. Bardolf were among the cannoniers serving in Normandy in 1435.

85. Line 3: *What, are* ANCIENT *Pistol and you friends yet!*—For *ancient* (defined by Cotgrave "An Ensigne, Auntient, Standard bearer") cf. The Knight of the Burning Pestle, v. 2: "March fair, my hearts! Lieutenant, beat the rear up—*Ancient*, let your colours fly" (Beaumont and Fletcher, Dyce's ed. ii. 218). But the best known of all *ancients* is of course Othello's *ancient*, Iago.

86. Line 6: *there shall be* SMILES.—It is rash to correct Nym's nonsense; but Dyce adopts Farmer's conjecture of *smites*. Nym may, however, be looking forward to the end of the war, which seems to be more in his thoughts than his quarrel with Pistol.

87. Line 10: *I will* DO *as I may.*—Dyce follows Mason in the needless change to *die*. Nym means to say that he will make the best of it, or submit to his fate.

88. Line 17: *that is my* REST.—A term taken from the old game of primero, equivalent to, "that is my stake, wager = resolve." Compare Comedy of Errors, iv. 3. 27: "he that sets up his *rest* to do more exploits;" and All's Well that Ends Well, ii. 1. 138: "Since you set up your *rest* 'gainst remedy." See Romeo and Juliet, note 186.

Outside Shakespeare note the Spanish Gipsy, iv. 2. 13, 14:

> Could I set up my *rest*
> That he were lost, or taken prisoner;

and same play, iv. 3. 133:

> Set up thy *rest*, her marriest thou or none.
> —Works (Dyce's edn.), vol. iv. pp. 171, 180.

89. Line 31: *Base* TIKE.—For *tike* (a Scandinavian word, Swedish *tik* = a bitch) cf. Lear, iii. 6. 73:

> Or bobtail *tike* or trundle-tail.

Tyke, in Yorkshire, is a common word for a hound (used also of a churlish fellow).

90. Line 43: ICELAND DOG.—Nares describes these animals as "shaggy, sharp-eared, white dogs, much imported formerly as favourites for ladies," and refers us to various passages where they are alluded to; *e.g.* Swetnam's Arraignment of Women, 1615: "But if I had brought little *dogges* from *Island*, or fine glasses from Venice, then I am sure that you would either have wooed me to have them, or wished to see them." So Massinger, the Picture, v. 1:

> So I might have my belly full of that
> Her *Island cur* refuses. —Works, p. 314.

The folios have *Island*, the old spelling of the word. In The Queen of Corinth, iv. 1, we find the form *Isling:*

> Hang hair like hemp, or like the *Isling curs.*
> —Beaumont and Fletcher, Works (Dyce's edn.), vol. v. p. 455.

91. **Line 48:** *Will you* SHOG *off?*—Cf. Beaumont and Fletcher's The Coxcomb, ii. 2:

> Come, prythee let 's *shog* off,
> And bowze an hour or two. —Works, vol. ii. p. 289.

Shog is a form of "jog;" it means "to shake" (Palsgrave); but in Westmoreland it means "to slink away."

92. Line 57: *Barbason.*—The name of this particular fiend or devil occurs in Merry Wives in the speech of Ford, ii. 2. 310–313, where he says: "Amaimon sounds well; Lucifer, well; *Barbason*, well; yet they are devils' additions, the names of fiends." In the list of devils given in Reginald Scot's Discovery of Witchcraft, bk. 15, chap. 2, no such fiend as *Barbason* appears; but there is *Barbatos*, who is said to be "a great countie or earle, and also a duke, he appeareth in *Signo sagitarii sylvestris*, with foure kings, which bring companies and great troupes" (Dr. B. Nicholson's reprint, p. 314). He is the fifth, and he comes next after "*Amon*, or *Aamon*," who was probably the same as "*Amaymon*, king of the east," who is mentioned in the next chapter.—F. A. M.

93. Line 66: *Therefore* EXHALE; *i.e.* "die," says Steevens; but Shakespeare, according to Mr. Aldis Wright, always uses the word in the sense of "draw out." For the latter we may compare Ben Jonson's The Poetaster, iii. 1: "Nay, I beseech you, gentlemen, do not *exhale* me thus" (Works, vol. ii. p. 444).

94. Line 78: *to the* SPITAL *go.*—For *spital* (spelt "spittle" in the folios), cf. The Little French Lawyer, iii. 2: "Thou *spital* of lame causes" (Beaumont and Fletcher (Dyce), vol. iii. p. 508).

95. Line 80: *the lazar kite*, &c.—Steevens quotes Gascoigne, Dan Bartholomew of Bathe, 1587: "Nor seldom seene in *kites* of Cressid's kind;" and Greene, Card of Fancy, 1601: "What courtesy is to be found in such *kites* of Cressid's kind?"

96. Line 86: *and* YOU, *hostess.*—The Ff. have *and your Hostesse.* The Qq. read, "*Boy.* Hostes you must come straight to my maister, and you Host Pistole."

97. Line 91: *yield the crow a pudding.*—Literally "become food for crows;" but by this extravagant expression the Hostess merely means to convey the idea that Falstaff's days are numbered.

98. Line 100: *Base is the slave that pays.*—Steevens pointed out that this irreproachable sentiment was apparently a proverb; or at least became one. He refers us to Heywood's Fair Maid of the West, 1631: "My motto shall be, Base is the man that pays."

99. **Line 122:** *As ever you* CAME *of* WOMEN, &c.—The Folio has "*come of women*," and the Qq. "*came of men.*" Knight and Collier follow the Folio.

100. Line **124:** *quotidian tertian.*—The dame mixes up the *quotidian* fever, the paroxysms of which recurred daily, and the *tertian*, in which the interval was three days.

101. **Line 132:** *he* PASSES *some* HUMOURS *and* CAREERS.—Curiously enough a double parallel to this line occurs in a single scene in The Merry Wives, where we have, i. 1. 169: "Be avised, sir, and *pass* good *humours;*" and line 184: "and so conclusions *passed* the *careires.*" The second phrase is perhaps a term borrowed from horsemanship, which Nares (under *Careires* or *Career*) illustrates by a passage in Harington's translation of Ariosto, xxxviii. 35:

> To stop, to start, *to pass carier*, to bound,
> To gallop straight, or round, or any way.

(The only difficulty in explaining this phrase lies in the fact that the word *carrire*, *carreer*, or *career* (the word being very variously spelt), must have had two distinct meanings. Baret (1573) gives under "a *Carryre*, the short tourning of a nimble horse now this wale, now that wale;" while Minsheu (edn. 1617) gives *Carriere* . . . a Lat: *currere: est propria locus cursibus equorum destinatus*, because it is a place of running. Later it was used simply = "a course, a race, a running full speed" (Phillips, 1706). Nares and Douce both say that *to run a career* was the same expression as *to pass a career;* but this may be doubted; for in the former phrase *career* probably has the more usual meaning of "a race at full speed." The meaning of the phrase *to pass a career* may be best explained by the following passage from Blundevill's The foure chiefest offices belonging to Horsemanship, &c., the first edition of which was published in 1580. In The Second Booke of the Art of Riding, ch. xxiii. "How and when to teach your horse to *passe* a swift *cariere*," Blundevill recommends: When a horse is "better broken, and made meet to be run, ride him into some fair plain sandy way void of al stübling stones & to acquaint him with yᵉ way pase him fair and softly yᵉ length of a good *Cariere*, which must bee measured, according as the horse is made. For if he be a mightie puissant horse, and great of stature: then the *Cariere* would bee the shorter. So likewise must it be, when you would haue him to boūd aloft in his *Cariere:* but if he be made like a jennet, or of a middle stature, then the *Cariere* path may be yᵉ longer, yet not ouerlong. At the end wherof let him stoppe and aduance, and at the second bound turn him faire and softly on the right hand, and so stay a little while. Then suddenly saying with a liuely voice, Hey, or Now, put him forward with both spurres at once, forcing him all yᵉ way to run so swiftly and so roundly as he can possibly, euen to the end, to the intent, he may stop on his buttocks. That done, turne him out on yᵉ left hand, and pase him forth faire and softly vnto the other end of the *Cariere* path, and there stop him and turn him againe on the right hand, as you did before, and so leaue" (edn. 1609, p. 33).

The derivation of the word is most probably from the French *Carrière*, which Cotgrave explains: "An high way, rode, or streete (Langued); also, a quarry of stones; also, a *carreere, on horse-backe;* and (more generally) any exercise, or place for exercise, on horse-backe; as, a horse race, or a place for horses to run in; and, their course, running, or full speed therein." (Nearly all these meanings are given to the word *Cariere* in the above passage from Blundevill.) Cotgrave also gives the phrase: *Donner carriere à son esprit*, which he explains: "To recreate his spirit; or, to set his wits a running, his conceit a gadding, his thoughts on a gallop;" which seems to be very near the meaning of Nym in this passage.—F. A. M.]

102. Line 134: *for,* LAMBKINS, *we will live.*—The folios have: "for (*Lambekins*) we will live;" the quartos: "for *lambkins* we . . ." The latter must mean "as *lambkins*," *i.e.* peaceably; so Malone explained. The text of Ff. gives good enough sense.

ACT II. Scene 2.

103. Line 8: *Nay, but the man that was his* BEDFELLOW.—This is taken from Holinshed, who says of Lord Scroop that he was "in such fauour with the king, that he admitted him sometime to be his *bedfellow*" (vol. iii. p. 70). But the custom of men sleeping together in Shakespeare's time even in the highest rank of life was common enough. We find constant allusions to this custom in old plays. The following, which is quoted by Nares from Beaumont and Fletcher's The Chances (ii. 3), best illustrates the custom:

> My kinsman, lady,
> My countryman, and fellow-traveller:
> *One bed contains us ever*, one purse feeds us.
> —Works, vol. i. p. 502.

This practice, which is so repugnant to modern ideas, was more or less necessitated in those days, when inns were few and far between, and bed-room accommodation for travellers very inadequate. Malone says: "This unseemly custom continued common till the middle of the last century, if not later. Cromwell obtained much of his intelligence during the civil wars from the mean men with whom he slept" (Var. Ed. vol. xvii. p. 305). The custom is alluded to in Pepys' Diary.—F. A. M.

104. Line 9: *dull'd and cloy'd with gracious favours.*—These words of Exeter's throw into strong relief the ingratitude of Cambridge. He has been the king's chosen friend, and the sun of princely favour has shone full upon his head. On him have been heaped so many gifts and tokens of fond friendship that "the sensitive palm of receiving" has become, as it were, *dulled*, and desire has grown *cloyed*. Yet in spite of all that friendship and favour should inspire him with, his heart finds room for the basest treachery.

105. Line 26: *there's not, I think,* &c.—Pope omits *I think*, which words make the line too long.

106. Line 35: *According to* THE WEIGHT.—So Ff. The Qq. have *their cause*, and Dyce reads *their weight*, which Camb. edd. give as an anonymous conjecture.

107. Line 43: *on his more advice*—.—Johnson explains this as "on his return to more coolness of mind," which is much the same as the explanation in our foot-note. *On more advice* may be rendered by our modern expression "on thinking better of it." For a similar use of *more advice* compare Merchant of Venice, iv. 2. 6, 7:

> My Lord Bassanio, *upon more advice*,
> Hath sent you here this ring:

and Two Gentlemen of Verona, ii. 4. 207:

> How shall I dote on her with *more advice*

But Shakespeare never uses the expression elsewhere precisely in the same manner as in the text. Collier's Old Corrector would substitute *our* for *his*; an unnecessary substitution, though plausible enough, and more in accordance with the usual use of the phrase. Mr. Aldis Wright (Clarendon Press edn. p. 127) suggests that *his* may here be used in an objective sense, and compares line 46 below "by *his* sufferance," *i.e.* "by allowing him to go unpunished."

108. Line 63: *ask for it*; *i.e.* "ask for my commission," *it* referring of course to the royal warrant.

109. Line 65: *And I, my royal sovereign.*—Some editors print *And me,* &c. The Qq. have "And *me* my *Lord.*"

110. Line 108: *did not* HOOP *at them.*—So Ff. For this form of the word *whoop*, see note on As You Like It, iii. 2. 203; "out of all *hooping.*"

111. Line 118: *But he that* TEMPER'D *thee.*—That is, he that moulded or made thee. Dyce adopts Johnson's conjecture of *tempted*, on the ground that the context requires it; but the temptation is sufficiently expressed as the passage stands. The emendation is plausible at first sight, but not really called for.

112. Line 123: *to* VASTY TARTAR *back*; *i.e.* Tartarus = hell. So Comedy of Errors, iv. 2. 32:

> No, he's in *Tartar* limbo.

Middleton has even a funnier form: "these are arguments sufficient to show the wealth of sin, and how rich the sons and heirs of *Tartary* are" (The Black Book, Works, viii. 22, Bullen's ed.). For *vasty* we may remember:

> To-night it doth inherit
> The *vasty* hall of death.
> —Matthew Arnold's *Requiescat*

113. Line 134: *in modest complement.*—"That is, in a corresponding outward appearance" (Schmidt). As to the words *complement* and *compliment* see Love's Labour's Lost, note 11.

114. Line 139: *To* MARK *the full-fraught man.*—The Ff. have *make*. The passage is not in the Qq. The correction is Theobald's, and commends itself.

115. Line 160: *earnest.*—It is this circumstance of their having received *earnest-money* for his assassination which most deeply moves the king's resentment.

116. Line 192: *Cheerly to sea,* &c.—"Let us put forth to sea gladly, and let our banners and pennons be displayed."

ACT II. Scene 3.

117. Line 2: *let me bring thee to* STAINES.—*Staines* was the first stage on the road to Southampton.

118. Line 11: *a* FINER *end.*—The reading of F. 1, F. 2 (F. 3, F. 4 omit *a*), and generally adopted. It is not in the Qq. Capell and Dyce read *fine*. Johnson thought the word a blunder for *final*.

119. Line 12: *christom.*—A blunder for *chrisom*. The *chrisom* was the white vesture put upon the child after baptism and worn till the mother came to be churched. It was also applied to the child, as we see from several passages; *e.g.* Your Five Gallants, iii. 5. 121: "it would

kill his heart i' faith; he 'd away like a *chrisom*" (Middleton, Works (Bullen's ed.), iii. 194). So in The Fancies Chaste and Noble, iv. 1: "And the boy was to any man's thinking a very *chrisome* in the thing you wot of" (Gifford's Ford, ii. 213).

120. Line 14: *fumble with the sheets.*—A phrase in common use apparently. Compare Beaumont and Fletcher's Spanish Curate, iv. 5:

> A glimmering before death; 't is nothing else, sir.
> *Do you see how he fumbles with the sheet?*
> —Works, vol. i. p. 174.

As an illustration of the whole passage Steevens quotes Thomas Lupton's Notable Things, book ix.: "If the forehead of the sicke waxe redde—and his nose waxe sharpe—if he *pull* strawes, or *the clothes of the bedde*—these are most certain tokens of death" (Var. Ed. vol. xvii. p. 318).

121. Line 16: *but one way.*—A proverbial and euphemistic expression for death. Various instances of its occurrence may be quoted: *e.g.* The Phœnix, i. 6. 66: "Newly deceased, I can assure your worship: the tobacco-pipe new dropt out of his mouth before I took horse; a shrewd sign; I knew there was *no way but one* with him" (Middleton's Works, Bullen's ed. i. p. 132). Compare, too, Witch of Edmonton, iv. 2:

> *Frank.* Do the surgeons say my wounds are dangerous then?
> *Car.* Yes, yes, and there's *no way* with thee *but one*.
> —Ford's Works, Gifford's ed. ii. p. 535.

So Marlowe's Tamburlaine, part i. v. 1. 200, 201:

> March on us with such eager violence,
> As if there were *no way but one* with us.
> —Works, p. 33.

122. Lines 17, 18: *a' babbled of green fields.*—The Folio has "*a Table* of greene fields." This emendation is Theobald's, and is generally adopted. Malone would read, "*upon a table* of green *fells;*" Smith, "*on* a table of green *frieze;*" and the Collier MS., *or as stubble on shorn fields.*

123. Line 23: *a' should not think of God.*—Malone remarks that Shakespeare may have been indebted to this story in Wits, Fits, and Fancies, 1595: "A gentlewoman fearing to be drowned, said, now Jesu receive our soules! Soft, mistress, answered the waterman; I trow, we are not come to that passe yet" (Var. Ed. vol. xvii. p. 320).

124. Line 29: *of sack.*—See note 41 on I. Henry IV.

125. Line 35: *carnation.*—Mrs. Quickly confuses the words *incarnate* and *carnation*, but the former was sometimes used in place of the latter in Shakespeare's time. Henderson quotes Questions of Love, 1566: "Yelowe, pale, redde, blue, whyte, graye, and *incarnate;*" and Reed cites also the Inventory of the Furniture to be provided for the Reception of the Royal Family, at the Restoration, 1660: "the rich *incarnate* velvet bed;" and "his majesty's *incarnate* velvet bed" (Var. Ed. vol. xvii. p. 321). Compare Merchant of Venice, note 127.

126. Line 51: "*Pitch and Pay.*"—A common proverbial expression of that day, signifying "to pay down ready money." We have it in Middleton's Blurt, Master Constable, i. 2. 171:

> But will you *pitch and pay*, or will your worship run?
> —Works (Dyce's edn.), vol. i. p. 242.

Steevens refers us (Var. Ed. xvii. 322) to Herod and Antipater, 1622:

> he that will purchase this,
> Must *pitch and pay*.

And Farmer (ibid.) to Tusser's Description of Norwich:

> A city trim . . . .
> Where strangers well may seem to dwell,
> That *pitch and pay*, or keep their day.

The meaning of the phrase is therefore established; its origin is doubtful.

ACT II. Scene 4.

127. Lines 9, 10:

> *as fierce*
> *As waters to the sucking of a gulf;*

i.e. "as dangerous as the waters that are drawn into a whirlpool."

128. Line 25: *Whitsun morris-dance.*—An ancient dance in which the performers were dressed in grotesque costume, with bells, &c. For a full description of the ancient English morris-dance see Douce's Illustrations of Shakespeare, Dissertation III.

129. Line 29: *fear attends her not; i.e.* "she is self-confident merely from ignorance and indifference."

130. Lines 37, 38:

> *the Roman Brutus,*
> *Covering discretion with a coat of folly.*

Malone cites Lucrece, 1807-1817:

> Brutus, who pluck'd the knife from Lucrece' side,
> Seeing such emulation in their woe,
> Began to *clothe his wit* in state and pride,
> Burying in Lucrece' wound his *folly's show*.
> He with the Romans was esteemed so
> As silly-jeering idiots are with kings,
> For sportive words and uttering foolish things.
> But now he throws that *shallow habit* by,
> Wherein deep policy did him disguise,
> And arm'd his long-hid wits advisedly,
> To check the tears in Collatinus' eyes.

131. Lines 41-44:

> *Well, 't is not so, my lord high constable;*
> *But though we think it so, it is no matter:*
> *In cases of defence 't is best to weigh*
> *The enemy more mighty than he seems.*

The weak, blustering nature of the Dauphin is well shown in these lines. He at first flatly contradicts the constable, and then, unwilling to own his mistaken conception of Henry's character, endeavours to cover his real timidity under commonplace remarks about assumptions it is best to make in certain cases.

132. Line 46: *projection.*—Plan, calculation. The construction in this place is somewhat confused, but the meaning, as Malone suggests, evidently is, "which proportions of defence, when weakly and niggardly projected, resemble a miser who spoils his coat," &c.

133. Line 57: *Whiles*, &c.—A second allusion to the battle of Cressy, but this time from the French point of view. Cf. i. 2. 108.

134. Line 57: *mountain sire.*—Theobald proposed moun-

ting, i.e. aspiring. The Collier MS. reads *mighty*. Coleridge suggested *monarch*. Steevens quotes, in explanation, from the Fairy Queen as follows:

> Where stretcht he lay upon the sunny side
> Of a great hill, himselfe *like a great hill*.
> —Bk. i. c. xi. st. 4.

Malone observes that the repetition of *mountain* is quite in the poet's manner.

135. Line 70: *Most* SPEND *their* MOUTHS.—One of the dramatist's technical touches; cf. Venus and Adonis, 695, 696:

> Then do they *spend their mouths:* Echo replies,
> As if another chase were in the skies.

136. Line 75: *our brother England*.—The Ff. have *brother of England*, as also in 115 below. The passage is not in the Qq.

137. Line 90: THIS *pedigree*.—Rowe and Dyce read "*his* pedigree."

138. Line 99: *Therefore in* FIERY *tempest is he coming*.—The early editors all have *fierce*, which was corrected by Walker. Some editors, however, retain *fierce*.

139. Line 120: *his* ORDINANCE.—Dyce and some others print *ordnance*, while saying that the word is a trisyllable; but it was often printed *ordinance* in the poet's day, and this was the original form of the word.

ACT III. Prologue.

140. Line 4: HAMPTON *pier*.—The Ff. have *Douer pier*. The chorus is not in the Qq.

141. Line 6: *young Phœbus* FANNING.—The Ff. have *fayning*, which Rowe corrected.

142. Line 10: THREADEN *sails*.—That is, made of thread. Compare A Lover's Complaint, 33:

> Some in her *threaden* fillet still did bide.

143. Line 33: *linstock*.—"The staff to which the match is fixed when the ordnance is fired" (Johnson). The old stage-direction, at the end of this line, in F. 1 has "*Alarume chambers go off*." *Chambers* were small cannon.

ACT III. Scene 1.

144. Line 7: SUMMON *up the blood*.—The Ff. have *commune*, corrected by Rowe. This scene is omitted in the Qq.

145. Line 14: *wasteful*.—Desolate, lying waste. A peculiarly apt expression in Shakespeare's time when commerce did not whiten every sea with her sails. *Ocean*, metrically a trisyllable. Compare Merchant of Venice, i. 1. 8:

> Your mind is tossing on the *ocean*.

146. Line 17: *you* NOBLEST *English*.—F. 1 has *noblish*, the other Ff. *noblest*. Malone substituted *noble*.

147. Line 24: MEN *of grosser blood*.—The first three Ff. have *me*, corrected in F. 4.

148. Line 31: *slips*.—Nooses in which the dogs were held until started for the game. To *let slip* was to loose the hound from the slip. Cf. I. Henry IV. i. 3. 278.

149. Line 32: STRAINING *upon the start*.—The Ff. have *straying*. The emendation in the text is Rowe's.

ACT III. Scene 2.

150. Line 3: *a* CASE *of lives*.—A musical allusion, as the Clarendon Press editor notes; musical instruments being often made in sets of four, which were kept in one *case*.

151. Line 4: *plain-song*.—In music "the simple melody, without any variations." Compare Midsummer Night's Dream, iii. 1. 134:

> The *plain-song* cuckoo gray;

and see note 160 on that play. See also Henry VIII. i. 3. 44, 45:

> An honest country lord, as I am, beaten
> A long time out of play, may bring his *plain-song*.

Nares reminds us of Ascham's Complaint: "I wish from the bottom of my heart that the laudable custom of England to teach children their *plainsong* and pricksong were not so decayed" (Toxophilus, p. 28).

152. Line 21: *breach*.—The quartos read *breaches*, and the folios *breach*. "Throughout the speeches of Fluellen the old copies sometimes mark the peculiarity of his pronunciation by using 'p' for 'b,' and 't' for 'd,' sometimes not; an inconsistency which Hanmer and others have attempted to correct" (Cambridge edn. vol. iv. p. 600, note vii.).

153. Line 22: *you* CULLIONS.—"A wretch. A coarse word. F. *couillon* (Ital. *coglione*)."—Skeat. We have the expression in The Taming of the Shrew, iv. 2. 20: "And makes a god of such a *cullion*." So II. Henry VI. i. 3. 43; and *cullionly*, "you whoreson *cullionly* barber-monger," in Lear, ii. 2. 36.

154. Line 23: *great duke*.—"It seems to us that there is some comic humour in making Pistol, almost beside himself with fright, endeavour to propitiate the captain by giving him high sounding titles" (Cambridge edn. *ut supra*).

155. Line 50: *carry coals*.—See Romeo and Juliet, note 3.

156. Line 90: *Captain* JAMES.—The Folio reading, and perhaps intentionally wrong. Dyce reads *Jamy*.

157. Line 123: *ay 'll* DO *gud service*.—The Ff. have *de*, which some editors retain; but it is almost certainly a misprint.

158. Lines 134, 135: *of my nation, &c.*—The Folio reading. Knight suggested that the type had been transposed, and reads the passage thus: "Of my nation! What ish my nation? What ish my nation? Who talks of my nation ish a villain, and a bastard, and a knave, and a rascal." Staunton's opinion is that "the incoherence of the original was designed to mark the impetuosity of the speaker," and in this view he is supported by the Cambridge editors.

ACT III. Scene 3.

159. Line 26: *As send* PRECEPTS *to the leviathan*; i.e. a "mandate," "summons," almost in the technical legal

sense of the latter. Schmidt refers us to II. Henry IV. v. 1. 14:

those *precepts* cannot be *serv'd*.

160. Line 32: HEADY *murder*.—F. 1 has *headly*, the other Ff. *headdy*, or *heady*. Malone proposed *deadly*, which Grant White accepts.

161. Line 35: DEFILE *the locks*.—The Ff. have *Desire*, which Rowe corrected.

162. Line 48: *thy soft mercy*.—The governor's response, with its military conciseness and straightforwardness, contains in the phrase, *soft mercy*, an indirect appeal to the clemency of the English king. "We are at your mercy" would be simply an appeal, and, to one of Henry's temperament, not particularly effective; but the addition of the adjective *soft* conveys a subtle compliment not unacceptable to the king, who would like to have it thought that he had a strain of compassion in his nature.

ACT III. Scene 4.

163.—Johnson says: "The scene is indeed mean enough, when it is read; but the grimaces of two French women, and the odd accent with which they uttered the English, made it divert upon the stage. It may be observed that there is in it not only the French language, but the French spirit. Alice compliments the princess upon her knowledge of four words, and tells her that she pronounces like the English themselves. The princess suspects no deficiency in her instructress, nor the instructress in herself. Throughout the whole scene there may be found French servility and French vanity" (Var. Ed. vol. xvii. p. 350). Grant White observes: "Shakespeare sought to enliven his History by humour; and his intention here was to excite mirth by the exhibition of a Frenchwoman in the ridiculous emergency of sudden preparation for amorous conquest of an Englishman. This could best be done by making her attempt to learn his language, in doing which she must of course speak French; and Shakespeare here, as in the subsequent scene between Pistol and the French soldier, instinctively preserved dramatic propriety at the expense of the mere verbal consistency of his work." We give a translation of the scene here, instead of in the foot-notes:—

Kath. Alice, you have been in England, and you speak the language well.

Alice. A little, madame.

Kath. I beg you, instruct me: I must learn to speak. What do you call *la main* in English?

Alice. *La main?* It is called *de hand*.

Kath. *De hand.* And *les doigts?*

Alice. *Les doigts?* Heavens, I forget *les doigts;* but I will try and recollect. *Les doigts!* I think they are called *de fingres;* yes, *de fingres* (*i.e.* the fingers).

Kath. *La main*, de hand: *les doigts*, de fingres. I think I am a good scholar; I have quickly learned two words of English. How do you call *les ongles?*

Alice. *Les ongles?* We call them *de nails*.

Kath. *De nails.* Listen; tell me if I say them right: *de hand, de fingres*, and *de nails*.

Alice. Quite right, madame: it is very good English.

Kath. Tell me the English for *le bras*.

Alice. *De arm*, madame.

Kath. And *le coude?*

Alice. *De elbow.*

Kath. *De elbow.* I will repeat all the words you have taught me so far.

Alice. I think it is too hard, madame.

Kath. Excuse me, Alice; listen: *de hand, de fingres, de nails, de arm, de bilbow.*

Alice. De elbow, madame.

Kath. O heaven, I am forgetting: *de elbow*. What do you call *le cou?*

Alice. *De neck*, madame.

Kath. *De nick*, and *le menton?*

Alice. *De chin.*

Kath. *De sin.* *Le col*, *de nick; de menton, de sin.*

Alice. With your leave, in all truth, you pronounce the words as correctly as the natives of England.

Kath. I have no fear about learning, with the grace of God, and in a little time.

Alice. Have you not already forgotten what I have taught you?

Kath. No, I will quickly tell you: *de hand, de fingres, de mails.*

Alice. *De nails*, madame.

Kath. *De nails*, de arm, *de ilbow*.

Alice. Pardon me, *de elbow*.

Kath. Thus then: *de elbow, de nick*, and *de sin*. What are *le pied* and *la robe?*

Alice. *De foot*, madame; and *de coun?*

Kath. *De foot* and *de coun*. O Heavens! these are words of a wicked, corruptible, gross and immodest sound, not fit for honourable ladies to use: I would not pronounce these words before the lords of France for all the world. Fauh! *de foot* and *de coun!* Nevertheless, I will repeat my lesson once again right through, etc.

Alice. Excellent, madame!

Kath. Enough for one time: let us go to dinner.

ACT III. Scene 5.

164.—The stage-direction of the Folio is, "Enter the King of France, the Dolphin, the Constable of France, and others," and the speeches beginning with lines 10 and 32 are assigned to "Brit." Since, however, the Duke of "Britaine" does not elsewhere appear in the play, the editors, following Theobald, here substituted Bourbon for "Brit." In line 41 Bourbon is mentioned as present among the lords, and the stage-direction of the Quarto also includes him. According to the Cambridge editors "Shakespeare probably first intended to introduce the Duke of Britaine, and then changed his mind, but forgot to substitute *Bour.* for *Brit.* before the two speeches."

165. Line 14: *nook-shotten*.—This is interpreted by Warburton and Schmidt to mean shooting out into capes and necks of land. A more probable meaning is that given by Knight and Grant White, who render it: "thrust into a corner apart from the world."

166. Line 15: WHERE *have they this mettle?*—Dyce reads *whence*.

167. Line 19: *A* DRENCH *for* SUR-REIN'D *jades*.—"Sur-reined" (= over-worked, for which the Quartos have

"swolne") occurs, according to Steevens, not infrequently in the dramatists; we are referred to Jack Drum's Entertainment, 1601:

> Writes he not a good cordial sappy style?—
> A *surreined* jaded wit, but he holds on.

Drench, as in I. Henry IV. ii. 4. 120:

> "Give my roan horse a *drench*."

168. Line 23: *like* ROPING *icicles*; *i.e.* dripping. Cf. iv. 2. 48:

> The gum *down-roping* from their pale-dead eyes.

169. Line 26: *Poor we* MAY *call them*.—The *may* was added in F. 2.

170. Line 33: *lavoltas*.—The lavolta is thus described by Sir John Davies, in his Orchestra (stanzas 70 and 71, Grosart's ed. 1869):

> Yet is there one the most delightful kind,
> A lofty jumping, or a leaping round,
> Where arm in arm, two dancers are entwin'd,
> And whirl themselves in strict embracements bound,
> And still their feet an anapest do sound:
> An anapest is all their musick's song,
> Whose first two feet is short, and third is long.
>
> As the victorious twins of Leda and Jove,
> That taught the Spartans dancing on the sands
> Of swift Eurotas, dance in heaven above;
> Knit and united with eternal hands,
> Among the stars their double image stands,
> Where both are carried with an equal pace,
> Together jumping in their turning race.

The *coranto*, or *corranto* (from the Italian *correre*, Latin *currere*, to run), was also a lively dance. Davies describes it as follows (stanza 69):

> What shall I name those *current* traverses,
> That on a triple dactyl foot do run,
> Close by the ground, with sliding passages,
> Wherein that dancer greatest praise hath won
> Which with best order can all order shun:
> For every where he wantonly must range,
> And turn and wind with unexpected change.

Compare All's Well, ii. 3. 49: "he's able to lead her a *coranto*;" Twelfth Night, i. 3. 136, 137: "go to church in a galliard and come home in a *coranto*."

171. Line 40: *Delabreth*.—The modern *D'Albret*, which will not satisfy the measure. This form of the name is taken from Holinshed.

172. Line 45: FOIX, *Lestrale*, &c.—Ff. have *Loys*, which Capell corrected.

173. Line 46: *lords, and* KNIGHTS.—Ff. have *kings*. The correction is Theobald's.

174. Lines 58, 59:

> *For I am sure, when he shall see our army,*
> *He'll drop his heart into the sink of fear.*

The Constable, while uttering these boastful lines, appears to have momentarily forgotten that he has not long before spoken of Henry as "terrible in constant resolution;" but he may have thought it best to fall in with the humour of the king, and outdo him, if possible, in bravado.

175. Line 60: *And for achievement offer us his ransom*.—"That is, *instead* of achieving a victory over us, make a proposal to pay us a certain sum as a ransom" (Malone).

ACT III. SCENE 6.

176. Line 4: *the bridge*.—After Henry had passed the Somme, the French attempted to break down the only bridge over the Ternoise, at Blangy, and thus cut off his passage to Calais; but Henry, learning their design, sent forward troops who put the French to flight, and guarded the bridge until the English had crossed.

177. Line 13: *an aunchient*.—The Ff. have "an *aunchient* Lieutenant;" the Q. has "an Ensigne."

178. Line 28: *Of buxom valour, hath, by cruel fate*.—This speech of Pistol's is printed in Ff. as prose, in Qq. as irregular verse. Both Qq. and Ff. read:

> *And* of buxom valour, &c.

We have followed Capell in omitting *and* for the sake of the metre. Pope omits *of*.

179. Line 30:

> *That goddess* BLIND,
> *That stands upon the* ROLLING RESTLESS STONE.

For a note on fortune as "the bountiful *blind* woman," see As You Like It, i. 2. 38. Pistol's alliterative effort is not, it would seem, original. Steevens reminds us of Gascoigne's

> O blissful concord, bredde in sacred brest
> Of him that guides the *restlesse rolling* sky.
> —Gascoigne's Jocasta, iv.

180. Line 41: *Fortune is Bardolph's foe, and frowns on him*.—The old editors missed an allusion here which Staunton was the first to point out, viz. that Pistol is referring to the ballad

> Fortune, my foe! why dost thou frown on me?

Compare—though the hint is vaguer—Merry Wives, iii. 3. 69, 70.

181. Line 42: *a pax*.—Altered to *pix* by Theobald. Johnson says the two words mean the same, but this is a complete mistake. The *pix*, or *pyx*, as it is usually written, is "a vase in which the Blessed Sacrament is preserved;" that is to say, not the large wafer called the Host, but the smaller consecrated wafer which is given to communicants at mass. "The *pyx* should be of silver, gilt inside, and covered with a silk veil." It is mentioned as early as the first half of the ninth century. (See Addis and Arnold's Catholic Dictionary, sub *Pyx*.) The *pax* is a totally different thing. It was the practice in the early church to give the kiss of peace. In the eastern church this was given at the end of the lections or readings, before the more solemn part of the mass began. In the western church it was always given after the consecration of the elements, and it was this ceremony which gave rise to the practice of separating the sexes in church. The kiss of peace was first given by the bishop to the priest, then by the priests to one another, lastly by the laity to each other. "It was only at the end of the thirteenth century that it gave way to the use of the 'osculatorium'—called also 'instrumentum' or 'tabella pacis,' 'pax,' 'pacificale,' 'freda' (from *Friede*), &c.—a plate with a figure of Christ on the cross stamped upon it, kissed first by the priest, then by the clerics and congregation. It was introduced into England by Archbishop Walter of York, in 1250. Usually now the *Pax* is not given at all in low

Masses, and in high Mass an embrace is substituted for the old kiss and given only to those in the sanctuary" (*ut supra, sub* KISS (*of peace*)). Those who propose to read *pix* instead of *pax*, in this passage, find their justification in the following passage from Hall (which Holinshed, as usual, copied): "And yet in this great necessitee the poore folkes wer not spoyled nor any thyng without paiment was of thē extorted, nor great offence was doen except one, whiche was that a foolishe souldier stale a *pixe* out of a churche and vnreuerently did eate the holy hostes within the same conteigned. For whiche cause he was apprehended, and the kyng would not once remoue till the vessel was restored & the offender strangled" (p. 64).—F. A. M.

182. Lines 60-62:

> *and* FIGO *for thy friendship!*
> Flu. *It is well.*
> Pist. *The fig of Spain!*

Figo is the obsolete Spanish form of *higo*, a fig, and *higa* is used in the same sense as the Italian *fica*, namely, of a contemptuous gesture made by putting the thumb between the two first fingers of the hand. (Compare II. Henry IV. v. 3. 124 and note thereon.) Florio gives under *Fica*, "any kind of fig; also a flirt with the fingers, made, or shewn to some in scorn or disgrace of them." *Figo* was undoubtedly used as we use a *fig* in such expressions as "a *fig* for your threats," to indicate something worthless. Douce has a long and interesting article on this passage (Illustrations of Shakespeare, pp. 302-308). Steevens thought that *The fig of Spain* alluded to the poisoned figs which were often given by Spaniards and Italians to the objects of their revenge. He quotes several passages from old plays in confirmation of his view, *e.g.* from Webster's Vittoria Corombona:

> I do look now for a *Spanish fig*, or an Italian sallet, daily.
> —Works (Dyce's edn.), vol. i. p. 93.

But it seems from a note of Reid's (Var. Ed. vol. xvii. p. 365) that *the Spanish fig* was also used in the sense of a contemptuous gesture.—F. A. M.

183. Lines 80, 81: *beard of the general's cut.*—The *cut of the beard* frequently seems to have denoted the profession of the wearer. See note on As You Like It, ii. 7. 155: "*beard of* formal *cut.*"

184. Lines 102-112.—Steevens suggests that Shakespeare may have remembered the description of the Sompnour in the Prologue to the Canterbury Tales.

185. Line 121: Tucket.—Obviously the Italian *toccata*, a prelude. Etymologically the word is the same as *toucher*, *toquer* (cf. *tocsin*), *touch*.

186. Line 121: *You know me by my* HABIT; *i.e.* "by my herald's coat," now commonly called "a tabard." (For an illustration of this *coat* or *tabard* see Planché's Cyclopædia of Costume, vol. i. p. 490.) The person of a herald, as Johnson says, being inviolable, he was obliged to wear a distinctive dress.

187. Line 124: *Thus says my king, &c.*—The attitude of the French towards England is made consistent throughout. Charles himself strikes the key-note of boastfulness and bluster, and all his subjects, from Dauphin to Herald, eagerly follow his lead.

ACT III. Scene 7.

188. Line 13: *on four* PASTERNS.—F. 1 has *postures*, corrected in F. 2. It is not in the Qq.

189. Lines 14, 15: *as if his entrails were hairs; le cheval volant, the Pegasus, qui a les narines de feu!*—The Dauphin's description of his horse is on a par with his bragging nature as represented in this play. Collier's MS. substituted *air* for *hairs;* but the speaker means that his horse bounds as if he were *stuffed with hair* like a tennis-ball. In the next line Ff. read *ches*, which Theobald printed as *chez;* but *chez* never means "with" in the sense demanded here. *Qui a*, the reading in the text, is Capell's emendation. *Chez* is nonsense. Heath suggests *voyez;* but it is possible the *ches* of the Folio is a misprint for *à les*, which was often used in old French instead of *aux*. —F. A. M.

190. Line 23: *the dull elements, &c.*—It was once a popular idea that everything was composed of the four elements—earth, air, fire, and water, and the proportion of these in the higher forms of life is indicated in Antony and Cleopatra, v. 2. 292:

> I am fire and air; my other *elements*
> I give to baser life.

See also Twelfth Night, ii. 3. 9, 10:

> Does not our life consist of the *four elements*?

In Shakespeare's 44th Sonnet this belief is thus referred to:

> . . . so much *of earth and water* wrought,
> I must attend time's leisure with my moan.

Tennyson alludes to this notion in the Two Voices:

> The *elements* were kindlier mixt.

191. Line 51: NAY, FOR *methought yesterday, &c.*—The Qq. have *Ma foi*, which some editors prefer, assuming the *Nay, for* of the Ff. to be a misprint.

192. Line 56: *like a* KERN *of Ireland.*—For *kern* (Irish *ceatharnach*, a soldier) see II. Henry VI. note 236, and Richard II. note 127.

193. Lines 64, 65: *wears his own hair.*—The practice of wearing false hair seems to have been peculiarly distasteful to Shakespeare. See Merchant of Venice, note 297, and Love's Labour's Lost, note 134.

194. Lines 69, 70.—"Dr. Nicholson informs me that this quotation of 2 Peter ii. 22 agrees, so far as it goes, word for word, with a Protestant version of the New Testament published by Antoine Cellier at Clarenton, 1669, and entitled 'Le N. Testament, c'est à dire, La Nouvelle Alliance de Nostre Seigneur Jesus Christ.'"—W. G. Stone in notes to his edition of Henry V. for the New Shakspere Society.

195. Lines 121, 122: *'tis a hooded valour; and when it appears, it will* BATE.—In falconry hawks were kept *hooded* until the moment they were to fly at the game. Johnson thus explains this passage: "The meaning is, the Dauphin's valour has never yet been loose upon an enemy, yet, when he makes his first essay we shall see how he will flutter." To *bate* was to flap the wings, as the bird did when unhooded; a technical term in falconry thus explained in The Gentleman's Academie (1595): "It is called *batting*" (*i.e. bating*) "in that she batteth

with herself without cause;" and just above we have "when she *batteth* or striveth to flee away."[1] Interesting too is the passage from Bacon's letters that Nares gives us: "wherein I would to God that I were *hooded*, that I saw less, or that I could perform: for now I am like a hawk, that *bates*, when I see occasion of service, but cannot fly because I am tied to another's fist." We may remember also Petruchio's—

> watch her, as we watch these kites
> That *bate*, and beat, and will not be obedient.
> —Taming of the Shrew, iv. 1. 198, 199.

ACT IV. Prologue.

196. Line 9: *umber'd*.—Schmidt explains this as "embrowned, darkened;" but, as Rolfe says, it seems better to understand it as referring to the effect of the fire-light on their faces. Malone remarks that *umber*, "mixed with water, produces such a dusky yellow colour as the gleam of fire by night gives to the countenance." Taken in this sense, it is an exceedingly *picturesque* word. For a note on its use as a dye, see As You Like It, i. 3. 114.

197. Line 12: *The armourers*, &c.—Compare Tennyson's Enid:

> An armourer,
> Who, with back turn'd, and bow'd above his work
> Sat riveting a helmet on his knee.

Douce says in his Illustrations of Shakespeare, p. 308: "This does not solely refer to the business of rivetting the plate armour before it was put on, but as to part when it was on. Thus the top of the cuirass had a little projecting bit of iron, that passed through a hole pierced through the bottom of the casque. When both were put on, the smith or armourer presented himself, with his rivetting hammer, *to close the rivet up*, so that the party's head should remain steady notwithstanding the force of any blow that might be given on the cuirass or helmet. This custom more particularly prevailed in tournaments"

198. Line 16: *drowsy morning* NAME.—The Ff. have *nam'd*, corrected by Tyrwhitt. The prologue is not in the Qq.

199. Lines 18, 19:

> *The confident and over-lusty French*
> *Do the low-rated English play at dice.*

Malone reminds us that this is a touch borrowed from Holinshed: "The Frenchmen in the mean while, as though they had been sure of victory, made great triumphe, for the captaines had determined before how to divide the spoil, and the souldiers the night before had *plaid the Englishmen at dice*" (Var. Ed. xvii. p. 385).

200. Line 27: PRESENTETH *them unto the gazing moon.*—The Ff. have *Presented*, which Steevens set right.

201. Line 39: *freshly looks*, &c.—See As You Like It, iii. 2. 243: "Looks he as freshly," &c. *Over-bears attaint*= "represses the anxiety that wears upon him" (Rolfe). Hudson explains it, "overcomes all disposition on the part of the soldiers to blame or reproach him for the plight he is in;" but this does not agree with the context. The king puts on a cheerful look himself, and thus revives the drooping spirits of his soldiers. Compare Virgil, Æn. i. 208:

> Talia voce refert, curisque ingentibus aeger,
> *Spem vultu simulat*, premit altum corde dolorem.

202. Line 45: *that mean and gentle all*, &c.—This, the Folio reading, is retained by Knight, Grant White, and the Cambridge editors. The interpretation of this passage seems to be, so that men, whether of inferior or superior rank in the English army, may behold some little touch of Harry in the night, as far as their unworthy or dull natures will enable them to appreciate it. Some editors adopt Theobald's:

> Then, *mean and gentle*,
> All behold;

which must, of course, be taken as an address to the audience, the *mean* being slightly inappropriate.

203. Lines 49-52:

> *we shall much disgrace*
> *With four or five most vile and ragged foils,*
> *Right ill-dispos'd in brawl ridiculous,*
> *The name of Agincourt.*

This is but one of the many apologies, made by the Chorus in this play, for the inadequacy of the scenic arrangements and general "mounting" of the piece. Surely those who object to the endeavours made by modern managers to give due artistic importance to the *mise-en-scène* of Shakespeare's plays, may find their best answer in the very marked way in which the poet himself deplores the poverty of the scenic resources at his command.—F. A. M.

ACT IV. Scene 1.

204. Line 23: *and fresh* LEGERITY.—Ff. 3 and 4 have the obvious correction *celerity*. For *legerity*, however, cf. Every Man Out of His Humour, ii. 1: "Ay, the *leigerity* for that, . . . and all the humours incident to the quality"

205. Line 40: *Trail'st thou the puissant pike?*—Farmer (Var. Ed xvii 390) cites Chapman, Revenge for Honour, i. 1:

> Fit for the *trayler of the puissant pike*.
> —Works, vol. iii. p. 289.

206. Line 66: *lower*.—The Quarto of 1600 has *lewer*, changed to *lower* in that of 1608; the Folio has *fewer*, which Steevens favours as a provincialism=lower. He adds: "In Sussex I heard one female servant say to another: Speak *fewer*, or my mistress will hear you."

207. Line 96: *Sir* THOMAS *Erpingham*.—The Ff. have *John*. The passage is not in the Qq.

208. Line 150: *when blood is their argument*; i.e "when engaged in battle."

209. Line 198: *the ill upon his own head*.—F. 4 has "the ill is upon his own head." The Qq. read *the fault on* or *the fault is on*. Dyce follows F. 4.

210. Line 243: *French crowns*.—A bald head was frequently termed a French crown, because the baldness was supposed to come from a certain disease called "the French disease;" but the pun here evidently relates to the double meaning of *crown*. The phrase is still further

[1] This part of the Gentleman's Academic is practically a reprint of Dame Juliana Berner's Boke of St. Albans, 1486.

played upon in the allusion in line 246 to the crime of clipping coin.

211. Line 262: *thy soul of adoration; i.e.* "the essential thing which men reverence in thee."

212. Line 277: *'T is not the* BALM.—Cf. Richard II. iii. 2. 55, and II. Henry IV. iv. 5. 115.

213. Line 280: *The* FARCED *title running 'fore the king.* —"The extended or swollen title prefixed to *the king*, as for example, *His Most Gracious Majesty*, the king" (John Hunter). *Farce* (French *farcir*, whence *forcemeat*, a good instance of popular etymology) seems to have been rather a favourite word with the Elizabethans; cf. Troilus and Cressida, v. 1. 61: "malice *farced* with wit;" again, Every Man Out of His Humour, v. 4: "if thou wouldst *farce* thy lean ribs with it" (Ben Jonson, Works, ii. 180); but the use of the word is common.

214. Line 292: *Doth rise and help* HYPERION *to his horse.* —*Hyperion* was one of the Titans, who by his sister Thia (Θεία) was the father of Helios, the sun. (Homer calls the mother of Helios Euryphaessa.) It is this *Hyperion* who gives his name to the magnificent poem of Keats, in which the description of Thea (as Keats calls her) attempting to console the fallen god Saturn, is familiar to every lover of English poetry. But Shakespeare uses *Hyperion* here, and in other passages (*e.g.* Troilus and Cressida, ii. 3. 207; Hamlet, iii. 4. 56), as Homer and other Greek poets use it, as the patronymic of Helios = Hyperionion. It may be noted that the name should be pronounced Hypèrion. Johnson admired this passage (280-292) very much; but it seems to me that the ultra-classical style of imagery employed is singularly out of place, considering both the subject (the life of an English labouring man) and the speaker.—F. A. M.

215. Line 308: *The sense of reckoning,* IF *th' opposed numbers.*—The Folio has *of*, amended by Tyrwhitt to *if*. The meaning of the passage is somewhat obscure, and the Cambridge editors (note xvi.) suggest that a line may have been lost, which with the help of the Quarto may be supplied as follows:

> Take from them now
> The sense of reckoning of the opposed numbers,
> *Lest that the multitudes which stand before them*
> Pluck their hearts from them.

216. Line 318: *chantries.*—Malone says: "One of these monasteries was for Carthusian monks, and was called *Bethlehem;* the other was for religious men and women of the order of St. Bridget, and was named *Sion*. They were on opposite sides of the Thames, and adjoined the royal manor of Sheen, now called Richmond" (Var. Ed. vol. xvii. p. 404).

217. Lines 320-322.—Heath (after censuring Warburton's interpretation of this passage, and his alteration of *all* to *call* in line 321) explains this passage thus: "I am sensible that everything of this kind (works of piety and charity) which I have done, or can do, will avail nothing towards the remission of this sin; since I well know that, after all this is done, true penitence and imploring pardon, are previously and indispensably necessary towards my obtaining it" (Revisal of Shakespeare's Text, p. 277).

ACT IV. SCENE 2.

218. Lines 2-6:

> Dau. Montez à cheval! *My horse!* varlet! laquais! *ha!*
> Orl. *O brave spirit!*
> Dau. Via! les eaux et la terre,—
> Orl. Rien puis? l'air et le feu,—
> Dau. Ciel! *cousin Orleans.*

It is a great pity that Shakespeare thought fit to insert the many little scraps of French which disfigure this play, at least when they are so much out of place as they are in this passage. To make his characters speak a composite language, half English, half (what is supposed to be) the language of their native country, is a dramatic mistake, of which he is very rarely guilty. Heath proposes to read, instead of "*monte* cheval" the reading of the old copies, "*mon* cheval." The reading in our text is Capell's. Lines 4-6, which are omitted in Qq., stand thus in F. 1:

> *Dolph. Via les ewes & terre*
> *Orleance. Rien puis le air & feu*
> *Dolph. Cein,* Cousin *Orleance.*

Heath remarks in his Revival of Shakespeare's Text (p. 277): "It is hardly worth while to mend this nonsense. But the dull duty of an editor . . . obliges him to think nothing beneath his attention which his author did not think it beneath him to write." He proposes to read:

> *Dau.* Voyez—*les eaux et la terre.*
> *Orl.* Bien—*puis l'air et le feu!*
> *Dau.* Le *ciel—cousin Orleans!*

which he thus explains: "We must suppose the Dauphin, seeing his horse curvet at some distance from the stage, cries out 'See, the waters and the earth'—he was going to say, how high he mounts above them! but is interrupted by Orleans, who answers, 'This is very well; but as to the other elements, the air and the fire, what say you to them?' To which the Dauphin replies, 'Ay, and the heaven too, cousin Orleans;' meaning by this rodomontade of his that his horse would even surmount that too if there were occasion" (*ut supra*, p. 278). This explanation is certainly ingenious, and has the merit of making sense of the passage. I doubt very much whether any Frenchman would ever have used such an expression as *Rien puis.* But, after all, this nonsense may only be an echo of the Dauphin's boasting description in act iii. sc. 7 above; compare especially lines 13-17 and 21-25.—F. A. M.

219. Line 11: *And* DOUT *them.*—The Ff. have *doubt:* Qq. omit the passage. The emendation is Rowe's. Grant White and Knight retain *doubt*, as meaning "to make to doubt, to terrify." The verb *dout* in this sense = "to do out," "to extinguish," is found in many provincial dialects of England at the present day. Steevens, on the authority of the Rev. H. Homer, says it was still used in Warwickshire in his day (Var. Ed. vol. xvii. p. 407). It is commonly used still in Devonshire, Wiltshire, Somersetshire; and in Yorkshire the substantive *dout* is used = "an extinguisher." It certainly would seem to be the right reading here; and it is remarkable that in the only other passage in Shakespeare in which this word occurs, on the authority of F. 1, it is there printed *doubt*, namely in Laertes' speech:

I have a speech of fire, that fain would blaze,
But that this folly *douts* it. —Hamlet, iv. 7. 191, 192.

Qq. and the other Ff. have *drowns* (substantially). The word *dout* would not be familiar to Londoners, and therefore the alteration in this passage to *drowns* is one very likely to have been made by the copyist or printer. Shakespeare uses the kindred words *don* = "do on" three times, and *doff* = "do off" eight times. These were, however, much more common than *dout;* but we may compare in Ophelia's song, iv. 5. 52, 53:

Then up he rose, and donn'd his clothes,
And *dupp'd* the chamber door.

The reading in all the old copies is *dupt.*—F. A. M.

220. Line 29: *To purge this field of such a* HILDING *foe.*—Compare Romeo and Juliet, ii. 4. 44: "Helen and Hero, *hildings;*" Cymbeline, ii. 3. 128: "a *hilding* for a livery;" and, as adjective, II. Henry IV. i. 1. 57: "He was some *hilding* fellow." The word is a shortened form of *hilderling* or *hinderling.* (As to its meaning and derivation, see Taming of the Shrew, note 70.)

221. Lines 36, 37:

For our approach shall so much DARE THE FIELD
That England shall couch down in fear and yield.

Johnson says (Var. Ed. vol. xvii. p. 408): "*To dare the field* is a phrase in falconry." This is scarcely correct, for there is no instance of the use of such a phrase in connection with falconry; but the use of the word *dare,* in the sense in which it is used here, is very common, and may be traced back to a very early period of English literature. In the Promptorium Parvulorum we have "DARYN', or drowpyn', or prively to be hydde (priuyly to hydyn, K. prevyly ben hyd, H.) *Latito, lateo,* CATH." The editor of the Camden Soc. edn. of this work gives a very interesting note, in which he quotes Palsgrave, who gives "to *dare,* prye or loke about me, *Je adeise alentour,* 'What *darest* thou on this facyon, me thynketh thou woldest catche larkes.'" He also gives an instance of the use of *dare* in the sense of "to crouch down," "to hide one's self" from Lydgate's Minor Poems, 174:

With woodecokkys leme for *to dare.*

Chaucer also uses *dare* in the same sense in the Shipman's Tale:

an olde appalled wight,
As ben thise wedded men, that lie and *dare,*
As in a fourme sitteth a wery hare;

and Cotgrave gives "*blotir,* to squat, ly close to the ground, like a *daring* larke, or affrighted fowle." In these last three cases the sense of the word is passive; but we have an instance of the active use of the word in Fletcher's Pilgrim, i. 1:

But there's another in the wind, some castrel,
That hovers over her, and *dares* her daily;
Some flick'ring slave.
—Beaumont and Fletcher's Works, p. 591.

And in Shakespeare's Henry VIII. iii. 2. 282, we have:

And *dare* us with his cap like larks.

It was chiefly in the capture of larks that *daring* was employed. Not only hawks were used, but also mirrors and pieces of scarlet cloth, &c. Nares gives a long quotation from The Gentleman's Recreation as to the method of taking woodlarks by terrifying with a hobby (a kind of hawk). It is evident that the allusion in our text is to the sport, if it may be so called, of *daring* larks. The Constable of France means to say that the English will crouch down in fear at the approach of the French, like larks that are *dared* by a hawk.—F. A. M.

222. Line 45: *fixed candlesticks.*—Ancient *candlesticks* were frequently made in the form of human figures holding in their hands the sockets for the lights. See the woodcut in the Var. Ed. xvii. 410.

223. Line 60: *I stay but for my* GUIDON.—The Ff. read "Guard: on," &c., which is defended by Malone on the ground that "*guard* means here nothing more than the *men of war* whose duty it was to attend on the Constable of France, and among those his *standard,* that is, his standard-bearer." The present reading is adopted by the Cambridge editors, Knight, Dyce, Rolfe, and others. It is given in the Cambridge edn. as an anonymous conjecture "*apud* Rann;" but it was made independently by Dr Thackeray, late provost of King's College, Cambridge, in his copy of Nares' Glossary (see Cambridge edn. note xvii. on this play). Cotgrave explains *guidon* as "a standard, ensigne, or banner . . . also he that beares it." This reading is confirmed by Holinshed.

ACT IV. SCENE 3.

224. Lines 11-14:

Bed. *Farewell, good Salisbury; and good luck go with thee!*
Exe. *Farewell, kind lord; fight valiantly to-day:*
And yet I do thee wrong to mind thee of it,
For thou art fram'd of the firm truth of valour.

The Ff. give lines 11, 13, and 14 to Bedford, and line 12 to Exeter. The transposition was made by Thirlby, and is confirmed by the Qq.

225. Line 40: *the feast of Crispian.*—Saint Crispin's Day, October 25th. "Crispin and Crispian were brothers who went with St. Denis from Rome to preach in France. They supported themselves by making shoes, and were supplied with leather by angels to make shoes for the poor. Being denounced as Christians, they were cruelly tortured, and then beheaded at Soissons. The Roman tradition fixes their death in A.D. 300, but other authorities give the date thirteen years earlier" (Christian Symbols, by Mrs. Clement, p. 83).

226. Line 44: *He that shall live this day, and* SEE *old age.*—The Folio reads:

He that shall *see* this day, and *live* old age.

The transposition was made by Pope, and is supported by the Quarto reading:

He that outlives this day and sees old age.

227. Line 48: *And say "These wounds I had on Crispin's day."*—This line is in the Qq. (but out of its proper place): the Ff. omit it.

228. Line 52: *Familiar in* HIS MOUTH.—The reading of the Ff. The Qq. have *their mouths,* for which Dyce zealously argues. Collier and Staunton also follow the Quartos, but most of the other editors adhere to the Folio reading.

229. Lines 57-59.—As Johnson very aptly observes, this prediction has not been verified; "the feast of *Crispin* passes by without any mention of Agincourt" (Var. Ed. vol. xvii. p. 437). In fact it may be doubted whether one in a thousand—we may say ten thousand—persons in England knows the date of the Battle of Agincourt at all, or which is St. *Crispin's* day; except in the latter case, of course, members of what used to be called the "gentle craft," *i.e.* shoemakers. In a curious book called The Shoemaker's Glory or Princely History of the Gentle-Craft (first published in 1598, and frequently reprinted) by Thomas Deloney, there is much said in glorification of Crispin and Crispianus, the two brothers, of whom a very different account is given to that quoted in note 225 above. But it is curious that, throughout this pamphlet, there is no mention made of the battle of Agincourt.—F. A. M.

230. Line 104: ABOUNDING *valour.*—The reading of the Ff. The Qq. have *abundant*. Theobald read *a bounding*, and Collier's MS. corrector has *rebounding*.

231. Line 105: *the* BULLET'S GRAZING.—Ff. read *bullets*. Hanmer first corrected this to *bullet's*. F. 1 has *crasing:* F. 2, F. 3, F. 4 *grasing*, which is evidently right.

232. Line 107: *Killing in* RELAPSE *of* MORTALITY; *i.e.* "at the very moment when their mortal elements are being dissipated into nothingness."

ACT IV. Scene 4.

233. Line 4: *Qualitie calmie custure me!*—So F. 1; F. 2, F. 3 have *Qualtity;* F. 4 reads *Quality*. This has been sometimes amended thus: *Quality! callino, custore me!* in accordance with Boswell's conjecture; he suggests that Pistol is here humming contemptuously an old Irish song called *Callino custore me*, the music of which is given in the Var. Ed. xvii. pp. 426, 427. In Mr. Alfred Perceval Graves's Irish Songs and Ballads, after mentioning that the air of Colleen Oge Asthore is *Callino Casturame*, quoting Stokes, Life of Petrie, he says: "It is evidently to this tune that Shakespeare alludes in the play of Henry V., act iv., scene 4, where Pistol, on meeting a French soldier, exclaims, 'Quality! *Calen, O custure me*' [the emendation of Malone] . . . *Calen O custure me* is an attempt to spell and pretty nearly represents the sound of 'Colleen oge astore,' and these words mean, 'young girl, my treasure.'" [I agree most strongly with Staunton in considering that this conjecture of Boswell's is "too preposterous." What on earth the refrain, *Callino castore me*, has to do with the context here, I cannot imagine. It seems to me too ridiculous to suppose that Pistol should sing the refrain of an Irish song which could have no possible earthly meaning in the situation, and which would indicate an indifference which he neither felt nor even wished to affect. It will be observed throughout the scene, that all his answers are very much to the point, even if he does not understand French. Though Warburton's emendations are generally very far-fetched, he certainly seems to have hit upon the right explanation of the wretched nonsense which is printed in F. 1. Pistol imitates the Frenchman's pronunciation of *quality*, and says, as Warburton reads, *cality—construe me*. This is exactly in keeping with Pistol's style of speaking, as in the very next speech he ridicules the Frenchman's pronunciation of *Seigneur Dieu*. It is quite possible that, originally, what Pistol said on the stage was *Qualitie, calitie* (mimicking the Frenchman), which in the hands of the copyist, or printer, became the egregious nonsense which the Cambridge editors, among others, are content to print. When we consider that throughout this play the French is printed, both in Qq. and Ff., in the most ridiculously blundering manner,—every conceivable mistake being introduced not only into the French of the Englishmen, who are supposed to speak the language badly, but into that of the Frenchmen, who are supposed to speak it correctly,—considering this, why should we go out of our way to hunt up the original song, which is totally opposed to the context, when such a very obvious correction, as that made by Warburton, stares one in the face, I cannot imagine. I have not altered the reading of the text because it is the reading of F. 1; but none the less do I feel bound to protest against the adherence to the old reading in such a case as this, though it is following the example of such able editors as those of the Cambridge Shakespeare.—F. A. M.]

234. Line 9: *on point of* FOX.—For this curious old word (=*sword*) cf. Bartholomew Fair, ii. 1: "What would you have, sister, of a fellow that knows nothing but a basket-hilt, and an old *fox* in't" (Ben Jonson, Gifford's ed. iv. p. 420). So the Captain, iii. 5:

> Put up your sword,
> I've seen it often; tis a *fox*.
> —Beaumont and Fletcher (Works, vol. i. p. 632).

235. Line 15: *Or I will fetch thy* RIM *out at thy throat.*—There has been some considerable difference of opinion as to what Pistol means here by *rim*, and several emendations have been proposed; but they are unnecessary. F. 1, F. 2, F. 3 have *rymme;* F. 4 has *rym*. Nares gives: "*Rim* or *Rym*. The peritoneum or membrane inclosing the intestines. 'The membrane of the belly.' Wilkins Real. Char. Alph. Index." (The work quoted is Bishop Wilkins' Essay towards a Real Character and a Philosophical Language, 1668.) He also quotes from another work, 1662. Johnson gives in his Dictionary (edn. 1756), under *Rim*, the following sentence in a passage from Sir Thomas Browne's Vulgar Errors: "as the peritoneum or *rim* of the belly may be broke." Skinner also gives (in the Etymologium, licensed 1668): "the inner *Rim* of the belly, *Peritonæum*." So that there can be no doubt as to the meaning of the word in the *latter* half of the seventeenth century. As to its use in Shakespeare's time, I cannot find the word given by any early Dictionary in this sense; nor does it occur in Batman on Bartholome (De Proprietatibus Rerum), where one might expect it. It is used twice in Chapman's Homer, in Iliad, bk. v. lines 536-538:

> The lance his target took,
> Which could not interrupt the blow, that through it clearly strook,
> And in his belly's *rim* was sheathed beneath his girdle-stead;

and in Iliad, bk. xiv. line 371, in describing the death of Satnius:

> And strook him in his belly's *rim*, &c.

In both cases the wound was fatal; but *rim* may mean nothing more in both passages but "the outside edge."

Steevens says that Holland "in his translation of Pliny's Natural History, several times mentions the *rim* of the paunch." I can only find one such mention, in bk. xxviii. ch. 9: "Even as the *rim* of the paunch, which is called in Latine *centipellis*" (vol. ii. p. 321). Now *centipellis* means "the second stomach of ruminating animals," and it is probably the coat of the stag's second stomach which Pliny means. Nares and Steevens both quote a passage from Sir Arthur Gorge's translation of Lucan (1614), bk. i.:

> The slender *rimme* too weak to part
> The boyling liver from the heart.

Here *rimme* must mean the midriff or diaphragm (Latin *præcordia*). Finally, in Sir Thomas Elyot's Castel of Helthe (first published in 1533), bk. iii. ch. 1, is a passage (quoted by Richardson *sub voce*): "Which ascendynge up into the head, and touchynge the *ryme*, wherein the brayne is wrapped." Here *ryme* evidently means the membrane of the brain.

Although it appears from the above that *rim*, in Shakespeare's time, was used in no *exact* anatomical sense, yet it is tolerably clear that no alteration of the text is necessary. Pistol meant by *rim* some vital part of the intestines. If any emendation were needed, perhaps *reins*= kidneys would be the most probable one.—F. A. M.

236. Line 19: BRASS, *cur!*—As the French word *bras* was pronounced, in Shakespeare's time, exactly as it is now pronounced (see Douce's note, quoted in Var. Ed. vol. xvii. p. 420), it would appear that Shakespeare did not know how to pronounce French, though he might be able to read it. But it is possible this joke was a bit of actor's "gag." The commentators in Var. Ed., in printing *braw* and *brawe* as representing the pronunciation of *bras*, do not show much knowledge of French orthoepy. —F. A. M.

237. Line 23: *moys.*—Johnson says: "*Moy* is a piece of money, whence *moi d'or* or *moi* of gold" (Var. Ed. vol. xiii. p. 430). But Dyce points out that this etymology of *moidore* is wrong, and that this coin did not exist in Shakespeare's time. He says *moy* is the same as *muid* (or *muy*), which Cotgrave gives as a measure = about five quarters English measure. Douce says "27 *moys* were equal to two tons" (Illustrations, p. 300). It may be noted that in writing *moy* for *moi* Shakespeare was not wrong, as Cotgrave gives *moy*= "me, I, myself."—F. A. M.

238. Line 30: *I'll fer him, and* FIRK *him.*—Cf. Middleton's A Game at Chess, iii. 1: "You shall have but small cause, for I'll *firk* you" (Works (Dyce's edn.), vol. iv. p. 570). The word is of not uncommon occurrence in Beaumont and Fletcher.

239. Line 75.—A passage from Mr. Symonds' Shakspere's Predecessors will serve as commentary on this and the next line. After mentioning the stock characters represented in the Moralities, Mr. Symonds continues: "Prominent among this motley company moved the Devil, leaping upon the stage dressed like a bear. His frequent but not inseparable comrade was the Vice—that tricksy incarnation of the wickedness which takes all shapes, and whose fantastic feats secure a kind of sympathy. The Vice was unknown in the English Miracles, and played no marked part in the French Moralities. He appears to have been a native growth, peculiar to the transitional epoch of our moral interludes. By gradual deterioration or amelioration, he passed at length into the Fool or Clown of Shakspere's comedy. But at the moment of which we are now treating, the Vice was a more considerable personage. He represented that element of evil which is inseparable from human nature. Viewed from one side he was eminently comic; and his pranks cast a gleam of merriment across the dulness of the scenes through which he hovered with the lightness of a Harlequin. Like Harlequin, he wore a vizor and carried a lathe sword. It was part of his business to belabour the Devil with this sword; but when the piece was over, after stirring the laughter of the people by his jests, and heaping mischief upon mischief in the heart of man, nothing was left for Vice but to dance down to Hell upon the Devil's back. The names of the Vice are as various as the characters which he assumed, and as the nature of the play required. At root he remains invariably the same—a flippant and persistent elf of evil. . . . The part of the Vice was by far the most original feature of the Moralities, and left a lasting impression upon the memory of English folk long after it had disappeared from the stage" (Shakspere's Predecessors, pp. 150, 151). A full account of *the Vice* will be found in note 305 of Richard III. Compare also Twelfth Night, iv. 2. 134-140.

ACT IV. SCENE 5.

240. Line 11: *Let's die in* HONOUR.—The Ff. omit *honour*, but the corresponding line in the Qq. has "Let's die with honour."

241. Line 16: *His fairest daughter is* CONTAMINATED.—The reading of the Ff. The Qq. have *contamuracke*. Dyce reads *contaminate*.

242. Line 18: *Let us on heaps go offer up our lives.*—Steevens and some others add from the Qq. the line:

> Unto these English, or else die with fame.

243. Line 22: *The devil take order now!*—The characters of Bourbon and Orleans are sharply contrasted here. At a time when every moment is of priceless value, Orleans debates the question of order in the attack that should be made at once; while Bourbon, smarting under the sense of defeat, indignantly casts such considerations to the winds.

ACT IV. SCENE 6.

244. Line 34: *mistful.*—The Ff. have *mixtful*, happily changed to *mistful* by Warburton.

245. Lines 35-38: Holinshed, copying almost verbatim from Hall, gives the following account of the circumstances which led to the king giving the cruel order to kill all the prisoners: "But when the outcrie of the lackies and boies, which ran awaie for feare of the Frenchmen thus spoiling the campe, came to the king's ears, he doubting least his enimies should gather togither againe, and begin a new field; and mistrusting further that the prisoners would be an aid to his enimies, or the verie enimies to their takers in déed if they were suffered to liue, contrarie to his accustomed gentleness, commanded by sound of trumpet, that euerie man (vpon paine of

death) should uncontinentlie slaie his prisoner. When this dolorous decree, and pitifull proclamation was pronounced, pitie it was to sée how some Frenchmen were suddenlie sticked with daggers, some were brained with pollaxes, some slaine with malls, other had their throats cut, and some their bellies panched, so that in effect, hauing respect to the great number, few prisoners were saued" (vol. iii. pp. 81, 82).

ACT IV. Scene 7.

246. Lines 5-11.—The description of the massacre of the prisoners, quoted above from Holinshed, scarcely warrants such approval of the king's conduct which Gower here gives. Some of the commentators have pointed out that there is an apparent contradiction here; and that the reason assigned for the massacre of the prisoners is not the same as that given in the last scene; but the fact is that Shakespeare was simply following Holinshed, as may be seen from the quotation given in the last note. When we examine the facts, as related in the more trustworthy chroniclers of the time, we find that there is really no contradiction; because there were two batches of prisoners. The first batch was taken before the attack on the camp by the French; the second was captured after those of the enemy, who had rallied, had been attacked by the English, and put to the rout. Henry's position was certainly a very desperate one, and justified very extreme measures; for his forces were so insignificant in number that they could not possibly defend their position and guard the prisoners too. It is possible that the threat, if even partly carried out, of killing the prisoners would effectively stop any attempt on the part of the French to renew the conflict; for so many princes and noblemen of distinction were captured, that the French must have known that their enemy held hostages whose lives were too valuable to be risked by any attempt to retrieve the fortunes of the day. It is certain that a large number of prisoners were killed on this occasion; it is equally certain a large number were spared. Hardyng, who was present at the battle, gives the following account (cc. xiiii. Chapiter):

> The feld he had and held it all that night,
> But when came woorde of [hoste and] enemies,
> For whiche thei slewe all prisoners doune right,
> Sauf dukes and erles in fell and cruell wise;
> And then the prees of enimies did supprise
> Their owne people, y^t mo were dede through pres,
> Then our menne might haue slain y^t tyme no lese.
>
> —Reprint, 1812, p. 375.

247. Line 51: *great-belly doublet.*—We have put a hyphen between the two words *great* and *belly*, for the same reason given by the Clarendon edd.; namely, that by so doing we are following the analogy of *thin-belly doublet* in Love's Labour's Lost. (See note 50 on that play.) In addition to the passage there quoted by Stubbes we may give the following extracts from Stubbes, who, speaking of these *great-belly doublets*, says: "Now, what handsomnes can be in these dubblettes . . . let wyse men iudge; For for my parte, handsomnes in them I see none, and much lesse profyte. And to be plaine, I neuer sawe any weare them, but I supposed him to be a man inclined to gourmandice, gluttonie, and suche like

"For what may these great bellies signifie els than that either they are suche, or els are affected that way? This is the truest signification that I could euer presage or diuyne of them. And this maye euerye one iudge of them that seeth them; for certaine I am there was neuer any kinde of apparell euer inuented that could more disproportion the body of man than these Dublets with *great bellies*" (New Shak. Soc. Reprint, p. 55).

248. Line 76: *To* BOOK *our dead, and then to bury them.*—For this sense of the verb *book* compare Sonnet cxvii. 9:

> *Book* both my wilfulness and errors down.

So II. Henry IV. iv. 3. 50. Collier's MS. Corrector gave *look*, which some editors have adopted, comparing As You Like It, ii. 5. 34: "He hath been all this day to *look* you," *i.e.* "for you."

249. Line 81: THEIR *wounded steeds.*—The Ff. have *with*, corrected by Malone. The line is not in the Qq.

250. Lines 102-104.—King Arthur is said to have won a great victory over the Saxons *in a garden where leeks did grow*, and Saint David ordered that every one of the king's soldiers should wear a leek in his cap in honour thereof. Hence the Welsh custom of wearing the emblem on St. David's Day, March 1st. Mr. Stone reminds us that a Welshman with a leek in his hat figures in the fourth plate of the Rake's Progress. Also that Peregrine Pickle's friend Cadwallader was "once maimed by a carman, with whom I quarrelled, because he ridiculed my leek on St. David's day; my skull was fractured by a butcher's cleaver, on the like occasion" (Peregrine Pickle, ii. xxxviii.). For some account of the origin of the custom see Brand's Popular Antiquities (edn. 1877, pp. 527-54).

251. Line 104: *Monmouth caps.*—Fuller, in his Worthies of Wales, says: "The best *caps* were formerly made at *Monmouth* where the Capper's chapple doth still remain."

252. Line 132: *who, if alive, &c.*—Capell and others read *a' live.*

253. Line 142: *quite from the answer of his degree.*—Johnson explains this: "A man of such station as is not bound to hazard his person to *answer* to a challenge from one of the soldier's *low degree*" (Var. Ed. vol. xvii. p. 440).

254. Line 161.—Shakespeare here alludes to a historical fact. Henry was felled to the ground by the Duke of Alençon, but recovered himself and slew two of the duke's attendants.

ACT IV. Scene 8.

255. Line 52: *Your majesty came, &c.*—Williams's defence of himself is a thoroughly manly one. He is not afraid to tell the king to his face that whatever indignities his majesty suffered at his hands were incident to his supposed condition, and could not rightfully be resented by the king as king.

256. Line 109: *Davy Gam, esquire.*—This gentleman, being sent by Henry, before the battle, to find out the strength of the enemy, made this report: "May it please you, my liege, there are enough to be killed, enough to be taken prisoners, and enough to run away." He saved the king's life in the field (Malone).

ACT V. Prologue.

257. Line 12: *whiffler*.—"An officer who walks first in processions, or before persons in high stations, on occasions of ceremony" (Hanmer). It seems to have been one of the duties of this person to clear the way before the king or high official whom he preceded. Steevens refers us to (amongst other passages) the Isle of Gulls, 1606: "And Manasses shall go before like a *whiffler*, and make way with his horns." Chapman has a graphic use of the word in his eulogistic lines prefixed to the Faithful Shepherdess:

> But as a poet, that 's no scholar, makes
> Vulgarity his *whiffler*, and takes
> Passage with ease;

and other instances of its occurrence might be quoted. Douce, undoubtedly, gives the right derivation of the word from *whiffle*, "a fife," *whifflers* being originally "those who preceded armies or processions as fifers" (Illustrations, p. 311). *Whiffler* = a trifler, a deceiver, is derived from the verb "to whiffle" = "to blow in gusts," "to veer about as the wind does."

258. Lines 30-34:

> *Were now the general of our gracious empress,*
> *As in good time he may, from Ireland coming,*
> *Bringing rebellion broached on his sword,*
> *How many would the peaceful city quit,*
> *To welcome him!*

This, as it turned out, was a most unfortunate prophecy. It refers, of course, to the well-known favourite of Queen Elizabeth, Robert Devereux, Earl of Essex, who, according to Stow, on March 27, 1599 "about two a clocke in the afternoone, . . . tooke horse in Seeding Lane, and from thence being accompanied with diuers Noble men and many others, himselfe very plainely attired, roade through Grace-streete, Cornehill, Cheapside, and other high streets, in all which places and in the fieldes, the people pressed exceedingly to beholde him, especially in the high wayes for more then foure myles space crying and saying, God blesse your Lordship, God preserue your Honour &c., and some followed him vntill the Euening, onely to behold him: when hee and his companie came foorth of London, the Skie was very calme and cleere, but before hee could get past Iseldon, there arose a great blacke cloude in the northeast, and sodainely came lightening and thunder, with a great shower of haile & raine, the which some helde as an ominous prodigie" (pp. 787, 788). It was under such auspicious circumstances that Essex set out on his expedition to Ireland, the object being to suppress the rebellion of Tyrone; but it would seem that, during the summer of that year, he became uneasy in his mind as to the decay of his influence with the queen; and, after many consultations with his friends, he took upon himself to return to England without leave, and came privately to the court at Nonsuch,[1] September 28th, 1599: "where hee prostrated himselfe beefore the Queene: who gaue him good wordes, and sayd hee was welcome: willed him to goe to his lodging, and rest him after so wearie a iournie: the second of October he was committed to the custodie of the Lorde Keeper" (pp. 788, 789). This was the beginning of the fall of Essex.—F. A. M.

259. Line 38: *The emperor's*.—The Folio reading. The conjectural emendation *emperor* has been adopted by several editors. The allusion is to the Emperor Sigismund, whose wife was Henry's second cousin. The "coming" referred to took place in May, 1416.

[1] This palace was at Cheam in Surrey, between Sutton and Epsom, about 15 miles from London.

ACT V. Scene 1.

260. Line 85: *huswife*.—This is the usual spelling of *housewife* in the Folio. Pistol uses the word contemptuously in the sense of hussy.

261. Line 80: *my* NELL *is dead*.—The early editions have *Doll*, which the Cambridge editors retain, assuming that the slip was "the author's own;" but this is extremely improbable.

262.—Johnson observes at the close of this scene: "The comick scenes of The History of Henry the Fourth and Fifth are now at an end, and all the comick personages are now dismissed. Falstaff and Mrs. Quickly are dead; Nym and Bardolph are hanged; Gadshill was lost immediately after the robbery; Poins and Peto have vanished since, one knows not how; and Pistol is now beaten into obscurity. I believe every reader regrets their departure."

ACT V. Scene 2.

263. Line 12: *brother* ENGLAND.—F. 1 has *Ireland*, which F. 2 corrects. This is not in the Qq.

264. Line 17: *The fatal* BALLS *of murdering* BASILISKS.—The word-play is more obvious if we remember the double meaning of *basilisk*: a fabulous snake, whose glance was fatal; and a large cannon. For the former see note 185, II. Henry VI., and compare (among many passages) Richard III. i. 2. 150, 151:

> *Glou.* Thine eyes, sweet lady, have infected mine.
> *Anne.* Would they were *basilisks*, to strike thee dead!

For the latter, compare I. Henry IV. ii. 3. 56:

> Of *basilisks*, of cannon, culverin.

265. Line 27: *Unto this* BAR *and royal interview*.—Johnson explains *bar* here as meaning "barrier," "place of congress." The actual place of conference was the cathedral of St. Peter at Troyes; but since, as Malone observes, St. Peter's Church would not admit of the French king and queen, &c., retiring, and then appearing again on the scene, the editors are united in supposing it to occur in a palace.

266. Line 49: *freckl'd cowslip*.—Compare Midsummer Night's Dream, ii. 1. 10-13:

> The *cowslips* tall her pensioners be:
> In their gold coats spots you see;
> Those be rubies, fairy favours,
> In those *freckles* live their savours.

267. Line 49.—The *burnet*, formerly prized as a salad plant, is the *Poterium Sanguisorba*.

268. Line 50: ALL *uncorrected*.—The Ff. have *withal*. This is not in the Qq.

269. Line 54: *And AS our vineyards.*—The Ff. have *all*, corrected by Roderick. It is not in the Qq.

270. Line 61: *diffus'd.*—The Folio has *defus'd;* as in Richard III. i. 2. 78. Schmidt would retain that form, explaining it as "shapeless." Warburton defines *diffus'd* as "extravagant;" Johnson as "wild, irregular, strange."

[There can be little doubt *defused* is the right form of the word in this passage, as well as in Richard III. i. 2. 78. (See note 81 on that play; in which note, by the way, the word should be spelt *defuse* in the quotation from Lear, i. 4. 2.) Shakespeare only once uses the form *diffused* in Merry Wives, iv. 4. 54, where it means "wild," "uncouth." He uses the verb *diffuse* in the sense of "to scatter," "to pour over" in The Tempest, iv. 1. 78, 79:

> Who with thy saffron wings upon my flowers
> *Diffusest* honey-drops, refreshing showers.

It may be noted that the Latin word *defundere* is very rare in the ante-Augustan period, and occurs neither in Cicero nor Cæsar. Horace uses it twice in the ordinary sense of "to pour out," Satire, ii. 2. 58; Odes, iv. 5. 34; and once, poetically, Epistles, i. 12. 29. It need scarcely be said that *diffundere*, from which *diffuse* is derived, is a totally different word and is common enough.—F. A. M.]

271. Line 77: *a* CURSORARY *eye.*—The Ff. have *curselarie*, the Qq. *cursenary*.

272. Line 84.—Neither *Clarence* nor *Huntington* appears in the Dramatis Personæ, as neither speaks a word. Huntington was John Holland, Earl of Huntington, who afterwards married the widow of Edmond Mortimer, Earl of March (Malone).

273. Line 161: *plain and uncoined constancy.*—Like a plain piece of metal bearing as yet no marks of the die.

274. Line 231: *très cher et devin.*—As the Cambridge editors remark, it is clear that the king is meant to speak bad French.

275. Line 241: *untempering.*—Unsoftening. Lacking the power to persuade in one's favour.

276. Line 263: *broken music.*—Mr. Chappell (Popular Music of the Olden Time, p. 246) formerly explained this as "the music of a stringed band;" but, according to Mr. W. A. Wright (Clarendon Press ed. of As You Like It, p. 89), he now gives the following explanation: "Some instruments, such as viols, violins, flutes, etc., were formerly made in sets of four, which when played together formed a 'consort.' If one or more of the instruments of one set were substituted for the corresponding ones of another set, the result was no longer a 'consort,' but 'broken music.'" In Troilus and Cressida, iii. 1. 52, and As You Like It, i. 2. 150, as here, there is a play upon the expression.

277. Line 265: *queen of all, Katharine.*—Dyce adopts Capell's *queen of all Katharines*, which is very plausible.

278. Lines 275, 276: d'une de votre seigneurie indigne serviteur.—The reading of the Cambridge edition. The Folio has it, "d'une *nostre Seigneur* indignie seruiteur," which is unintelligible. Pope reads: "d'une vostre indigne serviteur," a reading adopted also by the Variorum of 1821, Knight, Grant White, Hudson, and some other editors.

279. Line 348: *perspectively;* i.e. as through an optical contrivance called a *perspective*. For an account of *perspectives* see Richard II. note 150.

280. Line 350: *war hath* NEVER *entered.*—The early editions omit *never*, which Rowe inserted. Capell has *not*.

281. Line 361: *and* THEN *in sequel all.*—F. 1 omits *then*, which F. 2 supplies.

282. Line 369: *Præclarissimus.*—In the original treaty the word is correctly written *præcarissimus*, but the error occurs in Holinshed and was copied by Shakespeare.

283. Line 394: *the paction.*—"The old Folios have it *the pation*, which makes me believe the author's word was *paction*, a word more proper on the occasion of a peace struck up. A passion of two kingdoms for one another is an odd expression. An amity and political harmony may be fixed betwixt two countries, and yet either people be far from having a passion for the other" (Theobald).

284. Line 398: *Prepare we, &c.*—The Quartos of 1600 and 1608 end with this speech:

> *Hen.* Why then fair Katharine,
> Come give me thy hand:
> Our marriage will we present solemnize,
> And end our hatred by a bond of love.
> Then will I swear to Kate, and Kate to me,
> And may our vows once made, unbroken be.

285. Line 400: *surety of our* LEAGUE.—The Ff. have *leagues*, corrected by Walker.

286. Line 402.—The Cambridge editors observe: "The printer of the Second Folio, when he misread 'Sonet' for 'Senet,' probably supposed it to be the title of the poem of fourteen lines which the Chorus speaks, though the position of the word is ambiguous. The printer of the Fourth Folio and Rowe place it as if it belonged to the *Enter Chorus* rather than to the *Exeunt*. Pope omitted the word altogether, and it did not reappear till Mr. Dyce restored it." The *sennet* was a musical phrase given out by the trumpets to announce an arrival or departure; the word often occurs in stage-directions, taking forms the most diverse—*senet*, *cynet*, *signate*, *synnet*, and even *senate*. Cf. Clarendon Press note on Lear, i. 1. 34.

EPILOGUE.

287. Line 2: *bending.*—"Unequal to the weight of his subject and bending beneath it; or he may mean, as in Hamlet (iii. 2. 160), 'Here *stooping* to your clemency'" (Steevens). Schmidt also hesitates between these two explanations.

288. Line 7: *the world's best garden.*—France. Steevens observes that in the Taming of the Shrew, i. 1. 3, 4, a similar distinction is bestowed upon Lombardy:

> I am arriv'd for fruitful Lombardy,
> The *pleasant garden* of great Italy.

WORDS OCCURRING ONLY IN KING HENRY V.

NOTE.—The addition of sub., adj., verb, adv. in brackets immediately after a word indicates **that the word is** used as a substantive, adjective, verb, or adverb only **in the passage or passages cited.**

The compound words marked with an asterisk (*) are printed as two separate **words in F. 1.**

	Act	Sc.	Line
Abate[1] (intrans.)	ii.	1	79
	iv.	4	50
Accept (sub.)	v.	2	82
Accomplishment[2]		Prol.	30
Accrue	ii.	1	117
Acknowledgment	iv.	8	124
Admonishing[3]	iv.	1	9
Adulation	iv.	1	271
Advantageable	v.	2	88
Adventurously	iv.	4	79
Aggrieved[4]	iv.	7	170
Ale-washed	iii.	6	82
All-admiring	i.	1	39
All-watched	iv.	Prol.	38
Almshouses	i.	1	17
Appertinents	ii.	2	87
Attaint[5] (sub.)	iv.	Prol.	39
Avouchment	iv.	8	38
***Back-return**	v.	Prol.	41
Backward[6] (adj.)	iv.	3	72
*Barley-broth	iii.	5	19
*Before-breach	iv.	1	181
Betting[7] (intrans.)	ii.	1	99
Blessedly[8]	iv.	1	194
Bloody-hunting	iii.	3	41
Board[9]	ii.	1	35
Boastful	iv.	Prol.	10
Borderers	i.	2	142
Bound[10] (verb trans.)	v.	2	147
Bridled[11]	iii.	7	54

	Act	Sc.	Line
Brim[12] (adj.)	i.	2	150
Brokenly	v.	2	106
Bubukles[13]	iii.	6	108
Bungle (verb)	ii.	2	115
Barnet	v.	2	49
Candlesticks[14]	iv.	2	45
Cap (verb)	iii.	7	124
Captived	ii.	4	55
Cash (sub.)	ii.	1	120
Cavaliers[15]	iii.	Prol.	24
Charge[16] **(sub.)**	iii.	1	33
Charitably	iv.	1	149
Chartered	i.	1	48
Chases[17]	i.	2	206
Cheerer	v.	2	41
Choice-drawn	iii.	Prol.	24
Chrisom[18] (sub.)	ii.	3	12
Clipper	iv.	1	246
Closely	iv.	7	179
Clover	v.	2	49
Cock[19]	ii.	1	55
Cockpit		Prol.	11
Commissioners	ii.	2	61
Concavities	iii.	2	64
Congreeing	i.	2	182
Congreeted	v.	2	31
Contrariously	i.	2	206
Contrite[20]	iv.	1	313
Corroborate[21]	ii.	1	130
Coulter	v.	2	46
Countermines (sub.)	iii.	2	67

	Act	Sc.	Line
Courts[22]	i.	2	265
Cowarded	ii.	2	75
Crescive	i.	1	66
Crimson (sub.)	v.	2	324
Cruelly[23]	v.	2	216
Cudgelled	v.	1	93
Currance[24]	i.	1	34
Cursorary	v.	2	77
Dancing-schools	iii.	5	32
Decoct	iii.	5	20
Defend (intrans.)	i.	2	137
Defendant (adj.)	ii.	4	8
Defunction	i.	2	58
Demon[25]	ii.	2	121
Demonstrative	ii.	4	89
Down-roping	iv.	2	48
Enlinked	iii.	3	18
Enrounded	iv.	Prol.	36
Enscheduled	v.	2	73
*Even-pleached	v.	2	42
Ever-running	iv.	1	296
Executors[26]	i.	2	203
Exhibiters	i.	1	74
Fallow[27] (adj.)	v.	2	44
Farced	iv.	1	280
Fatally	ii.	4	54
Fat-brained	iii.	7	143
Ferret (verb)	iv.	4	30, 33
Fet[28]	iii.	1	18
Fig[29] (sub.)	iii.	6	62
Find-faults	v.	2	298
Fined[30] (verb)	iv.	7	72
Finely[31]	ii.	2	137
Fire-shovel	iii.	2	50
Firk	iv.	4	29, 33
Fluent	iii.	7	36
Fore-foot	ii.	1	71
Fore-rank	v.	2	97

	Act	Sc.	Line
Forespent[32]	ii.	4	36
Founder (sub.)	i.	2	42, 50
Fox[33]	iv.	4	9
Frankness	v.	2	313
Fumitory	v.	2	45
Galling[34]	v.	1	78
Gayness	iv.	3	110
Gentle (verb)	iv.	3	63
Gilt[35]	ii.	Prol.	26
Gimmal	iv.	2	49
Grafters	iii.	5	9
***Great-uncle**	i.	2	205
	iv.	7	96
Guidon	iv.	2	60
Gun-stones	i.	2	282
Haggled	iv.	6	11
Half-achieved	iii.	3	8
Havoc (verb)	i.	2	173
Hazard[36]	iii.	7	93, 95
Heart-grief	ii.	2	27
Hemp	iii.	6	45
Hold-fast (sub.)	ii.	3	54
*Honey-bees	i.	2	187
Honeyed	i.	1	50
Honour-owing	iv.	6	9
Horse-leeches	ii.	3	57
Howls (sub.)	iii.	3	39
Hydra-headed	i.	1	35
Imbar	i.	2	94
Impeachment[37]	iii.	6	151
Impounded	i.	2	160
Indigent	i.	1	16
Inheritrix	i.	2	51
Insteeped[38]	iv.	6	12
Interception	ii.	2	7
Intertissued	iv.	1	279
Intoxicates	iv.	7	39
Invoke[39]	i.	2	104
Irreconciled	iv.	1	160
Jacksauce	iv.	7	148
Jutty (verb)	iii.	1	13

1 Used as a transitive verb frequently, in various senses.

2 Lucrece, 716.

3 =exhorting. The verb is used only once elsewhere by Shakespeare, in I. Henry VI. v. 33, where it has more the sense of "to instruct."

4 Used by Fluellen in the dialectic form *Aggriefd*.

5 =anxiety. Also in Venus and Adonis, 741.

6 =unwilling. *Backward* is used frequently as an adverb, and three times as an adjective in other senses.

7 **Shakespeare uses the verb "to bet" (trans.) once elsewhere, in II. Henry IV. iii. 2. 50.**

8 **=holily. The adverb is used in one other** passage, Tempest, **i. 2. 63,** where it means "fortunately."

9 **=to furnish with food.**

10 **=to make to leap. Used frequently in the intransitive sense.**

11 **The verb is used figuratively in various passages in Shakespeare**; here=to put a *bridle* on a horse.

12 =overflowing. "Ample and brim fulness." Some editors wrongly print *brimfulness* as one word.

13 This is a mere corruption of *carbuncle*, or perhaps of *bubo* and carbuncle; used by Fluellen.

14 *Candlestick*, another form of the word, occurs in I. Henry IV. iii. 1. 131, and should have been given in the Words, &c., to that play.

15 *Cavaliero* (or *cavalero*) is used twice (Merry Wives, ii. 3. 78, and II. Henry IV. v. 3. 62); and *cavalery*, a vulgar corruption of the same word, in Mids. Night's Dream, iv. 1. 23.

16 =the order to attack. Also in Lucrece, 434.

17 =a term in tennis.

18 Used as adj. in corrupted form *christom* by Mrs. Quickly.

19 **Of a gun.**

20 **Lucrece, 1727.**

21 **Used by Pistol in a vague** sense.

22 =tennis-courts.

23 In figurative sense. **Used** elsewhere by Shakespeare in its ordinary sense.

24 =current.

25 ="a devil." **Used in Ant. and Cleo. ii. 3. 19="a genius,"** "guardian spirit."

26 =executioners.

27 =untilled. **28 =fetched.**

29 An expression of contempt. The verb in the sense of "to insult" occurs in II. Henry IV. **v.** 3. 124.

30 **Meaning doubtful; perhaps ="pledged as a fine:" used in other senses elsewhere.**

31 **=in minute parts.**

32 **=past.** 33 **=a sword.**

34 **Used with *at* =scoffing; the verb occurs frequently in other senses.**

35 **=money. Used frequently, in a figurative sense, elsewhere.**

36 **A term in tennis.**

37 **=hinderance. Occurs twice (Two Gent. i. 3. 15, and Richard III. ii. 2. 22) in another sense.**

38 ***Ensteeped* occurs in Othello,** ii. 1. 70.

39 **Sonnet, lxxviii. 1.**

WORDS PECULIAR TO KING HENRY V.

	Act	Sc.	Line
Kecksies	v.	2	52
Knobs	iii.	6	100
Lank-lean	iv.	Prol.	26
Lavoltas	iii.	5	33
Leap-frog	v.	2	142
Leashed		Prol.	7
Legerity	iv.	1	23
Linstock	iii.	Prol.	33
Literatured	iv.	7	157
Lob (verb)	iv.	2	47
Long-vanished	ii.	4	80
Low-rated	iv.	Prol.	19
Lute-case	iii.	2	46
May-morn	i.	2	120
Measure[1]	v.	2	140
Mercenaries	iv.	8	93
Mercifully	v.	2	214
Minding[2] (verb)	iv.	Prol.	53
Miscreate (adj.)	i.	2	16
Mistful	iv.	6	34
Morris-dance	ii.	4	25
Motionless	iv.	2	50
Mould[3]	iii.	2	23
New-store	iii.	5	31
New-tuned	iii.	6	80
Noble-ending	iv.	6	27
Nook-shotten	iii.	5	14
Observingly	iv.	1	5
O'erblows[4]	iii.	3	31
O'erglanced[5]	v.	2	78
O'erwhelm[6]	iii.	1	11
Ordure	ii.	4	39
Out-voice	v.	Prol.	11
Paction	v.	2	394
Pale-dead	iv.	2	48
Pasterns	iii.	7	13

[1] = metre. Occurs in other places in various senses.
[2] = thinking of.
[3] In the expression "men of mould" = men of clay.
[4] *Overblown* occurs several times in Shakespeare.
[5] *Overglance* occurs in Love's Labour's Lost, iv. 2. 125.
[6] = to hang down upon. Also in Venus and Adonis, 183.

	Act	Sc.	Line
Pavilioned	i.	2	129
Pax[7]	iii.	6	42, 47
Pennons	iii.	5	49
Perspectively	v.	2	347
Pettiness	iii.	6	136
Pilfering	i.	2	142
Poring[8]	iv.	Prol.	2
Portage[9]	iii.	1	10
Practic	i.	1	51
Prater	v.	2	166
Preachers	iv.	1	9
Predeceased[10]	v.	1	76
Prescript[11] (adj.)	iii.	7	49
Prick-eared	ii.	1	44
Privates[12]	iv.	1	255
Projection	ii.	4	46
Prologue-like		Prol.	33
Qualmish	v.	1	22
Rank[13] (verb intr.)	v.	2	374
Rawly	iv.	1	149
Re-answer	iii.	6	136
Red-faced	iii.	2	34
Reinforced (trans.)	iv.	6	36
Relapse[14]	iv.	3	107
Relish[15] (sub.)	iv.	1	114
Re-survey[16]	v.	2	81
Re-united	i.	2	85
Rim	iv.	4	15
Rise[17] (sub.)	iv.	1	289
Rivage	iii.	Prol.	14
Roping (adj.)	iii.	5	23
Rosed[18]	v.	2	323

[7] An ecclesiastical vessel. See note 181.
[8] = purblind. The verb "to pore" is used in its ordinary sense in Love's Labour's Lost, i. 1. 74, iv. 3. 298. [9] = port-hole.
[10] Lucrece, 1756.
[11] Used as a sub. in Hamlet, ii. 2. 142, and Ant. and Cleo. iii. 8. 5.
[12] = private persons.
[13] = to be coupled. The transitive verb is used frequently.
[14] = rebounding.
[15] = quality, sort.
[16] Sonn. xxxii. 3.
[17] Pilgrim, 194.
[18] In the expression "rosed over:" used as adj in Titus And. ii. 4. 24.

	Act	Sc.	Line
Sad-eyed	i.	2	202
Savagery[19]	v.	2	47
Scaffold[20]		Prol.	10
Self-glorious	v.	Prol.	20
Self-neglecting	ii.	4	75
Shales	iv.	2	18
Shog (verb)	ii.	1	47
	ii.	3	47
Shrill-shrieking	iii.	3	35
Slips[21] (sub.)	iii.	1	31
Slobbery (adj.)	iii.	5	13
Slovenry	iv.	3	114
Snatchers	i.	2	143
Soldier-breeder	v.	2	219
Sonance	iv.	2	35
Spirited	iii.	5	21
Spirituality	i.	2	132
Spirt	iii.	5	8
Spital	ii.	1	78
	v.	1	86
Sternage	iii.	Prol.	18
Stiffen	iii.	1	7
Stilly (adv.)	iv.	Prol.	5
Strait[22] (adj.)	iii.	7	57
Streamers	iii.	Prol.	6
Strossers	iii.	7	57
Sufferance[23]	ii.	2	159
Sumless	i.	2	165
Summered	v.	2	335
Sun-burning	v.	2	155
Superfluously	iii.	7	80
Sur-reined	iii.	5	19
Sutler	ii.	1	116
Swashers	iii.	2	30
Tardy-gaited	iv.	Prol.	20
Temporal[24]	i.	1	9

[19] = wild growth. Occurs in its ordinary sense in King John, iv. 3. 48.
[20] = a stage. Occurs in its ordinary sense in Rich. III. 4. 243.
[21] Of greyhounds.
[22] = tight, close.
[23] = death by execution.
[24] = secular; used repeatedly in its ordinary senses.

	Act	Sc.	Line
Tertian	ii.	1	124
Thatch (sub.)	iii.	5	24
Threaden[25] (adj.)	iii.	Prol.	10
Thrust (in) intrans.	v.	2	394
Tombless	i.	2	229
Torch-staves	iv.	2	46
Tucket	iv.	2	35
Umbered	iv.	Prol.	9
Uncoined	v.	2	160
Uncorrected	v.	2	50
Uncurbed	i.	2	244
Uneasiness	ii.	2	27
Unfought	iii.	5	12
Ungotten	i.	2	287
Unhidden	i.	1	86
Universe[26]	iv.	Prol.	3
Unraised		Prol.	9
Untempering	v.	2	241
Utility	v.	2	53
Uttermost[27] (adj.)	iii.	6	10
Valorously	iii.	2	125
Vaultages	ii.	4	124
Vigil	iv.	3	45
Wafer-cakes	ii.	3	53
Warming-pan	ii.	1	89
War-worn	iv.	Prol.	26
Well-foughten	iv.	6	18
Whelks	iii.	6	109
Whiffler	v.	Prol.	12
Wide-stretched	ii.	4	82
Wilfulness[28]	i.	1	35
Womby	ii.	4	124
Woodmonger	v.	1	69
Working-house	v.	Prol.	23
Worm-holes[29]	ii.	4	86
Worshipped[30]	i.	2	233
*Yoke-devils	ii.	2	106

[25] Complaint, 33.
[26] Sonn. cix. 13.
[27] Also in Pericles, v. 1. 76, where Q. 1 and Q. 2 have utmost.
[28] Sonn. cxvii. 9.
[29] Lucrece, 946.
[30] = honoured. The verb is used, in all its parts, frequently in the ordinary sense.

ORIGINAL EMENDATIONS ADOPTED.

None.

ORIGINAL EMENDATIONS SUGGESTED.

None.

THE MERRY WIVES OF WINDSOR.

NOTES AND INTRODUCTION

BY

P. A. DANIEL AND F. A. MARSHALL.

DRAMATIS PERSONÆ.[1]

SIR JOHN FALSTAFF.
FENTON, a young gentleman.
SHALLOW, a country justice.
SLENDER, cousin to Shallow.
FORD, }
PAGE, } two gentlemen dwelling at Windsor.
WILLIAM PAGE, a boy, son to Page.
SIR HUGH EVANS, a Welsh parson.
DOCTOR CAIUS, a French physician.
Host of the Garter Inn.
BARDOLPH, }
PISTOL, } followers of Falstaff.
NYM, }
ROBIN, page to Falstaff.
SIMPLE, servant to Slender
RUGBY, servant to Doctor Caius.

MISTRESS FORD.
MISTRESS PAGE.
ANNE PAGE, her daughter.
MISTRESS QUICKLY, servant to Doctor Caius.

Servants to Page, Ford, &c.

SCENE—Windsor, and the neighbourhood.

TIME OF ACTION.

Three days:—1. Act I.—2 and 3. Acts II. to V. (see Introduction, pp. 93-95 on the confusion of the time).

[1] First given by Rowe.

THE MERRY WIVES OF WINDSOR.

INTRODUCTION.

LITERARY HISTORY.

The earliest notice we have of this play is found in the entries in the Stationers' Registers under date 18th January, 1602:—

"John Busby Entred for his copie vnder the hand of master Seton | A booke called *An excellent and pleasant conceited commedie of Sir* JOHN FFAULSTOF *and the merry wyves of Windesor.* — vjd

Arthure Johnson Entred for his Copye by assignement from John Busbye, A booke Called *an excellent and pleasant conceyted Comedie of Sir* JOHN FFAULSTAFE *and the merye wyves of Windsor* . . . vjd."

—Arber's Transcript, iii. 199.

Mr. Arber notes on these entries that it is "quite clear" that the Merry Wives was printed by Busby before this date, but not entered in the Registers until he came to assign it to Johnson. I am not, however, aware of the existence of any evidence in support of this statement. If Busby printed, or caused to be printed, an edition of the play, not a single copy of it has come down to us. The earliest edition known is Johnson's, the title-page of which is as follows:—

"A | most pleasaunt and | excellent conceited Co- | medie, of Syr *John Falstaffe*, and the | merrie Wives of *Windsor.* | Entermixed with sundrie | variable and pleasing humors, of Sir *Hugh* | the Welch Knight, Justice *Shallow*, and his | wise Cousin M. *Slender.* | With the swaggering vaine of Auncient | *Pistoll*, and Corporall *Nym.* | By *William Shakespeare.* | As it hath bene diuers times Acted by the right Honorable | my Lord Chamberlaines seruants. Both before her | Maiestie, and elsewhere. | London | Printed by T. C. for Arthur Johnson, and are to be sold at | his shop in Powles Church yard, at the signe of the | Flower de Leuse and the Crowne. | 1602."

Johnson brought out a second edition, a mere reprint of the first, in 1619, but with a considerably modified title-page:—

"A | most pleasant and ex- | cellent Comedy, | *of Sir John Falstaffe, and the* | *merry Wives of Windsor.* | With the swaggering vaine of An | cient *Pistoll*, and Corporall *Nym.* | Written by W. SHAKESPEARE. | Printed for *Arthur Johnson*, 1619."

On the 29th January, 1630, we find, by an entry in the Stationers' Registers (Arber's Transcript, iv. 227), that Johnson assigned all his estate in The Merry Wives of Windsor to Master Meighen, who in this same year published a quarto edition with the following title:—

"The Merry Wives | of Windsor. | with the humours of Sir *John Falstaffe*, | as also, The swaggering vaine of Ancient | *Pistoll*, and Corporall *Nym.* WRITTEN BY *William Shakespeare.* | Newly corrected. | LONDON: | printed by *T. H.* for *R. Meighen* and are to be sold | at his Shop, next to the Middle-Temple Gate, and in | S. *Dunstan's* Church-yard in *Fleet-Street.* | 1630."

Meighen's title smacks somewhat of Johnson's Quartos; but the book itself has no connection with them. It is a mere reprint of the fuller version which was published for the first time in the Folio, 1623. It has a few, a very few, slight corrections of that text and a good many additional errors; but has no claim whatever to be considered an independent edition. Unless it was intended to mask Meighen's piratical reprint of the folio version, it is difficult to imagine the motive which induced the above-mentioned entry in the Stationers' Registers.

A reprint of this Quarto [Q. 3 of Cambridge

editors] is given in Steevens's Twenty Plays, &c., which contains also a reprint of Johnson's Second Quarto. Reprints of the First Quarto are easily accessible in the Cambridge Shakespeare and in Hazlitt's Shakespeare's Library, part ii. vol. ii., in which is a reprint of Halliwell's edition, published for the Shakespeare Society, 1842.

Facsimiles of it are included in Halliwell's series produced by Ashbee, and in Dr. Furnivall's Series, by Griggs and Praetorius. From the Introduction by me to the Facsimile in the latter series a large portion of the present introduction is derived.

Before entering on a consideration of the questions of the relation to each other of the Quarto and Folio versions of this play, and of the date of its production, the reader should have before him an account of the two traditions which are so inseparably connected with it. I therefore give in full the testimony of the witnesses on whose authority these traditions have come down to us.

1. The tradition that the play was written at the command of Queen Elizabeth.

In 1702 Mr. John Dennis [born 1657] published what he was pleased to consider an improved version of The Merry Wives under the title of The Comical Gallant; or The Amours of Sir John Falstaff. In the epistle dedicatory, speaking of Shakespeare's work, he says: "I knew very well that it had pleased one of the greatest queens that ever was in the world. . . . This comedy was written at her command, and by her direction, and she was so eager to see it acted, that she commanded it to be finished in fourteen days; and was afterwards, as tradition tells us, very well pleased at the representation."

In 1709 Rowe, in his Life of Shakespeare, says of Queen Elizabeth: "She was so well pleased with that admirable character of Falstaff in The Two Parts of Henry the Fourth, that she commanded him to continue it for one play more, and show him in love. This is said to be the occasion of his writing The Merry Wives of Windsor. How well she was obeyed, the play itself is an admirable proof."

In 1710 Gildon, in his Remarks on the Plays of Shakespeare, concludes his notice of The Merry Wives thus: "The Fairies, in the fifth Act, make a handsome compliment to the Queen in her Palace of Windsor, who had oblig'd Shakespear to write a Play of Sir John Falstaff in Love, and which I am very well assured he performed in a Fortnight; a prodigious thing, when all is so well contriv'd, and carried on without the least confusion."

These three are the only "authorities" for this tradition: later writers do but echo their statements. Whence they derived them is little more than matter of conjecture; though Rowe tells us that "for the most considerable part of the passages relating to his [Shakespeare's] life" he was indebted to Betterton, the celebrated actor, who is reported to have visited Warwickshire about the end of the seventeenth century for the purpose of collecting information regarding Shakespeare. That the tradition was in existence at the beginning of the last century must be admitted, and the truth of its main fact—that the play was written at the instance of the queen—no one now, I believe, is inclined to dispute. Though not capable of proof, it may receive some little independent support from the title-page of the Quarto given above, which expressly states that it was performed before her; and it is to be remarked that with this Quarto edition none of the above witnesses appear to have been acquainted, their references to the play being always to the Folio version (see Hunter, New Illustrations, &c., vol. i. p. 203).

2. The tradition that, in Justice Shallow, Sir Thomas Lucy is ridiculed in revenge for his prosecution of our poet as a deer-poacher.

The first record of this tradition is found in a certain blundering note, supposed to have been added by the Rev. Richard Davies, at some time between 1688 and 1708, to the Fulman Manuscripts, in which he states that Shakespeare was "much given to all unluckinesse in stealing venison and Rabbits, particularly from Sr Lucy, who had him oft whipt & sometimes Imprisoned, & at last made Him fly his Native Country to his great Advancem^t^ but His reveng was so great, that he is his Justice Clodpate, and calls him a great man & y^t^ in allusion to his name bore three lowses rampant for his Arms" (see Ingleby's Centurie of Prayse, 2nd ed., New Sh. Soc. p. 405). By "Justice Clodpate" and the "three lowses" Davies is supposed to mean "Justice Shallow" and his "dozen white luces."

In 1709 Rowe, in his Life of Shakespeare, writes: "In this kind of settlement [his married life] he continued for some time, till an extravagance he was guilty of forced him both out of his country and that way of living which he had taken up; . . . He had, by a misfortune common enough to young fellows, fallen into ill company, and amongst them, some that made a frequent practice of deer-stealing engaged him more than once in robbing a park that belonged to Sir Thomas Lucy, of Charlecote, near Stratford. For this he was prosecuted by that gentleman, as he thought, somewhat too severely; and in order to revenge that ill-usage, he made a ballad upon him. And though this, probably the first essay of his poetry, be lost, yet it is said to have been so very bitter, that it redoubled the prosecution against him to that degree that he was obliged to leave his business and family in Warwickshire for some time and shelter himself in London."

Further on, speaking of Falstaff, Rowe says: "Amongst other extravagances, in The Merry Wives of Windsor he [Shakespeare] has made him a deer-stealer, that he might at the same time remember his Warwickshire prosecutor under the name of Justice Shallow; he has given him very near the same coat of arms which Dugdale, in his Antiquities of that county, describes for a family there, and makes the Welsh parson descant very pleasantly upon them."

In this record of a tradition made from seventy to ninety years subsequent to the death of Shakespeare, we have absolutely all the evidence forthcoming on this subject:[1] a tradition interpreting the play, itself dependent for support on its interpretation of the play. The only solid bit of fact that we know to be so is that Sir Thomas Lucy gave for his arms *three luces argent*. No one pretends that there is any recognizable likeness between his known character and his supposed caricature in the Shallow of II. Henry IV., nor is he recognized there; it is only when Shallow is introduced in The Merry Wives with a "dozen white luces" in his coat, and a complaint about Falstaff's trespass on his deer-park, that Sir Thomas Lucy stands revealed as the object of the poet's satire.

These two traditions, it will be seen, are important, if we accept their main facts for truth, in their bearings on the date of the production of the play, and, consequently, on the question whether it first appeared a sketch, as in the Quarto, and was afterwards enlarged as in the Folio.

First as to date. According to the tradition Falstaff, and therefore his satellites, are *revivals* of the characters which appeared in the History-Plays. Now Nym makes his first appearance in these histories in Henry V., and unless he is to be regarded as an exception—and I cannot force myself to believe this—the chronology of Henry V. and The Merry Wives is definitely settled. The only argument—if argument it can be called—against this order of succession is that Falstaff, Bardolph, Nym, and Quickly are all reported dead in Henry V., and could not therefore with propriety be reproduced on the stage after that play. That argument would hold against their revival in a play or plays professing to represent a later phase of history; but in this play we are expressly informed that the adventures of Falstaff at Windsor take place while Prince Hal is still the madcap Prince of Wales. The very fact of Falstaff's death in Henry V. was probably the cause of his revival in The Merry Wives. In the epilogue to the second part of Henry IV. Shakespeare had promised that he would, in a play on the reign of Henry the Fifth, once more present to the laughter of his audience the great stage favourite, and we know that Henry V. followed close on Henry IV.; but Falstaff did not reappear, and in Henry V. we have only a pathetic account of his decease. The poet probably found that he had made a rash promise, and that it was im-

[1] I have not of course forgotten the lost ballad mentioned by Rowe, and subsequently "discovered," together with part of another ballad, purporting to be the real Simon Pure. These "discovered" verses, brutal and stupid as they are, present manifest signs of modern fabrication, and are not worth consideration.

possible any more, in the altered position of his royal hero, to bring Falstaff into any kind of companionship with him. "This disappointment," as Dr. Johnson remarks, "probably inclined Queen Elizabeth to command the poet to produce him once again, and to show him in love or courtship." And indeed it is much more likely that she should under these circumstances make this demand than that she should do so while Falstaff's reappearance was still in expectation. Hence the production of The Merry Wives; hence also reasonable grounds for deciding that the earliest limit to be assigned to it is the latter part of 1599, it being a well-established fact that Henry V. was produced in the middle of that year. The latest limit to its date is of course fixed by the entry in the Stationers' Register, 18th January, 1602; but the Shallow-Lucy tradition would require this limit to be put still further back; for Sir Thomas died in July, 1600, and it is impossible to suppose that Shakespeare would have waited till his butt was in the grave before he aimed his shafts at him. We need, however, scarcely take this matter into account in fixing the date of The Merry Wives; there was not likely to be any delay in complying with the queen's commands, and if therefore we place the first production of the play (say) at Christmas, 1599, we shall not, I believe, be far out as regards its date.

But the date of Sir Thomas Lucy's death is important as regards the "first sketch" theory and the date of the Folio version; for the "dozen white luces" by which he is supposed to be identified with Shallow are only found in the Folio; and if we accept the tradition we are forced to the conclusion that that version cannot be later than the first half of 1600; so that we get the "first sketch" and the "revised version" to pretty nearly the same date, and may begin to doubt whether the author did indeed produce two versions of the play; whether rather the two versions are not both derived from one and the same original, and differ only in the faithfulness of their reproduction of it. But, putting aside the Shallow-Lucy tradition altogether, other considerations lead to this same conclusion. Busby, who, on the 18th January, 1602, transferred his copyright in The Merry Wives to Johnson, was concerned, in partnership with Thomas Millington, in the publication in 1600 of a quarto edition of Henry V., which is now generally admitted to be a surreptitious and corrupted copy of a shortened version of that play; his copy of The Merry Wives has many of the characteristics of his Henry V., and the dates of his connection with these two Quartos suggests at once that he obtained his copies of them in the order in which the plays themselves were produced. Besides its obvious corruption, comparison with the Folio version proves that the quarto The Merry Wives, like the quarto Henry V., omits passages which must have existed in the original it professes to represent. In proof of this the nature of those scenes and parts of scenes which are not represented in the Quarto should be considered. Most of them are without doubt such as might be cut out without injury to the intelligibility of the story, and to that cause their absence from the Quarto may as fairly be attributed as, on the "first sketch" theory, their presence in the Folio is—or rather was—attributed to after elaboration; but some of them are provably absent from the Quarto through *omission*, and all, therefore, are liable to fall under that category.

In act i. sc. 4, for instance, Dr. Caius's anger against Parson Hugh is unintelligible in the Quarto, for there no information has been given him that Simple is the Parson's messenger; we must turn to the Folio if we want to understand why the doctor challenges the parson. Proof surely that there is *omission* in the Quarto.

Again, in act iv. sc. 5 Simple waits in the court-yard of The Garter the coming down of the supposed Mother Prat from Falstaff's chamber; he has two subjects on which to consult her—first, as to the chain of which Slender has been cozened; next, as to Slender's prospect of obtaining the hand of Anne Page. Sir John's "clerkly" answers lead poor Simple to expect that it will be his master's good fortune to win Mistress Anne, and he retires, saying, "I shall make my master glad with these tydings" ["I shall make my maister a glad man at these tydings," Quarto]. But in the Quarto there is no mention of Anne; and Simple, therefore, is made to say that he will make his master a glad man with the news that he has been cozened of his chain! His retiring speech could only apply to the Anne part of the consultation, and is clear proof that that part is *omitted* in the Quarto, not *added* in the Folio.

There is, however, this difference between the Quartos of Henry V. and The Merry Wives, that while the former is little else than a shortened and corrupted copy, the latter contains passages which cannot be considered even as corrupted renderings of Shakespeare's writing, but which may very well be regarded as the work of the note-taker employed by Busby to obtain his piratical copy, he clothing with his own words the bare ideas he had stolen.

Probably to these recomposed passages, more than to any other peculiarity of the Quarto—except, perhaps, its brevity—is due the idea that it represents a first sketch of the play.

As a specimen of what I take to be the note-taker's work I quote, for comparison with the Folio, the first fifteen lines of act iii. sc. 4 as given in the Quarto:—

> "*Fenton.* Tell me sweet *Nan*, how doest thou yet resolue,
> Shall foolish *Slender* haue thee to his wife?
> Or one as wise as he, the learned Doctor?
> Shall such as they enioy thy maiden hart?
> Thou knowst that I haue alwaies loued thee deare,
> And thou hast oft times swore the like to me.
>
> *Anne.* Good M. Fenton, you may assure yourselfe
> My hart is setled vpon none but you,
> Tis as my father and mother please:
> Get their consent, you quickly shall haue mine.
>
> *Fen.* Thy father thinks I loue thee for his wealth,
> Tho I must needs confesse at first that drew me,
> But since thy vertues wiped that trash away,
> I loue thee *Nan*, and so deare is it set,
> That whilst I liue, I nere shall thee forget."

This rewriting on the part of the note-taker may, I think, reasonably account for other passages greatly differing from the Folio version; such specially as the fairy speeches at Herne's Oak (act v. sc. 5).

Another feature which distinguishes the quarto Merry Wives from the quarto Henry V. is that it enables us to supply some manifest deficiencies of the Folio text, and occasionally presents superior readings of Folio passages which but for it might not have been suspected of corruption; and this fact is of great importance, proving as it does that the folio version, though, indeed, vastly superior to the Quarto, can only be regarded as an imperfect copy of the author's work. The Cambridge editors remark on it: "The fact that so many omissions [in the Folio text] can be supplied from such mutilated copies as the early Quartos, indicates that there may be many more omissions for the detection of which we have no clue."

Very few plays ever appeared on the stage exactly in the shape in which they left their authors' hands; alterations, rearrangements, curtailments, &c., to suit the real or fancied requirements of stage management, were their common fate. The author was not always responsible for these changes, nor were they always intelligently effected. To some such cause I incline to attribute the notable entanglement of the time-plot of The Merry Wives. This entanglement manifests itself principally in sc. 5 of act iii. If we follow the course of the play to this scene we find that it brings us to the afternoon of the second day of the action.

Day 1, (say) Monday, is represented by the scenes of act i., which serves as a kind of prologue; introduces all the characters to us, and prepares us for the events of the following acts.

Day 2, Tuesday, commences with act ii. The morning is occupied with the mock duel between Caius and Evans; with Falstaff's invitation to the first meeting with Mrs. Ford, and his escape from Ford's house in the buck-basket. Noon is marked by the dinner at Ford's which follows his fruitless search for the fat knight. In the afternoon, in act iii. sc. 4, we find Page and his wife returning home from this dinner; and from this scene Mrs. Quickly proceeds to the Garter Inn to invite Falstaff to the second meeting, which the Merry Wives had resolved on for "to-morrow, eight o'clock."

And now we come to act iii. sc. 5, where, while Falstaff is calling for sack to qualify the cold water he had swallowed when slighted into the Thames from the buck-basket, Mrs. Quickly arrives with the invitation to the second meeting.

Up to this point it seems quite clear that we have only yet arrived at the afternoon of Day 2; but when Mrs. Quickly speaks we find, to our surprise, that the invitation is for *this morning*—that is, as it seems, for the morning already passed, and for an earlier hour than that at which the first meeting took place; and this second meeting is to take place immediately, as Ford learns, when, directly after Mrs. Quickly's departure, he enters as Brook.

Here, then, in this scene 5 of act iii. we find the 1st and 2nd meetings shuffled in an impossible manner into one day; yet when in act iv. sc. 2 Ford, who follows close on Falstaff, again searches his house, while Falstaff escapes as Mother Prat, he exclaims: "Master Page, as I am a man, there was one conveyed out of my house *yesterday* in this basket; why may he not be there again?" And this *yesterday* must be Day 2, Tuesday; and of course, therefore, it must be Day 3, Wednesday, on which Ford refers to it.

In the Quarto version this complication also occurs, but with a difference. Mrs. Quickly, inviting Falstaff to the second meeting, does really tell him it is for the morrow, as the plot requires; but nevertheless when Ford (as Brook) comes in we learn that it is to take place immediately. This gross and palpable inconsistency suggests that in this scene 5 of act iii. we have two scenes run into one; and on examination it will be found that by merely drawing a line between the Quickly-Falstaff and the Ford-Falstaff portions of the scene we get in the Quarto, without the alteration of a syllable of the text, two scenes representing portions of two separate days—the afternoon of Tuesday and the morning of Wednesday—and the complication of the time-plot is thus absolutely cured. The like division, with the same excellent result, may be made in the Folio version, though there the alteration of two words in the Quickly portion of the scene is required: Mrs. Quickly, instead of "good *morrow*," should salute Falstaff with "good *even*," and instead of saying of Mrs. Ford's husband that he "goes *this morning* a-birding," she should say *in the morning* or *to-morrow morning*. Not a violent change, when the result is considered. It has not, however, been made in this edition, and for this reason. For stage purposes it would not be desirable to have the two scenes thus made follow one on the other immediately. A more marked division should be made between them, and that could only be done by transferring the Ford portion of the scene to act iv. and making it the 1st scene of that act and the commencement of Day 3, Wednesday. This would necessitate the renumbering of all the scenes of act iv.; and as it has been resolved that the acts, scenes, and lines of this edition shall be numbered in accordance with the Globe edition, the numbering of which is adopted by such important works as Schmidt's Lexicon, and is followed by most Shakespearian scholars, it was considered necessary for convenience of reference to retain the old division.

It should perhaps be noted that Mr. H. B. Wheatley, in his edition of The Merry Wives, 1886, has proposed another plan of righting the time-plot and at the same time preserving sc. 5 of act iii. as one scene. In consideration of the fact [see act ii. sc. 2, 295] that Ford (Brook) was to have visited Falstaff "soon at night," to learn from him the result of the first meeting on Day 2, Tuesday, he would make the whole sc. 5 of act iii. take place on the evening of that day; he would therefore adopt the changes I propose in the Quickly portion of the scene, and bring the Ford portion in accordance with it. As this plan would, however, involve the suppression or remodelling of a considerable portion of the dialogue between Falstaff and Ford, it is not likely to commend itself to an editor; though no doubt a stage-manager might easily effect it. An editor must be content to note the fact that Ford was to have visited Falstaff on Tuesday night, and did not do so till Wednesday morning: just as he also may note the fact that in act ii. sc. 1 Ford asks the Host to introduce him to Falstaff under the name of Brook, and then in the following scene introduces himself.

There is one more item of confusion in the time-plot of the play which must be noted; though not of so much importance as that discussed above. In act v. sc. 1, which, if the reader has followed the course of the action, he will necessarily see is the afternoon of the day [Wednesday] on which Falstaff had his second meeting with Mrs. Ford, Ford, still as Brook, visits him to ascertain whether he will come to the meeting at Herne's Oak, which has been arranged for his final exposure that night; but Ford, referring to the second meeting, asks him, "Went you not to her *yesterday*, sir, as you told me you had appointed?" And Falstaff is not surprised, but gives him an account of the cudgelling he had received, as Mother Prat, on the morning of the very day on which they are speaking. This *yesterday* must of course be altered to *this morning* to make the time-plot possible. This scene is not represented in the Quarto version.

There is another point which to me seems to indicate some omission in the Folio version; that is, the absence of any account of the plot by which the reconciled duellists Caius and Evans revenge themselves on the Host for having fooled them. Twice, at the ends of sc. 1 and 3 of act iii. [at the end of sc. 1 only in the Quarto], do they hint at something they intend, and in act iv. sc. 5, *after* the Host has lost his horses, they are curiously officious in cautioning him against the thieves: their threatened vengeance and the Host's loss were doubtlessly connected. We might, perhaps, even suppose that Pistol and Nym, who so unaccountably disappear from the play after the second scene of act ii., were their hired agents in this plot, and personated the "cousin-germans" who bring about its catastrophe; but this, I must admit, is somewhat idle speculation. The plot, if it ever had existence, is irrecoverably lost, and all that can be said with certainty is that something is wanting to render this part of the play intelligible.

All considerations then—the character of the publishers of the Quarto, its proved omissions, its recomposed passages, its retention of passages omitted in the Folio, the complication in both of the time-plot, and the necessity, as previously stated in connection with the traditions, of assigning but one date for the production of both Quarto and Folio versions—lead almost inevitably to the conclusion that there was but one original for both Quarto and Folio, and that we may with something like certainty fix the date of its production on the border line between 1599 and 1600.

It would of course be rash to assert positively that such a mere stage-copy as the Folio presents us with had never been touched after that date; but it may be confidently stated that not one of the supposed proofs advanced in support of this later revision is incompatible with that date. The points more especially relied on in proof of this later revision are:—

1. Falstaff's speech in act i. sc. 1. In the Folio it is, "Now, Master Shallow, you'll complain of me to the *king?*" in the Quarto, "You'll complain of me to the *council;*" and this reference to the *king* is supposed to imply a later date for the Folio than for the Quarto: the reign of James I. rather than that of Elizabeth. But as the time of the play is laid in the reign of Henry IV. the reference to *king* or *council* proves nothing, and those who put it forward should at least remember that in the Folio itself it is neutralized by Shallow's repeated references to the *council*. Firmer ground for supposing the play to have been revised in the reign of a king might have been found in the Folio, in act i. sc. 4, where Mrs. Quickly says of her master, "Here will be an old abusing of God's patience and the *king's English;*" though here again we must recollect that Mrs. Quickly is supposed to live under Henry IV.

2. Another argument in favour of a later date for the Folio version is founded on the reference, or rather the supposed reference, in act i. 1. 92, to the games instituted or revived by Capt. Robert Dover on the Cotswold Hills; but as it has been shown by the Rev. Joseph Hunter (New Illustrations, vol. i. p. 201) that these games were in existence at least as early as 1596, that argument may be set aside.

3. Then we have the supposed allusion to

the creation of knights by James I., at the commencement of his reign, in Mrs. Page's remark (act ii. sc. 1): "These knights will hack," &c.; but as James did not create any female knights, I do not think this allusion can be received. I agree with Staunton that "nothing like a satisfactory explanation of this passage has yet been given;" . . . "there must be in it a meaning more pertinent than this."

4. Lastly, we have Mrs. Quickly's account of the "coach after coach" in which Mrs. Ford's supposed suitors visited her; but as it was thought desirable, in 1601, to bring in a bill to restrain the excessive use of coaches within this realm (see vol. xx., Archæologia, p. 465), we may be pretty confident that they were not uncommon before that year, and therefore that no argument in favour of a later date for the Folio than for the Quarto can be founded on this speech of Mrs. Quickly's.

As regards the sources of the plot, there is no reason to believe that the general conduct of the play is due to any but the author's own invention; but it has been thought that, for Falstaff's attempted intrigue with Mrs. Ford, Shakespeare may have derived some hints from certain Italian stories which narrate how a lover unknowingly confides in the husband of his mistress, escapes the search made for him, and afterwards reveals the manner of his escape to the jealous, baffled husband. This kind of plot, however, is a commonplace of tales of love adventure, and it must be admitted that in other respects these tales show not the slightest affinity to The Merry Wives. The tales referred to will be found in vol. iii. of part i. of Shakespeare's Library, edited by Mr. W. C. Hazlitt, who has there reprinted the collection forming the Appendix to Mr. Halliwell's edition of Q. 1, published for the Shakespeare Society in 1842.

STAGE HISTORY.

Although this play was said to have been written by royal command, we have no record of its performance during Shakespeare's own lifetime other than the statement on the title-page of the First Quarto, 1602, that it had been "diuers times Acted by the right Honorable my Lord Chamberlaines seruants. Both before her Maiestie, and else-where." The entry in the Accounts of the Revels (see Cunningham's Extracts from the Accounts of the Revels at Court, 1842, p. 203) to the effect that the play was acted before the Court "by his Majesty's players," in 1604, is generally believed to be a forgery. The first authentic mention of the performance of this comedy is in a MS. list of plays acted "Before the King and Queene this yeare of our Lord 1638." This list was discovered by Mr. George Wright, the well-known archæologist, among the papers of the late Mr. Drinkwater Meadows, the celebrated comedian; and was by him reprinted, in facsimile, in his Archeologic and Historic Fragments in 1887. The authenticity of the document is beyond dispute; it appears to have been drawn up by the manager of the company known sometimes as "The Lady Elizabeth's Servants," sometimes as "the Queen of Bohemia's Players," who then occupied the Cockpit Theatre in Drury Lane. It appears, from this list, that The Merry Wives was acted at the Cockpit on November 15th, 1638. There are altogether eighteen plays mentioned in this list; the only other one of Shakespeare's being Julius Cæsar, which was acted two days previously, on November 13th.

The next authentic record of the performance of this comedy is in Pepys's Diary, where, under date December 5th, 1660, he says: "After dinner I went to the New Theatre and there I saw 'The Merry Wives of Windsor' acted, the humours of the country gentleman and the French doctor very well done, but the rest but very poorly, and Sir J. Falstaffe as bad as any" (vol. i. p. 226). He saw the comedy at least on two other occasions; on neither of which has he anything unusual to say about either the play or the acting. Under date September 27th, 1661, he writes: "to the Theatre, and saw 'The Merry Wives of Windsor,' ill done" (vol. i. p. 358), and on August 17th, 1667: "to the King's, and there saw 'The Merry Wives of Windsor:' which did not please me at all, in no part of it" (vol. iv. p. 468).

The next record of the performance of this play we find in Downes' Roscius Anglicanus, where it is mentioned as being one of four plays commanded to be acted at Court, at St. James's, during the period "from Candlemas, 1704, to the 23rd of April, 1706." The Merry Wives was "acted the 23rd of April, the Queen's Coronation-day." Downes gives the cast as follows: "Mr. Betterton, acting Sir John Falstaff; Sir Hugh, by Mr. Dogget; Mr. Page, by Mr. Vanbruggen; Mr. Ford, by Mr. Powel; Dr. Caius, Mr. Pinkethman; the Host, Mr. Bullock; Mrs. Page, Mrs. Barry; Mrs. Ford, Mrs. Bracegirdle: Mrs. Anne Page, Mrs. Bradshaw" (Edn. 1789, pp. 63, 64).

At Drury Lane, in 1702, a version of this play was produced entitled The Comical Gallant, or the Amours of Sir John Falstaff, by Dennis, which seems to have had little success and never to have been revived. The Dramatis Personæ are nearly the same as the original, except that one new character is added, the brother of Mrs. Ford, who is called the Host of the Bull; and our much respected acquaintance Doll Tearsheet is substituted for the Mistress Quickly of this comedy. It must be confessed that the chief occupation of the latter in this play is such as our friend Doll might have taken up, in her old age, without exciting in our minds any sense of moral incongruity. Fenton's character is made more important, while that of Ford is altered for the worse, and in act v. he has to submit to some very rough treatment as a punishment for his jealousy. Mrs. Page is made in act iii. to figure in male disguise as Captain Dingboy. The cast of this remarkable production does not seem to have been preserved. (See Genest, vol. ii. pp. 248–250.)

With the above exception this comedy seems to have escaped the hands of the mutilators of Shakespeare, and in this respect to have been more fortunate than most of his comedies. It was revived at Lincoln's Inn Fields on October 22, 1720; Quin acted Falstaff, Ryan Ford, Harper Dr. Caius, Bullock Slender, Boheme Shallow, Mrs. Cross Mrs. Ford, Mrs. Seymour Mrs. Page. The piece was very successful, and was acted eighteen times. From this time forward Merry Wives seems to have been a very popular comedy. During the first half of the eighteenth century it was acted at all three theatres, Drury Lane, Covent Garden, and Lincoln's Inn Fields; Quin being generally the representative of Falstaff. At Covent Garden, March 18, 1736, Delane played this part; and at the same theatre, March 27, 1740, for the benefit of Hippisley, with whom Sir Hugh Evans was a very favourite character, Stephens appeared as Falstaff. Stephens was a worthy citizen of London, a button-maker by trade, whose bulky form at least was well suited to the part. During the period from 1720 to 1760 we may note the first appearance of Theophilus Cibber as Slender at Drury Lane, December 6, 1734, Woodward afterwards taking the same rôle at Covent Garden, January 29th, 1742. The latter seems to have appeared in this part several times, even as late as 1768. We may also note that Mrs. Woffington appeared as Mrs. Ford at Covent Garden, as also at Drury Lane, November 29, 1743. At Drury Lane, September 22, 1750, Mrs. Pritchard took the part of Mrs. Ford. She frequently played this part to various Falstaffs, such as Howard, Stephens, Love, and Berry. It is worth remarking that at Covent Garden, in the season 1750–51, Shuter, who had already played Falstaff many times, took the parts of Shallow and Slender. It was in this comedy that Henderson appeared first as Falstaff at the Haymarket in 1777. Henderson was a most excellent representative of the much more important Falstaff of the Two Parts of Henry IV. (See Introduction to I. Henry IV. vol. iii. p. 333.) Down to the end of the eighteenth century this play continued to be popular. Few seasons passed without witnessing its revival, and during the first part of the present century its popularity does not seem to have diminished. Actors as various as Palmer, Shuter, Kean, and Cooke appeared as Falstaff; while among the representatives of Mrs. Ford we find well-known actresses, as Miss Farren, Miss Pope, Mrs. Mattocks, Miss Mellon, and Mrs. C. Kemble.

On April 25th, 1804, at Covent Garden, the great John Kemble appeared as Ford, and Genest justly censures him for omitting the *Sir* before the name of Hugh Evans, which title, apparently, Kemble forgot was given to clergymen as well as to knights.

Coming down to our own time, this comedy was included by Mr. Phelps in his series of Shakespearean Revivals at Sadler's Wells, when it was produced for the first time on March 9th, 1848. The Manager himself, of course, played Falstaff, with Mr. Marston as Ford. The other members of the cast were not remarkable. Probably the best representation of this play, on the whole, which has been given in the last twenty years, was at the Gaiety Theatre, in 1875, when Phelps again played Falstaff, with the rest of the cast as follows: Taylor as Slender, Arthur Cecil as Dr. Caius, E. Righton as Evans, Herman Vezin as Ford, Forbes Robertson as Fenton, Mrs. John Wood as Mrs. Page, Miss Rose Leclerq as Mrs. Ford, and Miss Furtado[1] as Anne Page. A song was introduced in the Forest scene, the words written specially for the occasion by Algernon Swinburne and set to music by Arthur (now Sir Arthur) Sullivan; it was sung by Miss Furtado. A very interesting performance of this play, given by a company of amateur ladies and gentlemen, took place at Oxford in the last week of May, 1888. I had not the pleasure of seeing the performance, but I am told the acting and the *mise-en-scene* were both excellent.—F. A. M.

CRITICAL REMARKS.

Although this comedy cannot be placed in the same rank as Much Ado About Nothing and As You Like It—belonging, as it does, more to the order of farce than to that of true comedy—it will still always be one of the most interesting of Shakespeare's plays; if for no other reason, because it is the only comedy the scene of which is laid entirely in England, and the characters of which are, avowedly, taken almost entirely from the English middle class. Though its historic period would be more than a century and a half before Shakespeare's own time, yet there can be little doubt that we may regard this play as affording a vivid sketch of contemporary manners in the reign of Queen Elizabeth. It is also remarkable as being the only one of Shakespeare's plays, so far as we know, that was, probably, written to order. If the tradition be correct, that it was written at the special request of Queen Elizabeth, and that it was finished in the short space of fourteen days, we can safely assign to those circumstances the cause of many of its merits and demerits. To the fact that it was not a spontaneous work is owing, most probably, the inconsistency, in many points, of the character of Falstaff as depicted in this play, with that so ably drawn in the Two Parts of Henry IV.; while, to the pressure, as regards time, under which the play was written, it is possible that we owe the rapidity and concentration of its action, as well as the absence of any of those episodes which the poet is very often tempted to introduce at the expense of the dramatist.

The Merry Wives belongs rather to farce than to comedy, not only on account of the nature of the incidents, many of which are decidedly farcical, but also because the characters, however distinct they may be, owe their individuality more to some peculiarity of manner, or of speech, than to the elaboration of their moral characteristics. The French doctor, the Welsh parson, Nym with his somewhat tedious "humours," the Host of the Garter with his favourite epithet *bully-rook*, and his affected sententiousness; even Slender himself, who is one of the cleverest pieces of portraiture in the play, all belong more to farce than to high comedy. The serious element, which is conspicuous in all the finer comedies of Shakespeare, is even more subordinate in this play than in The Comedy of Errors or The Taming of the Shrew. We see very little of the lovers Fenton and Anne Page, on whom are bestowed nearly all of the few touches of poetry found in this play. The Merry Wives themselves have little to do with sentiment. The jealousy of Ford, which has been held by some critics to be so serious as to be out of keeping with the rest of the story, is, truth to tell, almost ridiculous from its unreasonableness; certainly it contains nothing of the tragic

[1] This charming actress married the late Mr. John Clark, the well-known comedian of the Strand Theatre in the days when Miss Marie Wilton (now Mrs. Bancroft) was wasting her talents on burlesque. Mrs. Clark died young.

element. Falstaff himself is subdued to the quality of his surroundings; his humour is not so rich as in the Two Parts of Henry IV. He seems to have lost that unfailing readiness which he displayed alike in the tavern and on the battle-field: that adroit self-possession which stood him in such good stead when detected in some mendacious flight of boastfulness, or in some egregious piece of cowardice; and, most conspicuous deterioration of all, he no longer exhibits that splendid shamelessness which, in the former plays, we have been enforced, against our consciences, to admire rather than to censure in him. But, notwithstanding these comparative defects, The Merry Wives will ever remain one of the most perfect specimens of that lighter kind of comedy which, when treated by the hand of genius, we never can bring ourselves to call farce, though, strictly speaking, it may only deserve that title.

There can be no doubt that without Falstaff this play would never have existed, and that it was written only for the purpose of introducing that popular character among new scenes and in new situations. Therefore, in attempting to form any critical estimate of its merits, it is necessary first to determine what relations, if any, The Merry Wives was intended by its author to have with regard to Henry IV. A careful examination of the three plays convinces me that it was Shakespeare's deliberate intention to make the Falstaff of The Merry Wives, as much as possible, a distinct personage from the Falstaff of Henry IV. He seems to have taken the utmost pains to sever the incidents of this play, in which the characters with the same names as those in the Two Parts of Henry IV. appear, from any connection with the incidents of those two plays. The promise to continue the character of Falstaff in another play, made in the Epilogue to II. Henry IV., was a promise for which Shakespeare himself, probably, was not responsible. His fellow-actors, who had an interest in the theatre, were naturally anxious that a part which had proved so popular should be turned, if possible, to more account; especially as it would appear that they had recently produced a play which was not very successful.[1] Shakespeare might have, in a weak moment, consented to this proposal. But he was too much of an artist not to perceive that, after the cruel rebuff experienced by Falstaff in the last act of II. Henry IV., at the hands of his former comrade and patron, the only thing left for him was to die. It would have been cruel in the author to have tried to make any more fun out of the poor old knight, after he had been offered as the hugest of holocausts on the altar of offended propriety. "Sweet Hal," the "madcap" prince, could not accomplish his transformation into a respectable king without a violent paroxysm of indignant virtue; which, of course, must be at the cost of the humorous old sinner whom he had so long cherished in the warmth of his princely favour. But, having assisted at the moral regeneration of his patron by suffering so great and so public a humilation, the old knight could not be represented, by the author of his existence, as living on the royal bounty, and carrying on futile intrigues with the buxom matrons of Windsor. No; Shakespeare, if little of a courtier, was too much of a gentleman to refuse the request of his queen. He did, indeed, bring *a* Sir John Falstaff on the stage again. He represented him, not exactly in love perhaps, but in the pangs of unsuccessful gallantry. He surrounded him again with the shadows of Bardolph and Pistol, and with *a* Mrs. Quickly, not the old hostess of Eastcheap. He substituted the tiresome Nym for the lively Poins. He did all this, and contrived a very charming setting for these old names with new faces; but he could not do violence to his own artistic sense by exhibiting the immortal hero of the Gadshill robbery half smothered in a basket of dirty linen. The Jack Falstaff, formerly miscalled Oldcastle, who fought the hydra-headed rogues in buckram and played the king with such dignity before his scapegrace son, was laid to rest for ever, while the trumpets were sounding to call together the small but brave army, which the "royal Hal," the

[1] "Be it known to you, as it is very well, I was lately here in the end of a displeasing play, to pray your patience for it and to promise you a better" (lines 8–11).

once "sweet boy" who now knew his old comrade no longer, was leading to a victory destined to make his name immortal among the heroes of England. Broken in heart, no less than in health, the vain old man had passed away; little lamented save by the few who could not forget that they had lived on the prodigality of his sins; sincerely mourned only by the fiery-nosed follower, who wished that he were with his old master, "wheresome'er he is, either in heaven or in hell!" (Henry V. ii. 3. 7, 8). There was no bringing *that* Falstaff to life; and if such a feat of revivalism could have been done, would old Jack have condemned the faithful Bardolph to the degradation of serving as a tapster?

Flashes of the real Falstaff are occasionally seen in his namesake of The Merry Wives; for instance, when he boldly owns that he has beaten Master Shallow's men, killed his deer, and broken open his lodge. "I have done all this:—that is now answer'd" (i. 1. 118, 119); or when he says to Pistol: "think'st thou I'll endanger my soul gratis?" (ii. 2. 17, 18); or again in the same speech: "it is as much as I can do to keep the terms of my honour precise" (ii. 2. 24, 25); or when he declares that he abhors death by drowning, because "the water swells a man; and what a thing should I have been when I had been swelled" (iii. 5. 18, 19); or, again, when protesting that, "if his wind were long enough to say his prayers" he would repent (iv. 5. 104, 105); or when he prides himself on the skill with which he impersonates Herne the hunter: "Speak I like Herne the hunter?" (v. 5. 32, 33); or in that most characteristic if somewhat shocking speech of his: "I think the devil will not have me damn'd, lest the oil that's in me should set hell on fire" (v. 5. 40-42); or in his indignation at the clumsy chaff of Parson Evans: "'Seese' and 'putter'! have I lived to stand at the taunt of one that makes fritters of English?" (v. 5. 151-153). But we cannot recognize the Falstaff, that we know so well, in the old would-be gallant who lets himself be fooled so easily by two women; who bargains with Master Brook and tamely undertakes to play the pimp for him; or in the well-to-do knight who sits "at ten pounds a-week" (i. 3. 8) and apparently pays up; who has money to lend Pistol (ii. 2); nor when he is making a fine speech about Jove and Europa (v. 5. 1-7). Still less can we reconcile Mistress Ford's description of this Sir John with old Jack Falstaff: "and yet he would not swear; prais'd woman's modesty; and gave such orderly and well-behaved reproof to all uncomeliness, that I would have sworn his disposition would have gone to the truth of his words" (ii. 1. 58-63). The fat knight of the two older plays could never have been capable of such *sustained* hypocrisy as this description implies, any more than he would have made the speech about the fairies: "I was three or four times in the thought they were not fairies: and yet the guiltiness of my mind, the sudden surprise of my powers, drove the grossness of the foppery into a received belief, in despite of the teeth of all rhyme and reason, that they were fairies" (v. 5. 129-135).

Of the haste with which the play was written evidence will appear in some of the details of the main plot. Falstaff seems to have known Mrs. Ford very well, but Mrs. Page says that "he hath not been thrice in my company" (ii. 1. 25, 26). It is curious that, Mrs. Ford and Mrs. Page being represented as almost inseparable, Falstaff should have seen so very little of Mrs. Page, and should have been apparently so ignorant as regards her great friendship with Mrs. Ford; for surely he never would have written the same letter to both these matrons had he known they were on such very intimate terms. Again, the introduction of the episode in which Ford passes himself off as Brook, and gives Falstaff money in order to pimp for him with his own wife, is an incident which I cannot help regretting that Shakespeare ever introduced. It seems more like a reminiscence of the Cent Nouvelles, or of the much later Contes de la Reine de Navarre, than of the English country life which Shakespeare is depicting. It lowers Falstaff unnecessarily; and its only excuse is that it serves to create a situation which is, certainly, a tempting one to a dramatist, namely, the scene where Falstaff describes his reception by Mrs. Ford to her husband without knowing to whom he is speaking. We may observe here, incidentally, that nothing can well be meaner than the conduct of Ford in the last act, when he triumphs over Falstaff with an insolence which his own contemptible conduct certainly did not warrant; tells him that the twenty pounds of money which he, as Master Brook, had forced upon Falstaff must be paid, and that he has absolutely arrested his horses for the debt. Unless this was meant for a joke, it certainly makes Ford's character more despicable than it was before. Perhaps no more striking passage occurs in the play, allowing for its brevity, than Page's rebuke to this cankerworm of a husband (iv. 4. 11, 12):

> Be not as éxtreme in submission
> As in offence.

Ford is ready to suspect his wife without the slightest cause, and to resort to the meanest devices in order to spy upon her movements; but when convicted of something worse than folly, he is full of grovelling apologies. One feels that the creature's repentance is worth little; and that Mrs. Ford will do well to keep the whip hand over him for the rest of their married life.

The character of Page is one of the best things in the play. He is a thoroughly manly, sensible, sturdy Englishman of the middle class, with a shrewd mind and a warm heart. He treats the supposed intrigue of Falstaff in the right spirit; in fact one cannot bring one's self to believe that either of the husbands could have had much to fear from the awkward gambols of this leviathan lover. A very little womanly cunning and a very small stock of coquettishness would have served to keep the fat knight at a proper distance; though, no doubt, had either of the Merry Wives become widows, Falstaff would have made her "my lady" without any scruple. Indeed some such ending to his life, in which he might have been the unwieldy slave of some fair middle-aged tyrant in petticoats, would have conveyed quite as good a moral as the extreme humiliations to which he is subjected in this play. It almost seems as if some busybody had reproached Shakespeare for the lenient way in which he had dealt with the moral failings of old Jack Falstaff; and that, consequently, in the second Falstaff of The Merry Wives the fat old sinner was to be made, willy nilly, the means of pointing a moral. However, Shakespeare's mercy got the better of him in the end; after his ducking in the Thames, and the drubbing he got as the fat woman of Brentford, and the final beating and pinching in Windsor Park, we are happy to find that Mrs. Page, who bears no malice for the compliment paid to her matronly charms, invites the whole party, including Falstaff, to go home and spend a merry and friendly evening over the fire.

Of the other characters Slender and Parson Evans are most deserving of notice. Mr. Cowden Clarke has well compared Slender with Sir Andrew Aguecheek. One of the very best scenes in the play is that part of act i. scene 1 in which Sir Hugh Evans and Shallow introduce the subect of the proposed marriage between Anne Page and Slender. The obstinacy with which the latter stands on his dignity, and the absurd self-conceit with which he graciously promises to marry Anne, as if he had only to ask to be accepted, forms a very amusing contrast to his sheepishness in her presence; though, even then, his self-conceit does not desert him, as he trots out all his supposed accomplishments, and clumsily boasts of his wealth and his great courage. But, in spite of his affected reluctance to commence the courtship, and of his feeble efforts to maintain his self-importance, no sooner has he seen Anne Page than he falls hopelessly in love with her. When we next see him all he can say is "Sweet Anne Page!" But when it comes to the actual wooing of her, he again stands on his dignity, and affects indifference as to whether Anne accepts him or not. Anne certainly fully appreciates him when she says: "Good mother, do not marry me to yond fool" (iii. 4. 87, 88). As Slender is but a sketch, we see little enough of him; and after all he is a mere dim shadow by the side of such a finished portrait as Sir Andrew Aguecheek. Nor do the verbal mistakes that Slender makes—after the fashion of Dogberry—in the first scene in which he is introduced, seem very consistent with his character. It is quite natural that Slender should say many foolish things, and that he should misapply any proverb that he might quote; but such a mistake as "dissolved, and dissolutely" (i. 1. 259, 260) for "resolved and resolutely," seems scarcely worthy of him. Sir Hugh Evans is indeed a curious portrait of a parson. Considering the age in which he lived, one might think that Shakespeare intended to have a good-humoured laugh at the clergy of the Reformed Religion. But one would not have thought that Church had been established long enough to have many careless and easy-going members amongst its priesthood. Sir Hugh seems rather to belong to the eighteenth than to the sixteenth century. The First Quarto, with unconscious satire, calls him "the Welsh knight;" and, certainly, some of his occupations seem more those of a knight than of a parson. He is ready to fight a duel; but, on the other hand, he is ready to make peace between Shallow and Falstaff. He is ready to defy Dr. Caius before witnesses (iii. 1); but not until he has whispered in an aside: "I desire you in friendship, and I will one way or other make you amends" (iii. 1. 88–90). He is not above having a hand in match-making, which, perhaps, is a matter not without his province as a clergyman. He has many good points; he is forgiving enough to warn the Host of the Garter against the "cozen-germans" who had "cozen'd all the hosts of Readings, of Maidenhead, of Colebrook, of horses and money" (iv. 5. 79–81) in spite of the trick which the host played him about the duel, when, as Sir Hugh says: "he has made us his vlouting-stog" (iii. 1. 120,121). In fact he talks of revenge; but when it comes to the point, he exacts his vengeance in a purely Christian manner.

Shal. Sir Hugh, persuade me not; I will make a Star-Chamber matter of it: if he were twenty Sir John Falstaffs, he shall not abuse Robert Shallow esquire.—(Act i. 1. 1-4.)

THE MERRY WIVES OF WINDSOR.

ACT I.

SCENE I. *Windsor. Before Page's house.*

Enter JUSTICE SHALLOW, SLENDER, *and* SIR HUGH EVANS.

Shal. Sir Hugh, persuade me not; I will make a Star-Chamber matter of it: if he were twenty Sir John Falstaffs, he shall not abuse Robert Shallow, esquire.

Slen. In the county of Gloster, justice of peace and *coram*.[1]

Shal. Ay, Cousin Slender, and *cust-alorum*.[2]

Slen. Ay, and *rato-lorum*[3] too; and a gentleman born, master parson; who writes himself *armigero*,[4]—in any bill, warrant, quittance, or obligation, *armigero*.[4]

Shal. Ay, that I do; and have done any time these three hundred years.

Slen. All his successors gone before him hath done 't; and all his ancestors that come after him may: [they may give the dozen white luces[5] in their coat.[6]

Shal. It is an old coat.[6]

Evans. The dozen white louses do become an old coat[6] well; it agrees well, passant; it is a familiar beast to man, and signifies—love.

Shal. The luce[5] is the fresh fish; the salt fish is an old coat.

Slen.] I may quarter, coz?

Shal. You may, by marrying.

Evans. It is marring indeed, if he quarter it.

Shal. Not a whit.

Evans. Yes, py 'r lady; if he has a quarter of your coat, there is but three skirts for yourself, in my simple conjectures: but that is all one. If Sir John Falstaff have committed disparagements unto you, I am of the church, and will be glad to do my benevolence to make atonements and compremises between you.

[*Shal.* The Council[7] shall hear it; it is a riot.

[1] *Coram* (Latin) = in the presence of.

[2] *Cust-alorum*, a corruption of *Custos rotulorum*, a keeper of the rolls.

[3] *Rato lorum*, a corruption of *rotulorum*, i.e. (keeper) of the rolls.

[4] *Armigero*, ablative of *armiger* = one entitled to bear arms, a gentleman.

[5] *Dozen white luces*, the cognizance of the Lucy family; *luce* = pike (the fish).

[6] *Coat* = armorial bearings.

[7] *The Council*, i.e. Privy Council.

Evans. It is not meet the Council[1] hear a riot; there is no fear of Got in a riot: the Council,[1] look you, shall desire to hear the fear of Got, and not to hear a riot; take your vizaments[2] in that.]

Shal. Ha! o' my life, if I were young again, the sword should end it.

Evans. It is petter that friends is the sword, and end it: and there is also another device in my prain, which peradventure prings goot discretions with it:—there is Anne Page, which is daughter to Master George Page, which is pretty virginity.

Slen. Mistress Anne Page! She has brown hair, and speaks small like a woman.

Evans. It is that fery person for all the 'orld, as just as you will desire; and seven hundreds pounds of moneys, and gold, and silver, is her grandsire upon his death's-bed (Got deliver to a joyful resurrections!) give, when she is able to overtake seventeen years old: it were a goot motion[3] if we leave our pribbles and prabbles,[4] and desire a marriage between Master Abraham and Mistress Anne Page.

Shal. Did her grandsire leave her seven hundred pound?

Evans. Ay, and her father is make her a petter penny.

Shal. I know the young gentlewoman; she has good gifts.

Evans. Seven hundred pounds and possibilities is goot gifts.

Shal. Well, let us see honest Master Page. Is Falstaff there?

Evans. Shall I tell you a lie? I do despise a liar as I do despise one that is false, or as I despise one that is not true. The knight, Sir John, is there; and, I beseech you, be ruled by your well-willers. I will peat the door for Master Page. [*Knocks*] What, ho! Got pless your house here!

Page. [*Entering from house*] Who's there?

Evans. Here is Got's plessing, and your friend, and Justice Shallow; and here young Master Slender, that peradventures shall tell you another tale, if matters grow to your likings.

Page. I am glad to see your worships well. I thank you for my venison, Master Shallow.

Shal. Master Page, I am glad to see you: much good do it your good heart! I wish'd your venison better; it was ill kill'd.—How doth good Mistress Page?—and I thank you always with my heart, la! with my heart.

Page. Sir, I thank you.

Shal. Sir, I thank you; by yea and no, I do.

Page. I am glad to see you, good Master Slender.

Slen. How does your fallow[5] greyhound, sir? I heard say he was outrun on Cotsall.[6]

Page. It could not be judg'd, sir.

Slen. You'll not confess, you'll not confess.

Shal. That he will not.—'Tis your fault, 't is your fault:—'t is a good dog.

Page. A cur, sir.

Shal. Sir, he's a good dog, and a fair dog: can there be more said? he is good and fair.—Is Sir John Falstaff here?

Page. Sir, he is within; and I would I could do a good office between you.

Evans. It is spoke as a Christians ought to speak.

Shal. He hath wrong'd me, Master Page.

Page. Sir, he doth in some sort confess it.

Shal. If it be confess'd, it is not redress'd: is not that so, Master Page? He hath wrong'd me; indeed he hath;—at a word, he hath;—believe me: Robert Shallow, esquire, saith he is wrong'd.

Page. Here comes Sir John.

Enter SIR JOHN FALSTAFF, BARDOLPH, NYM, *and* PISTOL.

Fal. Now, Master Shallow,—you'll complain of me to the king?

Shal. Knight, you have beaten my men, kill'd my deer, and broke open my lodge.

Fal. But not kiss'd your keeper's daughter?

Shal. Tut, a pin![7] this shall be answer'd.

Fal. I will answer it straight; I have done all this:—that is now answer'd.

---

[1] *The Council*, *i.e.* Privy Council.

[2] *Vizaments*, *i.e.* advisements = consideration.

[3] *Motion* = proposal.

[4] *Pribbles and prabbles*, coined words = idle prattling and quarrelling.

[5] *Fallow*, pale red, or yellow.

[6] *On Cotsall*, *i.e.* on the Cotswold (hills).

[7] *A pin*, *i.e.* a matter of no consequence.

Shal. The Council[1] shall know this.

Fal. 'T were better for you if it were known in counsel. you'll be laugh'd at.

Evans. *Pauca verba*,[2] Sir John, goot worts.

Fal. Good worts![3] good cabbage.—Slender, I broke your head: what matter have you against me?

Slen. Marry, sir, I have matter in my head against you: and against your cony-catching[4] rascals, Bardolph, Nym, and Pistol; they carried me to the tavern and made me drunk, and afterward pick'd my pocket.

Bard. [*Threateningly to Slender, half drawing sword*] You Banbury cheese![5]

Slen. Ay, it is no matter.

Pist. [*Imitating Bardolph*] How now, Mephostophilus!

Slen. Ay, it is no matter.

Nym. [*Imitating Pistol*] Slice, I say! *pauca, pauca;*[6] slice! that's my humour.

Slen. Where's Simple, my man?—can you tell, cousin?

Evans. Peace, I pray you.—Now let us understand. There is three umpires in this matter, as I understand; that is, Master Page, *fidelicet* Master Page; and there is myself, *fidelicet* myself; and the three party is, lastly and finally, mine host of the Garter.

Page. We three, to hear it and end it between them.

Evans. Fery goot: I will make a prief[7] of it in my note-book; and we will afterwards 'ork upon the cause with as great discreetly as we can.

Fal. Pistol,—

Pist. [*Advancing*] He hears with ears.

Evans. The tevil and his tam! what phrase is this, "He hears with ear"? why, it is affectations.

Fal. Pistol, did you pick Master Slender's purse?

Slen. Ay, by these gloves, did he—or I would I might never come in mine own great chamber again else—of seven groats in mill-sixpences,[8] and two Edward shovel-boards,[9] that cost me two shilling and two pence a-piece of Yead[10] Miller, by these gloves.

Fal. Is this true, Pistol?

Evans. No; it is false, if it is a pick-purse.

Pist. [*Going up to Evans*] Ha, thou mountain-foreigner!—Sir John and master mine,
I combat challenge of this latten bilbo.[11]—
Word of denial in thy labras[12] here;
Word of denial: froth and scum, thou liest!

Slen. By these gloves, then, 't was he. [*To Nym.*

Nym. Be avis'd, sir, and pass good humours: I will say "marry trap" with you, if you run the nuthook's[13] humour on me; that is the very note of it.

Slen. By this hat, then, he in the red face had it; for though I cannot remember what I did when you made me drunk, yet I am not altogether an ass.

Fal. What say you, Scarlet and John?[14]

Bard. Why, sir, for my part, I say the gentleman had drunk himself out of his five sentences,—

Evans. It is his five senses: fie, what the ignorance is!

Bard. And being fap,[15] sir, was, as they say, cashier'd;[16] and so conclusions pass'd the careires.[17]

Slen. Ay, you spake in Latin then too; but 't is no matter: I'll ne'er be drunk whilst I live again, but in honest, civil, godly company, for this trick: if I be drunk, I'll be drunk with those that have the fear of God, and not with drunken knaves.

Evans. So Got 'udge me, that is a virtuous mind.

Fal. You hear all these matters denied, gentlemen; you hear it.

[*Pistol, Bardolph, and Nym retire up stage.*

---

1 *The Council*, i.e. the Privy Council.

2 *Pauca verba*, few words.

3 *Worts*, used punningly = colewort, cabbage.

4 *Cony-catching* = cheating.

5 *Banbury cheese*, a vulgar phrase applied to a lean person.

6 *Pauca*, *pauca*, i.e. *pauca verba*, few words.

7 *Prief*, i.e. brief = a memorandum.

8 *Mill-sixpences*, i.e. milled-sixpences.

9 *Edward shovel-boards*, coins used in the game of shovel-board.

10 *Yead* = Ned.

11 *Latten bilbo*, sword of base metal.

12 *Labras*, lips.

13 *Nuthook*, cant word for a bailiff.

14 *Scarlet and John*, an allusion to Bardolph's red face.

15 *Fap* = drunk.

16 *Cashier'd*, eased of his cash; had his pockets emptied.

17 *Pass'd the careires*. See note 13.

Enter ANNE PAGE, *with wine;* MISTRESS FORD *and* MISTRESS PAGE.

Page. Nay, daughter, carry the wine in; we'll drink within. [*Exit Anne Page.*

Slen. O heaven! this is Mistress Anne Page.

Page. How now, Mistress Ford!

Fal. Mistress Ford, by my troth, you are very well met: by your leave, good mistress. [*Kisses her.*

Page. Wife, bid these gentlemen welcome. [*Exeunt Falstaff, Mrs. Ford, and Mrs. Page into house.*
—Come, we have a hot venison-pasty to dinner: come, gentlemen, I hope we shall drink down all unkindness.

[*Exeunt into house all except Shallow, Slender, and Evans. Bardolph, Pistol, and Nym touch their sword hilts meaningly as they pass Slender.*

Slen. I had rather than forty shillings I had my Book of Songs and Sonnets here.

Enter SIMPLE.

How now, Simple! where have you been? I must wait on myself, must I? You have not the Book of Riddles about you, have you?

Sim. Book of Riddles! why, did you not lend it to Alice Shortcake upon All-hallowmas last, a fortnight afore Michaelmas?

Shal. Come, coz; come, coz; we stay for you. A word with you, coz; marry, this, coz;—there is, as 't were, a tender, a kind of tender, made afar off by Sir Hugh here. Do you understand me?

Slen. Ay, sir, you shall find me reasonable; if it be so, I shall do that that is reason.

Shal. Nay, but understand me.

Slen. So I do, sir.

Evans. Give ear to his motions,[1] Master Slender: I will description the matter to you, if you be capacity of it.

Slen. Nay, I will do as my cousin Shallow says: I pray you, pardon me: he's a justice of peace in his country, simple though I stand here.

Evans. But that is not the question: the question is concerning your marriage.

Shal. Ay, there's the point, sir.

Evans. Marry, is it; the very point of it: to Mistress Anne Page.

Slen. Why, if it be so, I will marry her upon any reasonable demands.

Evans. But can you affection the 'oman? Let us command to know that of your mouth or of your lips; for divers philosophers hold that the lips is parcel[2] of the mouth. Therefore, precisely, can you carry your good will to the maid?

Shal. Cousin Abraham Slender, can you love her?

Slen. I hope, sir, I will do as it shall become one that would do reason.

Evans. Nay, Got's lords and his ladies, you must speak positable, if you can carry her your desires towards her.

Shal. That you must. Will you, upon good dowry, marry her?

Slen. I will do a greater thing than that, upon your request, cousin, in any reason.

Shal. Nay, conceive me, conceive me, sweet coz: what I do is to pleasure you, coz. Can you love the maid?

Slen. I will marry her, sir, at your request: but if there be no great love in the beginning, yet heaven may decrease it upon better acquaintance, when we are married and have more occasion to know one another; I hope, upon familiarity will grow more contempt: but if you say, "marry her," I will marry her; that I am freely dissolved, and dissolutely.

Evans. It is a fery discretion answer; save the faul[3] is in the 'ort "dissolutely:" the 'ort is, according to our meaning, "resolutely:"—his meaning is goot.

Shal. Ay, I think my cousin meant well.

Slen. Ay, or else I would I might be hang'd, la!

Shal. Here comes fair Mistress Anne.

Re-enter ANNE PAGE *from house.*

Would I were young for your sake, Mistress Anne!

Anne. The dinner is on the table; my father desires your worships' company.

[1] *Motions* = proposals.

[2] *Parcel* = part.

[3] *Faul*, for fault.

Shal. I will wait on him, fair Mistress Anne.

Evans. 'Od's plessed will! I will not be absence at the grace.

[*Exeunt Shallow and Evans into house.*

Anne. Will't please your worship to come in, sir?

Slen. No, I thank you, forsooth, heartily; I am very well.

Anne. The dinner attends you, sir.

Slen. I am not a-hungry, I thank you, forsooth.—Go, sirrah, for all you are my man, go wait upon my cousin Shallow. [*Exit Simple.*] A justice of peace sometime may be beholding

Anne. I pray you, sir, walk in.—(Act i. 1. 292.)

to his friend for a man.—I keep but three men and a boy yet, till my mother be dead: but what though? yet I live like a poor gentleman born.

Anne. I may not go in without your worship: they will not sit till you come.

Slen. I' faith, I'll eat nothing; I thank you as much as though I did.

Anne. I pray you, sir, walk in.

Slen. I had rather walk here, I thank you. I bruis'd my shin th' other day with playing at sword and dagger with a master of fence,—three veneys[1] for a dish of stewed prunes; and, by my troth, I cannot abide the smell of hot meat since.—Why do your dogs bark so? be there bears i' th' town?

Anne. I think there are, sir; I heard them talk'd of.

Slen. I love the sport well; but I shall as soon quarrel at it as any man in England.—You are afraid, if you see the bear loose, are you not?

Anne. Ay, indeed, sir.

Slen. That's meat and drink to me, now. I have seen Sackerson loose twenty times, and have taken him by the chain; but, I warrant you, the women have so cried and shriek'd at it, that it pass'd:—but women, indeed, cannot abide 'em; they are very ill-favour'd rough things.

[1] *Veney*, a bout at fencing.

Re-enter PAGE *from house.*

Page. Come, gentle Master Slender, come; we stay for you.

Slen. I 'll eat nothing, I thank you, sir.

Page. By cock and pie, you shall not choose, sir! come, come.

Slen. Nay, pray you, lead the way.

Page. Come on, sir.

Slen. Mistress Anne, yourself shall go first.

Anne. Not I, sir; pray you, keep on.

Slen. Truly, I will not go first; truly, la! I will not do you that wrong.

Anne. I pray you, sir.

Slen. I 'll rather be unmannerly than troublesome. You do yourself wrong, indeed, la! [*Exeunt into house.*

[SCENE II. *The same.*

Enter SIR HUGH EVANS *and* SIMPLE.

Evans. Go your ways, and ask of Doctor Caius' house which is the way: and there dwells one Mistress Quickly, which is in the manner of his nurse, or his try nurse, or his cook, or his laundry, his washer, and his wringer.

Sim. Well, sir.

Evans. Nay, it is petter yet.—Give her this letter; for it is a 'oman that altogether 's acquaintance with Mistress Anne Page: and the letter is, to desire and require her to solicit your master's desires to Mistress Anne Page. I pray you, be gone: I will make an end of my dinner; there 's pippins and seese[1] to come. [*Exeunt.*]

SCENE III. *A room in the Garter Inn.*

Enter FALSTAFF, HOST, BARDOLPH, NYM, PISTOL, *and* ROBIN.

Fal. Mine host of the Garter,—

Host. What says my bully-rook? speak scholarly and wisely.

Fal. Truly, mine host, I must turn away some of my followers.

Host. Discard, bully-Hercules; cashier: let them wag; trot, trot.

Fal. I sit at[2] ten pounds a-week.

Host. Thou 'rt an emperor, Cæsar, Keisar, and Pheezar. I will entertain Bardolph; he shall draw, he shall tap: said I well, bully-Hector?

Fal. Do so, good mine host.

Host. I have spoke; let him follow.—Let me see thee froth and lime: I am at a word; follow. [*Exit.*

Fal. Bardolph, follow him. A tapster is a good trade: an old cloak makes a new jerkin; a wither'd serving-man a fresh tapster. Go; adieu.

Bard. It is a life that I have desired: I will thrive.

Pist. O base Hungarian wight! wilt thou the spigot wield? [*Exit Bardolph.*

Nym. He was gotten in drink: is not the humour conceited? His mind is not heroic, and there 's the humour of it.

Fal. I am glad I am so acquit of[3] this tinder-box: his thefts were too open; his filching was like an unskilful singer,—he kept not time.

Nym. The good humour is to steal at a minim's rest.

Pist. "Convey" the wise it call. "Steal!" foh! a fico for the phrase!

Fal. Well, sir, I am almost out at heels.

Pist. Why, then, let kibes[4] ensue.

Fal. There is no remedy; I must cony-catch;[5] I must shift.

Pist. Young ravens must have food.

Fal. Which of you know Ford of this town?

Pist. I ken the wight: he is of substance good.

Fal. My honest lads, I will tell you what I am about.

Pist. Two yards, and more.

Fal. No quips now, Pistol:—indeed, I am in the waist two yards about; but I am now about no waste; I am about thrift. Briefly, I do mean to make love to Ford's wife: I spy entertainment in her; she discourses, she carves, she gives the leer of invitation: I can construe the action of her familiar style; and the hardest voice of her behaviour, to be English'd rightly, is, "I am Sir John Falstaff's."

[1] *Seese*, i.e. cheese.

[2] *I sit at*, i.e. my expenses are. [3] *Acquit of*, rid of.
[4] *Kibes*, sores on the heel. [5] *Cony-catch*, i.e. cheat.

Pist. He hath studied her well, and translated her will, out of honesty into English.

[*Nym.* The anchor is deep: will that humour pass?]

Fal. Now, the report goes she has all the rule of her husband's purse—he hath a legion of angels.

[*Pist.* As many devils entertain; and, "To her, boy," say I.]

Nym. The humour rises; it is good: humour me the angels.

Fal. I have writ me here a letter to her: and here another to Page's wife, who even now gave me good eyes too, examin'd my parts with most judicious œillinds;[1] sometimes the beam of her view gilded my foot, sometimes my portly belly.—

Pist. [*Aside to Nym.*] Then did the sun on dunghill shine.

Nym. I thank thee for that humour.—

Fal. O, she did so course o'er my exteriors with such a greedy intention, that the appetite of her eye did seem to scorch me up like a burning-glass! Here's another letter to her: she bears the purse too; she is a region in Guiana, all gold and bounty. I will be 'cheator[2] to them both, and they shall be exchequers to me; they shall be my East and West Indies, and I will trade to them both. [*To Pistol, giving letter*] Go bear thou this letter to Mistress Page; [*to Nym, giving letter*] and thou this to Mistress Ford: we will thrive, lads, we will thrive.

Pist. Shall I Sir Pandarus of Troy become,
And by my side wear steel? then, Lucifer take all! [*Gives back the letter and stalks pompously away.*

Nym. I will run no base humour: here, take the humour-letter: [*giving back the letter*] I will keep the haviour of reputation. [*Goes to Pistol.*

Fal. [*To Robin*] Hold, sirrah, bear you these letters tightly;
Sail like my pinnace to these golden shores.— [*Exit Robin.*
Rogues, hence, avaunt! [*Drives them round stage*] vanish like hailstones, go;
Trudge, plod, away o' th' hoof; seek shelter, pack!
Falstaff will learn the humour of the age,
French thrift, you rogues; myself and skirted page. [*Exit.*

Pist. Let vultures gripe thy guts! for gourd[3] and fullam[4] hold,
And high[5] and low[5] beguile the rich and poor:
Tester[6] I'll have in pouch when thou shalt lack,
Base Phrygian Turk!

Nym. I have operations in my head, which be humours of revenge.

Pist. Wilt thou revenge?

Nym. By welkin and her star!

Pist. With wit or steel?

Nym. With both the humours, I:
I will discuss the humour of this love to Page.

Pist. And I to Ford shall eke unfold
How Falstaff, varlet vile,
His dove will prove, his gold will hold,
And his soft couch defile.

[*Nym.* My humour shall not cool: I will incense Page to deal with poison; I will possess him with yellowness,[7] for the revolt of mine is dangerous: that is my true humour.

Pist. Thou art the Mars of malcontents: I second thee; troop on!] [*Exeunt.*

SCENE IV. *A room in Doctor Caius's house.*

Enter MISTRESS QUICKLY *and* SIMPLE.

Quick. What, John Rugby!

Enter RUGBY.

I pray thee, go to the casement, and see if you can see my master, Master Doctor Caius, coming. If he do, i' faith, and find any body in the house, here will be an old[8] abusing of God's patience and the king's English.

Rug. I'll go watch.

Quick. Go; and we'll have a posset for't soon at night, in faith, at the latter end of a sea-coal fire. [*Exit Rugby.*] An honest, willing, kind fellow, as ever servant shall come in house withal; and, I warrant you, no

[1] *Œilliads*, glances.
[2] *'Cheator*=escheator, an official who collected forfeitures.

[3] *Gourd*, a cant term for false dice.
[4] *Fullam*, a kind of false dice.
[5] *High* for *high men*, *low* for *low men*; cant terms for loaded dice. [6] *Tester*, a coin of the value of sixpence.
[7] *Yellowness*, jealousy. [8] *Old*=great, abundant.

tell-tale nor no breed-bate:[1] his worst fault is, that he is given to prayer; he is something peevish[2] that way: but nobody but has his fault;—but let that pass.—Peter Simple you say your name is?

Sim. Ay, for fault of a better.

Quick. And Master Slender's your master?

Sim. Ay, forsooth.

Quick. Does he not wear a great round beard, like a glover's paring-knife?

Sim. No, forsooth: he hath but a little wee face, with a little yellow beard,—a cane-colour'd beard.

Quick. A softly-sprighted[3] man, is he not?

Caius. O diable, diable! vat is in my closet? Villainy! *larron!*—(Act i. 4. 70, 71.)

Sim. Ay, forsooth: but he is as tall a man of his hands[4] as any is between this and his head; he hath fought with a warrener.[5]

Quick. How say you?—O, I should remember him: does he not hold up his head, as it were, and strut in his gait?

Sim. Yes, indeed, does he.

Quick. Well, heaven send Anne Page no worse fortune! Tell Master Parson Evans I will do what I can for your master: Anne is a good girl, and I wish—

Re-enter Rugby.

Rug. Out, alas! here comes my master.

Quick. We shall all be shent.[6] [*Exit Rugby.*]—Run in here, good young man; go into this closet: he will not stay long. [*Shuts Simple in the closet.*]—What, John Rugby! John! what, John, I say! Go, John, go inquire for my master; I doubt he be not well, that he comes not home. [*Sings.*

And down, down, adown-a, &c.

Enter Doctor Caius.

Caius. Vat is you sing? I do not like dese

[1] *Breed-bate*, one who causes quarrels.
[2] *Peevish*, foolish.
[3] *Softly-sprighted*, i.e. soft-natured, gentle.
[4] *Tall . . . of his hands*, i.e. strong and active.
[5] *Warrener*, the keeper of a warren.
[6] *Shent*, scolded.

toys. Pray you, go and vetch me in my closet *une boitine verde*,—a box, a green-a box: do intend[1] vat I speak? a green-a box.

Quick. Ay, forsooth; I 'll fetch it you.—[*Aside*] I am glad he went not in himself: if he had found the young man, he would have been horn-mad.[2]— [*Goes to closet.*

Caius. *Fe, fe, fe, fe! ma foi, il fait fort chaud.*[3] *Je m'en vais à la cour,—la grande affaire.*[4]

Quick. [*Coming down from closet with green box*] Is it this, sir?

Caius. Oui; mets la dans mon pocket: *dépêche*,[5] quickly.—Vere is dat knave Rugby?

Quick. What, John Rugby! John!

Re-enter RUGBY.

Rug. Here, sir.

Caius. You are John Rugby, and you are Jack Rugby. Come, take-a your rapier, and come after my heel to de court.

Rug. 'T is ready, sir, here in the porch.

Caius. By my trot, I tarry too long.—'Od's me! *Qu'ai-j'oublié!*[6] dere is some simples in my closet, dat I vill not for de varld I shall leave behind. [*Going to closet.*

Quick. Ay me, he 'll find the young man there, and be mad!

Caius. O diable, diable! vat is in my closet? Villainy! *larron!*[7] [*Pulling Simple out.*]—Rugby, my rapier!

Quick. Good master, be content.

Caius. Verefore shall I be content-a?

Quick. The young man is an honest man.

Caius. Vat shall de honest man do in my closet? dere is no honest man dat shall come in my closet.

Quick. I beseech you, be not so phlegmatic. Hear the truth of it: he came of an errand to me from Parson Hugh.

Caius. Vell.

Sim. Ay, forsooth; to desire her to—

Quick. Peace, I pray you.

Caius. Peace-a your tongue.—Speak-a your tale.

Sim. To desire this honest gentlewoman, your maid, to speak a good word to Mistress Anne Page for my master in the way of marriage.

Quick. This is all, indeed, la! but I 'll ne'er put my finger in the fire, and need not.

Caius. Sir Hugh send-a you?—Rugby, *baillez me*[8] some paper.—[*To Simple*] Tarry you a little-a while.

[*Rugby brings paper; Caius goes to table at back, and writes.*

Quick. [*Aside to Sim.*] I am glad he is so quiet: if he had been thoroughly moved, you should have heard him so loud and so melancholy.—But notwithstanding, man, I 'll do you your master what good I can: and the very yea and the no is, the French doctor, my master,—I may call him my master, look you, for I keep his house; and I wash, wring, brew, bake, scour, dress meat and drink, make the beds, and do all myself,—

Sim. 'T is a great charge to come under one body's hand.

Quick. Are you avis'd o' that? you shall find it a great charge: and to be up early and down late;—but notwithstanding, to tell you in your ear,—I would have no words of it,—my master himself is in love with Mistress Anne Page: but notwithstanding that, I know Anne's mind,—that 's neither here nor there.

Caius. [*Coming down with letter to Simple*] You jack'nape,—give-a dis letter to Sir Hugh; by gar, it is a shallenge: I vill cut his troat in de park; and I vill teach a scurvy jack-a-nape priest to meddle or make:—you may be gone; it is not good you tarry here:—by gar, I vill cut all his two stones; by gar, he shall not have a stone to trow at his dog. [*Exit Simple.*

Quick. Alas, he speaks but for his friend.

Caius. It is no matter-a for dat:—do not you tell-a me dat I shall have Anne Page for myself?—by gar, I vill kill de Jack priest; and I have appointed mine host of de Jarteer to measure our weapon:—by gar, I vill myself have Anne Page.

Quick. Sir, the maid loves you, and all shall be well. We must give folks leave to prate: what, the good-jer![9]

1 *Do intend*, i.e. do you hear.
2 *Horn-mad*, mad with jealousy.
3 "My faith, it is very warm."
4 "I am going to the court—important business."
5 "Yes; put it in my pocket; make haste."
6 "What have I forgotten?"
7 *Larron*, thief.
8 *Baillez me*, i.e. give me.
9 *What, the good-jer!* See note 42.

Caius. Rugby, come to de court vit me.—By gar, if I have not Anne Page, I shall turn your head out of my door.—Follow my heels, Rugby.

Quick. You shall have Anne—[*Exeunt Caius and Rugby*]—fool's-head of your own! No, I know Anne's mind for that: never a woman in Windsor knows more of Anne's mind than I do; nor can do more than I do with her, I thank heaven.

Fent. [*Within*] Who's within there? ho!

Quick. Who's there, I trow?[1] Come near the house, I pray you.

Enter Fenton.

Fent. How now, good woman; how dost thou?

Quick. The better that it pleases your good worship to ask.

Fent. What news? how does pretty Mistress Anne?

Quick. In truth, sir, and she is pretty, and honest, and gentle; and one that is your friend, I can tell you that by the way; I praise heaven for it.

Fent. Shall I do any good, think'st thou? shall I not lose my suit?

Quick. Troth, sir, all is in his hands above: but notwithstanding, Master Fenton, I'll be sworn on a book, she loves you.—Have not your worship a wart above your eye?

Fent. Yes, marry, have I; what of that?

Quick. Well, thereby hangs a tale:—good faith, it is such another Nan;—but, I detest, an honest maid as ever broke bread:—we had an hour's talk of that wart:—I shall never laugh but in that maid's company!—But, indeed, she is given too much to allicholy[2] and musing: but for you—well, go to.

Fent. Well, I shall see her to-day. Hold, there's money for thee; let me have thy voice in my behalf: if thou see'st her before me, commend me.

Quick. Will I? i' faith, that we will; and I will tell your worship more of the wart the next time we have confidence; and of other wooers.

Fent. Well, farewell; I am in great haste now.

Quick. Farewell to your worship. [*Exit Fenton.*] Truly, an honest gentleman: but Anne loves him not; for I know Anne's mind as well as another does.—Out upon't! what have I forgot? [*Exit.*]

ACT II.

Scene I. *Before Page's house.*

Enter Mistress Page, *reading a letter, from house.*

Mrs. Page. What, have I scap'd love-letters in the holiday-time of my beauty, and am I now a subject for them? Let me see.

[Reads] "Ask me no reason why I love you; for though Love use Reason for his physician, he admits him not for his counsellor. You are not young, no more am I; go to, then, there's sympathy: you are merry, so am I; ha, ha! then there's more sympathy: you love sack, and so do I; would you desire better sympathy? Let it suffice thee, Mistress Page,—at the least, if the love of soldier can suffice,—that I love thee. I will not say, pity me,—'t is not a soldier-like phrase; but I say, love me. By me,

Thine own true knight,
By day or night,
Or any kind of light,
With all his might
For thee to fight, *John Falstaff.*"

What a Herod of Jewry[3] is this!—O wicked, wicked world!—one that is well-nigh worn to pieces with age to show himself a young gallant! What an unweigh'd[4] behaviour hath this Flemish drunkard pick'd—i' th' devil's name!—out of my conversation, that he dares in this manner assay me? Why, he hath not been thrice in my company!—What should I say to him?—I was then frugal of my mirth:—Heaven forgive me!—Why, I'll exhibit a bill in the parliament for the putting-down

[1] *I trow* = I wonder.
[2] *Allicholy* = melancholy.
[3] *Herod of Jewry* = a boasting, overbearing fellow.
[4] *Unweigh'd*, unthinking, inconsiderate.

of fat men. How shall I be reveng'd on him? for reveng'd I will be, as sure as his guts are made of puddings.

Enter Mistress Ford.

Mrs. Ford. Mistress Page! trust me, I was going to your house.

Mrs. Page. And, trust me, I was coming to you. You look very ill.

Mrs. Ford. Nay, I 'll ne'er believe that; I have to show to the contrary.

Mrs. Page. 'Faith, but you do, in my mind.

Mrs. Ford. Well, I do, then; yet, I say, I could show you to the contrary. O Mistress Page, give me some counsel!

Mrs. Page. What 's the matter, woman?

Mrs. Ford. O woman, if it were not for one trifling respect, I could come to such honour!

Mrs. Page. Hang the trifle, woman! take the honour. What is it?—dispense with trifles;—what is it?

Mrs. Ford. If I would but go to hell for an eternal moment or so, I could be knighted.

Mrs. Page. What? thou liest!—Sir Alice Ford! [These knights will hack; and so thou shouldst not alter the article of thy gentry.]

Mrs. Ford. [We burn daylight:]—here, read, read; [*giving her the letter*] perceive how I might be knighted.—I shall think the worse of fat men, as long as I have an eye to make difference of men's liking:[1] and yet he would not swear; prais'd woman's modesty; and gave such orderly and well-behaved reproof to all uncomeliness,[2] that I would have sworn his disposition would have gone to the truth of his words; but they do no more adhere and keep place together than the Hundredth Psalm to the tune of *Green sleeves.* What tempest, I trow,[3] threw this whale, with so many tons of oil in his belly, ashore at Windsor? How shall I be reveng'd on him? [I think the best way were to entertain him with hope, till the wicked fire of lust have melted him in his own grease.]—Did you ever hear the like?

Mrs. Page. [*Comparing the two letters*] Letter for letter, but that the name of Page and Ford differs!—To thy great comfort in this mystery of ill opinions, here 's the twin-brother of thy letter: [*giving her both letters*] but let thine inherit first; for, I protest, mine never shall. I warrant he hath a thousand of these letters, writ with blank space for different names,—

Mrs. Page. [*Comparing the two letters*] Letter for letter, but that the name of Page and Ford differs!—(Act ii. 1. 71-73.)

[sure, more,—and these are of the second edition: he will print them, out of doubt; for he cares not what he puts into the press, when he would put us two. I had rather be a giantess, and lie under Mount Pelion. Well, I will find you twenty lascivious turtles,[4] ere one chaste man.]

Mrs. Ford. [*Comparing the two letters*] Why,

[1] *Liking*=habit of body.

[2] *Uncomeliness*, impropriety.

[3] *I trow*, I wonder.

[4] *Turtles*, i.e. turtle-doves (considered emblems of chaste love).

this is the very same; the very hand, the very words. [*Giving her back her letter*] What doth he think of us?

Mrs. Page. Nay, I know not: it makes me almost ready to wrangle with mine own honesty. I'll entertain myself like one that I am not acquainted withal; for, sure, unless he know some strain[1] in me, that I know not myself, he would never have boarded me in this fury.

[*Mrs. Ford.* Boarding, call you it? I'll be sure to keep him above deck.

Mrs. Page. So will I: if he come under my hatches, I'll never to sea again.] Let's be reveng'd on him: let's appoint him a meeting; give him a show of comfort in his suit; and lead him on with a fine-baited[2] delay, till he hath pawn'd his horses to mine host of the Garter.

Mrs. Ford. Nay, I will consent to act any villany against him, that may not sully the chariness of our honesty. O, that my husband saw this letter! it would give eternal food to his jealousy.

Mrs. Page. Why, look where he comes;—and my good man too: he's as far from jealousy as I am from giving him cause; and that, I hope, is an unmeasurable distance.

Mrs. Ford. You are the happier woman.

Mrs. Page. Let's consult together against this greasy knight. Come hither. [*They retire.*

Enter Ford, Pistol, Page, *and* Nym.

Ford. Well, I hope it be not so.

Pist. Hope is a curtal[3] dog in some affairs: Sir John affects[4] thy wife.

Ford. Why, sir, my wife is not young.

Pist. He wooes both high and low, both rich and poor,
Both young and old, one with another, Ford;
He loves the gallimaufry:[5] Ford, perpend.[6]

Ford. Love my wife!

Pist. With liver burning hot. Prevent, or go thou,
Like Sir Actæon he, with Ringwood[7] at thy heels:—
O, odious is the name!

Ford. What name, sir?

Pist. The horn,[8] I say. Farewell.
Take heed; have open eye; for thieves do foot by night:
Take heed, ere summer comes, or cuckoo-birds do sing.—
Away, Sir Corporal Nym!—
Believe it, Page; he speaks sense. [*Exit.*

Ford. [*Aside*] I will be patient; I will find out this.

Nym. [*To Page*] And this is true; I like not the humour of lying. He hath wronged me in some humours: I should have borne the humour'd letter to her; but I have a sword, and it shall bite upon my necessity. He loves your wife; there's the short and the long. My name is Corporal Nym; I speak, and I avouch; 't is true: my name is Nym, and Falstaff loves your wife.—Adieu. I love not the humour of bread and cheese; and there's the humour of it. Adieu. [*Exit.*

Page. [*Aside*] "The humour of it," quoth 'a! here's a fellow frights humour out of his wits.

Ford. [*Aside*] I will seek out Falstaff.

Page. [*Aside*] I never heard such a drawling, affecting[9] rogue.

Ford. [*Aside*] If I do find it:—well.

Page. [*Aside*] I will not believe such a Cataian,[10] though the priest o' th' town commended him for a true man.

Ford. [*Aside*] 'T was a good sensible fellow:—well. [*Mistress Page and Mistress Ford come forward.*

Page. How now, Meg!

Mrs. Page. Whither go you, George? Hark you.

Mrs. Ford. How now, sweet Frank! why art thou melancholy?

Ford. I melancholy! I am not melancholy. Get you home, go.

Mrs. Ford. 'Faith, thou hast some crotchets in thy head now.—Will you go, Mistress Page?

---

[1] *Strain*, impulse, feeling.
[2] *Fine-baited*, subtly-seducing.
[3] *Curtal*, docked of the tail.
[4] *Affects*, i.e. loves.
[5] *Gallimaufry*, a mixture, a hotchpotch.
[6] *Perpend*, consider.
[7] *Ringwood*, the name of a dog.
[8] *Horn*, i.e. of a cuckold.
[9] *Affecting*=affected.
[10] *Cataian*=a cheat, a rogue.

Mrs. Page. Have with you.—You 'll come to dinner, George?—[*Aside to Mrs. Ford*] Look who comes yonder: she shall be our messenger to this paltry[1] knight.

Mrs. Ford. [*Aside to Mrs. Page*] Trust me, I thought on her: she 'll fit it.

Enter MISTRESS QUICKLY.

Mrs. Page. You are come to see my daughter Anne?

Quick. Ay, forsooth; and, I pray, how does good Mistress Anne?

Ford. I do not misdoubt my wife; but I would be loth to turn them together.—(Act ii. 1. 192, 193.)

Mrs. Page. Go in with us and see: we have an hour's talk with you.

[*Exeunt Mistress Page, Mistress Ford, and Mistress Quickly into house.*

Page. How now, Master Ford!

Ford. You heard what this knave told me, did you not?

Page. Yes: and you heard what the other told me?

Ford. Do you think there is truth in them?

Page. Hang 'em, slaves! I do not think the knight would offer it: but these that accuse him in his intent towards our wives are a yoke of his discarded men; very rogues, now they be out of service.

Ford. Were they his men?

Page. Marry, were they.

Ford. I like it never the better for that.—Does he lie at the Garter?

Page. Ay, marry, does he. If he should intend this voyage toward my wife, I would turn her loose to him; and what he gets more of her than sharp words, let it lie on my head.

Ford. I do not misdoubt my wife; but I would be loth to turn them together. A man may be too confident: I would have nothing lie on my head: I cannot be thus satisfied.

Page. Look where my ranting host of the Garter comes: there is either liquor in his pate, or money in his purse, when he looks so merrily.

Enter Host.

How now, mine host!

[1] *Paltry*, vile, contemptible.

Host. How now, bully-rook! thou 'rt a gentleman.—[*Calling off*] Cavaliero-justice, I say!

Enter SHALLOW.

Shal. I follow, mine host, I follow.—Good even and twenty, good Master Page! Master Page, will you go with us? we have sport in hand.

Host. Tell him, Cavaliero-justice; tell him, bully-rook.

Shal. Sir, there is a fray to be fought between Sir Hugh the Welsh priest and Caius the French doctor.—

Ford. Good mine host o' th' Garter, a word with you.

Host. What say'st thou, my bully-rook? [*They retire.*—

Shal. [*To Page*] Will you go with us to behold it? My merry host hath had the measuring of their weapons; and, I think, hath appointed them contrary places; for, believe me, I hear the parson is no jester. Hark, I will tell you what our sport shall be.

[*Shallow and Page retire up, conversing; Ford and Host come down.*—

Host. Hast thou no suit against my knight, my guest-cavalier?

Ford. None, I protest: but I 'll give you a pottle[1] of burnt sack to give me recourse to him, and tell him my name is Brook; only for a jest.

Host. My hand, bully; thou shalt have egress and regress;—said I well?—and thy name shall be Brook. It is a merry knight. [*Shallow and Page come down*]—Will you go, mynheers?

Shal. Have with you, mine host. [*Exit Host.*

Page. I have heard the Frenchman hath good skill in his rapier.

Shal. Tut, sir, I could have told you more. In these times you stand on distance, your passes, stoccadoes,[2] and I know not what: 't is the heart, Master Page; 't is here, 't is here. I have seen the time, with my long sword I would have made you four tall[3] fellows skip like rats. [*Re-enter Host.*

Host. Here, boys, here, here! shall we wag?

Page. Have with you.—I had rather hear them scold than see them fight.

[*Exeunt Host, Shallow, and Page.*

Ford. Though Page be a secure[4] fool, and stands so firmly on his wife's frailty, yet I cannot put off my opinion so easily: she was in his company at Page's house; and what they made there, I know not. Well, I will look further into 't: and I have a disguise to sound Falstaff. If I find her honest, I lose not my labour; if she be otherwise, 't is labour well bestowed. [*Exit.*

SCENE II. *A room in the Garter Inn.*

Enter FALSTAFF *and* PISTOL.

Fal. I will not lend thee a penny.

Pist. Why, then the world 's mine oyster,
Which I with sword will open.—
I will retort[5] the sum in equipage.[6]

Fal. Not a penny. I have been content, sir, you should lay my countenance to pawn: I have grated[7] upon my good friends for three reprieves for you and your coach-fellow[8] Nym; or else you had look'd through the grate, like a geminy[9] of baboons. I am damn'd in hell for swearing to gentlemen my friends, you were good soldiers and tall fellows; and when Mistress Bridget lost the handle of her fan, I took 't upon mine honour thou hadst it not.

Pist. Didst not thou share? hadst thou not fifteen pence?

Fal. Reason, you rogue, reason: think'st thou I 'll endanger my soul gratis? At a word, hang no more about me, I am no gibbet for you:—go:—a short knife and a throng;[10]—to your manor of Pickt-hatch[11] go.—You 'll not bear a letter for me, you rogue!—you stand upon your honour!—Why, thou unconfinable baseness,[12] it is as much as I can do to keep the terms of my honour precise: I, I, I myself sometimes, leaving the fear of heaven on the left hand, and hiding mine honour in my

1 *Pottle*, a large tankard, originally holding two quarts.
2 *Stoccadoes*, thrusts at fencing.
3 *Tall*, valiant.

4 *Secure*, unsuspecting.
5 *Retort*=return, give back.
6 *Equipage*, perhaps=service; property, accoutrements.
7 *Grated*=importuned.
8 *Coach-fellow*=companion.
9 *Geminy*, i.e. a twinned pair.
10 *Short knife*, the equipment of a pickpocket (see note 65).
11 *Pickt-hatch*, a notorious resort of bullies and thieves.
12 *Unconfinable baseness*=boundless rogue.

necessity, am fain to shuffle, to hedge, and to lurch;[1] and yet you, rogue, will ensconce your rags, your cat-a-mountain[2] looks, your red-lattice[3] phrases, and your bull-baiting[4] oaths, under the shelter of your honour! You will not do it, you!

Pist. I do relent:—what would thou more of man?

Fal. Well, go to; away; no more.

Enter ROBIN.

Rob. Sir, here's a woman would speak with you.

Fal. Let her approach.

Enter MISTRESS QUICKLY.

Quick. Give your worship good morrow.

Fal. Good morrow, good wife.

Quick. Marry, this is the short and the long of it; you have brought her into such a canaries as 't is wonderful.—(Act ii. 2. 60-62.)

Quick. Not so, an 't please your worship.

Fal. Good maid, then.

Quick. I 'll be sworn;
As my mother was, the first hour I was born.

Fal. I do believe the swearer. What with me?

Quick. Shall I vouchsafe your worship a word or two?

Fal. Two thousand, fair woman: and I 'll vouchsafe thee the hearing.

Quick. There is one Mistress Ford, sir:—I pray, come a little nearer this ways:—I myself dwell with Master Doctor Caius,—

Fal. Well, on: Mistress Ford, you say,—

Quick. Your worship says very true:—I pray your worship, come a little nearer this ways.

Fal. I warrant thee, nobody hears;—mine own people, mine own people.

Quick. Are they so? God bless them, and make them his servants!

Fal. Well: Mistress Ford;—what of her?

Quick. Why, sir, she 's a good creature.—Lord, Lord! your worship 's a wanton! Well, heaven forgive you, and all of us, I pray!—

Fal. Mistress Ford;—come, Mistress Ford,—

Quick. Marry, this is the short and the long

[1] *Lurch* = lurk.
[2] *Cat-a-mountain*, a wild cat; here = fierce.
[3] *Red-lattice* = ale-house.
[4] *Bull-baiting* = truculent, swaggering.

of it; you have brought her into such a canaries[1] as 't is wonderful. The best courtier of them all, when the court lay at Windsor, could never have brought her to such a canary.[1] Yet there has been knights, and lords, and gentlemen, with their coaches; I warrant you, coach after coach, letter after letter, gift after gift; smelling so sweetly—all musk—and so rushling, I warrant you, in silk and gold; and in such alligant[2] terms; and in such wine and sugar of the best and the fairest, that would have won any woman's heart; and, I warrant you, they could never get an eye-wink of her:—I had myself twenty angels given me this morning; but I defy all angels—in any such sort, as they say—but in the way of honesty:—and, I warrant you, they could never get her so much as sip on a cup with the proudest of them all: and yet there has been earls, nay, which is more, pensioners;[3] but, I warrant you, all is one with her.

Fal. But what says she to me? be brief, my good she-Mercury.

Quick. Marry, she hath receiv'd your letter; for the which she thanks you a thousand times; and she gives you to notify, that her husband will be absence from his house between ten and eleven.

Fal. Ten and eleven?

Quick. Ay, forsooth; and then you may come and see the picture, she says, that you wot of;—Master Ford, her husband, will be from home. Alas, the sweet woman leads an ill life with him! he 's a very jealousy man: she leads a very frampold[4] life with him, good heart.

Fal. Ten and eleven:—woman, commend me to her; I will not fail her.

Quick. Why, you say well. But I have another messenger to your worship. Mistress Page hath her hearty commendations to you, too:—and let me tell you in your ear, she 's as fartuous[5] a civil modest wife, and one, I tell you, that will not miss you morning nor evening prayer, as any is in Windsor, whoe'er be the other:—and she bade me tell your worship that her husband is seldom from home; but, she hopes, there will come a time—I never knew a woman so dote upon a man: surely, I think you have charms, la! yes, in truth.

Fal. Not I, I assure thee: setting the attraction of my good parts aside, I have no other charms.

Quick. Blessing on your heart for 't!

Fal. But, I pray thee, tell me this,—has Ford's wife and Page's wife acquainted each other how they love me?

Quick. That were a jest indeed!—they have not so little grace, I hope:—that were a trick indeed!—But Mistress Page would desire you to send her your little page, of all loves: her husband has a marvellous infection to the little page; and, truly, Master Page is an honest man. Never a wife in Windsor leads a better life than she does: do what she will, say what she will, take all, pay all, go to bed when she list, rise when she list, all is as she will: and, truly, she deserves it; for if there be a kind woman in Windsor, she is one. You must send her your page; no remedy.

Fal. Why, I will.

Quick. Nay, but do so, then: and, look you, he may come and go between you both: and, in any case, have a nay-word, that you may know one another's mind, and the boy never need to understand any thing; for 't is not good that children should know any wickedness: old folks, you know, have discretion, as they say, and know the world.

Fal. Fare thee well: commend me to them both: there 's my purse; I am yet thy debtor.—Boy, go along with this woman. [*Exeunt Mistress Quickly and Robin.*]—This news distracts me![6]

Pist. This pink[7] is one of Cupid's carriers:—
Clap on more sails; pursue; up with your fights;[8]
Give fire; she is my prize, or ocean whelm them all! [*Exit.*

Fal. Say'st thou so, old Jack? go thy ways; I 'll make more of thy old body than I have done. Will they yet look after thee? Wilt thou, after the expense of so much money, be

[1] *Canary*, a blunder for quandary.
[2] *Alligant*=elegant.
[3] *Pensioners*, gentlemen retainers at court.
[4] *Frampold*, quarrelsome.
[5] *Fartuous*, virtuous.
[6] *Distracts me* (with joy).
[7] *Pink*, with a double meaning=a small sailing-vessel; also, a procuress.
[8] *Fights*. See note 73.

now a gainer? Good body, I thank thee. Let them say 't is grossly done; so it be fairly done, no matter.

Enter BARDOLPH, *with a cup of sack.*

Bard. Sir John, there's one Master Brook below would fain speak with you, and be acquainted with you; and hath sent your worship a morning's draught of sack.

Fal. Brook is his name?

Bard. Ay, sir.

Fal. Call him in. [*Exit Bardolph.*] Such Brooks are welcome to me, that o'erflow such liquor.—Ah, ha! Mistress Ford and Mistress Page, have I encompass'd you? go to; *via!*[1]

Re-enter BARDOLPH, *with* FORD *disguised.*

Ford. 'Bless you, sir.

Fal. And you, sir. Would you speak with me?

Ford. I make bold to press with so little preparation upon you.

Fal. You 're welcome. What 's your will?—Give us leave, drawer. [*Exit Bardolph.*

Ford. Sir, I am a gentleman that have spent much; my name is Brook.

Fal. Good Master Brook, I desire more acquaintance of you.

Ford. Good Sir John, I sue for yours: not to charge you; for I must let you understand I think myself in better plight for a lender than you are: the which hath something embolden'd me to this unseason'd[2] intrusion; for they say, if money go before, all ways do lie open.

Fal. Money is a good soldier, sir, and will on.

Ford. Troth, and I have a bag of money here troubles me: if you will help to bear it, Sir John, take half, or all, for easing me of the carriage.

Fal. Sir, I know not how I may desire to be your porter.

Ford. I will tell you, sir, if you will give me the hearing.

Fal. Speak, good Master Brook: I shall be glad to be your servant.

Ford. Sir, I hear you are a scholar,—I will be brief with you;—and you have been a man long known to me, though I had never so good means, as desire, to make myself acquainted with you. I shall discover a thing to you, wherein I must very much lay open mine own imperfection: but, good Sir John, as you have one eye upon my follies, as you hear them unfolded, turn another into the register of your own; that I may pass with a reproof the easier, sith you yourself know how easy it is to be such an offender.

Fal. Very well, sir; proceed.

Ford. There is a gentlewoman in this town, her husband's name is Ford.

Fal. Well, sir.

Ford. I have long lov'd her, and, I protest to you, bestowed much on her; following her with a doting observance;[3] engross'd[4] opportunities to meet her; fee'd every slight occasion that could but niggardly give me sight of her; not only bought many presents to give her, but have given largely to many to know what she would have given; briefly, I have pursued her as love hath pursu'd me; which hath been on the wing of all occasions. But whatsoever I have merited, either in my mind or in my means, meed, I am sure, I have received none; unless experience be a jewel: that I have purchased at an infinite rate; and that hath taught me to say this;

"Love like a shadow flies when substance love pursues;
Pursuing that that flies, and flying what pursues."

Fal. Have you receiv'd no promise of satisfaction at her hands?

Ford. Never.

Fal. Have you importun'd her to such a purpose?

Ford. Never.

Fal. Of what quality was your love, then?

Ford. Like a fair house built on another man's ground; so that I have lost my edifice by mistaking the place where I erected it.

Fal. To what purpose have you unfolded this to me?

Ford. When I have told you that, I have told you all. Some say, that though she

[1] *Via*, a joyous exclamation.

[2] *Unseason'd* = unseasonable.

[3] *Observance* = attention.

[4] *Engross'd*, *i.e.* bought in the gross.

appear honest to me, yet in other places she enlargeth her mirth so far that there is shrewd[1] construction made of her. Now, Sir John, here is the heart of my purpose: you are a gentleman of excellent breeding, admirable discourse, of great admittance,[2] authentic[3] in your place and person, generally allowed[4] for your many war-like, court-like, and learned preparations,[5]—

Fal. O, sir!

Ford. Believe it, for you know it.—There is money; spend it, spend it; spend more; spend all I have; only give me so much of your time in exchange of it, as to lay an

Ford. O, understand my drift. She dwells so securely on the excellency of her honour, that the folly of my soul dares not present itself.—(Act II. 2. 251-254.)

amiable[6] siege to the honesty of this Ford's wife: use your art of wooing; win her to consent to you: if any man may, you may as soon as any.

Fal. Would it apply well to the vehemency of your affection, that I should win what you would enjoy? Methinks you prescribe[7] to yourself very preposterously.[8]

Ford. O, understand my drift. She dwells so securely[9] on the excellency of her honour, that the folly of my soul dares not present itself: she is too bright to be look'd against. Now, could I come to her with any detection in my hand, my desires had instance[10] and argument to commend themselves: I could drive her then from the ward of her purity, her reputation, her marriage-vow, and a thousand other her defences, which now are too-too strongly embattled against me. What say you to't, Sir John?

Fal. Master Brook, I will first make bold with your money; next, give me your hand;

[1] *Shrewd*, malicious.
[2] *Of great admittance* = admitted into high society.
[3] *Authentic*, i.e. having authority.
[4] *Allowed* = approved of.
[5] *Preparations* = accomplishments.
[6] *Amiable*, i.e. pertaining to love.
[7] *Prescribe*, i.e. a remedy.
[8] *Preposterously*, perversely, unnaturally.

[9] *Securely*, unsuspiciously.
[10] *Instance*, precedence.

and last, as I am a gentleman, you shall, if you will, enjoy Ford's wife.

Ford. O good sir!

Fal. I say you shall.

Ford. Want no money, Sir John; you shall want none.

Fal. Want no Mistress Ford, Master Brook; you shall want none. I shall be with her, I may tell you, by her own appointment—even as you came in to me, her assistant, or go-between, parted from me:—I say I shall be with her between ten and eleven; for at that time the jealous rascally knave, her husband, will be forth. Come you to me at night; you shall know how I speed.

Ford. I am blest in your acquaintance. Do you know Ford, sir?

Fal. Hang him, poor cuckoldly knave! I know him not:—yet I wrong him to call him poor; they say the jealous wittolly[1] knave hath masses of money; for the which his wife seems to me well-favour'd. I will use her as the key of the cuckoldly rogue's coffer; and there 's my harvest-home.

Ford. I would you knew Ford, sir, that you might avoid him, if you saw him.

Fal. Hang him, mechanical[2] salt-butter[3] rogue! I will stare him out of his wits; I will awe him with my cudgel: it shall hang like a meteor o'er the cuckold's horns. [Master Brook, thou shalt know I will predominate over the peasant, and thou shalt lie with his wife.—] Come to me soon at night:—Ford 's a knave, and I will aggravate his style;[4] thou, Master Brook, shalt know him for knave and cuckold:—come to me soon at night. [*Exit.*

Ford. What a damn'd Epicurean rascal is this!—My heart is ready to crack with impatience.—Who says this is improvident[5] jealousy? my wife hath sent to him, the hour is fix'd, the match is made. Would any man have thought this?—See the hell of having a false woman! My bed shall be abus'd, my coffers ransack'd, my reputation gnawn at; and I shall not only receive this villanous wrong, but stand under the adoption[6] of abominable terms, and by him who does me this wrong. Terms! names!—Amaimon sounds well; Lucifer, well; Barbason, well; yet they are devils' additions,[7] the names of fiends: but cuckold! wittol-cuckold![8] the devil himself hath not such a name. Page is an ass, a secure[9] ass: he will trust his wife; he will not be jealous. I will rather trust a Fleming with my butter, Parson Hugh the Welshman with my cheese, an Irishman with my aqua-vitæ bottle, or a thief to walk my ambling gelding, than my wife with herself: then she plots, then she ruminates, then she devises; and what they think in their hearts they may effect, they will break their hearts but they will effect. Heaven be prais'd for my jealousy!—Eleven o'clock the hour:—I will prevent this, detect my wife, be reveng'd on Falstaff, and laugh at Page. I will about it; better three hours too soon than a minute too late. Fie, fie, fie! cuckold! cuckold! cuckold! [*Exit.*

SCENE III. *A field near Windsor.*

Enter CAIUS *and* RUGBY.

Caius. Jack Rugby,—

Rug. Sir?

Caius. Vat is de clock, Jack?

Rug. 'T is past the hour, sir, that Sir Hugh promised to meet.

Caius. By gar, he has save his soul, dat he is no come; he has pray his Pible vell, dat he is no come: by gar, Jack Rugby, he is dead already, if he be come.

Rug. He is wise, sir; he knew your worship would kill him, if he came.

Caius. By gar, de herring is no dead so as I vill kill him. Take your rapier, Jack; I vill tell you how I vill kill him.

Rug. Alas, sir, I cannot fence.

Caius. Villainy, take your rapier.

Rug. Forbear; here 's company.

Enter Host, SHALLOW, SLENDER, *and* PAGE.

Host. 'Bless thee, bully doctor!

---

1 *Wittolly,* like a *wittol, i.e.* a willing cuckold.
2 *Mechanical,* having a trade, used in contempt.
3 *Salt-butter* = fed on coarse food.
4 *Aggravate his style, i.e.* add to his titles that of cuckold.
5 *Improvident,* heedless, rash.
6 *Stand under the adoption* = submit to the imposition.
7 *Additions,* titles.
8 *Wittol-cuckold,* one knowingly cuckolded.
9 *Secure,* unreflecting.

Shal. 'Save you, Master Doctor Caius!

Page. Now, good master doctor!

Slen. 'Give you good morrow, sir.

Caius. Vat be all you, one, two, tree, four, come for?

Host. To see thee fight, to see thee foin, to see thee traverse;[1] to see thee here, to see thee there; to see thee pass thy punto,[1] thy stock,[1] thy reverse,[1] thy distance,[1] thy montánt.[1] Is he dead, my Ethiopian? is he dead, my Francisco? ha, bully! What says my Æsculapius? my Galen? my heart-of-elder?[2] ha! is he dead, bully-Stale? is he dead?

Caius. By gar, he is de coward Jack priest of de varld; he is not show his face.

Host. Thou art [a Castalion-King-Urinal!] Hector of Greece, my boy!

Caius. I pray you, bear vitness that me

Host. Let him die: sheathe thy impatience, throw cold water on thy choler: go about the fields with me through Frogmore: I will bring thee where Mistress Anne Page is.—(Act ii. 3. 88-91.)

have stay six or seven, two, tree hours for him, and he is no come.

Shal. He is the wiser man, master doctor: he is a curer of souls, and you a curer of bodies; if you should fight, you go against the hair of[3] your professions.—Is it not true, Master Page?

Page. Master Shallow, you have yourself been a great fighter, though now a man of peace.

Shal. 'Bodikins, Master Page, though I now be old, and of the peace, if I see a sword out, my finger itches to make one. Though we are justices, and doctors, and churchmen, Master Page, we have some salt of our youth in us; we are the sons of women, Master Page.

Page. 'T is true, Master Shallow.

Shal. It will be found so, Master Page.—Master Doctor Caius, I am come to fetch you home. I am sworn of the peace: you have show'd yourself a wise physician, and Sir Hugh hath shown himself a wise and patient churchman. You must go with me, master doctor.

Host. Pardon, guest-justice.—A word, Mounseur Mock-water.

Caius. Mock-vater! vat is dat?

Host. Mock-water, in our English tongue, is valour, bully.

[1] Terms in fencing.
[2] *Heart-of-elder*, *i.e.* weak, faint.
[3] *Against the hair*=contrary to the nature of.

Caius. By gar, den, I have as mush mock-vater as de Englishman.—Scurvy jack-dog priest! by gar, me vill cut his ears.

Host. He will clapper-claw[1] thee tightly, bully.

Caius. Clapper-de-claw! vat is dat?

Host. That is, he will make thee amends.

Caius. By gar, me do look he shall clapper-de-claw me; for, by gar, me vill have it.

Host. And I will provoke him to't, or let him wag.

Caius. Me tank you for dat.

Host. And, moreover, bully,—But first, master guest, and Master Page, and eke Cavaliero Slender, go you through the town to Frogmore. [*Aside to them.*

Page. Sir Hugh is there, is he?

Host. He is there: see what humour he is in; and I will bring the doctor about by the fields. Will it do well?

Shal. We will do it.

Page, Shal., and Slen. Adieu, good master doctor. [*Exeunt Page, Shallow, and Slender.*

Caius. By gar, me vill kill de priest; for he speak for a jack-an-ape to Anne Page.

Host. Let him die: sheathe thy impatience, throw cold water on thy choler: go about the fields with me through Frogmore: I will bring thee where Mistress Anne Page is, at a farm-house a-feasting; and thou shalt woo her. Cried I aim? said I well?

Caius. By gar, me dank you for dat: by gar, I love you; and I shall procure-a you de good guest, de earl, de knight, de lords, de gentlemen, my patients.

Host. For the which I will be thy adversary toward Anne Page. Said I well?

Caius. By gar, 't is good; vell said.

Host. Let us wag, then.

Caius. Come at my heels, Jack Rugby. [*Exeunt.*

ACT III.

Scene I. *A field near Frogmore.*

Enter Sir Hugh Evans *and* Simple.

Evans. I pray you now, good Master Slender's serving-man, and friend Simple by your name, which way have you look'd for Master Caius, that calls himself doctor of physic?

Sim. Marry, sir, the pittie-ward,[2] the Park-ward: every way: old Windsor way, and every way but the town way.

Evans. I most fehemently desire you you will also look that way.

Sim. I will, sir. [*Retires.*

Evans. 'Pless my soul, how full of cholers I am, and trempling of mind!—I shall be glad if he have deceiv'd me:—how melancholies I am!—[I will knog his urinals about his knave's costard when I have goot opportunities for the 'ork.—'Pless my soul!—] [*Sings.*

"To shallow rivers, to whose falls
Melodious birds sing madrigals;
There will we make our peds of roses,
And a thousand fragrant posies.
To shallow—"

'Mercy on me! I have a great dispositions to cry.— [*Sings.*

"Melodious birds sing madrigals;—
When as I sat in Pabylon,—
And a thousand vagram[3] posies.
To shallow," &c.

Sim. [*Coming forward*] Yonder he is coming, this way, Sir Hugh.

Evans. He's welcome.— [*Sings.*

"To shallow rivers, to whose falls"—

Heaven prosper the right!—What weapons is he?

Sim. No weapons, sir. There comes my master, Master Shallow, and another gentleman, from Frogmore, over the stile, this way.

Evans. Pray you, give me my gown; or else keep it in your arms. [*Reads in a book.*

Enter Page, Shallow, *and* Slender.

Shal. How now, master parson! Good morrow, good Sir Hugh. Keep a gamester from

---

[1] *Clapper-claw* = beat, thrash.

[2] See note 81.

[3] *Vagram*, for vagrant.

the dice, and a good student from his book, and it is wonderful.

Slen. [*Aside*] Ah, sweet Anne Page!

Page. 'Save you, good Sir Hugh!

Evans. 'Pless you from his mercy sake, all of you!

Shal. What, the sword and the word! do you study them both, master parson?

Page. And youthful still, in your doublet and hose this raw rheumatic day?

Evans. There is reasons and causes for it.

Page. We are come to you to do a good office, master parson.

Evans. Fery well: what is it?

Page. Yonder is a most reverend gentleman, who, belike having received wrong by some person, is at most odds with his own gravity and patience that ever you saw.

Shal. I have lived fourscore years and upward; I never heard a man of his place, gravity, and learning, so wide of[1] his own respect.

Evans. What is he?

Page. I think you know him; Master Doctor Caius, the renowned French physician.

Evans. Got's will, and his passion of my heart! I had as lief you would tell me of a mess of porridge.

Page. Why?

Evans. He has no more knowledge in Hibbocrates and Galen,—and he is a knave besides; a cowardly knave as you would desires to be acquainted withal.

Page. I warrant you, he's the man should fight with him.

Slen. [*Aside*] O sweet Anne Page!

Shal. It appears so, by his weapons.—Keep them asunder:—here comes Doctor Caius.

Enter Host, Caius, *and* Rugby.

Page. Nay, good master parson, keep in your weapon.

Shal. So do you, good master doctor.

Host. Disarm them, and let them question: [*Page and Host take the rapiers from them*] let them keep their limbs whole, and hack our English.

Caius. I pray you, let-a me speak a word vit your ear. Vherefore vill you not meet-a me?

Evans. [*Aside to Caius*] Pray you, use your patience: in goot time.

Caius. By gar, you are de coward, de Jack-dog, John-ape.

Evans. [*Aside to Caius*] Pray you, let us not be laughing-stogs to other men's humours; I desire you in friendship, and I will one way or other make you amends.—[*Aloud*] I will knog your urinals about your knave's cogscomb for missing your meetings and appointments.

Caius. *Diable!*—Jack Rugby,—mine host de Jarteer,—have I not stay for him to kill him? have I not, at de place I did appoint?

Evans. As I am a Christians soul, now, look you, this is the place appointed: I'll be judgment by mine host of the Garter.

Host. Peace, I say, Guallia and Gaul, French and Welsh, soul-curer and body-curer!

Caius. Ay, dat is very good; excellent.

Host. Peace, I say! hear mine host of the Garter. Am I politic? am I subtle? am I a Machiavel? Shall I lose my doctor? no; he gives me the potions and the motions. Shall I lose my parson, my priest, my Sir Hugh? no; he gives me the proverbs and the no-verbs.—Give me thy hand, terrestrial; [*taking Caius' hand*] so.—Give me thy hand, celestial; [*taking Evans' hand*] so. [*Host joins their hands in token of reconciliation*]—Boys of art, I have deceiv'd you both; I have directed you to wrong places: your hearts are mighty, your skins are whole, and let burnt sack be the issue.—Come, lay their swords to pawn.—Follow me, lads of peace; follow, follow, follow.

Shal. Trust me, a mad host.—Follow, gentlemen, follow.

Slen. [*Aside*] O sweet Anne Page!

[*Exeunt Shallow, Slender, Page, and Host.*

Caius. Ha, do I perceive dat? have you make-a de sot of us, ha, ha?

Evans. This is well; he has made us his vlouting-stog.[2]—I desire you that we may be friends; and let us knog our prains together to be revenge on this same scall,[3] scurvy, cogging[4] companion,[5] the host of the Garter.

Caius. By gar, vit all my heart. He pro-

[1] *So wide of*, i.e. so wide of the mark of.

[2] *Vlouting-stog*, i.e. flouting-stock = laughing-stock.

[3] *Scall*, for scald = shabby, mean.

[4] *Cogging*, cheating.

[5] *Companion* = fellow.

mise to bring me vere is Anne Page; by gar, he deceive me too.

Evans. Well, I will smite his noddles. Pray you, follow.

[*Exeunt arm in arm, Rugby and Simple imitating them.*

SCENE II. *The street, in Windsor.*

Enter MISTRESS PAGE *and* ROBIN.

Mrs. Page. Nay, keep your way, little gallant; you were wont to be a follower, but now you are a leader. Whether had you rather lead mine eyes, or eye your master's heels?

Rob. I had rather, forsooth, go before you like a man than follow him like a dwarf.

Mrs. Page. O, you are a flattering boy: now I see you'll be a courtier.

Enter FORD.

Ford. Well met, Mistress Page. Whither go you?

Mrs. Page. Truly, sir, to see your wife. Is she at home?

Ford. Ay, and as idle as she may hang together, for want of company. I think, if your husbands were dead, you two would marry.

Mrs. Page. Be sure of that,—two other husbands.

Ford. Where had you this pretty weathercock?

Mrs. Page. I cannot tell what the dickens his name is my husband had him of.—What do you call your knight's name, sirrah?

Rob. Sir John Falstaff.

Ford. Sir John Falstaff!

Mrs. Page. He, he; I can never hit on 's name.—There is such a league between my good man and he!—Is your wife at home indeed?

Ford. Indeed she is.

Mrs. Page. By your leave, sir: I am sick till I see her. [*Exeunt Mrs. Page and Robin.*

Ford. Has Page any brains? hath he any eyes? hath he any thinking? Sure, they sleep; he hath no use of them. Why, this boy will carry a letter twenty mile, as easy as a cannon will shoot point-blank twelve score.[1] He pieces out his wife's inclination; he gives her folly motion[2] and advantage: and now she's going to my wife, and Falstaff's boy with her: —a man may hear this shower sing in the wind:—and Falstaff's boy with her!—Good plots!—they are laid; and our revolted wives share damnation together. Well; I will take him, then torture my wife, pluck the borrow'd veil of modesty from the so seeming Mistress Page, divulge Page[3] himself for a secure[4] and wilful Actæon; and to these violent proceedings all my neighbours shall cry aim.[5] [*Clock strikes.*] The clock gives me my cue, and my assurance bids me search: there I shall find Falstaff: I shall be rather prais'd for this than mock'd; for it is as positive as the earth is firm that Falstaff is there: I will go.

Enter PAGE, SHALLOW, SLENDER, *Host*, SIR HUGH EVANS, CAIUS, *and* RUGBY.

Shal., Page, &c. Well met, Master Ford.

Ford. Trust me, a good knot: I have good cheer at home; and I pray you all, go with me.

Shal. I must excuse myself, Master Ford.

Slen. And so must I, sir: we have appointed to dine with Mistress Anne, and I would not break with her for more money than I'll speak of.

Shal. We have linger'd about a match between Anne Page and my cousin Slender, and this day we shall have our answer.

Slen. I hope I have your good will, father Page.

Page. You have, Master Slender; I stand wholly for you:—but my wife, master doctor, is for you altogether.

Caius. Ay, by gar; and de maid is love-a me; my nursh-a Quickly tell me so mush.

Host. What say you to young Master Fenton? he capers, he dances, he has eyes of youth, he writes verses, he speaks holiday, he smells April and May: he will carry 't, he will carry 't; 't is in his buttons;[6] he will carry 't.

Page. Not by my consent, I promise you.

---

[1] *Twelve score*, i.e. twelve score yards.

[2] *Motion*, motive, incitement.

[3] *Divulge Page*, i.e. proclaim Page.

[4] *Secure*, wanting in circumspection.

[5] *Cry aim (to)* = approve of.

[6] *In his buttons* = in his capacity or power.

The gentleman is of no having:[1] he kept company with the wild prince and Pointz; he is of too high a region; he knows too much. No, he shall not knit a knot in his fortunes with the finger of my substance: if he take her, let him take her simply; the wealth I have waits on my consent, and my consent goes not that way.

Ford. I beseech you heartily, some of you go home with me to dinner: besides your cheer, you shall have sport; I will show you a monster.—Master doctor, you shall go;—so shall you, Master Page;—and you, Sir Hugh.

Shal. Well, fare you well:—we shall have the freer wooing at Master Page's.

[*Exeunt Shallow and Slender.*

Caius. Go home, John Rugby; I come anon.

[*Exit Rugby.*

Host. Farewell, my hearts: I will to my honest knight Falstaff, and drink canary with him. [*Exit.*

Ford. [*Aside*] I think I shall drink in pipe-wine[2] first with him; I'll make him dance.—Will you go, gentles?

All. Have with you to see this monster.

[*Exeunt.*

SCENE III. *A room in Ford's house.*

Enter MISTRESS FORD *and* MISTRESS PAGE.

Mrs. Ford. What, John! What, Robert!

Mrs. Page. Quickly, quickly:—is the buck-basket—[3]

Mrs. Ford. I warrant.—What, Robin, I say!

Enter Servants with a basket.

Mrs. Page. Come, come, come.

Mrs. Ford. Here, set it down.

Mrs. Page. Give your men the charge; we must be brief.

Mrs. Ford. Marry, as I told you before, John and Robert, be ready here hard by in the brew-house; and when I suddenly call you, come forth, and, without any pause or staggering, take this basket on your shoulders: that done, trudge with it in all haste, and carry it among the whitsters[4] in Datchet-mead, and there empty it in the muddy ditch close by the Thames side.

Mrs. Page. You will do it?

Mrs. Ford. I ha' told them over and over; they lack no direction.—Be gone, and come when you are call'd. [*Exeunt Servants.*

Mrs. Page. Here comes little Robin.

Enter ROBIN.

Mrs. Ford. How now, my eyas-musket![5] what news with you?

Rob. My master, Sir John, is come in at your back-door, Mistress Ford, and requests your company.

Mrs. Page. You little Jack-a-Lent,[6] have you been true to us?

Rob. Ay, I'll be sworn. My master knows not of your being here, and hath threaten'd to put me into everlasting liberty, if I tell you of it; for he swears he'll turn me away.

Mrs. Page. Thou 'rt a good boy: this secrecy of thine shall be a tailor to thee, and shall make thee a new doublet and hose.—I'll go hide me.

Mrs. Ford. Do so.—Go tell thy master I am alone.—Mistress Page, remember you your cue. [*Exit Robin.*

Mrs. Page. I warrant thee; if I do not act it, hiss me. [*Exit.*

Mrs. Ford. Go to, then: we'll use this unwholesome humidity, this gross watery pumpion;[7] we'll teach him to know turtles[8] from jays.[9]

Enter FALSTAFF.

Fal. "Have I caught" thee, "my heavenly jewel?" Why, now let me die, for I have liv'd long enough; this is the period of my ambition: [*kisses her hand*] O this blessed hour!

Mrs. Ford. O sweet Sir John!

Fal. Mistress Ford, I cannot cog,[10] I cannot prate, Mistress Ford. Now shall I sin in my wish,—I would thy husband were dead:

[1] *Having*, income, possessions.
[2] *Pipe-wine*, i.e. wine from the cask.
[3] *Buck-basket*, a basket for soiled linen.
[4] *Whitsters*, bleachers.
[5] *Eyas-musket*, a young sparrow-hawk.
[6] *Jack-a-Lent*, a stuffed puppet.
[7] *Pumpion*, a pumpkin.
[8] *Turtles*, used figuratively = chaste women.
[9] *Jays*, used figuratively = unchaste women.
[10] *Cog*, deceive, cheat.

I 'll speak it before the best lord, I would make thee my lady.

Mrs. Ford. I your lady, Sir John! alas, I should be a pitiful lady!

Fal. Let the court of France show me such another. I see how thine eye would emulate the diamond: thou hast the right arched beauty of the brow that becomes the ship-tire,[1] the tire-valiant,[1] or any tire[1] of Venetian admittance.[2]

Mrs. Ford. A plain kerchief, Sir John: my brows become nothing else; nor that well neither.

Fal. By the Lord, thou art a traitor to say so: thou wouldst make an absolute courtier; and the firm fixture of thy foot would give an excellent motion to thy gait in a semicircled

Fal. "Have I caught" thee, "my heavenly jewel?"—(Act iii. 3. 45, 46.)

farthingale. I see what thou wert, if Fortune thy foe were not, Nature thy friend. Come, thou canst not hide it.

Mrs. Ford. Believe me, there 's no such thing in me.

Fal. What made me love thee? let that persuade thee there 's something extraordinary in thee. Come, I cannot cog,[3] and say thou art this and that, like a many of these lisping hawthorn-buds, that come like women in men's apparel, and smell like Bucklersbury[4] in simple time;[5] I cannot: but I love thee; none but thee; and thou deserv'st it.

Mrs. Ford. Do not betray me, sir. I fear you love Mistress Page.

Fal. Thou mightst as well say I love to walk by the Counter-gate, which is as hateful to me as the reek[6] of a limekiln.

Mrs. Ford. Well, heaven knows how I love you; and you shall one day find it.

Fal. Keep in that mind; I 'll deserve it.

Mrs. Ford. Nay, I must tell you, so you do; or else I could not be in that mind.

Rob. [*Within*] Mistress Ford, Mistress Ford!

1 *Ship-tire*, a fanciful head-dress.
2 *Venetian admittance* = Venetian fashion.
3 *Cog*, deceive.
4 Bucklersbury, a street in London chiefly inhabited by druggists and herbalists.
5 *Simple time* = time for gathering simples or herbs.
6 *Reek*, smoke.

here 's Mistress Page at the door, sweating, and blowing, and looking wildly, and would needs speak with you presently.

Fal. She shall not see me: I will ensconce me behind the arras.

Mrs. Ford. Pray you, do so: she 's a very tattling woman.

[*Falstaff stands behind the arras.*

Re-enter MISTRESS PAGE *and* ROBIN.

What 's the matter? how now!

Mrs. Page. O Mistress Ford, what have you done? You 're sham'd, you 're overthrown, you 're undone for ever!

Mrs. Ford. What 's the matter, good Mistress Page?

Mrs. Page. O well-a-day, Mistress Ford! having an honest man to your husband, to give him such cause of suspicion!

Mrs. Ford. What cause of suspicion?

Mrs. Page. What cause of suspicion! Out upon you! how am I mistook in you!

Mrs. Ford. Why, alas, what 's the matter?

Mrs. Page. Your husband 's coming hither, woman, with all the officers in Windsor, to search for a gentleman that he says is here now in the house, by your consent, to take an ill advantage of his absence: you are undone.

Mrs. Ford. 'T is not so, I hope.

Mrs. Page. Pray heaven it be not so, that you have such a man here! but 't is most certain your husband 's coming, with half Windsor at his heels, to search for such a one. I come before to tell you. If you know yourself clear, why, I am glad of it; but if you have a friend here, convey,[1] convey him out. Be not amazed; call all your senses to you; defend your reputation, or bid farewell to your good life for ever.

Mrs. Ford. What shall I do?—There is a gentleman my dear friend; and I fear not mine own shame so much as his peril: I had rather than a thousand pound he were out of the house.

Mrs. Page. For shame! never stand "you had rather" and "you had rather:" your husband 's here at hand; bethink you of some conveyance:[2] in the house you cannot hide him.—O, how have you deceiv'd me!—Look, here is a basket: if he be of any reasonable stature, he may creep in here; and throw foul linen upon him, as if it were going to bucking: or,—it is whiting-time,[3]—send him by your two men to Datchet-mead.

Mrs. Ford. He 's too big to go in there. What shall I do?

Re-enter FALSTAFF.

Fal. Let me see 't, let me see 't, O, let me see 't!—I 'll in, I 'll in:—follow your friend's counsel:—I 'll in.

Mrs. Page. What, Sir John Falstaff! Are these your letters, knight?

Fal. I love thee, and none but thee; help me away: let me creep in here. I 'll never—

[*Goes into the basket; they cover him with foul linen.*

Mrs. Page. Help to cover your master, boy.—Call your men, Mistress Ford.—You dissembling knight! [*Exit Robin.*

Mrs. Ford. What, John! Robert! John!

Re-enter Servants.

Go take up these clothes here quickly:—where 's the cowl-staff? look, how you drumble![4]—Carry them to the laundress in Datchet-mead quickly, come.

[*They are going off with the basket, when—*

Enter FORD, PAGE, CAIUS, *and* SIR HUGH EVANS.

Ford. 'Pray you, come near: if I suspect without cause, why then make sport at me; then let me be your jest; I deserve it.—How now! whither bear you this?

Serv. To the laundress, forsooth.

Mrs. Ford. Why, what have you to do whither they bear it? You were best meddle with buck-washing.[5]

Ford. Buck! I would I could wash myself of the buck!—Buck, buck, buck! Ay, buck; I warrant you, buck; and of the season too, it shall appear. [*Exeunt Servants with the basket.*]—Gentlemen, I have dream'd to-night; I 'll tell you my dream. Here, here, here be

[1] *Convey*, remove secretly.

[2] *Conveyance*, trick, device.

[3] *Whiting-time*, bleaching-time.

[4] *Drumble* = are sluggish.

[5] *Buck-washing*, i.e. washing of soiled linen.

my keys: ascend my chambers; search, seek, find out: I 'll warrant we 'll unkennel the fox. —Let me stop this way first [*Locks the door*]. —So, now uncape.[1]

Page. Good Master Ford, be contented: you wrong yourself too much.

Ford. True, Master Page.—Up, gentlemen; you shall see sport anon: follow me, gentlemen. [*Exit.*

Evans. This is fery fantastical humours and jealousies.

Caius. By gar, 't is no de fashion of France; it is not jealous in France.

Page. Nay, follow him, gentlemen; see the issue of his search.

[*Exeunt Page, Caius, and Evans.*

Mrs. Page. Is there not a double excellency in this?

Mrs. Ford. I know not which pleases me better, that my husband is deceiv'd, or Sir John.

Mrs. Page. What a taking was he in when your husband asked what was in the basket!

Mrs. Ford. I am half afraid he will have need of washing; so throwing him into the water will do him a benefit.

Mrs. Page. Hang him, dishonest rascal! I would all of the same strain were in the same distress.

Mrs. Ford. I think my husband hath some special suspicion of Falstaff's being here; for I never saw him so gross in his jealousy till now.

Mrs. Page. I will lay a plot to try that; and we will yet have more tricks with Falstaff: his dissolute disease will scarce obey this medicine.

Mrs. Ford. Shall we send that foolish carrion Mistress Quickly to him, and excuse his throwing into the water; and give him another hope, to betray him to another punishment?

Mrs. Page. We will do it: let him be sent for to-morrow eight o'clock, to have amends.

Re-enter FORD, PAGE, CAIUS, *and* SIR HUGH EVANS.

Ford. I cannot find him: may be the knave bragg'd of that he could not compass.

Mrs. Page [*Aside to Mrs. Ford*] Heard you that?

Mrs. Ford. [*Aside to Mrs. Page*] Ay, ay, peace.—You use me well, Master Ford, do you?

Ford. Ay, I do so.

Mrs. Ford. Heaven make you better than your thoughts!

[*Retires up stage with Mrs. Page.*

Ford. Amen!

Mrs. Page. You do yourself mighty wrong, Master Ford.

Ford. Ay, ay; I must bear it.

Evans. If there be any pody in the house, and in the chambers, and in the coffers, and in the presses, heaven forgive my sins at the day of judgment!

Caius. By gar, nor I too; dere is no bodies.

Page. Fie, fie, Master Ford! are you not asham'd? What spirit, what devil suggests this imagination? I would not ha' your distemper in this kind for the wealth of Windsor Castle.

Ford. 'T is my fault, Master Page: I suffer for it.

Evans. You suffer for a pad conscience: your wife is as honest a 'omans as I will desires among five thousand, and five hundred too.

Caius. By gar, I see 't is an honest woman.

Ford. Well;—I promis'd you a dinner:—come, come, walk in the Park: I pray you, pardon me; I will hereafter make known to you why I have done this.—Come, wife;—come, Mistress Page.—I pray you, pardon me; pray heartily, pardon me.

Page. Let 's go in, gentlemen; but, trust me, we 'll mock him. I do invite you to-morrow morning to my house to breakfast: after, we 'll a-birding[2] together; I have a fine hawk for the bush. Shall it be so?

Ford. Any thing.

[*Evans.* If there is one, I shall make two in the company.

Caius. If dere be one or two, I shall make-a de turd.

Ford.] Pray you, go, Master Page.

Evans. I pray you now, remembrance to-morrow on the lousy knave, mine host.

[1] *Uncape*, perhaps = to uncouple hounds.

[2] *Birding* = shooting birds.

Caius. Dat is good; by gar, vit all my heart.

Evans. A lousy knave, to have his gibes and his mockeries! [*Exeunt.*

SCENE IV. *Before Page's house.*

Enter FENTON, ANNE PAGE, *and* MISTRESS QUICKLY.—QUICKLY *stands apart.*

Fent. I see I cannot get thy father's love;
Therefore no more turn me to him, sweet Nan.

Anne. Alas, how then?

Fent. Why, thou must be thyself.
He doth object I am too great of birth;
And that, my state being gall'd[1] with my expense,
I seek to heal it only by his wealth:
Besides, these other bars he lays before me,—
My riots past, my wild societies;
And tells me 't is a thing impossible
I should love thee but as a property.

Anne. May be he tells you true.

Fent. No, heaven so speed me in my time to come!
Albeit I will confess thy father's wealth
Was the first motive that I woo'd thee, Anne:
Yet, wooing thee, I found thee of more value
Than stamps in gold or sums in sealed bags;
And 't is the very riches of thyself
That now I aim at.

Anne. Gentle Master Fenton,
Yet seek my father's love; still seek it, sir:
If opportunity[2] and humblest suit
Cannot attain it, why, then—Hark you hither.
[*They converse apart.*

Enter SHALLOW *and* SLENDER.

Shal. Break their talk, Mistress Quickly: my kinsman shall speak for himself.

Slen. I 'll make a shaft[3] or a bolt on 't: 'slid, 't is but venturing.

Shal. Be not dismay'd.

Slen. No, she shall not dismay me: I care not for that,—but that I am afeard.

Quick. Hark ye; Master Slender would speak a word with you.

Anne. I come to him.—[*Aside*] This is my father's choice:
O, what a world of vile ill-favour'd faults
Looks handsome in three hundred pounds a-year!—

Quick. And how does good Master Fenton? Pray you, a word with you.—

Shal. She 's coming; to her, coz. O boy, thou hadst a father!

Slen. I had a father, Mistress Anne;—my uncle can tell you good jests of him.—Pray you, uncle, tell Mistress Anne the jest, how my father stole two geese out of a pen, good uncle.

Shal. Mistress Anne, my cousin loves you.

Slen. Ay, that I do; as well as I love any woman in Glostershire.

Shal. He will maintain you like a gentlewoman.

Slen. Ay, that I will, come cut and long-tail,[4] under the degree of a squire.

Shal. He will make you a hundred and fifty pounds jointure.

Anne. Good Master Shallow, let him woo for himself.

Shal. Marry, I thank you for it; I thank you for that good comfort.—She calls you, coz: I 'll leave you.

Anne. Now, Master Slender,—

Slen. Now, good Mistress Anne,—

Anne. What is your will?

Slen. My will! 'od's heartlings, that 's a pretty jest indeed! I ne'er made my will yet, I thank heaven; I am not such a sickly creature, I give heaven praise.

Anne. I mean, Master Slender, what would you with me?

Slen. Truly, for mine own part, I would little or nothing with you. Your father and my uncle hath made motions:[5] if it be my luck, so; if not, happy man be his dole! They can tell you how things go better than I can: you may ask your father; here he comes.

Enter PAGE *and* MISTRESS PAGE.

Page. Now, Master Slender:—love him, daughter Anne.—
Why, how now! what does Master Fenton here?

1 *Gall'd*, crippled.
2 *Opportunity*, making use of fitting occasions.
3 *I'll make a shaft, &c* = I 'll hit or miss.
4 *Come cut and long-tail* = whatever may happen.
5 *Motions*, i.e. propositions.

You wrong me sir, thus still to haunt my house:
I told you, sir, my daughter is dispos'd of.

Fent. Nay, Master Page, be not impatient.

Mrs. Page. Good Master Fenton, come not to my child.

Page. She is no match for you.

Fent. Sir, will you hear me?

Page. No, good Master Fenton.—
Come, Master Shallow; come, son Slender; in.—
Knowing my mind, you wrong me, Master Fenton.

[*Exeunt Page, Shallow, and Slender.*

Quick. Speak to Mistress Page.

Fent. Good Mistress Page, for that I love your daughter
In such a righteous fashion as I do,
Perforce, against all checks, rebukes, and manners,
I must advance the colours of my love,
And not retire: let me have your good will.

Anne. Good mother, do not marry me to yond fool.

Mrs. Page. I mean it not; I seek you a better husband.—

Quick. That 's my master, master doctor.—

Anne. Alas, I had rather be set quick i' th' earth,
And bowl'd to death with turnips!

Mrs. Page. Come, trouble not yourself.—Good Master Fenton,
I will not be your friend nor enemy:
My daughter will I question how she loves you,
And as I find her, so am I affected.
Till then farewell, sir: she must needs go in;
Her father will be angry.

Fent. Farewell, gentle mistress.—Farewell, Nan. [*Exeunt Mrs. Page and Anne.*

Quick. This is my doing now:—"Nay," said I, "will you cast away your child on a fool and a physician? Look on Master Fenton:"—this is my doing.

Fent. I thank thee; and I pray thee, once to-night
Give my sweet Nan this ring: there's for thy pains.

Quick. Now heaven send thee good fortune! [*Exit Fenton.*] A kind heart he hath: a woman would run through fire and water for such a kind heart. But yet I would my master had Mistress Anne; or I would Master Slender had her; or, in sooth, I would Master Fenton had her: I will do what I can for them all three; for so I have promis'd, and I'll be as good as my word; but speciously[1] for Master Fenton. Well, I must of another

Anne. Now, Master Slender.—(Act iii. 4. 56.)

errand to Sir John Falstaff from my two mistresses: what a beast am I to slack it! [*Exit.*

SCENE V. *A room in the Garter Inn.*

Enter FALSTAFF *followed by* BARDOLPH.

Fal. Bardolph, I say,—

Bard. Here, sir.

Fal. Go fetch me a quart of sack; put a toast in 't. [*Exit Bardolph.*] Have I lived to be carried in a basket, and to be thrown in the Thames like a barrow of butcher's offal? Well, if I be serv'd such another trick, I'll have

[1] *Speciously* = especially.

my brains ta'en out, and butter'd, and give them to a dog for a new-year's gift. The rogues slighted me[1] into the river with as little remorse as they would have drown'd a blind bitch's puppies, fifteen i' the litter: and you may know by my size that I have a kind of alacrity in sinking; if the bottom were as deep as hell, I should down. I had been drowned, but that the shore was shelvy and shallow,—a death that I abhor; for the water swells a man; [and what a thing should I have been when I had been swelled! I should have been a mountain of mummy.]

Re-enter BARDOLPH *with sack.*

Bard. Here 's Mistress Quickly, sir, to speak with you.

Fal. Come, let me pour in some sack to the Thames water; for my belly 's as cold as if I had swallowed snowballs for pills to cool the reins.[2] Call her in.

Bard. Come in, woman!

Enter MISTRESS QUICKLY.

Quick. By your leave; I cry you mercy:—give your worship good morrow.

Fal. Take away these chalices.[3] Go brew me a pottle[4] of sack finely.

Bard. With eggs, sir?

Fal. Simple of itself; I 'll no pullet-sperm[5] in my brewage. [*Exit Bardolph.*] How now!

Quick. Marry, sir, I come to your worship from Mistress Ford.

Fal. Mistress Ford! I have had ford enough; I was thrown into the ford; I have my belly full of ford.

Quick. Alas the day! good heart, that was not her fault: she does so take on with her men; they mistook their erection.

Fal. So did I mine, to build upon a foolish woman's promise.

Quick. Well, she laments, sir, for it, that it would yearn your heart to see it. Her husband goes this morning a birding;[6] she desires you once more to come to her between eight and nine: I must carry her word quickly: she 'll make you amends, I warrant you.

Fal. Well, I will visit her: tell her so; and bid her think what a man is: let her consider his frailty, and then judge of my merit.

Quick. I will tell her.

Fal. Do so. Between nine and ten, say'st thou?

Quick. Eight and nine, sir.

Fal. Well, be gone: I will not miss her.

Quick. Peace be with you, sir. [*Exit.*

Fal. I marvel I hear not of Master Brook; he sent me word to stay within: I like his money well.—O, here he comes.

Enter FORD *disguised.*

Ford. 'Bless you, sir!

Fal. Now, Master Brook,—you come to know what hath pass'd between me and Ford's wife?

Ford. That, indeed, Sir John, is my business.

Fal. Master Brook, I will not lie to you: I was at her house the hour she appointed me.

Ford. And how sped you, sir?

Fal. Very ill-favouredly, Master Brook.

Ford. How so, sir? Did she change her determination?

Fal. No, Master Brook; but the peaking[7] cornuto[8] husband, Master Brook, dwelling in a continual larum of jealousy, comes me in the instant of our encounter, after we had embrac'd, kiss'd, protested, and, as it were, spoke the prologue of our comedy; and at his heels a rabble of his companions, thither provok'd and instigated by his distemper, and, forsooth, to search his house for his wife's love.

Ford. What, while you were there?

Fal. While I was there.

Ford. And did he search for you, and could not find you?

Fal. You shall hear. As good luck would have it, come in one Mistress Page: gives intelligence of Ford's approach; and, in her invention[9] and Ford's wife's distraction, they convey'd me into a buck-basket.[10]

Ford. A buck-basket![10]

Fal. By the Lord, a buck-basket![10]—ramm'd

---

1 *Slighted me* = threw me heedlessly.
2 *The reins*, the kidneys.
3 *Chalices*, cups.
4 *Pottle*, a large tankard, originally holding two quarts.
5 *Pullet-sperm* = the embryo of a chicken.
6 *Birding* = shooting birds.
7 *Peaking* = sneaking.
8 *Cornuto*, a cuckold.
9 *Invention*, i.e. device.
10 *Buck-basket*, basket of soiled linen.

me in with foul shirts and smocks, socks, foul stockings, greasy napkins; that, Master Brook, there was the rankest compound of villanous smell that ever offended nostril.

Ford. And how long lay you there?

Fal. Nay, you shall hear, Master Brook, what I have suffer'd to bring this woman to evil for your good. Being thus cramm'd in the basket, a couple of Ford's knaves, his hinds,[1] were called forth by their mistress to carry me in the name of foul clothes to Datchet-lane: they took me on their shoulders; met the jealous knave their master in the door, who asked them once or twice what they had in their basket: I quak'd for fear, lest the lunatic knave would have search'd it; but fate, ordaining he should be a cuckold, held his hand. Well: on went he for a search, and away went I for foul clothes. But mark the sequel, Master Brook: I suffer'd the pangs of three several deaths; first, an intolerable fright, to be detected with a jealous rotten bell-wether; next, to be compass'd, like a good bilbo,[2] in the circumference of a peck, hilt to point, heel to head; and then, to be stopp'd in, like a strong distillation, with stinking clothes that fretted[3] in their own grease: think of that,—a man of my kidney,—think of that,—that am as subject to heat as butter; a man of continual dissolution and thaw;—it was a miracle to scape suffocation. And in the height of this bath, when I was more than half stew'd in grease, like a Dutch dish, to be thrown into the Thames, and cool'd, glowing hot, in that surge, like a horse-shoe; think of that,—hissing hot,—think of that, Master Brook. [*Throws himself into chair.*

Ford. In good sadness, sir, I am sorry that for my sake you have suffered all this. My suit, then, is desperate; you'll undertake her no more?

Fal. [*Rises*] Master Brook, I will be thrown into Etna, as I have been into Thames, ere I will leave her thus. Her husband is this morning gone a-birding:[4] I have receiv'd from her another embassy of meeting; 'twixt eight and nine is the hour, Master Brook.

Ford. 'T is past eight already, sir.

Fal. Is it? I will then address me to my appointment. Come to me at your convenient leisure, and you shall know how I speed; and the conclusion shall be crown'd with your enjoying her. Adieu. You shall have her, Master Brook; Master Brook, you shall cuckold Ford. [*Exit.*

Ford. Hum,—ha! is this a vision? is this a dream? do I sleep? Master Ford, awake! awake, Master Ford! there's a hole made in your best coat, Master Ford. This 't is to be married! this 't is to have linen and buck-baskets![5]—Well, I will proclaim myself what I am: I will now take the lecher; he is at my house; he cannot scape me; 't is impossible he should; he cannot creep into a halfpenny purse, nor into a pepper-box: but, lest the devil that guides him should aid him, I will search impossible places. Though what I am I cannot avoid, yet to be what I would not shall not make me tame: if I have horns to make me mad, let the proverb go with me,—I'll be horn-mad. [*Exit.*

ACT IV.

[Scene I. *The street.*

Enter Mistress Page, Mistress Quickly, *and* William.

Mrs. Page. Is he at Master Ford's already, think'st thou?

Quick. Sure he is by this, or will be presently: but, truly, he is very courageous mad about his throwing into the water. Mistress Ford desires you to come suddenly.

Mrs. Page. I'll be with her by and by; I'll but bring my young man here to school. Look, where his master comes: 't is a playing-day, I see.

1 *Hinds*, *i.e.* young serving-men.
2 *Bilbo*, a sword.
3 *Fretted* = rotted.
4 *Birding*, *i.e.* shooting birds.
5 *Buck-baskets*, basket of soiled linen.

Enter Sir Hugh Evans.

How now, Sir Hugh! no school to-day?

Evans. No; Master Slender is let the boys leave to play.

Quick. 'Blessing of his heart!

Mrs. Page. Sir Hugh, my husband says my son profits nothing in the world at his book. I pray you, ask him some questions in his accidence.

Evans. Come hither, William; hold up your head; come.

Mrs. Page. Come on, sirrah; hold up your head; answer your master, be not afraid.

Evans. William, how many numbers is in nouns?

Evans. William, how many numbers is in nouns?
Will. Two.—(Act iv. 1. 21-23.)

Will. Two.

Quick. Truly, I thought there had been one number more, because they say, 'Od's-nouns.

Evans. Peace your tattlings.—What is *fair*, William?

Will. *Pulcher.*

Quick. Polecats! there are fairer things than polecats, sure.

Evans. You are a very simplicity 'oman: I pray you, peace.—What is *lapis*, William?

Will. A stone.

Evans. And what is a stone, William?

Will. A pebble.

Evans. No, it is *lapis:* I pray you, remember in your prain.

Will. *Lapis.*

Evans. That is a good William. What is he, William, that does lend articles?

Will. Articles are borrowed of the pronoun, and be thus declined, *Singulariter, nominativo, hic, hæc, hoc.*

Evans. *Nominativo, hig, hag, hog;*—pray you, mark: *genitivo, hujus.* Well, what is your accusative case?

Will. *Accusativo, hinc*—

Evans. I pray you, have your remembrance, child; *accusativo, hung, hang, hog.*

Quick. Hang-hog is Latin for bacon, I warrant you.

Evans. Leave your prabbles, 'oman.—What is the focative case, William?

Will. *O,—vocativo, O.*

Evans. Remember, William; focative is *caret*.

Quick. And that's a good root.

Evans. 'Oman, forbear.

Mrs. Page. Peace!

Evans. What is your genitive case plural, William?

Will. Genitive case!

Evans. Ay.

Will. *Genitivo,—horum, harum, horum.*

Quick. 'Vengeance of Jenny's case! fie on her!—never name her, child, if she be a whore.

Evans. For shame, 'oman.

Quick. You do ill to teach the child such words:—he teaches him to hick and to hack, which they'll do fast enough of themselves, and to call whorum:—fie upon you!

Evans. 'Oman, art thou lunatics? hast thou no understandings for thy cases, and the numbers and the genders? Thou art as foolish Christian creatures as I would desires.

Mrs. Page. Prithee, hold thy peace.

Evans. Show me now, William, some declensions of your pronouns.

Will. Forsooth, I have forgot.

Evans. It is *qui, quæ, quod:* if you forget your *quies*, your *quæs*, and your *quods*, you must be preeches.[1] Go your ways, and play; go.

Mrs. Page. He is a better scholar than I thought he was.

Evans. He is a good sprag[2] memory. Farewell, Mistress Page.

Mrs. Page. Adieu, good Sir Hugh. [*Exit Sir Hugh.*]—Get you home, boy.—Come, we stay too long. [*Exeunt.*]

SCENE II. *A room in Ford's house.*

Enter FALSTAFF *and* MISTRESS FORD.

Fal. Mistress Ford, your sorrow hath eaten up my sufferance. I see you are obsequious[3] in your love, and I profess requital to a hair's breadth; not only, Mistress Ford, in the simple office of love, but in all the accoutrement, complement, and ceremony of it. But are you sure of your husband now?

Mrs. Ford. He's a-birding,[4] sweet Sir John.

Mrs. Page. [*Within*] What, ho, gossip Ford! what, ho!

Mrs. Ford. Step into the chamber, Sir John. [*Exit Falstaff.*

Enter MISTRESS PAGE.

Mrs. Page. How now, sweetheart! who's at home besides yourself?

Mrs. Ford. Why, none but mine own people.

Mrs. Page. Indeed!

Mrs. Ford. No, certainly.—[*Aside to her*] Speak louder.

Mrs. Page. Truly, I am so glad you have nobody here.

Mrs. Ford. Why?

Mrs. Page. Why, woman, your husband is in his old lunes[5] again: he so takes on yonder with my husband; so rails against all married mankind; so curses all Eve's daughters, of what complexion soever; and so buffets himself on the forehead, crying, "Peer out, peer out!"[6] that any madness I ever yet beheld seemed but tameness, civility, and patience, to this his distemper he is in now: I am glad the fat knight is not here.

Mrs. Ford. Why, does he talk of him?

Mrs. Page. Of none but him; and swears he was carried out, the last time he search'd for him, in a basket; protests to my husband he is now here; and hath drawn him and the rest of their company from their sport, to make another experiment of his suspicion: but I am glad the knight is not here; now he shall see his own foolery.

Mrs. Ford. How near is he, Mistress Page?

Mrs. Page. Hard by; at street end; he will be here anon.

Mrs. Ford. I am undone!—the knight is here.

Mrs. Page. Why, then, you are utterly sham'd, and he's but a dead man. What a woman are you!—Away with him, away with him! better shame than murder.

Mrs. Ford. Which way should he go? how should I bestow him? Shall I put him into the basket again?

[1] *Preeches*, *i.e.* breeched = flogged.
[2] *Sprag*, for sprack = quick, alert.
[3] *Obsequious*, devoted.
[4] *Birding* = shooting birds.

[5] *Lunes*, mad freaks.
[6] *"Peer out, peer out!"* an exclamation in a children's game.

Re-enter FALSTAFF.

Fal. No, I 'll come no more i' the basket. May I not go out ere he come?

Mrs. Page. Alas, three of Master Ford's brothers watch the door with pistols, that none shall issue out; otherwise you might slip away ere he came. But what make you here?

Fal. What shall I do?—I 'll creep up into the chimney.

Mrs. Ford. There they always use to discharge their birding-pieces.[1]

Mrs. Page. Creep into the kiln-hole.

Fal. Where is it?

Mrs. Ford. He will seek there, on my word. Neither press, coffer, chest, trunk, well, vault, but he hath an abstract[2] for the remembrance of such places, and goes to them by his note: there is no hiding you in the house.

Fal. I 'll go out, then.

Mrs. Page. If you go out in your own semblance, you die, Sir John. Unless you go out disguis'd,—

Mrs. Ford. How might we disguise him?

Mrs. Page. Alas the day, I know not! There is no woman's gown big enough for him; otherwise he might put on a hat, a muffler,[3] and a kerchief, and so escape.

Fal. Good hearts, devise something: any extremity rather than a mischief.

Mrs. Ford. My maid's aunt, the fat woman of Brainford, has a gown above.

Mrs. Page. On my word, it will serve him; she 's as big as he is: and there 's her thrumm'd hat,[4] and her muffler too.—Run up, Sir John.

Mrs. Ford. Go, go, sweet Sir John: Mistress Page and I will look some linen for your head.

Mrs. Page. Quick, quick! we 'll come dress you straight: put on the gown the while.

[*Exit Falstaff.*

Mrs. Ford. I would my husband would meet him in this shape: he cannot abide the old woman of Brainford; he swears she 's a witch; forbade her my house, and hath threaten'd to beat her.

Mrs. Page. Heaven guide him to thy husband's cudgel, and the devil guide his cudgel afterwards!

Mrs. Ford. But is my husband coming?

Mrs. Page. Ay, in good sadness, is he; and talks of the basket too, howsoever he hath had intelligence.

Mrs. Ford. We 'll try that; for I 'll appoint my men to carry the basket again, to meet him at the door with it, as they did last time.

Mrs. Page. Nay, but he 'll be here presently: let 's go dress him like the witch of Brainford.

Mrs. Ford. I 'll first direct my men what they shall do with the basket. Go up; I 'll bring linen for him straight. [*Exit.*

Mrs. Page. Hang him, dishonest varlet! we cannot misuse him enough.

We 'll leave a proof, by that which we will do,
Wives may be merry, and yet honest too:
We do not act that often jest and laugh;
'T is old, but true,—Still swine eat all the draff.

[*Exit.*

Re-enter MISTRESS FORD *with two Servants.*

Mrs. Ford. Go, sirs, take the basket again on your shoulders: your master is hard at door; if he bid you set it down, obey him: quickly, dispatch. [*Exit.*

First Serv. Come, come, take it up.

Sec. Serv. Pray heaven it be not full of knight again.

First Serv. I hope not; I had as lief bear so much lead.

Enter FORD, PAGE, SHALLOW, CAIUS, *and* SIR HUGH EVANS.

Ford. Ay, but if it prove true, Master Page, have you any way then to unfool me again?—Set down the basket, villains!—Somebody call my wife.—Youth in a basket!—O you panderly rascals! there 's a knot, a ging,[5] a pack, a conspiracy against me: now shall the devil be sham'd.—What, wife, I say! come, come forth! behold what honest clothes you send forth to bleaching!

Page. Why, this passes! Master Ford, you are not to go loose any longer; you must be pinion'd.

[1] *Birding-pieces*, fowling-pieces.
[2] *Abstract* = memorandum.
[3] *Muffler*, a kind of veil which covered the face.
[4] *Thrumm'd hat*, i.e. a hat made of thrums, or ends of a weaver's warp.
[5] *Ging* = gang, a number, company.

Evans. Why, this is lunatics! this is mad as a mad dog!

Shal. Indeed, Master Ford, this is not well; indeed.

Ford. So say I too, sir.

Re-enter MISTRESS FORD.

Come hither, Mistress Ford; Mistress Ford, the honest woman, the modest wife, the virtuous creature, that hath the jealous fool to her husband!—I suspect without cause, mistress, do I?

Mrs. Ford. Heaven be my witness you do, if you suspect me in any dishonesty.

Ford. Well said, brazen-face! hold it out.—Come forth, sirrah!

[*Pulling the clothes out of the basket.*

Page. This passes!

Ford. I'll prat her.—[*Beating him*] Out of my door, you witch.—(Act iv. 2. 195, 196.)

Mrs. Ford. Are you not ashamed? let the clothes alone.

Ford. I shall find you anon.

Evans. 'T is unreasonable! Will you take up your wife's clothes? Come away.

Ford. Empty the basket, I say!

Mrs. Ford. Why, man, why,—

Ford. Master Page, as I am an honest man, there was one conveyed out of my house yesterday in this basket: why may not he be there again? In my house I am sure he is: my intelligence is true; my jealousy is reasonable.—Pluck me out all the linen.

Mrs. Ford. If you find a man there, he shall die a flea's death.

Page. Here's no man.

Shal. By my fidelity, this is not well, Master Ford; this wrongs you.

Evans. Master Ford, you must pray, and not follow the imaginations of your own heart: this is jealousies.

Ford. Well, he's not here I seek for.

Page. No, nor nowhere else but in your brain.

[*Servants replace linen in basket, and carry it off.*

Ford. Help to search my house this one time. If I find not what I seek, show no colour for my extremity, let me for ever be your table-sport;[1] let them say of me, "As

[1] *Table-sport*, i.e. a subject for mirth.

jealous as Ford, that searched a hollow walnut for his wife's leman.[1]" Satisfy me once more; once more search with me.

Mrs. Ford. What, ho, Mistress Page! come you and the old woman down; my husband will come into the chamber.

Ford. Old woman! what old woman's that?

Mrs. Ford. Why, it is my maid's aunt of Brainford.

Ford. A witch, a quean, an old cozening quean! Have I not forbid her my house? She comes of errands, does she? We are simple men; we do not know what's brought to pass under the profession of fortune-telling. She works by charms, by spells, by th' figure, and such daubery[2] as this is, beyond our element: we know nothing.—Come down, you witch, you hag, you; come down, I say!

Mrs. Ford. Nay, good, sweet husband,—Good gentlemen, let him not strike the old woman.

Re-enter Falstaff *in women's clothes, led by* Mistress Page.

Mrs. Page. Come, Mother Prat; come, give me your hand.

Ford. I'll prat her.—[*Beating him*] Out of my door, you witch, you rag, you baggage, you polecat, you ronyon![3] out, out! I'll conjure you, I'll fortune-tell you. [*Exit Falstaff.*

Mrs. Page. Are you not asham'd? I think you have kill'd the poor woman.

Mrs. Ford. Nay, he will do it.—'Tis a goodly credit for you.

Ford. Hang her, witch!

Evans. By yea and no, I think the 'oman is a witch indeed: I like not when a 'oman has a great peard: I spy a great peard under her muffler.[4]

Ford. Will you follow, gentlemen? I beseech you, follow; see but the issue of my jealousy: if I cry out thus upon no trail, never trust me when I open again. [*Exit.*

Page. Let's obey his humour a little further: come, gentlemen.

[*Exeunt Page, Shallow, Caius, and Evans.*

Mrs. Page. Trust me, he beat him most pitifully.

Mrs. Ford. Nay, by th' mass, that he did not; he beat him most unpitifully methought.

Mrs. Page. I'll have the cudgel hallow'd, and hung o'er the altar; it hath done meritorious service.

Mrs. Ford. What think ye? may we, with the warrant of womanhood and the witness of a good conscience, pursue him with any further revenge?

Mrs. Page. The spirit of wantonness is, sure, scar'd out of him: if the devil have him not in fee-simple, with fine and recovery, he will never, I think, in the way of waste, attempt us again.

Mrs. Ford. Shall we tell our husbands how we have serv'd him?

Mrs. Page. Yes, by all means; if it be but to scrape the figures out of your husband's brains. If they can find in their hearts the poor unvirtuous fat knight shall be any further afflicted, we two will still be the ministers.

Mrs. Ford. I'll warrant they'll have him publicly sham'd: and methinks there would be no period to the jest, should he not be publicly sham'd.

Mrs Page. Come, to the forge with it; then shape it: I would not have things cool.

[*Exeunt.*

[Scene III. *A room in the Garter Inn.*

Enter Host and Bardolph.

Bard. Sir, the Germans desire to have three of your horses: the duke himself will be to-morrow at court, and they are going to meet him.

Host. What duke should that be comes so secretly? I hear not of him in the court. Let me speak with the gentlemen: they speak English?

Bard. Ay, sir; I'll call them to you.

Host. They shall have my horses; but I'll make them pay; I'll sauce[5] them: they have had my house a week at command; I have turn'd away my other guests: they must come off; I'll sauce[5] them. Come. [*Exeunt.*]

[1] *Leman*, lover.

[2] *Daubery*, pretence, trickery.

[3] *Ronyon*, a mangy woman.

[4] *Muffler*, a kind of veil which covered the face.

[5] *Sauce* = gratify, tickle.

Scene IV. *A room in Ford's house.*

Enter Page, Ford, Mistress Page, Mistress Ford, *and* Sir Hugh Evans.

Evans. 'T is one of the best discretions of a 'oman as ever I did look upon.

Page. And did he send you both these letters at an instant?

Mrs. Page. Within a quarter of an hour.

Ford. Pardon me, wife. Henceforth do what thou wilt;
I rather will suspect the sun with cold
Than thee with wantonness: now doth thy honour stand,
In him that was of late an heretic,
As firm as faith.

Page. 'T is well, 't is well; no more:
Be not as éxtreme in submission
As in offence.
But let our plot go forward: let our wives
Yet once again, to make us public sport,
Appoint a meeting with this old fat fellow,
Where we may take him, and disgrace him for it.

Ford. There is no better way than that they spoke of.

Page. How! to send him word they'll meet him in the Park at midnight? Fie, fie! he'll never come.

Evans. You say he has bin thrown in the rivers; and has bin grievously peaten, as an old 'oman: methinks there should be terrors in him that he should not come; methinks his flesh is punish'd, he shall have no desires.

Page. So think I too.

Mrs. Ford. Devise but how you'll use him when he comes,
And let us two devise to bring him thither.

Mrs. Page. There is an old tale goes, that Herne the hunter,
Sometime a keeper here in Windsor forest,
Doth all the winter-time, at still midnight,
Walk round about an oak, with great ragg'd horns;
And there he blasts the tree, and takes[1] the cattle,
And makes milch-kine yield blood; and shakes a chain
In a most hideous and dreadful manner:
You have heard of such a spirit; and well you know
The superstitious idle-headed eld[2]
Receiv'd, and did deliver to our age,
This tale of Herne the hunter for a truth.

Page. Why, yet there want not many that do fear
In deep of night to walk by this Herne's oak:
But what of this?

Mrs. Ford. Marry, this is our device;
That Falstaff at that oak shall meet with us,
Disguis'd like Herne, with huge horns on his head.

Page. Well, let it not be doubted but he'll come,
And in this shape: when you have brought him thither,
What shall be done with him? what is your plot?

Mrs. Page. That likewise have we thought upon, and thus.
Nan Page my daughter, and my little son,
And three or four more of their growth, we'll dress
Like urchins, ouphs,[3] and fairies, green and white,
With rounds of waxen tapers on their heads,
And rattles in their hands: upon a sudden,
As Falstaff, she, and I, are newly met,
Let them from forth a sawpit rush at once
With some diffused[4] song: upon their sight,
We two in great amazedness will fly:
Then let them all encircle him about,
And, fairy-like, to-pinch[5] the unclean knight;
And ask him why, that hour of fairy revel,
In their so sacred paths he dares to tread
In shape profane.

Mrs. Ford. And till he tell the truth,
Let the supposed fairies pinch him sound,
And burn him with their tapers.

Mrs. Page. The truth being known,
We'll all present ourselves, dis-horn the spirit,
And mock him home to Windsor.

[*Ford.* The children must
Be practis'd well to this, or they'll ne'er do 't.

Evans. I will teach the children their behav-

1 *Takes*, bewitches.

2 *Eld*, olden time.
3 *Ouphs*, elves, goblins.
4 *Diffused* = wild, uncouth.
5 *To-pinch* = pinch vindictively.

iours; and I will be like a jack-an-apes also, to burn the knight with my taber.

Ford. That will be excellent. I'll go buy them visards.

Mrs. Page. My Nan shall be the queen of all the fairies,
Finely attired in a robe of white.

Page. That silk will I go buy:—[*Aside*] and in that time
Shall Master Slender steal my Nan away,
And marry her at Eton.—Go send to Falstaff straight.

Ford. Nay, I'll to him again in name of Brook:
He'll tell me all his purpose: sure, he'll come.

Mrs. Page. Fear not you that. Go get us properties,
And tricking for our fairies.]

Evans. Let us about it: it is admirable pleasures and fery honest knaveries.

[*Exeunt Page, Ford, and Evans.*

Mrs. Page. Go, Mistress Ford,
Send Quickly to Sir John, to know his mind.

[*Exit Mrs. Ford.*

I'll to the doctor: he hath my good will,
And none but he, to marry with Nan Page.
That Slender, though well landed, is an idiot;
And he my husband best of all affects.
The doctor is well money'd, and his friends
Potent at court: he, none but he, shall have her,
Though twenty thousand worthier come to crave her. [*Exit.*

SCENE V. *The Court-yard of the Garter Inn.*

Enter Host and SIMPLE.

Host. What wouldst thou have, boor? what, thick-skin? speak, breathe, discuss; brief, short, quick, snap.

Sim. Marry, sir, I come to speak with Sir John Falstaff from Master Slender.

Host. There's his chamber, his house, his castle, his standing-bed,[1] and truckle-bed;[2] ['tis painted about with the story of the Prodigal, fresh and new. Go knock and call; he'll speak like an Anthropophaginian unto thee:] knock, I say.

Sim. There's an old woman, a fat woman, gone up into his chamber: I'll be so bold as stay, sir, till she come down; I come to speak with her, indeed.

Host. Ha! a fat woman! the knight may be robb'd: I'll call.—Bully-knight! bully Sir John! [speak from thy lungs military: art thou there? it is thine host, thine Ephesian, calls.]

Fal. [*Above*] How now, mine host!

Host. Here's a Bohemian-Tartar tarries the coming down of thy fat woman. [Let her descend, bully, let her descend; my chambers are honourable: fie! privacy? fie!]

Enter FALSTAFF.

Fal. There was, mine host, an old fat woman even now with me; but she's gone.

Sim. Pray you, sir, was't not the wise woman of Brainford?

Fal. Ay, marry, was it, mussel-shell:[3] what would you with her?

Sim. My master, sir, Master Slender, sent to her, seeing her go thorough the streets, to know, sir, [whether one Nym, sir, that beguil'd him of a chain, had the chain or no.

Fal. I spake with the old woman about it.

Sim. And what says she, I pray, sir?

Fal. Marry, she says that the very same man that beguil'd Master Slender of his chain cozen'd him of it.

Sim. I would I could have spoken with the woman herself; I had other things to have spoken with her too from him.

Fal. What are they? let us know.

Host. Ay, come; quick.

Sim. I may not conceal them, sir.

Host. Conceal them, or thou di'st.

Sim. Why, sir, they were nothing but] about Mistress Anne Page; to know if it were my master's fortune to have her or no.

Fal. 'Tis, 'tis his fortune.

Sim. What, sir?

Fal. To have her,—or no. Go; say the woman told me so.

Sim. May I be bold to say so, sir?

Fal. Ay, Sir Tike; who more bold?

[1] *Standing-bed*, a bed supported by legs.

[2] *Truckle-bed*, a bed on castors to run under another bed.

[3] *Mussel-shell* = open-mouthed.

Sim. I thank your worship: I shall make my master glad with these tidings. [*Exit.*

Host. Thou art clerkly, thou art clerkly, Sir John. Was there a wise woman with thee?

Fal. Ay, that there was, mine host; one that hath taught me more wit than ever I learn'd before in my life; and I paid nothing for it neither, but was paid for my learning.

Enter BARDOLPH.

Bard. Out, alas, sir! cozenage, mere cozenage!

Host. Where be my horses? speak well of them, varletto.

Bard. Run away with the cozeners: for so soon as I came beyond Eton, they threw me off, from behind one of them, in a slough of mire; and set spurs and away, like three German devils, three Doctor Faustuses. 71

[*Host.* They are gone but to meet the duke, villain: do not say they be fled; Germans are honest men.

Enter SIR HUGH EVANS.

Evans. Where is mine host?

Host. What is the matter, sir?

Evans. Have a care of your entertainments: there is a friend of mine come to town, tells me there is three cozen-germans that has cozen'd all the hosts of Readings, of Maidenhead, of Colebrook, of horses and money. I tell you for good will, look you: you are wise, and full of gibes and vlouting-stogs,[1] and 't is not convenient you should be cozened. Fare you well. [*Exit.*

Enter DOCTOR CAIUS.

Caius. Vere is mine host de Jarteer?

Host. Here, master doctor, in perplexity and doubtful dilemma.

Caius. I cannot tell vat is dat: but it is tell-a me dat you make grand preparation for a duke de Jarmany: by my trot, dere is no duke dat de court is know to come. I tell you for good vill: adieu.] [*Exit.*

Host. Hue and cry, villain, go!—Assist me, knight.—I am undone!—Fly, run, hue and cry, villain!—I am undone! 94

[*Exeunt Host and Bardolph.*

[1] *Vlouting-stogs* = flouting-stocks, *i.e.* laughing-stocks.

Fal. I would all the world might be cozen'd; for I have been cozen'd and beaten too. If it should come to the ear of the court, how I have been transformed, and how my transformation hath been wash'd and cudgell'd, they would melt me out of my fat drop by drop, and liquor fishermen's boots with me: I warrant they would whip me with their fine

Fent. Hark, good mine host:
To-night at Herne's oak, just 'twixt twelve and one,
Must my sweet Nan present the Fairy Queen.
—(Act iv. 6. 18-20.)

wits till I were as crest-fallen as a dried pear. I never prosper'd since I forswore myself at primero.[2] Well, if my wind were but long enough to say my prayers, I would repent.

Enter MISTRESS QUICKLY.

Now, whence come you?

Quick. From the two parties, forsooth. 107

Fal. The devil take one party, and his dam the other! and so they shall be both bestowed: I have suffer'd more for their sakes, more than the villanous inconstancy of man's disposition is able to bear.

Quick. And have not they suffer'd? Yes, I warrant; speciously[3] one of them; Mistress

[2] *Primero*, a game at cards.

[3] *Speciously* = especially.

Ford, good heart, is beaten black and blue, that you cannot see a white spot about her.

Fal. What tell'st thou me of black and blue? I was beaten myself into all the colours of the rainbow; and I was like to be apprehended for the witch of Brainford: but that my admirable dexterity of wit, my counterfeiting the action of an old woman, deliver'd me, the knave constable had set me i' the stocks, i' the common stocks, for a witch.

Quick. Sir, let me speak with you in your chamber: you shall hear how things go; and, I warrant, to your content. Here is a letter will say somewhat. Good hearts, what ado here is to bring you together! Sure, one of you does not serve heaven well, that you are so cross'd.

Fal. Come up into my chamber. [*Exeunt.*

[SCENE VI. *A room in the Garter Inn.*

Enter FENTON *and Host.*

Host. Master Fenton, talk not to me; my mind is heavy: I will give over all.

Fent. Yet hear me speak. Assist me in my purpose,
And, as I am a gentleman, I'll give thee
A hundred pound in gold more than your loss.

Host. I will hear you, Master Fenton; and I will at the least keep your counsel.

Fent. From time to time I have acquainted you
With the dear love I bear to fair Anne Page;
Who mutually hath answer'd my affection,
So far forth as herself might be her chooser,
Even to my wish: I have a letter from her
Of such contents as you will wonder at;
The mirth whereof so larded[1] with my matter,
That neither singly can be manifested
Without the show of both; fat Falstaff in 't
Hath a great scene. The image of the jest
I'll show you here at large. Hark, good mine host:
To-night at Herne's oak, just 'twixt twelve and one,
Must my sweet Nan present the Fairy Queen;
The purpose why, is here: in which disguise,
While other jests are something rank on foot,
Her father hath commanded her to slip
Away with Slender, and with him at Eton
Immediately to marry: she hath consented:
Now, sir,
Her mother, even strong against that match,
And firm for Doctor Caius, hath appointed
That he shall likewise shuffle her away,
While other sports are tasking of their minds,
And at the deanery, where a priest attends,
Straight marry her: to this her mother's plot
She seemingly obedient, likewise hath
Made promise to the doctor.—Now, thus it rests:
Her father means she shall be all in white;
And in that habit, when Slender sees his time
To take her by the hand, and bid her go,
She shall go with him: her mother hath intended,
The better to denote her to the doctor,—
For they must all be mask'd and visarded,—
That quaint in green she shall be loose enrob'd,
With ribands pendent, flaring[2] 'bout her head;
And when the doctor spies his vantage ripe,
To pinch her by the hand, and, on that token,
The maid hath given consent to go with him.

Host. Which means she to deceive? father or mother?

Fent. Both, my good host, to go along with me:
And here it rests,—that you'll procure the vicar
To stay for me at church 'twixt twelve and one,
And, in the lawful name of marrying,
To give our hearts united ceremony.

Host. Well, husband[3] your device; I'll to the vicar:
Bring you the maid, you shall not lack a priest.

Fent. So shall I evermore be bound to thee;
Besides, I'll make a present recompense.
[*Exeunt.*]

[1] *Larded, i.e.* garnished.

[2] *Flaring* = fluttering.

[3] *Husband* = perform carefully.

ACT V.

Scene I. *A room in the Garter Inn.*

Enter Falstaff *and* Mistress Quickly.

Fal. Prithee, no more prattling; go:—I'll hold.[1] This is the third time; I hope good luck lies in odd numbers. Away, go. They say there is divinity in odd numbers, either in nativity, chance, or death. Away.

Quick. I'll provide you a chain; and I'll do what I can to get you a pair of horns.

Fal. Away, I say; time wears: hold up your head, and mince.[2] [*Exit Mrs. Quickly.*

Enter Ford.

How now, Master Brook! Master Brook, the matter will be known to-night, or never. Be you in the Park about midnight, at Herne's oak, and you shall see wonders.

Ford. Went you not to her yesterday, sir, as you told me you had appointed?

Fal. I went to her, Master Brook, as you see, like a poor old man: but I came from her, Master Brook, like a poor old woman. That same knave Ford, her husband, hath the finest mad devil of jealousy in him, Master Brook, that ever govern'd frenzy. I will tell you:—he beat me grievously, in the shape of a woman; for in the shape of man, Master Brook, I fear not Goliath with a weaver's beam; because I know also life is a shuttle. I am in haste; go along with me: I'll tell you all, Master Brook. Since I pluck'd geese, played truant, and whipp'd top, I knew not what 't was to be beaten till lately. Follow me: I'll tell you strange things of this knave Ford; on whom to-night I will be reveng'd, and I will deliver his wife into your hand. Follow:—strange things in hand, Master Brook!—follow. [*Exeunt.*

Scene II. *Windsor Park.*

Enter Page, Shallow, *and* Slender.

Page. Come, come; we'll couch i' the castle-ditch till we see the light of our fairies.—Remember, son Slender, my daughter.

Slen. Ay, forsooth; I have spoke with her, and we have a nay-word how to know one another: I come to her in white, and cry "mum;" she cries "budget;" and by that we know one another.

Shal. That's good too; but what needs either your "mum" or her "budget"? the white will decipher[3] her well enough.—It hath struck ten o'clock.

Page. The night is dark; light and spirits will become it well. Heaven prosper our sport! No man means evil but the devil, and we shall know him by his horns. Let's away; follow me. [*Exeunt.*

Scene III. *A street leading to the Park.*

Enter Mistress Page, Mistress Ford, *and* Doctor Caius.

Mrs. Page. Master doctor, my daughter is in green: when you see your time, take her by the hand, away with her to the deanery, and dispatch it quickly. Go before into the Park: we two must go together.

Caius. I know vat I have to do. Adieu.

Mrs. Page. Fare you well, sir. [*Exit Caius.*] —My husband will not rejoice so much at the abuse of Falstaff as he will chafe at the doctor's marrying my daughter: but 't is no matter; better a little chiding than a great deal of heartbreak.

Mrs. Ford. Where is Nan now and her troop of fairies? and the Welsh devil Hugh?

Mrs. Page. They are all couch'd in a pit hard by Herne's oak, with obscur'd lights; which, at the very instant of Falstaff's and our meeting, they will at once display to the night.

Mrs. Ford. That cannot choose but amaze him.

Mrs. Page. If he be not amazed, he will be mock'd; if he be amaz'd, he will every way be mock'd.

---

[1] *Hold*, persevere.

[2] *Mince*, i.e. walk in a demure affected manner.

[3] *Decipher*, i.e. discover.

Mrs. Ford. We'll betray him finely.

Mrs. Page. Against such lewdsters[1] and their lechery
Those that betray them do no treachery.

Mrs. Ford. The hour draws on. To the oak, to the oak! [*Exeunt.*

[SCENE IV. *Windsor Park.*

Enter EVANS *with others as Fairies.*

Evans. Trib, trib, fairies; come; and remember your parts: be pold, I pray you; follow me into the pit; and when I give the watch-'ords, do as I pid you: come, come; trib, trib. [*Exeunt.*]

SCENE V. *Another part of the Park.*

Enter FALSTAFF *disguised as Herne, with a buck's head on.*

Fal. The Windsor bell hath struck twelve; the minute draws on. [Now, the hot-blooded gods assist me!—Remember, Jove, thou wast a bull for thy Europa; love set on thy horns:—O powerful love! that, in some respects, makes a beast a man; in some other, a man a beast.—You were also, Jupiter, a swan for the love of Leda:—O omnipotent love! how near the god drew to the complexion of a goose!—A fault done first in the form of a beast;—O Jove, a beastly fault!—and then another fault in the semblance of a fowl;—think on 't, Jove; a foul fault! When gods have hot backs, what shall poor men do? For me, I am here a Windsor stag; and the fattest, I think, i' th' forest.—Send me a cool rut-time, Jove, or who can blame me to piss my tallow?]—Who comes here? my doe?

Enter MISTRESS FORD *and* MISTRESS PAGE.

Mrs. Ford. Sir John! art thou there, my deer? my male deer?

Fal. My doe with the black scut[2]!—Let the sky rain potatoes; let it thunder to the tune of *Green sleeves*, hail kissing-comfits, and snow eryngoes;[3] let there come a tempest of provocation, I will shelter me here. [*Embracing her.*

Mrs. Ford. Mistress Page is come with me, sweetheart.

Fal. Divide me like a brib'd-buck, each a haunch: I will keep my sides to myself, my shoulders for the fellow of this walk, and my horns I bequeath your husbands. Am I a woodman,[4] ha? Speak I like Herne the hunter?—Why, now is Cupid a child of conscience; he makes restitution. As I am a true spirit, welcome! [*Noise of horns within.*

Mrs. Page. Alas, what noise?

Mrs. Ford. Heaven forgive our sins!

Fal. What should this be?

Mrs. Ford. } *Mrs. Page.* } Away, away! [*They run off.*

[*Fal.* I think the devil will not have me damn'd, lest the oil that's in me should set hell on fire; he would never else cross me thus.]

Enter SIR HUGH EVANS, *like a Satyr;* PISTOL, *as Hobgoblin;* MISTRESS QUICKLY, *like the Queen of Fairies, and* ANNE PAGE *and boys dressed like Fairies.*

Quick. Fairies, black, gray, green, and white,
You moonshine revellers, and shades of night,
You orphan-heirs of fixed destiny,
Attend your office and your quality.—
[Crier Hobgoblin, make the fairy O-yes.

Pist. Elves, list your names; silence, you airy toys.
Cricket, to Windsor chimneys shalt thou leap:
Where fires thou find'st unrak'd and hearths unswept,
There pinch the maids as blue as bilberry:
Our radiant queen hates sluts and sluttery.

Fal. They are fairies; he that speaks to them shall die:
I'll wink and couch: no man their works must eye. [*Lies down upon his face.*

Evans. Where 's Pead?—Go you, and where you find a maid
That, ere she sleep, has thrice her prayers said,
Rein up the organs of her fantasy;
Sleep she as sound as careless infancy:
But those as sleep and think not on their sins,
Pinse them, arms, legs, backs, shoulders, sides, and shins.

Quick.] About, about;

---

[1] *Lewdsters*, libertines.
[2] *Scut*, the tail of a deer.
[3] *Eryngoes*, the candied roots of the sea-holly.
[4] *Woodman*, a hunter, equivocatingly = a wencher.

Search Windsor Castle, elves, within and out:
Strew good luck, ouphs,[1] on every sacred room;
That it may stand till the perpetual doom,
In seat as wholesome as in state 't is fit,
Worthy the owner, and the owner it.
[The several chairs of order look you scour
With juice of balm and every precious flower:
Each fair instalment,[2] coat, and several crest,
With loyal blazon, evermore be blest!
And nightly, meadow-fairies, look you sing,
Like to the Garter's compass, in a ring:
Th' expressure[3] that it bears, green let it be,
More fertile-fresh than all the field to see;
And *Honi soit qui mal y pense* write
In emerald tufts, flowers purple, blue, and white;
Like sapphire, pearl, and rich embroidery,
Buckled below fair knighthood's bending knee:
Fairies use flowers for their charáctery.]
Away; disperse: but till 't is one o'clock,
Our dance of custom round about the oak
Of Herne the hunter let us not forget.

Evans. Pray you, lock hand in hand; yourselves in order set;
And twenty glow-worms shall our lanterns be,
To guide our measure round about the tree.—
But, stay; I smell a man of middle-earth.[4]

Fal. Heaven defend me from that Welsh fairy, lest he transform me to a piece of cheese!

[*Pist.* Vile worm, thou wast o'erlook'd[5] even in thy birth.

Quick. With trial-fire touch me his finger-end:
If he be chaste, the flame will back descend,
And turn him to no pain; but if he start,
It is the flesh of a corrupted heart.

Pist. A trial, come.

Evans. Come, will this wood take fire?

[*They put the tapers to his fingers, and he starts.*

Fal. O, O, O!]

Quick. [Corrupt, corrupt, and tainted in desire!—]
About him, fairies; sing a scornful rhyme;
And, as you trip, still pinch him to your time.

THE SONG.

Fie on sinful fantasy!
Fie on lust and luxury!
Lust is but a bloody fire,
Kindled with unchaste desire,
Fed in heart; whose flames aspire,
As thoughts do blow them, higher and higher.
Pinch him, fairies, mutually;
Pinch him for his villany;
Pinch him, and burn him, and turn him about,
Till candles and starlight and moonshine be out.

During this song the Fairies pinch Falstaff. Doctor Caius comes one way, and steals away a boy in green; Slender another way, and takes off a boy in white; and Fenton comes, and steals Mistress Anne. A noise of hunting is made within, and all the fairies run away. Falstaff pulls off his buck's head, and rises.

Enter PAGE, FORD, MISTRESS PAGE, *and* MISTRESS FORD.

They surround Falstaff.

Page. Nay, do not fly; I think we have watch'd you[6] now:
Will none but Herne the hunter serve your turn?

Mrs. Page. I pray you!—Come, hold up the jest no higher.—
Now, good Sir John, how like you Windsor wives?—
See you these, husband? do not these fair yokes[7]
Become the forest better than the town?

Ford. Now, sir, who 's a cuckold now?—Master Brook, Falstaff's a knave, a cuckoldly knave; here are his horns, Master Brook: and, Master Brook, he hath enjoy'd nothing of Ford's but his buck-basket,[8] his cudgel, and twenty pounds of money, which must be paid too, Master Brook; his horses are arrested for it, Master Brook.

Mrs. Ford. Sir John, we have had ill luck; we could never meet. I will never take you for my love again; but I will always count you my deer.

[1] *Ouphs*, elves, goblins.
[2] *Instalment*=the installing in a dignity, or office.
[3] *Expressure*, impression, trace.
[4] *Middle-earth, i.e.* the earth as opposed to the upper and lower regions, inhabited by fairies, &c.
[5] *O'erlook'd*, bewitched.
[6] *Watch'd you, i.e.* set a trap for your detection and so caught you.
[7] *Yokes*=the horns worn by Falstaff.
[8] *Buck-basket*, basket of soiled linen.

Fal. I do begin to perceive that I am made an ass.

Ford. Ay, and an ox too:[1] both the proofs are extant.

Fal. And these are not fairies? I was three or four times in the thought they were not fairies: and yet the guiltiness of my mind, the sudden surprise of my powers, drove the grossness of the foppery into a received belief, in despite of the teeth of all rhyme and reason, that they were fairies. See now how wit may be made a Jack-a-Lent,[2] when 't is upon ill employment!

Evans. Sir John Falstaff, serve Got, and leave your desires, and fairies will not pinse you.

Fal. Well, I am your theme: you have the start of me; I am dejected; I am not able to answer the Welsh flannel.—(Act v. 5. 171-172.)

Ford. Well said, fairy Hugh.

Evans. And leave you your jealousies too, I pray you.

Ford. I will never mistrust my wife again, till thou art able to woo her in good English.

Fal. Have I laid my brain in the sun, and dried it, that it wants matter to prevent so gross o'er-reaching as this? Am I ridden with a Welsh goat too? shall I have a coxcomb of frize? 'T is time I were chok'd with a piece of toasted cheese.

Evans. Seese is not goot to give putter; your pelly is all putter.

Fal. "Seese" and "putter"! have I lived to stand at the taunt of one that makes fritters of English? [This is enough to be the decay of lust and late-walking through the realm.]

Mrs. Page. Why, Sir John, do you think, though we would have thrust virtue out of our hearts by the head and shoulders, and have given ourselves without scruple to hell, that ever the devil could have made you our delight?

Ford. What, a hodge-pudding?[3] a bag of flax?

Mrs. Page. A puff'd man!

Page. Old, cold, wither'd, and of intolerable entrails?[4]

[1] *An ox too*, on account of his horns.

[2] *Jack-a-Lent*, a stuffed figure used as a mark, or target.

[3] *Hodge-pudding*, a pudding of mixed ingredients.

[4] *Intolerable entrails*=an enormous belly.

Ford. And one that is as slanderous as Satan?

Page. And as poor as Job?

Ford. And as wicked as his wife?

Evans. And given to fornications, and to taverns, and sack, and wine, and metheglins,[1] and to drinkings, and swearings and starings, pribbles and prabbles?[2]

Fal. Well, I am your theme: you have the start of me; I am dejected; I am not able to answer the Welsh flannel; ignorance itself is a-plummet o'er me: use me as you will.

Ford. Marry, sir, we'll bring you to Windsor, to one Master Brook, that you have cozen'd of money, to whom you should have been a-pander: over and above that you have suffer'd, I think to repay that money will be a biting affliction.

Mrs. Ford. Nay, husband, let that go to make amends;
Forgive that sum, and so we'll all be friends.

Ford. Well, here is my hand, all 's forgiven at last.

Page. Yet be cheerful, knight: thou shalt eat a posset to-night at my house; where I will desire thee to laugh at my wife, that now laughs at thee: tell her Master Slender hath married her daughter.

Mrs. Page. [*Aside*] Doctors doubt that: if Anne Page be my daughter, she is, by this, Doctor Caius' wife.

Enter Slender.

Slen. Whoa, ho! ho, father Page!

Page. Son, how now! how now, son! have you despatch'd?

Slen. Despatch'd!—I'll make the best in Glostershire know on 't; would I were hang'd, la, else!

Page. Of what, son?

Slen. I came yonder at Eton to marry Mistress Anne Page, and she 's a great lubberly boy. If it had not been i' th' church, I would have swing'd[3] him, or he should have swing'd[3] me. If I did not think it had been Anne Page, would I might never stir!—and 't is a postmaster's boy.

Page. Upon my life, then, you took the wrong.

Slen. What need you tell me that? I think so, when I took a boy for a girl. [If I had been married to him, for all he was in woman's apparel, I would not have had him.]

Page. Why, this is your own folly. Did not I tell you how you should know my daughter by her garments?

Slen. I went to her in white, and cried "mum," and she cried "budget," as Anne and I had appointed; and yet it was not Anne, but a postmaster's boy.

Evans. Jeshu! Master Slender, cannot you see put marry poys?

Page. O, I am vex'd at heart: what shall I do?

Mrs. Page. Good George, be not angry: I knew of your purpose; turn'd my daughter into green; and, indeed, she is now with the doctor at the deanery, and there married.

Enter Caius.

Caius. Vere is Mistress Page? By gar, I am cozen'd: I ha' married *un garçon*, a boy; *un paysan*, by gar, a boy; it is not Anne Page: by gar, I am cozen'd.

Mrs. Page. Why, did you not take her in green?

Caius. Ay, by gar, and 't is a boy: by gar, I'll raise all Windsor. [*Exit.*

Ford. This is strange. Who hath got the right Anne?

Page. My heart misgives me:—here comes Master Fenton.

Enter Fenton *and* Anne Page.

How now, Master Fenton!

Anne. Pardon, good father!—good my mother, pardon!

Page. Now, mistress,—how chance you went not with Master Slender?

Mrs. Page. Why went you not with master doctor, maid?

Fent. You do amaze her: hear the truth of it.
You would have married her most shamefully,
Where there was no proportion held in love.
The truth is, she and I, long since contracted,
Are now so sure that nothing can dissolve us.
Th' offence is holy that she hath committed;

[1] *Metheglins*, a beverage made from honey.
[2] *Pribbles and prabbles* = dissensions, recriminations.
[3] *Swing'd*, thrashed.

And this deceit loses the name of craft,
Of disobedience, or unduteous will;
Since therein she doth evitate[1] and shun
A thousand irreligious cursed hours,
Which forced marriage would have brought upon her.

Ford. Stand not amaz'd; here is no remedy:
In love the heavens themselves do guide the state;
Money buys lands, and wives are sold by fate.

Fal. I am glad, though you have ta'en a special stand to strike at me, that your arrow hath glanc'd.

Page. Well, what remedy?—Fenton, heaven give thee joy!—
What cannot be eschew'd must be embrac'd.

Fal. When night-dogs run, all sorts of deer are chas'd.

Mrs. Page. Well, I will muse no further.—Master Fenton,
Heaven give you many, many merry days!—
Good husband, let us every one go home,
And laugh this sport o'er by a country fire;
Sir John and all.

Ford. Let it be so.—Sir John,
[To Master Brook you yet shall hold your word;
For he to-night shall lie with Mistress Ford.]

[*Exeunt.*

[1] *Evitate*, avoid.

MAP TO ILLUSTRATE THE MERRY WIVES OF WINDSOR.

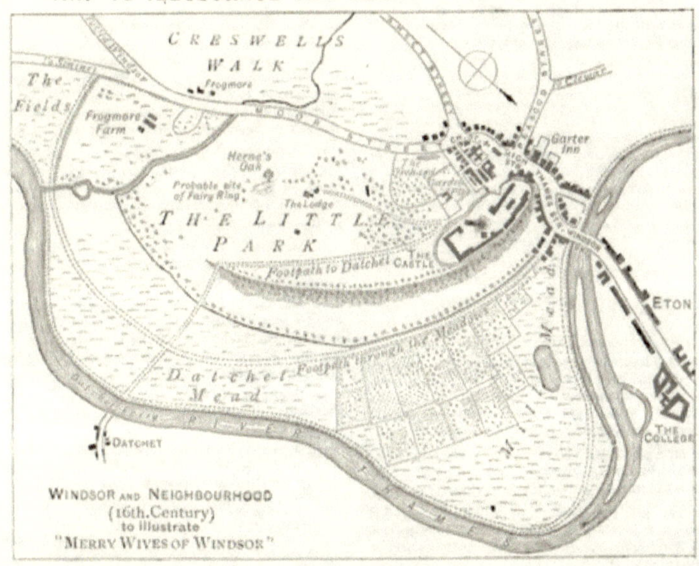

NOTES TO THE MERRY WIVES OF WINDSOR.

MEM.—Several lines from Q 1 have been admitted to our text which are not given in the *Globe* edition; in these cases the lines remain unnumbered and reference to them in these notes is marked by a parenthesis between the numbers of the *Globe* lines which immediately precede and follow the added matter: thus the Q. 1 passage inserted in act i. sc. 1—"they carried me to the tavern and made me drunk, and afterward pick'd my pocket"—is marked in the notes, "Lines 129 () 130."

ACT I. SCENE 1.

1. Lines 7, 8: cust-alorum . . . rato-lorum.—It seems scarcely probable that Shallow should corrupt *custos rotulorum* to *cust-alorum*, and Farmer therefore suggested that Shallow's speech should be: "Ay, cousin Slender, and *Custos*." Whereupon Slender, who had heard the words *custos rotulorum*, and supposes them to mean different offices, adds naturally: "Ay, and *ratolorum* too."

2. Line 22: *The luce is the fresh fish; the salt fish is an old coat.*—The meaning of this speech of Shallow's is not apparent; much has been written about it, but it remains unexplained.

3. Line 28: *Yes*, PY 'R LADY;—*per-lady* in the F. It may be here mentioned once for all that the Welsh and French peculiarities of Evans's and Caius's pronunciation of English, which are very arbitrarily given in the F., are in this edition reduced to something like uniformity, in accordance with the practice of most modern editors.

4. Line 46: GEORGE *Page*.—The F. has *Thomas Page;* but his wife always addresses him as *George* (see ii. 1. 153, 162, and v. 5. 213). Evans's blunder is therefore corrected by most editors.

5. Lines 59 and 63:

SHAL. *Did her grandsire leave her seven hundred pound?*

. . . .

SHAL. *I know the young gentlewoman; she has good gifts.*

These two speeches have the prefix *Slen.* in the F.; Capell first transferred them to Shallow, in whose mouth they seem more appropriate.

6. Lines 89-98.—The following extract from a little anonymous work published in 1558 entitled The institu-

cion of a Gentleman, may not be unacceptable as an illustration of the dialogue in our text:—

> But hunters sayinges are no Gospel, for sumtime they wil affirme and thereto binde an othe, that the fallowe dogge coild the whyte, when as euen dede [=indeed] the falow came behind.
>
> —[From the reprint 1859, sig. *g* 3 *recto*.

A difficulty has been raised as to the distribution of these speeches, and Mr. Hunter (New Illustrations, vol. i. p. 213), in view of the apparent improbability of Page, a Windsor man, running a dog on "Cotsall," proposed to give Slender's first speech to Page; but more than this, in my opinion, is required for the dramatic fitness of the dialogue, and I would propose to distribute it as follows:—

> *Page.* I am glad to see you, good Master Slender. How does your fallow greyhound, sir? I heard say he was outrun on Cotsall.
>
> *Slen.* It could not be judg'd, sir.
>
> *Page.* You'll not confess, you'll not confess.
>
> *Shal.* That he will not.—'T is your fault, 't is your fault:—'t is a good dog.
>
> *Slen.* A cur, sir.
>
> *Shal.* Sir, he's a good dog, &c

Page and Slender in fact should change places; there are several places in this play where, by the universal consent of the editors, changes in the distribution of the dialogue have been made; I believe this is only an additional instance of error in the original copies.

7. Lines 129 () 130: *they carried me to the tavern and made me drunk, and afterward pick'd my pocket.*—First restored to the text by Malone, from the early Q. edition.

8. Line 130: *You Banbury cheese!*—A *flat* and *thin* cheese, and therefore in Bardolph's opinion comparable with Slender. Steevens quotes the following passage in illustration:—

> Put off your clothes, and you are like a *Banbery cheese*,
> Nothing but paring.
>
> —Jacke Drums Entertainment, act iii. vol. ii. p. 173.
> Simpson's School of Shakspere.

9. Line 134: SLICE, *I say!*—Here we may suppose Nym to touch his sword significantly, or draw his hand across his throat, intimating thereby how he would like to serve his accusers; I should not have thought that any one acquainted with Nym's mode of expressing himself could have needed an explanation here any more than in Henry V. ii. 1. 23, where he darkly remarks that "men may sleep, and they may have their throats about them at that time; and some say knives have edges;" but Schmidt, I see, in his Shakespeare Lexicon, takes "Slice" to be an epithet of abuse addressed to Slender, telling him that he is *a* Slice, a mere paring; just as, four lines above, Bardolph calls him a "Banbury cheese." And again, Mr. H. B. Wheatley, in his edition of the Merry Wives, 1886, has the following extraordinary note on "Slice:"—"This has been explained as cut or be off [Cowden Clarke] but the explanation is not satisfactory. It is evidently an oath. Professor Hales suggests that it may be a corruption of God's liche or body (cf. ods bodikins)."

10. Line 158, 159: *of seven groats in mill-sixpences, and two Edward shovel-boards, that cost me two shilling and two pence a-piece.*—Slender has apparently forgotten that he is living in the reign of Henry IV.; *mill*, or *milled* sixpences were first coined in 1561. The Edward "shovel-boards" are said to be the broad shillings of Edward VI., so called from their being used for the old game of shovel or shove-board. Under the circumstances we need not therefore be surprised at the heavy premium Slender paid for his specimens of the coin. The joke of his having seven groats, twenty-eight pence, in sixpences may be paralleled by Bullcalf's possession of "four Harry ten shillings in French crowns," in 2 Henry IV. iii. 2. 236.

11. Line 170: *I will say "marry trap" with you.*—"Marry trap" may, I presume, be translated: "By St. Mary, catch, or take that!"—the *that* being a stab or a blow. "I will say tit for tat with you, I will give you as good as you bring."

12. Line 171: *if you run the nuthook's humour on me*; *i.e.* if you play the thief-taker with me. *Nuthook* was a slang term for an officer.

13. Line 184: *and so conclusions pass'd the careires.*—Slender thought this was Latin, as he didn't understand it; but it was not meant to be understood by him or any one else. [For the phrase *to pass carier* (or career) see Henry V. note 101.]

14. Lines 195–204: Enter Anne Page, with wine . . . *drink down all unkindness.*—For this passage the Q. has the following:—

> *Enter Mistresse* Foord, *Mistresse* Page, *and her daughter* Anne.
>
> *Pa.* No more now,
> I thinke it be almost dinner time,
> For my wife is come to meet us,
> *Fal.* Mistresse *Foord*, I thinke your name is,
> If I mistake not.
>
> *Syr* John kisses her
>
> *Mis. Ford.* Your mistake sir is nothing but in the
> Mistresse. But my husband's name is *Foord* sir.
> *Fal.* I shall desire your more acquaintance.
> The like of you good misteris *Page*.
> *Mis. Pa.* With all my hart sir *John*.
> Come husband will you goe?
> Dinner staies for us.
> *Pa.* With all my hart come along Gentlemen
>
> *Exit all but* Slender *and*
> *Mistresse* Anne.

15. Lines 211, 212: *upon All-hallowmas last, a fortnight afore Michaelmas.*—As *All-hallowmas* (All-saints) is nearly five weeks *after Michaelmas*, Theobald, who did not believe that Simple was intended to blunder here, substituted for "Michaelmas" *Martlemas* (Martinmas, Feast of St. Martin), which falls eleven days, or nearly a fortnight, after All-saints.

16. Lines 257, 258: *I hope, upon familiarity will grow more* CONTEMPT.—The F. has *content*; but it seems so probable that Slender should here misapply the old proverb of familiarity breeding *contempt*, that nearly all editors have followed Theobald's lead in adopting this word.

17. Lines 295, 296: *three veneys for a dish of stewed prunes.*—"Slender means to say that the wager for which he played was a dish of stew'd prunes, which was to be paid by him who received three *hits*. See Bullokar's English Expositor, 8vo, 1616: '*Venie*. A *touch* in the body at playing with weapons.' See also Florio's Italian Dictionary, 1598: '*Tocco*. A *touch* or feeling. Also a *venie* at fence; a *hit*'" (*Malone*).

18. Line 297: *I cannot abide the smell of hot meat since.*—As I do not know why Slender's mishap with his shin should have given him a distaste for hot meat, I fancy that others may be in a like state of ignorance. I therefore here give his speech as it is found in the Q.:—

> I cannot abide the smell of hot meate
> Nere since I broke my shin. Ile tel you how it came.
> By my troth. A Fencer and I plaid three venies
> For a dish of stewd prunes, and I with my ward
> Defending my head, he hot my shin. Yes faith.

19. Line 307: *Sackerson.*—The name of a famous bear of Paris-Garden, in Southwark. I believe the first mention of him (noted by Malone) is to be found in Sir John Davies's Epigrams, printed with Marlowe's Ovid's Elegies, without date, but it is supposed about 1596. It is certain that the book was, by order of the Archbishop of Canterbury and the Bishop of London, burnt at the Stationers' Hall on the 4th June, 1599.[1] I note this, as it proves that the mention of Sackerson in the F. edition of the Merry Wives—he is not named in the Q.—does not require a later date for the F. version than that which I assign to it, viz. Christmas, 1599.

Davies's Epigram, mentioned above, seems so applicable to Slender that I give it in full, from Dyce's one-volume edition of Marlowe's works, p. 363:

IN PUBLIUM. XLIII.

> Publius, a student at the Common-Law,
> Oft leaves his books, and, for his recreation,
> To Paris-garden doth himself withdraw;
> Where he is ravish'd with such delectation,
> As down amongst the bears and dogs he goes;
> Where whilst he skipping cries, "To head, to head,'
> His satin doublet and his velvet hose
> Are all with spittle from above be-spread:
> Then is he like his father's country hall,
> Stinking of dogs, and muted all with hawks;
> And rightly too on him this filth doth fall,
> Which for such filthy sports his books forsakes,
> Leaving old Ployden, Dyer and Brooke alone,
> To see old Harry Hunkes and Sacarson.

ACT I. Scene 3.

20. Line 15: *Let me see thee froth and* LIME.—So the Q.; the F. has *live*. Capell first restored the reading of the Q. to the text. The art of frothing beer needs no illustration: the following extracts from The Art and Mystery of Vintners and Wine-Coopers, &c., 1703, as regards the use of lime may be amusing:—"To correct Rankness, Egerness and pricking of Sacks and other sweet Wines, they take 20 or 30 of the whitest Limestones, and slack them in a Gallon of the Wine; then they add more Wine, and stir them together in a Half-tub, with a Parelling staff; next they pour this mixture into the Hogshead, and having again used the Parelling Instrument, leave the Wine to settle, and then rack it. This Wine I should guess to be no ill drink for gross Bodies and Rheumatic Brains; but hurtful to good Fellows of hot and dry constitutions, and meagre habits."

Again, here is a recipe: "*How to use a Butt of Sack when it is musty.* Take a gallon of Lime, and beat it small, and put it into the Butt; then take a Staff and beat it, and let it stand a day or two."

21. Lines 23, 24: *O base Hungarian wight! wilt thou the spigot wield?*—For *Hungarian* the Q. has *gongarian*. "This," says Steevens, "is a parody on a line taken from one of the old bombast plays, beginning,

> O base *Gongarian*, wilt thou the distaff wield?

I had," he says, "marked the passage down, but forgot to note the play." I believe no one since has been fortunate enough to light on the play which Steevens forgot to note: *Gongarian* has nevertheless been adopted in many of the best modern editions of Shakespeare; by Capell first. "*Hungarian*," as Dyce remarks, "is a cant term of doubtful origin; perhaps from *hungry*, perhaps from the free-booters of Hungary, or perhaps it is equivalent to gipsey." Several instances of its use are given in the notes to this passage in the Variorum Ed. 1821.

22. Lines 26 () 27: *His mind is not heroic, and there's the humour of it.*—From the Q. First inserted in the modern text by Theobald.

23. Lines 30, 31: *The good humour is to steal at a* MINIM'S *rest.*—Both Q. and F. have *at a minute's rest*. The reading of our text was first suggested by Dr. Johnson's friend, Bennet Langton, and first adopted by Singer. Its agreement with the preceding speech of Falstaff—"his filching was like an unskilful singer,—he kept not time"—commends it as a highly probable restoration of the text. "A *minim*," says Sir J. Hawkins, "was anciently, as the term imports, the shortest note in music. Its measure was afterwards, as it is now, as long as while two may be moderately counted. In Romeo and Juliet, ii. 4. 22, Mercutio says of Tybalt, that in fighting he 'rests me his minim rest, one, two, and the third in your bosom.'"

24. Line 49: *she* CARVES.—The collocation of this term best interprets it—"I spy entertainment in her; she discourses, she *carves*, she gives the leer of invitation," &c., *i.e.* by gesture, look, or action she encourages address. To carve to any person, that is, to send him a portion of a dish at table, was as usual a way of manifesting courtesy as "taking wine" with him, and from a superior or from a lady was accounted a great honour. Hence perhaps at last the term might come to mean merely, as Hunter expresses it (New Illustrations, vol. i. p. 216), "some form of action, which indicated the desire that the person to whom it was addressed should be attentive and propitious."

25. Lines 54, 55: *He hath studied her* WELL, *and translated her* WILL, *out of honesty into English.*—The F. has *will* in both places; the Q. has merely:

> He hath studied her well, out of honestie
> Into English.

The changes have been rung on both *well* and *will*, without, however, adding to the perspicuity of the speech. The reading I have adopted is that of Mr. Grant White, and I understand it to mean that Falstaff, having attentively considered Mrs. Ford, has translated her *will* out of its seeming honesty into a language that everyone may understand, into "plain English" in fact.

[1] See Arber's Transcript, iii. 678.

26. Line 50: *The* ANCHOR *is deep.*—Because Pistol in the preceding speech had talked of *translating*, Johnson conjectured that *anchor* here might be a misprint for *author*. Malone, however, retaining *anchor*, says: "Nym, I believe, only means to say, the scheme for debauching Ford's wife is *deep*—well laid." *Deep*, perhaps; but I should suppose that Nym meant to imply that by dropping anchor in *deep* water Falstaff had committed himself to a perilous venture.

27. Line 77: *I will be* 'CHEATOR *to them both.*—For *escheator*, an officer of the exchequer or treasury. The F. has *cheators*; perhaps a pun was intended.

28. Line 92: *away o'* TH' *hoof.*—The F. has *ith'*.

29. Line 93: *humour.*—Misspelt *honor* in F. A frequent misprint: it occurs twice in the first scene of Romeo and Juliet, in the first Q. edition.

30. Lines, 98, 99: *I have operations* IN MY HEAD, *which be humours of revenge.*—The F. omits *in my head*, which was restored to the text by Pope from the Q.

31. Line 101: *By welkin and her* STAR!—Meaning, I presume, by *star* the *sun*. Dyce, however, adopts the suggestion of Collier's MS. Corrector, and reads *stars*. The Q. has *Fairies*.

32. Lines 104, 105, 110: *Page . . . Ford . . . Page.*—These names are transposed in the F.; they are here given as in the Q., because, in act ii. scene 1, Nym addresses Page, and Pistol Ford. Steevens first made the correction.

33. Line 111: *for* THE REVOLT OF MINE *is dangerous.*—Understanding *revolt of mine* to be equivalent to *my revolt*, Pope altered the phrase to "*this* revolt of mine;" Theobald, who supposed Nym to allude to the "yellowness" with which he proposed to possess Page, read "the revolt of *mien*:" both readings have met with acceptance from several editors. [With regard to the latter reading *mien* does not occur in Shakespeare, though it is a conjectural reading in Two Gent. of Verona, ii. 4. 196; see note 52 on that play.] On the other hand, the Cambridge editors suggest that a word may have been missed by the printer; that we should read "the revolt of mine *anger* is dangerous," and they point out, as a cause of its omission, the fact that the letters of this word are included in the word "dangerous" which follows.

Perhaps, after all, we have here only one of Nym's terrific innuendos: he intends to undermine Falstaff, and darkly hints, in his fustian language, that, by the *revolt* or counterblast of his *mine*, he will "do" for his quondam master.

ACT I. Scene 4.

34. Line 15: PETER *Simple.*—Simple's Christian name is *John* in the Q. edition.

35. Line 23: *a little yellow beard,—a* CANE-*colour'd beard.*—The F. prints the word as "Caine," and Theobald having asserted that "*Cain* and *Judas*, in the tapestries and pictures of old, were represented with *yellow* beards,"—which is not true; for Judas at any rate has always a red beard—his reading "Cain-coloured" has been very generally adopted. The dialogue in the Q. is as follows:—

> *Quickly.* . . . And he has as it were a whay coloured beard.
> *Simple.* Indeed my maisters beard is *kane colored.*
> *Quickly. Kane colour*, you say well. &c.

This, I think, fully justifies Pope's rendering of the word: *cane*, a beard of the colour of *cane*. [Perhaps this was much the same coloured beard as the *straw-coloured* beard mentioned by Bottom in i. 2. 95, Mids. Night's Dream, and compare note 59 on that play.]

36. Line 27: *between this and* HIS HEAD. I incline to agree with Hunter (New Illustrations, vol. i. p. 210) that this "is nonsense." Staunton in a MS. note suggests that "his head" may be the corruption of the name of some place. The Q. affords us no assistance here, nor does any commentator venture on an explanation.

37. Line 47: une boitine verde.—This is printed in the F. *unboyteene verd*, and this, since Rowe's time, has, I believe, always been rendered by *un boitier vert*—*boitier* being supposed a small box for ointments; whereas it is a box of various compartments, holding instruments, dressings, &c., for surgical operations, something too large for the doctor to put in his pocket. The *boyteene* of the F. is evidently intended as the diminutive of *boite*.

38. Line 56: mets le dans mon *pocket*.—The F. has *mette le au mon pocket*; and so in all editions, I believe, it is allowed to stand. Perhaps I should have changed *mon* to *ma*; but the doctor may have thought the English word *pocket* to be masculine.

39. Line 57: dépêche, *quickly*.—*Quickly* is spelt with a small *q* in the F., and may therefore be only a repetition in English of *dépêche*. In iv. 4. 83 *quickly* is again spelt with a small *q*; but there it is by many editors taken as Mrs. Quickly's name.

40. Line 92: baillez.—Theobald; the F. has *ballow*. [It may be noted that the stage-business here is rather obscure as far as the original text is concerned. Mr. Daniel has well pointed out in note 37 above that "the green box" was not a small box to put in the pocket, but a regular box of surgical instruments, &c.; and it is equally necessary for the proper understanding of the scene to remember that Dr. Caius's closet was not a mere cupboard, but a sort of little study opening out of the large room. When he asked Rugby to bring him some writing paper it is most probable, as marked in all the acting editions, that he retired into this closet or study, where he wrote the letter, and then re-entered, after line 112, at the end of Mrs. Quickly's speech. I have marked the stage-direction in the text so as to avoid Caius going off the stage; but it is quite plain that he must be well out of hearing while Mrs. Quickly is talking to Simple. It must be remembered that the stage-directions in the best acting editions of old plays contain the stage-business, as marked in the old prompt copies which were used at the patent theatres, most of which "business" was based upon tradition, handed down from the end of the sixteenth and the beginning of the seventeenth centuries.—F. A. M.]

41. Lines 97, 98: *I'll do* YOU *your master what good I*

can.—As in our text *you* is a common colloquial redundancy. So, in ii. 2. 102, Mrs. Quickly says of Mrs. Page, she is one "that will not miss *you* morning nor evening prayer." F. 1 and Q. 3, 1630, for *you* have *yoe*, and this misprint was probably the cause of the "correction" *for* found in the later Ff.; a reading adopted by some editors.

42. Line 120: *what the good-jer!*—For some account of this obscure exclamation, see Much Ado, note 67.

43. Line 134: *You shall have Anne*—[Exeunt Caius and Rugby]—*fool's-head of your own!*—There is no stage-direction in the F., and the passage is given thus: "You shall have *An*-fooles head of your own." All modern editions, I believe, mark the exit of Caius and Rugby at the end of the preceding speech, and give Mrs. Quickly's speech thus: "You shall have *An* fool's-head of your own"—with what intention I know not.

Note that Anne is frequently in the F. spelt *An* (five times, including this instance, in this very scene), and the dash here clearly indicates a break in Mrs. Quickly's discourse. As I have arranged the passage, while the doctor is still within hearing, Mrs. Quickly continues to flatter him; as soon as he is clear off she utters a bit of her mind. (From my Notes and Conjectural Emendations, &c., 1870.)

ACT II. Scene 1.

44. Line 1: *have I scap'd.*—The *I* is omitted in the F.; it was first added in the Q. of 1630.

45. Line 5: *though Love use Reason for his* PHYSICIAN.—The F. has *precision*, a person of a precise, severe virtue; tho' the term was seldom used except in contempt for those who were supposed to be mere pretenders to sanctity. "Of this word," says Johnson, "I do not see any meaning that is very apposite to the present intention. Perhaps Falstaff said, 'Though love use reason as his *physician*, he admits him not for his counsellor.' This will be plain sense. Ask not the *reason* of my love: the business of *reason* is not to assist love, but to *cure* it. There may, however, be this meaning in the present reading [i.e. in *precision*]. *Though love*, when he would submit to regulation, may *use reason as his precisian*, or director, in nice cases, yet when he is only eager to attain his end, he takes not reason for *his counsellor*." Johnson's conjecture [*physician*], supported by an apt quotation by Dr. Farmer from the 147th Sonnet—"My reason the physician to my love"—met with very general approval, but no editor had the courage to admit it to the text till Dyce set the example: all since, I believe, have adopted it.

46. Line 23: *What* AN *unweigh'd behaviour.*—The third and fourth F. editions, followed by some editors, omit *an*: Capell read "What *one* unweighed behaviour," which seems to me *only* another way of putting what is clearly enough expressed in our text.

47. Line 24: I' TH' *devil's name!*—The F. has, in parenthesis, "(*with* (*The Deuills name*);" as this seems an obvious misprint I have corrected it as above.

48. Line 30: *for the putting-down of* FAT *men.*—The F. omits *fat*: it was first introduced by Theobald. There is nothing about exhibiting a bill in Parliament in what may be called the corresponding speech in the Q.; but there Mrs. Page is made to say: "I shall trust *fat* men the worse while I live for his sake;" a sentiment which in the F. finds its expression in a subsequent speech of Mrs. Ford's, line 55.

49. Line 51: *What? thou liest!—Sir Alice Ford!*—Few readers, I fancy, come upon this speech without receiving an unpleasant shock; it seems too much in the style of Doll Tearsheet for one of our Wives of Windsor. In the notes to Mr. Wheatley's edition I see that the late Mr. Stanford suggested, "What? thou *styled* Sir Alice Ford!" A happier suggestion, I think, was made by the late Howard Staunton, who in a MS. note proposed, "What? thou, *Alce!*—Sir Alice Ford!" For *Alce*, as a diminutive of Alice, see Taming of the Shrew, Induction, ii. 112, "*Alce* madam, or Joan madam?"

50. Line 58: *prais'd.*—So Theobald; F. has *praise.*

51. Line 63: *Hundredth Psalm.*—Rowe; *hundred Psalms*, F.

52. Line 110: *the gallimaufry*=the whole heterogeneous assembly, high, low, rich, poor, young and old. As *gallimaufry* was, however, a cant term for a woman, in allusion to her supposed contrariety of disposition, Pistol may mean to particularize Ford's wife, as Ford's answer—"Love my wife!"—seems to imply: and we should therefore perhaps read "*thy* gallimaufry."

53. Line 141: *and there's the humour of it.*—Added from Q. by Capell.

54. Line 143: *frights* HUMOUR *out of his wits.*—So the Q.; the F. for *humour* has *English*. Pope made the alteration in the modern text; and his example has been very generally followed.

55. Line 148: *Cataian.*—Properly a native of Catala, or Cathay, China. It had become a term of reproach, though in what sense, or for what reason is not known. Its meaning here must be gathered from the context, from which it appears that Page considered Nym to be an outlandish, lying rogue. Sir Toby Belch, in Twelfth Night, ii. 3. 80, calls Olivia a *Cataian*, but with what intention it is impossible to divine.

56. Lines 159, 160: *thou hast some crotchets in thy head now.—Will you go, Mistress Page!*—Printed in the F. in this fashion:— . . . "head, Now: will you go" . . . Some editors point as in our text; others have . . . "head.—Now, will you go" . . .

57. Line 203: *Good* EVEN *and twenty.*—Shallow forgets that the time of day is before ten o'clock in the morning.

58. Line 222: Ford.—This speech in the F. has the prefix *Shal.*; the corresponding speech in the Q. is correctly assigned to Ford.

59. Line 224: *tell him my name is* BROOK.—In the F. Ford's assumed name in his intercourse with Falstaff is invariably *Broome*; in the Q. it is always *Brooke*, and that the Q. is right is shown in the next scene, line 156, where Falstaff puns on the name: "Such *Brooks* are welcome

to me, that o'erflow such liquor." Pope was the first editor to restore *Brook*.

60. Line 228: *Will you go*, MYNHEERS?—The F. has: "will you goe *An-heires?*" The emendation of our text, though suggested by Theobald so far back as 1733, was not adopted till 1857, when Dyce introduced it in his text.

61. Line 237: *I would have made you* FOUR *tall fellows skip like rats*.—As, besides Shallow, who speaks this speech, only *three* personages, Ford, Page, and Mine Host are introduced in the F. text, it is argued that "you *four* tall fellows" could hardly be intended for them, and that "made you" is a colloquial redundancy (see note 41, i. 4. 97, 98) equivalent merely to "made." It has, however, I think, been suggested, though by whom or where I cannot now call to mind, that Slender also should be in company; as he certainly is in the scenes where Shallow and the others go to fetch the would-be duellists, Evans and Caius, home. Shallow's senile boast is matched by the dying Lear's utterances, v. 3. 276, 277:

> I have seen the day, with my good biting falchion
> I would have made them skip.

62. Lines 239, 240: *I had rather hear them scold than* SEE THEM *fight*.—The words *see them*, not in the F. or Q. texts, are due to Collier's MS. Corrector; they seem necessary to the sense, and are, I believe, now generally adopted.

63. Line 242: *and stands so firmly on his wife's frailty*.—Theobald altered *frailty* to *fealty*, and Collier's MS. Corrector to *fidelity*; but, as explained by Capell, Steevens, and others, it is the jealous Ford who speaks; to whose jaundiced mind all women's virtue is suspect. Staunton in his text adopted Theobald's alteration, yet afterwards, in his Addenda and Corrigenda, remarked: "An antithesis was possibly intended between *firmly* and *frailty*, the meaning being, 'who thinks himself so secure on what is a most brittle foundation.'"

ACT II. SCENE 2.

64. Line 3 () 4: *I will retort the sum in equipage*.—This line, not in the F., forms the whole of Pistol's speech in this place in the Q. It was first added to the modern text by Theobald. Pistol's meaning, as I understand it, is that he will give value for the sum by acting as part of Falstaff's retinue (*equipage*); will repay him, in fact, by his services. Warburton, whose opinion is supported by Farmer and Malone, explained *equipage* as Pistolese for *stolen goods*.

65. Line 18: *a short knife and a throng*.—A short knife concealed in the hand aided by a horn shield for the thumb served to nip or cut purses in a crowd. The purse, it is of course understood, was a pouch suspended from the girdle.

66. Line 19: *to your manor of Pickt-hatch, go*.—A polite way of telling Pistol to return to his old occupation of bully to a brothel. See notes, Variorum Shakespeare, 1821, vol. viii. p. 70, and vol. xxi. p. 140.

67. Line 24: *the fear of* HEAVEN.—The usual reading is *God*; from the Q.

68. Line 28: *your red-lattice phrases*.—Tavern or alehouse language. Formerly *lattices* appear to have supplied the place of windows to drinking dens or tap-rooms, letting in light and air, and screening the drinkers from observation; *red* seems to have been the most frequent colour, so that a *red-lattice* became the equivalent of a drinking-shop. The best illustration of this is found in II. Henry IV. ii. 2. 85–89, where the page, alluding to Bardolph's red face, says—"A' calls me e'en now, my lord, through a *red lattice*, and I could discern [= distinguish] no part of his face from the window; at last I spied his eyes, and methought he had made two holes in the ale-wife's new petticoat and peep'd through."

69. Line 28: *your* BULL-BAITING *oaths*.—The F. has *bold-beating*. The reading of our text, due to Hanmer, and adopted by many editors, is characterized by Sidney Walker (Crit. Exam., &c., vol. iii. p. 14) as a "certain conjecture."

70. Line 31: *I do* RELENT:—*what* WOULD *thou more of man?*—The Q. has *recant* and *woulst*; which latter grammatical correction, in the form of *would'st*, was adopted by Pope and many later editors. After this line there follows in the Q. a one-line speech by Falstaff, which I have ventured, on my own responsibility, to introduce into the text:—

> Well, go to; away; no more.

71. Line 79: *pensioners*.—A select body of gentlemen soldiers, who formed the body-guard of Henry VIII. and Queen Elizabeth. Tyrwhitt aptly illustrates the splendour of their corps by a quotation from Gervase Holles's Life of the First Earl of Clare. "I have heard the Earl of Clare say, that when he was pensioner to the queen he did not know a worse man of the whole band than himself; and that all the world knew he had then an inheritance of 4000 l. a-year." This corps is again referred to in Midsummer Night's Dream, ii. 1. 10:

> The cowslips tall her *pensioners* be.

See also note 66 on that play.

72. Line 142: *This* PINK *is one of Cupid's carriers*.—The F. has *Puncke*. Warburton made the alteration, and justified it by the nautical metaphor of which the whole of this speech of Pistol's consists. It may too be observed that, besides its proper meaning of a small vessel, *pink* was also a fancy term for the ladies whose profession is indicated by the coarser word of the F.

73. Line 145: *up with your* FIGHTS.—Waist-cloths hung round ships in battle to conceal the men from the enemy.

74. Line 157: *o'erflow*.—F. reads *ore'flowes*.

75. Line 174: *this* UNSEASON'D *intrusion*.—*Unseasoned* is, I believe, usually explained as *unreasonable*, *ill-timed*; I take it here to mean *not seasoned*, *not prepared* or *prefaced*.

76. Line 179: *take half, or all*.—The F. has "take all, or halfe." The obvious correction in our text is due to Collier's MS. Corrector.

77. Line 290: *mechanical salt-butter rogue!*—*Mechanical*; that is, handicraftsmen were supposed not to aspire to the luxury of fresh butter. So Pedro, in Fletcher's

play of The Maid in the Mill, act iii. 2, abuses his tailor: "Let him call at home in 's own house for *salt butter*."

78. Line 206: *I will aggravate his style*; i.e. I will add to his style or title of *knave* that of *cuckold*.

ACT II. Scene 3.

79. Line 50: *A* WORD, *Mounseur Mock-water*.—*Word* is omitted in the F.; it was restored to the text by Theobald from the Q.

80. Lines 92, 93: CRIED I AIM? *said I well?*—The F. has *Cride game*; the Q. *cried game*. Douce, on the evidence adduced in Warburton's and Steeven's notes (Var. Ed. 1821, vol. viii. p. 98), first proposed the reading of our text, and Dyce was the first editor who adopted it. For the expression *cry aim*, see King John, note 87.

ACT III. Scene 1.

81. Line 5: *the* PITTIE-WARD.—So F. 1 and the Q. of 1630 (Q. 3); F. 2, F. 3, and F. 4 have *pitty-wary*. Capell changed to *city-ward*, and Collier's MS. Corrector to *pit-way*. The emendations are not satisfactory, nor is any explanation forthcoming of the intention of the original.

[Capell's emendation is explained as "towards the *city* of London," which is, of course, plausible. It has occurred to me that *pittie-ward* might be a corruption of *pittes-ward*; that is to say, in the direction of the *pits*, supposing that there were in the neighbourhood any *clay pits* or *gravel pits*. It might assist us very much in deciphering the meaning of *pittie-ward* if we knew why "*Via de Pyttey* a *Pyttey*-gate, porta vocata Nether *Pittey*," mentioned in William de Worcestre's account of distances in the city of Bristol (and quoted by Steevens in his note, Var. Ed. vol. vii. p. 100), was so called. We have mention of a *sawpit* in iv. 4. 53, and again in v. 3. 14, 15 of a *pit* (probably the same) hard by Herne's oak. As for the attempted correction, if it be one, in F. 2, I fancy that may have arisen from the confusion between *ward* and *way*. This conjecture of mine is practically the same as the one in Collier's MS., though, in his Notes and Emendations, he does not attempt any explanation of *pit-way*. Anyone acquainted with the Berkshire country round Ascot and Windsor, knows that the *gravel-pits* are often recognized by the people of that neighbourhood as landmarks.—F. A. M.]

82. Line 17: *To shallow rivers*, &c.—Sir Hugh's snatches of song are from Marlowe's beautiful song, "Come live with me and be my love;" with this he, in his agitation, mixes a line of the old version of the 137th Psalm: "When we did sit in Babylon," &c. The Q. has in this place—"There dwelt a man in Babylon." This is the first line of The Ballad of Constant Susanna, the first stanza of which Percy gives in his Reliques. According to Warton (History of Poetry, p. 811, ed. 1870), it is the ballad licensed to T. Colwell in 1562. Stat. Reg., under the title of The godlye and constante wyfe Susanna. According to Collier (Extracts, &c., vol. i. p. 74) and Arber (Transcript, i. 210), the entry in Stat. Reg. is "constant *wyse*," not "constant *wyfe*." Sir Toby Belch sings this first line in Twelfth Night, ii. 3. 84.

83. Line 91: *urinals*.—So Capell, from the Q.; *urinal* is the reading of F.

84. Line 92: *for missing your meetings and appointments*.—Not in F.; introduced from Q. by Pope.

85. Line 99: GUALLIA *and Gaul*.—So Malone, adopting Farmer's emendation; the F. has *Gallia and Gaule*; the Q. *Gawle and Gawlia*.

86. Line 107: *Give me thy hand, terrestrial; so*.—Not in the F. Introduced from Q. by Theobald.

87. Line 113: *lads*.—So Warburton, from Q.; the F. has *Lad*.

ACT III. Scene 2.

88. Line 13: *as idle as she may hang together*; i.e. "as idle as it is possible to be without ceasing to be."

89. Line 71: *'tis in his buttons*.—Literally, in the person his *buttons* inclose, i.e. "it is in him, in his ability." Compare Marston, The Fawne, ii. 1. 66, ed. Bullen: "Thou art now *within the buttons* of the prince;" that is, "in his confidence, his inmost counsels." In the Variorum Shakespeare, 1821, several references to the flower called *bachelors' buttons*, and to the *buttons of a bachelor*, are collected; but they have no connection with the expression in our text.

90. Line 90: *pipe-wine*.—There is seemingly some play upon words here, the point of which is not very obvious. Mine host says he will to Falstaff, and drink canary with him; whereupon Ford promises himself that he will first drink in *pipe-wine* with him and make him dance. *Canary* is of course the name of a *dance* as well as of a *wine*. Ford intends to use his cudgel; and as *pipe-wine* I presume, is wine in the *wood*, this may be his figurative way of referring to it.

ACT III. Scene 3.

91. Line 22: *eyas-musket*.—A young male sparrow-hawk.

92. Line 27: *Jack-a-Lent*.—A puppet which, I presume, was supposed to represent Lent, and which was set up to be thrown at; as Jack only had a six-weeks' existence, his name was appropriate to the young page. See note on v. 5. 134.

93. Line 46: "*Have I caught*" THEE, "*my heavenly jewel?*"—So (except that it has no marks of quotation) the F.; the Q. omits *thee*. Tollet pointed out that this is the first line of the second song in Sidney's Astrophel and Stella (1591):

> Have I *caught my heavenly jewel*,
> Teaching sleep most fair to be? &c.

Dyce, who here follows the Q., supposes that "thee" was foisted into the F. text by some transcriber.

94. Line 65: BY THE LORD, *thou art a* TRAITOR *to say so*.—"The F. omits 'By the Lord,' and reads—Thou art a *tyrant*, &c., but the reading of the quarto appears to me far better" (*Malone*).

95. Lines 69, 70: *I see what thou wert, if Fortune thy foe were not, Nature thy friend*.—Here punctuated as in

F. 2, F. 3, and F. 4. F. 1 gives it—"If Fortune thy foe, *were not* Nature thy friend;" which seems nonsense. If our text is right we must understand: "Nature *being* thy friend."

96. Line 79: *Bucklersbury in simple time.*—A street branching off from the east end of Cheapside, at its junction with the Poultry, running down to Walbrook; it was formerly chiefly inhabited by druggists and grocers. The greater part of it has been improved out of existence by the new street running from the Mansion House to Blackfriars.

97. Line 85: *the Counter-gate.*—Stow (1500) tells us of two *Counters*, or *Compters*, in London in his time—the *Compter* in the Poultrie in the Ward of Cheap, and that in Wood Street in Cripplegate Ward.

98. Line 118: *'T is not so, I hope.*—Here Theobald introduced from the Q. an aside between Mrs. Ford and Mrs. Page—*Speak louder*—and his example has been followed by several editors. As Falstaff, however, is in the same room as the speakers, there is no need of this aside here, and the F. gives it more properly in act iv. 2. 16, where Falstaff has stepped into another chamber.

99. Lines 128, 129: *There is a gentleman my dear friend.*—With this punctuation, which is that of the F., my dear friend must apply to the gentleman, and not to Mrs. Page, to whom the speech is addressed. The evidence of the Q., such as it is, is in favour of this interpretation; there Mrs. Ford's speech is:

> *Mis. For.* Alas mistresse *Page*, what shall I do?
> Here is a gentleman my friend, how shall I do?

The usual punctuation has been to place a comma after *gentleman*, and then *my dear friend* would apply to Mrs. Page. Recent editors, however, have returned to the F., and Dyce, the Cambridge editors, Grant White, Hudson, give the passage as in our text.

100. Line 140: *I love thee,* AND NONE BUT THEE.—The words *and none but thee* were first introduced in the modern text by Malone from the Q., where Falstaff's speech is given thus:

> *Fal.* I loue thee, and none but thee:
> Helpe me to conuey me hence,
> Ile neuer come here more.

101. Line 175: *So, now* UNCAPE.—This is said to be a hunting term, though no evidence is forthcoming that it is so, nor are editors agreed as to its meaning. Warburton says it means to unearth a fox; Steevens, to let one out of a bag. Hanmer boldly substituted the word *uncouple*, meaning uncouple the dogs for the hunt, and that seems the obvious intention of the speaker. A writer in The Edinburgh Review, October, 1872, considers that *cape* may be taken as synonymous with *collar*, and therefore that "*uncape*, *uncollar*, or *uncouple* would each mean the same thing, and all would be easily, if not equally, intelligible."

102. Lines 102, 103: *What a taking was he in when your husband asked* WHAT *was in the basket!*—The F. has *who* was in the basket. I have, with Dyce and others, adopted Ritson's emendation. He says: "We should read—'*what* was in the basket!' for though in fact Ford had asked no such question, he could never suspect that there was either *man* or *woman* in it. The propriety of this emendation is manifest from a subsequent passage (iii. 5. 102-104), where Falstaff tells Master Brook—'the jealous knave . . . asked them once or twice *what* they had in their basket.'"

103. Line 205: *foolish carrion.*—The F. has *foolishion carion*. Corrected in F. 2.

104. Line 215: *Ay, ay, peace.*—Not in the F. Added to the modern text by Theobald from the Q.

ACT III. Scene 4.

105.—In the Q. this scene follows our scene 5. It is usually marked as "A room in Page's house." I make it to be "Before Page's house." It would have been a breach of maidenly propriety for Anne to admit her lover into the house; and the fact that the scene is really out of doors is distinctly proved by Page's speech, line 70: "Come, Master Shallow; come, son Slender; *in*;" and by Mrs. Page's speech, line 96: "she must needs go *in*." Moreover, the several arrivals of the personages of this scene without any kind of announcement, natural enough when the scene is out of doors, become rather awkward when the scene is supposed to be a particular room.

I have also departed from modern usage in making Mrs. Quickly (the confidant of the lovers) present at the commencement of the scene, instead of bringing her on in company with Shallow and Slender; in this respect I follow the Q. It will of course be remembered that in the F. in this play no entrances are marked; each scene is merely headed with a list of the actors who take part in it.

106. Line 7: *Besides, these other bars he lays before me.*—So punctuated by Sidney Walker (Crit. Exam., &c., vol. iii. p. 14); adopted by Dyce. The F. and most modern texts place the comma after *these*.

107. Line 14: *Was the first motive that I woo'd thee, Anne.*—Mr. Grant White (Riverside ed.) says of this line, that it is "Not S.'s grammar: mere carelessness in writing."

108. Line 24: *I 'll make a shaft or a bolt on 't*; *i.e.* a long arrow for a bow, or a short one for a cross-bow; a proverbial saying equivalent to "I 'll do it one way or another."

109. Line 47: *come cut and long-tail, &c.*—Slender of course means that he will maintain his proposed wife as like a gentlewoman as any one may who is of no higher degree than his own; "his meaning is goot," as Parson Evans observed in i. 1. 264, but he actually offers her no better position than that which any of the tag, rag, and bobtail might afford her. The origin of the term *cut and long-tail* is uncertain; its meaning, however, as clearly shown in numerous instances of its use, is—persons of all kind and degree.

110. Line 68: *happy man be his dole!*—Equivalent here to *let happiness be the portion of the winner.*

111. Lines 76, 77:

> Mrs. Page. *Good Master Fenton, come not to my child.*
> Page. *She is no match for you.*

I am not satisfied that these speeches are rightly assigned in the F.; both should, I think, be given to Page. From his entry, line 71, to his exit, line 80, the dialogue, it seems to me, should be confined to him and Fenton. If Mrs. Page is mixed up in it, there is no propriety in Quickly's suggestion to Fenton (line 81), that he should speak to Mistress Page; for, if the F. is right, Mrs. Page has already told Fenton her mind. There would be another advantage gained in keeping her out of the Fenton-Page bit: it would give her an opportunity of taking Mrs. Quickly aside, and in dumb-show communicating to her the message to Falstaff—the invitation to the second meeting with Mrs. Ford—which at the end of the scene Quickly sets off to deliver. Except during the Fenton-Page dialogue, it is difficult to imagine at what time Mrs. Quickly could have had any communication with her two mistresses.

112. Line 101: "*will you cast away your child on a fool* AND *a physician!*—A difficulty has been raised here: does Mrs. Quickly mean that her master is a *fool* as well as a *physician!* or does she refer the *fool* to Slender? Malone so understood her; and Johnson, with the same understanding, proposed to read: "a fool *or* a physician." *Physician* and *fool* are, however, for some occult reason, so constantly coupled that the point must remain doubtful. Take the following instance:—"As for *physicians, being fools*, I cannot blame them if they neglect wine and minister simples" (Aristippus. Randolph, Works, ed. Hazlitt, p. 20).

113. Line 103: *once to-night.*—This is usually interpreted as meaning *some time* to-night. I know of no other instance in which it is thus used. Schmidt explains it as being merely an emphatical expletive; but the other instances he gives do not seem to me to the point. I suspect it is simply a misprint for the familiar phrase, "soon at night," as in i. 4. 9.

ACT III. Scene 5.

114. Lines 4-6: *Have I lived to be carried in a basket, and to be thrown in the Thames like a barrow of butcher's offal?*—The F. has: "Have I liu'd to be carried in a Basket like a barrow of butchers Offall? and to be throwne in the Thames?" I have adopted here the arrangement of the Q., which only differs from my text by the words, "and thrown into," for "and *to be* thrown in." I suggested this alteration in my Introduction to the Facsimile of the Q., published in Dr. Furnivall's series of Shakspere-Quarto Facsimiles; and as the transposition has since been approved and adopted by Mr. H. B. Wheatley in his edition of the play, 1886, I venture also to adopt it here, retaining, however, the exact words of the F., which Mr. Wheatley rejects for those of the Q.

115. Line 9: *The rogues* SLIGHTED *me into the river.*—"Chucked me in contemptuously." The Q. has "*slided* me in."

116. Line 11: *a blind bitch's puppies.*—Theobald, whose lead has been generally followed, corrected this to "a bitch's blind puppies;" but I agree with Staunton that a colloquial inversion such as this may well be allowed to pass without editorial interference. The Q. agrees here with the F.

117. Line 67: *And* HOW *sped you, sir?*—Here as in the Q.; restored by Malone. The F. omits *how*. It is true that this speech, taken by itself, is perfectly good English and intelligible as it is given in the F.; but the context, Falstaff's reply to it—"*Very ill-favouredly*, Master Brook"—shows the necessity of the Q. reading.

118. Lines 86, 87: IN *her invention and Ford's wife's* DISTRACTION.—So the F., from which the Q. differs only in reading *by* for *in*. This variation is, quite needlessly, adopted by some editors; by Theobald first, I believe. Another less harmless change, made first by Hanmer, has also found its way into many modern editions: on the ground that Mrs. Ford was not really distracted, and that she had really prepared the buck-basket for Falstaff's disgrace, *distraction* has been altered to *direction*. It would almost seem that in making or adopting this change, editors had forgotten that it is Falstaff who speaks, Falstaff, who, if he had had the slightest suspicion that the *distraction* manifested by Mrs. Ford was only feigned, would probably never have got into the basket at all.

119. Line 90: *By the Lord, a buck-basket!*—So the Q.; adopted first by Malone. The F. has merely "*Yes:* a Buck-basket."

120. Line 111: *to be detected with.*—*With* is here used in the sense of *by*, and the whole phrase is equivalent to —*to be discovered by*. It may be noted, however, that *detected* was frequently used in the sense of suspected, accused, or impeached. See Notes on Measure for Measure, iii. 2. 130 in Variorum Ed. 1821, vol. ix. p. 126.

121. Line 154: *if I have horns to make* ME *mad.*—The F. has *one*. Dyce made the change, which I have adopted; it seems to me to agree better with the context than *one*.

ACT IV. Scene 1.

122.—This scene is altogether absent from the Q.

123. Line 11: *Master Slender is* LET *the boys leave to play.*—Collier's MS. Corrector reads *get*; certainly an improvement, and probably a restoration. Hudson adopts it in his Harvard edition. Slender could have no authority to *let* or allow the boys to play; but might very well *get* or obtain a holiday for them.

124. Line 49: accusativo, HUNG, hang, hog.—In the preceding speech William begins his *accusativo* with *hinc;* Evans now corrects him with *hung* (for *hunc*). The F., however, makes Evans say *hing* (for *hinc*); but Evans cannot be supposed to blunder here, and Pope accordingly made the correction in our text. Mr. Dyce and others carry the change further, and unnecessarily correct William's error too.

125. Line 63: Genitivo.—The F. has *Genitiue*, in italics.

126. Line 64: *Jenny's.*—It is *Ginyes* in the F.

127. Lines 72, 73: *and the numbers* AND *the genders.*—So Collier's MS. Corrector: the F. has "*of* the genders."

ACT IV. Scene 2.

128. Lines 21, 22: *your husband is in his old* LUNES *again.*—The F. has *lines;* the Q. in the corresponding passage has "his old *vaine.*" Theobald made the change —almost universally received—in our text. Mr. Knight, however, adheres to the F., understanding thereby "old courses, old humours, old vein." It is worthy of note that *lunes* occurs only once in the old editions of Shakespeare, and is not found elsewhere; Winter's Tale, ii. 2 30: "These dangerous, vnsafe *Lunes* i'th' King," &c. In Troilus and Cressida, ii. 3. 139, "His pettish *lunes*" is the modern reading, the original has *lines;* so also in Hamlet, iii. 3. 7, "his *lunes*" has, in some editions, been substituted for "his lunacies" of the F.

129. Line 59: Mrs. Page. *Creep into the kiln-hole.*—In the F. this forms part of a speech by *Mrs. Ford,* and when Falstaff asks "Where is *it?*" Mrs. Ford tells him that her husband will be sure to seek there! The suggestion that Falstaff should hide in the *kiln-hole* obviously belongs to *Mrs. Page,* and this is one instance in many of the wrong assignment of speeches in the old copies. Malone pointed out the error; but Dyce was the first to correct it.

130. Line 67: Mrs. Page. *If you go out, &c.*—Here, again, in the F., the speech is wrongly assigned to *Mrs. Ford.* Fortunately, however, in this instance the Q. comes to the rescue, and Malone made the necessary correction.

131. Line 78: *Brainford.*—In all modern editions, I believe, this name is changed to *Brentford.* I have restored the ancient name as it appears throughout in the old copies.

132. Line 105: *we cannot misuse* HIM *enough.*—*Him* is omitted in F. 1; the correction was made in F. 2.

133. Line 109: *eat.*—*Eats,* F.

134. Line 119: *I had as lief bear.*—So F. 2; F. 1 has "I had liefe *as* beare."

135. Line 121: *villains.*—The F. has *villaine;* but as two men bear the basket I presume there should be no difficulty in accepting Dyce's emendation; the odd thing is that it was never proposed before.

136. Line 123: *ging.*—The F. has *gin.* Corrected in F. 2.

137. Line 151: *as I am* AN HONEST MAN.—So in the Q.: the F. has merely *a man,* and so, I believe, all modern editions.

138. Lines 168, 169: *If I find not what I seek, show no colour for my extremity, let me for ever be, &c.*—The F., and some modern editions, by placing a colon or a semicolon after *extremity,* make it appear as if Ford urged his hearers to *show no colour for his extremity, i.e.* to show no reason for his *extreme* behaviour; which seems nonsense. The construction, of course, is: "If I find not what I seek, *if I* show no colour, &c., *then* let me, &c."

139. Line 191: *let him* NOT *strike.*—*Not* omitted in F. 1.

140. Line 194: *you* RAG.—*Ragge,* F. 1; *rag,* F. 2; *hagge,* Q. 3; *hag,* F. 3 and F. 4. Usually changed to *hag,* because in his preceding speech Ford has called the supposed Mother Prat a *hag.* But *rag* also was a term of abuse: why might not Ford vary the epithets he bestows on her?

141. Line 204: *I spy a great peard under* HER *muffler.* —*Her* in the Q.; the F. has *his.*

142. Line 237: *no period; i.e.* no *full stop,* no proper ending.

ACT IV. Scene 3.

143. Line 1: *the Germans desire.*—The F. has *the Germane desires;* Capell as in text.

144. Line 9: *them.*—So Theobald; *him* in F.

145. Line 12: *house.*—So the Q.; *houses,* F.

146. Line 13: *they must come off; i.e.* "they must pay soundly."

ACT IV. Scene 4.

147. Line 7: *I rather will suspect the sun with* COLD.—The F. has *gold;* Rowe made the correction.

148. Line 33: *makes.*—*Make,* F.

149. Lines 36-38:

> *The superstitious idle-headed* ELD
> *Receiv'd and did deliver to our age,*
> *This tale, &c.*

Eld is of course sometimes used for *elders, aged persons;* here, with Steevens, I take it to mean the *olden time;* and this agrees with the following line: the *olden time* delivered to *our time,* "our age." Compare "worm-eaten *elde,*" Pierce Peniless, p. 31, ed. Collier, Sh. Soc.: "musty *eld,*" Marston, What you Will, IV. 1. p. 396, vol. ii. ed. Bullen.

150. Lines 42 () 43: *Disguis'd like Herne, with huge horns on his head.*—This line is taken from the Q., which, however, has *Horne* for *Herne;* it is absolutely necessary for the intelligibility of Page's speech which follows it. It is, however, as the Cambridge editors remark, probable that Mrs. Ford gave a still fuller explanation of her device and the grounds on which the disguise was to be recommended to Falstaff. The lines in the Q. itself show this:

> Now for that Falstaffe hath bene so deceived
> As that he dares not venture to the house,
> Wee'le send him word to meet us in the field,
> Disguised like Horne with huge horns on his head.

Theobald introduced the two last lines in his edition; Malone the last line only, as in our text.

151. Lines 56, 57:

> *Then let them all encircle him about,*
> *And, fairy-like,* TO-PINCH *the unclean knight.*

There is no hyphen in *to pinch* in the F. Tyrwhitt suggested it, and Steevens first adopted it; since when it has maintained its place in the text, with the general consent of the editors, as marking an instance of the use of *to* as an intensitive prefix. Dr. Abbott, however, in his Shakespearian Grammar, par. 350, and Dr. Schmidt, Shakespeare-Lexicon, *s.v. To,* 7) maintain that this is one of many instances in which *to* is placed before the second infinitive, though omitted conformably to grammar before the first.

152. Line 60: Mrs. Ford. *And till he tell the truth, &c.*—The F. gives this speech to Ford.

153. Line 73: *and in that* TIME.—Theobald made the plausible emendation *tire;* Singer, *trim;* but as Page may mean that Slender shall steal away his daughter during *the time* of the proposed masque, neither of these changes can be considered absolutely necessary.

154. Line 76: *in name of Brook.*—The Q. 3 has "in *the* name," &c.

155. Line 83: *Send Quickly to Sir John.*—I adopt here Theobald's change of an adverb into a proper name; but it must be mentioned that in the F. *quickly* is not only printed with a small *q*, but in roman type, whereas proper names are almost invariably printed in italic. See note on "*dépêche*, quickly," i. 4. 57.

156. Line 87: *And* HE *my husband best of all affects.*—*He* for *him*.

157. Lines 88, 89:

> *The doctor is well money'd, and* HIS *friends*
> *Potent at court.*

This may be right; no editor seems to have questioned it; but it implies that all the doctor's friends are potent at court. Perhaps we should read—"and *has* friends," &c.

ACT IV. Scene 5.

158.—The locality of this scene is usually given as "A room in the Garter Inn." The dialogue would seem to imply that it was the court-yard of the inn; from which, as in many ancient inns still in existence, a staircase ascended to an open gallery giving access to the several rooms. I have accordingly marked it as "The Court-yard of the Garter Inn."

159. Line 31: *My master, sir, Master Slender.*—The F. has "My master (sir), my master *Slender.*" Steevens made the correction.

160. Line 45: Sim. *I may not conceal them, sir.*—Wrongly given to Falstaff in the F.; corrected by Rowe.

161. Line 55: *Ay, Sir Tike; who more bold?*—The F. has "I sir: *like* who more bold;" the Q., "*I* tike, who more bolde." The reading of our text, suggested by Dr. Farmer, was first adopted by Steevens, and has been very generally accepted. It is, however, rejected by some editors in favour of the F. Dyce, who interprets the F., "Ay, sir; like the boldest," says that Farmer's emendation is an "extraordinary reading;" Mr. Wheatley, who follows Dyce, says it is "absurd;" I adopt it, believing it to be excellent.

162. Line 58: Thou *art* clerkly.—The F. has *are*.

163. Line 80: *Readings.*—So the Q.; the F. has *Readins*.

164. Lines 105, 106: *if my wind were but long enough* TO SAY MY PRAYERS, *I would repent.*—The words *to say my prayers* were added to the text by Pope from the Q.

165. Lines 120-125: *I was like to be apprehended for the witch of Brainford: but that my admirable dexterity of wit, my counterfeiting the action of an* OLD WOMAN, *deliver'd me, the knave constable had set me i' the stocks, i' the common stocks, for a witch.*—Theobald pointed out that Falstaff's *admirable dexterity of wit* was the very thing that was likely to cause him to be stocked, and he accordingly changed *old woman* to *wood woman*, *i.e.* a crazy, frantic woman. I do not see how this would have helped Falstaff to escape the attention of the constable; the assumed feebleness of an old woman was perhaps his best safeguard. The Q. affords us no assistance here; all it has is:

> And in my escape like to a bene apprehended
> For a witch of *Brainford*, and set in the stockes.

ACT IV. Scene 6.

166. Lines 16, 17:

> *Without the show of both; fat Falstaff* IN 'T
> *Hath a great scene.*

The obvious incompleteness of this first line in the F., which ends it at *Falstaff*, is usually attempted to be cured by reference to the Q., which has the line:

> Wherein fat Falstaffe had a mightie scare,

and from this in the modern text the line is given:

> Without the show of both: *wherein* fat Falstaff.

The defect of the F. is more likely to have been caused by the dropping out of some word at the end of the line, and I have accordingly supplied the word *in 't*. F. 2, F. 3, and F. 4 make up the line by reading "fat *Sir John* Falstaff."

167. Line 27: *Her mother,* EVEN *strong against that match.*—"*Even* strong" is explained as equivalent to "as strong, with a similar degree of strength," *i.e.* Mrs. Page is as strong against the match with Slender as Mr. Page is strong for it. The explanation is somewhat forced. Pope altered to "*ever* strong." The Q. has, "*Now* her mother *still* against that match."

168. Line 39: *The better to* DENOTE *her to the doctor.*—The F. has *devote;* an obvious misprint, which, however, remained uncorrected till Steevens pointed it out.

169. Line 50: *And, in the lawful name of* MARRYING.—Sidney Walker (Crit. Exam. &c. vol. iii. p. 15) suggested *marriage*. *Marriage* would seem to be an unfortunate word in the printer's hands; in the Taming of the Shrew, iii. 2. 171, it has, I think, got corrupted to *many*—"after *many* ceremonies done"—for *many* read *marriage*.

ACT V. Scene 1.

170.—The first four short scenes of this act are omitted in the Q.

171. Line 14: Ford. *Went you not to her* YESTERDAY, *sir, &c.*—The reader will note that the time of this scene is the afternoon of the very day on which the Mother Prat business took place.

ACT V. Scene 2.

172. Line 4: *Remember, son Slender, my daughter.*—In the F. this sentence ends abruptly with *my*, with no period or pointing whatever: some word, or words, had

evidently dropped out at press. The editor, or printer of the second F. supplied the word *daughter*, as in our text. It does not seem to me a particularly satisfactory filling of the hiatus, as Page could scarcely think Slender so muddle-headed as to forget Anne; though he might seek to impress upon him the signs by which he was to recognize her. I conjecture, therefore, that the sentence should end with *my daughter's attire*, or *my daughter is in white*, or something to that effect.

ACT V. Scene 3.

173. Line 14: *the Welsh devil* Hugh.—The F. has *Herne*, an evident misprint; Theobald corrected to *Evans*; Capell to *Hugh*, as in our text.

ACT V. Scene 5.

174. Lines 20-24: *Let the sky rain potatoes, &c.*—Steevens notes: "Shakespeare, very probably, had the following artificial *tempest* in his thoughts, when he put the words on which this note is founded into the mouth of Falstaff. Holinshed informs us that in the year 1583, for the entertainment of Prince Alasco, was performed 'a verie statelie tragedie named Dido, wherein the queen's banket (with Œneas's narration of the destruction of Troie) was lively described in a marchpane patterne—*the tempest wherein it hailed small confects, rained rose-water, and snew an artificial kind of snow*, all strange, marvellous, and abundant.' Brantome, also describing an earlier feast given by the Vidam of Chartres, says—'Au desert, il y eut un *orage artificiel* qui, pendant une demie heure entiere, fit tomber une *pluie* d'eaux odorantes et un grôle de dragées.'"

175. Line 28: *Divide me like a brib'd-buck.*—*Bribed* has been variously interpreted; it is said to mean *begg'd*, and again to mean *divided* or *cut up*. A third interpretation which seems to suit the intention of the intrigue, is *stolen, obtained in a surreptitious manner;* which is exactly the position of the "male deer," Falstaff, to the Merry Wives—so at least the speaker, Falstaff himself, thinks. Tyrwhitt, in his glossary to Chaucer, sub voce *Briben*, cites *Rot. Parl.* 22 Edw. iv. n. 30, in which mention is made of persons who "have stolen and *bribed* signetts" [cygnets, or young swans]. Theobald altered to *bribe-buck*, i.e. a buck sent for a bribe, and his reading has been accepted by many editors.

176. Line 40: Stage-direction. Enter Sir Hugh, &c.—This is the only place in which the F. gives any stage-direction, and here it is merely "*Enter Fairies.*" In the Q. it stands thus:—

"*There is a noise of hornes, the two women run away.*
Enter Sir Hugh like a Satyre, and boyes drest like Fayries,
Mistresse Quickly, like the Queene of Fayries: they
Sing a song about him, and afterwards speake."

The stage-direction of our text is made up from this and from the prefixes to the speeches as given in the F., and there can be no pretence, as far as the prefixes to the speeches assigned to Quickly and Pistol are concerned, that they are blundered by the printer; for in the list of personages which heads the scene their names are included thus:—

"Scena Quinta.
Enter Falstaffe, Mistris Page, Mistris Ford, Evans, Anne Page, Fairies, Page, Ford, Quickly, Slender, Fenton, Caius, Pistoll."

No doubt Quickly and Pistol are out of their characters in this scene, and likely enough their presence by name is merely the result of a manager's *mem.* that the actors who took these parts in the earlier scenes were now to assume those of the *Fairy Queen* and *Hobgoblin*, or, as he is called in the Q., *Puck*. No doubt also her parents intended that Anne should present the *Fairy Queen*, and some editors accordingly assign the part to her; but as Anne intended to deceive her parents, and as the assumption of that part would have made her escape with Fenton more difficult, it seems to me best, on the whole, not to disturb the arrangement sanctioned by the F.

177. Line 43: *You orphan-heirs of fixed destiny.*—This line has been explained and expounded until its meaning has been lost. Warburton, whose lead is followed by many editors, altered *orphan* to *ouphen*, that is, elvish or fairy-like, on the ground that these spirits who were the heirs or children of Destiny could not be *orphans*, Destiny being still in existence. But this reasoning is founded, I believe, on a misapprehension, and we should, I think, understand these "heirs," to be not the heirs or children to or of Destiny, but heirs or children whose destiny is fixed. In a note on II. Henry IV. iv. 4. 122, Staunton has, I believe, suggested the true explanation, and *orphan heirs* may, I think, be taken as a synonym of the "unfather'd heirs" mentioned in that play; beings—

. . . . not the sonnes
Of mortall syre or other living wight,
But wondrously begotten, and begonne
By false illusion of a guilefull speight.
Fairie Queene, III. iii. 13.

Our *orphan-heirs* then, when all is said, are simply fairies, who, coming into existence without the law of Nature, are not subject to the changes of mortality, but are of a fixed and unchangeable being and destiny.

178. Line 45:

Crier Hobgoblin, make the fairy O-yes.
Pist. *Elves, list your names; silence, you airy toys.*

"These two lines were certainly intended to rhyme together, as the preceding and subsequent couplets do: and accordingly, in the old editions, the final words of each line are printed, *Oyes* and *toyes*. This, therefore, is a striking instance of the inconvenience which has arisen from modernizing the orthography of Shakespeare" (Tyrwhitt).

179. Line 53: *Where's Pead!*—So the Q.; the F. has *Bede*.

180. Line 55: Rein up *the organs of her fantasy.*—The F. has "raise up." Warburton as in our text. To *rein up* is to curb, restrain; and this seems the obvious sense of the passage. The advocates of the F., however, contend that by *raise up* is here to be understood; elevate above earthly and sensual dreams—a construction which, in connection with the context, is somewhat forced. "Raine," which would be the old spelling of *rein*, was easily corrupted to *raise*. The Q. affords no help here.

181. Line 63: *In* SEAT *as wholesome as in state 't is fit.*—For *seat* the F. has *state*, which seems an obvious instance of the familiar press error of repetition; the error frequently manifesting itself in the first occurrence of the repeated word. Hanmer substituted *site*, which of course has the same meaning as the correction of our text; I have, however, preferred *seat*, Sidney Walker's conjecture (Criticisms, &c. vol. i. p. 284), as it is nearer in form to the original.

182. Line 90: *And turn him to no pain.*—Equivalent to *put him to no pain.* See instances noted in Schmidt's Lexicon, s.v. *Turn*, vb. 1) trans. g).

183. Line 99: *a bloody fire*="a fire of the blood."

184. Line 106: Stage-direction. During this song, &c.—No stage-direction of any kind is given in the F.; that of our text is made up from the Q., somewhat altered to bring it into accordance with the action indicated in the text of the F. Theobald first introduced it in the modern editions. The song is not given in the Q., and the stage-direction in that version stands thus:—

"*Here they pinch him, and sing about him, and the Doctor comes one way and steales away a boy in red. And Slender another way he takes a boy in greene: And Fenton steales Misteris Anne, being in white. And a noyse of hunting is made within, and all the Fairies runne away. Falstaffe pulles of his bucks head, and rises up. And enters M. Page, M. Ford, and their wives, M. Shallow, Sir Hugh.*"

Shallow, who might have been expected to take part in this scene, is altogether absent in the F. version: in the Q. he has one short speech on his entrance—"God saue you sir John Falstaffe"—and with that his part ends.

185. Line 107: *I think we have* WATCH'D *you now.*—"Taken you in the fact by lying in wait for you." So in II. Henry VI. i. 4. 45, 58, where York and Buckingham surprise the Duchess of Gloucester, in the conjuration scene:—

> Beldam, I think we *watch'd* you at an inch.

and:

> Lord Buckingham, methinks, you *watch'd* her well.

See Schmidt's Lexicon, s.v. *Watch*, vb. 2) trans. c).

186. Line 111: *See you these, husband? do not these fair yokes, &c.*—*Yokes* spelt *yoakes* in the F.; the allusion is of course the buck's horns of Falstaff's disguise. F. 2, F. 3, however, have *okes*, F. 4 *oaks*, and Monk Mason having pointed out that the horns of a deer are called in French *les bois*, this last reading has been adopted by several editors. The resemblance of the horns to a yoke is, I take it, a sufficient justification of our text.

187. Line 118: *which must be paid too, Master Brook.*—The F., which, as stated in note 59, has *Broome* for *Brook*, reads *paid to Mr. Broome.* Capell made the correction in our text, which, however, it must be added, has not met with the acceptance of subsequent editors; though, as it seems to me, entirely justified by the context. The reason for this, I presume, is that in what may be called the corresponding speech in the Q. Ford says:

> There 's xx. pound you borrowed of M. Brooke Sir Iohn,
> And it must be paid to M. Ford Sir Iohn.

188. Line 134: *how wit may be made a Jack-a-Lent;* i.e. a mark for every fool to aim at. Falstaff probably felt himself as much degraded as Hilts reproaches Metaphor with being, to whom he says:—

> Thou, that when last thou wert put out of service,
> Travell'dst to Hamstead Heath on an Ash We'nesday,
> Where thou didst stand six weeks the *Jack of Lent*,
> For boys to hurl, three throws a penny, at thee,
> To make thee a purse.
>
> —See Ben Jonson's Tale of a Tub, IV. iii.

189. Line 173: *ignorance itself is* A-PLUMMET *o'er me;* i.e. is *directly* over me: I am at the lowest point of Fortune's wheel; ignorance, at the highest, triumphs over me." "A-plummet" is printed in the F., and in all editions till now, as a substantive with the indefinite article, and, being so taken, has given rise to a variety of unsatisfactory explanations and needless proposed alterations.

190. Lines 178 () 179: Mrs. Ford. *Nay, husband, . . . all's forgiven at last.*—These two speeches were first inserted in the modern text by Theobald, from the Q.

191. Lines 184–186: *Doctors doubt . . . Caius' wife.*—I am not aware that this speech has ever been questioned; but to me it seems to be a corruption of a couple of lines of verse, and that we should arrange and read:—

> Doctors doubt that: if Anne Page be my daughter,
> She is, by this *time*, Doctor Caius' wife.

192. Line 209: *I went to her in* WHITE.—Here the F. has *greene;* and in lines 215 and 221, where Mrs. Page should say *green*, the F. has *white*. Pope made the correction in accordance with what had been plotted in the preceding scenes.

193. Lines 212 () 213: Evans. *Jeshu! Master Slender . . . what shall I do?*—These two speeches were added to the modern text by Pope from the Q.

194. Line 221: *Why, did you* NOT *take her in green?*—The F. omits *not;* the correction was made by Rowe.

195. Lines 239, 240:

> *And this deceit loses the name of craft,*
> *Of disobedience, or unduteous* WILL.

For *will* the F. has *title*, which, considered with the context, seems meaningless. Mr. Collier's MS. Corrector has *guile*, and Dyce, in his second edition, altered to *wile.* The reading I have adopted is suggested in a MS. note by the late Howard Staunton, who supports it with the following quotation from Beaumont and Fletcher's play, Cupid's Revenge, i. 4:—

> The greatest curse the gods lay on our frailties
> Is *will* and disobedience in our issues.

WORDS OCCURRING ONLY IN THE MERRY WIVES OF WINDSOR.

NOTE.—The addition of sub., adj., verb, adv. in brackets immediately after a word indicates that the **word is** used as a substantive, adjective, verb, or adverb only in the passage or passages cited.

The compound words **marked with an asterisk** (*) are printed as two separate words in F. 1.

	Act	Sc.	Line
Accidence	iv.	1	16
Accusative	iv.	1	46
Admittance[1]	ii.	2	236
	iii.	3	61
Adversary[2]	ii.	3	98
Affection[3] (verb)	i.	1	234
All-hallowmas	i.	1	210
Alligant[4]	ii.	2	69
Anthropophaginian	iv.	5	10
Barrow	iii.	5	6
Beam (weaver's)	v.	1	25
Bilberry	v.	5	49
Bilbo	i.	1	166
	iii.	5	114
Birding	iii.	3	247
	iii.	5	46, 135
	iv.	2	8
Birding-pieces	iv.	2	59
Bodikins[5]	ii.	3	46
Body-curer	iii.	1	100
Bowled	iii.	4	91
Brazen-face	iv.	2	141
Breed-bate	i.	4	12
Brewage	iii.	5	33
Brew-house	iii.	3	11
Buck-basket	iii.	3	2
	iii.	5	88, 89, 90
	v.	5	117
Bucking	iii.	3	139
Buck-washing	iii.	3	167
***Bull-baiting**[6]	ii.	2	28
Bully-rook[7]	i.	3	2
	ii.	1	200, 207, 213
Burning-glass	i.	3	75
Cabbage	i.	1	124
Canary	ii.	2	61, 64
***Cane-coloured**[8]	i.	4	23
Careires	i.	1	185
Cashier	i.	3	6
Chooser	iv.	6	11
Clapper-claw	ii.	3	67
Cornuto	iii.	5	72
Counter-gate	iii.	3	85
Cowl-staff	iii.	3	156
Daubery	iv.	2	186
Deanery	iv.	6	31
	v.	3	3
	v.	5	216
Detection	ii.	2	255
Dickens[9]	iii.	2	19
Dis-horn	iv.	4	63
Distillation	iii.	5	116
Divulge	iii.	2	43
Drawling	ii.	1	146
Drumble	iii.	3	157
Edition	ii.	1	80
Egress	ii.	1	227
Embroidery	v.	5	75
Emerald[10] (adj.)	v.	5	74
Emulate (verb)	iii.	3	57
Englished	i.	3	52
Equipage[11]	ii.	2	304
Eryngoes	v.	5	24
Eschewed	v.	5	251
Evitate	v.	5	241
Eyas-musket	iii.	3	22
Eye-wink	ii.	2	72
Fairy-like	iv.	4	57
Fallow (adj.)	i.	1	91
Fap	i.	1	183
Farm-house	ii.	3	91
Fertile-fresh	v.	5	72
Fidelity	iv.	2	160
Fights[12]	ii.	2	142
Finally	i.	1	142
***Fine-baited**	ii.	1	98
*Finger-end	v.	5	88
Flannel	v.	5	173
Flaring	iv.	5	42
*Fool's-head	i.	4	135
Fortune-tell (verb)	iv.	2	106
Fortune-telling	iv.	2	185
Frampold	ii.	2	94
Fritters	v.	5	152
Fullam	i.	3	95
Gainer[13]	ii.	2	149
Geminy	ii.	2	10
Genders[14]	iv.	1	73
Genitive	iv.	1	59, 61
Giantess	ii.	1	81
Ging	iv.	2	123
Glover	i.	4	21
Gnawn	ii.	2	307
Go-between	ii.	2	273
Good-jer[15]	i.	4	129
Gourd	i.	3	95
Grated	ii.	2	7
Heartbreak	v.	3	12
Horse-shoe	iii.	5	125
Idle-headed	iv.	4	36
Instigated	iii.	5	78
Invitation	i.	3	50
Jack-a-Lent	iii.	3	27
	v.	5	136
*Jack-dog[16]	ii.	3	65
	iii.	1	85
***John-ape**	iii.	1	86
Kidney	iii.	5	18
*Kissing-comfits[17]	v.	5	23
Late-walking (sub.)	v.	5	154
Latten	i.	1	164
Laughing-stogs[18]	iii.	1	88
Laundress	iii.	3	157, 164
Laundry	i.	2	5
Lewdsters	v.	3	23
Long-tail	iii.	4	47
Lubberly	v.	5	194
Luce	i.	1	17, 22
Lurch[19]	ii.	2	26
Madrigals	iii.	1	18, 24
Meadow-fairies	v.	5	69
Mill-sixpences	i.	1	158
Moneyed	iv.	4	88
Montant	ii.	3	27
*Mum-budget[20]	v.	2	7, 10
	v.	5	210
Musk	ii.	2	67
Mussel-shell	iv.	5	29
Night-dogs	v.	5	252
***Orphan-heirs**	v.	5	43
Ouphs	iv.	4	49
	v.	5	61
Panderly	iv.	2	123
Paring-knife	i.	4	21
Passant	i.	1	20
Pepper-box	iii.	5	155
Pheezar[21]	i.	3	10
Phlegmatic	i.	4	79
Pipe-wine	iii.	2	91
Playing-day	iv.	1	9
Polecat	iv.	1	29, 30
	iv.	2	195
Posies	iii.	1	20, 26
Post-master	v.	5	199, 212
Precisian[22]	ii.	1	5
Presses[23] (sub.)	iii.	3	226
Pronoun	iv.	1	41, 77
Pullet-sperm	iii.	5	32
Pumpion	iii.	3	43
Rattles (sub.)	iv.	4	51
Regress	ii.	1	227
Resurrection	i.	1	54
Reverse[24]	ii.	3	27
Rut-time	v.	5	16
Salt-butter (adj.)	ii.	2	290
Sawpit	iv.	4	53
Scut	v.	5	21
Seemingly	iv.	6	33
Semicircled	iii.	3	68
Shelvy	iii.	5	16
Ship-tire	iii.	3	60
Shovel-boards	i.	1	159
Shuttle	v.	1	25
Skirted	i.	3	94
Slice	i.	1	134, 135

[1] Used in both passages in special and different senses (for which see foot-notes). In its ordinary sense the word occurs frequently.

[2] Used by Host in the sense of *advocate*.

[3] Evans for *affect*, *love*.

[4] Mrs. Quickly for *elegant* or *eloquent*.

[5] Used as an oath.

[6] Hanmer's conjecture in place of *bold-beating*, the reading of F. 1.

[7] Hyphened in F. 1 in all the four passages in which it occurs, except the first one.

[8] F. 1 reads *caine colour'd*.

[9] In the expression "**what the** dickens."

[10] Used **as a** substantive, Compl. 213.

[11] See note 64. **Used** in its ordinary sense, Sonn. xxxii. 12.

[12] Used in special sense. See note 73.

[13] Occurs in Sonn. lxxxviii. 9.

[14] In grammar.

[15] See note 42.

[16] Not hyphened in F. 1 in second passage, where it occurs alone; in first passage the three words *Jack dog priest* are all hyphened together.

[17] F. 1 has *kissing-comfits*, the hyphen having been, probably, misplaced.

[18] Evans's form of *laughing-stocks*.

[19] Here = "to lurk." It is used in Coriolanus ii. 2. 105 in a different sense.

[20] This word, which is an exclamation, occurs in all three passages, divided into two parts *mum* and *budget*.

[21] One of the Host's words, coined from "pheeze."

[22] This is the reading of F. 1; in our text Johnson's conjecture *physician* is adopted.

[23] = closets.

[24] A term in fencing.

EMENDATIONS ON MERRY WIVES OF WINDSOR.

	Act	Sc.	Line
Slough	iv.	5	69
Socks..........	iii.	5	91
Softly-sprighted	i.	4	25
Soul-curer	iii.	1	100
Spigot.........	i.	3	24
Sprag[1].........	iv.	1	84
Staggering (sub.)	iii.	3	13
Standing-bed..	iv.	5	7
Star-Chamber..	i.	1	2
Stoccadoes	ii.	1	234
Table-sport....	iv.	2	171

[1] = sprack.

	Act	Sc.	Line
Taking[2] (sub.)..	iii.	3	191
Tightly........	i.	3	89
	ii.	3	67
Tinder-box	i.	3	27
Tire-valiant....	iii.	3	60
To-pinch[3]	iv.	4	57
Trial-fire	v.	5	88
Tricking (sub.)	iv.	4	79
Turnips.......	iii.	4	91
Uncape	iii.	3	175
Uncomeliness..	ii.	1	59

[2] Occurs in Lucrece, 431.
[3] See note 151.

	Act	Sc.	Line
Unconfinable..	ii.	2	23
Unduteous	v.	5	240
Unfool	iv.	2	120
Unpitifully	iv.	2	215
Unraked	v.	5	48
Unweighed....	ii.	1	22
Veneys[4]	i.	1	296
Walnut[5].......	iv.	2	172

[4] Another form of venues, which occurs in Love's Lab. Lost, v. 1. 62.
[5] Walnut-shell occurs in Taming of Shrew, iv. 3. 66.

	Act	Sc.	Line
Warrener...	i.	4	28
Washer	i.	2	5
Wee..	i.	4	22
Well-behaved..	ii.	1	58
Well-willers.	i.	1	71
Whelm....	ii.	2	144
*Whiting-time.	iii.	3	140
Whitsters.	iii.	3	14
Wittol..	ii.	2	314
Wittolly.	ii.	2	283
Worts...	i.	1	124
Wringer.....	i.	2	6
Yellowness..	i.	3	111

ORIGINAL EMENDATIONS ADOPTED.

Note
37. i. 4. 47: *une boitine verde.*
38. i. 4. 56: *mets la dans.*
43. i. 4. 134: *You shall have Anne*—[Exeunt Caius and Rugby.]—*fool's-head of your own!*
47. ii. 1. 24: I' TH' *devil's name!*
70. ii. 2. 33: Fal. *Well, go to; away; no more.* (Introduced from Q.)

Note
114. iii. 5. 4-6: *like a barrow of butcher's offal* (transposed)
166. iv. 6. 16: *fat Falstaff* IN 'T.
180. v. 5. 174: *a-plummet.*
195. v. 5. 240: *unduteous* WILL. (Staunton MS.)

ORIGINAL EMENDATIONS SUGGESTED.

6. i. 1. 89-98: Redistribution of dialogue.
49. ii. 1. 51: *What! thou,* ALCE!—*Sir Alice Ford!* (Staunton MS.)
52. ii. 1. 119: THY *gallimaufry.*
111. iii. 4. 76, 77: Redistribution of dialogue.
113. iii. 4. 103: SOON AT *night.*
157. iv. 4. 88: *and* HAS *friends.*
172. v. 2. 4: *my daughter's* ATTIRE; or, *my daughter* IS IN WHITE.
191. v. 5. 184-186: Two lines of verse; the second reading: *She is by this* TIME *Doctor Caius' wife.*

MUCH ADO ABOUT NOTHING.

NOTES AND INTRODUCTION

BY

F. A. MARSHALL.

DRAMATIS PERSONÆ.

DON PEDRO, Prince of Arragon.
DON JOHN, his bastard brother.
CLAUDIO, a young lord of Florence.
BENEDICK, a young lord of Padua.
LEONATO, governor of Messina.
ANTONIO, his brother.
BALTHAZAR, a musician attendant on Don Pedro.
CONRADE, BORACHIO, } followers of Don John.
FRIAR FRANCIS.
DOGBERRY, a constable.
VERGES, a headborough.
OATCAKE, SEACOAL, } two Watchmen.
A Sexton.
A Boy.

HERO, daughter to Leonato.
BEATRICE, niece to Leonato.
MARGARET, URSULA, } gentlewomen attending on Hero.

Messengers, Watch, Attendants, &c.

SCENE—MESSINA.

HISTORIC PERIOD: Some time in the 14th century.[1]

TIME OF ACTION.

Daniel points out that according to Leonato, ii. 1. 374, 375, the time of action of this play should cover nine days, from Monday in one week to Tuesday in the next, with an interval of three days between Acts II. and III.; but, for stage purposes, the action may be supposed to take place on four consecutive days:—

Day 1: Act I. and Act II. Scenes 1 and 2.
Day 2: Act II. Scene 3 and Act III. Scenes 1-3.
Day 3: Act III. Scenes 4 and 5; Act IV.; Act V. Scenes 1, 2, and part of 3.
Day 4: Act V. part of Scene 3 and Scene 4.

[1] See note 2.

MUCH ADO ABOUT NOTHING.

INTRODUCTION.

LITERARY HISTORY.

This play was first printed in the year 1600. There is an entry in the Stationers' Register, under date August 4, without any year given, to the effect that As You Like It, Henry V., Every Man in his Humour, and Much Ado are "To be staied." It is evident that this entry belongs to the year 1600, as it follows that dated May 27, 1600, which entry makes mention of "My Lord Chamberlens mens plaies." A subsequent entry, dated August 23rd, 1600, headed "And. Wise Wm. Aspley" is to register two books, the one called "Muche Adoe about Nothinge," and the other the Second Part of the "History of King Henrie the iiii[th], with the Humors of Sir John Fallstaffe: wrytten by Mr. Shakespeare." Later on, in the same year, the first and only Quarto edition known of this play was printed with the following title-page: "*Much Adoe about Nothing.* As it hath been sundrie times publikely acted by the Right Honourable the Lord Chamberlaine his Servants. Written by William Shakespeare. Printed by V. J. [V. Simmes?] for Andrew Wise and William Aspley, 1600." It is a curious fact that we should have only one Q. edition of this play, which evidently, from the frequent allusions to it in contemporary writers, was a very popular one. It appears that when Andrew Wise assigned his copyrights, June 27th, 1603, "to Mathew Law," Aspley retained Much Ado and II. Henry IV., which were not, apparently, printed till the publication of the First Folio in 1623, of which Aspley was one of the publishers. In his admirable Introduction to the facsimile reprint of the Quarto Mr. Daniel says: "Wise appears to have been in business from 1594 to 1602. During the years 1597–1599 he published the first two Qo. editions of each of the three plays, *Richard II.*, *Richard III.*, and *1st Pt. of Henry IV.*, and, in 1602, a third edition of *Richard III.* On the 25th Jan. 1603 he transferred his right in all three to Matthew Law, by whom nine subsequent editions (2 of *Richard II.*; 3 of *Richard III.*, and 4 of *Henry IV. Pt. I*) were published prior to their appearance in the First Folio. In view of these numerous publications it is a singular but unexplained fact that no second quarto editions of two such popular plays as *Much Ado* and 2 *Henry IV.* should have been issued" (p. iii.). Aspley was in business from 1599 to 1630, "his name appears on the title-page of some copies of the *Sonnets*, 1609, as the bookseller" (*ut supra*). Perhaps he was a less speculative publisher than either Wise or Matthew Law. Mr. Daniel notices the very different circumstances under which the two plays, of which he appears to have retained the copyright, appeared in F. 1. As will be seen, it is highly probable that the Folio edition of this play was printed from the Q.; but it is very doubtful, to say the least, whether the Q. of II. Henry IV. was used at all in the printing of the Folio.

The question as to whether the Folio was printed from a copy of the Quarto only, or with the assistance of another MS. copy of the play, is so ably discussed by Mr. Daniel, in his Introduction to the facsimile Quarto already alluded to, that I must refer those who wish to investigate the question to that work. They will find that he gives nearly all the minute differences between the Quarto and the Folio; and I think that in face of the facts which he brings forward it is quite impossible to maintain that the latter was printed from any independent MS. If we suppose that it was printed from a copy in the possession of the theatre, it is pretty evident that the Quarto must have been printed from the same copy. As is usually the case, the Folio omits some passages which occur in the Quarto; and these possibly may be the result of alterations made, subsequent to the time when the Quarto was printed, either by the actor or by the stage manager, if there was such a person. I must venture to differ from Mr. Daniel most decidedly as to the omissions iii. 2. 33-37; iv. 2. 18-23 being the result of an accident. I believe them to have been "cuts" deliberately made; and, as I have pointed out in note 313, in the latter instance the only fault is that another sentence should have been also omitted; nor can I quite agree with him that some of the minor variations between Q. and F. 1 are the result of caprice or carelessness on the part of the printer. For instance, take the slight variation in i. 1. 314 (in Ff.):

How sweetly *do you* minister to love,

where the Quarto reads *you do:* the transposition of the words *you* and *do* is obviously an advantage to the rhythm of the line, the two *y*'s coming together in *sweetly* and *you* being avoided; and even where the alterations occur in prose passages, with very few exceptions the slight change made in the Folio is a change for the better. I am speaking now only of those alterations which Mr. Daniel has left without any mark against them. In other passages where the Folio differs from the Quarto there is no doubt, in many cases, that the variations are due to the blunders of the printers.

How is it, we may ask, that there was no independent MS. which the printers of the Folio could have consulted? Or are we to suppose that there was one, and that they were too idle or too negligent to do so? I think not. I will venture a conjecture that the state of the case was something like this. The Quarto of 1600 was printed from the theatre MS., which had been copied out in great haste, and in which several mistakes as to the names of the speakers, and not a few omissions in the stage-directions, were to be found. This stage copy, in course of time, the play being a popular one, became ragged and torn, and in parts defective; when, in order to save trouble, a printed copy of the Quarto was used instead of making a new copy of the play in MS.; and on this copy of the Quarto a few, very few, additions were made to the stage-directions; one or two cuts were marked, cuts which, undoubtedly, had been made some time after the production of the play; and, here and there, one or two slight corrections. The fact that the mistakes in the names prefixed to the speeches have been left may, possibly, be taken as a piece of indirect evidence in favour of the supposition that this copy had not been long in use in the theatre; that is to say, it was not long before the publication of the Folio that the theatre MS. was either destroyed, or seriously defaced, or lost. This theory accounts, to a considerable extent, for the close resemblance between the text of the Folio and Quarto, and for the fact of the corrections in the latter being so few. (See notes 308, 319.)

Of internal evidence as to the date of this play there is not much. Some commentators have seen an allusion to the campaign of the Earl of Essex in Ireland in 1599 in the opening scene of this play.[1] In Ben Jonson's Cynthia's Revels, which was acted, in 1600, by the children of Queen Elizabeth's chapel, and published in that year, one of the principal characters is called Amorphus, and he is described in the Induction as "Amorphus, or the Deformed." That the character described by Seacoal as "a vile thief," who "goes up and down like a gentleman" (iii. 3. 134, 135), and "wears a lock" (iii. 3. 183), was in any way suggested by this character I cannot see. Amorphus, in Ben Jonson's comedy, is a gourmet, a great traveller, and a mass of affectation who boasts of the female conquests he has made in his travels. It is worth remarking that, in the Palinode which ends the play (a kind of litany, the chorus of which is

[1] Chalmers, in § XII. of his "Supplemental Apology," in which he treats of the chronology of Shakespeare's dramas, says that we learn from Camden and Moryson "that there were complaints of the badness of the provisions which the contractors furnished to the English army in Ireland;" and he thinks there is an allusion to this in Beatrice's speech, i. 1. 51: "You had *musty victual*, and he hath holp to eat it."

"Good Mercury defend us"), Amorphus mentions several foppish affectations of dress, &c.; but, among these, he does not make any allusion to the wearing of love-locks. The passage (iii. 1. 9-11):

> like to favourites,
> Made proud by princes, that advance their pride
> Against that power that bred it,

is supposed to allude to Essex, who began to lose his head in the latter part of 1599; but Mr. Simpson would refer these words to Cecil. Hunter, in his New Illustrations of Shakespeare, vol. i. pp. 228-244, has a long disquisition in which he seeks to prove that, in the story of Benedick and Beatrice, Shakespeare was referring to the difficulty which was found in inducing William Herbert, the son of the second Earl of Pembroke, to marry. This is the same William Herbert who is supposed by many to be the "W. H." of the Sonnets. Hunter finds, in the attempts to bring Benedick and Beatrice together, a reference to the attempt made by Roland Whyte to bring about a marriage between William Herbert and the niece of the Lord Admiral; an attempt which was perfectly unsuccessful, as it was not till four or five years after that W. H. ultimately married one of the co-heiresses of Gilbert Talbot, Earl of Shrewsbury. Hunter's inferences seem very far-fetched; and the parallel, which he draws between Lord Herbert and Benedick, is not a very close one.

As to the sources whence Shakespeare derived the plot of this play, the device, by means of which Claudio is led to believe in the unchastity of Hero, is said to have been suggested by the story narrated by Dalinda in the fifth book of Ariosto's Orlando Furioso, a translation of which was published by Sir John Harington in 1591. Dalinda is in the service of Genevra, the daughter of the King of Scots. She has for some time been carrying on an intrigue with Polynesso, the Duke of Alban, who, after some time wearying of the maid, falls in love with the mistress. Genevra, however, has given her affections to a knight called Ariodante, and Polynesso, finding his suit with the Princess does not prosper, persuades Dalinda to dress herself up in Genevra's clothes and to receive him at night in Genevra's chamber, to which, it appears, he was in the habit of ascending by means of a ladder of ropes. Ariodante, or Ariodant as he is also called, is placed by the Duke on a spot opposite the window, from which he sees, as he thinks, Genevra receive Polynesso with every sign of affection. Lurcanio, the brother of Ariodante, is also a witness of Genevra's apparent faithlessness. Ariodante drowns himself, and Lurcanio accuses Genevra; but Rinaldo fights with Polynesso and kills him. Genevra's chastity is thus vindicated, and she is married to Ariodante, who turns out not to have been drowned after all. Spenser has made use of a very similar story in the Second Book of the Fairy Queen, C. 4, sts. 17-30; it is the story narrated by Phedon to Sir Guyon. Harington mentions, in the moral appended to the Fifth Book, that the same story had been related with different names by George Turbervile[1] "some few years past."

In the Revels Accounts for 1582 there is a record to the effect that "a Historie of Ariodante and Geneuora was showed before her Majestie on Shrove Tuesdaie at night, enacted by Mr. Mulcaster's children." We do not know if Shakespeare was at all indebted to this old play. It is probable that Shakespeare had read the story of Ariosto in some one of these translations, but he was undoubtedly indebted for the main part of the story of this comedy to a novel of Bandello's, the title of which is the Story of Timbreo of Cardona (see Hazlitt's Shak. Lib. vol. iii. pt. 1, pp. 104-136). This was the 22nd novel in Bandello; a French translation of it is given in the third volume of Belleforest. In it the Signor Scipio Attellano relates how "the Signor Timbreo di Cardona, being with the King Piero of Arragon, in Messina, fell in love with Fenicia Lionata, the daughter of Lionato de' Lionati, a gentleman of Messina, and the various accidents of fortune which happened before he took her for wife." This story is told at no inconsiderable length, and with as little of the spirit of comedy as it is possible to

[1] In his "Tragical Tales, translated by Turbervile in time of his troubles, out of sundry Italians," &c., 1587.

conceive. Timbreo is a knight and a baron, a great favourite with the King Piero, and of very noble family. He falls in love with Fenicia, whose father is of a good family but far from wealthy, and not holding any great position in Messina. Timbreo endeavours at first to make dishonourable love to Fenicia; she however rejects all his letters and presents, so that he at last determines to offer her marriage, which he does by deputy, through a gentleman of Messina, a friend of his; and it is very much insisted upon in the story that Timbreo is making rather a mésalliance. One Signor Girondo has also fallen in love with Fenicia; and, in order to break off the marriage, he devises what seems a very clumsy plot. He sends to Timbreo a young courtier, who declares that a friend of his is in the habit of visiting Fenicia at night; and, on Timbreo giving his solemn promise not to attack the supposed lover nor his informant, the latter agrees to place him where he can see the lover entering the window in Lionato's house. Girondo dresses up one of his servants, carefully perfuming him first, and then the young courtier, the perfumed servant, and another carrying a ladder, come close to where Timbreo is concealed; and he sees the supposed lover enter Lionato's house by a window, at which Fenicia sometimes sits in the daytime; but he does not see her nor any other woman. Considering that this window is in a part of the house which is not inhabited, it must be confessed that Timbreo shows himself even more credulous than Claudio, and much more so than the hero of Ariosto's story, Ariodante. The next day Timbreo sends to Lionato the same friend who had conducted his courtship, with instructions to break off the marriage on the ground that his betrothed has been false to him. Fenicia faints when the accusation is made, and afterwards falls into a swoon, in which she remains for some time, and is given up for dead by her parents and friends. It is only when her mother and aunt are beginning to lay out the body that she recovers; then she is sent away with her sister to her uncle's house some little distance from Messina. An elaborate mock funeral takes place; a coffin supposed to contain the body of Fenicia is followed to the church by a troop of weeping friends, and an epitaph in verse is placed on her tomb by her father. This incident may have suggested to Shakespeare the third scene of the fifth act; but there is no similarity between Claudio's epitaph and that of Lionato's in the story. It is a curious point in the novel, that the conduct of Timbreo is said to have been universally condemned, and his accusations against Fenicia disbelieved, by society in Messina; while in Shakespeare's comedy every one, except her own family and Benedick, seems to believe the charge against her. After Fenicia's supposed death Girondo is tortured with remorse; and Timbreo is much agitated by doubts which should have occurred to him before he ever made such a charge against his betrothed. The most dramatic part of the novel is the portion in which Girondo takes Timbreo to the church, and, before the tomb of Fenicia, confesses his deceit, imploring the man whom he has injured to kill him. Timbreo flings away the dagger which Girondo offers him, pardons his friend, and the two immediately set about making every compensation they can for the wrong that has been done to Fenicia. Lionato forgives them both; and, in answer to Timbreo's offer to do anything in the world, however difficult, in order to prove his repentance, Lionato only asks him that, when he intends to marry he will let him know, and provided he can find Timbreo a lady who shall please him, that he will choose her for his bride. A year passes away, during which time Fenicia completes her seventeenth year. She has grown so much and become so beautiful, that scarcely any one would have recognized her for the Fenicia who was supposed to have died. Lionato now thinks the time has come for him to complete his little plot. He tells Timbreo that he has found him a bride. The latter joyfully accepts the offer. He goes to the country house where are Fenicia and her sister Belfiore, who are living with their uncle and aunt. There Timbreo espouses Fenicia, under the name of Lucilla, without recognizing her. The story at this point is considerably spun out in the novel. The aunt tells Timbreo that Lucilla is

Fenicia. He humbly begs her pardon for the injury he has done her, and re-marries her under her own proper name. Girondo meanwhile has fallen in love with Belfiore, and all ends happily with a grand entertainment given by the king Piero to the two brides. It will be observed that we have nothing, in this story, of the comic element, no trace of Benedick or Beatrice; while the vile device, by which Don John succeeds in slandering Hero and breaking off the marriage with Claudio, much more resembles the corresponding incident in Ariosto than it does in Bandello's novel. But the two coincidences, first, that Timbreo and Claudio both make their proposals of marriage by deputy, and, secondly, that a servant is employed both by Girondo and Don John, are worth noticing. On the other hand, the Bastard is neither a friend of Claudio, nor is he in love with the lady whose character he injures so basely. All the characterization in this comedy is Shakespeare's own; and, as far as we know, all the portion of the story relating to Benedick and Beatrice is his invention.

In his Shakespeare in Germany Cohn seeks to establish some connection between this comedy and two old German plays; the first being the comedy of Vincentius Ladislaus by Duke Henry Julius of Brunswick; the second The Beautiful Phenicia by Jacob Ayrer. As to the first, the sole point of resemblance between Much Ado and Vincentius Ladislaus is that Vincentius is, what Beatrice wrongly calls Benedick, a boastful bragging coward; and, wonderful to relate, we find in the Duke's play that he speaks of his braggart master having had his name written on a bill and fastened up on a door (Shakespeare in Germany, p. xlvi), which Mr. Cohn considers a most happy illustration of Beatrice's speech "He set up his bills here in Messina" (i. 1. 39); as if the Elizabethan drama did not teem with references to this very common custom of setting up bills. Again, in the Duke's comedy the fool is the subject of a trick worthy of the clown of a modern pantomime; and this, forsooth, is supposed to have suggested the charming comedy scenes between Benedick and Beatrice. As to Ayrer's comedy, that is undoubtedly taken from the same source as Much Ado, namely, from Bandello's novel, which it resembles much more closely than does Shakespeare's play. Here again Mr. Cohn's eagle eye detects resemblances which might escape an ordinary observer. Benedick says "Cupid is a good hare-finder, and Vulcan a rare carpenter" (i. 1. 186, 187); and in Ayrer's comedy Cupid says of himself (p. lxxiii):

> Mein Vatter der zornig Vulcanus
> Der hat mir etlich Pfeil geschnit,

which he renders:

> For Vulcan now my wrathful sire
> Has a few arrows forged for me.

That any one could possibly have alluded to Vulcan, as the husband of Venus, without having read Ayrer's comedy, is, of course, incredible. Shakespeare makes Beatrice say (i. 1. 40-42): "my uncle's fool, reading the challenge, subscrib'd for Cupid, and challeng'd him at the bird-bolt." This, says Cohn, "reminds us of the fool . . . who is struck by Cupid's arrow." In Ayrer's play we have among the dramatis personæ Peter, King of Arragon, Tymborus, Count of Golison, Gerando, a knight, Lionito of Tonete and Veracundia, his wife, and their two daughters Phænicia and Belleflura. Venus and Cupid are introduced, as well as John the Clown and Malchus the Swaggerer, two stock characters in all old plays. The servant, who personates the supposed lover, is called Gerwalt. In the trick employed to deceive Tymborus, John the Fool is dressed up as a woman; and Gerwalt, disguised as a nobleman, makes love to John and calls him Phænicia. Shakespeare was wise in not stealing *this* farcical incident at any rate. Any one who reads Ayrer's play, or as much of it as is given by Cohn, will come to the conclusion that it is certainly taken from Bandello's novel of Timbreo and Fenicia; but that, in any other point, it has *no connection whatever* with Shakespeare's comedy. It may be added that the date of Ayrer's work is uncertain. It was first published in 1618; but Cohn supposes that it was first represented about 1595.

Much adoe aboute nothinge is mentioned

in the account of Lord Treasurer Stanhope, 1613, as having been one of fourteen plays presented before the Lady Elizabeth and the Prince Palatine. It is alluded to, in the same account, as *Benedicte and Betteris*. Burton, in his Anatomy of Melancholy (p. 161), says: "And many times those which at the first sight cannot fancy or affect each other, but are harsh and ready to disagree, offended with each other's carriage, [like *Benedict* and *Betteris* in the comedy][1] & in whom they finde many faults, by this living together in a house, conference, kissing; colling, & such like allurements, begin at last to dote insensibly one upon another" (Pt. 3, sec. 2, memb. 2, subs. 4). Leonard Digges, 1640, in his poem "Upon Master William Shakespeare" has:

> let but *Beatrice*
> And *Benedicke* be seene.

In Thomas Heywood's play The Fair Maid of the Exchange there are three passages which seem copied from passages in this play. (See Fresh Allusions to Shakspere, p. 48.) In Robert Armin's Dedication of The Italian Taylor, and his Boy, 1609, we have "pardon I pray you the boldnes of a Begger, who hath been writ downe for an Asse in his time" (*ut supra*, p. 59). This is a manifest allusion to Dogberry, which part Armin is said to have played. Of the two plays founded on Much Ado I have made reference, in the Stage History, to Davenant's Law against Lovers, which Pepys saw on the 18th February, 1661-2. He calls it a good play. It appears to have been published only in the collected edition of Davenant's plays, 1673, and never, separately, in Quarto. We shall have more to say about this play in the Introduction to Measure for Measure. Of the other play, partly founded on this comedy, mentioned in the Stage History, Universal Passion, by the Rev. James Miller (published in 1737), it is not necessary to say anything here.

STAGE HISTORY.

Of the early stage history of this play we know little or nothing. We can only conjecture that in Shakespeare's time it must have been a great favourite, from the many imitations of or allusions to the play, especially to the scenes in which Dogberry figures; but, incredible as it may seem, it appears that this charming and witty comedy remained entirely neglected for more than a hundred years after Shakespeare's death. There is no mention of it in Downes or in Pepys; and the only evidence that it was not forgotten is to be found in the fact that Davenant took the characters of Benedick and Beatrice, and put them into a play called A Law against Lovers, which appears to have been acted on February 18th, 1762, at Lincoln's Inn Fields. That play is partly an adaptation of Measure for Measure. It has very little merit, and I can find no record of it having been acted again. The Biographia Dramatica says that the play met with great success, a statement repeated by Halliwell in his Dictionary of Old Plays; but I cannot find any authority for this statement, nor does Langbaine say anything more in recommendation of Davenant's play than that the language was polished. On February 9th, 1721, at Lincoln's Inn Fields, Genest records "Not acted 30 years[2] Much ado about Nothing;" the names of the actors only are given; the cast probably being Benedick, Ryan; Leonato, Quin; Dogberry, Bullock; Beatrice, Mrs. Cross; Hero, Mrs. Seymour. This revival does not seem to have achieved any particular success, for the play was not repeated during this season, which was a remarkable one; for during it Rich ventured to revive four of Shakespeare's plays, Much Ado, King Lear, Measure for Measure, and Merry Wives, besides Dryden's version of Troilus and Cressida, and Cibber's Richard III. In fact, from this year we may date the commencement of the revival of Shakespeare's popularity on the stage. In September and October of this year no less than seven of Shakespeare's plays were produced, but Much Ado was not one of them. The next occasion on which this play, or rather a portion of it, seems to have been produced, was, in an extremely

[1] The words between brackets were added in the third edition, 1628.

[2] There is no record of any such performance as might be alluded to here in 1691-92, or indeed in any previous year.

disguised form, at Drury Lane, February 28th, 1737. This piece was called Universal Passion, by James Miller, a clergyman; the greater part of it was taken from Much Ado, and the rest, according to Genest, from Molière's Princess of Elis; the two plays being "badly jumbled together." . . . "Miller, in his Prologue, acknowledges his obligations to Shakespeare, but does not give the least hint about Molière—the scene lies at Genoa" (vol. iii. p. 493). Benedick figures as Protheus, "a nobleman of Genoa," = Quin: Claudio as Bellario, "a young Venetian lord," = W. Mills: Leonato as Gratiano, "the Duke of Genoa," = Milward: and Don John as Byron, "bastard-brother to the Duke," = Berry: Conrado becomes Gremio; Beatrice is transformed into Liberia, with songs = Mrs. Clive; Hero into Lucilla = Mrs. Butler: Margaret, into Delia = Mrs. Pritchard. Two characters with the ingenious and elegant names Porco and Asino are introduced, the latter was played by Macklin. Joculo, "the court jester," played by Theophilus Cibber, is another of the Rev. Miller's jokes. From the description that Genest gives of this precious work it does indeed seem to have been contemptible both in plot and dialogue. In the third act, the love between Protheus and Liberia is brought about by the same device as that employed against Benedick and Beatrice. In the fourth act there is the same plan used to cast suspicion on Lucilla (Hero), and there is a pretty close copy of the church scene in Much Ado. Protheus, instead of the Friar, proposes that Lucilla (Hero) shall be reported as dead. In the next act the scene between Benedick and Beatrice, which takes place in the church in Shakespeare's play, takes place in the street; Gratiano speaks some of the Duke's lines in Twelfth Night, and Bellario some from the Two Gentlemen of Verona; in fact this act is a fearful jumble of dialogue and incidents. The piece does not appear to have been much of a success; and there is no record of its repetition. On November 2, 3, 7, 1737, Much Ado was performed at Covent Garden, but no particulars are given as to the cast. On May 25th, 1739, at the same theatre, it was announced as "not acted this season," referring doubtless to the performances in the season of 1737, 1738, mentioned above. On this occasion the cast included Chapman as Benedick, Hallam as Claudio, Hippisley as Dogberry, Mrs. Vincent as Beatrice, and Mrs. Bellamy as Hero. On March 13th, 1746, at Covent Garden, Mrs. Pritchard took her benefit in this play, taking the part of Beatrice: Ryan was Benedick, Hippisley Dogberry, and Mrs. Hale Hero.

At last, in 1748, this much-neglected comedy was revived with some effect; and on the 14th November in that year Garrick played Benedick for the first time, Berry Leonato, Lee Claudio, and Mrs. Pritchard Beatrice. In other respects the cast was not a remarkably strong one, but the Benedick and Beatrice were admirable. Davies says "the excellent acting of Mrs. Pritchard in Beatrice was not inferior to that of Benedick. Every scene between them was a continual struggle for superiority; nor could the spectators determine which was the victor" (Davies' Life of Garrick, vol. i. p. 173); and Murphy says that "when Mrs. Pritchard resigned Beatrice in favour of her daughter, the play lost half its value" (Genest, vol. iv. p. 261). So successful was the comedy that it was acted eight times in succession, and no less than fifteen times during the season 1748–49. Garrick selected the part of Benedick in which to reappear after his marriage, which took place in June, 1749. On September 28th of that year Much Ado was presented at Drury Lane, with Mrs. Pritchard again as Beatrice. Davies says quite wrongly, that this was Garrick's first appearance as Benedick. Such speeches as "here you may see Benedick the married man," of course, went remarkably well on this occasion; but I think Mr. Fitzgerald is right in questioning the good taste of Garrick in perpetually inviting the public to take part in all his little domestic concerns. This was one of the many weaknesses in his character. There is no doubt that Benedick was one of Garrick's favourite parts; I think we might say positively that it was his favourite Shakespearean part, for it was the one which, throughout his managerial career, he never resigned to any other performer as long as he was at the theatre; and it was this character that he chose to impersonate in the memorable pageant at the celebrated Jubilee, 1769, which called forth so much ridicule from Garrick's enemies. The pageant was reproduced, on the stage, at Drury Lane on October 14th of that same year; Miss Pope representing Beatrice. During the last few years of his career as an actor, when his appearances were few and far between, Garrick managed to appear, at least once during each season, in this favourite character of his; and when he returned from abroad, Benedick was the first part he played, November 14th, 1765; that season being remarkable for the fact that foot-lights were then first used on the stage, an improvement which was introduced by Garrick himself. On November 6th, 1775, Mrs. Abington appeared for the first time as Beatrice at Drury Lane, with Garrick as Benedick; and on May 9th, 1776, he played the part for the last time, just a month before he took his final farewell of the stage on June 10th of the same year. Altogether, during his management, Garrick played Benedick over seventy times.

Among the actresses who played Beatrice with Garrick during these numerous performances, after Mrs. Pritchard had retired, were Miss Horton, on April 12th, 1755; Miss Pritchard, the daughter of the great actress, who made her first appearance as Beatrice on November 29th, 1756, but did not succeed in reminding the public of her great mother, except by her beauty, which was considerably in excess of her genius; Miss Macklin, the daughter of the great actor, who chose this part to appear in for her benefit, on March 27th, 1760, but does not seem to have produced any great impression. Of Mrs. Pritchard's successors, Miss Pope, always excepting Mrs. Abington, appears to have been the most successful. She played the part of Beatrice, for the first time, at Garrick's benefit on April 27th, 1762. During the absence of the great actor-manager abroad in 1764, the part of Benedick was assigned to William O'Brien, who appears to have been as great a favourite in society as on the stage, and was said to have given promise of being a worthy successor to Woodward in the heroes of high comedy. But his social success proved his professional ruin; for, having married the Earl of Ilchester's daughter, without the consent of her family, he was obliged to banish himself to America, and abandon his career on the stage. During the time that Garrick remained manager at Drury Lane no one appears to have disputed his right to claim the part of Benedick as his own special property, till, in the season 1772-73, an actor appeared at the Bath Theatre, first anonymously, then under the name of Courteney, and ultimately in his own name, which afterwards became so celebrated in the annals of the stage. This was Henderson; with whom, at the early part of his career at least, Benedick seems to have been rather a favourite character; but he never appears to have acted this part in London till after Garrick's retirement from the stage. He is said to have given an imitation of the Great Little Davy before his face, when Garrick was foolish enough to be offended, though he himself had requested Henderson to give the imitation. Perhaps the great actor was displeased because Henderson, having only seen him in his later years, would naturally, in his imitation, exaggerate that huskiness which had begun to affect the fine quality of Garrick's voice. It was not till February 10th, 1778, that Henderson appeared as Benedick at Drury Lane, when Miss Pope was Beatrice.

This comedy had been revived at Covent Garden for the first time for twenty years on November 8th, 1774, when Lee played Benedick, Hull Leonato, Wroughton Don Pedro, Lewis Claudio, Shuter Dogberry, Quick the Town Clerk, Mrs. Lessingham Hero, and Mrs. Barry Beatrice, her first performance of that character. It does not appear to have been very successful at this theatre, as there is no record of its having been repeated during this season. At the same theatre, on September 15th, 1777, Lewis made his first appearance as Benedick and Quin as Dogberry; Mrs. Bulkley being the Beatrice on that occasion.

We must pass over a great many performances now, and come to December 28th, 1779, when Mrs. Siddons appeared, at Bath, as Beatrice. One cannot imagine that this great tragedienne would shine to advantage in the brilliant comedy of Beatrice. Indeed, it may shock many persons, who look upon Sarah Siddons as the greatest Shakespearean actress that has appeared in the last hundred years, to learn that an analysis of her performances shows that she certainly had no preference for Shakespeare; and she was wise enough, after she had become famous, to abandon comedy altogether.

Mrs. Abington was so fond of the part of Beatrice that she continued to play it when she was above fifty years of age. She is said to have excelled in the sarcasm of the character. It was in the season 1797–98 that she played this part for the last time. Among the other celebrated actresses who shone in this part are included Miss Farren and Mrs. Jordan.

Charles Kemble seems to have been the best successor of Garrick in the character of Benedick. On May 30th, 1803, he made his first appearance as Benedick. He had frequently played Claudio to the Hero of Miss De Camp, who afterwards became Mrs. Charles Kemble. Elliston was also very fond of this part. He played it more in the style of Lewis, slurring over the more serious phases of the character which are developed in act iv.

Of the great representatives of Dogberry we may mention Quick, Moody, Munden, Suett, and Yates. Most of these actors seem to have first graduated in the part of the Town Clerk, who was probably the same as the Sexton, and also figured, perhaps, as one of the Watchmen.

Edmund Kean never seems to have attempted the character of Benedick; perhaps, after having triumphed where Garrick had failed most, in Othello, he did not care to challenge a comparison with his great predecessor in this character. Macready seems to have played Benedick—or "*Benedict*," as he will persist in calling it in his Reminiscences—in 1814, when he was twenty-one. According to his own account, the chief effect of his performance was to procure him the acquaintance of the Twiss family. In the season of 1843 he produced Much Ado at Drury Lane; his own criticism being that he "acted Benedick very well." The cast included Mr. Phelps, Mr. Anderson, Mr. Compton, Mr. Keeley, Mr. Ryder, with Mrs. Nesbitt as Beatrice. In spite of his own eulogy, Macready never seems to have had much success in this character. Phelps produced Much Ado About Nothing on November 17th, 1848. He did not play in the piece himself; the Benedick was Mr. H. Marston, with Miss Cooper as Beatrice. Charles Kean did not produce this comedy till his farewell season at the Princess's Theatre, 1858. This revival was very successful. The manager and his wife, of course, appeared as Benedick and Beatrice respectively; while in Frank Matthews and Meadows we had an opportunity of seeing the best representatives of Dogberry and Verges that the stage has given us, certainly for the last thirty years.

Coming down to our own times, Much Ado About Nothing has always been a great favourite both before and behind the curtain. Those of us, who only confess to middle age, can remember many excellent representations of this comedy. One of the most successful was at the St. James's Theatre, under the management of Miss Herbert, herself a most admirable Beatrice, with the advantage of a scarcely less admirable Benedick, Mr. Walter Lacy, and of Mr. Frank Matthews in his old part of Dogberry. At the Gaiety Theatre, in 1875, when the legitimate drama reigned supreme for some months in the temple of burlesque, this comedy was successfully revived with Miss Ada Cavendish as Beatrice and Mr. Herman Vezin as Benedick. Of the recent production of Much Ado at the Lyceum this is not the place to speak; suffice it to say that it proved one of the most successful of all the Shakespearean revivals; and that the success was well deserved not only by the perfection with which the piece was mounted, but by the excellence of the acting throughout.

CRITICAL REMARKS.

This delightful comedy is the most perfect specimen of what may, perhaps, be called Social Comedy that Shakespeare has left us. The Two Gentlemen of Verona, even if it may be classed in this category, is but a crude effort;

The Merchant of Venice has in it more of the tragic element; As You Like It, delightful comedy as it is, has something of the pastoral in it; The Merry Wives of Windsor deals with the middle class. Twelfth Night is the only comedy of Shakespeare which can compare with this play; but, in Twelfth Night, it must be confessed that the serious element is not so perfectly blended with that of high and low comedy as it is in Much Ado About Nothing. It is scarcely possible to imagine two characters, belonging to high comedy, more exhilarating than Benedick and Beatrice. Their witty encounters are, on the whole, singularly free from the element of coarseness. There is nothing of that vulgar insolence about their repartees which some authors of the past, and most of those who profess to write comedy in these days, mistake for wit. The word-combats between Benedick and Beatrice have none of the brutality of a prize-fight. They are like an exhibition of the most brilliant fencing; however sharply the foil seems to strike the breast of one of the combatants, we know that there will be no blood shed; and, although this play abounds with marks of carelessness in petty details, it is remarkable for the carefulness of its design. With regard to the principal characters, one sees from the first that Benedick and Beatrice feel no real malice against one another. On the contrary, it is plain that at least a strong liking for one another underlies all their chaff and their professions of hostility; so that their ultimate marriage is an event by no means improbable. Side by side with Benedick and Beatrice, both of whom have a strong element of eccentricity about them, Shakespeare has placed in admirable contrast,—all the more admirable because it is not, on the face of it, much of a contrast at all,—the characters of Claudio and Hero. Claudio, with all his reputation for courage, his superficial *bonhomie*, and his high spirits, is far below Benedick in all the nobler qualities of manhood. Benedick may sneer at women, ridicule marriage, laugh at lovers, affect the cynic and woman-hater, but he would be incapable of the atrocious meanness that Claudio shows in disgracing the woman, whom he had pretended to love, in the presence of her father and at the very altar. No; Benedick might laugh at lovers' sighs; but he would have thought twice before he brought tears to a woman's eyes. He would not have cared how much he wounded her vanity with his gibes, but he would not stab her heart by an act of cruelty. Who could be a greater contrast to Beatrice with her reckless tongue, her fearless courage, her energetic self-assertion, than the somewhat timid and pliable Hero? The latter is perfectly ready to resent her wrongs in the silence of an assumed death; whereas Beatrice would have made the whole world ring with the clamour of her indignation, and never rested until she had found the means of active vengeance. Yet there could be no sincerer love than that between these two; and Hero could find no gentler comforter, in the time of her great sorrow, than the bold outspoken cousin who would be content with nothing short of the death of her calumniator.

Mrs. Jameson, in her Characteristics of Women, talks of Beatrice as a spirited portrait of the "fine lady" of Shakespeare's time. Surely there could be nothing more unlike a "fine lady" than Beatrice. The "fine lady" is always a conventional creature of fashion; selfish, an imitator of others, with just courage enough to do what is evil, as long as there are plenty of others in her own rank to keep her company; but far too great a coward to do a good action, because she knew it to be right, though others might think it foolish. In this play Shakespeare, as in many others, displays his utter contempt for the morality of fashionable society. Beatrice is what she is, with her little faults and her great virtues, precisely because she is *not* "a fine lady." Witty, handsome, self-conscious, fond of admiration, she may be; but, when it is a question of right or wrong, she is guided by the dictates of her conscience and by the noble impulses of an uncorrupted heart; she shows qualities which, perhaps from want of practice, are not often to be found in "fine ladies." As has been pointed out in the notes, when Hero is accused Beatrice never hesitates, though she has no positive evidence with which to disprove the accusation of Claudio and the Princes. Her belief in her cousin's loyalty and purity never falters for a moment. Her nature is a higher one than Benedick's; and, at this crisis, it is she that inspires him to take the nobler side, and not his own impulse. It is exactly such a crisis as this, when Claudio brutally repudiates his bride in the church, that tries our natures most severely. It is then that we find out of what stuff we really are made. It is not a time for weighing and balancing evidence; it is not a question even of judgment of character or knowledge of human nature. It is a question our heart must decide; and if through all the meannesses, the deceits, and crimes of the world we have kept our hearts pure, it is then we discover their value. Such an accusation, brought against one whom we have known hitherto to be true and good, may be supported by the strongest evidence, and may be credited by the most highly respectable members of society; but, if we have really that noblest of all virtues, true charity, we shall not believe the accusation; we shall do as Beatrice does, without waiting to sift the evidence we shall reject it with indignation. True, we may sometimes be wrong, but we shall be much oftener right; and even if we do err on the side of generosity, it cannot cost us one-hundredth part of the pain that we must feel—if we are worth anything at all—when we find we have wrongly believed such an accusation. One may be forgiven for suspecting that, in order to bring out more strongly the unconventional character of Beatrice, Shakespeare has intensified the odious character of the thoroughly worldly and conventional Claudio. There is no more bitter satire, in any of his plays, on the thoroughly superficial nature of the "young man of the world." Even his namesake in Measure for Measure is not so odiously mean as Beatrice's "Count Confect." Isabella's brother yields, for a moment, to fearful temptation, when brought face to face with an ignominious death in the very flower of his youth; but the precious Count Sugarplum in this play has no such excuse for his despicable meanness. It is as well to go through the history of Claudio's love affair, as it is told in this play, in order fully to appreciate his character. He falls in love with the daughter of Leonato, Governor of Messina, to whose hand he could scarcely hope to aspire except for the fact that he had distinguished himself in the war, and that he was fortunate enough to have a strong advocate in his patron, Don Pedro, who uses his influence in his favour. Claudio accepts Don Pedro's offer to woo Hero as his deputy; he then believes, on the very slightest evidence, in fact on the mere statement of Don John, of whose character he could scarcely be ignorant—that his friend and patron has betrayed him in the basest manner possible. It would appear, from this instance, that it was in the nature of this wretchedly unstable creature to be quite as unjust to those of his own sex, as he was afterwards to one of the other. Having through the kind offices of the friend, whose honour he had been so prompt to suspect, become affianced to Hero, and the marriage having been, at his own request, appointed at the very earliest date possible, he is told by this same Don John, whose truthfulness he had the strongest reason to suspect from what had already happened, that his love is little better than a strumpet, a fact which Don John is careful to announce with as little delicacy as possible. He goes, without one word of remonstrance, to witness the alleged proof of her profligacy; remarking, with singular generosity, that if he sees any reason to doubt her chastity, he will shame her "in the congregation" where he should wed her on the morrow. He goes, in the company of a man with whom he should not have had any intercourse whatever, namely, Don John, and sees some one making love, apparently, to his betrothed. He does not take any pains to identify the lover; nor does he make the slightest effort to find out whether he is the victim of a deception or not; though surely the probability of Hero's being chaste was, to say the least, quite as great as that of Don John telling the truth under any circumstances. Next morning this fine young gentleman, this excellent count, goes to the church, cries out the supposed shame of his betrothed bride in the presence of her father, her friends, and the priest who is going to marry them, and of the whole congregation; then, leaving her senseless on the floor of the church, he marches off in an outburst of virtuous indignation, supported by his fashionable friends and his princely patron. The only two who have the charity and good sense to believe in the innocence of Hero are the priest and Beatrice, the latter of whom succeeds in converting Benedick to her views. The next thing Claudio hears of his affianced bride is that she is dead, news which he seems to take with the most notable resignation. When he meets the father of the maiden whom his brutal insult is supposed to have killed, he certainly has the decency to refuse to accept a challenge from him; but not a gleam of remorse seems to come over his mind, and the possibility of his having wronged the girl never occurs to him. He is ready to chaff Benedick, though he finds that gentleman in anything but a humour to stand any chaff; still, with a singular want of tact, and brazen shamelessness, he persists in his elaborate attempts at facetiousness, though it is evident that Benedick is perfectly serious in calling him a villain. When the fact is made known to him, immediately afterwards, that he has been the willing victim of the clumsiest trick ever devised, his idea of atoning for the atrocious crime he has committed is the utterance of that beautiful sentiment:

> Sweet Hero! now thy image doth appear
> In the rare semblance that I lov'd it first.
> —v. 1. 259, 260.

He immediately accepts, without a moment's hesitation, the offer made him by Leonato of the hand of his niece; though it strikes one Claudio must have been singularly blinded by self-conceit not to have reflected that, if Hero were really dead, the very last thing that Leonato could possibly have wished was the introduction of such an extremely undesirable relative as Claudio into his family circle. But we must not be unjust towards this noble-hearted young man; his repentance does not stop short here; he announces his intention of mourning that night with Hero; and having borrowed a book of poems, or having procured from somebody of more intelligence than himself some verses, he goes to hang an epitaph on the tomb of his dead love.

> Done to death by slanderous tongues
> Was the Hero that here lies. —v. 3. 3, 4.

It does not seem to have occurred to the young gentleman, when reading these lines out of the scroll, that one of the most slanderous tongues of all was his own. However he fulfils this function of sorrow and repentance, which is neither a very long nor a very laborious one; and the next morning he is quite ready to be married to a woman whom he has never seen. Perhaps Shakespeare was anxious to bring the play to an end, and was loth to dwell more than necessary on the painful part of the story he was telling; otherwise he might have here introduced one redeeming point in the character of Claudio. He might have made him scruple, even at the bidding of the father of the woman he had so grievously wronged, to marry a perfect stranger within so short a time after the death of his betrothed, for which death he could not but have felt himself in part responsible. He might have said, with all respect to Leonato, that he could not transfer his affections, at sight, from Hero to her cousin; and, in this case, one could imagine there might have been a very charming scene between Claudio and the supposed daughter of Antonio, in which he might gently but earnestly urge his respect for the memory of her whom he had so deeply injured as a reason for his not being ready to espouse the young lady, however charming, whom he had never before seen. The exhibition of such a redeeming point in his character might have reconciled Hero to her marriage, and might have afforded her some plausible ground for forgiving the abominable wrong that Claudio had done her. As matters stand in the play, it certainly requires one fully to realize the marvellous loyalty of women to the objects of their love, the happy blindness which they exhibit for the faults, the vices, and even the crimes of the fortunate individual to whom they have given their hearts; it requires one to remember all this before one can bring one's self to believe that, after what she had experienced,

Hero could ever bear to look at Claudio again.

As to the other characters, of Leonato and Antonio there is not much to say. The skilful touches introduced in act v. scene 1 have been pointed out in the notes. Don John is the link between Falconbridge and Edmund (in King Lear) in the Gallery of Bastards that Shakespeare has drawn. He has none of the gay self-assertion which distinguishes Falconbridge, while his villainy is meaner than that of Edmund; he does not defy all laws human and divine with the audacity that the illegitimate son of Gloucester does. He hates mankind and womankind; but it is with the sullen and cowardly hatred of the cur which snaps at your heels, not with the ferocity of the tiger that flies at your throat. When his miserable plot has succeeded but too well, he slinks away from the scene of his triumph. He has neither the shamelessness nor the courage to meet the consequences of his own act. Borachio, whom he uses as a tool, has more manliness than his employer. When detected and brought to bay, he has the generosity to confess freely the evil that he has done, and the humanity, if one may use the word, to make his confession so full and complete as to exonerate the unfortunate victim of the plot to which he has lent himself. One feels that he deserves to win Margaret as his wife, and to live happily with her ever afterwards. Conrade is a less marked character; but we should not fail to notice the clever touch of nature which makes both these men, who are mere dependents of Don John, behave to him all through the play with more familiarity than they would dare to show towards a man of more noble character. They are both ready, more or less, to do his dirty work; but they treat him less as a superior than as an equal.

Side by side with the brilliant high comedy of Benedick and Beatrice we have the admirable low comedy of Dogberry and Verges, and of the various parochial officials of Messina. Many people have been inclined to attach rather too great importance to the scenes in which Dogberry figures. It has always been easier to find a low comedian, who could make the most of the good-natured pompousness and self-conceit of the chief constable, than to find a high comedian who could do full justice to Benedick, or an actress who could combine the sparkling vivacity of Beatrice in the first three acts with the passionate intensity that she shows in the fourth act. The humour of Dogberry is, after all, not of a very original pattern; or rather, perhaps, we should say that what originality the conception had at first has been seriously discounted by the many imitations, which have been perpetrated of this popular character; some of which—notably Mrs. Malaprop in Sheridan's Rivals—have acquired almost as much fame and popularity as the original. Every one must have been struck with the sublime self-conceit of Dogberry; but we have had very much the same trait of character, quite as admirably treated, in Bottom the Weaver. The perfect unconsciousness and good faith, with which Dogberry misapplies words, is found in a lesser degree in other characters in Shakespeare; for instance in Gobbo, Mrs. Quickly, and the Second Gravedigger in Hamlet. But there is a feature in Dogberry's character which does not seem to have been much noticed by critics; and that is the extreme kindliness of heart which coexists with his intense vanity. He has a monstrously high opinion of himself. He is intensely indignant at being called an ass, though his sense of injury is considerably tempered by the unassailable conviction that no one could ever possibly conceive the term to be properly applied in his case; but there is not in him the slightest malice, though such a quality is but too often found combined with vanity. The Head Constable is, in Dogberry's eyes, an official of almost regal importance; but he does not show any inclination to abuse his office by any exhibition of over-severity against offenders whom he may apprehend. He has a kindly sympathy, we had almost said affection, for them; at any rate his pity for them is akin to love. Even when Conrade and Boracchio show their contempt for him in the most insolent manner, he does not seem to cherish any vindictive feeling against them.

He does not try to exaggerate their offence, or to amplify, by any effort of invention, the evidence against them; there is no spice of *odium officiale*, if one may use the expression, or of cruelty in his disposition. A kindlier-hearted constable never carried bill or lanthorn; and, in spite of all his egregious self-conceit and the ridiculous way in which he airs his supposed knowledge, we take leave of him without one harsh thought. We have not the heart to sneer at him; even though he may not be "as pretty a piece of flesh as any in Messina," we doubt if a kindlier-natured piece of humanity existed there.

Delightful as the dialogue of this comedy is, both in its gayest and most serious moods, occasionally, as has been pointed out in the notes, it is disfigured by obscurities, the result of too much aiming after antithesis, or of those jingling alliterations which so often jar upon one's ear in some of the writers of the Elizabethan age. I am not aware that any critic has pointed out previously what certainly strikes me, namely, that Shakespeare was inspired, to some extent, in the prose dialogue of this comedy by hearing or reading the so-called comedies of Lilly. It seems as if he had said to himself: "I have already, in Love's Labour's Lost, ridiculed the affectations of Lilly; I will now try, taking his style to a certain extent as a model, whether by putting these epigrams and antitheses into the mouth of men and women of our own time, instead of into the mouths of classical personages, and by making their wit seem spontaneous and natural, I cannot write a comedy, the prose language of which shall be as finished as that of Lilly without being so tedious." If this was indeed Shakespeare's idea, if he was incited, by the example of Queen Elizabeth's favourite Lilly, to make this effort to show that prose could be rhythmical without being laboured, and that sentences could be balanced without being affected, then we owe a debt of gratitude to the author of Euphues, which perhaps we may, hitherto, not have been inclined to acknowledge. Anyone, who will read Lilly's comedies through carefully, and compare with them some of the prose portions of the dialogue in this comedy, will see that there is more ground for this conjecture of mine than, at first sight, would appear probable.

In spite of all its blemishes, in spite of passages unnecessarily coarse, which we should be glad to see omitted, Much Ado will remain one of the most perfect comedies in our language, and one of the most favourite of all Shakespeare's plays within the theatre and out of it.

Balthasar sings. Sigh no more, ladies, sigh no more,
Men were deceivers ever.—(Act ii. 3. 63, 64.)

MUCH ADO ABOUT NOTHING.

ACT I.

SCENE I. *Before the house of Leonato.*

Enter LEONATO, *with a Messenger and others.*

Leon. I learn in this letter that Don Pedro of Arragon comes this night to Messina.

Mess. He is very near by this:[1] he was not three leagues off when I left him.

Leon. How many gentlemen have you lost in this action?

Mess. But few of any sort,[2] and none of name.

Leon. A victory is twice itself when the achiever brings home full numbers. [*Enter* BEATRICE, HERO, MARGARET, *and Ladies.*] I find here that Don Pedro hath bestowed much honour on a young Florentine called Claudio.

Mess. Much deserv'd on his part, and equally remember'd by Don Pedro. He hath borne himself beyond the promise of his age; doing, in the figure of a lamb, the feats of a lion: [he hath, indeed, better better'd expectation than you must expect of me to tell you how.

[1] *By this*, i.e. by this time. [2] *Sort* = rank.

Leon. He hath an uncle here in Messina will be very much glad of it.

Mess. I have already deliver'd him letters, and there appears much joy in him; even so much, that joy could not show itself modest enough without a badge of bitterness.

Leon. Did he break out into tears?

Mess. In great measure.[3]

Leon. A kind[4] overflow of kindness:[5] there are no faces truer than those that are so wash'd. How much better is it to weep at joy than to joy at weeping!]

Beat. I pray you, is Signior Montanto return'd from the wars or no?

Mess. I know none of that name, lady: there was none such in the army of any sort.[6]

Leon. What[7] is he that you ask for, niece?

Hero. My cousin means Signior Benedick of Padua.

Mess. O, he's return'd; and as pleasant[8] as ever he was.

Beat. [He set up his bills here in Messina,

[3] *In great measure*, i.e. abundantly. [4] *Kind* = natural. [5] *Kindness*, tenderness. [6] *Sort*, rank. [7] *What* = who. [8] *Pleasant*, merry, facetious.

and challeng'd Cupid at the flight; and my uncle's fool, reading the challenge, subscrib'd for Cupid, and challeng'd him at the bird-bolt.]—I pray you, how many hath he kill'd and eaten in these wars? But how many hath he kill'd? for, indeed, I promis'd to eat all of his killing.

Leon. Faith, niece, you tax Signior Benedick too much; but he'll be meet with you,[1] I doubt it not.

Mess. He hath done good service, lady, in these wars.

Beat. You had musty victual,[2] and he hath holp to eat it: he's a very valiant trencher-man; he hath an excellent stomach.

Mess. And a good soldier too, lady.

Beat. And a good soldier to a lady:—but what is he to a lord?

Mess. A lord to a lord, a man to a man; stuff'd with all honourable virtues.

Beat. It is so, indeed; he is no less than a stuff'd man: but for the stuffing,—well, we are all mortal.

Leon. You must not, sir, mistake my niece. There is a kind of merry war betwixt Signior Benedick and her: they never meet but there's a skirmish of wit between them.

Beat. Alas, he gets nothing by that! In our last conflict four of his five wits went halting off, and now is the whole man govern'd with one: so that if he have wit enough to keep himself warm, let him bear it for a difference[3] between himself and his horse; for it is all the wealth that he hath left, to be known a reasonable creature.—Who is his companion now? He hath every month a new sworn brother.

Mess. Is't possible?

Beat. Very easily possible: he wears his faith but as the fashion of his hat; it ever changes with the next block.

Mess. I see, lady, the gentleman is not in your books.

Beat. No; an he were, I would burn my study. But, I pray you, who is his companion? Is there no young squarer[4] now that will make a voyage with him to the devil?

[1] *He'll be meet with you*, he'll be even with you.
[2] *Victual*=victuals.
[3] *Difference*, a term in heraldry.
[4] *Squarer*, quarreller.

Mess. He is most in the company of the right noble Claudio.

Beat. O Lord, he will hang upon him like a disease: he is sooner caught than the pestilence, and the taker runs presently[5] mad. God help the noble Claudio! if he have caught the Benedick, it will cost him a thousand pound ere he be cur'd.

Mess. I will hold friends with you, lady.

Beat. Do, good friend.

Leon. You will never run mad, niece.

Beat. No, not till a hot January.

Mess. Don Pedro is approach'd.

Enter DON PEDRO, DON JOHN, CLAUDIO, BENEDICK, *and* BALTHAZAR.

D. Pedro. Good Signior Leonato, you are come to meet your trouble: the fashion of the world is to avoid cost, and you encounter it.

Leon. Never came trouble to my house in the likeness of your grace: for trouble being gone, comfort should remain; but when you depart from me, sorrow abides, and happiness takes his leave.

D. Pedro. You embrace your charge too willingly.—[*Turning towards Hero*] I think this is your daughter.

Leon. Her mother hath many times told me so.

Bene. Were you in doubt, sir, that you ask'd her?

Leon. Signior Benedick, no; for then were you a child.

D. Pedro. You have it full,[6] Benedick; we may guess by this what you are, being a man.—Truly, the lady fathers herself.[7]—Be happy, lady; for you are like an honourable father.

[*Retires to a little distance with Leonato: they converse apart.*

Bene. If Signior Leonato be her father, she would not have his head on her shoulders for all Messina, as like him as she is.

Beat. I wonder that you will still[8] be talking, Signior Benedick: nobody marks you.

Bene. What, my dear Lady Disdain! are you yet living?

[5] *Presently*, immediately.
[6] *You have it full*, i.e. you are fully answered.
[7] *Fathers herself*, i.e. is so like her father you cannot mistake her parentage.
[8] *Still*, continually.

Beat. Is it possible disdain should die while she hath meet food to feed it as Signior Benedick? Courtesy itself must convert[1] to disdain, if you come in her presence.

Bene. Then is courtesy a turncoat.—But it is certain I am loved of[2] all ladies, only you excepted: and I would I could find in my heart that I had not a hard heart; for, truly, I love none.

Beat. A dear happiness[3] to women: they would else have been troubled with a pernicious suitor. I thank God and my cold blood, I am of your humour for that: I had rather hear my dog bark at a crow than a man swear he loves me.

Bene. God keep your ladyship still in that mind! so some gentleman or other shall scape a predestinate scratched face.

Beat. Scratching could not make it worse, an 't were such a face as yours were.

Bene. Well, you are a rare parrot-teacher.

Beat. A bird of my tongue is better than a beast of yours.

Bene. I would my horse had the speed of your tongue, and so good a continuer. But keep your way, o' God's name; I have done.

Beat. You always end with a jade's trick: I know you of old.

D. Pedro. [*Coming forward with Leonato*] This is the sum of all: Leonato,—Signior Claudio and Signior Benedick,—my dear friend Leonato hath invited you all. I tell him we shall stay here at the least a month; and he heartily prays some occasion may detain us longer: I dare swear he is no hypocrite, but prays from his heart.

Leon. If you swear, my lord, you shall not be forsworn.—[*To Don John*] Let me bid you welcome, my lord: being reconciled to the prince your brother, I owe you all duty.

D. John. I thank you: I am not of many words, but I thank you.

Leon. Please it your grace lead on?

D. Pedro. Your hand, Leonato; we will go together.

[*Exeunt all except Benedick and Claudio.*

Claud. Benedick, didst thou note the daughter of Signior Leonato?

[1] *Convert* = be converted or changed. [2] *Of* = by.
[3] *A dear happiness* = a precious piece of good fortune.

Bene. I noted her not; but I look'd on her.

Claud. Is she not a modest young lady?

Bene. Do you question me, as an honest man should do, for my simple true judgment; or would you have me speak after my custom, as being a professed tyrant[4] to their sex?

Bene. Why, i' faith, methinks she 's too low for a high praise, too brown for a fair praise, and too little for a great praise. —(Act i. 1. 173-175.)

Claud. No; I pray thee speak in sober judgment.

Bene. Why, i' faith, methinks she 's too low for a high praise, too brown for a fair praise, and too little for a great praise: only this commendation I can afford her,—that were she other than she is, she were unhandsome; and being no other but as she is, I do not like her.

Claud. Thou thinkest I am in sport: I pray thee tell me truly how thou likest her.

[4] *Tyrant* = a pitiless censor.

Bene. Would you buy her, that you inquire after her?

Claud. Can the world buy such a jewel?

Bene. Yea, and a case to put it into. But speak you this with a sad[1] brow? or do you play the flouting Jack[2] [to tell us Cupid is a good hare-finder, and Vulcan a rare carpenter]? Come, in what key shall a man take you, to go in[3] the song?

Claud. In mine eye she is the sweetest lady that ever I look'd on.

Bene. I can see yet without spectacles, and I see no such matter: there's her cousin, an she were not possess'd with a fury, exceeds her as much in beauty as the first of May doth the last of December. But I hope you have no intent to turn husband, have you?

Claud. I would scarce trust myself, though I had sworn the contrary, if Hero would be my wife.

Bene. Is't come to this, in faith? Hath not the world one man but he will wear his cap with suspicion?[4] Shall I never see a bachelor of threescore again? Go to, i' faith; and thou wilt needs thrust thy neck into a yoke, wear the print of it, and sigh away Sundays. Look; Don Pedro is returned to seek you.

Re-enter Don Pedro.

D. Pedro. What secret hath held you here, that you followed not to Leonato's?

Bene. I would your grace would constrain me to tell.

D. Pedro. I charge thee on thy allegiance.

Bene. You hear, Count Claudio: I can be secret as a dumb man, I would have you think so; but on my allegiance,—mark you this, on my allegiance.—He is in love. With who?—now that is your grace's part.—Mark how short his answer is;—with Hero, Leonato's short daughter.

Claud. If this were so, so were it utter'd.

Bene. Like the old tale, my lord: "it is not so, nor 't was not so; but indeed, God forbid it should be so."

Claud. If my passion change not shortly, God forbid it should be otherwise.

D. Pedro. Amen, if you love her; for the lady is very well worthy.

Claud. You speak this to fetch me in,[5] my lord.

D. Pedro. By my troth, I speak my thought.

Claud. And, in faith, my lord, I spoke mine.

Bene. And, by my two faiths and troths, my lord, I spoke mine.

Claud. That I love her, I feel.

D. Pedro. That she is worthy, I know.

Bene. That I neither feel how she should be loved, nor how she should be worthy, is the opinion that fire cannot melt out of me: I will die in it at the stake.

D. Pedro. Thou wast ever an obstinate heretic in the despite of beauty.

Claud. And never could maintain his part but in the force of his will.

Bene. That a woman conceived me, I thank her; that she brought me up, I likewise give her most humble thanks: but that I will have a recheat[6] winded in my forehead, or hang my bugle in an invisible baldrick,[7] all women shall pardon me. Because I will not do them the wrong to mistrust any, I will do myself the right to trust none; and the fine[8] is (for the which I may go the finer), I will live a bachelor.

D. Pedro. I shall see thee, ere I die, look pale with love.

Bene. With anger, with sickness, or with hunger, my lord; not with love: [prove that ever I lose more blood with love than I will get again with drinking, pick out mine eyes with a ballad-maker's pen, and hang me up at the door of a brothel-house for the sign of blind Cupid.]

D. Pedro. Well, if ever thou dost fall from this faith, thou wilt prove a notable argument.

Bene. If I do, hang me in a bottle[9] like a cat, and shoot at me; and he that hits me, let him be clapp'd on the shoulder, and call'd Adam.

---

1 *Sad*, serious.
2 *The flouting Jack* = the mocking rascal.
3 *To go in* = to join with you in.
4 *With suspicion*, i.e. with the suspicion of having horns under it.

5 *To fetch me in*, i.e. to draw me into a confession.
6 *Recheat*, a term of the chase; the call sounded on the horn to bring the dogs back.
7 *Baldrick*, a belt, usually worn across the body.
8 *Fine*, conclusion.
9 *A bottle*, i.e. a small wooden barrel.

D. Pedro. Well, as time shall try:
"In time the savage bull doth bear the yoke."

Bene. The savage bull may; but if ever the sensible Benedick bear it, pluck off the bull's horns, and set them in my forehead: and let me be vilely painted; and in such great letters as they write, "Here is good horse to hire," let them signify under my sign, "Here you may see Benedick the married man."

Claud. If this should ever happen, thou wouldst be horn-mad.

D. Pedro. Nay, if Cupid have not spent all his quiver in Venice, thou wilt quake for this shortly.

Bene. I look for an earthquake too, then.

D. Pedro. Well, you will temporize with the hours. In the mean time, good Signior Benedick, repair to Leonato's: commend me to him, and tell him I will not fail him at supper; for indeed he hath made great preparation.

Bene. I have almost matter enough in me for such an embassage; and so I commit you,—

Claud. To the tuition of God: From my house (if I had it),—

D. Pedro. The sixth of July: Your loving friend, Benedick.

Bene. Nay, mock not, mock not. The body of your discourse is sometimes guarded[1] with fragments, and the guards[2] are but slightly basted on neither: ere you flout[3] old ends any further, examine your conscience: and so I leave you. [*Exit.*

Claud. My liege, your highness now may do me good.

D. Pedro. My love is thine to teach: teach it but how,
And thou shalt see how apt it is to learn
Any hard lesson that may do thee good.

Claud. Hath Leonato any son, my lord?

D. Pedro. No child but Hero; she's his only heir.
Dost thou affect her, Claudio?

Claud. O, my lord,
When you went onward on this ended action,[4]
I look'd upon her with a soldier's eye,
That lik'd, but had a rougher task in hand
Than to drive liking to the name of love:
But now I am return'd, and that war-thoughts
Have left their places vacant, in their rooms
Come thronging soft and delicate desires,
All prompting me how fair young Hero is,
Saying, I lik'd her ere I went to wars—

D. Pedro. [*Interrupting*] Thou wilt be like a lover presently,
And tire the hearer with a book[5] of words.

[*Enter* BORACHIO, *who hides and listens.*

If thou dost love fair Hero, cherish it;
And I will break with her[6] and with her father,
And thou shalt have her. Was't not to this end
That thou began'st to twist so fine a story?

Claud. How sweetly do you minister to love,
That know love's grief by his complexion!
But lest my liking might too sudden seem,
I would have salv'd[7] it with a longer treatise.[8]

D. Pedro. What need the bridge much broader than the flood?
The fairest grant is the necessity.
Look, what will serve is fit: 't is once,[9] thou lovest;
And I will fit thee with the remedy.
I know we shall have revelling to-night:
I will assume thy part in some disguise,
And tell fair Hero I am Claudio;
And in her bosom I'll unclasp[10] my heart,
And take her hearing prisoner with the force
And strong encounter of my amorous tale:
Then after to her father will I break;[11]
And the conclusion[12] is, she shall be thine.
In practice let us put it presently. [*Exeunt.*

[SCENE II. *A room in Leonato's house.*

Enter, severally, LEONATO *and* ANTONIO.

Leon. How now, brother! Where is my cousin, your son? hath he provided this music?

Ant. He is very busy about it. But, brother, I can tell you strange news, that you yet dreamt not of.

Leon. Are they good?

[1] *Guarded*, ornamentally trimmed.
[2] *Guards*, ornamental trimmings.
[3] *Flout*, make fun of.
[4] *Went onward*, &c., *i.e.* started on the campaign just brought to a close.

[5] *A book*, *i.e.* a quantity.
[6] *Break with her*, *i.e.* break the subject to her.
[7] *Salv'd*, palliated, excused.
[8] *Treatise*, discourse.
[9] *Once*=once for all.
[10] *Unclasp*, *i.e.* lay bare.
[11] *Break*, *i.e.* break the matter.
[12] *Conclusion*, *i.e.* result.

Ant. As the event stamps them: but they have a good cover; they show well outward. The prince and Count Claudio, walking in a thick-pleached[1] alley in my orchard,[2] were thus much overheard by a man of mine: the prince discovered to Claudio that he loved my niece

D. John. I had rather be a canker in a hedge than a rose in his grace.—(Act I. 3. 28, 29.)

your daughter, and meant to acknowledge it this night in a dance; and if he found her accordant,[3] he meant to take the present time by the top,[4] and instantly break with you of it.

Leon. Hath the fellow any wit that told you this?

Ant. A good sharp fellow: I will send for him; and question him yourself.

Leon. No, no; we will hold it as a dream till it appear itself: but I will acquaint my daughter withal, that she may be the better prepared for an answer, if peradventure this be true. Go you and tell her of it.—[*Exit Antonio.—Antonio's son, with some Musicians, crosses the stage.—To Antonio's son*] Cousin, you know what you have to do.—[*To the leader of the Musicians*] O, I cry you mercy,[5] friend; go you with me, and I will use your skill.—Good cousin, have a care this busy time. [*Exit.*]

SCENE III. *Another room in Leonato's house.*

Enter DON JOHN *and* CONRADE.

Con. What the good-year, my lord! why are you thus out of measure sad?

D. John. There is no measure in the occasion that breeds it, therefore the sadness is without limit.

Con. You should hear reason.

D. John. And when I have heard it, what blessing bringeth it?

Con. If not a present remedy, yet a patient sufferance.

D. John. I wonder that thou, being (as thou say'st thou art) born under Saturn, goest about to apply a moral medicine to a mortifying mischief. I cannot hide what I am: I must be sad when I have cause, and smile at no man's jests; eat when I have stomach, and wait for no man's leisure; sleep when I am drowsy, and tend on[6] no man's business; laugh when I am merry, and claw[7] no man in his humour.

Con. Yea, but you must not make the full show of this till you may do it without controlment. You have of late stood out against your brother, and he hath ta'en you newly into his grace; where it is impossible you should take true root but by the fair weather that you make yourself: it is needful that you frame the season for your own harvest.

D. John. I had rather be a canker[8] in a hedge than a rose in his grace; and it better fits my blood to be disdain'd of all than to

[1] *Thick-pleached*, thickly interwoven.
[2] *Orchard, i.e.* garden.
[3] *Accordant*, of the same kind; favourable to his suit.
[4] *By the top*=by the forelock.
[5] *I cry you mercy*=I ask your pardon.
[6] *Tend on, i.e.* wait on=care for.
[7] *Claw, i.e.* flatter.
[8] *Canker, i.e.* dog-rose.

fashion a carriage to rob love from any: in this, though I cannot be said to be a flattering honest man, it must not be denied but I am a plain-dealing villain. I am trusted with a muzzle, and enfranchis'd with a clog; therefore I have decreed not to sing in my cage. If I had my mouth, I would bite; if I had my liberty, I would do my liking: in the mean time let me be that I am, and seek not to alter me.

Con. Can you make no use of your discontent?

D. John. I make all use of it, for I use it only.[1]—Who comes here?

Enter BORACHIO.

What news, Borachio?

Bora. I came yonder from a great supper: the prince your brother is royally entertained by Leonato; and I can give you intelligence of an intended marriage.

D. John. Will it serve for any model to build mischief on? What is he for a fool[2] that betroths himself to unquietness?

Bora. Marry, it is your brother's right hand.

D. John. Who, the most exquisite Claudio?

Bora. Even he.

D. John. A proper squire! And who—and who—which way looks he?

Bora. Marry, on Hero, the daughter and heir of Leonato.

D. John. A very forward March-chick! How came you to this?

Bora. [Being entertain'd for a perfumer, as I was smoking a musty room, comes me the prince and Claudio, hand in hand, in sad conference:] I whipt me behind the arras; and there heard it agreed upon, that the prince should woo Hero for himself, and having obtain'd her, give her to Count Claudio.

D. John. Come, come, let us thither: this may prove food to my displeasure. That young start-up[3] hath all the glory of my overthrow: if I can cross him any way, I bless myself every way. You are both sure, and will assist me?

Con. To the death, my lord.

D. John. Let us to the great supper: their cheer is the greater that I am subdued. Would the cook were of my mind!—Shall we go prove what 's to be done?

Bora. We 'll wait upon your lordship.

[*Exeunt.*

ACT II.

SCENE I. *A hall in Leonato's house.*

Enter LEONATO, ANTONIO, HERO, BEATRICE, *and others.*

Leon. Was not Count John here at supper?

Ant. I saw him not.

Beat. How tartly that gentleman looks! I never can see him but I am heart-burn'd an hour after.

Hero. He is of a very melancholy disposition.

Beat. He were an excellent man that were made just in the midway between him and Benedick: the one is too like an image, and says nothing; and the other too like my lady's eldest son, evermore tattling.

Leon. Then half Signior Benedick's tongue in Count John's mouth, and half Count John's melancholy in Signior Benedick's face,—

Beat. With a good leg and a good foot, uncle, and money enough in his purse, such a man would win any woman in the world,—if he could get her good-will.

Leon. By my troth, niece, thou wilt never get thee a husband, if thou be so shrewd[4] of thy tongue.

Ant. In faith, she 's too curst.[5]

Beat. Too curst is more than curst: I shall lessen God's sending that way; for it is said, "God sends a curst[5] cow short horns;" but to a cow too curst he sends none.

[1] *Use it only*, i.e. adopt no other disposition.

[2] *What is he for a fool?* i.e. what kind of fool is he?

[3] *Start-up*=upstart.

[4] *Shrewd*, bitter, malicious.

[5] *Curst*=vicious, as used nowadays of animals.

Leon. So, by being too curst, God will send you no horns.

Beat. Just,[1] if he send me no husband; for the which blessing I am at him upon my knees every morning and evening. Lord, I could not endure a husband with a beard on his face: I had rather lie in the woollen.

Leon. You may light on a husband that hath no beard.

Beat. What should I do with him? dress him in my apparel, and make him my waiting-gentlewoman? He that hath a beard is more than a youth; and he that hath no beard is less than a man: and he that is more than a youth is not for me; and he that is less than a man, I am not for him: [therefore I will even take sixpence in earnest of the bear-herd, and lead his apes into hell.

Leon. Well, then, go you into hell?

Beat. No; but to the gate; and there will the devil meet me, like an old cuckold, with horns on his head, and say, "Get you to heaven, Beatrice, get you to heaven; here's no place for you maids:" so deliver I up my apes, and away to Saint Peter: for the heavens![2] he shows me where the bachelors sit, and there live we as merry as the day is long.]

Ant. Well, niece [*to Hero*], I trust you will be ruled by your father.

Beat. Yes, faith; it is my cousin's duty to make courtesy, and say, "Father, as it please you:"—but yet for all that, cousin, let him be a handsome fellow, or else make another courtesy, and say, "Father, as it please me."

Leon. Well, niece, I hope to see you one day fitted with a husband.

Beat. Not till God make men of some other metal than earth. Would it not grieve a woman to be overmaster'd with a piece of valiant dust? to make an account of her life to a clod of wayward marl? No, uncle, I'll none: Adam's sons are my brethren; and, truly, I hold it a sin to match in my kindred.

Leon. Daughter, remember what I told you: if the prince do solicit you in that kind, you know your answer.

Beat. The fault will be in the music, cousin, if you be not wooed in good time: if the prince be too important,[3] tell him there is measure[4] in every thing, and so dance out the answer. For, hear me, Hero:—wooing, wedding, and repenting, is as a Scotch jig, a measure, and a cinque-pace: the first suit is hot and hasty, like a Scotch jig, and full as fantastical; the wedding, mannerly-modest, as a measure,[5] full of state and ancientry;[6] and then comes repentance, and, with his bad legs, falls into the cinque-pace[7] faster and faster, till he sink into his grave.

Leon. Cousin, you apprehend passing shrewdly.[8]

Beat. I have a good eye, uncle; I can see a church by daylight.

Leon. The revellers are entering, brother: make good room.

Enter DON PEDRO, CLAUDIO, BENEDICK, BALTHAZAR, DON JOHN, BORACHIO, MARGARET, URSULA, *and others, masked.*

D. Pedro. Lady, will you walk about with your friend?[9]

Hero. So[10] you walk softly, and look sweetly, and say nothing, I am yours for the walk; and especially when I walk away.

D. Pedro. With me in your company?

Hero. I may say so, when I please.

D. Pedro. And when please you to say so?

Hero. When I like your favour; for God defend[11] the lute should be like the case!

D. Pedro. My visor is Philemon's roof;
within the house is Jove.

Hero. Why, then, your visor should be thatch'd.

D. Pedro. Speak low, if you speak love.
[*Takes her aside.*

[*Balth.* Well, I would you did like me.

Marg. So would not I, for your own sake; for I have many ill qualities.

Balth. Which is one?

Marg. I say my prayers aloud.

1 *Just*=just so. 2 *For the heavens!*=by Heaven!

3 *Important*=importunate.

4 *Measure*, used here in the double sense, first, of moderation; secondly, of a *dance-measure*.

5 *A measure*, i.e. a grave dance.

6 *Ancientry*, old-fashioned manners.

7 *Cinque-pace*, a lively kind of dance.

8 *Passing shrewdly*, with mischievous wit enough.

9 *Friend*=lover. 10 *So*=provided that.

11 *Defend*=forbid.

Balth. I love you the better: the hearers may cry, Amen.

Marg. God match me with a good dancer!

Balth. Amen.

Marg. And God keep him out of my sight when the dance is done!—Answer, clerk.

Balth. No more words: the clerk is answered.

[*They retire among the other maskers.*]

Urs. [*Coming forward*] I know you well enough; you are Signior Antonio.

Ant. At a word, I am not.

Urs. I know you by the waggling of your head.

Ant. To tell you true, I counterfeit him.

Urs. You could never do him so ill-well, unless you were the very man. Here's his dry hand up and down:[1] you are he, you are he.

Ant. At a word,[2] I am not.

Urs. Come, come, do you think I do not know you by your excellent wit? can virtue hide itself? Go to, mum, you are he: graces will appear, and there's an end.

[*They retire to back of stage.*

Beat. [*Coming forward, following* **Benedick**] Will you not tell me who told you so?

Bene. No, you shall pardon me.

Beat. Nor will you not tell me who you are?

Bene. Not now.

Beat. That I was disdainful, and that I had my good wit out of the *Hundred Merry Tales:*—well, this was Signior Benedick that said so.

Bene. What's he?

Beat. I am sure you know him well enough.

Bene. Not I, believe me.

Beat. Did he never make you laugh?

Bene. I pray you, what is he?

Beat. Why, he is the prince's jester: a very dull fool; only his gift is in devising impossible[3] slanders: none but libertines delight in him; and the commendation is not in his wit, but in his villany; for he both pleases men and angers them, and then they laugh at him and beat him. I am sure he is in the fleet:[4] I would he had boarded[5] me.

Bene. When I know the gentleman, I'll tell him what you say.

Beat. Do, do: he'll but break a comparison or two on me; which, peradventure, not mark'd, or not laugh'd at, strikes him into melancholy; and then there's a partridge' wing saved, for the fool will eat no supper that night. [*Music within.*] We must follow the leaders.

Bene. In every good thing.

Beat. Nay, if they lead to any ill, I will leave them at the next turning.

[*Dance. Then exeunt all except Don John, Borachio, and Claudio.*

D. John. Sure my brother is amorous on Hero, and hath withdrawn her father to break with him about it. The ladies follow her, and but one visor remains.

Bora. And that is Claudio: I know him by his bearing.[6]

D. John. Are you not Signior Benedick?

Claud. You know me well; I am he.

D. John. Signior, you are very near[7] my brother in his love: he is enamour'd on Hero; I pray you, dissuade him from her, she is no equal for his birth: you may do the part of an honest man in it.

Claud. How know you he loves her?

D. John. I heard him swear his affection.

Bora. So did I too; and he swore he would marry her to-night.

D. John. Come, let us to the banquet.

[*Exeunt Don John and Borachio.*

Claud. Thus answer I in name of Benedick,
But hear these ill news with the ears of Claudio.
'T is certain so;—the prince wooes for himself.
Friendship is constant in all other things
Save in the office and affairs of love:
Therefore all[8] hearts in love use their own tongues;
Let every eye negotiate for itself,
And trust no agent; for beauty is a witch,
Against whose charms faith melteth into blood.[9]
This is an accident of hourly proof,
Which I mistrusted not. Farewell, therefore, Hero!

Re-enter BENEDICK.

Bene. Count Claudio?

---

[1] *Up and down*, i.e. exactly. [2] *At a word*, i.e. in short.
[3] *Impossible*, i.e. so extravagant that they cannot be believed.
[4] *In the fleet*, i.e. in the company. [5] *Boarded*, accosted.

[6] *Bearing*, i.e. demeanour.
[7] *Near*=intimate with. [8] *All*, i.e. let all.
[9] *Blood*=sensual passion.

Claud. Yea, the same.

Bene. Come, will you go with me?

Claud. Whither?

Bene. Even to the next willow, about your own business, count. What fashion will you wear the garland of? about your neck, like an usurer's chain? or under your arm, like a lieutenant's scarf? You must wear it one way, for the prince hath got your Hero.

Claud. I wish him joy of her.

Bene. Why, that's spoken like an honest drover: so they sell bullocks. But did you think the prince would have served you thus?

Claud. I pray you, leave me.

Bene. Ho! now you strike like the blind man: 't was the boy that stole your meat, and you 'll beat the post.

Claud. If it will not be, I 'll leave you. [*Exit.*

Bene. Alas, poor hurt fowl! now will he creep into sedges.—But, that my Lady Beatrice should know me, and not know me! The prince's fool?—Ha! it may be I go under that title because I am merry.—Yea, but so I am apt to do myself wrong; I am not so reputed; it is the base, though bitter, disposition of Beatrice that puts the world into her person,[1] and so gives me out. Well, I 'll be revenged as I may.

Re-enter DON PEDRO.

D. Pedro. Now, signior, where 's the count? did you see him?

Bene. Troth, my lord, I have played the part of Lady Fame. I found him here as melancholy as a lodge in a warren: I told him, and I think I told him true, that your grace had got the good-will of this young lady; and I offered him my company to a willow-tree, either to make him a garland, as being forsaken, or to bind him up a rod, as being worthy to be whipp'd.

D. Pedro. To be whipp'd! What 's his fault?

Bene. The flat transgression of a school-boy, who, being overjoyed with finding a bird's nest, shows it his companion, and he steals it.

D. Pedro. Wilt thou make a trust a transgression? The transgression is in the stealer.

Bene. Yet it had not been amiss the rod had been made, and the garland too; for the garland he might have worn himself, and the rod he might have bestowed on you, who, as I take it, have stolen his bird's nest.[2]

D. Pedro. I will but teach them[3] to sing, and restore them to the owner.

Bene. If their singing answer your saying, by my faith, you say honestly.

D. Pedro. The Lady Beatrice hath a quarrel to[4] you: the gentleman that danc'd with her told her she is much wrong'd by you.

Bene. O, she misus'd[5] me past the endurance of a block! an oak but with one green leaf on it would have answered her; my very visor began to assume life and scold with her. She told me,—not thinking I had been myself,—that I was the prince's jester, and that I was duller than a great thaw; huddling jest upon jest, with such impossible conveyance,[6] upon me, that I stood like a man at a mark, with a whole army shooting at me. She speaks poniards, and every word stabs: [if her breath were as terrible as her terminations,[7] there were no living near her; she would infect to the north star.] I would not marry her, though she were endowed with all that Adam had left him before he transgressed: she would have made Hercules have turn'd spit, yea, and have cleft his club to make the fire too. Come, talk not of her: you shall find her the infernal Até in good apparel. I would to God some scholar would conjure her; for certainly, while she is here, a man may live as quiet in hell as in a sanctuary; and people sin upon purpose, because they would go thither; so, indeed, all disquiet, horror, and perturbation follow her.

D. Pedro. Look, here she comes.

Bene. Will your grace command me any service to the world's end? I will go on the slightest errand now to the Antipodes that you can devise to send me on; I will fetch you a toothpicker now from the furthest inch of Asia; bring you the length of Prester John's

[1] *Puts the world into her person*, i.e. speaks as if she represented the opinion of the world in general.

[2] *Nest* here includes the nestlings in the nest.

[3] *Them*, i.e. the nestlings.

[4] *Quarrel to*, i.e. a difference with.

[5] *Misus'd* = abused, reviled.

[6] *Impossible conveyance*, incredible dexterity.

[7] *Terminations* = words, expressions.

foot; fetch you a hair off the great Cham's beard; do you any embassage to the Pigmies; —rather than hold three words' conference with this harpy. You have no employment for me?

D. Pedro. None, but to desire your good company.

Re-enter CLAUDIO, BEATRICE, HERO, *and* LEONATO.

Bene. O God, sir, here's a dish I love not: I cannot endure my Lady Tongue. [*Exit.*

D. Pedro. Come, lady, come; you have lost the heart of Signior Benedick.

Beat. Indeed, my lord, he lent it me awhile; and I gave him use[1] for it,—a double heart for his single one: marry, once before he won it of me with false dice, therefore your grace may well say I have lost it.

D. Pedro. You have put him down, lady, you have put him down.

Beat. So I would not he should do me, my lord, lest I should prove the mother of fools. —I have brought Count Claudio, whom you sent me to seek.

D. Pedro. Why, how now, count? wherefore are you sad?

Claud. Not sad, my lord.

D. Pedro. How then? sick?

Claud. Neither, my lord.

Beat. The count is neither sad, nor sick, nor merry, nor well; but civil, count,—civil[2] as an orange, and something of that jealous complexion.

D. Pedro. I' faith, lady, I think your blazon[3] to be true; though, I'll be sworn, if he be so, his conceit is false.—Here, Claudio, I have wooed in thy name, and fair Hero is won: I have broke with her father, and, his good-will obtained, name the day of marriage, and God give thee joy!

Leon. Count, take of me my daughter, and with her my fortunes: his grace hath made the match, and all grace say Amen to it!

Beat. Speak, count, 't is your cue.

Claud. Silence is the perfectest herald of joy: I were but little happy, if I could say how much.—Lady, as you are mine, I am yours: I give away myself for you, and dote upon the exchange.

Beat. Speak, cousin; or, if you cannot, stop his mouth with a kiss, and let not him speak neither.

Bene. Will your grace command me any service to the world's end?—(Act ii. 1. 271, 272.)

D. Pedro. In faith, lady, you have a merry heart.

Beat. Yea, my lord; I thank it, poor fool, it keeps on the windy side[4] of care.—My cousin tells him in his ear that he is in her heart.

Claud. And so she doth, cousin.

Beat. Good Lord, for alliance!—Thus goes

[1] *Use*, interest.

[2] *Civil*, a play on *civil* and *Seville*.

[3] *Blazon* = explanation.

[4] *On the windy side*, i.e. to windward.

every one to the world but I, and I am sunburn'd; I may sit in a corner, and cry Heigh-ho for a husband!

[*D. Pedro.* Lady Beatrice, I will get you one.

Beat. I would rather have one of your father's getting. Hath your grace ne'er a brother like you? Your father got excellent husbands, if a maid could come by them.]

D. Pedro. Will you have me, lady?

Beat. No, my lord, unless I might have another for working-days: your grace is too costly to wear every day. But, I beseech your grace, pardon me: I was born to speak all mirth and no matter.

D. Pedro. Your silence most offends me, and to be merry best becomes you; for, out of question, you were born in a merry hour.

Beat. No, sure, my lord, my mother cried; but then there was a star danc'd, and under that was I born.—Cousins, God give you joy!

Leon. Niece, will you look to those things I told you of?

Beat. I cry you mercy, uncle.—By your grace's pardon. [*Exit.*

D. Pedro. By my troth, a pleasant-spirited lady.

Leon. There 's little of the melancholy element in her, my lord: she is never sad but when she sleeps; and not ever sad then; for I have heard my daughter say, she hath often dream'd of unhappiness, and wak'd herself with laughing.

D. Pedro. She cannot endure to hear tell of a husband.

Leon. O, by no means: she mocks all her wooers out of suit.

D. Pedro. She were[1] an excellent wife for Benedick.

Leon. O Lord, my lord, if they were but a week married, they would talk themselves mad!

D. Pedro. Count Claudio, when mean you to go to church?

Claud. To-morrow, my lord: time goes on crutches till love have all his rites.

Leon. Not till Monday, my dear son, which is hence a just seven-night;[2] and a time too brief, too, to have all things answer my mind.

D. Pedro. Come, you shake the head at so long a breathing:[3] but I warrant thee, Claudio, the time shall not go dully by us. I will, in the interim, undertake one of Hercules' labours; which is, to bring Signior Benedick and the Lady Beatrice into a mountain of affection the one with the other. I would fain have it a match; and I doubt not but to fashion it, if you three will but minister such assistance as I shall give you direction.

Leon. My lord, I am for you, though it cost me ten nights' watchings.

Claud. And I, my lord.

D. Pedro. And you too, gentle Hero?

Hero. I will do any modest office, my lord, to help my cousin to a good husband.

D. Pedro. And Benedick is not the unhopefullest husband that I know. Thus far can I praise him; he is of a noble strain,[4] of approved valour, and confirm'd honesty. I will teach you how to humour your cousin, that she shall fall in love with Benedick;—and I, with your two helps, will so practise on Benedick, that, in despite of his quick wit and his queasy[5] stomach, he shall fall in love with Beatrice. If we can do this, Cupid is no longer an archer: his glory shall be ours, for we are the only love-gods. Go in with me, and I will tell you my drift. [*Exeunt.*

SCENE II. *Before Leonato's house.*

Enter DON JOHN *and* BORACHIO.

D. John. It is so; the Count Claudio shall marry the daughter of Leonato.

Bora. Yea, my lord; but I can cross it.

D. John. Any bar, any cross, any impediment will be medicinable[6] to me: I am sick in displeasure to[7] him; and whatsoever comes athwart his affection[8] ranges evenly with mine. How canst thou cross this marriage?

Bora. Not honestly, my lord; but so covertly that no dishonesty shall appear in me.

D. John. Show me briefly how.

[1] *She were*, *i.e.* she would be.

[2] *A just seven-night*, *i.e.* exactly a week.

[3] *Breathing*, delay.

[4] *Strain*, descent, race.

[5] *Queasy*, squeamish, fastidious.

[6] *Medicinable* = medicinal.

[7] *To* = towards, with.

[8] *Affection*, desire.

Bora. I think I told your lordship, a year since, how much I am in the favour of Margaret, the waiting-gentlewoman to Hero.

D. John. I remember.

Bora. I can, at any unseasonable instant of the night, appoint her to look out at her lady's chamber-window.

D. John. What life is in that, to be the death of this marriage?

Bora. The poison of that lies in you to temper.[1] Go you to the prince your brother; spare not to tell him that he hath wronged his honour in marrying the renowned Claudio (whose estimation[2] do you mightily hold up)

Bora. The poison of that lies in you to temper.—(Act ii. 2. 21, 22.)

to [a contaminated stale,[3]] such a one as Hero.

D. John. What proof shall I make of that?

Bora. Proof enough to misuse[4] the prince, to vex Claudio, to undo Hero, and kill Leonato. Look you for any other issue?

D. John. Only to despite[5] them, I will endeavour any thing.

Bora. Go, then; find me a meet hour to draw Don Pedro and the Count Claudio alone: tell them that you know that Hero loves me; [intend[6] a kind of zeal both to the prince and Claudio, as,—in love of your brother's honour, who hath made this match, and his friend's reputation, who is thus like to be cozen'd with the semblance of a maid,]—that you have discover'd thus. They will scarcely believe this without trial: offer them instances;[7] which shall bear no less likelihood than to see me at her chamber-window; hear me call Margaret, Hero; hear Margaret term me Borachio; and bring them to see this the very night before the intended wedding,—for in the mean time I will so fashion the matter that Hero shall be absent, and there shall appear such seeming truth[8] of Hero's disloyalty, that jealousy shall be call'd assurance, and all the preparation overthrown.

[1] *To temper*, i.e. to mix = to arrange.
[2] *Estimation* = good qualities, titles to esteem.
[3] *Stale* = harlot.
[4] *Misuse* = deceive.
[5] *To despite*, to annoy.
[6] *Intend* = pretend.
[7] *Instances*, proofs.
[8] *Truth* = true proofs.

D. John. Grow this[1] to what adverse issue it can, I will put it in practice. Be cunning in the working this, and thy fee is a thousand ducats.

Bora. Be you constant in the accusation, and my cunning shall not shame me.

D. John. I will presently[2] go learn their day of marriage. [*Exeunt.*

SCENE III. *Leonato's garden. Evening.*

Enter BENEDICK, *a Boy following.*

Bene. Boy,—

Boy. Signior?

Bene. In my chamber-window lies a book: bring it hither to me in the orchard.

Boy. I am here already, sir.

Bene. I know that; but I would have thee hence, and here again. [*Exit Boy.*]—I do much wonder that one man, seeing how much another man is a fool when he dedicates his behaviours to love, will, after he hath laugh'd at such shallow follies in others, become the argument of his own scorn by falling in love: and such a man is Claudio. I have known when there was no music with him but the drum and the fife; and now had he rather hear the tabor and the pipe: I have known when he would have walk'd ten mile a-foot to see a good armour; and now will he lie ten nights awake, carving the fashion of a new doublet. He was wont to speak plain and to the purpose, like an honest man and a soldier; and now he is turn'd orthography;[3] his words are a very fantastical banquet,—just so many strange dishes. May I be so converted, and see with these eyes? I cannot tell; I think not: I will not be sworn but love may transform me to an oyster; but I'll take my oath on it, till he have made an oyster of me, he shall never make me such a fool. One woman is fair,—yet I am well; another is wise,—yet I am well; another virtuous,—yet I am well: but till all graces be in one woman, one woman shall not come in my grace. Rich she shall be, that's certain; wise, or I'll none; virtuous, or I'll never cheapen[4] her; fair, or I'll never look on her; mild, or come not near me; noble, or not I for an angel; of good discourse, an excellent musician, and her hair shall be of what colour it please God.—Ha, the prince and Monsieur Love! I will hide me in the arbour.
[*Withdraws into the arbour.*

Enter DON PEDRO, CLAUDIO, *and* LEONATO, *followed by* BALTHAZAR *carrying a lute.*

D. Pedro. Come, shall we hear this music?
Claud. Yea, my good lord.—How still the evening is,
As hush'd on purpose to grace harmony!
D. Pedro. See you where Benedick hath hid himself?
Claud. O, very well, my lord: [the music ended,
We'll fit the kid-fox[5] with a pennyworth.]
D. Pedro. Come, Balthazar, we'll hear that song again.
Balth. O, good my lord, tax not so bad a voice
To slander music any more than once.
D. Pedro. It is the witness[6] still of excellency
To put a strange face on[7] his own perfection:—
I pray thee, sing, and let me woo[8] no more.
[*Balth.* Because you talk of wooing, I will sing;
Since many a wooer doth commence his suit
To her he thinks not worthy; yet he wooes,
Yet will he swear he loves.
D. Pedro. Nay, pray thee, come;
Or, if thou wilt hold longer argument,
Do it in notes.
Balth. Note this before my notes,—
There's not a note of mine that's worth the noting.
D. Pedro. Why, these are very crotchets that he speaks;
Note notes, forsooth, and nothing![9]]
[*Balthazar plays the air.*

Bene. [*Aside*] Now, "Divine air!" now is his soul ravish'd!—Is it not strange that

---

[1] *Grow this*, i.e. let this grow.
[2] *Presently*, immediately.
[3] *Orthography*, i.e. orthographer; here=one who uses fine words.

[4] *Cheapen* = bid for.
[5] *Kid-fox.* See note 146.
[6] *Witness* = proof.
[7] *To put a strange face on* = to ignore, to seem not to know.
[8] *Woo* = press.
[9] *Nothing*, formerly pronounced *noting*; hence the pun here on *no-thing* and *noting*.

sheeps' guts should hale souls out of men's bodies?—Well, a horn for my money, when all's done.

BALTHAZAR *sings.*

Sigh no more, ladies, sigh no more,
Men were deceivers ever;
One foot in sea, and one on shore;
To one thing constant never:
Then sigh not so,
But let them go,
And be you blithe and bonny;
Converting all your sounds of woe
Into Hey nonny, nonny.

Sing no more ditties, sing no moe
Of dumps[1] so dull and heavy;
The fraud of men was ever so,
Since summer first was leavy.
Then sigh not so, &c.

D. Pedro. By my troth, a good song.

Balth. And an ill singer, my lord.

D. Pedro. Ha, no, no, faith; thou sing'st well enough for a shift.

Bene. [*Aside*] An he had been a dog that should have howl'd thus, they would have hang'd him: and I pray God his bad voice bode no mischief! I had as lief have heard the night-raven, come what plague could have come after it.

D. Pedro. Yea, marry, dost thou hear, Balthazar? I pray thee, get us some excellent music; for to-morrow night we would have it at the Lady Hero's chamber-window.

Balth. The best I can, my lord.

D. Pedro. Do so: farewell. [*Exeunt Balthazar and Musicians.*]—Come hither, Leonato. What was it you told me of to-day,—that your niece Beatrice was in love with Signior Benedick?

Claud. O, ay:—stalk on, stalk on; the fowl sits [*Aside to Pedro.*]—I did never think that lady would have loved any man.

Leon. No, nor I neither; but most wonderful that she should so dote on Signior Benedick, whom she hath in all outward behaviours seemed ever to abhor.

Bene. [*Aside*] Is't possible? Sits the wind in that corner?

Leon. By my troth, my lord, I cannot tell what to think of it; but that she loves him with an enraged affection,—it is past the infinite[2] of thought.

D. Pedro. May be she doth but counterfeit.

Claud. Faith, like enough.

Leon. O God, counterfeit! There was never counterfeit of passion came so near the life of passion as she discovers it.

D. Pedro. Why, what effects of passion shows she?

Claud. [*Aside*] Bait the hook well; this fish will bite.

Leon. What effects, my lord! She will sit you,—you heard my daughter tell you how.

Claud. She did, indeed.

D. Pedro. How, how, I pray you? You amaze me: I would have thought her spirit had been invincible against all assaults of affection.

Leon. I would have sworn it had, my lord; especially against Benedick.

Bene. [*Aside*] I should think this a gull, but that the white-bearded fellow speaks it; knavery cannot, sure, hide himself in such reverence.

Claud. [*Aside*] He hath ta'en the infection: hold it up.[3]

D. Pedro. Hath she made her affection known to Benedick?

Leon. No; and swears she never will: that's her torment.

Claud. 'T is true, indeed; so your daughter says: "Shall I," says she, "that have so oft encounter'd him with scorn, write to him that I love him?"

Leon. This says she now when she is beginning to write to him; for she'll be up twenty times a night; and there will she sit in her smock till she have writ a sheet of paper:—my daughter tells us all.

Claud. Now you talk of a sheet of paper, I remember a pretty jest your daughter told us of.

Leon. O,—when she had writ it, and was reading it over, she found Benedick and Beatrice between the sheet?—

Claud. That.[4]

[1] *Dumps*, low spirits; perhaps here = melancholy subjects.

[2] *Infinite* = infinite reach.

[3] *Hold it up*, keep it up.

[4] *That* = "yes, that is it."

Leon. O, she tore the letter into a thousand halfpence;[1] railed at herself, that she should be so immodest to write to one that she knew would flout her: "I measure him," says she, "by my own spirit; for I should flout him, if he writ to me; yea, though I love him, I should."]

Claud. Then down upon her knees she falls, weeps, sobs, beats her heart, tears her hair, prays, curses;—"O sweet Benedick! God give me patience!"

Leon. She doth indeed; my daughter says so: and the ecstasy[2] hath so much overborne her, that my daughter is sometime afeard she will do a desperate outrage to herself: it is very true.

D. Pedro. It were good that Benedick knew of it by some other, if she will not discover it.

Claud. To what end? He would but make a sport of it, and torment the poor lady worse.

D. Pedro. An he should, it were an alms[3] to hang him. She's an excellent-sweet lady; and, out of all suspicion, she is virtuous.

Claud. And she is exceeding wise.

D. Pedro. In every thing but in loving Benedick.

[*Leon.* O, my lord, wisdom and blood[4] combating in so tender a body, we have ten proofs to one that blood[4] hath the victory. I am sorry for her, as I have just cause, being her uncle and her guardian.

D. Pedro. I would she had bestow'd this dotage[5] on me: I would have daff'd[6] all other respects, and made her half myself.] I pray you, tell Benedick of it, and hear what he will say.

Leon. Were it good, think you?

Claud. Hero thinks surely she will die; for she says she will die, if he love her not; and she will die, ere she make her love known; and she will die, if he woo her, rather than she will bate one breath of her accustom'd crossness.

D. Pedro. She doth well: if she should make tender of her love, 't is very possible he 'll scorn it; for the man, as you know all, hath a contemptible[7] spirit.

Claud. He is a very proper[8] man.

D. Pedro. He hath indeed a good outward happiness.[9]

Claud. 'Fore God, and in my mind, very wise.

D. Pedro. He doth indeed show some sparks that are like wit.

Leon. And I take him to be valiant.

D. Pedro. As Hector, I assure you: [and in the managing of quarrels you may say he is wise; for either he avoids them with great discretion, or undertakes them with a most Christian-like fear.

Leon. If he do fear God, he must necessarily keep the peace: if he break the peace, he ought to enter into a quarrel with fear and trembling.

D. Pedro. And so will he do; for the man doth fear God, howsoever it seems not in him by some large[10] jests he will make.] Well, I am sorry for your niece. Shall we go seek Benedick, and tell him of her love?

Claud. Never tell him, my lord: let her wear it out with good counsel.[11]

Leon. Nay, that 's impossible: she may wear her heart out first.

D. Pedro. Well, we will hear further of it by your daughter: let it cool[12] the while. I love Benedick well; and I could wish he would modestly examine himself, to see how much he is unworthy so good a lady.

Leon. My lord, will you walk? dinner is ready.

Claud. [*Aside*] If he do not dote on her upon this, I will never trust my expectation.

D. Pedro. [*Aside*] Let there be the same net spread for her; and that must your daughter and her gentlewomen carry.[13] The sport will be, when they hold one an opinion of another's dotage,[14] and no such matter:[15] that 's the scene that I would see, which would be merely a dumb-show. Let us send her to call him in to dinner.

[*Exeunt Don Pedro, Claudio, and Leonato.*

[1] *Halfpence* = very small pieces.
[2] *Ecstasy*, madness.
[3] *An alms*, i.e. a charity.
[4] *Blood* = passion.
[5] *Dotage* = doting love.
[6] *Daff'd*, put aside.
[7] *Contemptible* = contemptuous.

[8] *Proper*, handsome.
[9] *Outward happiness* = prepossessing appearance.
[10] *Large* = broad.
[11] *Counsel* = reflection.
[12] *Cool* = rest.
[13] *Carry* = carry out.
[14] *Dotage*, i.e. doting love.
[15] *And no such matter* = when there is no such thing.

BENEDICK *advances from the arbour.*

Bene. This can be no trick: the conference was sadly[1] borne. They have the truth of this from Hero. They seem to pity the lady: it seems her affections have their full bent.[2] Love me! why, it must be requited. I hear how I am censur'd:[3] they say I will bear myself proudly, if I perceive the love come from her; they say too that she will rather die than give any sign of affection.—I did never think to marry:—I must not seem proud:—happy are they that hear their detractions,[4] and can put them to mending. They say the lady is

Beat. Against my will I am sent to bid you come in to dinner.—(Act ii. 3. 256, 257.)

fair,—'t is a truth, I can bear them witness; and virtuous,—'t is so, I cannot reprove[5] it; and wise, but for loving me,—by my troth, it is no addition to her wit;[6] nor no great argument[7] of her folly, for I will be horribly in love with her. I may chance have some odd quirks and remnants of wit broken on me, because I have rail'd so long against marriage: but doth not the appetite alter? a man loves the meat in his youth that he cannot endure in his age. Shall quips and sentences,[8] and these paper-bullets of the brain, awe a man from the career of his humour? no, the world must be peopled. When I said I would die a bachelor, I did not think I should live till I were married.—Here comes Beatrice. By this day, she's a fair lady: I do spy some marks of love in her.

[1] *Sadly*, seriously.

[2] *Have their full bent*, i.e. are at their greatest tension; a metaphor originally taken from archery.

[3] *How I am censur'd*, i.e. what their opinion is of me.

[4] *Their detractions*, i.e. the faults found with them by their detractors.

[5] *Reprove* = disprove, deny.

[6] *Wit*, i.e. wisdom.

[7] *Argument* = proof.

[8] *Sentences*, i.e. sententious sayings.

Enter BEATRICE.

Beat. Against my will I am sent to bid you come in to dinner.

Bene. Fair Beatrice, I thank you for your pains.

Beat. I took no more pains for those thanks than you take pains to thank me: if it had been painful, I would not have come.

Bene. You take pleasure, then, in the message?

Beat. Yea, just so much as you may take upon a knife's point, and choke a daw withal.—You have no stomach, signior: fare you well. [*Exit.*

Bene. Ha! "Against my will I am sent to bid you come in to dinner,"—there's a double meaning in that. "I took no more pains for those thanks than you took pains to thank me,"—that's as much as to say, Any pains that I take for you is as easy as thanks.—If I do not take pity of her, I am a villain; if I do not love her, I am a Jew. I will go get her picture. [*Exit.*

ACT III.

SCENE I. *Leonato's garden.*

Enter HERO, MARGARET, *and* URSULA.

Hero. Good Margaret, run thee to the parlour;
There shalt thou find my cousin Beatrice
Proposing[1] with the prince and Claudio:
Whisper her ear, and tell her, I and Ursula
Walk in the orchard, and our whole discourse
Is all of her; say that thou overheard'st us;
And bid her steal into the pleached[2] bower,
Where honeysuckles, ripen'd by the sun,
Forbid the sun to enter;—like to favourites,
Made proud by princes, that advance their pride
Against that power that bred it:—there will she hide her,
To listen our propose. This is thy office:
Bear thee well in it, and leave us alone.

Marg. I'll make her come, I warrant you, presently. [*Exit.*

Hero. Now, Ursula, when Beatrice doth come,
As we do trace[3] this alley up and down,
Our talk must only be of Benedick.
When I do name him, let it be thy part
To praise him more than ever man did merit:
My talk to thee must be, how Benedick
Is sick in love with Beatrice. [Of this matter
Is little Cupid's crafty arrow made,
That only wounds by hearsay.] Now begin:

Enter BEATRICE, *behind.*

[*Aside*] For look where Beatrice, like a lapwing, runs
Close by the ground, to hear our conference.

Urs. [*Aside*] The pleasant'st angling is to see the fish
Cut with her golden oars the silver stream,
And greedily devour the treacherous bait:
So angle we for Beatrice; who even now
Is couched in the woodbine coverture.
Fear you not my part of the dialogue.

Hero. [*Aside*] Then go we near her, that her ear lose nothing
Of the false sweet bait that we lay for it.—
[*They advance to the bower.*
[*Aloud*] No, truly, Ursula, she is too disdainful;
I know her spirits are as coy and wild
As haggards[4] of the rock.

Urs. But are you sure
That Benedick loves Beatrice so entirely?

Hero. So says the prince and my new-trothèd lord.

Urs. And did they bid you tell her of it, madam?

Hero. They did entreat me to acquaint her of it;
But I persuaded them, if they lov'd Benedick,
To wish[5] him wrestle with affection,
And never to let Beatrice know of it.

[1] *Proposing*, conversing.
[2] *Pleached*, interwoven.
[3] *Trace* = pace.
[4] *Haggards*, i.e. wild, untrained hawks.
[5] *Wish* = bid.

Urs. Why did you so? Doth not the gentleman
Deserve as full[1] as fortunate a bed
As ever Beatrice shall couch upon?
Hero. O god of love! I know he doth deserve
As much as may be yielded to a man:
But nature never fram'd a woman's heart
Of prouder stuff than that of Beatrice;
Disdain and scorn ride sparkling in her eyes,
Misprising[2] what they look on; and her wit
Values itself so highly, that to her
All matter else seems weak: she cannot love,
Nor take no shape nor project of affection,
She is so self-endear'd.[3]
Urs. Sure, I think so;
And therefore certainly it were not good
She knew his love, lest she make sport of it.
Hero. Why, you speak truth. I never yet saw man

Urs. [*Aside*] She's lim'd, I warrant you: we've caught her, madam.—(Act iii. 1. 104.)

How wise, how noble, young, how rarely[4] featur'd,
But she would spell him backward:[5] if fair-fac'd,[6]
She'd swear the gentleman should be her sister;
If black,[7] why, Nature, drawing of an antic,[8]
Made a foul blot; [if tall, a lance ill-headed;
If low,[9] an agate very vilely cut;
If speaking, why, a vane blown with all winds;
If silent, why, a block moved with none.
So turns she every man the wrong side out;
And never gives to truth and virtue that
Which simpleness[10] and merit purchaseth.]
Urs. Sure, sure, such carping is not commendable.
Hero. No, nor to be so odd, and from all fashions,[11]
As Beatrice is, cannot be commendable:
But who dare tell her so? If I should speak,
She'd mock me into air; O, she would laugh me
Out of myself, press me to death with wit!
Therefore let Benedick, like cover'd fire,
Consume away in sighs, waste inwardly:
It were a better death than die with mocks,
Which is as bad as die with tickling.[12]
Urs. Yet tell her of it: hear what she will say.
Hero. No; rather I will go to Benedick,
And counsel him to fight against his passion.
And, truly, I'll devise some honest slanders
To stain my cousin with: one doth not know
How much an ill word may empoison liking.
Urs. O, do not do your cousin such a wrong!
She cannot be so much without true judgment

1 *Full*=fully. 2 *Misprising*, despising.
3 *Self-endear'd*=in love with herself.
4 *How rarely*, however excellently.
5 *Spell him backward*, misconstrue him.
6 *Fair-fac'd*, pale-complexioned.
7 *Black*, dark-complexioned. 8 *An antic*, a buffoon.
9 *Low*, short. 10 *Simpleness*, simplicity.
11 *From all fashions*, i.e. averse to all fashions=unconventional, eccentric.
12 *Tickling*, pronounced as a trisyllable.

(Having so swift[1] and excellent a wit
As she is priz'd[2] to have) as to refuse
So rare a gentleman as Signior Benedick.

Hero. He is the only man of Italy,
Always excepted my dear Claudio.

Urs. I pray you, be not angry with me, madam,
Speaking my fancy: Signior Benedick,
For shape, for bearing, argument,[3] and valour,
Goes foremost in report through Italy.

Hero. Indeed, he hath an excellent good name.

Urs. His excellence did earn it, ere he had it.—
When are you married, madam?

Hero. Why, every day,[4] to-morrow. Come, go in:
I 'll show thee some attires; and have thy counsel
Which is the best to furnish me to-morrow.

Urs. [*Aside*] She's lim'd,[5] I warrant you: we 've caught her, madam.

Hero. [*Aside*] If it prove so, then loving goes by haps:
Some Cupid kills with arrows, some with traps.
[*Exeunt Hero and Ursula.*

BEATRICE *advances.*

Beat. What fire is in mine ears? Can this be true?
Stand I condemn'd for pride and scorn so much?
Contempt, farewell! and maiden pride, adieu!
No glory lives behind the back of such.
And, Benedick, love on; I will requite thee,
Taming my wild heart to thy loving hand:
If thou dost love, my kindness shall incite thee
To bind our loves up in a holy band;
For others say, thou dost deserve, and I
Believe it better than reportingly.[6] [*Exit.*

SCENE II. *A room in Leonato's house.*

Enter DON PEDRO, CLAUDIO, LEONATO, *and* BENEDICK.

D. Pedro. I do but stay till your marriage be consummate,[7] and then go I toward Arragon.

Claud. I 'll bring[8] you thither, my lord, if you 'll vouchsafe[9] me.

D. Pedro. Nay, that would be as great a soil in the new gloss of your marriage, as to show a child his new coat, and forbid him to wear it. I will only be bold with Benedick for his company; for, from the crown of his head to the sole of his foot, he is all mirth: he hath twice or thrice cut Cupid's bow-string, and the little hangman dare not shoot at him; he hath a heart as sound as a bell, and his tongue is the clapper,—for what his heart thinks, his tongue speaks.

Bene. Gallants, I am not as I have been.

Leon. So say I: methinks you are sadder.

Claud. I hope he be in love.

D. Pedro. Hang him, truant! there 's no true drop of blood in him, to be truly touch'd with love: if he be sad, he wants money.

Bene. I have the toothache.

D. Pedro. Draw it.

Bene. Hang it!

Claud. You must hang it first, and draw it afterwards.

D. Pedro. What! sigh for the toothache?

Leon. Where is but a humour or a worm?

Bene. Well, every one can master a grief but he that has it.

Claud. Yet say I he is in love.

D. Pedro. There is no appearance of fancy[10] in him, unless it be a fancy that he hath to strange disguises; as, to be a Dutchman to-day, a Frenchman to-morrow; or in the shape of two countries at once, as, a German from the waist downward, all slops,[11] and a Spaniard from the hip upward, no doublet. Unless he have a fancy to this foolery, as it appears he hath, he is no fool for fancy, as you would have it appear he is.

Claud. If he be not in love with some woman, there is no believing old signs. He brushes his hat o' mornings: what should that bode?

D. Pedro. Hath any man seen him at the barber's?

Claud. No, but the barber's man hath been seen with him; and the old ornament of his cheek hath already stuff'd tennis-balls.

---

1 *Swift*, ready. 2 *Priz'd*, estimated.
3 *Argument*, conversation.
4 *Every day*, i.e. without delay, forthwith.
5 *Lim'd*, i.e. snared with bird-lime.
6 *Reportingly*, on mere report.
7 *Consummate* = consummated.
8 *Bring*, accompany. 9 *Vouchsafe*, allow.
10 *Fancy*, i.e. love; with a play on the double meaning of the word. 11 *Slops*, wide loose breeches.

Leon. Indeed, he looks younger than he did, by the loss of a beard.

D. Pedro. Nay, he rubs himself with civet:[1] can you smell him out by that?

Claud. That 's as much as to say, the sweet youth 's in love.

D. Pedro. The greatest note of it is his melancholy.

[*Claud.* And when was he wont to wash his face?

D. Pedro. Yea, or to paint himself? for the which, I hear what they say of him.]

Claud. Nay, but his jesting spirit, which is now crept into a lute-string, and govern'd by stops.[2]

D. Pedro. Indeed, that tells a heavy tale for him. Conclude, conclude he is in love.

Claud. Nay, but I know who loves him.

D. Pedro. That would I know too: I warrant, one that knows him not.

Claud. Yes, and his ill conditions;[3] and, in despite of all, dies for him.

D. Pedro. She shall be buried—with her face upwards.

Bene. Yet is this no charm for the toothache.—Old signior, walk aside with me: I have studied eight or nine wise words to speak to you, which these hobby-horses must not hear.

[*Exeunt Benedick and Leonato.*

D. Pedro. For my life, to break with him about Beatrice.

Claud. 'T is even so. Hero and Margaret have by this played their parts with Beatrice; and then the two bears will not bite one another when they meet.

Enter Don John.

D. John. My lord and brother, God save you!

D. Pedro. Good den, brother.

D. John. If your leisure serv'd, I would speak with you.

D. Pedro. In private?

D. John. If it please you: yet Count Claudio may hear; for what I would speak of concerns him.

D. Pedro. What 's the matter?

D. John. [*To Claudio*] Means your lordship to be married to-morrow?

D. Pedro. You know he does.

D. John. I know not that, when he knows what I know.

Claud. If there be any impediment, I pray you discover it.

D. John. You may think I love you not: let that appear hereafter, and aim better at me[4] by that I now will manifest. For my brother, I think he holds you well; and in dearness of heart[5] hath holp to effect your ensuing marriage,—surely suit ill spent and labour ill bestowed.

D. Pedro. Why, what 's the matter?

D. John. I came hither to tell you; and, circumstances shorten'd[6]—for she hath been too long a talking of—the lady is disloyal.

Claud. Who, Hero?

D. John. Even she; Leonato's Hero, your Hero, every man's Hero.

Claud. Disloyal!

D. John. The word is too good to paint out[7] her wickedness; I could say she were worse: think you of a worse title, and I will fit her to it. Wonder not till further warrant: go but with me to-night, you shall see her chamber-window enter'd, even the night before her wedding-day: if you love her then, to-morrow wed her; but it would better fit your honour to change your mind.

Claud. May this be so?

D. Pedro. I will not think it.

D. John. If you dare not trust that you see, confess not that you know: if you will follow me, I will show you enough; and when you have seen more, and heard more, proceed accordingly.

Claud. If I see any thing to-night why I should not marry her to-morrow, in the congregation, where I should wed, there will I shame her.

D. Pedro. And, as I wooed for thee to obtain her, I will join with thee to disgrace her.

D. John. I will disparage her no further till you are my witnesses: bear it coldly[8] but till midnight, and let the issue show itself.

D. Pedro. O day untowardly[9] turned!

---

[1] *Civet*, a perfume made from the civet-cat.
[2] *Stops*, the divisions on the finger-board of a lute.
[3] *Conditions*, qualities.

[4] *Aim better at me*, better guess my disposition.
[5] *Dearness of heart*, i.e. affection for you.
[6] *Circumstances shorten'd* = to omit details.
[7] *Out*, thoroughly.
[8] *Bear it coldly*, endure it calmly.
[9] *Untowardly*, unfortunately.

Claud. O mischief strangely thwarting!

D. John. O plague right well prevented!
So will you say when you have seen the sequel.
[*Exeunt.*

SCENE III. *A street.*

Enter DOGBERRY *and* VERGES, SEACOAL, OATCAKE, *and* WATCH.

Dog. Are you good men and true?

Verg. Yea, or else it were pity but they should suffer salvation, body and soul.

Dog. Nay, that were a punishment too good for them, if they should have any allegiance in them, being chosen for the prince's watch.

Verg. Well, give them their charge, neighbour Dogberry.

Dog. First, who think you the most desartless man to be constable?

Verg. Hugh Oatcake, sir, or George Seacoal; for they can write and read.

Dog. Come hither, neighbour Seacoal. God hath bless'd you with a good name: to be a well-favour'd man is the gift of fortune; but to write and read comes by nature.

Sea. Both which, master constable,—

Dog. You have: I knew it would be your answer. Well, for your favour, sir, why, give God thanks, and make no boast of it; and for your writing and reading, let that appear when there is no need of such vanity. You are thought here to be the most senseless and fit man for the constable of the watch; therefore bear you the lantern. This is your charge:—you shall comprehend all vagrom[1] men; you are to bid any man stand, in the prince's name.

Sea. How if 'a will not stand?

Dog. Why, then, take no note of him, but let him go; and presently call the rest of the watch together, and thank God you are rid of a knave.

Verg. If he will not stand when he is bidden, he is none of the prince's subjects.

Dog. True, and they are to meddle with none but the prince's subjects.—You shall also make no noise in the streets; for for the watch to babble and talk is most tolerable and not to be endured.

Sea. We will rather sleep than talk: we know what belongs to a watch.

Dog. Why, you speak like an ancient and most quiet watchman; for I cannot see how sleeping should offend: only, have a care that your bills[2] be not stol'n.—Well, you are to call at all the ale-houses, and bid those that are drunk get them to bed.

Sea. How if they will not?

Dog. Why, then, let them alone till they are sober: if they make you not then the better answer, you may say they are not the men you took them for.

Sea. Well, sir.

Dog. If you meet a thief, you may suspect him, by virtue of your office, to be no true man; and, for such kind of men, the less you meddle or make[3] with them, why, the more is for your honesty.

Sea. If we know him to be a thief, shall we not lay hands on him?

Dog. Truly, by your office, you may; but I think they that touch pitch will be defil'd: the most peaceable way for you, if you do take a thief, is to let him show himself what he is, and steal out of your company.

Verg. You have been always call'd a merciful man, partner.

Dog. Truly, I would not hang a dog by my will, much more a man who hath any honesty in him.

Verg. If you hear a child cry in the night, you must call to the nurse and bid her still it.

Sea. How if the nurse be asleep and will not hear us?

Dog. Why, then, depart in peace, and let the child wake her with crying; for the ewe that will not hear her lamb when it baes will never answer a calf when he bleats.

Verg. 'T is very true.

Dog. This is the end of the charge: [*To Seacoal*]—you, constable, are to present[4] the prince's own person: if you meet the prince in the night, you may stay him.

Verg. Nay, by'r lady, that I think 'a cannot.

Dog. Five shillings to one on't, with any man that knows the statues, he may stay him:

[1] *Vagrom*, i.e. vagrant.

[2] *Bills*, a kind of halberd, carried by watchmen.

[3] *Make*, have to do.

[4] *Present*, i.e. represent.

marry, not without the prince be willing; for, indeed, the watch ought to offend no man; and it is an offence to stay a man against his will.

Verg. By 'r lady, I think it be so.

Dog. Ha, ah-ha! Well, masters, good night: an there be any matter of weight chances, call up me: keep your fellows' counsels and your own; and good night.—Come, neighbour.

Sea. Well, masters, we hear our charge: let us go sit here upon the church-bench till two, and then all to bed.

Dog. One word more, honest neighbours. I pray you, watch about Signior Leonato's door; for the wedding being there to-morrow, there is a great coil[1] to-night. Adieu: be vigitant, I beseech you. [*Exeunt Dogberry and Verges.*

Sea. We charge you, in the prince's name, stand!—(Act iii. 3. 176, 177.)

Bora. [*Without*] What, Conrade!—

Sea. [*Aside*] Peace! stir not.

Bora. [*Without*] Conrade, I say!—

Enter Borachio *and* Conrade.

Con. Here, man; I am at thy elbow.

[*Bora.* Mass, and my elbow itch'd; I thought there would a scab[2] follow.

Con. I will owe thee an answer for that:] and now forward with thy tale.

Bora. Stand thee close, then, under this pent-house, for it drizzles rain; and I will, like a true drunkard, utter all to thee.

Sea. [*Aside*] Some treason, masters: yet stand close.

Bora. Therefore know I have earned of Don John a thousand ducats.

Con. Is it possible that any villany should be so dear?

Bora. Thou shouldst rather ask, if it were possible any villain should be so rich; for when rich villains have need of poor ones, poor ones may make what price they will.

Con. I wonder at it.

Bora. That shows thou art unconfirm'd.[3] [Thou knowest that the fashion of a doublet, or a hat, or a cloak, is nothing to a man.

[1] *Coil*, confusion.

[2] *Scab*, a play on the word; it meant, as well as a sore, a low fellow.

[3] *Unconfirm'd*, i.e. inexperienced.

Con. Yes, it is apparel.

Bora. I mean, the fashion.

Con. Yes, the fashion is the fashion.

Bora. Tush! I may as well say the fool's the fool. But seest thou not what a deformed thief this fashion is?

Sea. [*Aside*] I know that Deformed; 'a has been a vile thief this seven year; 'a goes up and down like a gentleman: I remember his name.

Bora.] Didst thou not hear somebody?

Con. No; 't was the vane on the house.

Bora. [Seest thou not, I say, what a deformed thief this fashion is? how giddily he turns about all the hot bloods[1] between fourteen and five-and-thirty? sometime fashioning them like Pharaoh's soldiers in the reechy[2] painting, sometime like god Bel's priests in the old church window, sometime like the shaven Hercules in the smirch'd[3] worm-eaten tapestry, where his codpiece seems as massy as his club?

Con. All this I see; and I see that the fashion wears out more apparel than the man. But art not thou thyself giddy with the fashion too, that thou hast shifted out of thy tale into telling me of the fashion?

Bora. Not so, neither: but] know that I have to-night wooed Margaret, the Lady Hero's gentlewoman, by the name of Hero: she leans me out at her mistress' chamber-window, bids me a thousand times good night,—I tell this tale vilely:—I should first tell thee how the prince, Claudio, and my master, planted and plac'd and possess'd[4] by my master Don John, saw afar off in the orchard this amiable encounter.

Con. And thought they Margaret was Hero?

Bora. Two of them did, the prince and Claudio; but the devil my master knew she was Margaret; and partly by his oaths, which first possess'd[4] them, partly by the dark night, which did deceive them, but chiefly by my villany, which did confirm any slander that Don John had made, away went Claudio enraged; swore he would meet her, as he was appointed, next morning at the temple, and there, before the whole congregation, shame her with what he saw o'ernight, and send her home again without a husband.

Sea. We charge you, in the prince's name, stand!

Oat. Call up the right master constable. [We have here recovered the most dangerous piece of lechery that ever was known in the commonwealth.

Sea. And one Deformed is one of them: I know him; 'a wears a lock.[5]

Con. Masters, masters,—

Oat. You'll be made bring Deformed forth, I warrant you.]

Con. Masters,—

Sea. Never speak: we charge you let us obey you to go with us.

[*Conrade and Borachio are secured.*

[*Bora.* We are like to prove a goodly commodity, being taken up of these men's bills.

Con. A commodity in question,[6] I warrant you.—Come, we'll obey you.] [*Exeunt.*

[SCENE IV. *A room in Leonato's house.*

Enter HERO, MARGARET, *and* URSULA.

Hero. Good Ursula, wake my cousin Beatrice, and desire her to rise.

Urs. I will, lady.

Hero. And bid her come hither.

Urs. Well. [*Exit.*

Marg. Troth, I think your other rabato[7] were better.

Hero. No, pray thee, good Meg, I'll wear this.

Marg. By my troth, 's[8] not so good; and I warrant your cousin will say so.

Hero. My cousin's a fool, and thou art another: I'll wear none but this.

Marg. I like the new tire within excellently, if the hair were a thought[9] browner; and your gown's a most rare fashion, i' faith. I saw the Duchess of Milan's gown that they praise so.

Hero. O, that exceeds, they say.

Marg. By my troth, 's[8] but a night-gown[10] in

---

[1] *Bloods*, *i.e.* young fellows.

[2] *Reechy*, blackened with smoke.

[3] *Smirch'd*, soiled.

[4] *Possess'd*, influenced.

[5] *A lock*, *i.e.* a love-lock. See note 229.

[6] *In question*, *i.e.* under trial judicially, or perhaps in custody.

[7] *Rabato*, a kind of ruff for the neck.

[8] *'s*—it is.

[9] *A thought*, *i.e.* a little: as we should say, a shade browner.

[10] *Night-gown*, *i.e.* dressing-gown.

respect of yours,—cloth-o'-gold, and cuts,[1] and lac'd with silver, set with pearls down sleeves, side sleeves,[2] and skirts round underborne[3] with a bluish tinsel: but for a fine, quaint, graceful, and excellent fashion, yours is worth ten on't.

Hero. God give me joy to wear it! for my heart is exceeding heavy.

Marg. 'T will be heavier soon by the weight of a man.

Hero. Fie upon thee! art not asham'd?

Marg. Of what, lady? of speaking honourably? Is not marriage honourable in a beggar? Is not your lord honourable without marriage? I think you would have me say, "saving your reverence, a husband:" an bad thinking do not wrest true speaking, I'll offend nobody: is there any harm in "the heavier for a husband?" None, I think, an it be the right husband and the right wife: otherwise 't is light, and not heavy: ask my Lady Beatrice else; here she comes.

Enter BEATRICE.

Hero. Good morrow, coz.

Beat. Good morrow, sweet Hero.

Hero. Why, how now! do you speak in the sick tune?

Beat. I am out of all other tune, methinks.

Marg. Clap's into *Light o' love;* that goes without a burden: do you sing it, and I'll dance it.

Beat. Ye *Light o' love* with your heels!—then, if your husband has stables enough, you'll see he shall lack no barns.[4]

Marg. O illegitimate construction! I scorn that with my heels.

Beat. 'T is almost five o'clock, cousin; 't is time you were ready.—By my troth, I am exceeding ill:—heigh-ho!

Marg. For a hawk, a horse, or a husband?

Beat. For the letter that begins them all, H.[5]

Marg. Well, an you be not turn'd Turk, there's no more sailing by the star.

Beat. What means the fool, trow?[6]

Marg. Nothing I; but God send every one their heart's desire!

Hero. These gloves the count sent me; they are an excellent perfume.

Beat. I am stuff'd, cousin; I cannot smell.

Marg. A maid, and stuff'd! there's goodly catching of cold.

Beat. O, God help me! God help me! how long have you profess'd apprehension?[7]

Marg. Ever since you left it. Doth not my wit become me rarely?

Beat. It is not seen enough; you should wear it in your cap.—By my troth, I am sick.

Marg. Get you some of this distill'd Carduus Benedictus,[8] and lay it to your heart: it is the only thing for a qualm.

Hero. There thou prick'st her with a thistle.

Beat. Benedictus! why Benedictus? you have some moral[9] in this Benedictus.

Marg. Moral! no, by my troth, I have no moral meaning; I meant, plain holy-thistle. You may think perchance that I think you are in love: nay, by'r lady, I am not such a fool to think what I list; nor I list not to think what I can; nor, indeed, I cannot think, if I would think my heart out of thinking, that you are in love, or that you will be in love, or that you can be in love. Yet Benedick was such another, and now is he become a man: he swore he would never marry; and yet now, in despite of his heart, he eats his meat without grudging: and how you may be converted, I know not; but methinks you look with your eyes as other women do.

Beat. What pace is this that thy tongue keeps?

Marg. Not a false gallop.

Re-enter URSULA.

Urs. Madam, withdraw: the prince, the count, Signior Benedick, Don John, and all the gallants of the town, are come to fetch you to church.

Hero. Help to dress me, good coz, good Meg, good Ursula. [*Exeunt.*]

---

[1] *Cuts*, shaped edges.
[2] *Side sleeves*, hanging sleeves.
[3] *Underborne*, trimmed.
[4] *Barns*, a pun upon *barns* and *bairns* (children).
[5] *H*, i.e. ache, which was formerly pronounced *aiche*.
[6] *Trow*, i.e. trow ye? = think ye?
[7] *Profess'd apprehension* = set up as a wit.
[8] *Carduus Benedictus*, the holy thistle; a plant supposed to be a cure for all diseases, including the plague.
[9] *Moral* = hidden meaning.

[SCENE V. *Another room in Leonato's house.*

Enter LEONATO, *with* DOGBERRY *and* VERGES.

Leon. What would you with me, honest neighbour?

Dog. Marry, sir, I would have some confidence with you that decerns[1] you nearly.

Leon. Brief, I pray you; for you see it is a busy time with me.

Dog. Marry, this it is, sir,—

Verg. Yes, in truth it is, sir.

Leon. What is it, my good friends?

Dog. Goodman Verges, sir, speaks a little off the matter:[2] an old man, sir, and his wits

Dog. Goodman Verges, sir, speaks a little off the matter: an old man, sir, and his wits are not so blunt as, God help, I would desire they were.—(Act iii. 5. 10-13.)

are not so blunt as, God help, I would desire they were; but, in faith, honest as the skin between his brows.

Verg. Yes, I thank God I am as honest as any man living that is an old man and no honester than I.

Dog. Comparisons are odorous: *palabras*, neighbour Verges.

Leon. Neighbours, you are tedious.

Dog. It pleases your worship to say so, but we are the poor duke's officers; but truly, for mine own part, if I were as tedious as a king, I could find in my heart to bestow it all of your worship.

Leon. All thy tediousness on me, ha!

Dog. Yea, an 't were a thousand pound more than 't is; for I hear as good exclamation on your worship as of any man in the city; and though I be but a poor man, I am glad to hear it.

Verg. And so am I.

Leon. I would fain know what you have to say.

Verg. Marry, sir, our watch to-night,[3] excepting[4] your worship's presence, have ta'en a

[1] *Decerns*, a blunder for *concerns*.

[2] *Off the matter*, i.e. away from the subject.

[3] *To-night*, i.e. last night.

[4] *Excepting*, a blunder for *saving*.

couple of as arrant knaves as any in Messina.

Dog. A good old man, sir; he will be talking: as they say, When the age is in, the wit is out: God help us! it is a world to see!—Well said, i'faith, neighbour Verges:—well, God's a good man; an two men ride of a horse, one must ride behind.—An honest soul, i'faith, sir; by my troth, he is, as ever broke bread: but God is to be worshipp'd: all men are not alike,—alas, good neighbour!

Leon. Indeed, neighbour, he comes too short of you.

Dog. Gifts that God gives.

Leon. I must leave you.

Dog. One word, sir: our watch, sir, have indeed comprehended two auspicious persons, and we would have them this morning examined before your worship.

Leon. Take their examination yourself, and bring it me: I am now in great haste, as it may appear unto you.

Dog. It shall be suffigance.

Leon. Drink some wine ere you go: fare you well.

Enter a Messenger.

Mess. My lord, they stay for you to give your daughter to her husband.

Leon. I 'll wait upon them: I am ready.

[*Exeunt Leonato and Messenger.*

Dog. Go, good partner, go, get you to Francis Seacoal; bid him bring his pen and inkhorn to the gaol: we are now to examine those men.

Verg. And we must do it wisely.

Dog. We will spare for no wit, I warrant you; here 's that [*Touching his forehead*] shall drive some of them to a non-come:[1] only get the learned writer to set down our excommunication, and meet me at the gaol. [*Exeunt.*]

ACT IV.

Scene I. *The Inside of a Church.*

Enter Don Pedro, Don John, Leonato, Friar Francis, Claudio, Benedick, Hero, Beatrice, *and Attendants.*

Leon. Come, Friar Francis, be brief; only to the plain form of marriage, and you shall recount their particular duties afterwards.

F. Fran. You come hither, my lord, to marry this lady?

Claud. No.

Leon. To be married to her:—friar, you come to marry her.

F. Fran. Lady, you come hither to be married to this count?

Hero. I do.

F. Fran. If either of you know any inward impediment why you should not be conjoined, I charge you, on your souls, to utter it.

Claud. Know you any, Hero?

Hero. None, my lord.

F. Fran. Know you any, count?

Leon. I dare make his answer,—none.

Claud. O, what men dare do! what men may do! what men daily do, not knowing what they do!

Bene. How now! interjections? [Why, then, some be of laughing, as, Ha, ha, he!]

Claud. Stand thee by, friar.—Father, by your leave:
Will you with free and unconstrained soul
Give me this maid, your daughter?

Leon. As freely, son, as God did give her me.

Claud. And what have I to give you back, whose worth
May counterpoise this rich and precious gift?

D. Pedro. Nothing, unless you render[2] her again.

Claud. Sweet prince, you learn[3] me noble thankfulness.—
There, Leonato, take her back again:
Give not this rotten orange to your friend;
She 's but the sign and semblance of her honour.—
Behold how like a maid she blushes here!
O, what authority and show of truth

[1] *To a non-come*, *i.e.* to be "non compos mentis" = (drive them) out of their wits; or a blunder for *non-plus*.
[2] *Render*, give back. [3] *Learn*=teach.

Can cunning sin cover itself withal!
[Comes not that blood[1] as modest evidence
To witness simple virtue? Would you not swear,
All you that see her, that she were a maid,
By these exterior shows? But she is none:
She knows the heat of a luxurious[2] bed;]
Her blush is guiltiness, not modesty.

Leon. What do you mean, my lord?

Claud. Not to be married, not to knit my soul
To an approved[3] wanton.

Leon. Dear my lord—
[*He pauses from emotion*] If you, in your own proof,[4]
Have vanquish'd the resistance of her youth,
[And made defeat of her virginity,—]

Claud. [I know what you would say: if I have known her,
You 'll say she did embrace me as a husband,
And so extenuate the 'forehand sin:]
No, Leonato,
I never tempted her with word too large;[5]
But, as a brother to his sister, show'd
Bashful sincerity and comely love.

Hero. And seem'd I ever otherwise to you?

Claud. Out on thy seeming! I will write against it:
You seem to me as Dian in her orb,
As chaste as is the bud ere it be blown;
But you are more intemperate in your blood
Than Venus, [or those pamper'd animals
That rage in savage sensuality.]

Hero. Is my lord well, that he doth speak so wide?[6]

Claud. Sweet prince, why speak not you?

D. Pedro. What should I speak?
I stand dishonour'd, that have gone about
To link my dear friend to a common stale.[7]

Leon. Are these things spoken? or do I but dream?

D. John. Sir, they are spoken, and these things are true.

Bene. This looks not like a nuptial.

Hero. True!—O God!

Claud. Leonato, stand I here?
Is this the prince? is this the prince's brother?
Is this face Hero's? are our eyes our own?

Leon. All this is so: but what of this, my lord?

Claud. Let me but move one question to your daughter;
And, by that fatherly and kindly[8] power
That you have in her, bid her answer truly.

Leon. I charge thee do so, as thou art my child.

Hero. O, God defend me! how am I beset!—
What kind of catechising call you this?

Claud. To make you answer truly to your name.

Hero. Is it not Hero? Who can blot that name
With any just reproach?

Claud. Marry, that can Hero;
Hero itself can blot out Hero's virtue.
What man was he talk'd with you yesternight
Out at your window betwixt twelve and one?
Now, if you are a maid, answer to this.

Hero. I talk'd with no man at that hour, my lord.

D. Pedro. Why, then are you no maiden.—Leonato,
I 'm sorry you must hear: upon mine honour,
Myself, my brother, and this grieved count
Did see her, hear her, at that hour last night
Talk with a ruffian at her chamber-window;
[Who hath indeed, most like a liberal[9] villain,
Confess'd the vile encounters[10] they have had
A thousand times in secret.]

D. John. [Fie, fie! they are not to be nam'd, my lord,
Not to be spoke of;
There is not chastity enough in language,
Without offence to utter them.]—Thus, pretty lady,
I 'm sorry for thy much misgovernment.[11]

Claud. O Hero, what a Hero hadst thou been,
If half thy outward graces had been plac'd
About the thoughts and counsels of thy heart!
But fare thee well, most foul, most fair! farewell,
Thou pure impiety and impious purity!
For thee I 'll lock up all the gates of love,
And on my eyelids shall conjecture[12] hang,

[1] *Blood*, i.e. blush. [2] *Luxurious*, wanton, lustful.
[3] *Approved*, i.e. proved. [4] *Proof*, i.e. trial of her.
[5] *Large* = licentious.
[6] *Wide*, i.e. wide of the truth. [7] *Stale*, harlot.
[8] *Kindly*, natural. [9] *Liberal*, licentious.
[10] *Encounters*, meetings.
[11] *Misgovernment*, misconduct.
[12] *Conjecture*, suspicion.

To turn all beauty into thoughts of harm,
And never shall it more be gracious.[1]

Leon. Hath no man's dagger here a point for me? [*Hero swoons.*

Beat. Why, how now, cousin! wherefore sink you down?

D. John. Come, let us go. These things, come thus to light,
Smother her spirits up.

[*Exeunt Don Pedro, Don John, Claudio, and Attendants.*

Bene. How doth the lady?

Beat. Dead, I think:—help, uncle:—
Hero! why, Hero!—uncle!—Signior Benedick! —friar!

Leon. O Fate, take not away thy heavy hand!
Death is the fairest cover for her shame
That may be wish'd for.

Beat. How now, cousin Hero!

F. Fran. Have comfort, lady.

Leon. Dost thou look up?

F. Fran. Yea, wherefore should she not?

Leon. Wherefore! Why, doth not every earthly thing
Cry shame upon her? Could she here deny
The story that is printed in her blood?[2]—
Do not live, Hero; do not ope thine eyes:
For, did I think thou wouldst not quickly die,
Thought I thy spirits were stronger than thy shames,
Myself would, on the rearward of reproaches,
Strike at thy life. Griev'd I, I had but one?
Chid I for that at frugal nature's frame?[3]
O, one too much by thee! [Why had I one?
Why ever wast thou lovely in my eyes?
Why had I not with charitable hand
Took up a beggar's issue at my gates,
Who smirched thus and mir'd[4] with infamy,
I might have said, "No part of it is mine;
This shame derives itself from unknown loins"?
But mine, and mine I lov'd, and mine I prais'd,
And mine that I was proud on; mine so much
That I myself was to myself not mine,
Valuing of her; why, she]—O, she is fall'n
Into a pit of ink, that the wide sea
Hath drops too few to wash her clean again,
[And salt too little which may season give
To her foul-tainted flesh]!

Bene. Sir, sir, be patient.
For my part, I am so attir'd in wonder,
I know not what to say.

Beat. O, on my soul, my cousin is belied!

Bene. Lady, were you her bedfellow last night?

Beat. No, truly, not; although, until last night,
I have this twelvemonth been her bedfellow.

Leon. Confirm'd, confirm'd! O, that is stronger made
Which was before barr'd up with ribs of iron!
Would the two princes lie? and Claudio lie,
Who lov'd her so, that, speaking of her foulness,
Wash'd it with tears? Hence from her! let her die.

F. Fran. Hear me a little;
For I have only silent been so long,
And given way unto this course of fortune,
By noting of the lady: I have mark'd
A thousand blushing apparitions start
Into her face; a thousand innocent shames
In angel whiteness beat away those blushes;
And in her eye there hath appear'd a fire,
To burn the errors that these princes hold
Against her maiden truth. Call me a fool;
Trust not my reading nor my observation,
Which with experimental seal[5] doth warrant
The tenour of my book;[6] trust not my age,
My reverence, calling, nor divinity,
If this sweet lady lie not guiltless here
Under some biting error.

Leon. Friar, it cannot be.
Thou see'st that all the grace that she hath left
Is that she will not add to her damnation
A sin of perjury; she not denies it:
Why seek'st thou, then, to cover with excuse
That which appears in proper nakedness?

F. Fran. Lady, what man is he you are accus'd of?

Hero. They know that do accuse me; I know none:
If I know more of any man alive
Than that which maiden modesty doth warrant,

[1] *Gracious*, lovely, attractive.
[2] *In her blood*, i.e. in her blushes.
[3] *Frame*, i.e. order, disposition of things.
[4] *Mir'd*, soiled with mud.
[5] *Experimental seal*, i.e. the seal of experience.
[6] *Of my book*, i.e. of what I have read.

Let all my sins lack mercy!—O my father,
Prove you that any man with me convers'd
At hours unmeet, or that I yesternight
Maintain'd the change of words with any creature,
Refuse me, hate me, torture me to death!

F. Fran. There is some strange misprision[1] in the princes.

Bene. Two of them have the very bent[2] of honour;
And if their wisdoms be misled in this,
The practice[3] of it lies in John the bastard,
Whose spirits toil in frame[4] of villanies.

Leon. I know not. If they speak but truth of her,
These hands shall tear her; if they wrong her honour,
The proudest of them shall well hear of it.
Time hath not yet so dried this blood of mine,
Nor age so eat up my invention,
Nor fortune made such havoc of my means,
Nor my bad life reft me so much of friends,
But they shall find, awak'd in such a cause,
Both strength of limb and policy of mind,
Ability in means and choice of friends,
To quit me of them thoroughly.

F. Fran. Pause awhile,
And let my counsel sway you in this case.
Your daughter here the princes left for dead:
Let her awhile be secretly kept in,
And publish it that she is dead indeed;
Maintain a mourning ostentation,
And on your family's old monument
Hang mournful epitaphs, and do all rites
That appertain unto a burial.

Leon. What shall become of this? what will this do?

F. Fran. Marry, this, well carried, shall on her behalf
Change slander to remorse;—that is some good:
[But not for that dream I on this strange course,
But on this travail look for greater birth.]
She dying, as it must be so maintain'd,
Upon the instant that she was accus'd,
Shall be lamented, pitied, and excus'd
Of every hearer: for it so falls out,
That what we have we prize not to the worth
Whiles we enjoy it; but being lack'd and lost,
Why, then we rank the value, then we find
The virtue that possession would not show us
Whiles it was ours. So will it fare with Claudio:
When he shall hear she died upon his words,
Th' idea of her life shall sweetly creep
Into his study of imagination;
And every lovely organ of her life
Shall come apparell'd in more precious habit,
More moving, delicate, and full of life,
Into the eye and prospect of his soul,
Than when she liv'd indeed; [then shall he mourn
(If ever love had interest in his liver),
And wish he had not so accused her,—
No, though he thought his accusation true.]
Let this be so, and doubt not but success
Will fashion the event in better shape
Than I can lay it down in likelihood.
[But if all aim but this be levell'd false,
The supposition of the lady's death
Will quench the wonder of her infamy:]
And if it sort not well, you may conceal her
(As best befits her wounded reputation)
In some reclusive[5] and religious life,
Out of all eyes, tongues, minds, and injuries.

Bene. Signior Leonato, let the friar advise you:
And though you know my inwardness[6] and love
Is very much unto the prince and Claudio,
Yet, by mine honour, I will deal in this
As secretly and justly as your soul
Should with your body.

Leon. Being that I flow in grief,
The smallest twine may lead me.

F. Fran. 'Tis well consented: presently away;
[For to strange sores strangely they strain the cure.—]
Come, lady, die to live: this wedding-day
Perhaps is but prolong'd:[7] [have patience and endure.]

[*Exeunt Friar Francis, Hero, and Leonato.*

Bene. Lady Beatrice, have you wept all this while?

Beat. Yea, and I will weep a while longer.

---

[1] *Misprision*, misapprehension.

[2] *The very bent*, the very highest degree, or, according to some, the true natural disposition.

[3] *Practice*, contrivance.

[4] *Frame*, devising.

[5] *Reclusive* = secluded.

[6] *Inwardness*, intimacy, confidential friendship.

[7] *Prolong'd* = deferred.

Bene. I will not desire that.

Beat. You have no reason; I do it freely.

Bene. Surely I do believe your fair cousin is wrong'd.

Beat. Ah, how much might the man deserve of me that would right her!

Bene. Is there any way to show such friendship?

Beat. A very even[1] way, but no such friend.

Bene. May a man do it?

Beat. It is a man's office, but not yours.

Bene. I do love nothing in the world so well as you: is not that strange?

Beat. As strange as the thing I know not. It were as possible for me to say I lov'd nothing so well as you: but believe me not; and

Bene. Lady Beatrice, have you wept all this while?—(Act iv. 1. 257.)

yet I lie not; I confess nothing, nor I deny nothing.—I am sorry for my cousin.

Bene. By my sword, Beatrice, thou lov'st me.

Beat. Do not swear by it, and eat it.

Bene. I will swear by it that you love me; and I will make him eat it that says I love not you.

Beat. Will you not eat your word?

Bene. With no sauce that can be devised to it. I protest I love thee.

Beat. Why, then, God forgive me!

Bene. What offence, sweet Beatrice?

Beat. You have stay'd me in a happy hour:
I was about to protest I loved you.

Bene. And do it with all thy heart.

Beat. I love you with so much of my heart, that none is left to protest.

Bene. Come, bid me do anything for thee.

Beat. Kill Claudio.

Bene. Ha! not for the wide world.

Beat. You kill me to deny it. Farewell.

Bene. Tarry, sweet Beatrice.

[*She is going, he holds her by the arm.*

Beat. I am gone, though I am here:—[*Struggling to free herself*] there is no love in you:—nay, I pray you, let me go.

Bene. [*Still holding her*] Beatrice,—

[1] *Even*, plain.

Beat. In faith, I will go.

[*She tears herself away from him.*

Bene. We'll be friends first.

Beat. You dare easier be friends with me than fight with mine enemy.

Bene. Is Claudio thine enemy?

Beat. Is he not approved in the height[1] a villain, that hath slander'd, scorn'd, dishonour'd my kinswoman?—O that I were a man!—What, bear her in hand[2] until they come to take hands; and then, with public accusation, uncover'd slander, unmitigated rancour,—O God, that I were a man! I would eat his heart in the market-place.

Bene. Hear me, Beatrice,—

Beat. Talk with a man out at a window!—a proper saying!

Bene. Nay, but, Beatrice,—

Beat. Sweet Hero!—she is wrong'd, she is slander'd, she is undone.

Bene. Beat—

Beat. Princes and counties! Surely, a princely testimony, a goodly count, count comfect; a sweet gallant, surely! O that I were a man for his sake! or that I had any friend would be a man for my sake! But manhood is melted into courtesies, valour into compliment, and men are only turned into tongue, and trim[3] ones too: he is now as valiant as Hercules that only tells a lie, and swears it.—I cannot be a man with wishing, therefore I will die a woman with grieving. [*Going.*

Bene. Tarry, good Beatrice. By this hand, I love thee.

Beat. Use it for my love some other way than swearing by it.

Bene. Think you in your soul the Count Claudio hath wrong'd Hero?

Beat. Yea, as sure as I have a thought or a soul.

Bene. Enough, I am engag'd;[4] I will challenge him. I will kiss your hand, and so leave you. By this hand, Claudio shall render me a dear account. As you hear of me, so think of me. Go, comfort your cousin. I must say she is dead: and so, farewell. [*Exeunt.*

[1] *In the height*, in the highest degree.
[2] *Bear her in hand*, keep her in (false) hope.
[3] *Trim*, nice (used ironically).
[4] *Engag'd*, pledged (to fight him).

SCENE II. *A Prison.*

Enter DOGBERRY, VERGES, *and Sexton, in gowns; and the Watch, with* CONRADE *and* BORACHIO.

Dog. Is our whole dissembly appear'd?

Verg. O, a stool and a cushion for the sexton.

Sex. Which be the malefactors?

Dog. Marry, that am I and my partner.

Verg. Nay, that 's certain; we have the exhibition[5] to examine.

Sex. But which are the offenders that are to be examined? let them come before master constable.

Dog. Yea, marry, let them come before me.

[*Conrade and Borachio are brought forward.*

—What is your name, friend?

Bora. Borachio.

Dog. Pray, write down—Borachio.—Yours, sirrah?

Con. I am a gentleman, sir, and my name is Conrade.

Dog. Write down—master gentleman Conrade.—[Masters, do you serve God?

Con. } *Bora.* } Yea, sir, we hope.

Dog. Write down—that they hope they serve God:—and write God first; for God defend but God should go before such villains!—] Masters, it is proved already that you are little better than false knaves; and it will go near to be thought so shortly. How answer you for yourselves?

Con. Marry, sir, we say we are none.

Dog. A marvellous witty fellow, I assure you; but I will go about with him.[6]—Come you hither, sirrah: a word in your ear, sir: I say to you, it is thought you are false knaves.

Bora. Sir, I say to you we are none.

Dog. Well, stand aside.—'Fore God, they are both in a tale. Have you writ down—that they are none?

Sex. Master constable, you go not the way to examine: you must call forth the watch that are their accusers.

Dog. Yea, marry, that 's the eftest[7] way.—

[5] *Exhibition*, used blunderingly as = permission.
[6] *I will go about with him*, i.e. "I 'll manage him.
[7] *Eftest*, quickest; or, perhaps a blunder for *deftest*.

Let the watch come forth.—Masters, I charge you, in the prince's name, accuse these men.

First Watch. This man said, sir, that Don John, the prince's brother, was a villain.

Dog. Write down—Prince John a villain. —Why, this is flat perjury, to call a prince's brother villain.

Bora. Master constable,—

Dog. Pray thee, fellow, peace: I do not like thy look, I promise thee.

Sex. What heard you him say else?

Sec. Watch. Marry, that he had received a thousand ducats of Don John for accusing the Lady Hero wrongfully.

Dog. Flat burglary[1] as ever was committed.

Verg. Yea, by the mass, that it is.

Sex. What else, fellow?

First Watch. And that Count Claudio did mean, upon his words, to disgrace Hero before the whole assembly, and not marry her.

Dog. O villain! thou wilt be condemn'd into everlasting redemption for this.

Sex. What else?

Sec. Watch. This is all.

Sex. And this is more, masters, than you can deny. Prince John is this morning secretly stolen away; Hero was in this manner accus'd, in this very manner refus'd, and upon the grief of this suddenly died.—Master constable, let these men be bound, and brought to Leonato's: I will go before and show him their examination. [*Exit.*

Dog. Come, let them be opinion'd.

Verg. Let them be in the hands—

Con. Off, coxcomb!

Dog. God 's my life, where 's the sexton? let him write down—the prince's officer, coxcomb. —Come, bind them.—Thou naughty varlet!

Con. Away! you are an ass, you are an ass.

Dog. Dost thou not suspect my place? dost thou not suspect my years?—O that he were here to write me down an ass!—but, masters, remember that I am an ass; though it be not written down, yet forget not that I am an ass. —No, thou villain, thou art full of piety, as shall be proved upon thee by good witness. I am a wise fellow; and, which is more, an officer; and, which is more, a householder; and, which is more, as pretty a piece of flesh as any in Messina; and one that knows the law, go to; and a rich fellow enough, go to; and a fellow that hath had losses, and one that hath two gowns, and every thing handsome about him. —Bring him away.—O that I had been writ down an ass! [*Exeunt.*

ACT V.

Scene I. *Leonato's garden.*

Enter Leonato *and* Antonio.

Ant. If you go on thus, you will kill yourself;
And 't is not wisdom thus to second grief
Against yourself.

Leon. I pray thee, cease thy counsel,
Which falls into mine ears as profitless
As water in a sieve: give not me counsel;
Nor let no comforter delight mine ear
But such a one whose wrongs do suit with[2] mine.
Bring me a father that so lov'd his child,
Whose joy of her is overwhelm'd like mine,
And bid him speak of patience;
[Measure his woe the length and breadth of mine,
And let it answer every strain for strain,[3]
As thus for thus, and such a grief for such,
In every lineament, branch, shape, and form:
If such a one will smile, and stroke his beard,
And, sorry wag, cry "hem" when he should groan,
Patch grief with proverbs, make misfortune drunk
With candle-wasters,[4]—bring him yet to me,
And I of him will gather patience.

[1] *Burglary*, a blunder for perjury.

[2] *Suit with*, i.e. match with, equal.

[3] *Strain for strain*, feeling for feeling.

[4] *Candle-wasters*, i.e. bookworms.

But there is no such man: for,] brother, men
Can counsel and speak comfort to that grief
Which they themselves not feel; but, tasting it,
Their counsel turns to passion;[1] [which before
Would give preceptial medicine[2] to rage,
Fetter strong madness in a silken thread,
Charm ache with air, and agony with words:]
No, no; 't is all men's office to speak patience
To those that wring[3] under the load of sorrow,
But no man's virtue nor sufficiency
To be so moral[4] when he shall endure
The like himself. Therefore give me no counsel:
My griefs cry louder than advertisement.[5]

Ant. Therein do men from children nothing differ.

Leon. I pray thee, peace,—I will be flesh and blood;

Leon. I pray thee, cease thy counsel,
Which falls into mine ears as profitless
As water in a sieve.—(Act v. 1. 3-5.)

For there was never yet philosopher
That could endure the toothache patiently,
[However they have writ the style of gods,
And made a push at[6] chance[7] and sufferance.[8]]

Ant. Yet bend not all the harm upon yourself;
Make those that do offend you suffer too.

Leon. There thou speak'st reason: nay, I will do so.
My soul doth tell me Hero is belied;
And that shall Claudio know; so shall the prince,
And all of them that thus dishonour her.

Ant. Here come the prince and Claudio hastily.

Enter Don Pedro *and* Claudio.

D. Pedro. Good den, good den.

Claud. Good day to both of you.

Leon. Hear you, my lords,—

D. Pedro. We have some haste, Leonato.

Leon. Some haste, my lord!—well, fare you well, my lord:—
Are you so hasty now?—well, all is one.

D. Pedro. Nay, do not quarrel with us, good old man.

Ant. If he could right himself with quarrelling,
Some of us would lie low.

Claud. Who wrongs him?

Leon. Who!
Marry, thou dost wrong me; thou dissembler, thou:— [*Claudio lays his hand on his sword.*
Nay, never lay thy hand upon thy sword;
I fear thee not.

[1] *Passion*, emotion.
[2] *Preceptial medicine*, i.e. the medicine of precepts.
[3] *Wring*=writhe.
[4] *Moral*, ready to moralize.
[5] *Advertisement*, admonition, moral exhortation.
[6] *Made a push at*=defied.
[7] *Chance*, here used of fortune in a bad sense.
[8] *Sufferance*=suffering.

Claud. Marry, beshrew my hand,
If it should give your age such cause of fear:
In faith, my hand meant nothing to[1] my sword.

Leon. Tush, tush, man; never fleer[2] and jest at me:
I speak not like a dotard nor a fool,
As, under privilege of age, to brag
What I have done, being young, or what would do,
Were I not old. Know, Claudio, to thy head,[3]
Thou hast so wrong'd mine innocent child and me,
That I am forc'd to lay my reverence[4] by,
And, with grey hairs and bruise[5] of many days,
Do challenge thee to trial of a man.[6]
I say thou hast belied mine innocent child;
Thy slander hath gone through and through her heart,
And she lies buried with her ancestors,—
O, in a tomb where never scandal slept,
Save this of hers, fram'd[7] by thy villany!

Claud. My villany!

Leon. Thine, Claudio; thine, I say.

D. Pedro. You say not right, old man.

Leon. My lord, my lord,
I 'll prove it on his body, if he dare,
Despite his nice fence[8] and his active practice,[9]
His May of youth and bloom of lustihood.[10]

Claud. Away! I will not have to do with you.

Leon. Canst thou so daff me?[11] Thou hast kill'd my child:
If thou kill'st me, boy, thou shalt kill a man.

Ant. He shall kill two of us, and men indeed:
But that 's no matter; let him kill one first;—
Win me and wear me,—let him answer me.—
Come, follow me, boy! come, sir boy, follow me:
Sir boy, I 'll whip you from your foining[12] fence;
Nay, as I am a gentleman, I will.

Leon. Brother,—

Ant. Content yourself.[13] God knows I lov'd my niece;
And she is dead, slander'd to death by villains,
That dare as well answer a man indeed,[14]
As I dare take a serpent by the tongue;
Boys, apes, Jacks,[15] braggarts, milksops!—

Leon. Brother Anthony,—

Ant. Hold you content. What, man! I know them, yea,
And what they weigh, even to the utmost scruple,—
Scambling,[16] out-facing, fashion-monging[17] boys,
That lie, and cog,[18] and flout,[19] deprave,[20] and slander,
Go anticly,[21] show outward hideousness,
And speak off half a dozen dangerous[22] words,
How they might hurt their enemies, if they durst;
And this is all.

Leon. But, brother Anthony,—

Ant. Come, 't is no matter:
Do not you meddle; let me deal in this.

D. Pedro. Gentlemen both, we will not wake[23] your patience.
My heart is sorry for your daughter's death:
But, on my honour, she was charg'd with nothing
But what was true, and very full of proof.[24]

Leon. My lord, my lord,—

D. Pedro. I will not hear you.

Leon. No?—Come, brother, away.—I will be heard.

Ant. And shall, or some of us will smart for it.

[*Exeunt Leonato and Antonio.*

D. Pedro. See, see; here comes the man we went to seek.

Enter BENEDICK.

Claud. Now, signior, what news?

Bene. Good day, my lord.

D. Pedro. Welcome, signior: you are almost come to part almost a fray.

Claud. We had like to have had our two noses snapp'd off with two old men without teeth.

---

[1] *To*, *i.e.* with regard to, or to do with (my sword).
[2] *Fleer* = sneer.
[3] *To thy head*, *i.e.* to thy face.
[4] *Reverence*, my right to be treated with reverence (as an old man).
[5] *Bruise*, used figuratively = the wear and tear.
[6] *To trial of a man*, *i.e.* to a combat, man to man.
[7] *Fram'd*, devised, invented.
[8] *Fence*, skill in fencing.
[9] *Practice*, exercise.
[10] *Lustihood*, physical vigour.
[11] *Daff me*, *i.e.* put me off.
[12] *Foining*, thrusting.
[13] *Content yourself*, *i.e.* calm yourself.
[14] *A man indeed*, *i.e.* one who is indeed a man.
[15] *Jacks*, a term of contempt.
[16] *Scambling* = scrambling.
[17] *Fashion-monging*, foppish.
[18] *Cog*, cheat = our modern "gammon."
[19] *Flout*, mock.
[20] *Deprave*, practise detraction.
[21] *Anticly*, fantastically.
[22] *Dangerous* = threatening.
[23] *Wake* = rouse.
[24] *Full of proof*, fully proved.

D. Pedro. Leonato and his brother. What think'st thou? Had we fought, I doubt[1] we should have been too young for them.

Bene. In a false quarrel there is no true valour. I came to seek you both.

Claud. We have been up and down to seek thee; for we are high-proof[2] melancholy, and would fain have it beaten away. Wilt thou use thy wit?

Bene. It is in my scabbard: shall I draw it?

D. Pedro. Dost thou wear thy wit by thy side?

Claud. Never any did so, though very many have been beside their wit.—I will bid thee draw, as we do the minstrels; draw, to pleasure us.

D. Pedro. As I am an honest man, he looks pale.—Art thou sick, or angry?

Claud. What, courage, man! What though care kill'd a cat, thou hast mettle enough in thee to kill care.

Bene. Sir, I shall meet your wit in the career,[3] an you charge it against me. I pray you choose another subject.

Claud. Nay, then, give him another staff: this last was broke cross.[4]

D. Pedro. By this light, he changes more and more: I think he be angry indeed.

Claud. If he be, he knows how to turn his girdle.[5]

Bene. Shall I speak a word in your ear?

Claud. God bless me from a challenge!

Bene. You are a villain;—I jest not:—I will make it good how you dare, with what you dare, and when you dare.—Do me right,[6] or I will protest your cowardice. You have kill'd a sweet lady, and her death shall fall heavy on you. Let me hear from you.

Claud. Well, I will meet you, so I may have good cheer.

D. Pedro. What, a feast? a feast?

Claud. I' faith, I thank him; he hath bid me to a calf's-head and a capon;[7] the which if I do not carve most curiously,[8] say my knife's naught.[9]—[Shall I not find a woodcock[10] too?

Bene. Sir, your wit ambles well; it goes easily.

D. Pedro. I 'll tell thee how Beatrice prais'd thy wit the other day. I said, thou hadst a fine wit: "True," says she, "a fine little one." "No," said I, "a great wit:" "Right," says she, "a great gross one." "Nay," said I, "a good wit:" "Just," said she, "it hurts nobody." "Nay," said I, "the gentleman is wise:" "Certain," said she, "a wise gentleman."[11] "Nay," said I, "he hath the tongues:"[12] "That I believe," said she, "for he swore a thing to me on Monday night, which he forswore on Tuesday morning; there 's a double tongue; there 's two tongues." Thus did she, an hour together, trans-shape[13] thy particular virtues: yet at last she concluded with a sigh, thou wast the prop'rest[14] man in Italy.

Claud. For the which she wept heartily, and said she car'd not.

D. Pedro. Yea, that she did; but yet, for all that, an if she did not hate him deadly,[15] she would love him dearly:—the old man's daughter told us all.

Claud. All, all; and, moreover, God saw him when he was hid in the garden.]

D. Pedro. But when shall we set the savage bull's horns on the sensible Benedick's head?

Claud. Yea, and text underneath, "Here dwells Benedick, the married man"?

Bene. Fare you well, boy: you know my mind. I will leave you now to your gossip-like humour: you break jests as braggarts do their blades, which, God be thank'd, hurt not. —My lord, for your many courtesies I thank you: I must discontinue your company: your brother the bastard is fled from Messina: you have among you kill'd a sweet and innocent lady. For my Lord Lackbeard there, he and I shall meet: and till then peace be with him. [*Exit.*

D. Pedro. He is in earnest.

[1] *Doubt*=suspect.

[2] *High-proof*, i.e. in a high degree.

[3] *In the career*, i.e. in tilting, as at a tournament.

[4] *Broke cross*, i.e. broke athwart or across the opponent's body: an expression taken from tilting.

[5] *To turn his girdle*, i.e. to challenge (us). See note 354.

[6] *Do me right*, i.e. give me satisfaction.

[7] *And a capon*, perhaps a pun, i.e. a (fool's) *cap on*.

[8] *Curiously*, i.e. cleverly. [9] *Naught*, good for nothing.

[10] *A woodcock*, i.e. a fool.

[11] *A wise gentleman*, used ironically as we use "a wiseacre." [12] *He hath the tongues*, i.e. he is a good linguist.

[13] *Trans-shape*, caricature. [14] *Prop'rest*, handsomest.

[15] *Deadly*, i.e. mortally.

Claud. In most profound earnest; and, I 'll warrant you, for the love of Beatrice.

D. Pedro. And hath challeng'd thee?

Claud. Most sincerely.

D. Pedro. What a pretty thing man is when he goes in his doublet and hose, and leaves off his wit!

Claud. He is then a giant to an ape: but then is an ape a doctor[1] to such a man.

D. Pedro. But, soft you, let me be: pluck up,[2] my heart, and be sad![3] Did he not say, my brother was fled?

Enter DOGBERRY, VERGES, *and the Watch, with* CONRADE *and* BORACHIO.

Dog. Come, you, sir: if justice cannot tame you, she shall ne'er weigh more reasons in her balance: nay, an you be a cursing hypocrite once, you must be look'd to.

D. Pedro. How now! two of my brother's men bound! Borachio one!

Claud. Hearken after[4] their offence, my lord.

D. Pedro. Officers, what offence have these men done?

Dog. Marry, sir, they have committed false report; moreover, they have spoken untruths; secondarily, they are slanders; sixth and lastly, they have belied a lady; thirdly, they have verified unjust things; and, to conclude, they are lying knaves.

D. Pedro. First, I ask thee what they have done; thirdly, I ask thee what 's their offence; sixth and lastly, why they are committed; and, to conclude, what you lay to their charge.

Claud. Rightly reason'd, and in his own division;[5] and, by my troth, there 's one meaning well suited.

D. Pedro. Who have you offended, masters, that you are thus bound to your answer? this learned constable is too cunning[6] to be understood: what 's your offence?

Bora. Sweet prince, let me go no further to mine answer: do you hear me, and let this count kill me. I have deceived even your very eyes: what your wisdoms could not discover, these shallow fools have brought to light; who, in the night, overheard me confessing to this man, how Don John your brother incensed[7] me to slander the Lady Hero; how you were brought into the orchard, and saw me court Margaret in Hero's garments; how you disgrac'd her, when you should marry her: my villany they have upon record; which I had rather seal with my death than repeat over to my shame. The lady is dead upon mine and my master's false accusation; and, briefly, I desire nothing but the reward of a villain.

D. Pedro. Runs not this speech like iron through your blood?

Claud. I have drunk poison whiles he utter'd it.

D. Pedro. But did my brother set thee on to this?

Bora. Yea, and paid me richly for the practice[8] of it.

D. Pedro. He is compos'd and fram'd of treachery:—
And fled he is upon this villany.

Claud. Sweet Hero! now thy image doth appear
In the rare semblance that I lov'd it first.

Dog. Come, bring away the plaintiffs: by this time our sexton hath reformed Signior Leonato of the matter: and, masters, do not forget to specify, when time and place shall serve, that I am an ass.

Verg. Here, here comes master Signior Leonato, and the sexton too.

Re-enter LEONATO *and* ANTONIO, *with the Sexton.*

Leon. Which is the villain? let me see his eyes,
That, when I note another man like him,
I may avoid him: which of these is he?

Bora. If you would know your wronger, look on me.

Leon. Art thou the slave that with thy breath hast kill'd
Mine innocent child?

Bora. Yea, even I alone.

Leon. No, not so, villain; thou beliest thyself;

---

[1] *A doctor, i.e.* a learned person.
[2] *Pluck up*=rouse thyself.
[3] *Sad*, serious.
[4] *Hearken after, i.e.* inquire into.
[5] *Division*=arrangement, order.
[6] *Cunning*, clever.
[7] *Incensed* instigated.
[8] *Practice*, carrying out.

Here stand a pair of honourable men,
A third is fled, that had a hand in it.—
I thank you, princes, for my daughter's death:
Record it with your high and worthy deeds;
'T was bravely done, if you bethink you of it.

Claud. I know not how to pray your patience;
Yet I must speak. Choose your revenge yourself;
Impose me to[1] what penance your invention
Can lay upon my sin: yet sinn'd I not
But in mistaking.

D. Pedro. By my soul, nor I:
And yet, to satisfy this good old man,
I would bend under any heavy weight
That he 'll enjoin me to.

Leon. I cannot bid you bid my daughter live,—
That were impossible: but, I pray you both,
Possess[2] the people in Messina here
How innocent she died; and if your love
Can labour aught in sad invention,
Hang her an epitaph upon her tomb,
And sing it to her bones,—sing it to-night:—
To-morrow morning come you to my house;
And since you could not be my son-in-law,
Be yet my nephew: my brother hath a daughter,
Almost the copy of my child that 's dead,
And she alone is heir to both of us:
Give her the right you should have giv'n her cousin,
And so dies my revenge.

Claud. O noble sir,
Your over-kindness doth wring tears from me!
I do embrace your offer; and dispose
For henceforth of poor Claudio.

Leon. To-morrow, then, I will expect your coming;
To-night I take my leave.—This naughty man
Shall face to face be brought to Margaret,
Who, I believe, was pack'd[3] in all this wrong,
Hir'd to it by your brother.

Bora. No, by my soul, she was not;
Nor knew not what she did when she spoke to me;
But always hath been just[4] and virtuous
In any thing that I do know by[5] her.

Dog. Moreover, sir (which indeed is not under white and black), this plaintiff here, the offender, did call me ass: I beseech you, let it be remember'd in his punishment. [And also, the watch heard them talk of one Deformed: they say he wears a key in his ear, and a lock hanging by it; and borrows money in God's name,—the which he hath us'd[6] so long and never paid, that now men grow hard-hearted, and will lend nothing for God's sake: pray you, examine him upon that point.]

Leon. I thank thee for thy care and honest pains.

Dog. Your worship speaks like a most thankful and reverend youth; and I praise God for you.

Leon. There 's for thy pains.

Dog. God save the foundation!

Leon. Go, I discharge thee of thy prisoner, and I thank thee.

Dog. I leave an arrant knave with your worship; which I beseech your worship to correct yourself, for the example of others. God keep your worship! I wish your worship well; God restore you to health! I humbly give you leave to depart; and if a merry meeting may be wished, God prohibit it!—Come, neighbour.

[*Exeunt Dogberry, Verges, and Watch.*

Leon. Until to-morrow morning, lords, farewell.

Ant. Farewell, my lords: we look for you to-morrow.

D. Pedro. We will not fail.

Claud. To-night I 'll mourn with Hero.

[*Exeunt Don Pedro and Claudio.*

Leon. Bring you these fellows on. We 'll talk with Margaret,
How her acquaintance grew with this lewd[7] fellow. [*Exeunt.*

SCENE II. *Another part of Leonato's garden.*

Enter, severally, BENEDICK *and* MARGARET.

Bene. Pray thee, sweet Mistress Margaret, deserve well at my hands by helping me to the speech of[8] Beatrice.

---

[1] *Impose me to, i.e.* sentence, or put me to.
[2] *Possess*=inform.
[3] *Pack'd, i.e.* implicated, mixed up.
[4] *Just, i.e.* upright.
[5] *By*=of, about.
[6] *Hath us'd, i.e.* has practised.
[7] *Lewd*, depraved.
[8] *To the speech of*=to speech with.

Marg. Will you, then, write me a sonnet in praise of my beauty?

Bene. In so high a style, Margaret, that no man living shall come over it;[1] for, in most comely truth, thou deservest it.

[*Marg.* To have no man come over me![2] why, shall I always keep below stairs?

Bene. Thy wit is as quick as the greyhound's mouth,—it catches.

Marg. And yours as blunt as the fencer's foils, which hit, but hurt not.

Bene. A most manly wit, Margaret; it will not hurt a woman: and so, I pray thee, call Beatrice: I give thee the bucklers.[3]

Marg. Give us the swords; we have bucklers of our own.

Bene. If you use them, Margaret, you must put in the pikes[4] with a vice;[5] and they are dangerous weapons for maids.]

Marg. Well, I will call Beatrice to you, who, I think, hath legs.

Bene. And therefore will come.

[*Exit Margaret.*

The God of love, [*Singing.*
That sits above,
And knows me, and knows me,
How pitiful I deserve,—

I mean in singing; but in loving,—Leander the good swimmer, Troilus the first employer of panders, and a whole book full of these quondam carpet-mongers,[6] whose names yet run smoothly in the even road of a blank verse,—why, they were never so truly turned over and over as my poor self in love. Marry, I cannot show it in rhyme; I have tried: I can find out no rhyme to "lady" but "baby,"—an innocent rhyme; for "scorn," "horn,"—a hard rhyme; for "school," "fool,"—a babbling rhyme; very ominous endings: no, I was not born under a rhyming planet, nor I cannot woo in festival terms.[7]

Enter BEATRICE.

Sweet Beatrice, wouldst thou come when I called thee?

Beat. Yea, signior, and depart when you bid me.

Bene. O, stay but till then!

Beat. "Then" is spoken; fare you well now: and yet, ere I go, let me go with that I came for; which is, with knowing what hath pass'd between you and Claudio.

Bene. [Only foul words; and thereupon I will kiss thee.

Beat. Foul words is but foul wind, and foul wind is but foul breath, and foul breath is noisome; therefore I will depart unkiss'd.

Bene. Thou hast frighted the word out of his right sense, so forcible is thy wit. But I must tell thee plainly,] Claudio undergoes[8] my challenge; and either I must shortly hear from him, or I will subscribe[9] him a coward. And, I pray thee now, tell me for which of my bad parts didst thou first fall in love with me?

Beat. For them all together; which maintain'd so politic a state of evil, that they will not admit any good part to intermingle with them. But for which of my good parts did you first suffer love for me?

Bene. Suffer love,—a good epithet! I do suffer love indeed, for I love thee against my will.

Beat. In spite of your heart, I think; alas, poor heart! If you spite it for my sake, I will spite it for yours; for I will never love that which my friend hates.

Bene. Thou and I are too wise to woo peaceably.

Beat. It appears not in this confession: there's not one wise man among twenty that will praise himself.

Bene. An old, an old instance,[10] Beatrice, that liv'd in the time of good neighbours. If a man do not erect in this age his own tomb ere he dies, he shall live no longer in monument[11] than the bell rings and the widow weeps.

Beat. And how long is that, think you?

Bene. Question:[12]—why, an hour in clamour, and a quarter in rheum:[13] therefore is it most

---

[1] *Come over it*, i.e. excel it.
[2] *Come over me*, a play on words = marry me.
[3] *I give thee the bucklers*, i.e. I confess myself defeated.
[4] *Pikes*, a central spike, screwed into the buckler or shield. [5] *Vice*, screw.
[6] *Carpet-mongers*, i.e. carpet-knights.
[7] *Festival terms*, i.e. not in everyday language.
[8] *Undergoes*, i.e. is under = has received.
[9] *Subscribe*, proclaim in writing.
[10] *Instance*, proverbial saying.
[11] *Live no longer in monument*, i.e. his memory shall endure no longer. [12] *Question* = that is the question.
[13] *Rheum*, i.e. tears.

expedient for the wise (if Don Worm, his conscience, find no impediment to the contrary) to be the trumpet of his own virtues, as I am to myself. So much for praising myself, who, I myself will bear witness, is praiseworthy: and now tell me, how doth your cousin? 91

Beat. Very ill.

Bene. And how do you?

Beat. Very ill too.

Bene. Serve God, love me, and mend. There will I leave you too, for here comes one in haste.

Claud. Now, unto thy bones good night!—
Yearly will I do this rite.—(Act v. 3. 22, 23.)

Enter URSULA.

Urs. Madam, you must come to your uncle. Yonder 's old coil[1] at home: it is prov'd my Lady Hero hath been falsely accus'd, the prince and Claudio mightily abus'd;[2] and Don John is the author of all, who is fled and gone. Will you come presently?[3] 102

Beat. Will you go hear this news, signior?

Bene. I will live in thy heart, die in thy lap, and be buried in thy eyes; and moreover I will go with thee to thy uncles.[4] [*Exeunt.*

[1] *Old coil* = "the devil to pay."
[2] *Abus'd*, deceived. [3] *Presently*, immediately.
[4] *Uncles*, *i.e.* Leonato and Antonio.

SCENE III. *The Monument of Leonato—within the Church.*

Enter DON PEDRO, CLAUDIO, *and Attendants, with music and tapers.*

Claud. Is this the monument[5] of Leonato?

Atten. It is, my lord.

Claud. [*Reads from a scroll*]

"Done to death by slanderous tongues
Was the Hero that here lies:
Death, in guerdon[6] of her wrongs,
Gives her fame which never dies.
So the life that died with shame
Lives in death with glorious fame."

[5] *Monument*, family tomb. [6] *Guerdon*, recompense.

Hang thou there upon the tomb,
[*Fixing up the scroll.*
Praising her when I am dumb.—
Now, music, sound, and sing your solemn hymn.

Song.

Pardon, goddess of the night,
Those that slew thy virgin knight;[1]
For the which, with songs of woe,
Round about her tomb they go.
Midnight, assist our moan;
Help us to sigh and groan,
Heavily, heavily
Graves, yawn, and yield your dead,
Till death be uttered,
Heavily, heavily.

Claud. Now, unto thy bones good night!—
Yearly will I do this rite.

D. Pedro. Good morrow, masters; put your torches out:
The wolves have prey'd; and look, the gentle day,
Before the wheels of Phœbus, round about
Dapples the drowsy east with spots of grey.
Thanks to you all, and leave us: fare you well.

Claud. Good morrow, masters: each his several way.

D. Pedro. Come, let us hence, and put on other weed;
And then to Leonato's we will go.

Claud. And Hymen now with luckier issue speed
Than this for whom we render'd up this woe!
[*Exeunt.*

SCENE IV. *A hall in Leonato's house.*

Enter LEONATO, ANTONIO, BENEDICK, BEATRICE, MARGARET, URSULA, FRIAR FRANCIS, *and* HERO.

F. Fran. Did I not tell you she was innocent?

Leon. So are the Prince and Claudio, who accus'd her
Upon[2] the error that you heard debated:
But Margaret was in some fault for this,
Although against her will, as it appears
In the true course of all the question.[3]

Ant. Well, I am glad that all things sort[4] so well.

Bene. And so am I, being else by faith[5] enforc'd
To call young Claudio to a reckoning for it.

Leon. Well, daughter, and you gentlewomen all,
Withdraw into a chamber by yourselves,
And when I send for you, come hither mask'd:
The prince and Claudio promis'd by this hour
To visit me.—You know your office, brother:
[*Exeunt Ladies.*
You must be father to your brother's daughter,
And give her to young Claudio.

Ant. Which I will do with cónfirm'd[6] countenance.

Bene. Friar, I must entreat your pains, I think.

F. Fran. To do what, signior?

Bene. To bind me, or undo me; one of them.—
Signior Leonato, truth it is, good signior,
Your niece regards me with an eye of favour.

Leon. That eye my daughter lent her: 't is most true.

Bene. And I do with an eye of love requite her.

Leon. The sight whereof I think you had from me,
From Claudio, and the prince: but what 's your will?

Bene. Your answer, sir, is enigmatical:
But, for[7] my will, my will is, your good-will
May stand with ours, this day to be conjoin'd
In the state of honourable marriage:—
In which, good friar, I shall desire your help.

Leon. My heart is with your liking.

F. Fran. And my help.—
Here comes the prince and Claudio.

Enter DON PEDRO *and* CLAUDIO, *with Attendants.*

D. Pedro. Good morrow to this fair assembly.

Leon. Good morrow, prince; good morrow, Claudio:
We here attend you. Are you yet[8] determin'd
To-day to marry with my brother's daughter?

Claud. I'll hold my mind, were she an Ethiop.

Leon. Call her forth, brother; here 's the friar ready. [*Exit Antonio.*

---

[1] *Virgin knight*, i.e. virgin servant.
[2] *Upon*, on the ground of.
[3] *Question*, investigation.
[4] *Sort*, turn out.
[5] *By faith*, i.e. in order to be true to his word.
[6] *Cónfirm'd*, unmoved.
[7] *For*, as for.
[8] *Yet*, still.

D. Pedro. Good morrow, Benedick. Why, what 's the matter,
That you have such a February face,
So full of frost, of storm, and cloudiness?
Claud. I think he thinks upon the savage bull.—
[Tush, fear not, man; we 'll tip thy horns with gold,
And all Europa shall rejoice at thee;
As once Europa did at lusty Jove,
When he would play the noble beast in love.
Bene. Bull Jove, sir, had an amiable low;
And some such strange bull leap'd[1] your father's cow,
And got a calf in that same noble feat
Much like to you, for you have just his bleat.
Claud.] For this I owe you: here come other reckonings.

Re-enter Antonio, *with* Hero, Beatrice, *and the Ladies veiled.*

Which is the lady I must seize upon?
Ant. This same is she, and I do give you her.
Claud. Why, then she 's mine.—Sweet, let me see your face.
Leon. No, that you shall not, till you take her hand
Before this friar, and swear to marry her.
Claud. Give me your hand before this holy friar:
I am your husband, if you like of me.
Hero. And when I liv'd, I was your other wife: [*Unveiling.*
And when you lov'd, you were my other husband.
Claud. Another Hero!
Hero. Nothing certainer:
One Hero died defil'd;[2] but I do live,
And surely as I live, I am a maid.
D. Pedro. The former Hero! Hero that is dead!
Leon. She died, my lord; but whiles her slander liv'd.
F. Fran. All this amazement can I qualify;[3]
When after that the holy rites are ended,
I 'll tell you largely[4] of fair Hero's death:
Meantime let wonder seem familiar,
And to the chapel let us presently.

[1] *Leap'd, i.e.* covered.
[2] *Defil'd, i.e.* by slander.
[3] *Qualify,* moderate.
[4] *Largely,* at large, fully.

Bene. Soft and fair, friar.—Which is Beatrice?
Beat. [*Unveiling*] I answer to that name.
What is your will?
Bene. Do not you love me?
Beat. Why, no; no more than reason.
Bene. Why, then your uncle, and the prince, and Claudio have been deceiv'd; they swore you did.
Beat. Do not you love me?
Bene. Troth, no; no more than reason.
Beat. Why, then my cousin, Margaret, and Ursula
Are much deceiv'd; for they did swear you did.
Bene. They swore that you were almost sick for me.
Beat. They swore that you were well-nigh dead for me.
Bene. 'T is no such matter.—Then you do not love me?
Beat. No, truly, but in friendly recompense.
Leon. Come, cousin, I 'm sure you love the gentleman.
Claud. And I 'll be sworn upon 't that he loves her;
For here 's a paper, written in his hand,
A halting sonnet of his own pure brain,
Fashion'd to Beatrice.
Hero. And here 's another,
Writ in my cousin's hand, stol'n from her pocket,
Containing her affection unto Benedick.

Bene. A miracle! here 's our own hands against our hearts.—Come, I will have thee; but, by this light, I take thee for pity.

Beat. I would not deny you;—but, by this good day, I yield upon great persuasion; and partly to save your life, for I was told you were in a consumption.

Bene. Peace! I will stop your mouth. [*Kissing her.*

D. Pedro. How dost thou, Benedick, the married man?

Bene. I 'll tell thee what, prince; a college of wit-crackers cannot flout[5] me out of my humour. Dost thou think I care for a satire or an epigram? No: if a man will be beaten with brains, he shall wear nothing handsome about him. In brief, since I do purpose to

[5] *Flout,* jeer.

marry, I will think nothing to any purpose that the world can say against it; and therefore never flout[1] at me for what I have said against it; for man is a giddy thing, and this is my conclusion.—For thy part, Claudio, I did think to have beaten thee; but in that[2] thou art like to be my kinsman, live unbruis'd, and love my cousin.

Claud. I had well hop'd thou wouldst have denied Beatrice, that I might have cudgell'd thee out of thy single life, to make thee a double-dealer;[3] which, out of question, thou

D. Pedro. How dost thou, Benedick, the married man?—(Act v. 4. 99, 100.)

wilt be, if my cousin do not look exceeding narrowly to thee.

Bene. Come, come, we are friends.—Let's have a dance ere we are married, that we may lighten our own hearts and our wives' heels.

Leon. We'll have dancing afterward.

Bene. First, of my word; therefore play, music!—Prince, thou art sad; get thee a wife, get thee a wife: there is no staff more reverend than one tipp'd with horn.

[*Enter a Messenger.*

Mess. My lord, your brother John is ta'en in flight,
And brought with armed men back to Messina.

Bene. Think not on him till to-morrow: I'll devise thee brave punishments for him.—] Strike up, pipers! [*Dance.*

[*Exeunt.*

[1] *Flout*, jeer.

[2] *In that*, inasmuch as.

[3] *Double-dealer*, i.e. one who is unfaithful to his wife.

NOTES TO MUCH ADO ABOUT NOTHING.

ACT I. Scene 1.

1.—The stage-direction in both Q. and Ff. is "*Enter Leonato gouernour of Messina*, Innogen *his wife, Hero his daughter, and Beatrice his neece, with a messenger.*" This character, called *Innogen*, the wife of Leonato and mother of Hero, is not again mentioned throughout the play, nor is any allusion made to her death. It is impossible to believe that Shakespeare would have left the mother of Hero among the characters as a mere dummy. As has been already noted in the Introduction, scarcely any attempt seems to have been made in the Folio to correct the mistakes of the Quarto. The fact that the name of *Innogen* (probably a misprint for *Imogen*) was left, by an oversight, in the stage-direction is interesting; as it shows that Shakespeare had, at first, the intention of introducing this character, but that as he worked out the play he found there was no room for her, so he dropped her altogether. In this he showed his usual dramatic tact; for one cannot conceive how Hero's mother could have been introduced in any of the important scenes without diminishing their effect; and the nature of the story would not permit of her being a very subordinate character.

2. Lines 1, 2: *Don Pedro of Arragon comes this night to Messina.*—None of the commentators seem to have paid any attention to the question as to what is supposed to be the historical period of this play. The Kingdom of The Two Sicilies, including the Island of Sicily and the Kingdom of Naples on the mainland, was first established, in 1131, under Roger, the second Count of Sicily, who took the title of Roger I., King of The Two Sicilies. In 1266 Charles I. of Anjou, brother of Louis IX., became king of The Two Sicilies. In 1282, in consequence of an insurrection known as the Sicilian Vespers, Sicily became independent, and the two kingdoms were again separated; the house of Anjou retaining that of Naples, while that of Sicily went to the house of Arragon. This arrangement continued till 1435, when Alphonso I., king of Sicily, re-united the two crowns. He reigned till 1458, when another separation took place, and a bastard prince of the house of Arragon, whose name was John, assumed the crown of Sicily; under his successor, the celebrated Ferdinand II. of Spain and III. of Naples, the husband of Isabella, Naples and Sicily were again reunited (in 1501) under the crown of Spain; and they continued to be part of the Austro-Spanish Empire established by Charles V. till 1700. Shakespeare did not probably wish to be very particular about the exact historic period of the play; but it would certainly seem that the events here supposed to take place must have occurred when the island was still under the house of Arragon; probably, during some time in the first half of the fifteenth century. It is worth noting that Shakespeare probably took the name of Don John the Bastard from John of Arragon the Bastard, who was King of Sicily from 1458 to 1479.

3. Line 8: *But few of any* sort, *and none of name.*—This line, it will be seen, whether intentionally or not, is in perfect blank verse metre. *Sort* is a word used in several senses. Here perhaps "rank" is the best explanation we can give of it. The word is originally derived from the Latin *sortem*, the accusative of *sors* = "lot," "destiny." (See Merchant of Venice, note 62.) Thence it naturally came to mean "condition," "class," and so "kind," "species," "manner." For its use = "company," see Mids. Night's Dream, note 171. Wedgwood compares the use of *lot* in vulgar language.

4. Lines 16, 17: *he hath, indeed, better better'd expectation than you must expect of me to tell you how.*—This is one of those passages, not a few in this play, in which, as Seymour rightly observes, sense is sacrificed to "the charm of a jingle" (vol. i. p. 72); if, indeed, the word "charm" can be applied to such an annoying trick.

5. Lines 22, 23: *joy could not show itself modest enough without a* badge *of bitterness.*—Compare Macbeth, i. 4. 33-35:

> My plenteous joys,
> Wanton in fulness, seek to hide themselves
> In drops of sorrow.

Warburton, whose notes are rarely much to the purpose, has a very ingenious criticism on this passage: "Of all the transports of joy, that which is attended with tears is least offensive; because, carrying with it this mark of pain, it allays the envy that usually attends another's happiness" (see Var. Ed. vol. vii. p. 6). This explains the epithet *modest*; for the figurative use of *badge* compare Sonnet xliv. 14: "heavy tears, *badges* of either's woe." *Badge* originally meant a ring or collar worn as a mark of distinction. In Shakespeare's time it was usually applied to the silver *badges* worn by the servants of the nobility; and, as livery coats were uniformly of a blue colour, they required some such distinction. Compare Rape of Lucrece, line 1054:

> A *badge* of fame to slander's livery.

6. Line 30: *Signior Montanto.*—The reason why Beatrice chooses this name for Benedick is, perhaps, because it was a term used in the fencing schools. It is the same as that referred to in The Merry Wives, ii. 3. 26, 27: "to see thee pass thy punto, thy stock, thy reverse, thy distance, thy *montant*;" and in its Spanish form in Ben Jonson's Every Man in his Humour, v. 1: "I would teach these nineteen the special rules, as your punto, your reverso, your stoccata, your imbroccato, your passada, your montanto" (Works, vol. i. p. 121). *Montanto*, in Spanish, is a two-handed sword, or broadsword, used by fencing masters. The word does not seem to be used in Italian at all.

7. Line 38: *as* PLEASANT *as ever he was.*—For the use of *pleasant* in this sense of "merry" compare Lucrece, Arg. 8: "In that *pleasant* humour they all posted to Rome;" and Love's Labour's Lost, iv. 1. 131: "By my troth, most *pleasant.*" It frequently occurs in the titles of plays, and of books belonging to the class called "Facetiæ."

8. Line 39: *He set up his bills.*—It appears to have been the custom for fencing masters, when they first settled in a town, to *set up their bills;* that is to say, to post up, in public places, *printed bills* announcing their address and advertising their accomplishments with various weapons. It is most probable that, in these bills, they directly or indirectly challenged anyone who chose to come and have a bout with them, either with the broad-sword, or cudgels, or foils. In this sense they might be called challenges; but these *bills* were more of the nature of advertisements—what we should term "posters." It appears to have been the custom to fix bills of this description in certain parts of St. Paul's Cathedral. In Ben Jonson's Every Man out of his Humour, in a scene laid in The Middle Aisle of St. Paul's (iii. 1) we have:

> *Shift.* (*coming forward.*) This is rare, I have *set up my bills* without discovery.

Later on, in the same scene, these *bills* are again referred to, some of them being given in full (Works, vol. ii. pp. 91–98).

9. Line 40: *challeng'd* Cupid AT THE FLIGHT.—There seems to be some difficulty as to ascertaining the exact meaning of this expression. Steevens in his note (Var. Ed. vol. vii. p. 8) says: "*Flight* (as Mr. Douce observes to me) does not here mean an arrow, but a sort of shooting called *roving,* or shooting at long lengths." See also several references given by Steevens in his note on this passage. An interesting account of *roving,* or rural archery, will be found in The Book of Archery. It would appear, however, from the account given there that *roving* was the highest branch of archery, as it involved shooting at objects "barely within the range of his lightest *flight-shaft*" (p. 407). This would evidently involve, on the part of the archer, not only perfect practice with his bow, as regards what Ascham calls "fair shooting"—that is to say, sending the arrow from the bow clean and straight—but also the power of judging distance, which, as everyone knows who has practised rifle shooting, is a most difficult thing. *Flight* was also applied to a certain kind of arrow. The Book of Archery (p. 301) says: "Old English archers carried into the field a sheaf of twenty-four barbed arrows, buckled within their girdles. A portion of these, about six or eight, were longer, lighter, and winged with narrower feathers than the rest. With these *flight* shafts, as they are termed, they could do execution further than with the remaining heavy sheaf arrows."

10. Line 42: *challeng'd him at the* BIRD-BOLT.—This was a short blunt arrow used for killing birds. Douce gives representations of these *bird-bolts* (p. 102). In The Book of Archery, plate 16, figure 12, is a more exact representation of such a "blunt arrow;" and in figure 8, same plate, is given "an ornamental case for *bird-bolts* in the time of Queen Elizabeth." They were about half the length of an ordinary arrow. Such arrows would usually stun a bird, and not inflict such a wound as to injure it for the purposes of the table. Those who were adepts at the long-bow looked down upon the cross-bow as being so much easier a weapon to handle. Douce says (p. 102): that fools, "for obvious reasons were only entrusted with blunt arrows; hence the proverb *A fool's bolt is soon shot.*" This, I think, is decidedly an error, as the proverb only refers to the fact that *a fool* generally shoots in too great a hurry, and will fire all his arrows and ammunition away without producing much effect. These blunt arrows were only used, apparently, for small birds. Against wild-fowl and herons they would be of no use. In the case of the larger birds the sportsman generally employed barbed and double-headed arrows.

11. Lines 43, 44: *I pray you, how many hath he kill'd and eaten in these wars?*—Compare Lilly's Endimion, ii. 2:

> *Top.* . . . Let me see, be our enemies fat?
> *Epi.* Passing fat: and I would not change this life to be a lord; and yourselfe passeth all comparison, for other captaines *kill* and *beate,* and there is nothing you *kill, but you also eate.*
> —Works, vol. i. p. 24.

Compare also Henry V. iii. 7. 99, 100:

> *Ram.* He longs to eat the English.
> *Con.* I think he will *eat all he kills.*

12. Line 48: *he'll be meet with you.*—Steevens says that this is a very common expression in the midland counties. Halliwell, in his Provincial and Archaic Dictionary, says that it is still in use. See Middleton's The Witch, ii. 1: "Now I'll be meet with 'em" (Works, vol. iii. p. 302). Compare also the expression *to meet with*="to be even with," *e.g.* in A Match at Midnight, iii. 1: "I know the old man's gone to meet with an old wench that will *meet with* him" (Dodsley, vol. xiii. p. 62).

13. Line 56: *stuff'd with all honourable virtues.*—Compare Romeo and Juliet, iii. 5. 183:

> *Stuff'd,* as they say, *with honourable parts.*

Steevens quotes, on the authority of Edwards's MS., from Mede's Discourses on Scripture, referring to Adam, "he whom God had *stuffed with so many excellent qualities*" (Var. Ed. vol. vii. p. 10).

14. Line 60: *but for the stuffing,—well, we are all mortal.*—Q. Ff. have *stuffing well,* a punctuation which renders the passage nonsense. Theobald first made the alteration. The passage, however, is so stopped in Davenant's Law against Lovers, i. 1 (Works, vol. v. p. 120, edn. 1870). Beatrice breaks off abruptly here, apparently because she has used the expression "*stuff'd* man" in the line above, that being one of the many synonyms of a cuckold; at least so Farmer says, in his note, on the strength of a passage in Lilly's Mydas, v. 1, where Petulus and Licio are going through an inventory of Motto's movables:

> *Pet.* Item, one paire of hornes in the bride chamber, on the bed's head.
> *Licio.* The beast's head, for Motto is *stuft* in the head, and these are among unmoveable goods.
> —Works, vol. ii. p. 58.

I cannot find the expression used, in this sense, anywhere else; but if that be the meaning of the phrase here, Beatrice would naturally pull herself up, remembering that, as Benedick was not married, he could scarcely be a cuckold; and the sense of the commonplace end to her speech, *well, we are all mortal* would be that, as he was mortal, he might yet be married.

15. Line 66: *four of his* FIVE WITS *went halting off, and now is the whole man govern'd with one.*—Compare Sonnet cxli. 9, 10:

> But my *five wits* nor my five senses can
> Dissuade one foolish heart from serving thee;

and Lear, iii. 4. 59: "Bless thy *five wits!*" In the Interlude of Every Man, which was published in the early part of the reign of Henry VIII., we have the five *wits* among the characters:

> Also ye must call to mind
> Your *Five Wits* as your councillors.
> —Dodsley, vol. i. p. 130.

16. Line 69: *if he have wit enough to keep himself warm.*—This is a common proverbial expression. Compare Taming of Shrew, ii. 1. 268, 269:

> *Pet.* Am I not wise?
> *Kath.* Yes; *keep you warm;*

and Heywood's Wise-woman of Hogsdon, ii. 1: "You are the Wise-woman, are you? and *have wit to keepe your selfe warme enough,* I warrant you" (Works, vol. v. p. 295).

17. Lines 69, 70: *let him bear it* FOR A DIFFERENCE *between himself and his horse.*—Compare Hamlet, iv. 5. 183: "you must wear your rue *with a difference.*" This word *difference* is rather loosely defined in ordinary dictionaries. In Sloane-Evans's Grammar of British Heraldry (pp. 43–50) will be found a very full account of Heraldic *Differences,* which, he says, may be defined as "Extraordinary Additaments, whereby bearers of the same Coat Armour may be distinguished, and their nearness to the representative of the family demonstrated." They were divided into two classes, ancient and modern. The ancient ones were used to distinguish between tribes and nations as well as individual persons, and consisted of various "Bordures" which went round the edge of the shield; of these there were fourteen different kinds. The modern *Differences* came into use about the time of Richard II., and consisted of nine different signs and marks, of which the first was the label, being the badge of the eldest son and heir during his father's lifetime. The others were the Crescent, Mullet, Martlet, Annulet, Fleur-de-Lis, &c., which were borne by the second, third, fourth, fifth, sixth, &c., sons.

18. Line 73: *He hath every month a new* SWORN BROTHER.—Compare Richard II. v. 1. 20, 21:

> I am *sworn brother*, sweet,
> To grim Necessity;

and I. Henry IV. ii. 4. 7: "I am *sworn brother* to a leash of drawers." When two knights became *brothers,* or companions in arms, they usually recorded their friendship or brotherhood with some semi-barbarous ceremony, such as being bled and mixing their blood together. In his article on this phrase, Nares says: "Robert de Oily, and Roger de Ivery, are recorded as *sworn brothers* (fratres jurati) in the expedition of the Conqueror to England, and they shared the honours bestowed upon either of them." They were also called *fratres conjurati,* and the term was sometimes applied to those who were sworn to defend the king against his enemies.

19. Line 77: *it ever changes with the next block.*—That is, the wooden *block* on which hats are made. The word is still used in this sense. It occurs in Shakespeare in only one other passage, in Lear, iv. 6. 187: "this' a good *block.*" In other senses Shakespeare uses the word frequently.

20. Lines 78, 79: *the gentleman is not* IN YOUR BOOKS.—The origin of this phrase seems to be doubtful. Some suppose that it is connected with the custom of great men keeping *books* with the names of their retainers and members of their household. Others, with more probability, suppose that it refers to the *memorandum book* or tables which it was the custom for everyone to carry. The allusions to this custom are frequent in Shakespeare and other authors, *e.g.* the well-known passage in Hamlet, i. 5. 107:

> My *tables,*—meet it is I set it down.

But one would think that these *tables* or memoranda books would be used more for recording events and engagements, or as a commonplace book, than as records of the names of those with whom the writer of the memoranda was familiar, or on good terms. In the present day we generally say that a person is "in one's *good books,*" or "in one's *bad books,*" and this would certainly seem to refer to the *books* or ledger of a tradesman; the *good books* being the pages which recorded the good debts, and therefore trustworthy debtors; the *bad books* those in which the bad debts were entered. As in Shakespeare's time it was not the custom to give credit, except to those persons who were well known, it is very probable that, after all, this phrase may have had, originally, a commercial origin; and that to say a person was *in your books* meant merely that he was such a one as you could trust, and to whom you would give credit. It may be worth mentioning that it seems, to judge from some books of Shakespeare's period which have come down to us, to have been the custom for the owner of a *book* to write or scribble, on the title-page and elsewhere, the name of some friend or some favourite author; in which custom those who prefer a far-fetched derivation may, perhaps, find the origin of the phrase. Beatrice's answer, "No; an he were, *I would burn my study,*" seems to favour some connection between the phrase and the books in one's library.

21. Line 81: *young* SQUARER.—Compare Mids. Night's Dream, note 72. This is the only place where Shakespeare uses the substantive = "quarreller." For the verb compare Antony and Cleopatra, iii. 13. 41:

> Mine honesty and I begin to *square.*

22. Line 95: Enter Don Pedro, Don John, &c.—Q. Ff. have "John the *Bastard.*" See above, note 2.

23. Lines 98-102.—This speech of Leonato's is a very graceful compliment. In confirmation of the suggestion made in our Introduction (p. 180) that Shakespeare, while writing the prose portions of this play, had Lilly's style very much in his mind, compare the following speech in Lilly's Endimion, ii. 1: "*End.* You know (faire Tellus) that the sweet remembrance of your love, is the onely companion of my life, and thy presence, my paradise; so that I am not alone when nobodie is with mee, and in heaven itselfe when thou art with me" (Works, vol. i

p. 20). Although there are no identical phrases common to the two speeches, yet in the style there is considerable similarity.

24. Line 103: *You embrace your* CHARGE *too willingly.*—Johnson says that *charge* means "burden, incumbrance" (Var. Ed. vol. vii. p. 15); but Douce explains it "the person committed to your care." As Don Pedro has alluded above (line 96) to the probable cost of entertaining him, the word *charge* is, perhaps, used advisedly = "the person whom you will be at the *charge* of entertaining." The royal progresses, in which the sovereign used to indulge in Shakespeare's time, no doubt conferred great honour upon the persons her majesty visited; but they were also a source of considerable expense.

25. Line 100: *You have it full.*—Schmidt explains this phrase = "you are the man, you will do it," and compares this with the passage in Taming of Shrew, i. 1. 203: "I *have it full.*" But surely, there, the meaning is, "I have the plan complete;" while here it is no more nor less than a polite form of the vulgar expression *You have got it hot;* meaning that Leonato's courteous retort to Benedick's rather impertinent question was a reproof which hit him *full* in the face.

26. Lines 113-115: *If Signior Leonato be her father, she would not have his head on her shoulders for all Messina, as like him as she is.*—The meaning of this speech is not quite clear, though none of the commentators seem to have felt any difficulty about it. Perhaps Benedick means to say that Hero would not exchange her young head for her father's old and gray-haired one.

27. Line 125: *Courtesy itself must* CONVERT *to disdain.*—Shakespeare uses *convert* in the intransitive sense elsewhere, principally in his earlier works, *e.g.* in Lucrece, line 592: "stones dissolv'd to water do *convert;*" and Richard II. v. 1. 66:

The love of wicked men *converts* to fear.

28. Line 131: *troubled with a* PERNICIOUS *suitor.*—Grey proposed to read *pertinacious*, a very unnecessary change, and a word never used by Shakespeare; while *pernicious* is a very favourite word of Shakespeare's.

29. Line 137: *an 'twere such a face as yours* WERE.—That anachronistic personage, the Old Corrector, omitted *were;* but his godfather, Mr. Collier, restored it, on the ground that it was certainly the language of Shakespeare's day. Dyce doubts if the old text is right, and certainly the omission of *were* would be an improvement.

30. Lines 140, 141: *A bird of my* TONGUE *is better than a beast of yours.*—Seymour suggests that for *tongue* we should read *teaching*. But Benedick's answer seems to show that the text is right. Beatrice probably means by *a bird of my tongue*, "a bird that *my tongue* has taught." Benedick's answer would have no meaning if Seymour's conjecture were adopted.

31. Lines 147-149: THIS *is the* sum *of all: Leonato,—Signior Claudio and Signior Benedick,—my dear friend Leonato hath invited you all.*—Q. reads "*That* is." The Cambridge edd. punctuate this sentence thus: *That is the sum of all, Leonato. Signior Claudio and Signior Benedick, my dear friend Leonato hath invited you all.*—They have a note (II.) in which they say: "The punctuation which we have adopted seems to be the only one which will make sense of this passage without altering the text. We must suppose that, during the 'skirmish of wit' between Benedick and Beatrice, from line 93 to 125, Don Pedro and Leonato have been talking apart and making arrangements for the visit of the Prince and his friends." We have inserted the necessary stage-direction, in order to show that Don Pedro and Leonato are supposed to be talking apart during the wordy encounter of Benedick and Beatrice. This is consonant with the arrangement adopted on the stage; but we have not followed the punctuation of the Cambridge edd., as Q. Ff. all agree in punctuating the passage much as in our text. The speaker is addressing Claudio and Benedick, and he breaks off his sentence to call their attention to Leonato. It will be noted that he does not include Don John. Hanmer suggested reading *Don John* instead of the first *Leonato*. But perhaps Don Pedro deliberately omitted to address Don John; for, though reconciled, they were not on very cordial terms. See below, scene 3, lines 22-24.

32. Line 171: *a professed* TYRANT *to their sex.*—For this use of *tyrant* compare Measure for Measure, ii. 4. 169: "I 'll prove a *tyrant* to him."

33. Line 183: *Yea, and a* CASE *to put it into.*—Benedick plays here upon the word *case*, which does not only mean a jewel *case*, but also "a dress." Compare I. Henry IV. i. 2. 201: "I have *cases* of buckram for the nonce." In Nabbes's Covent Garden, iii. 3; Spruce, alluding to his dress, says: "I have this onely *case* for my Carkasse: and 't will not be quite paid for til the next quarter" (Bullen's Old Plays, New Series, vol. I. p. 48).

34. Lines 184, 185: *do you play the* FLOUTING JACK, *to tell us Cupid is a good hare-finder, and Vulcan a rare carpenter?*—*Jack* appears always to have been used in a contemptuous sense, or, at best, applied to a pert fellow, as *Jack-a-dandy*. In Merry Wives, iii. 1. 120, and iv. 5. 83, Sir Hugh Evans uses *vlouting-stog* (*i.e. flouting-stock*) = laughing-stock. The latter part of this passage has puzzled commentators of old; but perhaps the simple explanation is the right one. He means "Do you mean to laugh at us by telling us that *blind Cupid* is a good *finder of hares*, and that *Vulcan* the clumsy blacksmith is a good *carpenter!*" There possibly may be a double meaning in *harefinder;* but if so, it is scarcely worth the trouble of deciphering it. See Romeo and Juliet, note 96.

35. Lines 191-194.—Here is a dramatic hint at Benedick's concealed liking for Beatrice, which is afterwards so cleverly developed into love.

36. Lines 200-202: *Hath not the world one man but he will wear his cap with suspicion!*—The explanation given in our foot-note is probably the right one. Henderson quotes a passage from Painter's Palace of Pleasure: "All they that *weare hornes* be pardoned to *weare* their *cappes* upon their heads" (Var. Ed. vol. vii. p. 19).

37. Line 204: *sigh away Sundays.*—Warburton says this was a proverbial expression; but no other instance of its use has been found. Steevens thought it was an allusion to the Puritans' Sabbath. Possibly it may be; but it seems more likely that it refers to the wholesome restraint which

husbands enjoy on Sunday; on which day, in Shakespeare's time as in our own, gay young bachelors would amuse themselves in spite of ecclesiastical prohibition.

38. Lines 217-220:

Claud. *If this were so, so* WERE *it* UTTER'D.

Bene. *Like the old tale, my lord: "it is not so, nor 't was not so; but indeed, God forbid it should be so."*

This passage, at first sight, is not very intelligible, especially the speech of Claudio. Johnson thought there was something omitted in the previous dialogue; but, in order to make the sense clearer, he suggested that Claudio's speech should break off abruptly at *were*, and that *utter'd* should belong to Benedick's speech. Steevens explained Claudio's speech thus: "if I had really confided such a secret to him, yet he would have blabbed it in this manner" (Var. Ed. vol. vii. p. 20). But surely his words cannot bear that meaning. He simply means to make an indirect and rather ungracious confession that what Benedick says is true. The meaning is: "If this he says were true, so would it be told." The *were* here can hardly be optative —"I would wish it were so told;" for Claudio could not have thought Benedick's manner of telling his secret a very agreeable one. Benedick replies to this half-sullen confession of Claudio's by comparing it with the words *uttered* in some well-known old tale. These words would have been almost incomprehensible to us, if it had not been that Blakeway was able to recall this identical tale as told to him when a child by an old aunt. His version is probably pretty much the same as that which was current in Shakespeare's time. The story belongs to the Bluebeard class, and is generally known as the Story of Mr. Fox. From the notes to Grimm's Fairy Tales (vol. ii. pp. 164-167, edn. 1804) it would appear that the same story is to be found in Danish and Hungarian. It may be compared with "Bloudie Jacke of Shrewsbury" in the Ingoldsby Legends, and with the story of Captain Murderer given in Dickens' most amusing article, "Nurses' Stories," published in The Uncommercial Traveller. These stories all resemble one another in the main point, namely, that the hero of them was in the habit of marrying as many young ladies as he could get hold of, and of murdering them very soon after marriage. Captain Murderer disposed of his victims' remains in a pie, which he ate with some ceremony and great delectation. Bloudie Jack, in the old story, only kept the toes and fingers of his wives, and gave the rest of them to a big dog. Blakeway's story will be found in the Var. Ed. (vol. vii. pp. 163-165); and it is quoted at length by Rolfe. The girl who finds out Mr. Fox is called Lady Mary. Like the heroines of similar stories she conceals herself under a staircase, and sees Mr. Fox dragging a young lady down the staircase, to the balusters of which she clings. Mr. Fox cuts off her hand with a gold bracelet on it, which falls into the lap of Lady Mary. (In the other stories it is the wedding-ring finger, with the ring on it, that the murderer cuts off.) She takes the opportunity, when Mr. Fox is dining at a house in company with her two brothers, to tell the story; saying after each incident, *It is not so, nor it was not so* to Mr. Fox, who, as he gets interested, repeats, *It is not so, nor it was not so, and God forbid it should be so.* This would make us incline to believe that we should read, *So were it* NOT *uttered*, in Claudio's speech in the line above. But, perhaps, all that Benedick intends by his allusion is to say that Claudio's half-denial of being in love was worth no more than Mr. Fox's protestation in the old story.

It may be worth remarking that Barham, curiously enough, thought Bloudie Jack to be an original story.[1] (See a letter of his in Life of R. H. Barham, vol. ii. p. 98.)

39. Lines 221, 222: *If my passion change not shortly, God forbid it should be otherwise.*—This speech is not very clear. Claudio probably means: "If a change does not come over my feelings, God forbid it should be otherwise than that I am in love with her and hope to marry her."

40. Line 230: *force of his will.*—Warburton detected here an allusion to the theological definition of heresy, which is *wilful* adherence to heterodox opinion (Var. Ed. vol. vii. p. 21). Schmidt's explanation, though not quite so refined, is, perhaps, more probable; that Claudio uses *will* here in the sense of "carnal passion," "lust." There are many "strokes of wit" in this play which will not bear inquiring into too curiously.

41. Lines 242, 243: RECHEAT *winded in my forehead.*—*Recheat* is from the French *requete*, old French *requeste*. It was sometimes written *rechate*. It was the call sounded on the hunting-horn, or bugle, to recall the hounds from the fox, or other game. There were regular notes for it. See a note in the Var. Ed. vol. v. p. 21, where Steevens quotes a sheet in the British Museum, containing the ancient hunting notes of England, from which it would appear that there were several kinds of *recheats*. It is alluded to in the Return from Parnassus (ii. 5): "when you blow the death of your fox in the field or couert, then must you sound 3. notes, with 3. windes, and *recheat:* marke you sir, vpon the same with 3. windes" (Macray's Reprint, pt. ii. p. 106).

42. Lines 245, 246: *and the* FINE *is (for the which I may go the finer).*—For FINE = conclusion, compare All 's Well, iv. 4. 35: "still the *fine's* the crown." This is another silly jingle, with which we may compare Hamlet, v. 1. 115: "is this the *fine* of his *fines?*"

43. Line 250: *If I do, hang me in a bottle like a cat, and shoot at me.*—The reference here is to a cruel practice which, according to Douce (quoted in the Var. Ed. vol. iii. p. 23), though the passage is not in his Illustrations of Shakespeare, 1839), was still kept up at Kelso in Scotland, where it is called "*Cat* in barrel." A *cat* was placed in a small wooden barrel, or in a basket, and shot at by archers.

44. Line 260: *let him be clapp'd on the shoulder, and call'd Adam.*—No doubt, in spite of the acrimonious note of Ritson in his Remarks Critical, &c., 1783 (published anonymously), this refers to *Adam* Bell, the well-known outlaw, so famous, in the North of England, with his two companions Clym of the Clough and William

[1] The purport of the passage is rather doubtful. It is not clear whether Barham means that he believed the stanza to be new, or the story. He alludes to it again (pp. [illegible]); but, at any rate, he does not seem to have been aware that it was virtually the same story as that alluded to here, or that a similar one existed in other countries.

Cloudsley. There is a long ballad in Percy's Reliques on this subject. (Series i. book ii.)

45. Line 263: "*In time the savage bull doth bear the yoke.*"—This line is slightly misquoted from Kyd's Spanish Tragedy (licensed 1592). It appears that the line was taken from Watson's Ecatompathia, 1582, and occurs in Sonnet xlvii.

46. Lines 267, 268: *in such great letters as they write, "Here is good horse to hire."*—This shows us that, in Shakespeare's time, announcements, on the outside of ale-houses and such like places, were written in as primitive a fashion as they were in Pompeii, or as they are in some of the villages of southern Italy nowadays; and that printed bills were the exception and not the rule.

47. Line 274: *if Cupid have not spent all his quiver in* VENICE.—*Venice*, in Shakespeare's time, was a modern Corinth, the paradise of pleasure-seekers, especially of those given to the worship of Venus. Writers of the Elizabethan age testify to the number and beauty of its courtezans, professional and amateur. Borde in his Boke to the Introduction to Knowledge (chap. xxiv.) says: "whosoeuer y^t hath not seene the noble citie of *Venis*, he hath not sene ye bewtye and ryches of thys worlde."

48. Lines 283–286:

Claud. *To the tuition of God: From my house (if I had it),—*

D. Pedro. *The sixth of July: Your loving friend, Benedick.*

Claudio is ridiculing the old-fashioned mode of terminating letters, especially dedicatory ones. Reed quotes from Barnaby Googe in his dedication to the first edition of Palingenius, 1560: "And thus *committyng* your Ladiship with all yours to the *tuicion* of the moste mercifull *God*, I ende. From Staple Inne at London, the eighte and twenty of March" (Var. Ed. vol. vii. p. 25). Reed says that this mode of ending letters had become obsolete in Shakespeare's time; but though it might be considered affected, it was not obsolete. See Malone's note on same passage (*ut supra*, p. 26).

49. Lines 288, 289: *The body of your discourse is sometimes* GUARDED *with fragments.*—*Guarded* means, as explained in our foot-note, "ornamented with some trimming or border." Compare Merchant of Venice, ii. 2. 163, 164:

> Give him a livery
> More *guarded* than his fellows'.

But *guards* were also used for other ornaments, such as embroidery, or "clocks" on hose. See Love's Labour's Lost, note 112.

50. Lines 290, 291: *ere you flout* OLD ENDS *any further, examine your conscience: and so I leave you.*—It is not very clear whether Benedick refers to the old way of finishing letters, which they were laughing at, or whether he refers to the quotation from The Spanish Tragedy (line 263 above). It is evident that he affects to be very solemn in his leave-taking, and to resent their laughter at his denunciations of marriage. At present he is very serious on this subject, having no idea of living to see himself rightly called "Benedick the married man."

51. Line 299: *When you went onward on this ended* ACTION.—Compare Lucrece, line 1504:

> *Onward* to Troy with the blunt swains he goes.

Action here means something more than a single battle. We have explained it in the foot-note = "campaign." Schmidt explains it as a "warlike enterprise." Compare King John, ii. 1. 233:

> Forwearied in this *action* of swift speed;

referring to the campaign in which Angiers was taken by John, and Arthur was made prisoner.

52. Line 307: *Saying, I lik'd her ere I went to wars——* It is evident that Claudio is going to say more, something to the effect that "now that liking has grown into love," &c.; Don Pedro, however, interrupts him. This mode of punctuating the passage is adopted by Collier, Halliwell, and Rolfe.

53. Line 309: *And tire the hearer with a* BOOK OF WORDS.—Perhaps there is some reference here to the rather tedious *Books of Words* often provided for masquers in their entertainments. (Compare Romeo and Juliet, note 46.) It is possible that, when no book was provided, the masquers improvised dialogues, which were, perhaps, no less tedious than the written words. Certainly nothing could well be more so than the *Books of Words* to most masques.

54. Line 311: *And I will* BREAK WITH *her.*—For a similar use of this phrase compare Two Gent. i. 3. 44: "now will we *break with* him;" and King John, iv. 2. 227:

> I faintly *broke with* thee of Arthur's death.

The expression occurs more than once in this play. Compare ii. 1. 162; iii. 2. 76. The same phrase is also used without an objective = to break faith, in Merry Wives, iii. 2. 57:

> I would not *break with* her for more money.

55. Line 313: *to twist so fine a* STORY.—Walker suggests that *story* is not the right reading (vol. iii. p. 29). Lettsom conjectured *string*. But surely the expression may be compared with the phrase so common in our time "to *spin* a yarn;" the idea having been taken from the *twisting* together of the threads from off the distaff of a spinning-wheel.

56. Line 317: *I would have* SALV'D *it with a longer treatise.*—For a similar figurative use of *salve* compare Coriolanus, iii. 2. 70–72:

> you may *salve* so,
> Not what is dangerous present, but the loss
> Of what is past.

57. Lines 318, 319:

What need the bridge much broader than the flood?
The fairest GRANT *is the necessity.*

Many emendations have been made on the latter somewhat obscure line. Hanmer for *grant* substituted *plea*. Collier's Old Corrector altered it to *ground*. The Cambridge edd. give an anonymous conjecture *garanto*. Warburton explains the passage: "no one can have a better reason for granting a request than the necessity of its being granted" (Var. Ed. vol. vii. p. 27). Mason makes *grant* = concession (*ut supra*), and Steevens explains it "The fairest grant is *to* necessity; *i.e.* necessitas quod cogit defendit" (*ut supra*). Let us, however, look at the whole passage. Don Pedro says:

What need the bridge much broader than the flood?

i.e. "Why need your apologies be so much more ample than the case requires?" Then he goes on, "the kindest answer I can make to your request is to give what you *most urgently need the necessity*, i.e. my influence on your behalf;" and he goes on: *Look, what will serve is fit*, that is to say, "What will answer the purpose," or "What will gain your object is the best thing to do." This seems a more straightforward and a clearer explanation than any of those given above, although it involves an elliptical construction. For a similar use of *necessity* compare Winter's Tale, i. 2. 22:

Were there *necessity* in your request.

Shakespeare uses it frequently in the sense of "cogency," "imperative need." The substantive *grant* does not occur very often; it is used = the *grant* of a request in III. Henry VI. iii. 3. 130:

Your *grant*, or your denial, shall be mine;

and again: II. Henry IV. iv. 2. 40:

With *grant* of our most just and right desires.

But if this interpretation of the passage be thought too far-fetched, we must suppose that all Don Pedro means to say is: "The best excuse for you is that everyone *must* be in love some time or other" (*the necessity*). But this explanation strikes one as not quite satisfactory. Don Pedro takes a serious interest in Claudio's love affair, and is anxious to forward it; he recognizes that he stands in need, perhaps, of some recommendation to Leonato, and that his, *i.e.* Don Pedro's, good word would help him more than anything else. Except for the recent success which he had made in the campaign under Don Pedro, it may be doubted whether Claudio could have ventured to aspire to the hand of the daughter of the governor of Messina.

ACT I. Scene 2.

58. Line 1: *How now, brother! Where is my* COUSIN, *your son?*—*Cousin* was used very loosely in Shakespeare's time for any kinsman. For instance, in King John, iii. 3. 17, Eleanor uses it when addressing her grandson; and below, in the same scene, line 71, John uses *it*, as here, for "nephew." *Niece* and *nephew* were both used in a similarly lax manner. See Two Gent. note 91; and I. Henry VI. note 135.

59. Line 4: *I can tell you* STRANGE *news*.—So Q.; Ff. omit *strange*.

60. Lines 4, 5:

NEWS, *that you yet dreamt not of.*
Leon. ARE THEY *good?*

Shakespeare uses *news* both as a singular and plural noun. See Tempest, v. 1. 220: "What *is the news*?" and ii. 1. 180 of this play: "*these* ill *news*," where again he uses it in the plural.

61. Line 6: *As the* EVENT *stamps them*.—So F. 2, F. 3, F. 4; Q. F. 1 have *events*.

62. Line 9: *walking in a thick*-PLEACHED *alley in my* ORCHARD.—Shakespeare uses *pleached* in Henry V. v. 2. 42: "hedges even-*pleach'd*;" in Antony and Cleopatra, iv. 14. 73: "with *pleach'd* arms;" and in this play, iii. 1. 7: "steal into the *pleached* bower." In The Lover's Complaint, line 205, we have:

With twisted metal amorously *impleach'd*.

The verb *to pleach*, or *to plash*—the latter being the more usual form—is connected with middle English *plechan* = to propagate a vine. The old French was *plessier*, and the modern French *plesser*, which Cotgrave renders "To *plash* . . . plait young branches, one within an other; also, to thicken a hedge, or cover a walke, by *plashing*." These are probably all derived from the Latin *plectere*. *To plash* is still used as a term in modern gardening.

Shakespeare does not ever use *orchard* in the modern sense of a garden devoted to fruit-trees, as distinguished from a flower-garden. The fact is, that, in olden times, a flower-garden and what we call a kitchen-garden were all one. Such gardens may still be seen attached to monasteries. At the Dominican Monastery near Woodchester, in Gloucestershire, there is a very fine specimen of a *thick-pleached* alley of filbert trees. Such alleys, alas! are quite out of fashion in modern gardens.

63. Line 10: *were thus* MUCH *overheard by a man of mine*.—Ff. omit *much*, perhaps rightly, as being unnecessary, and, on the same ground, the omission of *strange* (line 4 above) might be justified.

64. Line 16: *to take the present time by the top*.—Compare All's Well, v. 3. 39:

Let's take the instant *by the forward top*.

Compare the common expression, "To take time by the forelock." For *break with him*, see above, note 54.

65. Line 21: *we will hold it as a dream till it* APPEAR *itself*.—Dyce, very plausibly, suggests that we should read *approve*, and compares Coriolanus, iv. 3. 9: "your favour is well *approv'd* by your tongue," where, he says, "the Folio has *appear'd*, but the sense requires *approv'd*." Schmidt says it is used there adjectively = "apparent." It is possible that, after all, the reading in the text requires no alteration. The sense may be "We will look upon it as a dream till it makes itself visible," *itself* having the force of "the very person."

66. Lines 24, 25: [Exit Antonio.—Antonio's son, with some Musicians, crosses the stage.—To Antonio's son] COUSIN, *you know what you have to do*.—It is evident that *Antonio* is intended to go off the stage at this point, and that these words are addressed to somebody else; most probably, as Dyce suggests, to *Antonio's* son. For *cousin* see note 58 above.

There is no stage-direction in the original either for Antonio's exit, or for the entry of anybody else. The only direction prefixed to the scene in Q. Ff. is *Enter Leonato and an old man brother to Leonato*. Capell inserted here the stage-direction, *Enter several persons, bearing things for the Banquet*, for which the Cambridge edd. substituted *Enter Attendants*.

Q. Ff. read *cousins*. We have followed Dyce in reading *cousin*, as Q. Ff. both have "good *cousins*" just below, line 29, and it is much more probable that Antonio should address his *nephew* than that he should address one of the attendants.

ACT I. SCENE 3.

67. Line 1: *What the good-year!*—This expression, according to some commentators, is equivalent to "a slight curse." Good-year is supposed, generally, to be a corruption of *goujere* (Fr.) = the venereal disease; and the expression would therefore be equivalent to "What the pox on it!" Blakeway quotes Roper's Life of More: "When Sir Thomas More was confined in the Tower, his wife visited him, and began reproving him: '*What the good yeare*, Mr. Moore, I marvell that you will now soe playe the foole?'" (Var. Ed. vol. v. p. 29). Halliwell (in his Folio Shakespeare) quotes from Holyband's French Littleton, ed. 1609, a passage where the expression is used in its literal sense, "God give you a good morrow and a *good yeare*.—Dieu vous doit bon jour et *bon an*." He also gives several similar examples. The same expression, *What the good year!* occurs in three other passages in Shakespeare: in Merry Wives, i. 4. 129, where it is spelt in F. 1 *good-ier*; and in II. Henry IV. ii. 4. 64, 191, where, in the Quarto, it is spelt in the first passage *good-yere*, and in the second *goodeare*, and in F. 1 *good-yere* in both passages. In the passage in our text it is spelt *good yeare*. In Lear, v. 3. 24:

> The *good-years* shall devour them, flesh and fell,

F. 1 has *good yeares*; Qq. have simply *good*. It therefore remains doubtful whether we are to consider the word, in this passage, as a corruption of *goujere*, or whether we are to consider it as *good year*. In the three instances where this same expression occurs quoted above, Mistress Quickly[1] is the speaker on each occasion; and therefore it is highly probable that the expression is intended to have there its vulgar sense. In the passage in our text Conrade is the speaker; and, though he is addressing Don John, his superior, still, as he does not seem to have been a gentleman distinguished by any remarkable politeness, it is quite possible that he would use the coarser of the two expressions. In the passage from King Lear there can be no doubt that *good-yeare* means the same disease as the French *goujere*.

68. Line 4: *There is no measure in the occasion that breeds* IT.—Q. Ff. omit *it;* added by Theobald.

69. Lines 11-19.—Don John's sentiments in this speech epitomize the principles of a thoroughly selfish man. Johnson has a note in which he remarks: "This is one of our author's natural touches. An envious and unsocial mind, too proud to give pleasure, and too sullen to receive it, always endeavours to hide its malignity from the world and from itself, under the plainness of simple honesty, or the dignity of haughty independence" (Var. Ed. vol. vii. p. 30).

70. Line 19: CLAW *no man in his humour.*—It does not appear that Shakespeare uses *claw* elsewhere in this sense = to flatter, except it be in Love's Labour's Lost, where Nathaniel, after complimenting Holofernes on his verses, says (iv. 2. 64-66): "A rare *talent*," and Dull remarks: "If a *talent* be a *claw*, look how he *claws* him with a *talent*." There it would certainly seem that *claw* is used in the double sense. Palsgrave has: "I *clawe*, as a man or a beest dothe a thyng softely with his nayles. *Je grattigne*, prim. conj. *Clawe* my backe and I wyll *clawe* thy toe; *gratigne* mon dos et je te *gratigneray* ton orteyl." Cotgrave has: "To *claw* gently. *Galloner;*" and under *Galloner*, "To stroake, cherish, *claw*, or clap on the backe;" and Minsheu has: "*Clawebacke*, vide *Adulador*," *i.e.* a flatterer.

71. Lines 28, 29: *I had rather be a* CANKER *in a hedge than a* rose IN *his* GRACE.—*Canker* here is supposed to mean the dog-rose, the sense in which certainly Shakespeare seems sometimes to use it, as in I. Henry IV. i. 3. 175, 176:

> To put down Richard, that sweet lovely rose,
> And plant this thorn, this *canker*, Bolingbroke.

There is also the following passage in Middleton's Fair Quarrel, iii. 2:

> he held out a rose,
> To draw the yielding sense, which come to hand,
> He shifts and gives a *canker*.
> —Works, vol. iii. p. 501.

It is not very easy to see how CANKER-*rose* came to be applied to the dog-rose. In some dialects *canker-rose* means the red poppy, both from its colour and from its being a noxious weed in wheat-fields. Grose gives: "CANKER, a poisonous fungus, resembling a mushroom. Glou. Likewise the dog-rose. Devon. Called also the *canker-rose*." One does not see why the dog-rose should have so ill a name, as it grows generally in hedges where it does no harm. The word *canker* does not ever seem to have borne any sense except that of "a sore," or "a disease in trees," or "a fungus." It is possible that the reason why this name was given to the dog-rose—of which, by the way, there are twenty-three different species in England—is that this shrub is very subject to a disease which in Cumberland I have often heard called the *canker*, and which anyone who walks along a country hedgerow may notice for himself. In this disease the calyx becomes abnormally developed; and the bud, instead of growing into a flower, remains a large green mossy-looking lump which produces neither flower nor seed. It would seem that this use of the word *canker* is by no means confined to the North. Johnson would read "rose *by* his grace;" but he first hazarded the conjecture "rose in his *garden*." It is evident that Don John refers to Conrade's speech above (line 22), where he reminds him that his brother has taken him "newly into his *grace*."

72. Line 41: *I make all use of it, for I use it* ONLY.—This Steevens explains "I make nothing else my counsellor" (Var. Ed. vol. vii. p. 31). But surely it is not necessary to attach this meaning to the phrase. What Don John means is that he makes *all use* of his discontent, because it is the only humour that he ever does *use* or employ.

73. Line 50: *What is he for a fool?*—For this phrase compare Ram Alley, iv. 1:

> *Lady Som.* What is he for a man?
> *Serv.-Man.* Nothing for a man, but much for a beast.
> —Dodsley, vol. x. p. 355.

Shakespeare does not seem to have used this expression except in this instance. Compare Ben Jonson's Silent Woman, iii. 1: "*What is he for a vicar?*" (Works, vol. iii.

[1] It is doubtful, to say the least, whether the Mistress Quickly of the Merry Wives and of Henry IV. are the same person.

p. 397). Gifford in his note on this passage says: "This is pure German, or, as the authorized phrase seems to be, Saxon, in its idiom, and is very common in our old writers. Was ist das für ein?" Compare also Ben Jonson's Every Man out of his Humour, iii. 1: "*What is he for a creature?*" (Works, vol. ii. p. 105). Though not exactly the same expression, we may compare Comedy of Errors, ii. 2. 190: "I cross me *for a sinner*."

74. Line 54: *And who—and who—which way looks he?*—None of the commentators seem to have paid any attention to this passage, which is not very intelligible, except Walker, who gives four instances from Shirley's plays of similar repetition; three being the very same phrase. Dyce says that Grant White pronounced the second *and who* to be an accidental repetition. But whether it be an accidental repetition or not, there does not seem to be any sense in the sentence as commonly punctuated. Don John has already asked (line 52), "*Who*, the most exquisite Claudio?" to which Borachio answers "Even he." But there can be no sense in his asking *again* who Claudio is. As we have printed the passage, the meaning would be that Don John is going to ask *And who—and who is the lady?* when he changes his mind and puts the question in another form. It may be that *And who and who?* is a misprint for *And how and how?* but even then there does not seem much sense in it.

75. Line 58: *A very forward* MARCH-CHICK.—This is usually explained as a *chicken* hatched in *March*. Amongst poultry farmers it is not usual to set eggs under the hens until the spring; but the earlier they are set, the more valuable the chickens are for the market and for laying purposes, as the pullets bred early in the year come on to lay in the winter months when eggs are scarcest.

76. Lines 60, 61: *Being entertain'd for a perfumer, as I was* SMOKING *a musty room.*—Steevens says in his note on this passage: "The neglect of cleanliness among our ancestors, rendered such precautions too often necessary" (Var. Ed. vol. vii. p. 32). But it is not at all certain that the *smoking*, or *fumigation*, of the rooms was necessitated by any special want of cleanliness. In a very interesting reprint by Dr. Furnivall, Bokes of Nurture and Keruynge, there is given at pp. 141, 142, in an extract from Sir John Harington's Schoole of Saleme, 2nd Part (1624): "Take your meate in the hotte time of Summer in cold places, but in the Winter let there bee a bright fire, and take it in hotte places, your parlors or chambers being *first purged and ayred with suffumigations*, which I would not haue you to enter before the suffumigation bee plainely extinct, lest you draw the fume by reason of the odour." It would seem that the object of these *fumigations* was to air a room which had not been used regularly for some time.

77. Lines 67–70: *That young start-up hath all the glory of my overthrow: if I can cross him any way, I bless myself every way.*—It does not quite appear what ground Don John had, further than his sullen discontented nature, for his hatred of Claudio; or in what particular Claudio could be said to have caused his overthrow. It looks as if the ground of complaint was very much the same as that which Iago had against Cassio; and that Claudio, by gaining Don Pedro's favour, had been raised over the head of Don John in the army. We are told that Don John had been taken "newly into his grace" after having "stood out against" him, perhaps upon this very subject of Claudio's promotion. See Conrade's speech above, lines 22–24. Anyhow, it is clear that the reconciliation, however brought about, was not a very sincere one.

ACT II. Scene 1.

78.—The stage-direction at the beginning of this scene stands thus in Q. and Ff.: "*Enter Leonato, his brother, his wife, Hero his daughter, and Beatrice his niece, and a kinsman.*" See above, note 1.

79. Lines 4, 5: *I never can see him but I am heart-burn'd an hour after.*—This expression, more forcible than elegant, well describes the disagreeable sensation known as *heartburn*, which arises from an excess of acidity, and causes the food after a meal, when only half digested, to rise in the stomach.

80. Lines 10, 11: *the other too like my lady's eldest son, evermore tattling.*—None of the commentators apparently have noticed that this is, most probably, an allusion to some well-known anecdote or "Merry Tale." In answer to an inquiry of mine, Mr. Halliwell-Phillipps writes that I am "undoubtedly right" in my conjecture, but that he cannot give me any clue to the anecdote in question. "I do not think," he adds, "it could have escaped me had I met with the jest, but so much of the lighter literature of the time has unfortunately perished."

81. Line 33: *I had rather lie in the woollen.*—This expression is usually explained to mean "I had rather lie between blankets," *i.e.* without sheets; as people, in Shakespeare's time, generally slept naked, this would be more disagreeable than in modern times, when night-shirts are universally worn. But there may also be a reference to a totally different matter. It appears that it was the custom in England to bury persons in *woollen* material; but that the employment of linen material gradually increased to such an extent, that an act was passed in the reign of Charles II. (30 Car. II. stat. 1, cap. 3, sec. 3) providing that no corpse should be buried in anything but *woollen* material, or in a coffin lined with anything but sheep's *wool*. This was done to encourage the *woollen* trade. The act was repealed in 1815 (see Notes and Queries, 4th Series, ix. p. 284). In some churches a register was kept of persons "Bury'd in Wollen," and "Not Bury'd in Wollen" (*ut supra*, xi. 84).

82. Lines 42, 43: *I will even take sixpence in earnest of the* BEAR-HERD, *and lead his apes into hell.*—Q. Ff. read *Berrord*; F. 3, F. 4 *Bear-herd*. Collier, who is followed by many modern editors, altered it, unnecessarily, to *bear-ward*. *Bear-herd* occurs in Taming of Shrew, Induction, ii. 21, also in II. Henry IV. i. 2. 192. In the other passages in which the word occurs, II. Henry VI. v. 1. 149, 210, the spelling is *bearard*. Certainly the spelling there seems to warrant the reading of *bear-ward*, which, though not found in Shakespeare, occurs in Elizabethan writers. See (as well as regards the superstition that old maids, to

whom Beatrice refers, had to *lead apes in hell*) Taming of the Shrew, note 72.

83. Lines 50, 51: *and away to Saint Peter:* FOR THE HEAVENS!—Q. Ff. punctuate thus, except that they have a comma after *heavens*. We have followed Staunton in putting a note of exclamation after *heavens*, in order to mark more clearly that the expression is an oath which was in common use in Shakespeare's time. We have an example of it in Merchant of Venice, ii. 2. 13: "*for the heavens*, rouse up a brave mind." Cotgrave has a curious use of this phrase; under *Haut* he gives "*Faire haut le bois*, to make a stand; also, to tipple, carouse *for the heavens*." Nares says it is merely a corrupted form of "'fore the heavens." Schmidt, curiously enough, takes *for* here = "bound for," "on the way to," while, in the passage from Merchant of Venice, he seems to take it as = "for the sake of," "for the love of."

84. Line 62: *till God make men of some other* METAL *than earth*.—*Metal* is used here, of course, not in its scientific sense, but, figuratively, as the material of which a thing is made. Shakespeare is rather fond of using *metal* in this sense. Compare All's Well, i. 1. 141: "That you were made of, is *metal* to make virgins;" Lear, i. 1. 71:

> Of the self-same *metal* that my sister is.

85. Line 65: *a clod of wayward* MARL.—This is the only passage in which Shakespeare uses this word, either in his plays or poems. *Marl* properly means a rich kind of earth, consisting partly of lime, partly of clay, which has been used in agriculture for enriching poorer soil since the time of the Romans; as is evident from a passage in Pliny (bk. xvii. chap. vi.) thus translated by Holland: "The Britaines and Frenchmen have devised another meanes to manure their ground, by a kind of lime-stone or clay, which they call *Marga*, [*Marle*.] And verily they have a great opinion of the same, that it mightily enricheth it and maketh it more plentifull. This *marle* is a certaine fat of the ground, much like unto the glandulous kernels growing in the bodies of beasts, and it is thickned in manner of marow or the kernell of fat about it" (pt. i. p. 505). Chaucer uses *marle-pit* in The Miller's Tale (line 3460). Milton uses the word *marle* in Paradise Lost with what seems to be singular inappropriateness, for the soil by the shore of the burning lake (i. 295, 296):

> He walk'd with to support uneasy steps
> Over the burning *marl*.

86. Line 73: *if the prince be too* IMPORTANT.—For *important* used as = "importunate," compare Comedy of Errors, v. 1. 138: "At your *important* letters;" and Lear, iv. 4. 26:

> My mourning and *important* tears hath pitied.

87. Line 81: *full of state and* ANCIENTRY.—Q. F. 1, F. 2, have *auncientry;* F. 3, F. 4, *ancientry*. These readings are worth noting, perhaps, as guides to the pronunciation of the word in the time of Shakespeare. *Ancient* was very often pronounced *auncient*. *Ancientry* is used in one other passage in Shakespeare; in Winter's Tale, iii. 3. 63: "wronging the *ancientry;*" where it means "old people." Schmidt explains the meaning of the word in the text as "the port and behaviour of old age;" but it seems rather to mean what may be termed "old-fashionedness."

88. Line 82: *cinque-pace*.—This dance is thus alluded to by Sir John Davies, st. 67:

> *Five* was the number of the music's feet,
> Which still the dance did with *five paces* meet.

The *cinque-pace* is only mentioned in one other passage in Shakespeare, viz. in Twelfth Night, i. 3. 139. I am indebted to Mr. Julian Marshall for the following information: The *Galliard* consisted of five paces or bars in the first strain, and was therefore called a *Cinque Pace*. Every Pavan had its *Galliard*, a lighter air, made out of the former; and the tunes are common in old music-books. An instance is given in Grove's Dictionary, vol. i. p. 578.

89. Lines 82, 83: *falls into the cinque-pace faster and faster, till he* SINK *into his grave*.—Collier altered *sink* into *cinque-pace* or *sink a pace*. We cannot see the necessity for the alteration. Perhaps Collier was thinking of a passage in Marston's Insatiate Countess, act ii.:

> Thinke of me as of the man
> Whose dancing dayes you see are not yet done.
> *Len.* Yet, you *sinke a pace*, sir.
>
> —Works, vol. iii. p. 125.

We certainly do not wish to increase the number of verbal jingles in this play, nor is the rhythm of the passage improved by Collier's alteration.

90. Line 90: *Lady, will you walk about with your* FRIEND?—For this use of the word *friend* compare Merry Wives, iii. 3. 124, where Mrs. Page, addressing Mrs. Ford, says: "If you have a *friend* here," *i.e.* a lover; and, as applied to one of the other sex, Love's Labour's Lost, v. 2. 404, where Biron, addressing Rosaline, jocularly asks her never to "come in vizard to my *friend*." We may compare the French *cher ami* and *chère amie* used in a somewhat similar sense. See Romeo and Juliet, note 145.

91. Lines 97, 98: *God defend the lute should be like the* CASE!—She means "God forbid his face should be as ugly as is his mask or *visor!*"

92. Lines 99-101:

> D. Pedro. *My visor is* PHILEMON'S ROOF; *within the house is* JOVE.
> Hero. *Why, then, your visor should be* THATCH'D.
> D. Pedro. *Speak low, if you speak love.*

In line 99 *Jove* is the reading of Q.; Ff., by an evident mistake, have *love*. The two latter speeches should clearly be printed not as separate lines, but as forming a single line corresponding in metre with Don Pedro's speech above. The story alluded to is that of Baucis and Philemon, which is found in Ovid's Metamorphoses (bk. viii. lines 626-724). Jupiter and Mercury were wandering about Phrygia, disguised as ordinary mortals, and they could find no one to receive them into their house but two old peasants, Philemon and his wife Baucis. In reward for the kind treatment received in the *thatched* cottage of Philemon, Jupiter saved the old couple from a sudden flood, which took place in their neighbourhood, by transporting them to an adjacent hill out of reach of the waters. Then, having changed their cottage into a temple, dedicated to himself, of which at their request he made them the guardians, he granted them, in accordance with their request, the privilege of dying at the same moment. After death they were metamorphosed into trees. In As You Like It (iii. 3. 10, 11) Shakespeare, apparently, alludes again to the same story: "O knowledge ill-inhabited,—worse than Jove in a *thatch'd* house!" The expression *thatched* was probably, in both cases, suggested by Golding's translation of the line:

> Parva quidem, stipulis et cannâ tecta palustri.
> —Ovid Metamorph. viii. 630.
>
> The *roofe* thereof was *thatched* all with straw and fennish reede.

Dyce, in a note on this passage, asks whether Shakespeare, in these two lines, does not quote some poem which has now perished. The conjecture is a very probable one.

93. Lines 105, 106.—These, and the two next speeches of Balthazar, are given by mistake in Q. Ff. to Benedick. Theobald was the first to give them rightly to Balthazar.

94. Line 114: *Answer*, CLERK.—Referring to Balthazar's *Amen* above (lines 110, 112). *Clerk* is used here, and in three other passages in Shakespeare, in the sense of the "parish *clerk*," *i.e.* the person who reads the responses in church. See Taming of Shrew, iv. 4. 94; Richard II. iv. 1. 173; and Sonnet lxxxv. 6:

> And like unletter'd *clerk* still cry "Amen."

The latter passage would seem to militate against the most probable origin of the use of *clerk* in this sense, namely, that some scholar among the congregation was appointed to say the responses on behalf of all. In the English Church before the Reformation, as now in the Roman Catholic Church, the responses at the mass were said by the "server," who was generally a layman; and his successor, in the Protestant Church, was the *clerk*.

95. Line 120: *I know you by the* WAGGLING *of your head*.—This word, which occurs only here in Shakespeare, is found in May's translation of Lucan's Pharsalia, 1627 (bk. v.):

> Nor that the crow *waggling* along the shore
> Diues downe, and seemes t' anticipate a shoure.

96. Line 122: *so ill-well*.—This expression, which, at first sight, seems an awkward one, is really very forcible. Ursula means, "You could never imitate him *with such cruel fidelity* (*so ill well*) if you were not the man yourself." Steevens compares the expression in The Merchant of Venice (i. 2. 63), "a *better bad* habit of frowning."

97. Line 122: *Here's his* DRY HAND UP AND DOWN.—A *dry hand* was always supposed to be a sign of a cold and chaste nature, as a *moist* palm was of the contrary. For *up and down* compare our modern expression *all the world over*.

98. Line 125: *At a word*.—Schmidt gives as the German equivalent to this, *kurz und gut*. Compare Merry Wives, i. 1. 108, 109: "He hath wrong'd me; indeed he hath;—*at a word*, he hath."

99. Lines 134, 135: *that I had my good wit out of the* HUNDRED MERRY TALES.—This refers to the earliest jest-book printed in the English language, of which there is extant only one perfect copy, in the library at Gottingen. For some time the commentators thought the book referred to was either a translation of *Les Cent Nouvelles Nouvelles*, or a translation of Boccaccio's Decameron; but at last an imperfect copy of the work was discovered by Professor Conybeare, and this copy was edited by Singer in 1814, and was included in Hazlitt's Collection of Shakespeare Jest Books, 1864. It was made up of a number of mutilated leaves, and was very defective. It was once in the possession of Mr. Halliwell-Phillipps; but I do not know where it is to be found at present. The Gottingen copy, which is dated 1526, has been twice reprinted: once in 1866 by Dr. Hermann Oesterley; and more recently (1887), a limited number of copies, reproduced in facsimile by photolithography, and edited by Mr. Carew Hazlitt, have been published. This is a very handsome edition; and as the only reproduction of the unique original, is very valuable to lovers of old English literature. It would seem that the Gottingen copy, and that discovered by Professor Conybeare, belonged to different editions, some tales being included in the former which are not found in the latter; while three tales, found in the imperfect edition, are not found in the perfect edition of 1526. In his preface to the edition of 1887 Mr. Hazlitt suggests that the author of the *Hundred Merry Tales* was John Heywood, chiefly known by his Book of Epigrams, and by some Interludes which were printed by Rastell, who also printed the *Hundred Merry Tales*. Hazlitt conjectures that Sir Thomas More might have helped John Heywood in making this collection. The stories are, many of them, very simple, and comparatively few of them coarse. Many of the jokes, such as they are, turn upon points connected with the ritual of the old Church before Protestantism was established in England; and some of these stories might certainly be attributed to Sir Thomas More. To all the tales quaint morals are appended. It does not appear that either Beatrice or Benedick was indebted to this collection of *facetiæ* for any of their wit.

100. Lines 143–147: *only his gift is in devising* IMPOSSIBLE *slanders: none but libertines delight in him; and the commendation is not in his wit, but in his villany; for he both pleases men and angers them, and then they laugh at him and beat him*.—It must be confessed that this is a most pungent description of the licensed slanderer, and might seem to anticipate certain forms of journalism developed in modern times. The meaning of the passage is quite clear, though some of the commentators have treated it as obscure. In such a person as Beatrice describes *none but libertines*—that is to say, people more or less unscrupulous in their moral conduct—*delight*; and it is not the *wit* of the slanderer so much as his ill-nature that pleases them. When that ill-nature, as almost invariably happens sooner or later, is turned against their own selves, what they formerly found so full of amusement now *angers* them; and they are the first to take summary vengeance on the slanderer. Scarcely a day passes but the truth of this description is practically illustrated. The man or woman of the world, who chuckles over some malicious and cowardly insult directed against an acquaintance, or even against a dear friend, will be furious, the very next day, at some attack, perhaps less malicious, directed against himself or herself.

101. Line 148: *I would he had* BOARDED *me*.—This word, adapted from the French *aborder*, seems to have meant originally "to come close to," "to accost;" and

hence "to *board* a ship," that is, to come alongside a ship for the purpose of taking it by force; at least it is the only meaning given by Palsgrave. Shakespeare uses the word in both senses pretty frequently. Here, as Beatrice has compared the company to a fleet, it comes natural enough, and it is used, with the same reminiscence of its nautical meaning, in Love's Labour's Lost, ii. 1. 218:

> I was as willing to grapple as he was *to board.*

102. Line 160.—The dance here introduced is, in the acting version, generally introduced earlier in the scene, before line 90, when Don Pedro, Claudio, and the rest enter.

103. Line 169: *you are very* NEAR *my brother* IN HIS LOVE.—Compare Richard III. iii. 4. 13:

> Lord Hastings, you and he are *near in love.*

104. Line 170: *he is* ENAMOUR'D ON *Hero.*—*Enamoured* is used with the preposition *on* in II. Henry IV. i. 3. 102; and with *upon* in I. Henry IV. v. 2. 70, 71:

> Cousin, I think thou art *enamoured*
> *Upon* his follies.

It is used with *of* in Mids. Night's Dream, iii. 1. 141; iv. 1. 82; and Romeo and Juliet, iii. 3. 2.

105. Line 184: *Therefore all hearts in love use their own tongues.*—Some commentators understand *let* before *all*, making *use* the imperative. Abbott suggests that it may be a subjunctive used optatively.

106. Line 186: *And trust no agent;* FOR *beauty is a witch.*—Pope would omit *for;* but the irregularity of metre is not displeasing, and the word *for* is almost necessary.

107. Line 187: *Against whose charms faith melteth into* BLOOD.—The meaning is, *against* (that is, "in the face of") *whose charms, faith* (*i.e.* "loyalty") "is dissolved into sensual passion." Such is, undoubtedly, the meaning of *blood* here. The imagery is founded upon the superstition that witches, or other persons who practised witchcraft, were in the habit of making wax figures of those whom they wished either to injure or to influence. In the 16th chap. of book xii. of his Discoverie of Witchcraft, in the second section, which treats of "A charme teaching how to hurt whom you list with images of wax &c.," Reginald Scot says: "To obteine a womans love, an image must be made in the houre of *Venus*, of virgine wax, in the name of the beloved, whereupon a character is written, & is warmed at a fier, and in dooing therof the name of some angell must be mentioned" (Nicholson's Reprint, p. 209). It is probable that to some such supposed practice the reference here is made.

108. Line 189: *Which I mistrusted not. Farewell,* THEREFORE, *Hero!*—Here again Pope would get rid of the redundant syllable by reading *then* instead of *therefore;* an obvious emendation, which Collier's Old Corrector adopted; but there is a considerable pause after the full stop, so that the extra syllable is not at all unrhythmical, and, in fact, helps the speaker to linger on the *Farewell.*

109. Lines 195–197: *to the next* WILLOW . . . *What fashion will you wear the garland of? about your neck, like an usurer's chain? or under your arm, like a lieutenant's scarf?*—For the WILLOW as an emblem of unhappy love, see III. Henry VI. note 231; and compare the well-known and pathetic song of Desdemona (Othello, iv. 3). The symbolical use of the *willow* as an emblem of grief and mourning must be of very ancient date, as we find a reference to it in the beautiful psalm, "By the rivers of Babylon" (Psalm cxxxvii. 2).

Usurer's chain refers to the gold chains worn by the more wealthy merchants of that day, many of whom were bankers, and lent out money at interest. For the *wearing of the scarf under the arm,* see Love's Labour's Lost, note 75.

110. Line 201: *spoken like an honest drover: so they sell bullocks.*—There is probably an allusion here to some popular saying. Benedick may mean that Claudio seems as ready to get rid of Hero, as a *drover* is to get rid of his restive beasts.

111. Lines 209, 210: *Alas, poor hurt fowl! now will he creep into sedges.*—This is one of those touches which shows how well Shakespeare was acquainted with a country life. Every one who has gone wild-fowl shooting knows how a wounded bird will *creep into sedges,* and what a difficult thing it is to dislodge it.

112. Lines 214, 215: *it is the base,* THOUGH *bitter, disposition of Beatrice that puts the world into her person, and so gives me out.*—Johnson proposed to read: "it is the *base,* THE *bitter,*" and other emendations have been proposed; but both Q. and F. 1 have "THOUGH *bitter*" between brackets; and therefore it seems evident that the reading of the text is the right one. The meaning, perhaps, is that to the *base* disposition we generally attribute a cringing and sycophantic demeanour, but that Beatrice, on the contrary, adds to her *baseness* the fault of *bitterness.*

113. Line 222: *as melancholy as a lodge in a warren.*—Rabbit *warrens* were generally in a wild part of the country, and the *lodge,* in which the keeper of the *warren* lived, was a lonely habitation enough. Compare in The Man in the Moone Telling Strange Fortunes, 1609, p. 3: "By the solitarinesse of the house I judged it *a lodge* in a forest" (Percy Reprint, 1849).

114. Line 223: *that your grace had got the good-will of* THIS *young lady.*—Some editors alter *this* to *the,* on the ground that *this* would imply the presence of Hero in the scene; but it is possible that Benedick was meant to indicate, by a gesture in the direction of the room where Hero was supposed to be, to whom he referred; or, as the entertainment was given at Leonato's, *this* may more probably mean "the young lady of the house."

115. Lines 241, 242: *If their singing answer your saying, by my faith, you say honestly.*—This speech of Benedick's is not very clearly expressed. It is an instance of an epigrammatic style of answer obtained at the cost of intelligibility. What he means to say is, that if the young birds, when restored to their owner, had suffered no greater injury than being taught to sing, he would believe Don Pedro was speaking the truth; that is, in saying that he made love to Hero, not on his own account, but on account of Claudio.

116. Line 243: *The Lady Beatrice hath a quarrel* TO

you.—For an instance of this same construction, see Twelfth Night, iii. 4. 247: "I am sure no man hath any *quarrel to me.*"

117. Line 246: *she* MISUS'D *me past the endurance of a* BLOCK!—For this use of *misused*=abused, compare Taming of Shrew, ii. 1. 159, 160:

> with twenty such vile terms,
> As she had studied to *misuse* me so.

For *block*, explained by Schmidt to mean "a stupid or insensible fellow," compare Richard III. iii. 7. 42:

> What tongueless *blocks* were they!

The expression was taken, probably, from the *blocks* on which hats were made. See above, note 19.

118. Line 251: *duller than a great thaw.*—This is Benedick's expansion of what Beatrice said. She simply called him "a very dull fool." *A great thaw* might be called *dull*, either because of the fog and dull weather which generally accompany it, or because it puts an end to all the sports that take place on the ice during a frost.

119. Line 252: *huddling jest upon jest, with such* IMPOSSIBLE CONVEYANCE, *upon me.*—All sorts of emendations have been proposed for the word *impossible* here, but surely quite unnecessarily. We have had *impossible* used above (line 143) in a somewhat similar sense; and compare Merry Wives, iii. 5. 151: "I will search *impossible* places," and Twelfth Night, iii. 2. 76: "such *impossible* passages of grossness." *Impossible* here has simply the force of "what you would scarcely think *possible.*" The exact meaning of *conveyance* it is more difficult to determine. Malone probably is right in saying that it is used in the sense of the sleight of hand of a juggler; and it is worth noting that Scot in the 13th book of his Discoverie of Witchcraft (chapters xxiv. to xxxi.), in which he treats of jugglery and sleight of hand, constantly uses the verb *to convey* in the technical sense of "to pass;" and the title of chap. xxiv. is "Of *conveiance* of monie." But it may also imply the idea of dishonesty, as well as its simple primitive sense of the act of transferring anything or *conveying* anything. Benedick means to say that Beatrice heaped upon him, or flung at him, ridiculous jests with such inconceivable rapidity, and such unfairness at the same time, that he felt like a man being shot at with a deadly weapon.

120. Line 254: *She speaks poniards, and every word stabs.*—Compare the well-known line in Hamlet, iii. 2. 414:

> I will *speak daggers* to her, but use none;

and King John, ii. 1. 463:

> He gives the bastinado with his tongue.

For a similar use of the word *stab* compare II. Henry VI. iv. 1. 66:

> First let my words *stab* him, as he hath me.

121. Lines 256, 257: *if her breath were as terrible as* HER *terminations, there were no living near her; she would infect to the north star.*—So Q.; Ff. omit *her*, which probably led Walker to make the curious conjecture "her *minations.*" Benedick purposely uses an extravagant, and perhaps not a very elegant word. With regard to the last sentence Dyce gives a very curious quotation (note 23) from the "Protesilaos of Anaxandrides (apud Athenæus, book iv. sect. 7), which describes the wedding-feast of Iphicrates on his marriage with the daughter of Kotys, king of Thrace:

> [illegible]
> [illegible]
> That purple tapestry strew'd the market-place,
> And thence extended *to the northern star.*

122. Line 263: *the infernal Atè in good apparel.*—This phrase gave rise to a curious note of Warburton's; he says it was "a pleasant allusion to the custom of ancient poets and painters, who represent the *Furies in rags*" (Var. Ed. vol. vii. p. 45). But, as Steevens pointed out, unfortunately *Atè* is not one of the Furies, but the Goddess of Revenge or Discord.

123. Lines 265–267: *for certainly, while she is* HERE, *a man may live as quiet in hell as in a sanctuary.*—This passage is very vague, and is another instance of the obscurity which arises from the speaker trying to be over-clever. Staunton (in a note on this passage) thinks that the obscurity may have arisen "from the author having first written *in hell*, and afterwards substituted *in a sanctuary*, without cancelling the former, so that, as in many other cases, both got into the text." The sentence would have been perfectly clear if the author had written "for certainly a man may live as quiet in hell as in a sanctuary *where she is.*" Perhaps if, instead of *here* we were to read *there*, it would convey very much the same meaning; but it may be that the poet advisedly wrote *here*, meaning *here in this world.*

124. Lines 274–276: *I will fetch you a toothpicker now from the furthest inch of Asia, &c.*—Asia was then the great land of marvels; the further east the traveller got the more wonderful the stories he ventured to tell. Africa was comparatively little known. It was in Asia that nearly all of the extraordinary prodigies, of which Mandeville gave an account, were to be found. *Prester John* was a semi-legendary potentate, to whom constant allusion is made in old plays. A somewhat similar feat to this one proposed in jest by Benedick was accomplished by Sir Huon of Bordeaux. The task prescribed him was to "goe to the citie of Babylon to the Admiral Gaudisse," and to bring his "hand full of the heare of his beard, and foure of his greatest teeth" (Huon of Bourdeaux, ch. 17).

125. Line 283: *I cannot endure* MY *Lady Tongue.*—So Q.; F. 1 has "*this* Lady Tongue," which F. 2 altered to "*this Lady's* tongue."

126. Lines 286–288: *he lent it me awhile; and I gave him use for it,—a double heart for his single one.*—This speech of Beatrice is not very intelligible: though none of the commentators seem to have thought it required any explanation; but I have little doubt she alludes here to some game or popular custom; perhaps to one resembling Philippine.

127. Line 305: CIVIL *as an* ORANGE, *and something of* THAT JEALOUS *complexion.*—So Q.; Ff. read *a* for *that.* As to *civil*, see Cotgrave, who defines *aigre-douce* as a "*civile* orange, or orange that is betweene sweet and sower." *Jealous complexion*, of course, refers to the yellowness which was the colour of jealousy. See Winter's Tale, ii. 3. 106–108:

'mongst all colours
No *yellow* in't, lest she suspect, as he does,
Her children not her husband's.

Steevens quotes from Nashe's Four Letters Confuted, 1592: "For the order of my life, it is *as civil as an orange*" (Var. Ed. vol. vii. p. 47); and we have the very same phrase in the chap-book "Mother Bunch" (Reprint, p. 2). *Civil* here no doubt means "bitter," as the rind of the *Seville orange* is very bitter. Staunton thought that if this sense of the word had become at all general, it might explain some passages in which it occurs apparently as a misprint for *cruel*, *e.g.* in Romeo and Juliet. (See note 5 of that play.) *Civil* occurs very frequently in act iv. scene 2 of Beaumont and Fletcher's Comedy, The Scornful Lady, where it seems to mean "respectable" in opposition to what we call "Bohemian."

128. Line 308: *I think* your BLAZON *to be true.*—According to Mr. Sloane-Evans "*Blazon* is derived from the French *Blazonner*, Angl.—*To lay out, or open.* Hence, in a secondary meaning, *To give an account of.* It has been defined, either as a description of Arms in apt and significant terms; or, a display of the virtues of their bearers" (British Heraldry, p. 1). The greater part of his work is called The Art of Blazon. The meaning here is: "I think your description of Claudio to be true; that you have 'displayed' him in his right colours in saying that his complexion is *yellow* or jealous." There may also be a reference to the second definition of the word *blazon* given above.

129. Line 327: *it keeps on the windy side of care.*—Beatrice means that it (her heart) keeps to *windward* of care. When two sailing boats are racing, it is of course the object of each to get to *windward* of the other, because the vessel which is on that side gets the first advantage of any breeze as it springs up. Of course when there were nothing but sailing ships, it would be the great object of every vessel to get this advantage in an encounter at sea. If the idea were that *care* was a *shore* which Beatrice's heart wished to avoid, it would be, as a rule, worse for her to be to *windward*, as she would then run the risk of being driven on a lee shore.

130. Line 328: *tells him in his ear that he is in* HER *heart.*—So Q.; Ff. have "my heart."

131. Line 330: *Good lord, for alliance!*—Staunton explains this expression as equivalent to "Heaven send me a husband!" Boswell thought it meant "Good Lord, how many alliances are forming! Every one is likely to be married but me" (Var. Ed. vol. vii. p. 48).

132. Line 331: *Thus* GOES *every one* TO THE WORLD *but I, and I am* SUN-BURN'D.—It appears that the expression *go to the world*, which puzzled the early commentators, was a popular phrase for "going to be married." Compare All's Well, i. 3. 19-21, where the clown says: "if I may have your ladyship's good-will *to go to the world*, Isbel the woman and I will do as we may." *Sun-burn'd* or *sun-burnt* means simply "homely-looking." Compare Troilus and Cressida, i. 3. 282, 283:

The Grecian dames are *sun burnt* and not worth
The splinter of a lance.

133. Lines 342, 343: *I beseech your grace, pardon me: I was born to speak all mirth and no matter.*—This apology of Beatrice's is very graceful, and quite redeems her from the imputation of rudeness to which her somewhat free utterances might have exposed her.

134. Line 372: *time goes on crutches till love have all his rites.*—Compare Rosalind's speech in As You Like It, iii. 2. 331-335: "Marry, he (*i.e.* Time) trots hard with a young maid between the contract of her marriage and the day it is solemnized: if the interim be but a se'nnight, *Time's pace* is so hard that it seems the length of seven year."

135. Line 377: *a time too brief, too, to have all things answer* MY *mind.*—So Q.; Ff. omit *my*.

136. Lines 381-383: *to bring Signior Benedick and the Lady Beatrice into a mountain of affection the one with the other.*—Johnson thought this a strange expression, and suggested "to bring . . . into a *mooting* of affection; to bring them not to any more *mootings* of contention, but to a *mooting* or conversation of love. This reading is confirmed by the preposition *with*; 'a mountain *with* each other,' or 'affection *with* each other,' cannot be used, but 'a *mooting* with each other is proper and regular" (Var. Ed. vol. vii. p. 50). But no alteration seems necessary. It is one of those exaggerated phrases common enough. It simply means a huge affection, as we might say "a heap of love."

ACT II. Scene 2.

137. Line 21: *The poison of that lies in you* TO TEMPER.—Shakespeare uses this verb (= to mix) in connection with poisons in three other passages: in Romeo and Juliet, iii. 5. 98; Hamlet, v. 2. 339; Cymbeline, v. 5. 250.

138. Line 24: *whose* ESTIMATION *do you mightily hold up.*—This word is only used twice by Shakespeare in its usual sense = "the act of estimating." He generally uses it in the sense of "that which entitles a person to esteem." Compare All's Well, v. 3. 3, 4:

As mad in folly, lack'd the sense to know
Her *estimation* home.

And, generally, in the sense of reputation; as in The Two Gent. of Verona, ii. 4. 55, 56:

I know the gentleman
To be of worth and worthy *estimation*;

in which sense it is common.

139. Line 44: *hear me call Margaret, Hero; hear Margaret term me* BORACHIO.—Q. Ff. read "hear Margaret term me *Claudio*." There is nothing to lead one to believe that there is a misprint here; but the difficulty is an obvious one: and, believing the author to have made a slip, we have adopted Theobald's emendation of *Borachio* for *Claudio* after serious consideration. It may be remarked that this is not only a question of verbal alteration; it is a question of making what is a very important incident in the plot—in fact one may almost say the main incident on which the play turns—intelligible to the audience. Borachio begins by saying: "Tell them that you know that Hero loves me;" he says nothing as to his being called Claudio by her, nor is there any subsequent mention of this fact in the account given of the scene by Borachio. Compare iii. 3. 153-157. Nor does

Claudio make any allusion to it when he denounces Hero in the church, iv. 1. 84, 85; nor does *Borachio* in his confession, v. 1. 235–251. If Margaret was intended, while personating Hero, to call *Borachio* by the name of *Claudio*, it could only have been, as Malone suggests (Var. Ed. vol. vii. p. 54), because, in her assumed character, she wished to pass off her lover Borachio as her engaged husband Claudio, in case of anyone overhearing her talk. But of what possible use could such a deception have been? If a man was heard talking with Hero the night before her marriage under such suspicious circumstances, it could scarcely have made matters much better, if there had been anyone by, to hear her call him *Claudio*, because it would have given very serious ground for suspicion that she and Claudio had anticipated the marriage ceremony. But let us examine the question as to the effect which this notable device of *Borachio* was to have on *Claudio* and Don Pedro. To see her, as he thought, talking with another man, with whom it was evident she was carrying on an intrigue, and calling that man *Claudio*, would have given *Claudio* one of two impressions: either that he was so much in her mind that she had called her lover *Claudio* by mistake; or that, for some time past, this lover had been, as it were, impersonating him: surely such a detail in the plot would not have been passed over, either by him or by Don Pedro, in total silence. We should certainly have expected, if such really had been the case—that is to say, if Claudio had heard *Borachio* called by the name of *Claudio*—that he would have made some remark thereon. But though we do not see the scene absolutely in action, we have no less than three different accounts of it in the course of the play; and in none of these accounts is there anything to justify us in the belief that *Borachio* was called by the name of *Claudio*. It would appear that the whole incident did not occupy much space of time; that no attempt was made by Claudio or Don Pedro to identify the supposed lover of Hero at the time; and, for the dramatic purpose required, it is obvious that it would produce a much more violent impression upon Claudio to hear Hero use the name of *Borachio* than to hear her use his own name.

But there is another point which requires consideration as between Margaret and Borachio. Is it more probable that he would have induced her to take part in this deception, if it was arranged that she was to call him *Claudio?* I think not; because it would have made her suspect at once that something wrong was intended. The Cambridge edd. suggest, in their note on this passage (note xii. vol. ii.), that "the author meant that Borachio should persuade her to play, as children say, at being Hero and Claudio." There certainly is some probability that such might have been the original intention of the dramatist. It has been already pointed out that the incident is not represented, it is only described; and it is quite possible that, in making up the plot in his own mind, Shakespeare might have pictured Borachio as saying something like this to Margaret: "I want you to put on your mistress's clothes and to talk to me to-night out of the window; I will call you *Hero*, and you can call me *Claudio;* and we can fancy that we are engaged to be married." Such a proposal, though not very probable, and one for which there could be no apparent object, might, from its very childish absurdity, disarm Margaret's suspicions; but it is at least quite as probable that she was persuaded merely to put on Hero's dress out of womanly vanity, to see how she looked when dressed as her mistress; and that Borachio only called her *Hero* at the moment, when he saw that *Claudio* and the others were present. On the whole it seems to us that the reasons for retaining the reading of Q. Ff. involve an explanation too subtle for an audience to grasp at such a moment. If the actor were to speak the words *hear Margaret term me* CLAUDIO without any explanation, nine out of ten of the audience would come to the conclusion that he had made some blunder.

140. Line 50: *seeming* TRUTH *of* HERO'S *disloyalty.*—*Truth* is here used in a somewhat peculiar sense = "true or genuine proof." Ff. have *truths. Hero's* is the reading of Q. Ff., unnecessarily changed to *her* by Capell.

ACT II. SCENE 3.

141. Lines 17, 18: *now will he lie ten nights awake, carving the fashion of a new doublet.*—This is probably a reference to the well-known wood-cut of the naked Englishman with a pair of shears in his hand, which figures at the head of the first chapter of Andrew Borde's Boke of Knowledge, having under it some verses commencing as follows:

> I Am an Englysh man, and naked I stand here
> Musyng in my mynd, what rayment I shal were
> For now I wyll were thys and now I wyl were that
> Now I wyl were I cannot tel what.

See Merchant of Venice, note 57.

142. Line 19: *now he is turn'd* ORTHOGRAPHY.—This is the reading of Q. Ff. Rowe altered it to *orthographer;* Capell proposed *orthographist.* Many modern editors follow Rowe; but no alteration is necessary. It is an instance of the use of the abstract for the concrete, which is common enough in Shakespeare. Some instances of a very similar use of this by no means uncommon poetical license may be given: *blasphemy* = blasphemer, Tempest, v. 1. 218; *chastity* = chaste woman, Cymbeline, ii. 2. 14; *counsel* = counsellors, Rich. III. ii. 3. 20; *enchantment* = enchanter, Winter's Tale, iv. 4. 445; *encounters* = encounterer, Love's Labour's Lost, v. 2. 82; *information* = informer, Coriolanus, iv. 6. 53; *reports* = reporter, Antony and Cleopatra, ii. 2. 47. Compare Love's Labour's Lost, note 20.

143. Line 35: NOBLE, *or not I for an* ANGEL.—Similar puns on the names of the coins, *noble* and *angel*, are common enough. Compare Richard II. v. 5. 67, 68, and note 322. For the coin *angel*, see Merchant of Venice, note 180.

144. Line 36: *and her hair shall be of what colour it please God.*—As to the practice of wearing false hair, here alluded to, see Love's Labour's Lost, note 131; and Merchant of Venice, note 227.

145. Line 38: Enter Don Pedro, Claudio, and Leonato, followed by Balthazar CARRYING A LUTE.—In the Quarto the stage-direction here is: *Enter Prince Leonato Claudio and music;* and, lower down, line 44, *Enter Balthazar with music.* In Ff. the stage-direction is *Enter Prince,*

Leonato, Claudio, and JACKE WILSON; the latter being the singer who acted Balthazar. It would seem, from the stage-direction of the Quarto, that musicians came on with Don Pedro and the others; but the unnecessary repetition of *with music* at Balthazar's entrance shows that there was some confusion here. From Don Pedro's speech (line 45) "we'll hear that song again," it appears that Balthazar has already sung a song. It does not speak of any other music being heard; that is to say, if we take *music* in lines 39 and 43 to refer to the song as about to be sung. Most modern editors put the stage-direction *music* before Benedick's speech, line 60; the Cambridge edd. put *air* for *music*. It is possible that Balthazar was intended to be accompanied in his song by one or more musicians on stringed instruments; but it is more probable that the accompaniment was intended to be played by himself, or rather to appear to be so played, being really furnished by the orchestra; because in Don Pedro's speech below (lines 86-89) he asks Balthazar to get them "some excellent music" for the next night. He would scarcely say that if any musicians were present.

According to Burney (quoted in Var. Ed. vol. vii. p. 59) the name *Balthazar* was perhaps taken "from the celebrated Baltazarino, called de Beaujoyeux," an Italian violinist, in great "favour at the court of Henry II. of France 1577." But we have had the same name in the Merchant of Venice and Romeo and Juliet, in both cases as that of a servant.

146. Lines 43, 44:

> *the music ended,*
> *We'll fit* THE KID-FOX *with a pennyworth.*

This is the reading of both Q. and Ff., in which *kid-fox* is also hyphened, and the *k* is very distinct; so that there is no doubt that, however unintelligible, we must accept this as the reading of the old copies. The obvious and plausible emendation "HID *fox*" was first made by Warburton, and was followed by Dyce without a word of comment. Steevens also proposed the same reading, basing it on the well-known passage in Hamlet, iv. 2. 32, 33: "*Hide fox*, and all after," which seems to refer to some popular form of the game of "Hide and Seek," or "I spy," as it is called in some schools. But, unfortunately, no passage has been found, in any writer of the Elizabethan or ante-Elizabethan period, giving any account of such a game, or of the expression *hid fox* or *hide fox*. With regard to the proposed emendation of "*hid* fox," it may be worth noting that in a song, called The Concealment, in the collection entitled The Merry Drollerie (1661), there is a refrain:

> Nay, that were a folly, the *fox* is unholy,
> And yet he hath the grace to *hide*.
> —Ebsworth's Reprint, pt. ii. p. 15.

Ritson suggested that "*kid*-fox" might mean nothing more than "young fox." But it is impossible to accept this suggestion, unless some instance can be brought forward of so very singular a use of the word *kid*. Such an expression as *dog-fox* may be admissible; but what there can be in common between a *kid* and a young fox it is impossible to imagine. *Kid*, in its well-known slang sense of a child, does not appear to have been used in Shakespeare's time; nor does the sense of to *kid* = to cheat, which might give a clue to the meaning of "*kid*-fox," appear to have existed at that period. If "HID-*fox*" were the right reading, we should not expect to find the words hyphened, unless such an expression was in use in the game of Hide and Seek as a regularly recognized phrase. A more plausible explanation of "KID-*fox*" has been given by supposing that *kid* here has the same meaning as it has in Chaucer, who uses the word *kid* or *kidde* = "discovered;" but the expression seems to have had no such meaning in the literature of Shakespeare's time. It is possible that "*kid* fox" may have been in use in the game of "Hide Fox," if there was such a game; and that it might have been employed by the children, when they *discovered* the hiding-place of the fox. It is evident, from the context, that Benedick was not successfully hiding (see line above), and that the two others saw him immediately after their entry, so that "*kid*-fox," in this last sense, would be appropriate enough, quite as appropriate as "*hid*-fox."

147. Line 50: *I pray thee, sing, and let me woo no more.*—For *woo*, in this sense = "entreat," "urge," compare Cymbeline, iii. 6. 69, 70:

> Were you a woman, youth,
> I should woo hard but be your groom;

and Othello, iii. 3. 293: "*Woo'd* me to steal it."

148. Line 59: *Note notes, forsooth, and* NOTHING!—It would appear that *nothing* was pronounced *noting* sometimes. We have it rhyming to *doting* in Sonnet xx. 10-12:

> Till Nature, as she wrought thee, fell *a-doting*,
> And by addition me of thee defeated,
> By adding one thing to my purpose *nothing*.

Probably it was usually pronounced *no-thing* in two syllables; the short pronunciation of the word, in use nowadays, is only a vulgarism, and was then unknown.

149. Lines 60-62: *Is it not strange that sheeps' guts should hale souls out of men's bodies?*—We are so accustomed to talk of *catgut* in connection with fiddle-strings, that the word *sheeps' guts* here seems strange; but it is nevertheless perfectly accurate. I am again indebted to Mr. Julian Marshall for the following note on this point: "Fiddle-strings were never made from the intestines of cats, always from those of sheep or goats, preferably the former; but the best are made from the guts of lambs at a certain period of their development, September being about the time when the string-making trade is most active. The best strings are made at Rome, or in Italy; next, in France; last, in England. The reason is supposed to be that in Italy the manufacture is carried on in the open air, which is not done here, nor in France, I think." The derivation of *catgut* is very uncertain, the only one given in any dictionary that I can find is in Worcester, on the authority of Notes and Queries (no reference given), namely, that it is a corruption of *gut-cord*; but is it not more probably a corruption of KIT-GUT, from *kit*, a small fiddle?

150. Line 71: *Hey nonny, nonny.*—This refrain, like many refrains to songs, has no meaning. It occurs in a song called "The Shepheards lamentation for the losse of his Love" in the collection entitled The Choice Drollery, 1656, every verse of which ends with *Hy nonny*

nonny no (Ebsworth's Reprint, pp. 65–67). Compare Ophelia's song in Hamlet, iv. 5. 165:

Hey non nonny, nonny, hey nonny;

and a somewhat similar refrain in As You Like It, in the Second Page's song, v. iii. 18:

With a *hey*, and a ho, and a *hey nonino*.

There seems to be a reference to this song in Beaumont and Fletcher's Scornful Lady, iii. 2, where the Captain says to the Steward, "Be *blithe and bonny* Steward."

151. Line 84: *I had as lief have heard the night-raven.*—Compare III. Henry VI. note 333. Harting says (p. 102) that Goldsmith, in his Animated Nature, calls the bittern the *night-raven*, and speaks thus of it from his personal experience: "I remember, in the place where I was a boy, with what terror the bird's note affected the whole village; they considered it as the presage of some sad event, and generally found, or made one to succeed it. If any person in the neighbourhood died, they supposed it could not be otherwise, for the *night-raven* had foretold it; but if nobody happened to die, the death of a cow or a sheep gave completion to the prophecy."

152. Line 96: *stalk on, stalk on; the fowl sits.*—This is an allusion to the use of the painted figure of a horse or bull for stalking wild-fowl and other game. In a Cavalier's Note Book, by William Blundell, written at the latter end of the seventeenth century (edited by the Rev. T. E. Gibson, 1880), is given an interesting description of this device: "The use of *stalking-horses* is great and notably advantageous in some parts. Horses are easily taught. Some do use to have a painted horse carried upon a frame. But, doubtless, a bust is more easy and not less useful. I know some to have stalked so near to partridges that the birds have pecked at the horses' legs. Let your painted horse or cow have one side of a different colour to the other" (pp. 106, 107).

153. Line 107: *it is past the* INFINITE *of thought.*—Warburton made a great difficulty over this passage, and wanted to substitute *definite* for *infinite;* but the meaning is very simple. Speaking, intentionally, in an exaggerated style Leonato means to say that Beatrice's affection is so violent, that it is past the power of thought to conceive the depth or vehemence of her love. *Infinite* is used = *infinity* in two other passages in Shakespeare; in Two Gent. of Verona, ii. 7. 70: "instances of *infinite* of love;" and Troilus and Cressida, ii. 2. 29: "the past-proportion of his *infinite*."

154. Line 114: *She will sit you,—you heard my daughter tell you how.*—Leonato breaks off abruptly after *sit you.* He is probably going to say, "She will sit you ever so long, writing letters to Benedick." Compare what he says below, lines 137, 138: "there *will she sit* in her smock till she have writ a sheet of paper."

155. Line 146: *she tore the letter into a thousand* HALFPENCE.—Theobald thought that this only meant "pieces of the same bigness." Compare As You Like It, iii. 2. 372: "they were all like one another as *half-pence* are." *Halfpence* in Elizabeth's time were of silver, and a very small coin, smaller (according to Rolfe) than an American half-dime. Silver pennies are still issued once a year, on Maundy Thursday. Copper coins were not *regularly* issued in England till 1672; though they were coined first in 1609, and more numerously in 1665. In Ireland they were issued as early as 1339; in Scotland, 1466; in France, 1530. The silver pennies were originally stamped with a cross, so that they could be broken into half or quarter pieces.

156. Lines 153, 154: *tears her hair, prays,* CURSES;—"*O sweet Benedick! God give me patience!*"—Collier's MS. substituted for *curses, cries.* Certainly *curses* seems rather out of place here. Grant White and Hudson both adopt Collier's emendation. Halliwell suggests that perhaps Shakespeare wrote *curses, prays.* It is scarcely necessary to alter the text here. In both Q. and Ff. there is only a comma after *curses;* but by putting a break the sense becomes quite clear. The speaker is evidently pretending to quote Beatrice's own words, and imitating her manner; and his action supplies, as it were, the place of the words *and then she cries,* or some such expression.

157. Line 177: *I would have* DAFF'D *all other respects.*—This verb is the same as *doff* = do off. Shakespeare uses this form again in Lover's Complaint, 297:

There my white stole of chastity I *daff'd*.

It occurs again in this play, v. 1. 78: "Canst thou so *daff* me?" *i.e.* put me off; and in I. Henry IV. iv. 1. 96:

that *daff'd* the world aside,
And bid it pass.

It probably was either a later or a provincial form of *doff;* as, in two or three of the places in which it occurs, F. 2 alters it to *doff; e.g.* in Antony and Cleopatra, iv. 4. 13, and Othello, iv. 2. 176. The word *daff* = "a fool" is used by Chaucer. *Daff* would seem also to mean to cheat, and the noun *daff* is used for a coward.

158. Line 189: *a* CONTEMPTIBLE *spirit.*—This is the only instance of the use of this word = "scornful," "disdainful." It does not occur again in Shakespeare except in I. Henry VI. i. 2. 75:

To shine on my *contemptible* estate;

where he uses it in its ordinary sense of "despicable," "mean." In II. Henry VI. i. 3. 86, and John ii. 1. 384, he uses *contemptuous* in the sense first given = "disdainful." Steevens quotes from Darius, a tragedy by Lord Sterline, 1603: "in a proud and *contemptible* manner," where *contemptible* "certainly means contemptuous;" and from Drayton's 24th Song of his Polyolbion, where the passage refers to a hermit who

The mad tumultuous world *contemptibly* forsook,
And to his quiet cell by Crowland him betook.
—Var. Ed. vol. vii. pp. 66, 67.

159. Line 195: *And I take him to be valiant.*—This line is given by Q. to Claudio. We follow Ff. in giving it to Leonato.

160. Line 208: *let her* WEAR *it* OUT *with good counsel.*—This is a very forcible expression, the meaning being "let her efface gradually," *i.e.* conquer "her passion solely by good counsel," that is, by wise reflection. There is no precisely similar use of *wear out* in Shakespeare. Perhaps we may compare Cymbeline, i. 4. 68: "this gentleman's opinion by this *worn out*."

161. Line 214: *to see how much he is unworthy so good a lady.*—So Q.; Ff. read "unworthy *to have* so good a lady." But *to have* is unnecessary.

162. Line 241: *'t is so, I cannot* REPROVE *it.*—Compare Venus and Adonis, 787: "that I cannot *reprove;*" and II. Henry VI. iii. 1. 40:

Reprove my allegation, if you can;

the only two other instances in which Shakespeare uses the word in this sense = "to disprove.

163. Line 258.—The change in Benedick's manner towards Beatrice is very marked; so marked, in fact, that it seems strange that she does not perceive it. Benedick finds it easier to drop his satire than Beatrice. It is a touch which shows how well Shakespeare knew human nature, that when they meet in the church scene (iv. 1), although Beatrice "has taken the infection," and the occasion is still such a serious one, she cannot entirely drop her bantering manner.

164. Line 272: *if I do not love her, I am a Jew.*—Compare I. Henry IV. ii. 4. 198: "or I am *a Jew else, an Ebrew Jew.*"

ACT III. Scene 1.

165. Line 3: PROPOSING *with the prince and Claudio.*—This use of *propose* in the sense of "to converse" comes from the French *propos*, which is used for "talk," "speech;" though the verb *proposer* never seems to be used in the sense of *causer* = to converse. This is the only passage in which Shakespeare uses the verb *propose* in this sense. In the three other instances in which it is used by him, viz. in III. Henry VI. v. 5. 20; Othello, i. 1. 25; and in the well-known passage in Hamlet, i. 5. 152:

Propose the oath, my lord,

the word is used in its proper sense of "to lay before," "to set forth;" as we now say when a person *proposes* a toast. There is one passage from Othello where Shakespeare uses this verb in a somewhat similar sense, though there it has more of a technical meaning than here, where Iago, speaking of Cassio, says:

Wherein the toged consuls can *propose*
As masterly as he. —i. 1. 25, 26.

The meaning is that Cassio knew nothing practically about military tactics; and the word, perhaps, might be paraphrased as = "to explain theories or problems." Below, line 12, according to the reading of the Quarto, we have the noun *propose* used in the same sense of "conversation;" Ff. read *purpose*.

166. Line 4: WHISPER *her ear, and tell her.*—For this use of the verb *whisper* compare All 's Well, ii. 3. 75:

The blushes in my cheeks thus *whisper* me;

and Winter's Tale, i. 2. 437:

Your followers I will *whisper* to the business.

167. Line 8: *Where* HONEYSUCKLES, *ripen'd by the sun.*—On the question of the identity of the *honeysuckle* and *woodbine* compare below, line 30:

Is couched in the *woodbine* coverture;

and see Mids. Night's Dream, note 223.

168. Line 12: *To listen our* PROPOSE. *This is thy office.*—So Q.; F. 1 reads *purpose*, and F. 2, F. 3, F. 4 read "To listen *to our purpose.*" There is no instance of Shakespeare using the verb *purpose* with the accent on the last syllable; and the reading of Q. here is probably the right one. Compare note 165 above.

169. Lines 24, 25:

For look where Beatrice, like a lapwing, runs
Close by the ground, to hear our conference.

See Comedy of Errors, note 101. This refers to the habit of the female green plover[1] (*Vanellus cristatus*), called *lapwing* "from its peculiar mode of flight,—a slow flapping of its long wings, and *Peewit* from its cry which the sound of the word *peewit* closely resembles" (Yarrell, vol. ii. p. 418). When disturbed on its nest the female bird runs close to the ground a short distance without uttering any cry, while the male bird keeps flying round the intruder, uttering its peculiar cry very rapidly and loudly, and trying, by every means, to draw him in a contrary direction from the nest. The *lapwing* is again alluded to by Shakespeare in Measure for Measure, i. 4. 32, 33:

With maids to seem the *lapwing* and to jest,
Tongue far from heart;

in Comedy of Errors, iv. 2. 27:

Far from her nest the *lapwing* cries away;

and in Hamlet, v. 2. 193, 194: "This *lapwing* runs away with the shell on his head." The latter passage refers, however, to quite a different matter in connection with this bird's history, namely, that their young run almost as soon as hatched. Harting remarks (p. 222) that it is rather curious that Shakespeare has not alluded to this bird under its popular name of *Peewit*, and that he never refers to it by the name of *wype*, a name for this bird which is frequently used in old household books and in privy-purse expenses. In a note Harting gives the modern Swedish name of the bird as *wipa*. The Promptorium Parvulorum gives the name of the bird in Latin as *Upupa*. Singular enough, in Russell's Boke of Nurture (1460–70) the Plover is never called anything else but the Plover or Lapwing (Furnivall's Reprint, p. 27); but in the Collectanea Curiosa (1781), in "The Charges of my Lord of Leiyster" [chancellor of the University of Oxford] "his dinner the vth day of September 1570," we find as one of the items "For iij Pewetes, to Goodman Cortyse of Staddome, xs." (vol ii. p. 7). This would seem to show that they were not always to be bought as cheap as they are now, but were rather an expensive delicacy.

170. Lines 35, 36:

I know her spirits are as coy and wild
As HAGGARDS *of the rock.*

There seems to be some considerable incertitude as to the exact meaning of the word *haggard*. According to some authorities *haggard* would seem to be a distinct species of hawk. Turberville in his Book of Falconry, 1575, says that "the *haggard* doth come from foreign parts a stranger and a passenger;" and Simon Latham (Falconry in two Books, 1615–18) says, speaking of the *haggard*, "that the tassel gentle her natural and chiefest companion, dares not

[1] Yarrell only gives the *Green Plover* as a synonym for the Golden Plover (*Charadrius pluvialis*).

come near that coast where she useth, nor sit by the place where she standeth" (Var. Ed. vol. vii. p. 71). Drake (vol. i. p. 270) says: "A *haggard* is a species of hawk wild and difficult to be reclaimed, and which, if not well trained, flies indiscriminately at every bird." I cannot find any mention of this term in Gervase Markham's "The Gentlemans Academie, or, The Booke of S. Albons,"[1] 1595. In his reprint of the "Booke for Kepinge of Sparhawkes" (about 1575) Harting in the Glossary (*sub* "Eyess") quotes D'Arcussia in his "Fauconnerie," 1605, who, among the five different names assigned to hawks, gives "(5) *Agar* (mot Hébreu qui signifie, estranger), if she has once moulted." He adds "hence our word *Haggard* applied to a wild-caught old hawk" (p. 42). Under *Haggard*, however, he gives "*adj.* living in a hedge (hag); hence wild. Technically a hawk that has been caught after assuming its adult plumage" (p. 43). In his Ornithology of Shakespeare he thus explains this word: "By '*haggard*' is meant a wild-caught and unreclaimed mature hawk, as distinguished from an 'eyess,' or nestling; that is, a young hawk taken from the 'eyrie' or nest" (p. 57). It must be confessed that we have a choice of derivations, if not of meanings, for the word. Shakespeare uses the term *haggard* twice in Taming of the Shrew, iv. 1. 196:

> Another way I have to man my *haggard*;

again, iv. 2. 38, 39:

> which hath as long lov'd me
> As I have lov'd this proud disdainful *haggard*;

in Twelfth Night, iii. 1. 71, 72:

> And, like the *haggard*, check at every feather
> That comes before his eye.

It is pretty certain, from the last quotation, that the sense in which Shakespeare uses the word is that of "an untrained hawk," and *not* of any particular species. (Compare a passage in Beaumont and Fletcher's Scornful Lady, v. 3, in a speech of the Elder Loveless.) The first quotation from the Taming of the Shrew confirms this; in the second case the meaning of the word might be doubtful. *Haggard* is used adjectively in Othello, iii. 3. 260-263:

> If I do prove her *haggard*,
> Though that her jesses were my dear heart-strings,
> I 'ld whistle her off and let her down the wind,
> To prey at fortune;

where it would appear to mean "wild," "unfaithful." Of other instances of the use of the word *haggard* we have in The Spanish Tragedy or The Second Part of Hieronymo, act i.:

> In time all *haggard* hawks will stoop to lure.
> —Dodsley, vol. v. p. 35.

The substantive *haggardness* occurs in Lyly, Euphues, 1579: "Though the Fawlcon be reclaimed to the fist, she retyreth to her *haggardnesse*: . . . education can haue no shewe, where the excellencye of Nature doth beare sway" (Arber's Reprint, p. 41). Compare also The City Nightcap (licensed Oct. 1624), act iv.: "What, have ye not brought this young wild *haggard* to the lure yet?" (Dodsley, vol. xiii. p. 161); in Massinger, The Maid of Honour, ii. 2:

> A proud *haggard*,
> And not to be reclaim'd!
> —Works, p. 262.

in Lingua (1607), ii. 5:

> with a wondrous flight
> Of falcons, *haggards*, hobbies, terselets,
> Lasards[2] and goshawks, sparhawks, and ravenous birds.
> —Dodsley, vol. ix. p. 379.

In all these quotations, with the exception of the last passage from Lingua, it is pretty clear that *haggard* means "a hawk that is untamed or untrained;" but in the last quotation it would seem to mean a particular species, as it is included among a list of the various kinds of hawks.

As to the expression *haggards of the rock*, in The Gentlemans Academie, in the section "To what Honour all Hawkes do belong" (p. 14, E ii), we find, assigned to a duke, "a Falcon *of the Rocke*." This, one would think, meant a Peregrine Falcon; but in the very next paragraph we find that an earl may claim "a falcon peregrine;" and in the two preceding paragraphs the gerfalcon is said to belong to a king, and the "Falcon gentle, and a Tercel gentle" to a prince. Of the various members of the family of Falconidæ used for hunting purposes, the Gerfalcon and the Peregrine Falcon build only on rocks. The Merlin builds generally on the ground, but sometimes on rocks, and is still called in parts of the country the Stone Falcon. Yarrell says: "It is not, however, improbable that the habit of sitting on a bare stone or portion of rock, by which this species has acquired the name of Stone Falcon, is common to it at all ages, and in other countries. In France it is called *Le Rochier* and *Faucon de Roche*; and in Germany *Stein-Falke*. This bird occasionally builds on rocks" (vol. i. p. 50). The Hobby and the Goshawk invariably build on trees, as also the Sparrowhawk. Yarrell says: "Young Peregrines of the year, on account of the red tinge of their plumage, are called, the female, a Red Falcon, and the male, a Red Tiercel, to distinguish them from older birds, which are called *Haggards*, or Intermewed Hawks" (vol. i. p. 35).

It would appear from the numerous quotations given above, that the word *haggard* was used by later writers in somewhat a lax sense. It certainly meant, generally speaking, a hawk more or less wild and untrained; and, probably from the fact that the females of some species were wilder than others, the word *haggard* came to be used by some writers of one species of *Falcon* only, but it never seems to be used of the male bird.

171. Line 42: *To* WISH *him wrestle with affection.*—For this use of the verb to *wish*, compare I. Henry VI. ii. 5. 96: "the rest I *wish* thee gather;" and All's Well, ii. 1. 134.

172. Line 45: *Deserve as* FULL *as fortunate a bed.*—So Q., F. 1, F. 2. Some adopt the punctuation of F. 3, F. 4, and place a comma after *full*, making *full* an adjective used in the same sense as in Othello, i. 1. 66:

> What a *full* fortune does the thick-lips owe;

but it seems better to take it as an adverb = *fully*. Compare Two Gentlemen of Verona, iv. 4. 191:

> Were *full* as lovely as is this of hers;

and Sonnet liv. 5:

> The canker-blooms have *full* as deep a dye.

---

[1] This is really a new edition of Juliana Barnes' celebrated Boke of Hawkynge, &c. (1486).

[2] *Lasard*, *i.e.* a *Lanner*, the female of a certain kind of falcon (*Falco Lanarius*).

It is only fair to say that there does not seem any precisely similar instance of *as* being used redundantly as it is here. We have in this same play an instance of the duplicated *as* in i. 1. 116: "*as* like him *as* she is" = "however much she may be like him;" and it is used redundantly before *how* in As You Like It, iv. 3. 142:

> *As*, how I came into that desert place.

173. Line 61: *she would spell him* BACKWARD.—This is said to be an allusion to the practice, attributed to witches, of uttering prayers backward. (See Comedy of Errors, note 109.) Though this is one of the commonest superstitions connected with witches, the origin of it is not very clear. I can find no mention of it in Scot's Discoverie of Witchcraft. It may be that the practice of saying prayers *backward* was supposed to be an insult directed against God, and prompted by the devil. One of the commonest tests applied to suspected witches was to say the Lord's Prayer and the Apostle's Creed through—a ridiculous test, because, as most of the accused witches were very ignorant people, they were very likely to make mistakes.

174. Lines 61-67.—The following passages in Lyly's Euphues, The Anatomie of Wit, 1579, bear a strong similarity to these lines, and may have suggested them to Shakespeare: "Woemen deeme none valyaunt vnlesse he be too venterous . . . they accompt one a dastard if he be not desperate, a pynch penny if he be not prodiggall, if silent a sotte, if fulle of wordes a foole" (Arber's Reprint, p. 100). Again: "If he be cleanelye, then terme they him proude, if meane in apparell a slouen, if talle a lungis, if shorte, a dwarfe, if bolde, blunt: if shamefast, a cowarde" (*ut supra*, p. 115). Steevens (Var. Ed. vol. vii. p. 73) quotes the latter of these two passages as well as one which resembles the former, but which I cannot identify.

175. Lines 63, 64:

> *If* BLACK, *why, Nature, drawing of an antic,*
> *Made a foul blot.*

The use of the word *black* for dark-compexioned people is very common in Shakespeare and in writers of his period. Indeed, it makes us doubt whether Othello is intended to be as *black* as he is very often painted. Douce says in a note quoted in the Var. Ed. vol. vii. p. 73: "A *black man* means a man with a dark or thick beard, not a swarthy or dark-brown complexion;" but what authority he has for this statement I do not know. Certain it is that *black* is far oftener applied to a person with a complexion no darker than a brunette than it is to negroes. Compare Two Gent of Verona, v. ii. 8-12:

> *Thu.* What says she to my face?
> *Pro.* She says it is a fair one.
> *Thu.* Nay then, the wanton lies; my face is *black*.
> *Pro.* But pearls are fair; and the old saying is,
> *Black* men are pearls in beauteous ladies' eyes.

and see Love's Labour's Lost, note 132.

176. Line 65: *If* LOW, *an* AGATE *very vilely cut.*—For the use of *low*, as applied to a person's height, see Mids. Night's Dream, iii. 2. 295:

> Because I am so dwarfish and so *low*.

For *agate*, which Warburton would absurdly have changed to *aglet*, compare Love's Labour's Lost, ii. 1. 236:

> His heart, like an *agate*, with your print impress'd;

and II. Henry IV. i. 2. 18, 19, where Falstaff refers to his little page, "I was never mann'd with an *agate* till now."

Agate here refers to the cut stones which were worn in Shakespeare's time. Florio gives under *Formaglio*, "any such, jewel, brooch, or tablet of gold, that yet some wear in their hats, or hanging at some chain or ribband with *Agate* stones, cut or graven with the heads or images of famous men or women;" so that, if a man were short, Beatrice compared him to one of the figures on *agate* stones very badly cut. There is no reference, as Steevens suggested, to the grotesque natural veining often found in *agates*.

177. Line 72: *No*, NOR *to be so odd.*—Q. Ff. read *not*. Rowe proposed to read *for*. Capell's emendation *nor* is generally accepted by most editors.

178. Line 76: PRESS ME TO DEATH *with wit.*—This is an allusion to that fearful punishment, known as the *peine forte et dure*, inflicted on persons accused of treason or felony, who "stood *mute* by malice," and refused to answer the questions put to them. It consisted of piling heavy weights on the body of the unfortunate victim till he was *pressed to death*. In Stow's Annals, under the year 1605, in the reign of James I., we find this paragraph: "Walter Calluerly, of Calluerly in Yorkeshire Esquier, murdred 2. of his young children stabbed his wife into the bodie with full purpose to haue murdred her, & instantly went frō his house to haue slaine his youngest child at Nurse, but was preuented. For which fact at his triall in Yorke, hee stood mute, & was iudged to bee *prest to death*, according to which iudgment hee was executed at the castell of Yorke the 5. of August" (pp. 870, 871); and compare Measure for Measure, v. 1. 528: "Marrying a punk, my lord, is *pressing* to death, whipping, and hanging." As late as 1792 a man, refusing to plead on a charge of burglary at Wells, was condemned and executed; and it was not till 1827 that an act was passed, directing the court to enter a plea of not guilty when the prisoner, "dumb by malice," refused to plead.

179. Line 79: *It were a* BETTER *death* THAN *die with mocks.*—So Q., except that it has *then* instead of *than*, a common misprint. F. 1 reads "*than to* die;" F. 2, F. 3, F. 4 (omitting *than*):

> It were a bitter death *to* die with mocks.

Bitter is obviously either an error or an officious correction.

180. Line 80: *die with* TICKLING.—Whether any person was ever *tickled to death*, except the unfortunate lady whose husband's effigy figured in Mrs. Jarley's Waxworks, is not known. It certainly was in the reign of Elizabeth that the monster who *tickled* his wife to death was supposed to flourish.

For the somewhat similar word *tacklings* used as a trisyllable, compare III. Henry VI. v. 4. 18:

> The friends of France our shrouds and *tacklings*.

181. Line 86: *empoison.*—This word only occurs once again in Shakespeare, viz. in Coriolanus, v. 6. 11:

> As with a man by his own alms *empoison'd*.

182. Lines 100, 101:

> *When are you married, madam?*
> Hero. *Why,* EVERY DAY, *to-morrow.*

I have adopted Mr. P. A. Daniel's explanation of the phrase *every day* = "immediately, without delay as the French *incessamment*" (See New Shak. Soc. Trans., 1877–79, pt. ii. p. 145). But I cannot see that the passage he quotes from Middleton's Your Five Gallants is conclusive. In the Var. Ed. (vol. vii. p. 77) the line is thus punctuated:

> Why, every day;—to-morrow: Come, go in;

which does not render the sense much more intelligible. Staunton's explanation, which Dyce adopts, is that Hero means: "I am married (*i.e.* a married woman) *every day* [after] to-morrow;" but this is hardly satisfactory. It seems curious that Ursula should not know on what day her mistress is going to be married. *Why* may be equivalent here to *Why, did you not remember?*

183. Line 107: *What fire is in mine ears? Can this be true?*—Surely there can be no doubt that Beatrice refers to the very common superstition that persons' ears burn when some one is speaking about them. Steevens (Var. Ed. vol. vii. p. 77) quotes from The Castell of Courtesie, &c., 1582, p. 73:

> *Of the burning of the eares.*
> That I doe credite giue
> vnto the saying old,
> Which is, *when as the eares doe burne,*
> *some thing on thee is told.*

Chapman alludes to this same popular belief in the 22nd Book of the Iliad:

> Now *burnes* my ominous *eare*
> With whispering, "Hector's self conceit hath cast away his host."
> —Works, vol. ii. p. 211.

This superstition seems to be common to the folk-lore of many different parts of the world. According as it is the *right ear* or the *left ear*, which tingles or burns, so are you being praised or abused; though, in some parts, the sides are reversed, and the *left* burns when you are praised, the *right* when someone speaks ill of you.

184. Line 110: *No glory lives behind the back of such.*—That is to say, people who are proud and scornful are never praised behind their backs; and, therefore, when listening, are not likely to hear any good of themselves. Mr. Collier's Old Corrector could not leave this simple sentence alone, but altered it to:

> No glory lives *but in the lack of such.*

185. Line 112: *Taming my wild heart to thy loving hand.*—A simile evidently taken from falconry, and probably suggested to Beatrice through having heard herself compared to a "wild haggard of the rock." See above, line 36, and note 170.

It will be noted that this soliloquy of Beatrice's is very inferior to that of Benedick's, and that it is written in alternate rhyme. Perhaps Shakespeare intentionally made the difference between the two soliloquies as marked as possible. Women are not, as a rule, given to self-analysis so much as men. Being accustomed to act on impulse, they do not care to prove, even to themselves, that their conduct is logical.

ACT III. Scene 2.

186. Line 4: *if you'll* VOUCHSAFE ME.—For this construction of the verb *vouchsafe* compare Comedy of Errors, v. 1. 282: "*vouchsafe me* speak a word." In the text the infinitive is understood, and there is no instance of such a use of the verb, except it be in Love's Labour's Lost, v. 2. 888, where Armado is interrupted while saying "Sweet majesty, *vouchsafe me.*"

187. Line 6: *the new* GLOSS *of your marriage.*—Compare Macbeth, i. 7. 33, 34:

> Golden opinions from all sorts of people,
> Which would be worn now in their *newest gloss;*

and Othello, i. 3. 227, 228: "to slubber the *gloss* of your new fortunes."

188. Lines 10, 11: *he hath twice or thrice* CUT *Cupid's* BOW-STRING.—In Hansard's Book of Archery, 1840, we find (p. 107): "To rush upon an archer and sever his bow-string by the stroke of a sword, or otherwise, seems to have been a common expedient in ancient battles, either to place an enemy *hors du combat*, or check the impetuous valour of a brave companion in arms." He gives an instance taken from Hubbard's History of the troubles of New England, 1673, of an incident of this kind: "at which time an Indian, drawing an arrow, would have killed me, had not one Davis, my sergeant, rushed forwards and *cut the bowstring* with (his) courtlace (*i.e.* cutlas)." Compare Mids. Night's Dream, note 62.

189. Line 11: *the little* HANGMAN.—See Two Gent. of Verona, note 106. This name may have been given to Cupid, because, as the God of Love, he is instrumental in tying the *fatal knot* of so many people. Compare III. Henry VI. iii. 3. 55: "With nuptial *knot*;" and Antony and Cleopatra, ii. 2. 128, 129:

> to knit your hearts
> With an unslipping *knot.*

190. Line 21: *I have the* TOOTHACHE.—Boswell quotes from Beaumont and Fletcher's The False One, ii. 3:

> Oh, this sounds mangily,
> Poorly, and scurvily, in a soldier's mouth!
> You had best be troubled with the *tooth-ache* too,
> For lovers ever are. —Works, vol. i. p. 376.

191. Line 24: *You must* HANG *it first, and* DRAW *it afterwards.*—The allusion is to the punishment for treason, to be *hanged, drawn*, and quartered. Under the barbarous law which was enforced in Shakespeare's time, *drawing* of the entrails took place while the wretched victim was still alive.

192. Line 27: *Where is but a humour or a* WORM?—The idea that the toothache was caused by a *worm* is a very old one, and still lingers in parts of Scotland. (See Romeo and Juliet, note 51.) In Batman upon Bartholomew (bk. v. chap. 20), we have: "And if *Wormes* be the cause, full sore ache is bred; for they eating, pearce into the subtill sinew, and make the teeth to ake, and grieue them very sore" (p. 45). Batman's book is one that Shakespeare must almost certainly have read, and he might have been thinking of this passage. Chettle in Kind Hart's Dream, speaking of the practices of "tooth-drawers," says: "Another sort get hot wiers, and with them they burne out

the *worme* that so torments the greeued" . . . "Others there are that perswade the pained to hold their mouths open ouer a basen of water by the fire side, and to cast into the fire a handfull of henbane seede, the which naturally hath in euery seede a little *worme*; the seedes breaking in the fire, vse a kind of cracking, and out of them, it is hard, among so many, if no *worme* fly into the water: which *wormes* the deceiuers affirme to haue fallen from the teeth of the diseased" (Reprint, New Shak. Soc. p. 50).

193. Lines 33–37: *as, to be a Dutchman to-day, a Frenchman to-morrow; or in the* SHAPE *of two countries at once, as, a German from the waist downward, all* SLOPS, *and a Spaniard from the hip upward,* NO *doublet.*—The greater part of this passage (from *or in the* to *doublet*) is omitted in Ff., probably because some great German or Spanish ambassadors or personages were in England at the time it was played. In Dekker's Seuen deadly Sinnes of London, in the chapter entitled: "Apishnesse: Or The fift dayes Triumph" is the following passage: "For an English-mans suite is like a traitors bodie that hath been hanged, drawne, and quartered, and is set vp in seuerall places: his Codpeece is in *Denmarke*, the collor of his Duble [t], and the belly in *France:* the wing and narrowe sleeue in *Italy;* the short waste hangs ouer a *Dutch* Botchers stall in *Vtrich:* his huge *Sloppes* speakes *Spanish: Polonia* giues him the Bootes: the blocke for his heade alters faster then the Feltmaker can fitte him, and thereupon we are called in scorne *Blockheades*. And thus we that mocke euerie Nation, for keeping one fashion, yet steale patches from euerie one of them, to peece out our pride, are now laughing-stocks to them, because their cut so scurrily becomes us" (Arber's Reprint, pp. 36, 37).

It is probable that *shape* here has the technical sense which it had in the language of the theatre, viz. a characteristic dress or disguise. For instance, in Middleton's Part of the Entertainment to King James &c. we have "The Four Elements, in proper *shapes*, artificially and aptly expressing their qualities &c." (Works, vol. v. p. 209); and again in Massinger's The Bondman, v. 3:

> Look better on this virgin, and consider,
> This *Persian shape* laid by, and she appearing
> In a *Greekish dress*, such as when first you saw her.
> —Works, p. 131.

See also Love's Labour's Lost, note 112.

Shakespeare uses *slops* in the plural in only one other passage, viz. in II. Henry IV. i. 2. 34: "the satin for my short cloak and my *slops*." For *slop* in the singular see Love's Labour's Lost, note 112. Planché in his Cyclopædia of Costume (p. 469), under *slop*, says: "The '*slop*' above mentioned is a body-garment, a *hauseline*, a jacket or cassock, 'cut' so short that it exposed the tight-fitting, particoloured hose to an extent deservedly incurring the reprobation of the clergy." He also gives an extract from the wardrobe accounts of the reign of Edward IV. which proves that there were then a kind of shoes which were called *slops*, and says that Tarleton, the great clown in Shakespeare's time, was known by "his great clownish *slop*." There is little doubt that the wide breeches, so useful to the clown of modern pantomime as a storehouse for stolen goods, are lineal descendants of the old *slops* or wide Dutch breeches.

For "*no* doublet" Mason proposed to read "*all* doublet," which he said corresponds with the actual dress of the old Spaniards; but Malone explains the words as meaning "all cloak." The Spanish cloak often figures in old plays as a means of disguise; the cloak would conceal the doublet.

194. Line 41: *He brushes his hat o' mornings.*—Is this one of the old signs of being in love? If so, no commentator seems to have found any passage in any contemporary work which describes it as such.

195. Lines 46, 47: *the old ornament of his cheek hath already stuff'd tennis-balls.*—Undoubtedly it was the custom in old times, both in France and in England, *to stuff tennis-balls with hair*. (See Mr. Julian Marshall's Annals of Tennis, pp. 11 and 72.) To the allusions given in the Var. Ed. (vol. vii. p. 81) we may add this from Dekker's Gull's Hornbook: "A Mohammedan cruelty therefore is it to *stuff* breeches and *tennis-balls* with that, which, when 'tis once lost, all the hare-hunters in the world may sweat their hearts out, and yet hardly catch it again" (Reprint, 1812, p. 96). In fact *hair* was used generally for *stuffing*. Compare Coriolanus, ii. 1. 97–99: "your beards deserve not so honourable a grave as to *stuff* a botcher's cushion, or to be entombed in an ass's pack-saddle."

196. Line 50: *he rubs himself with* CIVET.—This appears to have been a favourite perfume in Shakespeare's time. It rather resembles musk in smell, and was made from the secretion of the anal glands of the *Civetta viverra*. Shakespeare alludes to it in As You Like It, iii. 2. 69, 70: "*civet* is of a baser birth than tar,—the very uncleanly flux of a cat;" and in Lear, iv. 6. 132, 133: "Give me an ounce of *civet*, good apothecary, to sweeten my imagination."

197. Lines 55, 56:

> *And when was he wont to wash his face?*
> D. Pedro. *Yea, or to paint himself?*

From the first of these two lines some commentators have conjectured that *washing* was not much practised in Shakespeare's time. Certainly much indulgence in it would have been dangerous to many of the ladies, or at least to their complexions; but is not the meaning of *wash* here, to *wash* with some preparation for beautifying the complexion?

Stubbes devotes nearly four pages (64–67) to a denunciation of the "oyles, liquors, unguents, and waters" used by women for colouring their faces. He calls all these things "sibber-sawces;" but he seems to think that they were made from "goodly condiments and holsome confections," which certainly is not the case with many of the modern face washes. Stubbes apparently makes no allusion to the habit of men painting their faces; but no doubt effeminate men did so in Shakespeare's time, as they do sometimes nowadays.

198. Lines 59, 60: *his jesting spirit, which is now crept into a lute-string, and govern'd by* STOPS.—Q. Ff. read "*now* governed." Walker (vol. ii. p. 214) proposed "*new*

governed," which Dyce adopts. *Now*, as Walker points out, is often confused with *new*. He gives several instances, and refers to that passage, among others, in Taming of the Shrew, iii. 2. 60, "*new*-repaired with knots," where we have adopted the emendation "*new*-repaired" instead of "*now* repaired;" but here we prefer to omit the *now*, which looks very much as if it had been repeated through a printer's mistake.

The *lute* being generally used to accompany love songs Claudio says Benedick's "jesting spirit *is crept into a lute-string*." *Stops* mean here the divisions on the finger-board of the *lute*, showing where the finger is to be pressed in order to produce certain notes.

199. Line 71: *She shall be buried—with her face* UPWARDS.—It is hardly credible that in the Var. Ed. (vol. vii. p. 82) there is absolutely a page of notes on this passage. Theobald gravely suggested that we should read "with *heels upwards*," or "*face downwards*." The meaning of the line is very obvious; and one would think that the tone of the conversation could scarcely have left a doubt on this point, namely, that the *grave* Beatrice was to be *buried* in was the marriage-bed.

200. Line 72: *Yet is this no* CHARM FOR THE TOOTHACHE.—The following charm is given in Chettle's Kind Harts Dream: "First he (*i.e.* the tooth-drawer) must know your name, then your age, which in a little paper he sets downe: on the top are these words *In verbis, et in verbis, et in lapidibus sunt virtutes;* vnderneath he writes in capitall letters *A AB ILLA HVRS GIBBELLA*, which he sweres is pure Chalde and the names of three spirites that enter into the bloud and cause rewmes, and so consequently the toothache. This paper must be likewise three times blest, and at least with a little frank-incense burned, which being thrice vsed, is of power to expell the spirites, purifie the bloud, and ease the paine." He concludes: "for this I find to be the only remedy for the tooth paine, either to haue patience, or pull them out" (New Shak. Soc. Reprint, pp. 58, 59).

201. Line 74: *which these* HOBBY-HORSES *must not hear*.—*Hobby-horse*, as a term of contempt, is generally applied to women. See Love's Labour's Lost, note 59; Winter's Tale, i. 1. 276; and Othello, iv. 1. 160. In the last passage the meaning of the word, as applied to women, is quite obvious; but, when applied to men, it seems to have had reference rather to the tricks which the person who played the hobby-horse in the ancient morris-dance was accustomed to perform. *Hobby-horse* is applied to a man in the following passage in The Duchess of Suffolk by Thomas Drew, 1631, c. 4. b:

> Clu. Answere me *hobbihorse*,
> Which way crost he you saw enow?
> Ien. Who doe you speake to sir,
> We haue forgot the *hobbihorse*.

A great deal of useful information about the *hobby-horse* will be found in act iv. scene 1 of Beaumont and Fletcher's A Woman Pleased (Works, vol. ii. p. 193).

202. Line 100: AIM BETTER AT ME *by that I now will manifest*.—This is a curious expression. We may compare The Two Gent. of Verona, iii 1 45:

> That my discovery be not *aimed at*;

where *aimed at* means, as we have explained it in a foot-note, "guessed." Don John evidently means to convey the notion, in his usual sullen manner, that he has been misjudged by Claudio; and the sentence may be paraphrased: "Make a better guess at my nature and real disposition than you have hitherto done."

203. Line 110: *Leonato's Hero, your Hero, every man's Hero*.—This passage is imitated by Dryden in his All for Love: "Your Cleopatra, Dolabella's Cleopatra, every man's Cleopatra."

204. Line 112: *The word is too good to paint* OUT *her wickedness*.—Compare Venus and Adonis, line 290:

> In limning *out* a well-proportion'd steed.

205. Line 115: *you shall see her chamber-window enter'd*.—It would seem that Don John promises here rather more than was performed, for when this notable device was originally planned between him and Borachio, the latter only undertook that Margaret should appear at the window (see act ii. scene 2). Nor, in the account given by Borachio afterwards in the next scene, is anything said about his actual entrance through the window, but only that he talked with Margaret; and all that Claudio asks in the church scene (iv. 1. 84, 85) is:

> What man was he talk'd with you yesternight
> Out at your window betwixt twelve and one?

206. Line 132: *bear it coldly*.—Compare this with our modern expression: "Take it coolly."

ACT III. Scene 3.

207. Enter DOGBERRY and VERGES, SEACOAL, OATCAKE, and Watch.—Q. Ff. have *Enter Dogberry and his compartners with the Watch*. Most editors have *Enter Dogberry and Verges with the Watch;* but as we are told in the course of the scene that the names of the First and Second Watchmen were *Hugh Oatcake* and *George Seacoal*, there is no reason why we should not give them their names as we give to *Verges* his name. Later on in this act, at the beginning of what is scene 5 in modern editions—the division of the scenes not being marked in the old copies—we have "*Enter Leonato and the Constable and the Head Borough*," evidently meaning Dogberry and *Verges*. As is frequently the case in the Qq., as well as in Ff., the prefixes to the speeches of the minor characters are very confusing. For instance, we have the prefix of *Verges* in Q.; *Verg.* in Ff. to the second speech in this scene; and to most of the speeches ordinarily assigned to *Verges* we have his name prefixed. To the speech beginning "*Hugh Oatcake*, sir" (line 11), Q. Ff. have *Watch* 1. as a prefix, which we have changed to *Verges*. The speech beginning, "Both which, master constable" (line 17) is given to the Second Watchman (Watch 2) in Q. Ff. It is evident from *Dogberry's* speech that the speaker's name was *Seacoal;* but to most of the speeches given to this character there is simply the prefix *Watch* in the rest of the scene, up to line 72. It would appear from *Dogberry's* speech (lines 21-24) that *Seacoal* was appointed *constable of the watch* for the night; and we have given him the speeches which belong to that character whether they have the prefix *Watch*, *Watch* 1, or *Watch* 2.

As to the names *Dogberry* and *Verges*, Halliwell says in a note that "*Dogberry* occurs as a surname in a charter of the time of Richard II. and *Varges* as that of a usurer in *MS. Ashmol.* 38, where this epitaph is given: 'Here lyes father *Varges*, who died to save charges.'" *Dogberry* is the vulgar name for the *dogwood* (*Cornus sanguinea*), a common shrub in our hedgerows, called *dogwood*, not in any way from the animal *dog*, but because the wood, being very hard, was used for skewers; and therefore the shrub had its name—for it is rather a shrub than a tree—from the French *dague*, a dagger, or perhaps we should say from the same root as that word. *Verges* is the provincial corruption for *verjuice*.

208. Line 11: GEORGE *Seacoal*.—Halliwell would read *Francis*, supposing this *Seacoal* to be the same as the one mentioned in iii. 5. 62; but it appears that the latter was the sexton, and it is doubtful whether he was the same person as the *Seacoal* mentioned here. On the other hand, there is so much stress laid upon the fact that this *George* could both read and write, and as such mistakes with regard to Christian names are far from uncommon in Shakespeare and other dramatists, Halliwell's proposed alteration is very reasonable.

209. Line 23: *the most senseless and fit man for the* CONSTABLE OF THE WATCH.—It would seem that one of the watchmen was chosen each night to be *constable of the watch;* and that he acted as leader of the watchmen in the absence of the head constable, and that to him belonged the honour of bearing the lanthorn. In Samuel Rowley's play, When You See Me You Know Me, 1632, D. 2. b, there is a stage-direction: "*Enter the* CONSTABLE *and Watch: Prichall the Cobler beeing one bearing a Lanthorne;*" and it appears from the scene that "the Cobler" on this occasion acted, in the absence of the *constable*, as the commanding officer of the watch.

210. Lines 27-31.—This passage is imitated very closely in "An Excellent Pleasant New Comedy," called "Lady Alimony," iii. 5 (1650):

> *Watch.* Report goes, that there be spirits that patrol familiarly in this sentry; what shall we say to them, if they pass by?
> *Con.* Bid them stand.
> *Watch.* But what if they either cannot or will not?
> *Con.* Let them take themselves to their heels, and thank God you are well rid of them. —Dodsley, vol. xiv. p. 333.

And it may be noted that the stage-direction at the beginning of that scene is, "*Enter* CONSTABLE *and Watch in rug gowns, bills, and dark lanthorns.*"

211. Line 30.—*We will rather* SLEEP *than talk.*—This joke about the watchmen *sleeping* seems to have been a very favourite one with the old dramatists. In Glapthorne's Wit in a Constable, v. 1, Busy, the Constable, says:

> for your selves you have
> Free leave for th' good oth' common wealth to
> *Sleepe* after eleven.
> —Works, vol. i. p. 227.

And further on, in the same act, two constables sing a song, the chief burden of which is that constables *sleep* for the good of the commonwealth; and in When You See Me You Know Me, in the same scene as the one alluded to above, one of the watch is named *Dormouse*, who goes to *sleep* almost before his watch begins. In Lady Alimony, v. 1, the constable says: "if I hold constable long, the deputy of the ward will return me one of the Seven *Sleepers*" (Dodsley, vol. xiv. p. 332). In fact it would seem that the principal occupation of the watchman was to *sleep* on his "bulk" or bench.

212. Line 43: *have a care that your* BILLS *be not* STOL'N.—In When You See Me You Know Me, D. 3. b. King Henry VIII. goes in disguise with Sir William Compton and *steals* all the *bills* of the watchmen. The king says:

> The watch has giuen vs leaue to arme our selues,
> They feare no dawnger, for they sleepe secure:
> Goe carrie those *bils* we *tooke* to Baynards Castle.

213. Line 55: *the less you* MEDDLE OR MAKE *with them.*—Compare Troilus and Cressida, i. 1. 14: "I'll not *meddle nor make* no further." For this speech and the next speech of Dogberry's we may compare the speech of Busy in Glapthorne's Wit in a Constable, v. 1:

> Next, if a thiefe chance to passe through your watch,
> Let him depart in peace; for should you stay him,
> To purchase his redemption he 'le impart
> Some of his stolne goods, and you 're apt to take them,
> Which makes you accessary to his theft,
> And so fit food for Tiburne. —Works, vol. i. p. 227.

214. Line 60: *they that touch pitch will be defil'd.*—This proverbial saying is a very ancient one. It is found in Ecclesiasticus, xiii. 1: "He that *toucheth pitch*, shall be *defiled* with it."

215. Line 69: *If you hear a child cry*, &c.—Steevens thought that "part of this scene was intended as a burlesque on The Statutes of the Streets, imprinted by Wolfe in 1595" (Var. Ed. vol. vii. p. 55). He gives some of the regulations, of which these two seem the most apposite: "22. No man shall blowe any horne in the night, within this citie, or whistle after the houre of nyne of the clock in the night, under paine of imprisonment;" and "30. No man shall, after the hour of nyne at night, keepe any *rule*,[1] whereby any such suddaine outcry be made in the still of the night, as making any affray, or beating his wyfe, or servant, or singing, or revyling in his house, to the disturbance of his neighbours, under payne of iiis. iiiid." &c.

216. Line 79: *This is the end of the* CHARGE.—It appears to have been the custom of the head constable to *charge* the watch every night. In When You See Me You Know Me, D. 2. b, the Constable says:

> I need not to repeat *your charge* againe:
> Good neighbours, vse your greatest care I pray,
> And if vnruly persons trouble yee,
> Call and ile come: so sirs goodnight.

In Glapthorne's Wit in a Constable, v. 1, the Constable gives a charge, a portion of which we have already quoted; and one of the watchmen says:

> I have edified
> More by your *charge* I promise you, than by
> Many a mornings exercise.
> —Works, vol. i. p. 226.

217. Line 84: THAT *knows the* STATUES.—So F. 1; Q., F. 2,

---

[1] *Rule* here means "conduct," "regulation." Compare Twelfth Night, ii. 3. 132; and *night-rule*, Mids. Night's Dream, iii. 2. 5.

F. 3, F. 4 have *statutes*. Probably Dogberry was intended to mistake the word, and the reading of F. 1 is right.

218. Lines 90, 91: *Ha, ah-ha! Well, masters, good night: an there be any matter of weight chances*, CALL UP ME.—The exclamation at the beginning of this speech shows that Dogberry, however unconscious he is of the liberties which he takes with his mother tongue, is perfectly conscious of his own wit. It seems to have been another part of the routine for the head constable, after he had charged the watch, to retire. In Glapthorne's Wit in a Constable, Busy uses almost the same words as here, v. 1 (p. 229):

> and if any businesse
> Be of importance, *call me*.

219. Line 92: *keep your fellows' counsels and your own*.—In that amusing pamphlet Shakespeare's Legal Acquirements Considered, the author, Lord Campbell, brings forward many quotations to support the theory that Shakespeare had been a clerk in an attorney's office. Amongst them this sentence in Dogberry's speech is noted as being "the very words of the oath administered by the Judges marshal to the grand jury at the present day" (p. 46). Lord Campbell says (p. 45): "There never has been a law or custom in England to '*give a charge*' to constables; but from time immemorial there has been '*a charge to grand juries*' by the presiding judge." But the extracts we have given in the last note seem to prove that there was such a custom of *giving a charge* to the Watch on behalf of the head constable; unless we are to suppose that all the scenes in which constables and watchmen are brought on the stage owe their origin to this scene of Shakespeare's. Lord Campbell thinks that Shakespeare here ridicules the charge which Justice Shallow might have given to the grand jury. He may be stretching a point here; but as to Shakespeare's fondness for legal phraseology, see Mids. Night's Dream, note 11.

220. Lines 94, 95: *let us go sit here upon the church-bench till* TWO, *and then all to bed*.—It would seem from this that the Watch were off duty at *two o'clock*. We have already quoted a passage from one of Busy's speeches, in Wit in a Constable, which seems to show that this Constable's watchmen had an easy time of it, as they were allowed to sleep after 11. The old watchmen, who were the guardians of the night in towns before the establishment of the police, used to proclaim the hour of the morning and the state of the weather up to daybreak.

221. Line 104: Enter BORACHIO and CONRADE.—*Borachio* and *Conrade* are generally made to enter before at line 102; but *Borachio's* two first speeches are better spoken without. The night is dark, and *Borachio*, who has evidently taken a glass or two, cannot at first find his companion.

222. Line 110: *Stand thee close, then, under this* PENT-HOUSE.—For *pent-house* see Love's Labour's Lost, note 55.

223. Line 111: *I will, like a true drunkard, utter all to thee*.—The name *Borachio* seems to have been used for a drunkard, as we find from a poem entitled "To *Borachioes*" in a volume of rare poetical pieces (*Annæ-dicata*) by George Tooke, 1654, the last verse of which begins:

> Up then ye base *Borachioes*, call excesse.
> But an insidious *Circe*. —C. i. b.

Another peculiar use of the word is to be found in Greene's Looking Glass for London and England: "whereupon, offering a *borachio* of kisses to your unseemly personage" (Works, p. 133), where it would seem to mean "a quantity." Further on in the same play it is used in the sense of bottle (p. 140): "these *borachios* of the richest wine." The word is evidently a corruption of the Spanish *borracho* (not *bóracho*), drunk, which comes from *borracha*, a leather bag or bottle for wine, which is itself derived from *bórra*, a goat skin, such bottles being generally made of goat skins. *Borachio*, or *boracho*, would seem to have been used as a common term of abuse on the part of the Spaniards against the English, as appears from a passage in Dick of Devonshire, i. 2,[1] where an English merchant, speaking of the Spaniards at the time of the Armada, says:

> These were the times in which they calld our nation
> *Borachos*, Lutherans and Furias del Inferno.
> —Bullen's Old Plays, vol. ii. p. 14

224. Line 120: *if it were possible any* VILLAIN *should be so rich*.—Q. Ff. read *villanie*. Warburton first suggested the substitution of *villain*, which seems the right word. Walker supports this emendation very decidedly. We have followed Dyce in adopting it.

225. Line 124: *unconfirm'd*.—Shakespeare only uses this word in one other passage = "inexperienced," in Love's Labour's Lost, iv. 2. 19: "*unconfirmed* fashion," in the speech of Holofernes.

226. Line 137: *'t was the vane on the house*.—So Q., F. 2, F. 3, F. 4; F. 1 reads *veine*; Walker would here read *rain*, referring to "it drizzles rain" in Borachio's speech above (line 111). Dyce rejects this emendation, because in Q. we find in that line *rain* written *raine*, and in this passage we have *vane* properly spelt. According to the Cambridge edd. (see their note xvii. on this play) Mr. Halliwell-Phillipps had seen a copy of F. 1 which had *raine* in this passage.

227. Lines 142–146: *sometime fashioning them like Pharaoh's soldiers in the reechy painting, sometime like god Bel's priests in the old church window, sometime like the shaven Hercules in the smirch'd worm-eaten tapestry*.—I suppose that Borachio is represented as thinking of a picture of the crossing of the Red Sea by Pharaoh and his army. A picture would easily become discoloured by smoke in those days, when the old-fashioned chimneys mostly drew downwards if there was any wind. *God Bel's priests in the old church window* alludes to some representation in stained glass of the story of *Bel* and the Dragon. In Beaumont and Fletcher's Scornful Lady, iv. 1, we have "and say you look like one of *Ball's priests* in a hanging" (Works, vol. i. p. 94).

Warburton suggested that by the shaven Hercules was meant Samson, and he has a long rigmarole note upon the passage; but Steevens very properly observed that if it were Samson who was represented, he would be equipped probably with a jawbone and not with a club; and he

[1] The date of this play is uncertain; it was probably written after 1626.

suggested that by the *shaven Hercules* is meant Hercules, when shaved to make him look like a woman, while he was in the service of Omphale. But though Hercules is said to have put on woman's attire to please Omphale, and to have led a very effeminate life, there is no mention of his having been shaved. Sidney, in his Defence of Poesie, speaking of the difference between "delight" and "laughter," says: "Yet deny I not, but that they may goe well together, for as in *Alexanders* picture well set out, wee delight without laughter, . . . so in Hercules, painted with his great beard, and furious countenance, in woman's attire, spinning at Omphales commaundement, it breedeth both delight and laughter" (Arber's Reprint, p. 66). In the Illustrations of The Twelve Labours of Hercules given in Smith's Classical Dictionary, *Hercules* is represented with a beard in every case but in three of his Labours, viz.: iii. Hercules and the Arcadian Stag; xi. Hercules and the Hesperides; xii. Hercules and Cerberus.

228. Line 162: *And thought* THEY *Margaret was Hero!*—So Q.; Ff. have *thy*. There is not really much to choose between the two readings. All the old copies have a note of interrogation after the sentence. Borachio is a long time telling his story, and it is evident that Conrade is naturally impatient; so that it is very likely that, if Borachio paused at this point, he would interpose a suggestion rather than a question, especially as the point of the story must have been clear to him. On this account I should prefer to put a break at the end of Borachio's speech, and to adopt the reading of F. 1 *without* the note of interrogation.

229. Line 182: *'a wears a lock.*—This is an allusion to the custom of wearing a long lock of hair, which was generally tied with ribbon and worn under the left ear. There seems to have been some confusion, in the minds of the commentators, as to the exact fashion to which allusion is here made. For instance, reference is made in Malone's note to the portrait of the Earl of Dorset by Vandyck, which was, of course, painted some considerable time after this play was written. *Love-locks* were worn in the reign of Charles I. According to Planché the *love-lock* was "a long ringlet of hair worn on the left side of the head, and allowed to stream down the shoulder, sometimes as far as the elbow" (Cyclopædia of Costume, vol. i. p. 246). It was against this fashion that Prynne wrote his quarto volume entitled The Unloveliness of Love Locks. In Lilly's Mydas (1591), iii. 2, we have "a low curle on your head like a bull, or dangling locke like a spaniell? . . . your *love-lockes* wreathed with a silken twist, or shaggie to fall on your shoulders?" (Works, vol. ii. p. 30). This kind of *love-lock* was probably the one which was generally adopted by men of fashion in the reign of Charles I. But it appears that a kind of *love-lock* would seem to have been used by some persons, who especially affected French fashions, in the time of Queen Elizabeth, as we see from the following passage in Greene's Quip for an Upstart Courtier (1592), quoted by Planché, where a barber asks a customer: "Sir, will you have your worship's hair cut after the Italian manner? . . . Or will you be Frenchified, with a *lovelock* down on your shoulders, wherein you may weave your mistress's favour?" Dekker, in his Gull's Hornbook, 1609, when speaking of the practice of the beaux of that day of sitting on the stage during the performance of a play, says that one of the advantages is the chance of displaying "the best and most essential parts of a gallant, good clothes, a proportionable leg, white hand, the *Persian lock*, and a tolerable beard" (Reprint, 1812, pp. 36, 37). *Persian*, very probably, was a misprint for Parisian. In Arden of Feversham, 1592, Bradshaw, describing the man who had brought him the stolen plate, says:

> His chin was bare, but on his vpper lippe
> A *mutchado*, which he wound about his eare.
> —Bullen's Reprint, p. 36.

From this it would seem that the fashion of wearing the moustaches long was carried to such an extreme by some people that they curled the ends round their ears.

It is perhaps worth noticing that Prynne, in his Histriomastix (quoted by Nares *sub Lock* or *Love-lock*) speaks of these *love-locks* as "growne now too much in fashion with comly pages, youthes, and lewd, effeminate, *ruffianly* persons" (p. 209). Now "that Deformed," according to the worthy Seacoal was "a vile thief," and would come under the last category.

It is curious that the only survival of this custom, apparently, should be among the so-called dangerous classes. It was the practice of thieves, in our own time, to wear the hair very short with the exception of one lock, called a "Newgate knocker," which curled round the ear.

230. Lines 187, 188:

> Con. *Masters,*—
> Sea. *Never speak: we charge you,* &c.

This is Theobald's arrangement, followed by most modern editors. In Q. Ff. both these speeches are given to *Conrade*, evidently by mistake.

231. Lines 190, 191: *We are like to prove a goodly* COMMODITY, *being* TAKEN UP *of these men's* BILLS.—There is so much play upon words here that it can hardly be explained in a foot-note. *Commodity* was a term used for any kind of merchandise. See Merchant of Venice, note 45.

To take up, besides its ordinary meaning = "to arrest," meant to obtain goods on credit. The pun on the word *bills* is obvious. In connection with this passage it may be as well to quote Greene's Looking Glass for London and England, where Thrasybulus says to the usurer: "this is the day wherein I should pay you money that I *took up* of you alate in a *commodity*" (Works, p. 120); and again a little further on "my loss was as great as the *commodity I took up*." It appears to have been a common practice for a borrower, then as now, to accept a considerable portion of the loan in goods; and it is very possible that Conrade is referring to this use (well known in Shakespeare's time) of the phrase *take up a commodity*.

232. Line 192: *in question.*—There are only two other examples of the use of this expression in Shakespeare; one = "in or on a judicial trial," in Winter's Tale, v. 1. 197, 198: "who now has these poor men *in question*;" the other in II. Henry IV. i. 2. 68, 69: "He that was *in question* for the robbery." Schmidt gives the meaning as "on judicial trial." In the last passage it would almost seem to mean

"under suspicion;" and in the passage from Winter's Tale it might very well be rendered "in custody" or "under examination."

ACT III. Scene 4.

233. Line 7: *rabato.*—*Rabato* is thus described by Planché (p. 416): "a falling band or ruff, so called from the verb *rabattre* to put back." They are often alluded to in the old dramatists. They were supported by wires known as *rabato* wires. These were called *poting-sticks*, or *poking-sticks*. (See Winter's Tale, iv. 4. 228.) Cotgrave under *rabat* has "also, a *Rabatoe* for a womans ruffe; also, a falling band." From this and other passages it is evident that the word *rabato* came also to be applied to the wire that supported the ruff as well as to the ruff itself.

234. Lines 13, 14: *I like the new* TIRE *within excellently, if the hair were a thought browner.*—It would appear from this that besides being worn, as it is now, mixed with the natural hair, *false hair* was worn inside the *tire* or head-dress. In Planché's Dictionary of Costume (p. 277) appears the following, which will afford the clearest explanation of this passage: "A list of her 'attiers,' as they are termed, is curious, as it informs us that the word *caul* was applied to false hair, of which Queen Elizabeth wore a constant change, but generally of a red colour (see p. 246): 'Item, one *cawle* of hair set with pearles in number xliij. Item, one do. set with pearles of sundry sort and bigness, with seed pearle and seven buttons of gold, in each button a rubie."

235. Lines 18-22: *cloth-o'-gold, and* CUTS, *and lac'd with silver, set with* PEARLS DOWN SLEEVES, SIDE SLEEVES, *and* SKIRTS *round underborne with a bluish* TINSEL.—We have here a very interesting description of a lady's *dress* for grand occasions. The details given here of Hero's wedding dress are, doubtless, more interesting to those of her own sex than to male readers; but they give us a very good idea of the extravagance in costume which prevailed in Shakespeare's time. The *cuts* mentioned were the shaped edges of the *skirt* and *long sleeves*. These *cuts* were also called *dags*, and were made in different shapes to resemble letters of the alphabet, leaves of plants and flowers, &c. In 1407 Henry IV. issued a sumptuary edict against these *cuts* or *slashes*; but, though the penalty of imprisonment and fine was inflicted on any tailor who should make any gown or garment ornamented with these *dags*, the penalty could not have been very strictly exacted, for we find the same fashion prevailing both in men's and women's dresses down to the time of Elizabeth (see Planché's Cyclopædia of Costume, *sub Dagges*). The dress here described as having sleeves embroidered with *pearls* is after the fashion of the dress worn by Elizabeth in the engraving of her visit to Blackfriars, June 15, 1601, a copy of which is given in Harrison's Description of England (Shakespeare Society Reprint), and in Planché's Cyclopædia; it appears to have been somewhat similar to the one described by Hentzner (p. 49) in his account of the queen going to prayers at Greenwich, which he says was "of white Silk, bordered with *pearls* of the size of beans, and over it a mantle of black silk, shot with silver threads." *Pearls* seem to have been a good deal used in the sixteenth century to ornament sleeves.

Side sleeves were long hanging sleeves which were worn over the tight-fitting sleeves, and which either formed part of the upper dress or could be detached from the shoulder at the pleasure of the wearer. The word *side* in some of our north-country dialects still retains the sense of "long," "trailing." Compare *side*-coats, *i.e.* the long coats worn by young children. These *hanging sleeves* were most extravagantly decorated, and at last were allowed to reach such a length that they became a positive nuisance, as they trailed along the ground; many allusions to which occur in our old writers. Occleve, who lived just after Chaucer, in a passage of considerable length, part of which we quote, ridicules this fashion in his "Pride and Waste Clothynge of Lordis mene which is ayens ther Astate" (lines 64-72):

> What is a lord withoute his mene?
> I put case that his foos hym assayle
> Sodenly in the strete: what help shall he,
> Whos *sleves* encombrous so *syde* trayle,
> Do to his lorde? he may hym not avayle.
> In such a case he nys but a woman;
> He may not stande hym in stede of a man.
> His armes twoo have righte ynow to doo,
> And somewhat more, his sleves vp to hold.
> —Early English Text Soc. Reprint, pp. 106, 107.

From this it would appear that men, and not women, were the chief offenders; and in the fourth year of the reign of Henry IV. there was an act passed against these long trailing sleeves, which applied only to men. Stubbes (Anatomie of Abuses, p. 74), writing of women's dress, describes some gowns as having "sleeves hanging down to their skirts, trayling on the ground, and cast ouer their shoulders, like cow-tailes."

For *tinsel* used in dress compare Marston's What You Will, i. 1:

> A Florentine cloth-of-silver jerkin, sleeves
> White satin cut on *tinsel*, then long stock.
> —Bullen's ed. of Marston, vol. ii. p. 337.

236. Lines 32, 33: *I think you would have me say,* "SAVING YOUR REVERENCE, A HUSBAND."—This is generally printed with the word *husband* only between quotation marks. The Cambridge edd. print the whole passage in quotation marks, and point out that Q. and Ff. punctuate the passage thus: "say, saving your reverence, 'a *husband*.'" It seems to me that they are quite right in their conjecture that "Margaret means that Hero was so prudish as to think that the mere mention of the word '*husband*' required an apology" (vol. ii. p. 93, note xx). The sentence should be delivered with an elaborate curtsey, as if apologizing for alluding to such a word as a *husband*. Certainly Margaret has not been over-delicate in her speech, three lines above, in which she alludes to the fact that her young mistress would soon be a bride.

237. Lines 43, 44: *Clap's into* LIGHT O' LOVE; *that goes without a burden.*—See Two Gent. of Verona, note 20. The air of this song is given in the Var. Ed. vol. vii. p. 98.

238. Line 46: YE LIGHT O' LOVE *with your heels!*—So Q. Ff.; Rowe altered *Ye* into *Yes*; while Dyce, and other modern editors, read "*Yea*, light o' love." It seems quite clear to me that the old copies are right. My only doubt is whether we should not read "light o' *loves*." The

sense in which this word was used is quite clear from the following passage in Fletcher's Wild Goose Chase, iv. 1:

> That she's an English whore! a kind of fling-dust,
> One of your London *light o' loves*, a right one!
> Come over in thin pumps, and half a petticoat.
> —Works, vol. i. p. 556.

239. Line 51: *I scorn that with my heels.*—Compare Merchant of Venice, note 122. Margaret evidently refers to the first sentence of Beatrice's last speech.

240. Line 56: *For the letter that begins them all*, H.—This pun on the letter *H* and *ache*, which was pronounced as if spelt *aiche*, seems to have been a rather favourite one; but this pronunciation appears to have been confined to the noun and not to have applied to the verb, which is often spelt *ake*, *e.g.* in Lilly's Mydas, iii. 2: "my teeth ake" (Works, vol. ii. p. 28). Heywood's Epigram on the letter *H* is quoted by Steevens and other editors. The Epigram is the 59th of the "fourth hundred of Epigrammes."

> *H* is worst among letters in the crossrow,
> For if thou finde him either in thyne elbow,
> In thyne arme, or leg, in any degree,
> In thy hed, or teeth, in thy toe or knee,
> Into what place so euer *H* may pyke him,
> Where euer thou finde *ache*, thou shalt not like him.

Compare also the Epigram (494) on the letter *H* in Wits Recreations:

> Nor Hauk, nor Hound, nor Horse, those letters *hhh*,
> But *ach* its self, 't is *Brutus* bones attaches.
> —Reprint, vol. ii. p. 137.

John Kemble may have been ridiculed for his adherence to the old pronunciation of *ache* in Shakespeare, but he was perfectly justified, as is shown by the well-known passage in The Tempest, i. 2. 370:

> Fill all thy bones with *aches*, make thee roar.

It is said that one night when the manager had to announce from the stage the fact of Kemble being too ill to appear, a wag in the pit cried out: "Kemble's head *ai-ches*."

241. Line 57: *an you be not* TURN'D TURK.—Compare Hamlet, iii. 2. 287: "if the rest of my fortunes *turn Turk* with me." Greene, in his Tu Quoque, uses this expression: "This it is to *turn Turk*, from an absolute and most complete gentleman, to a most absurd, ridiculous, and fond lover."

242. Line 62: *These* GLOVES *the count sent me; they are an excellent* PERFUME.—*Perfumed gloves* are alluded to in Winter's Tale. Among the articles Autolycus offers for sale are "*Gloves* as sweet as damask roses" (iv. 4. 222); and below in the same play Mopsa says to the Clown: "you promised me a tawdry-lace and a pair of *sweet gloves*" (iv. 4. 252, 253). Nares quotes from the continuator of Stow: "The queene [Elizabeth] had a payre of *perfumed gloves*, trimmed onlie with foure tuftes or roses of culler'd silke. The queene took such pleasure in those gloves, that she was pictured with those gloves upon her hands" (p. 868). Elizabeth was very particular about the perfumes for her gloves; the one which she used most being called the "Earl of Oxford's perfume," "because Edward Vere, earl of Oxford, had brought it, with other refinements, from Italy" (Nares, sub. *Gloves*).

243. Line 64: *stuff'd.*—This is the only instance in which Shakespeare uses this word, in the same sense as we use it nowadays, of being *stuffed* with a cold. I cannot find any instance of a similar use of the word in any writer of Shakespeare's time. Probably the word is used here for the sake of the very poor pun which Margaret makes in the next speech.

244. Line 68: *how long have you profess'd* APPREHENSION?—*Apprehension* is used here, apparently, in the sense of "wit." Shakespeare uses it = "the faculty of observation" in Henry V. iii. 7. 145: "If the English had any *apprehension*, they would run away;" and perhaps in the well-known passage in Hamlet, ii. 2. 319: "in *apprehension* how like a god!" He never uses the word in the modern sense of "fear."

245. Line 73: *Carduus Benedictus.*—This plant, called the *Blessed Thistle*, is a native of the South of Europe. Hunter quotes from Paradisus Terrestris, 1629, p. 471: "the *Carduus Benedictus*, or the Blessed Thistle, is much used in the time of any infection or plague, as also to expel *any evil symptom from the heart* at all other times." He also quotes from Abel Redivivus, 4to, 1651, p. 44: "About the beginning of the year 1527 Luther fell suddenly sick of a congealing of blood *about his heart*, which almost killed him; but by the drinking of the water of Carduus Benedictus, whose virtues then were not so commonly known, he was perfectly helped" (Hunter, vol. i. pp. 253, 254). Certainly these quotations are very appropriate to Margaret's advice, "lay it to your hearts." This plant had the credit of being good for any disease under the sun, from the plague to a toothache.

246. Line 78: *you have some* MORAL *in this Benedictus*—Compare Taming of the Shrew, iv. 4. 79: "to expound the meaning or *moral* of his signs and tokens;" and Richard II. iv. 1. 290:

> Mark, silent king, the *moral* of this sport;

and Henry V. iii. 6. 35. This use of the word is taken from the *morals* appended to fables and such stories as these in the Gesta Romanorum, in which the meaning of the allegory or the hidden *moral* lesson of the story was explained.

247. Line 90: *he eats his meat without* GRUDGING.—Malone explains this, "and yet now, in spite of his resolutions to the contrary, he *feeds on love*, and likes his food" (Var. Ed. vol. vii. p. 101).

I confess I do not quite see how the passage can be made to bear this meaning. Loss of appetite has always been supposed to be among the signs of love. Johnson thought that it might mean "he is content to live by eating like other mortals, and will be content, notwithstanding his boasts, like other mortals, to have a wife" (Var. Ed. vol. vii. p. 100); that is to say, to marry. If "to eat the leek" had become, at this time, a proverbial expression, which is scarcely probable, *he eats his leak without grudging* would be very appropriate. It is more than likely that we have here another indelicate allusion from Mistress Margaret. Compare the dialogue between the Lady and Welford in Beaumont and Fletcher's Scornful Lady, act v. sc. 4, especially Welford's speech beginning, "He that fares well is" (Works, vol. i. p. 104).

248. Line 100: *Help to dress me.*—As Mr. Daniel points out, in his Time Analysis of this play, this scene is supposed to take place early *in the morning* of Hero's wedding-day (see Beatrice's speech above, line 52), the night having intervened between this scene and the first scene of the act. Certainly it would seem that five o'clock in the morning (see line 52 above) was rather early to set out for church, even for a wedding.

ACT III. Scene 5.

249.—The stage-direction at the beginning of this scene in Q. F. 1 is "Enter Leonato and the constable and Headborough." By *Headborough*, evidently, *Verges* is meant. It would seem therefore that the *Headborough* was not the chief constable, but perhaps the next in authority to him, and undoubtedly superior to the *Thirdborough* (see Taming of the Shrew, note 4). Perhaps we get the explanation of the rank of these various guardians of the peace in the Dramatis Personæ to Ben Jonson's Tale of a Tub, among whom we find "Toble Turfe, high constable of Kentish-town; In-and-In Medlay, of Islington, cooper and *head-borough;* Rasi' Clench, of Hamstead, farrier and petty constable; To-Pan, tinker, or metal-man of Belsise, *third-borough.*"

250.—To illustrate the confusion which exists both in the Quarto and First Folio of this play as to the prefixes to the speeches of the various characters, it may be noted that in this scene, in Q. and F. 1, are the following prefixes. To the first speech of Dogberry's both Q. F. 1 have *Const Dog.* The prefix to the speech at line 8 is *Headb.* The prefix to the speech beginning line 10 is *Con. Dog.*, &c., till we come to the speech, line 56, which has the prefix *Constable;* but the speech beginning line 62 has again the prefix *Dogb.* The next speech has the prefix *Verges.* The next speech of Dogberry has the full prefix *Dogberry* in Q., and *Dogb.* in F. 1. In scene 2 of the next act, as we shall see, we have the matter further complicated by the names of the actors being given, in many instances, instead of the names of the characters.

251. Line 13: *honest as the skin between his brows.*—This would seem a proverbial expression, though I cannot find it in Bohn, or in the numerous proverbs of John Heywood. Reed gives two instances of its use in Gammer Gurton's Needle, v. 2 (1575): "I am as true, I would thou knew, as *skin betwene thy brows*" (Dodsley, vol. iii. p. 244); and in Cartwright's Ordinary, v. 4: "I am as honest *as the skin* that is between thy brows" (Dodsley, vol. xii. p. 310).

252. Line 18: *Comparisons are odorous.*—Compare in Sir Gyles Goosecappe, iv. 2, 1603:

> by heaven a most edible *Caparison:*
> *Ru. Odious* thou woodst say, for *Caparisons are odious.*
> *Foul.* So they are indeed, sir *Cut.*, all but my Lords.
> *Goos.* Be *Caparisons odious*, sir Cut; what, like flowers!
> *Rud.* O asse they be *odorous.*
> *Goos.* A botts a that stinking word *odorous*, I can never hitt on 't.
> —Bullen's Old Plays, vol. iii. p. 65.

We have here also the original of Mrs. Malaprop's "*Caparisons* are odious."

253. Line 18: *palabras.*—This is probably elliptical for the Spanish phrase *pocas palabras*, "few words," which is said to be pretty well the equivalent of our slang phrase "shut up." This expression seems to have been used even among the common people in England, having been imported probably by our sailors from Spain. Compare Taming of Shrew, Induction, i. 5, where Sly uses the corrupt form *paucas pallabris.* In the Spanish Tragedy, act iv., *Pocas palabras* occurs in its correct form (Dodsley, vol. v. p. 139). Neuman and Baretti's Spanish Dictionary does not give the phrase at all; but it gives *palábras* as an interjection = "I say, a word with you."

Palábras also meant the superstitious words used by sorcerers. The word still survives in English, in the form of "palaver."

254. Line 22: *we are the* POOR *duke's officers.*—Compare Measure for Measure, ii. 1. 47, 48: "I am the *poor* duke's constable."

255. Line 23: *if I were as* TEDIOUS *as a king.*—It is difficult to follow Dogberry's meaning here. In the other cases his mistakes are quite clear and natural enough; but what he supposes *tedious* or *tediousness* to mean I cannot imagine. He seems to mistake these two words as somehow connected with wealth.

256. Line 33: *our watch* TO-NIGHT, *excepting your worship's presence, have ta'en a couple of as arrant knaves as any in Messina.*—*To-night* here, as Mr. Daniel points out in his Time Analysis of this play, means the night before, as we should say last night, as it does in several other passages in Shakespeare, *e.g.* in Merry Wives, iii. 3. 171: "I have dream'd *to-night;*" Merchant of Venice, ii. 5. 18: "I did dream of money-bags *to-night;*" and King John, iv. 2. 85.

257. Line 37: *When the age is in, the wit is out.*—An obvious mistake for the proverb: "when the *ale* is in the wit is out." See Heywood's Epigrams and Proverbs (edn. 1598), O. 4:

> ALE AND WIT. 163.
>
> When *ale is in, wit is out:*
> When *ale is out, wit is in.*
> The first thou shewest out of doubt,
> The last in thee hath not bin.

258. Line 64: *we are* NOW TO EXAMINE *those men.*—Q. has *to examination*, a mistake Dogberry was not very likely to have made, as just above (line 52) he has used the word *examined* rightly. It was probably a mistake inserted gratuitously by the actor.

ACT IV. Scene 1.

259. Lines 12, 13: *If either of you know any* INWARD IMPEDIMENT *why you should not be conjoined.*—These words are very much the same as those used in the ceremony of marriage in the liturgy of the English Church. The marriage service in the Church of Rome is different. The sacrament of matrimony in that church commences with the priest asking first of the bridegroom: "Wilt thou take N., here present, for thy lawful wife, according to the rite of our holy Mother the Church?" Then he addresses the same question to the bride, putting the bridegroom's name of course instead of the bride's, and each answers: "I will." Then the bridegroom, "holding her by the right hand with his own right hand, plights

her his troth," and says much the same words as are used in the Anglican ritual: "I, N., take thee, N., to my wedded wife, to have and to hold, from this day forward, for better, for worse, for richer, for poorer, in sickness and in health, till death us do part, *if holy Church will it permit;* and thereto I plight thee my troth." The words italicized imply that there is no impediment either "of consanguinity, affinity, or spiritual relationship," nor of course any such impediment as being already married, or solemnly pledged to marry another. It will be noticed that Friar Francis uses here the expression, "any *inward* impediment," which probably means any impediment only known to the parties themselves. In Addis and Arnold's Catholic Dictionary we have under Impediments of Marriage: "Impediments are of two kinds. They may render marriage unlawful merely, in which case they are called 'mere impedientia;' or they may nullify it, in which case they are known as 'dirimentia.'" It is unnecessary to give here a list of all these impediments. It is sufficient to say that if the story against Hero had been true, and she had been, in any way, pledged to marry her supposed lover, she would have been bound to confess that fact as an impediment to marriage under the law of the old Church. It must be remembered that the Order of Matrimony so called, that is, the conferring of the sacrament of matrimony in the Church of Rome, is partly the old service of Betrothal or Espousal, and has nothing to do with what is called the "Mass for the Bride and Bridegroom," at which the nuptial benediction is generally given. Neither the celebration of Mass nor the bestowal of the benediction is necessary to the sacrament of marriage.

260. Line 21: *not knowing what they do.*—So Q. Ff. omit these words.

261. Lines 22, 23: *How now! interjections! Why, then, some be of laughing, as, Ha, ha, he!*—This is a quotation from some old English grammar. Compare Lilly's Endimion, iii. 3:

> *Tophas.* Unrigge me. Hey ho!
> *Eps.* What's that?
> *Tophas.* An *interjection*, whereof *some are of* mourning: as *eho, vah.*
> —Works, vol. i. p. 35.

There are other grammatical jokes in the same scene.

262. Line 42: *luxurious.*—Shakespeare uses *luxurious* in this sense = "lustful," in Henry V. iv. 4. 20: "*luxurious* mountain goat;" and Macbeth, iv. 3. 58:

> *Luxurious*, avaricious, false, deceitful;

and, in the canonical sense of "lust," "lasciviousness," *luxury* is used pretty frequently, *e.g.* Hamlet, i. 5. 82, 83:

> Let not the royal bed of Denmark be
> A couch for *luxury* and damned incest.

Compare Troilus and Cressida, v. 2. 55.

263. Lines 44-47:

> Leon. *What do you mean, my lord?*
> Claud. *Not to be married, not to knit my soul*
> *To an approved wanton.*
> Leon. *Dear my lord—*
> [He pauses from emotion] *If you in your own proof, &c.*

These lines are printed thus in Q. Ff.:

> *Leonato.* What do you meane, my Lord?
> *Clau.* Not to be married,
> Not to knit my soule to an approued wanton.
> *Leon.* Deere my Lord, if you in your owne proofe.

It may be observed that *Not to knit* is the reading of F. 1, while F. 2, F. 3, F. 4 read *Not knit*. Steevens proposed to read:

> *Nor* knit my soul to an approved wanton.

The arrangement in our text is substantially the same as Walker proposed, but we adopted it independently. The insertion of the stage-direction in line 46 explains why that line is imperfect. It seems natural that Leonato should be somewhat overcome by his emotion when he suggests that his daughter has yielded to the solicitation of Claudio before her marriage; and it gets rid of the very awkward line as it stands in the ordinary arrangement of the text:

> Dear my lord, if you in your own proof.

264. Line 57: *Out on* THY *seeming! I will* WRITE AGAINST IT.—Q. Ff. read *thee* for *thy*. The misprint *thee* for *thy* is common enough. Grant White adheres to the reading of the old copies, and puts a note of exclamation after *thee*. For the expression *write against*, compare Cymbeline, ii. 5. 32: "I'll *write against* them," which appears to be the only other passage in which Shakespeare uses this expression. Schmidt explains it simply = declare; but surely it means something more, and refers to the practice of *writing* pamphlets *against* people.

265. Line 58: *You* SEEM *to me as Dian in her orb.*—So Q. Ff.; Hanmer altered *seem* to *seem'd;* but the change does not seem necessary. Although the past tense might seem more natural, there is a force in the use of the present; it implies that Hero still bore that outward semblance of innocence to which, according to Claudio's belief, her conduct had given the lie.

266. Line 63: *Is my lord well, that he doth speak so* WIDE?—Collier altered *wide* to *wild*. Compare Troilus and Cressida, iii. 1. 97: "No, no, no such matter; you are *wide;*" and Lear, iv. 7. 50: "Still, still, far *wide!*" There can be no doubt as to the meaning of the phrase = "*wide* of the mark;" it is here equivalent to "far away from the truth."

267. Line 64: *Sweet prince, why speak not you?*—Q. Ff. give this speech to *Leonato*. It seems more proper that Claudio should call upon the *Prince* to confirm his statement; and, as Dyce points out, the very expression *Sweet prince* has been used by him in addressing Don Pedro above (line 30).

268. Line 69: *This looks not like a* NUPTIAL.—Shakespeare uses this word in the singular as we should use the plural form *nuptials* = marriage. Compare Measure for Measure, iii. 1. 222: "the *nuptial* appointed;" and Love's Labour's Lost, iv. 1. 78: "The catastrophe is a *nuptial*."

269. Line 75: *And, by that fatherly and* KINDLY *power.*—Compare II. Henry IV. iv. 5. 84:

> Washing with *kindly* tears his gentle cheeks;

and Timon of Athens, ii. 2. 226:

> 'T is lack of *kindly* warmth they are not *kind*.

Compare als · the use of *kindless* in Hamlet, ii. 2. 600, as = "contrary t. nature," "unnatural:"

> Remorseless, eacherous, lecherous, *kindless* villain!

The adverb *kindly* is used in the same way in Taming of Shrew, Ind. i. 66:

> This do, and do it *kindly*, gentle sirs.

270. Line 77: *I charge thee do so, as thou art my child.*—So Q. F. 2; F. 1 has *I charge thee doe;* and F. 3, F. 4, "I charge thee *to* do;" both omit *so*.

271. Line 83: *Hero* ITSELF *can blot out Hero's virtue.*—So Q. Ff. Rowe substituted *herself* for *itself*, which certainly seems the more natural expression; but *it* is sometimes applied to persons, *e.g.* in Mids. Night's Dream, ii. 1. 171, 172:

> Will make or man or woman madly dote
> Upon the next live creature that *it* sees;

where *it* applies to man or woman. We have one other instance, however, where *it* appears to apply to women generally, in Cymbeline, iii. 4. 160: "Woman *it* pretty self." Neither of these instances seems to me satisfactory, any more than the explanation that Claudio means by "Hero *itself*" the name of Hero, using *it* as an abstraction; for surely it is only a *personal* act, on the part of Hero herself, that can blot out her virtue. However, as the sense is clear, we have not altered the text.

272. Lines 93-95:

> *Who hath indeed, most like a* LIBERAL *villain,*
> *Confess'd the vile encounters they have had*
> *A thousand times in secret.*

This use of *liberal* = "licentious" was a natural extension of its original sense of "free," "frank;" but it is not very common in Shakespeare. Some of the instances quoted by Schmidt are certainly not apposite, *e.g.* Love's Labour's Lost, v. 2. 743:

> The *liberal* opposition of our spirits.

The only other passage where the sense of the word seems almost exactly similar to that which it bears here is in Hamlet, iv. 7. 171:

> That *liberal* shepherds give a grosser name;

for we might almost paraphrase it, in both these passages, as "gross of speech."

None of the commentators seem to have noticed that this statement of Don Pedro's is scarcely reconcilable with the facts of the case. When could Borachio have confessed these *vile encounters?* Certainly not when he was talking to Margaret, who was pretending to be Hero; for had they spoken to him then, Claudio would at once have discovered the fraud. As he was arrested almost immediately afterwards by the constables, he could not have had time to make any confession in the interim. Perhaps Don Pedro is speaking on the authority of Don John, to whom one lie more or less was a matter of perfect indifference, and who might, after the discovery of Hero's supposed misconduct, have volunteered the information that Borachio had confessed to him "these *vile encounters*." Certainly Don Pedro, and Claudio, for whom there is less excuse, accept all the evidence against Hero with the most perfect ingenuousness. As usual, in cases of slander, it is not thought necessary to cross-examine the witness. As long as he or she speaks evil against one of his or her fellow-creatures, we are ready to accept the evidence however weak it may be. It is only when good is spoken of them that we give way to a spirit of honest scepticism.

273. Lines 96-100.—The assumption of a high moral tone, in this speech of Don John's, is very characteristic. One would have thought that Don Pedro, at least, knew him well enough to be able to detect his hypocrisy. The malice of this scoundrelly liar is well shown in the mocking profession of sympathy for Hero, with which the speech concludes.

274. Line 103: *About the thoughts and counsels of* THY *heart.*—This is Rowe's emendation. Q. Ff. read *the*.

275. Line 106: *For thee I'll lock up all the gates of love.*—This excellent resolution of Claudio does not seem to have been persevered in very long. In the first scene of the next act he receives the news of Hero's death with admirable resignation; but scarcely has he discovered the monstrous wrong he has done her, when he is ready to marry another young lady, whom he has never seen before, at the bidding of Leonato. Perhaps this was *his* idea of repentance.

276. Line 109: *And never shall it more be* GRACIOUS.—This sense of *gracious*, as applied to beauty, means that which finds *grace* or favour in one's eyes. Compare John, iii. 4. 81, where Constance, speaking of Arthur, says:

> There was not such a *gracious* creature born.

277. Lines 112, 113:

> *These things, come thus to light,*
> SMOTHER *her spirits* UP.

Shakespeare does not often use *smother* with *up*, and in a figurative sense only once, in this passage. Compare I. Henry IV. i. 2. 221-223:

> Yet herein will I imitate the sun,
> Who doth permit the base contagious clouds
> To *smother up* his beauty from the world.

278. Line 128: *rearward of reproaches.*—Compare Sonnet xc. 5, 6:

> Ah, do not, when my heart hath 'scap'd this sorrow,
> Come in the *rearward* of a conquer'd woe.

279. Line 130: *Chid I for that at frugal nature's* FRAME?—It seems pretty clear that *frame* here has the sense we have given it in the foot-note, that is to say, "order" or "disposition of things." Schmidt would give to *frame* the extraordinary sense of "a mould for castings," making the passage mean, "Did I grumble against the niggardness of nature's casting-mould?" *i.e.* "in giving me one child only;" while Mason thinks that Leonato refers "to the particular formation of himself, or of Hero's mother, rather than to the universal system of things" (Var. Ed. vol. vii. p. 112). Collier's Old Corrector settled the difficulty by calmly substituting *frown*.

280. Line 135: *Who smirched thus and* MIR'D *with infamy.*—So Q.; Ff. have *smear'd*. Shakespeare only uses the verb *mire* in one other passage, in Timon of Athens, iv. 3. 147:

> Paint till a horse may *mire* upon your face;

where it is used in a different sense, that of a horse sinking in the mud.

281. Lines 138-141:

> *But mine, and mine I lov'd, and mine I prais'd,*
> *And mine that I was proud on; mine so much*
> *That I myself was to myself not mine,*
> *Valuing of her.*

This passage is certainly not over-clear, though it would scarcely be improved by the adoption of Warburton's proposed emendation:

> But mine, *as* mine I lov'd, *as* mine I prais'd
> *As* mine that I was proud on.

The construction is not an unusual one, the relative *that* being understood: "mine *that* I lov'd," &c. There is a good deal of unnecessary jingle in the whole passage, the latter part of which is even more obscure than the former. Perhaps it is for that reason that the commentators avoid any attempt to explain it. The sentence may perhaps be thus paraphrased: "So much and so dear a possession of mine, that I regarded myself as nothing in comparison with her, so greatly did I value and esteem her." It is a great pity that the sentiment, which is a very beautiful one, could not have been expressed in clearer language.

282. Line 146: *attir'd in wonder.*—Compare Lucrece, 1601:

> Why art thou thus *attir'd in* discontent?

Compare also, for a similar expression, Psalm cix. 18: "he *clothed* himself *with cursing* like as with his garment."

283. Line 154: *Would the* TWO *princes lie? and Claudio lie?*—Ff. omit *two*.

284. Lines 157-162:

> *Hear me a little;*
> *For I have only silent been so long,*
> *And given way unto this course of fortune,*
> *By noting of the lady: I have mark'd*
> *A thousand blushing apparitions start*
> *Into her face.*

In Q. this passage comes at the bottom of page G 1 (*r*) and is printed as prose; the last line being marked with a comma after *lady*, and after *mark'd* A is the catch letter. The rest of the speech is properly printed as verse. F. 1 prints the passage also in prose, but puts a full stop after *mark'd*. The Cambridge edd. think the type was "accidentally dislocated," and some words lost in the process of resetting; they say the whole passage would therefore stand as follows (vol. ii. p. 93, note xxi.):

> Hear me a little; for I have only been
> Silent so long and given way unto
> This course of fortune . . .
> By noting of the lady I have mark'd, &c.

The usual punctuation:

> And given way unto this course of fortune,
> By noting of the lady: I have mark'd, &c.,

makes but indifferent sense.

I have only been silent may mean "I alone have been silent."

We have arranged the passage as it is usually arranged, adopting in line 158 the transposition, first made by Grant White, of *silent been* instead of *been silent*, which is the reading of Q. Ff. If we take *by* to = "because of," the meaning will be perfectly clear. The Friar says "I have only been silent *because of* noting, or carefully watching the lady." This is the sense of *by* described by Schmidt as "the idea of instrumentality passing into that of causality." Though we have no exactly similar instance of its use with the gerund, or present participle, yet the sense of the preposition is quite the same as this in Cymbeline, iii. 4. 56, 57:

> All good seeming,
> *By* thy revolt, O husband, shall be thought, &c.

This course of fortune = "this sequence of events," "this chapter of accidents." In line 161 Q. Ff. read "*To start*" making the line an alexandrine:

> *To* start into her face, a thousand shames.

We have followed Reed's arrangement.

285. Line 162: *shames.*—Shakespeare frequently uses the plural of *shame* where we should use the singular. Compare Sonnet cxii. 6:

> To know my *shames* and praises from your tongue;

and above, in this very scene, line 127:

> Thought I thy spirits were stronger than thy *shames*.

286. Line 167: *Trust not my reading nor my* OBSERVATION.—Q. Ff. have the plural *observations;* the emendation is Hanmer's.

287. Line 170: *My* REVERENCE, CALLING, *nor divinity.*—Collier, quite unnecessarily, altered this to *reverend calling*, which Dyce adopts; but as instances of *reverence* = "the qualities or character entitled to be revered," we have in this play, v. 1. 64:

> That I am forc'd to lay my *reverence* by;

and, as applied to a priest, in Twelfth Night, v. 1. 154:

> Father, I charge thee, by thy *reverence*.

288. Line 172: BITING *error.*—Here again Collier, quite unnecessarily, alters *biting* to *blighting*. It appears to me that *biting* is the much more expressive epithet of the two, for it exactly expresses the malicious nature of the *error*, or false evidence, on which Hero has been condemned.

289. Line 187: *misprision.*—Shakespeare uses this word, in the sense of "mistake," in five other passages beside this. Compare Sonnet lxxxvii. 11, 12:

> So thy great gift, upon *misprision* growing,
> Comes home again, on better judgement making.

Once only he uses it in the sense of "contempt," in All's Well, ii. 3. 159.

290. Line 188: *Two of them have the very* BENT *of honour.*—Schmidt gives, as the second meaning of *bent*, "inclination," "disposition." It is much the same as the second meaning given in our foot-note; but, in the other passages that he quotes, *e.g.* Romeo and Juliet, ii. 2. 143:

> If that thy *bent* of love be honourable,

the word seems to have more the sense of "tendency." Johnson explains it: "the bow has its full *bent*, when it is drawn as far as it can be," most probably = "the utmost degree;" and comparing the passage in this play, ii. 3. 232: "her affections have their full *bent*," he says that the expression is derived from archery (Var. Ed. vol. vii. p. 115). Compare, in this sense, the passage in Hamlet, ii. 2. 30, 31:

> And here give up ourselves, *in the full bent*
> To lay our service freely at your feet.

291. Line 190: *The practice of it* LIES *in John the bastard.*—Q. Ff. have *lives.* The emendation is Walker's.

292. Lines 199, 200:

> *But they shall find, awak'd in such a* CAUSE,
> *Both strength of limb and policy of mind.*

The old copies read "in such a *kind*," making a rhymed couplet, which is very awkward here, coming as it does in the middle of a passage of blank verse. Capell first suggested the emendation printed in our text, on which Collier's Old Corrector also hit. Apart from the objection to the rhyme, *kind* seems to have no particular sense. Dyce thinks that the close occurrence of *find* and *mind* in the passage led to the corruption *kind*.

293. Line 204: *Your daughter here the* PRINCES *left for dead.*—The old copies have *princess;* but Hero is never called by the title *princess;* nor does one quite see how she could be, for her father was not a prince any more than was her intended husband; while Don Pedro and Don John are called *princes*, lines 154 and 165 above.

294. Line 230: *More* MOVING, DELICATE, *and full of life.*—All the editors, including the Cambridge, hyphen these two adjectives, I cannot tell why, as they are not hyphened in the old copies, and they seem to be much more expressive when used as separate and independent epithets. For *moving* = "that which excites the emotions," compare Measure for Measure, ii. 2. 36: "Heaven give thee *moving* graces!" and Richard II. v. 1. 47:

> The heavy accent of thy *moving* tongue.

The sense of *delicate* here is probably that of "delicious." Compare above, in this play, i. 1. 305:

> Come thronging soft and *delicate* desires.

If the words are hyphened the meaning must be either "delicately-moving" or "graceful." For the *liver* as the supposed seat of love, see Love's Labour's Lost, note 113.

295. Line 247: *inwardness.*—This is the only passage in which Shakespeare uses this word as a substantive; but he uses the adjective *inward* = "familiar," "intimate." Compare Richard III. iii. 4. 8:

> Who is most *inward* with the noble duke?

296. Line 251: *Being that I* FLOW IN *grief.*—Compare Romeo and Juliet, ii. 4. 41: "the numbers that Petrarch *flowed in;*" and Troilus and Cressida, v. 2. 41: "You *flow to* great distraction."

297. Lines 253-256.—These four lines of rhyme, with a marked alliteration in the second of them, seem rather out of place, and could well be spared.

298. Line 257, &c.—This scene between Benedick and Beatrice, admirable as it is from a dramatic point of view, cannot but seem out of place in a church; and the incongruity of the surroundings is emphasized in modern times, when the resources of the scenic artist are so much more extensive than they were in the Elizabethan era. This incongruity, probably, did not strike Shakespeare, as there would be little or nothing in his time to indicate that the dialogue was taking place in a church, and almost in front of the sacred altar. But there is not the slightest necessity for the scene taking place in front of the *high altar*, as the marriage ceremony was, evidently, not intended to be what is called a nuptial mass. In the revival of this play at the Lyceum Theatre, a small detail might easily have escaped attention in this scene. The ceremony was supposed to take place before one of the side altars, the lamp belonging to which was *not* alight, as a sign that the sacred Host was supposed not to be on the altar, which to Roman Catholics would make a very great difference.

299. Line 291: *Kill Claudio.*—There are few speeches more dramatic, in the whole of Shakespeare, than these two words. Great actresses have differed as to the mode of speaking them. It seems to me that they ought to be spoken with the utmost passion, in fact almost hissed into Benedick's ears. It is in this scene that the real intensity of Beatrice's character comes out for the first time. Her whole nature revolts against the meanness of Claudio's conduct. With the true instinct of a loyal heart she spurns the lying slander against her cousin, not stopping to inquire into the evidence, such as it was, much less receiving with a greedy ear the foul imputation on another woman's fair fame. True, the night before, almost for the first time, her cousin and she were not bedfellows; therefore the story of these precious princes might possibly not be a lie; but she, with true nobleness of disposition, looks at the great moral fact—greater far than any gobbets of circumstantial evidence that slander could scrape together—that her cousin was, to her knowledge, a pure and loyal girl. What the man who had won her cousin's love, who was bound by every tie of affection, and by every quality of his manhood, to defend her character *should* have done, Beatrice, woman as she is, *does* without one moment's hesitation. At the same time that she, without any effort or self-consciousness, displays the generosity, courage, and greatness of soul that Claudio should have shown, had he been worthy of the name of man, she feels such an overwhelming scorn and loathing for the cowardly wretch who has outraged, with such brutal publicity, her innocent cousin, that she naturally cries for his blood. Death is the only punishment which seems to her adequate for such an outrage. In these two simple words *Kill Claudio* her indignation bursts forth; afterwards she gives her reasons for this indignation, reasons not thought out or laboured, but which flashed upon her mind simultaneously with the events which had occurred in such rapid succession. It is the privilege of such natures as that of Beatrice, undeformed by conventionality, unpoisoned by the lethal drug of worldliness, when any great question of right or wrong arises, not to have to reason out, with well-balanced arguments *pro* and *con*, the course they adopt, but to spring naturally to their conclusion.

300. Line 295: [She is going, he holds her by the arm.] *I am gone, though I am here:*—[Struggling to free herself].—The stage-direction we have inserted will explain the meaning of this sentence, to which some commentators have given a very strained interpretation. All that Beatrice means is that, although Benedick does detain her by force, she is, in spirit, *gone.* After his refusing her request she does not wish to have anything more to say to him.

301. Line 303: *Is he not approved in the height a villain?*

—Compare Henry VIII. i. 2. 214: "He's traitor *to the height;*" and Comedy of Errors, v. 1. 200:

> Even in the strength and *height* of injury.

Compare also the expression in Hamlet, i. 4. 21: "our achievements, though perform'd *at height.*"

302. Line 300: *bear her in hand.*—Compare Measure for Measure, i. 4. 51, 52:

> Bore many gentlemen, myself being one,
> *In hand* and hope of action;

and see Taming of Shrew, note 146.

303. Line 309: *I would* EAT HIS HEART *in the market-place.*—Steevens quotes from Chapman's Iliad, book 22nd:

> Hunger for slaughter, and a hate that eates thy heart, *to eate*
> *Thy foe's heart.*

Ferocious as this sentiment of Beatrice may seem, it is not unnatural by the light of what I have suggested above in note 299. The very lack of all manliness in Claudio makes *her* more than virile in her ferocity.

304. Line 316: Bene. *Beat*—.—This is as Theobald printed it. Q. F. 1 have *Beat!* F. 2, F. 3 *Bett!* F. 4 *But!* Steevens conjectured *But Beatrice.* We prefer, however, to leave the mere fragment of a word, as the storm of Beatrice's indignation must sweep down everything before it.

305. Line 317: *a goodly count,* count *confect.*—So Q. substantially; F. 1 has *a goodly count, comfect.* Some modern editors hyphen the two words *count comfect,* unnecessarily I think. Beatrice uses the expression in supreme contempt = "count sugar-plum." Grant White would see a play upon the words *count* and the French word *conte,* in the sense of a story made up. He explains this sense of the passage as being "further evident from the inter-dependence of the whole exclamation, 'Surely a princely *testimony,* a goodly count,'—the first part of which would be strangely out of place if there were no pun in the second. In Shakespeare's time the French title *Count* was pronounced like *conte* or *compte,* meaning a fictitious story, a word which was then in common use." It is quite possible that Grant White is right, as the words which follow *sweet gallant* certainly seem to show that Beatrice is playing upon words.

306. Line 323: *men are only* TURNED *into tongue.*—The non-elision in F. 1 of the final *ed* in *turned* is here, I am convinced, intentional. The unpleasant alliteration of *turn'd into tongue* is very much modified by pronouncing the final syllable of *turned.*

307. Line 336.—Benedick is at last convinced; but mark, it has taken all Beatrice's wonderful energy, all the shock caused by the noble fury of her indignation, to bring this result about. To Benedick, with his opinion of women,—such as is, it must be confessed, held by many men, who, as they pass the best part of their lives in trying to corrupt the other sex, console themselves for any failure by thinking that nature has done their work for them,—the idea of Hero's having carried on a low intrigue up to the very night before her marriage presents no difficulty, and makes no demand upon his credulity. It is one of the many subtle touches in this scene, the way in which his newly-born love of Beatrice causes him to detain her, but for which detention he would never have heard her eloquent vindication of her cousin. The nobler part of Benedick's nature is now awakened, and the viler part of it paralysed. Henceforth he is not only ready to challenge Claudio, but he firmly believes that he is challenging him in the cause of truth and justice. But a little before this, when unredeemed by love, he would have cracked his coarse jests over Hero's supposed unchastity, and laughed at the very idea of challenging anyone, much less his friend, in such a quarrel.

ACT IV. Scene 2.

308.—In this scene the prefixes to the speeches afford ample proof how careless was the editing of this play in the First Folio. Instead of the names of the characters the names of the actors are prefixed, and, in one or two cases, even these are wrong. There are in all thirty-nine speeches in this scene, counting line 19, which is given both to Conrad and Borachio, as one speech. It will be more convenient to refer to the speeches rather than to the lines. The prefix to speech 1, Dogberry's, is both in Q. and Ff. *Keeper,* generally supposed to be a misprint for *Kemp.* The prefix to speech 2 is *Cowley;* to speech 3, *Sexton;* to speech 4, *Andrew.* This has been supposed to be another name, perhaps a nickname, given to Kemp on account of his playing so often the Merry Andrew. This explanation seems to be a little far-fetched; Kemp's Christian name was *William;* and there is no actor among those mentioned in F. 1 whose Christian name is *Andrew.* The prefix to the next speech, the 5th, is *Cowley;* to the 6th speech, *Sexton;* to the 7th speech, *Kemp;* to the 8th, *Bor.;* to the 9th, *Ke.* in Q., *Kemp* in F. 1; to the 10th, *Con.;* to the 11th, *Ke.* in Q., *Kee* in F. 1; to the 12th, omitted in F. 1, *both;* to the 13th, omitted in F. 1, *Kem.;* to the 14th, *Con.;* to the 15th, *Kemp;* to the 16th, *Bor.;* to the 17th, *Kemp;* to the 18th, *Sexton* in Q., *Sext.* in F. 1; to the 19th, *Kemp;* to the 20th, *Watch 1;* to the 21st, *Kemp;* to the 22nd, *Borachio* in Q., *Bora.* in F. 1; to the 23rd, *Kemp;* to the 24th, *Sexton;* to the 25th, *Watch 2;* to the 26th, *Kemp;* to the 27th, *Const.;* to the 28th, *Sexton;* to the 29th, *Watch 1;* to the 30th, *Kemp;* to the 31st, *Sexton;* to the 32nd, *Watch;* to the 33rd, *Sexton;* to the 34th, *Constable* in Q., *Const.* in F. 1; the next two speeches, 35th and 36th, are made one by mistake both in Q. and F. 1, Q. gives the speech to *Cowley,* F. 1 to *Sexton;* to the 37th, *Kem.;* to the 38th, *Cowley;* to the 39th, *Kemp.*

I think it better to give the full details of this scene, because they may help us to settle two questions: the first, whether F. 1 was not simply transcribed from a printed copy of the Quarto, with a few cuts; the second, how the names of the actors came to be prefixed to the speeches in this scene, and not in any other part of the play. With regard to the first question, it will be noted that, with one or two slight exceptions, the prefixes given to the speeches are substantially the same both in Q. and F. 1, the only important exception being that of the two speeches, 35th and 36th, lines 70, 71, which, being hopelessly bungled together in both Q. and F. 1, are given in the former to *Cowley, i.e.* Verges, and in the latter to *Sex.* or *Sexton,* who has just left the stage. In fact, except in the omission in F. 1 of speech 12 and part of speech 13 (an omission evidently due to the frequent mention of the name of God), Q. F. 1 are substantially the same in this scene; and it is a powerful argument in favour of the theory that F. 1 is but a transcription of the Quarto that these prefixes should be retained in both. There is no other way to account for such a strange similarity in error, unless we suppose that both were transcribed from the same stage copy.

As to the second question, how it is that the names of the actors are found prefixed to the speeches in this scene and not elsewhere in the play, this is a difficult question to answer. There is an instance in The Taming of the Shrew, in Induction i. (see note 9 on that play), where the name *Sinklo* is prefixed to a speech, the speech of one of the characters who has no other designation but *a Player*. *Sinklo* also figures in a stage-direction in III. Henry VI. iii. 1, as one of the Two Keepers; and in II. Henry IV. v. 4 as *a Beadle*. This actor's name does not appear in the list of the principal actors given in F. 1. He was probably an unimportant member of the company who took only very small parts. It will be seen that in all these three cases, where Sinklo's name appears, it was substituted for a character such as *a Player*, *a Keeper*, *a Beadle*, to which there were assigned no specific names; but in the case of the scene before us it is quite different. Both Kemp and Cowley were important members of the company, and the proper prefixes of their respective characters are given to almost all their speeches. But it is to be noted that in act iii. scene 5 they are called in the stage-direction, prefixed to the scene, *Constable* and *Headborough;* and in the stage-direction at the beginning of act iii. scene 3, Verges's name does not appear, only *Dogberry and his compartner*, although in that scene Verges's name is prefixed to all his speeches. It seems to me that the most probable explanation of this confusion as to the prefixes is, that when first the play was written and the parts distributed to the actors, Shakespeare had not yet decided upon the names which he would give to Dogberry and Verges; and in the copy used by the prompter it is possible that, in order to prevent any confusion in some scenes—in this one, for instance—he had written the names of the actors instead of such vague titles as *Constable*, *Headborough*, &c. When the names Dogberry and Verges were decided upon, they were prefixed to the speeches belonging to these characters in part of the MS. but not throughout. It may be noted that it would be much easier for the prompter, who had to see that the various actors were "called," as the technical expression is, in time for their various entrances, if he wrote down in his MS. the names of the actors of small parts such as *Keepers*, *Beadles*, *Officers*, and *Constables*, because then he could scarcely make any mistake as to the actor whom he had to call, and this may account for such things as the occurrence of the name *Sinklo* in the stage-directions already alluded to. Again, it is possible that this portion of the MS. had got torn or otherwise defaced; perhaps the margin containing the names of the speakers had been torn away, and it had been re-copied by the prompter or some other member of the company, who put the name of the actor instead of the name of the character which he represented. Unfortunately we know so very little about the interior life of the theatre in Shakespeare's time, that we are almost ignorant how rehearsals were conducted, whether pieces were read to the company or not, and how parts were distributed. It is possible, in the case of actors who were regularly cast for a certain line of business, like Kemp, who always played the clown or comic character, that their own names were written on the part instead of the names of the characters they played. In such a case, a copyist supplying any deficiencies in the MS. prepared for the press from the actors' "parts"—which he would do, probably, in case of the stage copy being injured—would naturally write the name of the actor and not the name of the character.

309. Enter Dogberry, &c.—The stage-direction in Q. F. 1 is *Enter the Constables, Borachio, and the Towne Clearke; in gownes*. Here we have another proof of the confusion as to the designation of the characters in this piece; by the *Town Clerk* is evidently meant the *Sexton*, who takes down the examination of the prisoners. The stage-direction from Lady Alimony (1659) has already been quoted above (note 210) which says "Enter &c. in their *rug gowns*." According to a passage quoted by Malone from the Black Book, 4to, 1604: "—when they mist thei *constable*, and sawe the *black gowne* of his office lye full in a puddle—" (Var. Ed. vol. vii. p. 122), the constables wore a *black gown* of office. Probably it was these *gowns*, and not the *rug gowns* which they wore when on their active duties, that were intended to be worn in this scene. The slovenly nature of the stage-direction will be noticed, as according to its wording Borachio, as well as the *Constable* and *Town Clerk*, would be in a gown; and all mention of Conrade is omitted.

310. Line 2: *O, a stool and a cushion for the sexton.*—Malone (Var. Ed. vol. vii. p. 122) points out that here perhaps was another cut at that favourite butt of all the Elizabethan dramatists, The Spanish Tragedy (act iv.):

> *Hieron.* What are you ready? Balthazar!
> Bring a *chair and a cushion* for the king.
>
> —Dodsley, vol. v. p. [illegible]

It is worth noting that Malone misquotes this passage, making, by a curious mistake, *Balthazar* the name of the speaker of the second line quoted, whereas it is clear that the whole speech is addressed to Balthazar by Hieronimo.

311. Lines 3, 4:

> Sex. *Which be the malefactors?*
> Dog. *Marry, that am I and my partner.*

This looks suspiciously like what is technically termed a piece of *gag*. It is difficult to understand for what word Dogberry can have mistaken *malefactors*. If this line was not introduced by the actor, Shakespeare may have intended Dogberry to claim the title of *malefactor*, because it was a long word which he did not understand, but which he thought from its very length would add to his and his fellow constable's dignity.

312. Line 6: *we have the* EXHIBITION *to examine.*—Steevens explains this as a blunder for *examination to exhibit*, and refers to Leonato's words in iii. 5. 53: "Take their *examination* yourself." He might also have referred to the words of the Sexton below, line 68: "I will go before and show him their *examination*." But is it not rather doubtful whether Verges would have known the legal sense of the phrase *to exhibit!* It seems to me more probable that he is using *exhibition* in the sense of "allowance," or "permission," knowing that *exhibition* was used in the sense of "a money allowance," as we have it in The Two Gent. of Verona. See note 33 on that play.

313. Lines 19-23.—This passage, as has already been observed, is omitted in Ff. (see above, note 308) on account of the act, so often alluded to, passed in 3rd James i. chap. 21; but when the cut was made, by some mistake the sentence above was retained in Dogberry's part, probably because the person who had charge of the play-house copy was misled by the *Masters* in the second sentence commencing *Masters, it is proved already.* This mistake occasioned the absurdity noticed by Theobald, through which Dogberry asks a question without waiting for the answer. If we omit all between the word *Conrade,* line 16, and the sentence beginning *Masters it is proved,* line 23, the speech will read all right; and the omission of the passage, which contains the name of the Deity no less than five times, is certainly an improvement, at least as far as the reading aloud of the play, or its performance on the stage, is concerned.

314. Line 28: *but I will go about with him.*—This expression *to go about* is generally applied in such a phrase as "*to go about* your business," *i.e.* "to occupy one's self," "to undertake anything;" so we have it in Venus and Adonis, line 319:

> His testy master *goeth about* to take him;

and in this very play above, iv. 1. 65, 66:

> I stand dishonour'd, that have *gone about*
> To link my dear friend to a common stale;

where it almost has the meaning of "have taken pains," "have laboured." Hamlet uses it, in a rather peculiar sense, in the scene between Rosencrantz and Guildenstern, iii. 2. 361, 362: "why do you *go about* to recover the wind of me?" where it seems to imply a circuitous method of attaining an object. The passage in our text is the only instance, as far as I can find, of this expression being used "*to go about with a person.*" It would probably be best translated into our modern vernacular by "I'll tackle you."

315. Line 37: *that's the* EFTEST *way.*—Rowe suggested *easiest* for *eftest.* Theobald supposed that it was a blunder for *deftest;* but it is more probable that Dogberry is intended here to use the old word (of A. Sax. origin) *eft. Eft* has the sense of "quickly," and is frequently so used by Spenser, although its more proper meaning was "afterwards."

316 Lines 70, 71:

> Verg. *Let them be in the hands—*
> Con. *Off, coxcomb!*

These two lines, as has already been stated, are printed as one speech in Q. and F. 1; Q. gives them to Cowley, the actor who played Verges; while F. 1 gives them to the Sexton, who has just gone off. The line is thus printed in the old copies; Q. has "Let them be in the hands of coxcombe;" F. 1 has "Let them be in the hands of *Coxcombe.*" Probably there is some corruption here, besides the mistake of making the two speeches one. Several emendations have been proposed: "*Ver.* Let them be *in the hands of*—*Con.* Coxcomb!" (Malone); "*Ver.* Let them be *in hands. Con.* Off, coxcomb!" (Capell); "Let them *bind their hands;*" afterwards withdrawn (Tyrwhitt). "*Ver.* Let them be *bound. Con. Hands off,* Coxcomb!" (Collier MS.). Shakespeare never uses the expression *Hands off.* It may be that, originally, Verges was going to say, "Let them be *in the hands of the law;*" but that when he got as far as *of,* Conrade interrupted him with "*Off,* coxcomb!" or "*Of a* coxcomb." But *off* and *of* are very often confounded, and the usually accepted reading we have given in our text is as satisfactory as any.

317. Line 85: *as pretty a piece of flesh as any in Messina.*—Compare Twelfth Night, i. 5. 30, 31: "thou wert as witty *a piece of* Eve's *flesh* as any in Illyria."

318. Line 87: *a fellow that hath had* LOSSES.—It is scarcely conceivable that the Old Corrector absolutely changed *losses* to *leases.* He did not add "copyholds" and "freeholds," which he might as well have done, when he tried to rob us of one of the most delightful bits of Shakespeare's humour. Human nature is much the same, nowadays, as it was in Shakespeare's time; and the pride which people take in referring to "better days" is but a piece of the same kind of vanity as that which Dogberry here exhibits. Indeed some people take such a delight in recounting their losses that one cannot grudge them the pleasure, since it seems a sort of compensation for their misfortunes.

ACT V. SCENE 1.

319.—In both Q. and F. 1 the stage-direction, at the beginning of this scene, is *Enter Leonato and his brother.* There are altogether ten speeches assigned to Antonio before he and Leonato "go off." The prefix to these ten speeches in Q. is *Brother,* with the exception of the last speech (line 109), which has the abbreviation *Bro.* prefixed to it. In F. 1 the 1st and 3rd have the prefix *Brother* in full, the 2nd, *Broth.;* the 4th and 5th, *Brot.;* the 6th, *Bro.;* the 7th, and 8th, *Brot.;* the 9th—and here is a difference worth recording—has the prefix *Ant.;* the 10th has the same prefix as the Q., *Bro.* I have thought it worth while to point out the discrepancies between Q. and F. 1 in Antonio's speeches, trifling as they may appear to be, because we may possibly find in them some indirect evidence as to the question whether F. 1 was simply printed from a copy of the Q., or from a separate MS. (See above, note 308.) The only really important difference between the Q. and F. 1, which would seem to show that F. 1 was printed at least from a corrected copy of the Q., is the fact of the prefix in line 100, in F. 1, being *Ant., i.e.* an abbreviation of Antonio's name, while to the other many speeches the prefix is practically identical in both editions.

It is possible that the copy of the Q. from which F. 1 was printed had a few corrections made on it, and that this prefix *Ant.,* instead of *Brother,* to the speech referred to above, was one of those corrections, it having been obviously suggested by the fact that Leonato calls him there by his name; but still this is not a very satisfactory explanation, for Leonato also calls his brother by his name above (line 91). On the other hand, we may note that in both Q. and F. 1 there is the same variation in the spelling of the name *Antonio*, which in line 91 is spelt *Anthony*, and in line 100 *Antonie*, in both copies. The use of the form *Anthony* is rather out of place, and may be compared with the obvious mistake in i. 1. 9 and 10, where *Don Pedro* is called *Don Peter*.

It would certainly seem that *Antonio* was one of the characters in this play to whom the author had not assigned any name when he commenced this comedy. (See above, note 308.) In act i. scene 2, Q. F. 1 have *Enter Leonato and an old man brother to Leonato;* and the prefix to Antonio's speeches is simply *Old*. In act ii. scene 1 the stage-direction is *Enter Leonato his Brother, &c.*, and the prefix to his speeches throughout is *Brother* in both Q. and F. 1. In line 116 he is, for the first time, named *Anthonio* by Ursula, and the prefix to his speeches with Ursula, lines 119, 121, 125, is *Antho.* in Q.; *Anth.* in F. 1.

320. Lines 3-32.—For a comparison between portions of this speech of Leonato's with the speech of Adriana in the Comedy of Errors, see note 27 on that play.

321. Line 6: *Nor let no* COMFORTER *delight mine ear.*—So Q.; F. 1 has *comfort;* F. 2 *comfort els;* F. 3, F. 4 *comfort else.*—It is rather remarkable that the editors of F. 2, when trying to correct the faulty line in F. 1, should not have resorted to the Q. rather than have accepted the reading of F. 1; or was the addition of the *else* made by the actors, and taken by the editors of F. 2 from the then theatre copy?

322. Line 10: *And bid him speak of patience.*—So Q. Ff.; most editors adopt the emendation of Hanmer, who added the words *to me* after *speak* in order to make the line metrically complete. With all due deference to Dyce, and other commentators, who have adopted this supposed improvement without any question, I must beg to differ from them as to there being either any necessity for an addition to the line, or as to such an addition being, in any way, an improvement on the text of the old copies. We have had a great many *mine's* and *me's* already in this passage; *e.g.* line 5, *me;* line 6, *mine;* again, line 7, *mine;* line 8, *me;* line 9, *mine;* and, in the next line, we have *mine;* so that unless there were any necessity for it, I do not think the poet would have wished to add the words *to me* in this line. There is another reason for the omission of these words, and that is, that we require the emphasis to be put on the *him* in this line. Anyone who will read the whole sentence beginning with *Bring me a father*, will see, if he has any ear for rhythm, that by omitting the words *to me*, the conclusion of the sentence is both more forcible and more rhythmical. The *to me* is really unnecessary. We must remember that the slurring slovenly style of pronouncing our beautiful native tongue, which prevails nowadays, was not prevalent in Shakespeare's time, when *patience* was not pronounced *pay-shense*, but distinctly as a trisyllable.

323. Line 12: *And let it answer every* STRAIN *for* STRAIN.—The sense of *strain* in this line is, perhaps, rendered as nearly as possible by the word given in our foot-note, viz. "feeling." *Strain*, in this sense, is by no means uncommon in Shakespeare, *e.g.* in II. Henry IV. iv. 5. 171:

> Or swell my thoughts to any *strain* of pride;

and Coriolanus, v. 3. 149:

> Thou hast affected the fine *strains* of honour.

This sense of the word is not connected with its peculiar sense = "note" or "tune," but with the original meaning of an "effort." We have had the word used above in this play, ii. 1. 394, in the sense of "natural" or "inherited disposition," where Don Pedro, speaking of Benedick, says "he is of a noble *strain*."

324. Lines 15-18:

> *If such a one will smile, and stroke his beard,*
> *And,* SORRY *wag, cry "hem" when he should groan,*
> *Patch grief with proverbs, make misfortune drunk*
> *With* CANDLE-WASTERS.

This very difficult passage, which has, with some reason, puzzled all the commentators, can only be understood by a careful consideration of the context. What does Leonato intend to say? He may express himself obscurely, but his meaning is obvious enough. We may thus paraphrase his speech. "I do not want sententious comfort. I want some one who has suffered what I have suffered to come and talk to me. If you can find anyone who has loved his child as I have loved mine, and whose joy and pride in her has been overwhelmed by such a catastrophe as that which has overtaken my daughter; and if this man will talk to me of patience—if this man will be calm and sententious, and will attempt to mend my grief with proverbial sayings, and to drug my sense of unhappiness with essays upon resignation—the work of those who waste candles in sitting up to labour out such dull and tedious performances—if such a one will attempt to console me thus, and preach to me patience, I will listen to him; but you cannot find such a man, for it is only those who have not to bear sorrow that can preach patience; directly we have to endure sorrow ourselves our patience goes to the winds." To come to the special difficulties in this passage: first, as to the well-known crux in line 16, the reading of Q., F. 1, F. 2 is as follows:

> And *sorrow*, wagge, crie hem when he should groan.

The correction of F. 3, F. 4 seems, at first sight, scarcely worth notice. The former reads: "And *hallow*, wag, cry hem;" the latter reads the same, except that it has *hollow* instead of *hallow*. This attempt at an emendation may be interpreted in two ways: "And *hallow* wag," *i.e.* "and cry out *wag* (=go your way);" or it may be meant for "And *hollow* wag," *hollow* being used, as it frequently is by Shakespeare, in the sense of "insincere. It is possible that the alteration in F. 3 was originally made by one of the actors. Of the many—far too many—proposed emendations emanating from various commentators, it will be sufficient to say that they will be found duly recorded in the Cambridge edn. The one we have adopted in the text, which occurred to me, independently, many years ago, is the same as a conjecture by Steevens, which, for some mysterious reason or other, he subsequently abandoned. The other emendation, which is most generally accepted, is that of Capell, "BID *sorrow wag*, cry *hem;* and the next most received one is that of Johnson, which Steevens adopted: "CRY, *sorrow wag! and hem.*" Johnson, before adopting this arrangement of the words had pointed out that the text, as it stands in the old copies, would make sense if we read, *And sorrow wag! cry; hem;* but on account of the harshness of the order in which the words *and* and *cry* are placed he adopted the arrangement given above, which Steevens thoroughly approved of and followed. The meaning of the sentence is: "And cry 'away with sorrow'!" or "sorrow avaunt!" Steevens supports this reading by quoting the use of the phrase *care away*, from Acolastus, comedy, 1540: "I may now say, *Care awaye!*" and "*Now grievous sorrowe and care awaye!*" also from Barnaby Googe's "third Eglog:"

> Som chesnuts have I there in store,
> With cheese and pleasaunt whaye;
> God sends me vittayles for my need,
> And I synge *Care awaye!*

Steevens tells us also he was assured that *Sorrow go by!* is "a common exclamation of hilarity even at this time, in Scotland" (Var. Ed. vol. vii. p. 129). There does not seem to me to be much force in the comparison between the expression *sorrow wag!* and such a very natural expression as "care away!" or "sorrow away!" or "away with sorrow!" or in the more common form, "away with melancholy!" With regard to the word *to wag*, in the sense of "to go one's way," it is remarkable that it is used no less than four times in The Merry Wives (always by the Host of the Garter), i. 3. 7: "let them *wag*; trot, trot;" ii. 1. 238: "Here, boys, here, here! shall we *wag!*" and also ii. 3. 74, 101. We have it once in As You Like It, ii. 7. 23, in the proverbial expression: "how the world *wags*," where I do not think it has the same meaning exactly that it has in Merry Wives. However, it is worth remarking that Shakespeare only uses *wag*, in this sense, in the four passages cited; and, from his putting the expression into the mouth of the Host, it would seem that he considered it rather an affected one. As to the imaginary comforter that Leonato is describing, he might perhaps be termed an affected prig; and the use of the verb *wag*, in this rather unusual sense, would not be out of place. Both because it involves very little alteration in the text, and also makes very fair sense, Johnson's emendation is a very plausible one. The reason why we have preferred the one printed in the text is, that it involves even less alteration of the reading of the old copies, and because the misprint of *sorrow* for *sorry* is a very probable one, although no other instance of such a misprint seems to occur in Shakespeare. In Dymock's translation of Il Pastor Fido (1602) *shadow* appears to be used in two passages = *shady*: in act ii. scene 5:

> About noone time among these *shadow* trees
> Come you without your nimphs.
> (F. 3, back, F. 4.)

Again, in act iii. scene 5:

> unto my garden there
> Where a *shadow* hedge doth close it in. (I. 1.)

It is possible that in those two passages *shadow* may be used as an adjective; but it looks more like a misprint. We must remember that all words like pretty, heavy, sorry, were formerly spelt *prettie, heavie, sorrie* (we have an instance in F. 1, Love's Labour's Lost, v. 2. 720); and if anyone will compare the two words *sorrie* and *sorrow*, in the handwriting of any MS. of Shakespeare's time, he will see how easily they might be mistaken for one another. The expression *sorry wag* seems to me very applicable to the type of character that Leonato is describing: one utterly devoid of sympathy, unable to enter into the griefs, or indeed into any of the higher feelings of the sufferer. Such a man *smiles, strokes his beard, cries hem*, offers for consolation stale proverbs and conventional exhortations to patience, gathered from the laborious writings of scholars who consume the midnight oil, and are learned in everything but human nature.

The second difficulty, which I am inclined to think almost greater than the first, is as to the meaning of *candle-wasters* in this passage—in fact as to the meaning of the last sentence altogether. In the paraphrase of the speech given above I have taken *candle-wasters* to mean "students" or "book-worms;" in fact those who sit up late at night reading or writing. On account of the occurrence of the word *drunk* in the sentence, the meaning generally accepted for *candle-wasters* is, as Malone says, "men who waste candles while they pass the night in drinking" (Var. Ed. vol. vii. p. 130); that is to say, "drunkards" or "revellers;" but we have no instance of the use of *candle-wasters* in such a case, while we have a very striking instance of its use in the sense of "one who burns the midnight oil," as we say. Thus we have in Ben Jonson's Cynthia's Revels, iii. 2: "spoiled by a whoreson book-worm, a *candle-waster*" (Works, vol. ii. p. 277); and in The Antiquary, act iii. 1: "he should catch more delicate court-ear, than all your head-scratchers, thumb-biters, *lamp-wasters* of them all" (Dodsley, vol. xiii. p. 460). Both the above passages are quoted by Whalley (Var. Ed. vol. vii. p. 130); but we may add the following expression from the Prologue to Wily Beguiled: "*cotton-candle* eloquence" (Dodsley, vol. ix. p. 221). It has been suggested in connection with the word *drunk* that Shakespeare might have been thinking of one of the practices of extravagant lovers, namely that of drinking off flap-dragons (see Love's Labour's Lost, note 152), which is alluded to in II. Henry IV. ii. 4. 267: "and drinks off *candles' ends* for *flap-dragons*." In a passage, however, in The Return from Parnassus (iv. 3), students are described as:

> *Drinking* a long lank *watching candle's* smoke,
> Spending the marrow of their flow'ring age
> In fruitless poring on some worm-eat leaf.
> —Dodsley, vol. ix. p. 200.

This passage confirms one in the opinion that *candle-wasters* here should be interpreted in some such sense as we have given to the word, in the paraphrase of Leonato's speech above.

325. Line 28: WRING *under the load of sorrow.*—This intransitive use of the verb *to wring* = "to writhe," or, perhaps, "to be wrung," is found in two other passages in Shakespeare; in Henry V. iv. 1. 252, 253:

> Of every fool, whose sense no more can feel
> But his own *wringing!*

and, more appositely, in Cymbeline, iii. 6. 79: "He *wrings* at some distress." This elliptical use of the verb is one of which Shakespeare and the writers of his time were rather fond.

326. Line 30: *moral* = "moralizing."—Compare Lear, iv. 2. 58: "a *moral* fool." Schmidt also takes the passage in As You Like It, ii. 7. 28, 29:

> When I did hear
> The motley fool thus *moral* on the time,

to be another instance of the use of the adjective in this sense, though generally *moral*, in that passage, is considered to be a verb. I have not been able to find a similar use of the word in any other author.

327. Line 32: *My griefs cry louder than* ADVERTISEMENT.—This use of *advertisement* = "exhortation" is given by Baret in his Alvearie (1573), *sub voce:* "A warning: an admonition: an *aduertisemét*." The vulgarized use of the word has become so common in this, which may be considered, emphatically, "the age of *advertisements*," that the original meaning of the word has been almost, if not entirely, lost. In Sherwood's dictionary, which is bound up with Cotgrave (1650), *monition* is given as one of the French equivalents to *advertisement*. But the verb, *to advertise* would seem by that time to have nearly lost all connection with the idea of moral advice, and only to have retained the sense of "to give notice" or "information," "to notify," through which sense it came to have its modern meaning. The only explanation of this line is given by Seymour, who explains it "my griefs are too violent to be expressed in words." Seymour's explanation is plausible enough; but it would seem from the answer of Antonio, in the next line,

> Therein do men from children nothing differ,

that the meaning is "My griefs cry louder than your moral exhortations;" that is to say, "The voice of my grief makes itself heard so loudly in my own breast, that I cannot hear the moral consolations that you offer;" but Antonio takes the more literal sense of the word *cries*, and endeavours to ridicule his brother out of his excessive dwelling on his unhappiness, by comparing him to a child who *cries* so loudly that it cannot hear the remonstrances, or good advice, of its instructor.

328. Lines 37, 38:

> *However they have writ the* STYLE OF GODS,
> *And made a* PUSH *at chance and sufferance.*

Warburton thought this referred to the extravagant titles the Stoics gave their wise men (Var. Ed. vol. vii. p. 131). Steevens, more probably, explains it "in the style of gods," *i.e.* "in exalted language," as if they were divine beings above the level of ordinary men (*ut supra*).

The phrase *made a push at* seems to have given the commentators some trouble. Pope altered *push* to *pish*, which, with due deference to him, is an alteration for the worse. The meaning undoubtedly is the one we have given in the foot-note. Compare I. Henry IV. iii. 2. 66, 67:

> stand the *push*
> Of every beardless vain comparative;

and Troilus and Cressida, ii. 2. 137:

> To stand the *push* and enmity of those;

from which it is evident that the expression *make a push at* means here "attack," "defy."

329. Line 52:

> *Who wrongs him?*
> Leon. *Who!*

We have followed Dyce in adopting Walker's addition of the word *Who!* at the end of this line in order to complete it. Hanmer printed "*wrongeth* him," and Capell, "Who wrongs him, *sir?*" but Walker's emendation seems to us much the best, as it is very natural Leonato should repeat the word *Who!*

330. Line 57: *my hand meant nothing* TO *my sword.*—None of the commentators notice this phrase, though it is rather an obscure one. It may either mean "I had no intention of drawing my sword in touching it;" that is to say, it was a mere mechanical action; or, perhaps, the meaning is, "My hand laid *to my sword* meant nothing."

331. Line 65: *And, with grey hairs and* BRUISE *of many days.*—This is a very expressive phrase. It would be difficult to express more forcibly the effect of old age, which makes us feel, both in mind and body, as if we had been sorely *bruised*. Shakespeare only uses the word *bruise* in two other passages: II. Henry IV. iv. 1. 100:

> That feel the *bruises* of the days before,

where it is also used figuratively, though not in precisely the same sense as in the text; and (in the literal sense) in I. Henry IV. i. 3. 57, 58:

> the sovereign'st thing on earth
> Was parmaceti for an inward *bruise*.

Compare with this passage II. Henry VI. v. 3. 3, and see note 338 on that play.

332. Line 66: *Do challenge thee to* TRIAL *of a man.*—Compare Richard II. i. 1. 81:

> Or chivalrous design of knightly *trial*.

333. Line 75: *Despite his nice fence and his active* PRACTICE.—*Practice* is explained by some commentators as = "experience." Surely the sense we have given it in the foot-note is the right one. Leonato would have had more experience than Claudio; but he could not have had such active habits, and he could not have exercised his skill in fencing very much of late. Compare Hamlet, v. 2. 220, 221, where Hamlet says, apropos of his approaching combat with Laertes: "since he went into France, I have been in continual *practice*."

334. Line 76: *His May of youth and bloom of* LUSTIHOOD.—Shakespeare only uses this word in one other passage, in Troilus and Cressida, ii. 2. 49, 50:

> reason and respect
> Make livers pale, and *lustihood* deject.

335. Line 78: *Canst thou so* DAFF *me?*—See above, note 157.

336. Lines 80-101.—The sudden anger of Antonio at this point is one of the cleverest touches in the whole of this charming comedy. Leonato has been working himself up into a towering passion, and his brother, who, during the first part of the scene, has been endeavouring to argue him into patience, not only abandons that useless endeavour, but, taking up the cudgels for his slandered niece, works himself into a genuine passion. The contempt of the brave old man for the boy Claudio, and the fearless scorn which the representative of the old school pours upon the head of the representative of the new school, are admirably expressed; but what is best of all, in this outburst of Antonio, is the true knowledge of

human nature shown by the poet. Whenever any good-hearted but quick-tempered man gets into a passion, there is only one sure way of calming him; and that is either really to be angry one's self, or to make believe to be angry as naturally as possible. Brother Antony knew this; and sure enough, directly he begins to rave against Claudio, Leonato recovers his temper and begins to try and soothe him. How much can be done with a very small part by a good actor, was seen when Mr. Howe played the part of Antonio at the revival of this play at the Lyceum in 1882.

337. Line 83: *Come, follow me, boy! come,* SIR BOY, FOLLOW *me.*—Q. Ff. read *come, sir boy, come follow me.* Capell, whose emendation we have followed, omitted the second *come.* Pope reads, *come boy follow me.* There would seem to be something especially irritating in the application of the term *boy* to grown-up men. Antonio, doubtless, repeats advisedly the phrase *sir boy* here and in the next line. Compare Coriolanus, v. 6. 101, where Aufidius in his quarrel with Coriolanus says:

> Name not the god (*i.e.* Mars), thou *boy* of tears;

and Coriolanus answers, line 104: "*Boy!* O slave!" and again, line 113: "*Boy!* false hound!"

338. Line 84: *I'll whip you from your* FOINING *fence.*—Baret gives under "to *Foine*, to pricke, to stinge," and gives as the Latin equivalent "Pungo, & Cõpungo." It seems to have been used in fencing, as meaning "to thrust." Cotgrave gives under "Coup d'estoc, A thrust, *foine*, stab." Compare Lear, iv. 6. 251: "no matter vor your *foins*." The verb is used in three other passages: in Merry Wives, ii. 3. 24; II. Henry IV. ii. 1. 17; ii. 4. 252. In the latter passage it is used in a very equivocal sense.

339. Line 89: *That dare as well answer a man indeed.*—We have adopted Warburton's suggestion of placing a comma after *indeed* here, giving to the words *a man indeed* the sense of "one who is *indeed* a man." In Hamlet, iii. 4. 60:

> A combination and a form *indeed*,

the word is used in the same emphatic or intensitive sense.

340. Line 91: *Boys, apes,* JACKS, *braggarts, milksops!*—This word is often used as a term of contempt. Compare Merchant of Venice, iii. 4. 77:

> A thousand raw tricks of these bragging *Jacks*;

and our modern *Jack-in-office.* We have followed Hanmer in transposing the position of *braggarts* and *Jacks.* Q. Ff. read *apes, braggarts, Jacks.* Dyce puts an accent on the last syllable of *braggarts* in order to make the rhythm of the verse correct; but surely this is not allowable, as the word *braggart* occurs nine times in verse in Shakespeare, and on every occasion it is accented on the first syllable, *e.g.* in All's Well, iv. iii. 270, 372.

341. Line 94: SCAMBLING, OUT-FACING, FASHION-MONGING *boys.*—For *scambling* see King John, note 252; for *out-facing* compare As You Like It, i. 3. 123, 124:

> As many other mannish cowards have
> That do *outface* it with their semblances.

Fashion-monging is the reading of Q. F. 1; F. 2, F. 3, F. 4 read "fashion-*mongring*." Dyce (note 72) quotes Mr. Arrowsmith, Shakespeare's Editors and Commentators, p. 34: "*monging* is the present participle regularly inflected from the Anglo-Saxon verb 'mangian,' to traffick." From this verb comes the noun *monger* found in such words as *fishmonger.* Compare Romeo and Juliet, ii. 4. 34: *fashion-mongers.*

342. Line 95: *That lie, and* COG, *and flout,* DEPRAVE, *and slander.*—Schmidt defines *to cog* = "to cheat, to deceive, especially by smooth lies;" and compare the passage in Merry Wives, iii. 3. 76: "Come, I cannot *cog*, and say thou art this and that," &c. The word seems to come nearest, in sense, to our modern word "to gammon." Afterwards *to cog* came especially to be applied to loading, or otherwise falsifying dice. The verb *to deprave* is used in only one other passage in Shakespeare, in Timon, i. 2. 145:

> Who lives that 's not *depraved* or *depraves*?

343. Line 96: *Go anticly, show outward hideousness.*—Q. Ff. read "*and* show." We have adopted Spedding's emendation in omitting *and*, which is clearly unnecessary, and spoils the line. Steevens quotes an expression in Gower's speech in Henry V. iii. 6. 81: "a *horrid* suit of the camp;" the whole passage being: "and what a beard of the general's cut and a *horrid* suit of the camp will do among foaming bottles and ale-wash'd wits, is wonderful to be thought on." There is no doubt it was the practice of these braggarts to assume the most warlike dress and accoutrements they could.

344. Line 101: *Do not you meddle; let me* DEAL IN *this.*—Compare above in this play, iv. 1. 249, 250. *With* is the preposition generally used with *deal;* but we have the same expression = "have to do with," in I. Henry VI. v. 5. 56: "*dealt in* by attorneyship;" and again in The Tempest, v. 1. 270, 271:

> That could control the moon, make flows and ebbs,
> And *deal in* her command without her power.

345. Line 102: *we will not* WAKE *your patience.*—There have been several proposed emendations for *wake*, which certainly does not seem to be quite the right word here. Warburton proposed *wrack;* Hanmer *rack;* Talbot conjectured *waste.* Johnson explained it: "will not longer force them to *endure* the presence of those whom, though they look on them as enemies, they cannot resist" (Var. Ed. vol. vii. p. 135). Henley explains it thus: "The ferocity of wild beasts is overcome by not suffering them to sleep;" and therefore the sentence means "we will forbear any further provocation" (Var. Ed. vol. vii. p. 135). I confess I do not quite understand this explanation. Steevens compares the well-known passage in Othello, iii. 3. 362, 363:

> Thou hadst been better have been born a dog
> Than answer my *wak'd* wrath!

But surely there is a good deal of difference between *wrath* and *patience.* One naturally speaks of *waking* a person's wrath, but not of *waking* his patience. There can hardly be two things more opposite than *wrath* and *patience;* but we find somewhat similar expressions elsewhere in Shakespeare; for instance, in Richard II. i. 3. 131-133:

> set on you
> To *wake* our peace, which in our country's cradle
> Draws the sweet infant breath of gentle sleep;

Richard III. i. 3. 288, where Margaret is speaking of the effect of curses:

> And there *awake* God's gentle-sleeping peace;

and Coriolanus, iii. 1. 98, 99:

> *awake*
> Your dangerous lenity;

which last passage bears a very strong resemblance to the one in our text, because there is no mention in the other two passages, as quoted, of sleep; but the idea is essentially the same as here, viz. that by provocation the *passive* quality of non-resistance is turned into the *active* quality of resistance.

346. Lines 106-109:

> Leon. *My lord, my lord,—*
> D. Pedro. *I will not hear you.*
> Leon. *No?—Come, brother, away.—I will be heard.*
> Ant. *And shall, or some of us will smart for it.*

Hanmer, whom Dyce follows, arranges these lines as follows:—

> Leon. *My lord, my lord,—*
> D. Pedro. *I will not hear you.*
> Leon. *No?—*
> *Come, brother, away.—I will be heard.*
> Ant. *And shall,*
> *Or some of us will smart for 't.*

The one objection to this arrangement is that line 109 is left imperfect, while line 108 is not very rhythmical. The arrangement of the old copies, it seems to me, better suits the sense of the words.

347. Line 109: [Exeunt Leonato and Antonio.—The stage-direction in F. 1 is "*Exeunt ambo*" after Leonato's speech, "I will be heard," and "*Enter Benedick*" after line 107; in Q. "*Enter Benedick*" comes before line 110. It is pretty clear that F. 1 was printed from the theatre copy, for nearly all the entrances are marked too early.

348. Line 114: *you are* ALMOST *come to part* ALMOST *a fray.*—Is not the first *almost* here a printer's error, or is the repetition intentional? Most commentators seem to think that the second *almost* ought to be omitted; but I cannot help thinking that it is the first which is redundant. The phrase *almost* is used by Don Pedro in a somewhat contemptuous sense, which is quite consistent with the tone adopted by him and Claudio. Another objection to the repetition of *almost* is that the sentence makes a blank verse, which, as it occurs in prose, is objectionable.

349. Line 120: *In a false quarrel there is no true valour.*—Compare II. Henry VI. iii. 2. 233-235:

> Thrice is he arm'd *that hath his quarrel just*,
> And he but naked, though lock'd up in steel,
> Whose conscience with injustice is corrupted.

350. Lines 128, 129: *I will bid thee* DRAW, *as we do the minstrels;* DRAW, *to pleasure us.*—There seems to be a difference of opinion here, among the commentators, as to whether *draw* means to *draw* an instrument out of its case, or to *draw* the bow along the strings of the viol. Douce suggests that there is an allusion to the itinerant sword-dancers. It will be easier to decide the exact meaning of *draw* here, when we can find any passage in which the direction is used to *minstrels to draw* either their instruments out of the case, or their bows.

351. Line 132: *care kill'd a cat.*—This seems to have been a common proverb. In his Complete Alphabet of Proverbs (p. 335) Bohn gives it in the form "Care will kill a cat; yet there's no living without it;" but at page 76 of the same work it is given in the simple form: "Care will kill a cat." The proverb is alluded to in Ben Jonson's Every Man in his Humour, i. 3: "hang sorrow, care 'll kill a cat" (Works, vol. i. p. 33).

352. Line 135: *I shall* MEET *your wit* IN THE CAREER, *an you charge it against me.*—The allusions in this and the following speech are to tilting. *To meet in the career* is to meet in the full charge.

353. Line 139: *give him another staff: this last was broke cross.*—Claudio keeps up the metaphor from the tilting-field. It was considered a disgrace when the spear, used in tilting, was broken across the body of the adversary instead of being snapped by the force of the charge, after having struck him full.

354. Line 142: *he knows how to turn his girdle.*—There seems to be no doubt that the reference here is to the practice of turning the large *buckle* of the *girdle* behind one, previously to challenging anyone to a personal encounter; but for what reason the *girdle* was turned does not seem quite clear. Holt White explains it: "Large belts were worn with the buckle before, but for wrestling the buckle was turned behind, to give the adversary a fairer grasp at the girdle. To turn the buckle behind, therefore, was a challenge" (Var. Ed. vol. vii. p. 138). I confess I do not understand this explanation. In wrestling the object is to try and get a good hold on one's adversary, which is done by putting the arms round him and trying to join your hands in the middle of his back. How it would help matters to have a great *buckle* there I do not know; surely it would render it more difficult to get a good hold, and perhaps that may be the real explanation of the practice, if such a practice existed among wrestlers. In the case of combatants going to fight with fists, one could understand the turning round of the *buckle*, in order that it might not cut one's opponent's hands, though he would have to hit rather low down to come in contact with it, but still it would not be hitting "below the belt," and we must remember that these large *buckles* came quite as high as what I believe in sporting parlance is called the "bread-basket." Halliwell explains the passage "you may change your temper or humour, alter it to the opposite side;" but Grant White and Hunter think that the *girdle* was turned round in order to get at the sword hilt.

355. Line 156: *he hath bid me to a* CALF'S-HEAD *and a* CAPON.—Schmidt thinks that there is a pun intended here in *capon*, as = "cap on," i.e. coxcomb, and that Claudio means to say a *calf's head* with a fool's cap on; but *capon* was frequently used as a term of contempt, and figures among the humorous terms of abuse used by Dromio of Syracuse, in Comedy of Errors, iii. 1. 32.

356. Line 172: *trans-shape thy particular virtues.*—Compare Webster's Cure for a Cuckold: "O to what a monster would this *trans-shape* me" (Works, vol. iv. p. 17).

357. Lines 181, 182: *God saw him when he was hid in the*

garden.—This is of course a reference to ii. 3, where Benedick is hid in the arbour, and it is also a rather profane allusion to the story of Adam and Eve.

358. Line 184: *the savage bull's horns on the sensible Benedick's head*.—An allusion to Benedick's speech above, in i. 1. 264-266.

359. Line 203: *when he goes* IN HIS DOUBLET AND HOSE.—It is pretty certain that the meaning here is simply "without his cloak;" it being the custom to take off the cloak before fighting a duel. Compare Merry Wives, iii. 1. 46, where Page says to Sir Hugh Evans, who is awaiting the arrival of Doctor Caius with hostile intent: "in your *doublet and hose* this raw rheumatic day!" This seems to be the more probable meaning of the phrase than to suppose that it refers to the negligence in the matter of dress which is said to characterize lovers, and of which Rosalind makes such fun in As You Like It, iii. 2. 392-403.

360. Line 207: *soft you*, LET ME BE: *pluck up, my heart, and be sad!*—Hanmer proposed to read *let be*, a phrase which occurs in Winter's Tale, v. 3. 61: *Let be, let be*, used in a deprecatory sense and = "Forbear speaking to me; leave me alone." The same phrase, with the same meaning, occurs in Antony and Cleopatra, iv. 4. 6, and is applied by Antony to Cleopatra when she attempts to help him on with his armour. Compare also Matthew xxvii. 49: "*Let be*, let us see whether Elias will come to save him."

As to *pluck up, my heart*, compare Taming of Shrew, iv. 3. 38: "*Pluck up* thy spirits."

361. Line 211: *she shall ne'er weigh more reasons in her balance*.—Some commentators think that there may be a pun here on *reasons* and *raisins*, as in I. Henry IV. ii. 4. 264-266: "Give you a *reason* on compulsion! if *reasons* were as plenty as blackberries, I would give no man a *reason* upon compulsion, I." It seems that *reason* was in Shakespeare's time pronounced *rayson*, as if it were an anglicized form of the French *raison*; in fact, the word was often spelt so, *e.g.* in Tragical Discourses (fol. 56): "wherin certeinly she had *raison*;" ten lines lower down the word is spelt *reason*.

362. Line 242: *Don John your brother* INCENSED *me to slander the Lady Hero*.—For a similar use of the verb *incense* compare Merry Wives, i. 3. 109: "I will *incense* Page to deal with poison;" Winter's Tale, v. 1. 61, 62:

> and would *incense* me
> To murder her I married.

Nares supposes that the word has the same sense here as in Henry VIII. v. 1. 43, 45:

> *Incens'd* the lords o' the council, that he is
> . . . . .
> A most arch heretic,

in which passage, and in Richard III. iii. 1. 152, where Buckingham suggests that the young prince, York, was "*incensed* by his subtle mother" to taunt his uncle, the meaning is "to instruct," "to inform," a sense which it still bears in Staffordshire.

363. Lines 293, 294:

> *Hang her an epitaph upon her tomb,*
> *And sing it to her bones.*

Blakeway gives an extract from "La Monnoie en Bayle, au mot Aretin (Pierre), note G:" referring to this practice: "C'est la coutume parmi les Catholiques d'attacher a quelque colonne, ou ailleurs, près du tombeau des morts, et surtout des morts de reputation, des inscriptions funebres en papier" (Var. Ed. vol. vii. p. 144); *i.e.* "It is the custom among the Catholics to attach to some column, or elsewhere, near the tomb of the dead, and especially of dead celebrities, funeral inscriptions on paper." An instance of this practice is exemplified in Ben Jonson's well-known lines on the Countess of Pembroke, commencing "Underneath this sable hearse," which were intended to be hung as an epitaph on her tomb.

364. Line 299: *And she alone is heir to both of us*.—This is one among the many proofs of the carelessness with which this play was written. The author forgot that already, in i. 2. 1, Leonato, speaking to Antonio, says: "Where is my cousin, your *son*?"

365. Lines 301-304.—Nothing perhaps makes the character of Claudio more contemptible than the prompt fickleness with which he transfers his affections to order, even at the very moment when he has just discovered how cruelly he had wronged his first love, whom he supposed to be dead.

366. Line 308: *Who, I believe, was* PACK'D *in all this wrong*.—Compare Comedy of Errors, v. 1. 219, 220:

> That goldsmith there, were he not *pack'd* with her,
> Could witness it;

i.e. "if he were not in conspiracy with her." Compare the passage in the Taming of the Shrew, v. 1. 121 and note 202 on that play. The noun *pack* is used for "a gang of conspirators" in Comedy of Errors, iv. 4. 105:

367. Lines 309-312.—As if Shakespeare was determined to heap contempt upon the head of Claudio he makes Borachio, villain as he is, a striking contrast to the young count in generosity of character. He will not allow, hardened ruffian though he be, the woman who unconsciously aided him in his conspiracy to suffer any unjust blame.

368. Line 318: *he wears a key in his ear, and a lock hanging by it*.—This looks very suspiciously like a piece of gag on the part of Master Kemp. In iii. 3. 182 Seacoal has already spoken about this Deformed wearing a *lock* (see note 229). The *key in the ear* may be a satire on the fashion of wearing roses in the *ears*, alluded to in King John. (See note 43 on that play.) But the joke on the *lock* and the *key* is very much on a par with some of those attributed to Kemp.

369. Line 319: *borrows money in* GOD'S NAME; *i.e.* "he is a common beggar;" to ask for money *in God's name*, or for *God's sake*, being the usual adjuration of beggars when begging for alms. Minsheu (1599) has under *Pordioséros*: "men that *ask for God's sake*, beggers." Halliwell says that "this phrase was used in the counterfeit passports of the beggars, as appears from Dekker's English Villanies.

370. Line 327: *God save the foundation!*—This was the recognized mode of thanksgiving employed by those who received alms at the gates of religious houses.

ACT V. Scene 2.

371. Line 2: *deserve well at my hands by* HELPING ME TO THE SPEECH OF *Beatrice*.—We have a similar phrase in another passage in Shakespeare, in Winter's Tale, iv. 4. 786: "if I may *come to the speech of* him."

It seems rather doubtful where this scene is supposed to take place. In Mr. Irving's arrangement of the play it formed part of scene 1, which seems the most sensible plan, as it would certainly seem to be intended to take place out of doors and near Leonato's house. Pope was the first to assign any locality to the last scene (v. 1), which he described as "before Leonato's house." He placed this scene "In Leonato's house." Reed rightly placed it "In Leonato's garden;" for it is clear from line 98 below, where Ursula says "Yonder's old coil *at* home," that the scene did not take place in the house. At the same time there is an objection to placing it in the same part of the garden as the previous scene, namely, that Benedick, after the angry leave he had taken of Claudio and Don Pedro, would hardly risk meeting them again; but this objection is of very little force where there is what is called a "full set scene" to represent the garden, occupying the whole of the stage. We have, however, in order not to interfere with the usual division into scenes of this act, placed this scene as in another part of Leonato's garden.

372. Lines 9, 10: *To have no man come over me! why, shall I always* KEEP BELOW STAIRS?—The meaning of this latter phrase is not very clear. The conversation between Margaret and Benedick is not very edifying at this point; still, it is as well to try and make some sense of it. Theobald simply altered it to "keep *above* stairs." Steevens proposed to read "keep *men* below stairs," *i.e.* "never suffer them to come into her bed-chamber." Singer made a very similar conjecture: "keep *them* below stairs." Schmidt explains the phrase, "in the servants' room," and so presumably "never get married." This conjecture seems rather founded on the arrangement in modern houses, by which servants' rooms are in the basement; but that portion of the house, if it existed at all in Elizabethan times, was used for cellarage only, the servants' rooms being on the ground floor. Probably the meaning is: "Shall I never get up to the bridal-chamber?" There is possibly also some double meaning in the expression to which the clue is wanting.

373. Lines 26-29: *The god of love, &c.*—This is (according to Ritson) the beginning of an old song by "W. E." (William Elderton).

374. Line 33: *carpet-mongers.*—The same as *carpet-knights*, the title given to those knights who received their knighthood at court and not on the battle-field, and for accomplishments which could be better displayed in the lists of Cupid than in tournaments or in battle. In Fenton's Tragical Discourses (1567) we have "a crew of Venesyan and *carpet knights*" (fol. 39, b.). It appears to have been used generally as a term of contempt. Cotgrave gives under Muguet, "an effeminate youngster, a spruce *Carpet-knight.*" Shakespeare does not use this term anywhere; but he describes such a person very well in Twelfth Night, iii. 4. 257, 258: "He is knight, dubbed with unhatched rapier and on *carpet* consideration." Shakespeare uses many compounds of the word *monger*, such as *ballad-monger*, I. Henry IV. iii. 1. 130; *barber-monger*, Lear, ii. 2. 36, &c.; and compare *fashion-monging* above, in the last scene, line 94. A *carpet-monger* is well described in Richard III. i. 1. 12, 13:

> He capers nimbly in a lady's chamber
> To the lascivious pleasing of a lute.

375. Line 41: *I cannot woo in* FESTIVAL *terms.*—Compare Merry Wives, iii. 2. 69: "he speaks *holiday;*" and I. Henry IV. i. 3. 46, 47:

> With many *holiday* and lady terms
> He question'd me.

376. Line 47: *let me go with that I came* FOR.—Q. Ff. omit *for;* but it seems necessary for the sense. Pope was the first to add this word, an emendation which most editors have adopted. The Cambridge edd. adhere to the reading of the old copies. They give in a note (xxvi.), as an instance of the same construction, "*i.e.* the non-repetition of the preposition," a line from the following passage in Marston's Fawne, i. 2:

> I will revenge us all upon you all
> *With* the same stratagem we still are caught,
> Flatterie it selfe. —Works, vol. i. pp. 24, 25.

But the preposition there to be repeated is the same. Here it is a different one; for "*with* that I came *with*" would make no sense at all. Their instance would very well apply if the preposition *with* was omitted in the following sentence.

377. Line 57: *Claudio* UNDERGOES *my challenge.*—Schmidt explains *undergoes* here "in a bad sense, = to suffer, to bear;" but it seems rather to have the sense of "is under = has received," which we have given it in our foot-note; that is to say, "he *goes*, or *is under* my challenge to which he has not yet replied;" for no hostile meeting had absolutely been arranged between Benedick and Claudio. We may compare, generally, King John, v. 2. 99, 100.

> Is 't not I
> That *underge* this charge?

378. Line 77: *an old* INSTANCE.—For this sense of *instance*, compare As You Like It, ii. 7. 156:

> Full of wise saws and modern *instances;*

and Troilus and Cressida, v. 10. 40, 41: "what verse for it? what *instance* for it?"

379. Lines 79-82: *If a man do not erect in this age his own tomb ere he dies, he shall live no longer in* MONUMENT *than the* BELL RINGS *and the widow weeps.*—So Q. Ff. read *monuments* and *bells ring. In monument* is almost equivalent here to "in men's memory," *monument* being that which is erected to preserve one's memory in the minds of men. We may, perhaps, compare the well-known line in Horace, Ode xxx. bk. iii. line 1:

> Exegi *monumentum* ære perennius.

380. Line 85: *an hour in clamour, and a quarter in* RHEUM.—Shakespeare uses *rheum* for tears in two or three other places. Compare especially Coriolanus, v. 6. 46: "a few drops of women's *rheum.*"

381. Line 86: *Don* WORM, *his conscience.*—Compare

Richard III. i. 3. 222: "The *worm* of conscience." Some theologians interpret "the worm that dieth not" as meaning the human conscience, which shall reproach us for ever, in a future state, if we do not listen to its voice here.

382. Line 98: *Yonder's* OLD COIL *at home.*—Perhaps the colloquial expression we have given in the foot-note, "The devil to pay," is the nearest rendering of the expression *old* coil. Cotgrave has under *Faire le diable de l'auvert*, "To keep an *old coyle*, horrible stirre." *Old* is often used as a colloquial intensitive. Compare Merchant of Venice, iv. 2. 15: "We shall have *old* swearing;" and see Comedy of Errors, note 64, and Two Gent. of Verona, note 23.

383. Line 100: *I will go with thee to thy* UNCLES.—So Q. Ff. Modern editors generally print the word *uncle's*, and Rowe altered it to *uncle*, a slight alteration very frequently adopted, and in support of which we may refer to line 97 above, where Ursula says: "you must go to your *uncle*." But as it is generally agreed that this scene takes place in the garden of Leonato's house, if not within the precincts of the house itself, there does not seem to be much sense in Benedick's saying "I will go . . . to thy *uncle's*." On the other hand some may think that the expression of Ursula just above, in line 98, "Yonder's old coil *at home*," may seem to imply that they were not in the grounds of the house itself; but this may be explained by comparing it to our common form of expression "up at the house," which we use under exactly similar circumstances. For instance, if a message is brought to anyone who is in the grounds belonging to a country house, it is very common to say "You are wanted *up at the* house." We have adopted the reading of the old copies without printing it *uncle's*, and I think that the explanation given in the foot-note is probably the right one. Benedick would be very likely to know that the two brothers, Leonato and Antonio, were together. At any rate that fact was present in the dramatist's mind, and would account for his writing *uncles* instead of *uncle*.

ACT V. SCENE 3.

384. Line 3: *Done to death.*—This expression is now obsolete, but was common enough in the sixteenth century. Shakespeare uses it in only one other passage, II. Henry VI. iii. 2. 179: "who should *do* the duke *to death*?" Chapman has it in the Argument to the 22nd Book of the Iliad:

> Hector (in Chi) *to death is done*
> By pow'r of Peleus angry sonne.
> —Vol. i. p. 208.

Steevens says that *to do to death* is merely an old translation of the French *Faire mourir*. Surely the literal translation of that would be "to make to die." The fact is that the verb *to do* had many more senses in Shakespeare's time even than it has now. We have in III. Henry VI. i. 4. 108 the peculiar expression: "take time *to do him dead*."

385. Line 10: *Praising her when I am* DUMB.—So Ff.; Q. has "when I am *dead*;" a reading which, but for the necessity of a rhymed or quasi-rhymed line here, we might prefer. It may be supposed that *dumb* was pronounced, as it is now in the North, "*doom*."

386. Line 13: *Those that slew thy virgin knight.*—Steevens has expended a great deal of unnecessary erudition in a note on this passage, in which he seeks to make out that *virgin knight* means *virgin hero* without any intention of a pun; the expression being taken from that of a *virgin* or *maiden knight*, applied to a *knight* who had not yet achieved any adventure; and he goes further in seeking to prove from certain lines in Spenser that "an ideal order," called Knights of Maidenhed, "was supposed as a compliment to Queen Elizabeth's virginity" (Var. Ed. vol. ii. 154). Many ideal compliments have been offered up at the same durable shrine; but it may be doubted if this was one. *Knight* originally meant "servant," and *virgin knights* means nothing more than "virgin servants of Diana." Compare All's Well, i. 3. 120: "Dian no queen of *virgins*, that would suffer her poor *knight* surprised."

387. Lines 20, 21:

> *Till death be uttered,*
> *Heavily, heavily.*

So Q. Ff. read here *Heavenly, heavenly*, a reading which Knight, Staunton, and Grant White all adopt. The last-named editor gives a singular interpretation to the passage; viz. "that death is to be uttered (*i.e.* expelled, outer-ed) by the power of Heaven." So far from the sense demanding the reading of Ff., that of Q. is infinitely preferable, the meaning being "till death be expressed, commemorated in song;" but Schmidt takes it to mean, "the cry '*graves, yawn*,' etc. shall be raised till death." But, in any case, *heavenly* can have little meaning, while, for the use of *heavily* in this passage, we may compare the well-known passage in Hamlet, ii. 2. 309: "and indeed it goes so *heavily* with my disposition," where F. 1 misprints *heavenly for heavily;* and also Sonnet xxx. 10:

> And *heavily* from woe to woe tell o'er,

and again, Sonnet, l. 11:

> Which *heavily* he answers with a groan.

388. Lines 30-33:

> D. Pedro. *Come, let us hence, and put on other* WEED;
> *And then to Leonato's we will go.*
> Claud. *And Hymen now with luckier issue* SPEED
> *Than this for whom we render'd up this woe!*

F. 1 read *weedes* and *speeds;* F. 2, F. 3, F. 4 *speed*. Theobald adopted the conjecture of Thirlby, *speed's*, i.e. *speed us*, on the ground that Claudio could not know what the issue of his coming marriage was to be, and that therefore the verb should be in the subjunctive. Many editors, including the Cambridge, have adopted this emendation; but though it is a very plausible one, I cannot help agreeing with Malone in his objection to it, though not on the same ground that "it is so extremely harsh" (Var. Ed. vol. vii. p. 155); but rather that it must be perfectly valueless, as a guide to the sense or construction, when the line is spoken; for, unless the actor says *speed us* in full, it is impossible to make any clear distinction between *speeds* and *speed's*. I have therefore ventured to alter *weed* to the singular, and to adopt the reading *speed*, feeling that Claudio's wish should be in the optative. *Weed* is used, apparently as a plural noun, in a passage in Pericles, iv. 1. 14:

> No, I will rob Tellus of her *weed*;

where it certainly might be paraphrased as "clothing," which is the sense that we require here. But more instances of this use of the word are to be found given under "Weeds," in Richardson's Dictionary, *e.g.* from Robert of Gloucester:

> Hiy sende her feble messagers in povere monne *weed*;

from Chaucer, A Ballade in Com. of our Lady:

> Thy mantel of mercy on our misery sprede
> And er wo awake wrap vs vnder thy *wede*;

and from Spenser, Fairy Queen, bk. ii. c. 8. st. 16:

> To spoyle the dead of *weed*
> Is sacrilege, and doth all sinnes exceed.

It may be that Shakespeare intended *speeds* to be in the indicative mood, because Claudio knew that there was not likely to be any such interruption to his marriage, on this occasion, as there was before. But the *And*, at the beginning of the line, certainly makes one think that the sentence is meant to express a wish.

In the last line there seems to me a fault that none of the commentators have pointed out; and that is the first *this*, which is certainly very weak, and coming immediately after *than* is extremely cacophonous; the repetition of the word again, in the same line, being, to say the least, very clumsy. Might not we read *hers*, that is, "her marriage," referring, of course, to Hero?

ACT V. Scene 4.

389.—Enter Leonato, &c., Margaret, &c.—Most of the modern editors omit Margaret's name, though it occurs both in Q. and Ff. here, and also when Antonio re-enters, with the ladies masked, after line 52 below. There is no reason for the omission of her name here; for, as Dyce pertinently observes, there is nothing said of her at the beginning of this scene which would prevent her being present. Leonato lets her off with a very slight rebuke (lines 4, 5 below), which he might well emphasize by turning towards her. Her presence later on in the scene seems to us to be implied by Beatrice's speech (line 78).

390. Line 6: *In the true course of all the* QUESTION.—There is no doubt that *question* here means "investigation;" though Schmidt, curiously enough, gives it as "subject, matter, cause."

391. Lines 22, 23:

> *Your niece regards me with an eye of favour.*
> Leon. *That eye my daughter lent her: 't is most true.*

Leonato means to say that by means of the harmless plot carried out against Beatrice by his daughter, Hero, and her waiting-women, Beatrice has been brought to regard Benedick with favour, just as he had been brought to love her through the plot conducted by Don Pedro, Claudio, and Leonato himself. So Leonato says (line 25) to Benedick:

> The sight whereof I think you had from me;

that is, "The sight *of an eye of love* I think you had from me." It is noticeable that in his answer, line 27, Benedick overlooks this suggestion with the most dignified blindness:

> Your answer, sir, is enigmatical.

392. Lines 41, 42:

> *such a February face,*
> *So full of frost, of storm, and cloudiness.*

It is needless to explain this expression to anyone who has experienced the delights of February, 1888. It may be some satisfaction, to those who have suffered from the amenities of that month and its successor, to recollect that, in Shakespeare's time, matters do not seem to have been much better.

393. Lines 43, 44:

> *I think he thinks upon the savage bull.—*
> *Tush, fear not, man; we'll tip thy horns with gold.*

This is another reference to i. 1. 263–266 above.

394. Line 45: *And all* EUROPA *shall rejoice at thee.*—For some reason, best known to himself, Steevens wanted to amend this passage by printing "And all *our Europe, &c.*" in support of which utterly unnecessary alteration he brought forward the line in Richard II. i. 4. 35:

> As were *our* England in reversion his.

But the meaning of the passage would be destroyed by Steevens's proposed emendation, as it is, evidently, the author's desire to mark the reference to the story of Jupiter and *Europa*.

395. Lines 48–51.—It is plain Benedick is not quite reconciled yet to Claudio. The facility with which that plausible young gentleman transfers his affections, at the bidding of his father-in-law that was to be, does not quite satisfy Benedick's notions of honour. His answer to Claudio's chaff here is certainly not polite, and it was probably written by the author, deliberately, in rhyme, in order that it might be robbed of some of its offensiveness by being put into the same form as the rhymed epigrams, such as those of Heywood, which were great favourites in Shakespeare's day.

396. Line 54: *This same is she, and I do give you her.*—In Q. Ff. this line is given by evident mistake, though the mistake may have been that of the author, to *Leonato*. It is plain from lines 14–16 above in Leonato's own speech that this line should belong to *Antonio*; as it was he, and not *Leonato*, that was to give the veiled Hero to Claudio.

It is worth while remarking here the extreme levity of Claudio's behaviour. Having hung up his rhymed epitaph on the grave of the woman whom he believed he had helped to kill, he does not seem, at this point, to have the slightest thought or memory of his dead love.

397. Line 59: *I am your husband, if you like of me.*—This construction is pretty frequent in Shakespeare. Compare Tempest, iii. 1. 57: "Besides yourself, *to like of*;" and Love's Labour's Lost, i. 1. 107:

> But *like of* each thing that in season grows.

398. Line 63: *One Hero died* DEFIL'D; *but I do live.*—Ff. omit *defil'd*, and Collier substituted *belied*. It is pretty evident from the next line that the word *defil'd* must have been omitted accidentally from F. 1.

399. Lines 75, 76: *Why, then your uncle, and the prince, and Claudio have been deceiv'd; they swore you did.*—So Ff. (except that the final *ed* in *deceiv'd* is not elided; Q. prints the passage as verse:

> Why, then your uncle and the prince and Claudio
> Have been deceived, they swore you did.

In order to make the verse complete Capell inserted the word *for* before *they swore you did*; while Hanmer printed the line *for they did swear you did*, making it correspond with line 79 below. If there is to be any emendation, this is much the more plausible one; but I think that F. 1 is quite right in printing the passage as prose. It is most likely that Benedick, after the words, *have been deceiv'd*, would turn round to Claudio, the Prince, and Leonato for confirmation of his words; he would be met, on their part, by an explosion of smothered laughter, upon which he would turn away and say with emphasis, and rather in a tone of vexation, "*they swore you did.*"

400. Lines 80-82:

Bene. *They swore* THAT *you were almost sick for me.*
Beat. *They swore* THAT *you were well-nigh dead for me.*
Bene. *'T is no* SUCH *matter.—Then you do not love me?*

So Q.; Ff. omit *that* in lines 80, 81, and *such* in line 82. I am not at all certain, although nearly all editors adopt the reading of Q., that F. 1 is not right here. It looks very much as if *that* in the first two lines, and *such* in the last line, had been put in to make the verse complete. It must be remembered that Benedick and Beatrice find out now, for the first time, the trick that has been played upon them; and the fun of the scene is that this discovery very nearly leads to a quarrel between them. Beatrice, who has really learned to love Benedick, is at heart less annoyed than he is, because her love is much stronger than her vanity; but in Benedick's case, he being a man, the wound to his vanity, or self-love, is more acutely felt. In this frame of mind,—he, in real vexation, and she, in vexation more or less assumed,—the sharper the sentences they speak the better; and the omissions in Ff. certainly seem to improve the lines, which are then easier to speak in a petulant tone than if they were verses, made complete by the addition of the word *that*.

As for line 82 the reading of Q. makes the sense different to that in F. 1. Benedick (according to Ff.) says: '*T is no matter*, *i.e.* "It is not a matter of the slightest importance what they swear." According to Q. he says: "The statement that I was well-nigh dead for love of Beatrice is not true in any sense." In either case the point is, "you do not love me;" and that point he is eager to reach; but according to the reading of the Q. he stops to deny the statement that he was *well-nigh dead* with love for Beatrice. Here again it seems to me that the reading of Ff. is the better one.

401. Line 98: *Peace! I will stop your mouth.* [Kissing her.—This line, in Q. Ff., is given to Leonato. Theobald was the first to make the obvious suggestion that it should be given to Benedick, and he added at the same time the stage-direction [*Kissing her.*

402. Line 110: *double-dealer.*—There is an obvious play upon the word here, which Shakespeare only uses in one other passage, in Twelfth Night, v. 1. 37, 38: "I will be so much a sinner, to be a *double-dealer;*" said by the Duke to the Clown when asked to give the latter another gold coin.

403. Lines 125, 126: *there is no staff more reverend than one tipp'd with* HORN.—Malone thinks that there was some allusion here to the ancient trial by Wager of Battle or Combat. Stow gives an account in his Annals, under the thirteenth year of Queen Elizabeth, of the ceremonies observed at a trial of this kind (in a civil action) which was to have taken place, but which was stopped before the two champions, chosen by the plaintiffs and defendants, actually came to blows; he says: "The names of these two champions were, Henry Nailor for the plaintiff, George Thorne for the defendant. The combat was to have been fought in Tuthill Fields, Westminster." Stow says: "the gauntlet that was cast downe by George Thorne was borne before the sayd Nailor upon a sword's poynt, and his baston (a *staffe* of an elle long, made Taper-wise, *tipt with horne*,) with his shield of hard leather, was borne after him by Askam a yeoman of the Queenes gard." Minsheu, under the word *Combat*, gives a more elaborate account of this ceremony.

Reed quotes "Britton, Pleas of the Crown, c. xxvii. f. 18: 'Next let them go to combat with *two bastons tipped with horn* of equal length'" (Var. Ed. vol. vii. p. 169). The probability is that there is no special reference here to the combat between Nailor and Thorne, nor to any other instance of the Wager of Battle, but to the simple fact that horn was commonly used to tip staves with in the place of what is now called the ferrule. Of course there is an obvious play on the word *horn*, in the sense of a cuckold's *horn*.

WORDS OCCURRING ONLY IN MUCH ADO ABOUT NOTHING.

NOTE.—The addition of sub., adj., verb, adv. in brackets immediately after a word indicates that the word is used as a substantive, adjective, verb, or adverb only in the passage or passages cited.

The compound words marked with an asterisk (*) are printed as two separate words in F. 1.

	Act	Sc.	Line
Accordant	i.	2	15
Achiever	i.	1	9
Anticly	v.	1	96
Baldrick	i.	1	244
Blazon[1] (sub.)	ii.	1	307
Blent (sub.)	v.	4	51
Bluish	iii.	4	22

[1] = explanation. See note 128.

	Act	Sc.	Line
Brothel-house	i.	1	256
Bugle[2]	i.	2	244
Burglary[3]	iv.	2	52
Candle-wasters	v.	1	18
Carpet-mongers	v.	2	33

[2] = a hunting horn.

[3] Dogberry's blunder for *perjury*.

	Act	Sc.	Line
*Church-bench	iii.	3	95
Clapper	iii.	2	13
Claw[4] (verb)	i.	3	18
Cloudiness	v.	4	42
Contemptible[5]	ii.	3	189

[4] = to flatter.

[5] = scornful; used in modern sense of *despicable* in I. Henry VI. i. 2. 75.

	Act	Sc.	Line
Continuer	i.	1	143
Conveyance[6]	ii.	1	253
Covertly	ii.	2	9
Cross[7] (adv.)	v.	1	139
Crossness	ii.	3	180

[6] = skill of a juggler; frequently used in other senses.

[7] = athwart.

WORDS PECULIAR TO MUCH ADO ABOUT NOTHING.

	Act	Sc.	Line
Dearness	iii.	2	101
Desartless[1]	iii.	3	9
Despite (verb)	ii.	2	31
Drover	ii.	1	202
Eftest	iv.	2	38
Employer	v.	2	31
Endings[2]	v.	2	39
Enigmatical	v.	4	27
Epigram	v.	4	104
Excommunication[3]	iii.	5	69
Experimental	iv.	1	168
Fashion-monging	v.	1	94
Featured[4]	iii.	1	60
February (adj.)	v.	4	41
Flight[5]	i.	1	39
Frame[6] (sub.)	iv.	1	191
Giddily[7]	iii.	3	140
Gossip-like (adj.)	v.	1	188
Greedily	iii.	1	28
Gull[8] (sub.)	ii.	3	123
Hare-finder	i.	1	186
Hearsay[9]	iii.	1	23
Hideousness	v.	1	96
*High-proof (adj.)	v.	1	123
*Holy-thistle	iii.	4	80
Householder[10]	iv.	2	84
Huddling[11] (trans.)	ii.	1	252
*Ill-headed	iii.	1	64
*Ill-well	ii.	2	122
Interjections	iv.	1	22
Inwardness	iv.	1	247
Kid-fox	ii.	3	44
Kind[12] (adj.)	i.	1	26
Lackbeard	v.	1	195
Largely[13]	v.	4	69
Leaped[14]	v.	4	49
Love-god[15]	ii.	2	403
Low (sub.)	v.	4	48
Lute-string	iii.	2	59
March-chick	i.	3	59
Marl	ii.	1	66
Meet[16] (adv.)	i.	1	47
Mired[17] (verb)	iv.	1	135
Misgovernment	iv.	1	100
Misuse[18] (verb)	ii.	2	28
Necessarily	ii.	3	201
*New-trothed	iii.	1	38
Night-raven	ii.	3	85
Orange	ii.	1	305
	iv.	1	33
Orthography[19]	ii.	3	22
Over-kindness	v.	1	302
*Parrot-teacher	i.	1	138
Perfumer	i.	3	61
Pipers	v.	4	132
Pitiful (adverbially)	v.	2	20
*Pleasant-spirited	ii.	1	355
Praiseworthy	v.	2	90
Preceptial	v.	1	24
Predestinate (adj.)	i.	1	135
Prohibit	v.	1	335
Quiver (sub.)	i.	1	274
Rabato	iii.	4	6
Recheat	i.	1	243
Reclusive	iv.	1	244
Reportingly	iii.	1	116
Secondarily	v.	1	222
*Self-endeared	iii.	1	56
Side[20] (adj.)	iii.	4	21
Snapped (verb tr.)	v.	1	116
Sole[21]	iii.	2	10
Squarer	i.	1	82
Stalk[22] (verb)	ii.	3	95
Start-up	i.	3	68
Stuffing (sub.)	i.	1	59
Style[23]	v.	1	37
	v.	2	6
Taker[24]	i.	1	88
Tartly	ii.	1	3
Tax[25] (verb)	ii.	3	46
Terminations	ii.	1	257
*Thick-pleached	i.	2	10
Thirdly	v.	1	223
Tinsel	iii.	4	22
Toothpicker	ii.	1	275
Trans-shape	v.	1	172
Trencher-man	i.	1	51
Tuition	i.	1	283
Twine (sub.)	iv.	1	252
Underborne[26]	iii.	4	21
Underneath[27] (adv.)	v.	1	185
Unhopefullest	ii.	1	392
Unkissed	v.	2	53
Unmitigated	iv.	1	306
Untowardly	iii.	2	134
Upwards (adv.)	iii.	2	71
Vagrom	iii.	3	25
Vice[28]	v.	2	21
Waggling	ii.	1	119
Warren	ii.	1	222
War-thoughts	i.	1	303
Watchings (sub.)	ii.	1	387
Winded[29] (verb)	i.	1	243
Wit-crackers	v.	4	102
Woollen (sub.)	ii.	1	33

[1] Dogberry's form of *desertless*.

[2] Of words.

[3] Dogberry's blunder for *examination*.

[4] Sonn. xxix. 6.

[5] = a kind of light arrow.

[6] = contrivance. Compare iv. 1. 130 and note 279.

[7] = inconstantly. Used once again (=heedlessly) in Twelfth Night, ii. 4. 87.

[8] = a trick. Used frequently elsewhere = a dupe.

[9] Sonn. xxi. 13.

[10] Used only once elsewhere, in I. Henry IV. iv. 2. 17, where, perhaps, it means "one of a household."

[11] Used intrans. in Merchant of Venice, iv. 1. 28.

[12] = natural. Also in Lucrece, 1423.

[13] = fully.

[14] Used, sexually, of a bull.

[15] Sonn. cliv. 1.

[16] = even.

[17] = soiled with mud.

[18] = to deceive; used frequently in other senses.

[19] Here = orthographer; used in its ordinary sense in Love's Labour's Lost, v. 1. 22.

[20] Used in the phrase "side sleeves." See note 238.

[21] Of the foot. Used several times in Shakespeare of the bottom of the shoe.

[22] In sporting sense. Also in Lucrece, 365.

[23] Of composition. Used three times in the Sonn. in this sense (xxxii. 14, lxxviii. 11, lxxxiv. 12); used frequently in other senses in Shakespeare.

[24] Of a disease. Used twice in the sense of one who swallows anything: Sonn. cxxix. 8; Rom. and Jul. v. 1. 62.

[25] = to lay a burden on. Used literally, in its fiscal sense, II. Henry VI. iii. 1. 116; and frequently in the sense of "to censure, to accuse."

[26] = trimmed. In the sense of "to endure;" the verb occurs in John iii. 1. 65 and Richard II. i. 4. 29.

[27] The preposition is of common use in Shakespeare.

[28] A screw; used in the sense of a carpenter's **vice** (figuratively), II. Henry IV. ii. 1. 24.

[29] = to blow.

ORIGINAL EMENDATIONS ADOPTED.

Note

74. i. 3. 54: *And who—and who—which way looks he?*

203. iv. 1. 44–47:

Leon. *What do you mean, my lord?*

Claud. *Not to be married, not to knit my soul*
To an approved wanton.

Leon. *Dear my lord—*

[He pauses from emotion.] *If you, in your own proof*, &c.

So Walker; except the stage-direction.

324. v. 1. 16: *And*, SORRY *way, cry "hem" when he should groan.*

So Steevens's conjecture, afterwards abandoned.

ORIGINAL EMENDATIONS SUGGESTED.

Note

123. ii. 1. 265–267: *for certainly, while she is* THERE, *a man may live as quiet in hell as in a sanctuary.*

228. iii. 3. 160–162: *saw afar off in the orchard this amiable encounter—*

Con. *And thought thy Margaret was Hero.*

316. iv. 2. 70, 71:

Verg. *Let them be in the hands—*

Con. *Of* A *coxcomb.*

348. v. 1. 114: *You are come to part almost a fray.*

AS YOU LIKE IT.

NOTES AND INTRODUCTION

BY

A. WILSON VERITY.

DRAMATIS PERSONÆ.

DUKE, living in banishment.

FREDERICK, his brother, and usurper of his dominions.

AMIENS, }
JAQUES, } lords attending on the banished Duke.

LE BEAU, a courtier attending on Frederick.

CHARLES, wrestler to Frederick.

OLIVER, }
JAQUES, } sons of Sir Roland de Bois.
ORLANDO, }

ADAM, }
DENIS, } servants to Oliver.

TOUCHSTONE, a clown.

SIR OLIVER MARTEXT, a vicar.

CORIN, }
SILVIUS, } shepherds.

WILLIAM, a country fellow, in love with Audrey.

A person representing Hymen.

ROSALIND, daughter to the banished Duke.

CELIA, daughter to Frederick.

PHEBE, a shepherdess.

AUDREY, a country wench.

Lords, Pages, and Attendants, &c.

SCENE—First (and in act ii. sc. 3), near Oliver's house; afterwards, partly in the usurper's court, and partly in the Forest of Arden.

HISTORIC PERIOD: during the fourteenth century.

TIME OF ACTION (according to Daniel).

The action of the play covers ten days, with intervals, the divisions being as follows:—

Day 1: Act I. Scene 1.
Day 2: Act I. Scenes 2 and 3; and Act II. Scene 1.
Day 3: Act II. Scene 2.—An interval of a few days; the journey to Arden.
Day 4: Act II. Scene 4.
Day 5: Act II. Scenes 5, 6, and 7.—An interval of a few days.
Day 6: Act III. Scene 2.—Interval.
Day 7: Act III. Scene 3.
Day 8: Act III. Scenes 4 and 5; Act IV. Scenes 1, 2, and 3; and Act V. Scene 1.
Day 9: Act V. Scenes 2 and 3.
Day 10: Act V. Scene 4.

The third scene of Act II. must be referred to the second day, and the first scene of Act III. to the third day.

AS YOU LIKE IT.

INTRODUCTION.

LITERARY HISTORY.

The date of As You Like It can be fixed with approximate closeness: it was probably written in 1600, the evidence in favour of that date being as follows. On the registers of the Stationers' Company occurs this entry:

4 Augusti	
As you like yt/a booke	To be staied.
Henry the ffift/a booke	
Euery man in his humour/a booke	
The commedie of mucho A doo about nothing a booke/	

Unfortunately the year is not given; the date, however, of the previous entry is May 27, 1600, and we know that the other plays mentioned in the list were printed in 1600 and 1601; it seems, therefore, a fair inference to conclude that the undated entry should be referred to 1600, and that year in all likelihood saw the production of this most delightful comedy. Of other incidental points of testimony that support this conjecture several are worth noting. As You Like It is not mentioned in Mere's Palladis Tamia: hence it cannot have been printed prior to 1598. Again, in act iii. scene 5 we have the oft-quoted line from Marlowe's Hero and Leander: "Who ever loved that loved not at first sight?" Marlowe's poem was published in 1598. There are other less satisfactory pieces of internal evidence: *e.g.* in i. 2. 94: "for since the little wit that fools have was silenc'd," Mr. Fleay finds an allusion to "the burning of satirical books by public authority, 1st June, 1599." Malone, too, has pointed out that the expression "like Diana in the fountain" (iv. 1. 134) may be a reference to the "curiously-wrought tabernacle of grey marble, and in the same an image alabaster of Diana, and water conveyed from the Thames prilling from her naked breast," which, according to Stow—whose words we have just quoted—was set up in 1596.

Combining these individual points, and emphasizing the importance of the entry on the stationers' registers, we may, I think, with tolerable safety assign the composition and production of As You Like It to the year 1600; with 1599 (late) as a possible, though not very plausible, alternative.

It will have been noticed that the play was "stayed;" *i.e.* a proviso was made against its being printed. Mr. Aldis Wright ingeniously suggests that this may have been because the piece was not properly finished, and he points out that even in its present state, or rather as given in the Folio of 1623—where, by the way, it seems to have been first published—there are slight signs of hurry and carelessness. For instance: in the first scene the second son of Sir Rowland is called Jaques; at the end he is introduced as the "second brother," for fear, no doubt, that he might be confounded with the melancholy Jaques; this is unlike Shakespeare's usually careful method. Again, in i. 2. 284, Le Beau's reply to Orlando: "but yet indeed the *taller* is his daughter," is a significant slip; for in the very next scene Rosalind says of herself: "because that I am more than common tall." And there are other trifling touches that point the same way.

To turn now to the source of the play. For the main incidents of his comedy-romance Shakespeare drew (with his accustomed freedom) upon a novel by Lodge. Lodge's story—itself a partial reminiscence of the Tale of Gamelyn, often ascribed to Chaucer—was published in 1590 and again in 1592; the full title being, "Rosalynde; Euphues Golden Legacie: found after his death in his cell at Silexedra. Bequeathed to Philautus Sonnes, noursed up with their Father in England." In the introduction Lodge tells us that he "fell from books to arms," and sailed with Captain Clarke to the island of Terceras and the Canaries; writing his euphuistic pastoral to beguile the dulness of the voyage; so that, in his own charming phrase, "every line was writ with a surge, and every humorous passion counter-checkt with a storme. *If You Like it*, so; and yet I will be yours in duty, if you will be mine in favour." The words italicized need no comment. It may be worth while to observe that in the editions of Lodge's novel prior to 1598 the name Rosalind does not appear on the title-page, the addition being subsequently made on account, no doubt, of the popularity of Shakespeare's play. How closely Shakespeare followed his authority, the extracts from Rosalynde which I have given in the notes will sufficiently show. As to points of divergence, the two dukes are not brothers in the novel; the episode of Aliena's rescue from robbers is omitted in the play; in Lodge's version of the forest scenes Rosalind and Celia pass for a lady and her page; and—most important variation—Audrey, Jaques, and Touchstone are altogether creations of the dramatist.

To the history of the play there is nothing further to be added, except indeed to mention the tradition that Shakespeare himself acted the part of Adam, a tradition which is pleasant enough and upon which every one will remember Coleridge's comment, but which may be a tradition *et præterea nihil.*

STAGE HISTORY.

Of seventeenth-century performances of As You Like It no record exists; Downes and Pepys, authorities most copious and valuable, are silent about it, and we may reasonably conclude that the play was not among the Shakespearian dramas which after the Restoration fell on the evil days of revivals and merciless mutilations. In 1723, however, this immunity ceased:

> Omnes eodem serius ocius
> Cogimur;

and the Tempest, Troilus and Cressida, and others having known the hand of the restorer, the turn of As You Like It came. A certain Charles Johnson—of whom we are only told that he was fat "and famous for writing a play every year and being at Buttons every day"—produced at Drury Lane, with a strong cast that included Cibber (Jaques), Wilks (Orlando), Booth (the banished Duke), Theophilus Cibber (Le Beau), and Mrs. Booth (Rosalind), a by no means "respectful perversion" of Shakespeare's faultless comedy. The new piece was called Love in a Forest, and from Genest's account of it—which I venture to borrow—we get a good idea of the splendid courage of the last-century adapters of Shakespeare, and, still more, of the callousness of literary opinion which tolerated such massacres of the flawless and innocent. "Love in a Forest," says Genest, iii. 100, "altered from As You Like It: this is a bad alteration of Shakespeare's play by Charles Johnson—he entirely omits the characters of Touchstone, Audrey, William, Corin, Phœbe and Sylvius, except that the last, in act 2nd, speaks about 18 lines which belong to Corin. Johnson supplies the deficiency from some of Shakespeare's other plays, adding something, but not a vast deal, of his own. Act 1st. The wrestling between Orlando and Charles is turned into a regular combat in the lists—Charles accuses Orlando of treason, several speeches are introduced from Richard II. Act 2nd. When Duke Alberto enters with his friend, the speech about the wounded stag is very properly taken from the first Lord and given to Jaques—in the next scene between the same parties, notwithstanding Touchstone is omitted, yet Jaques gives the description of his meeting with a fool—much, however, of his part in this scene is left out very injudiciously, as is still the case when As You Like It is acted. Act 3rd. The verses which Cælia ought to read are omitted, and Touchstone's burlesque verses are given her instead—when Orlando and Jaques enter, they begin their conversation as in the original, and end it with part of the 1st Act of Much Ado, Jaques speaking what Benedick says about women—when Rosalind and Cælia come forward, Jaques walks off with Cælia—

Rosalind omits the account of Time's different paces— Jaques returns with Cælia and makes love to her—after which he has a soliloquy patched up from Benedick and Touchstone, with some additions from C. Johnson. Act 4th begins with a conversation between Jaques and Rosalind, in which he tells her of his love to Cælia—in the scene between Orlando and Rosalind considerable omissions are made, and Viola's speech ('she never told her love') is inserted—Robert (Jaques) de Bois brings the bloody napkin to Rowland, instead of Oliver, who does not appear after the 1st act. Robert says that he (not Oliver) was the person rescued from the lioness—that Oliver had killed himself—the act concludes with the 2nd scene of Shakespeare's 5th act, in which Rosalind desires all the parties on the stage to meet her to-morrow. Jaques and Cælia are made in some way to supply the place of Sylvius and Phœbe. Act 5th consists chiefly of the burlesque Tragedy of Pyramus and Thisbe from Midsummer Night's Dream; this is represented before the Duke, while Rosalind is changing her dress, instead of Touchstone's description of the quarrel. When Rosalind returns the play ends much as in the original—except that Jaques marries Cælia instead of going in quest of Duke Frederick—and that the Epilogue is omitted."—Genest, Some Account of the English Stage, vol. iii. p. 100-102.

It is a comfort to know that this preposterous pasticcio (dedicated, by the way, to "The Worshipful Society of Freemasons") only held the stage for six nights.

In 1740, for the first time, As You Like It was restored to the boards; produced on December 20th, it was acted some twenty-five times, a considerable success in those days. The cast was excellent: Jaques, Quin; Silvius, Woodward; Celia, Mrs. Clive; and Rosalind, Mrs. Pritchard — not to mention others. This revival (Genest iii. 627) took place at Drury Lane, and two years later, January 8, 1742, we find Covent Garden following the lead of its rival; the Rosalind again being Mrs. Pritchard, with Ryan as Jaques (Genest, iv. 5). Mrs. Pritchard was great as Rosalind, her chief competitor being Peg Woffington, who made her entry in the part at Drury Lane, in 1747; the Touchstone on that occasion was Macklin, with Kitty Clive as Celia. We may note in passing that it was while playing in As You Like It that Peg Woffington was struck down by paralysis; garrulous Tate Wilkinson gives us a graphic account of the painful "last scene of all."

Excluded by unfriendly space, I cannot describe in detail all the revivals mentioned by Genest; here, however, are the dates. October 22, 1767, at Drury Lane: Touchstone, King; Orlando, Palmer; Celia, Mrs. Baddeley; Rosalind, Mrs. Dancer (*i.e.* Barry), whom some people preferred to Mrs. Pritchard and Mrs. Woffington. April 5, 1771, at Covent Garden; January 24, 1775, Covent Garden, the play-bill announcing that the "cuckoo song," from Love's Labour's Lost, would be introduced; December 17, 1779, Covent Garden; July 4th, 1783, Haymarket; April 30th, 1785, Drury Lane. This last was a very important event: it was the début in the part of Rosalind of the great Mrs. Siddons. Was she a success? Who could say? The town was divided, and the friendships of a lifetime were dissolved, over this vexing question. Her biographer Boaden boldly says (ii. 167): "Rosalind was one of the most delicate achievements of Mrs. Siddons. The common objection to her comedy, that it was only the smile of tragedy, made the express charm of Rosalind—her vivacity is understanding, not buoyant spirits." There is much truth in this: unfortunately play-goers had grown accustomed to the stage Rosalind of the romping type, and even those who prided themselves on being nothing if not critical were dissatisfied with what seemed coldness and want of spontaneity in the great actress. Hear, for instance, the *dicta plusquam Johnsoniana* of the epically eloquent Miss Seward: "For the first time I saw the justly celebrated Mrs. Siddons in comedy, in Rosalind; but though her smile is as enchanting as her frown is magnificent, as her tears are irresistible, yet the playful scintillations of colloquial wit, which most mark that character, suit not the dignity of the Siddonian countenance." Genest, vi. 341, writes to the same effect: "Mrs.

Siddons did not add to her reputation by her performance of Rosalind, and when Mrs. Jordan had played the character, few persons wished to see Mrs. Siddons in it." This brings us to the greatest of eighteenth-century Rosalinds: in point of popularity, if not of actual merit, Mrs. Jordan seems to have been unrivalled; it was Eclipse first, and the rest, if not nowhere, at least next by a very long interval indeed. Her first appearance in the part was on April 13, 1787, for her own benefit; and she was triumphantly successful. "Her laugh and her voice," says Boaden (Life of Kemble, i. 428), were irresistible;" Shakespeare himself, to quote Campbell's magnificent compliment, would have gone behind the scenes to congratulate her. It was always one of Mrs. Jordan's favourite and best parts, and we should like to have been present at a certain *première* at Drury Lane on May 12, 1797, when the play-bill read as follows: Touchstone, Bannister, junior; Orlando, Barrymore; Jaques, Palmer; Rosalind, Mrs. Jordan; Celia, Miss Mellon; Audrey, Miss Pope. Miss Pope, by the way, often played Rosalind.

To follow the fortunes of As You Like It in this century were a long story. It must be sufficient to mention that Kemble played, in 1805, Jaques to the Orlando of Charles Kemble; that Miss Tree was a not inglorious Rosalind; that as actress and critic Helen Faucit has interpreted the same part with equal mastery and magic; and that As You Like It was among the Shakesperean revivals of Macready.[1]

Turning to quite modern times, we may mention the production of the play at the Opera Comique Theatre in 1875, when Mrs. Kendal first appeared as Rosalind, the Orlando being Mr. Kendal, with Mr. Herman Vezin as Jaques; ten years later very much the same cast was representing As You Like It at the St. James Theatre; and in the interval—in 1880—had taken place the brilliantly successful revival at the Imperial Theatre. On the last occasion the Rosalind was Miss Litton.

In concluding we may mention, as an unconsidered trifle of some interest, that, thanks to the effort of the Pastoral Players, Rosalind and Orlando have met and made love, if not in a veritable forest of Arden—where are such fairy lands to be found?—at least, *sub Jove frigido.*

CRITICAL REMARKS.

As You Like It is not one of Shakespeare's greatest plays; it is merely one of his most delightful works, delightful alike to reader and to critic, if only on account of its perfect simplicity of motive. We are out in the open air; we hear the wind rustling in the fragrant leaves of the fairy-land of Arden; and we are far too lazy and too genially contented to think of purposes, and leading ideas, and things philosophic. We take the play as it is, without peering beneath the surface for subtle significance, and never once does Touchstone's query rise to our lips—"hast any philosophy in thee?" only the most Teutonic of Teutons would look for a *tendenz* in this fantastic study of an impossible Arcadia, a pastoral Utopia which "never was on sea or land." For As You Like It is, I take it, from beginning to end, purely ideal; the characters, or some of them, we may possibly have met, but their life and environment exist only in the fine frenzy of the poet. And we need not wonder that it should be so, not at any rate if we remember when the play was written. It came immediately after the great historic trilogy. Shakespeare had sounded forth to all the world the silver note of patriotism, had carried men's minds back from a splendid present to an equally splendid and imperishable past, and made an incomparable appeal to the old and eternally fresh sentiment—*pro focis et aris.* And now he hangs up his arms in the temple of the goddess of war, and steeps himself in the freshness and fairness of a life where sorrow and sin are not, where truth is on every shepherd's tongue, where the time fleets by as it did in the golden days of Saturn, where destiny herself deigns to smile, and where the thought of each and all is—"Come live with me and be my love." Such the *mise-en-scène*, such the atmosphere of careless

[1] See Macready's Diaries, vol. ii. p. 203, where Sir Frederick Pollock gives the cast: Rosalind, Mrs. Nisbett; Celia, Mrs. Stirling; William, Compton; Adam, Phelps; the banished Duke, Ryder, etc.

buoyancy, and with what art is the latter maintained throughout! True, we are told of "the uses of adversity." But Adversity here, as some one has said, is really a fourth Grace, less celebrated by the poets because so seldom seen, but none the less a true sister of the classic Three. She lays the lightest of chastening hands on her children, just revealing "the humorous sadness" of existence, and no more; she is not the pitiless goddess whose stoney glare chills and kills the gazer; she is in perfect harmony with the tone of a play in which no deep chord of passion is ever struck.

Of the characters who live and move in this fairy and fantastic world of romance, a world all touched with the tints of young desire and the purple light of love, it is difficult to speak; they are so familiar to us. Yet a word must be said; and first of Rosalind. She is wit and womanliness in equal proportions; and her womanliness is the spiritualized tenderness that Thackeray gives us. Hence the difficulty of rendering the part aright. It is so easy for an actress to sink the intellectual side of the character and emphasize merely the *abandon* and buoyancy which find vent in the forest scenes; it is so easy, too, to make those scenes a series of boisterous romps. Thus the last-century Rosalind appears to have been a tousselled hoyden, for whom the part was pure comedy, and comedy of no very dignified type; and when Mrs. Siddons restored that element of intellectual refinement and sobriety which is essential to the character, the verdict of critics and public was: "cold, unemotional; we prefer Mrs. Jordan." Yet this swash-buckler Rosalind, forever reminding us of her hose and doublet, though too often, perhaps, the stage Rosalind, is emphatically not the Rosalind of Shakespeare. The latter is never a mere boy, a "moonish youth, longing and liking, proud, changeable, fantastic;" under the mask of careless abandonment to every passing freak of fancy she preserves gracious and intact her perfect womanliness and dignity; so that when at last the little comedy has played to its close, and the time comes for all disguise to be laid aside, she moves quite naturally into her new position as bride and princess. She was at home in the forest glade. She will be no less so at the court.

The contrast between Rosalind and Aliena is too obvious to require comment: who runs may read; Shakespeare in his earlier plays is fond of placing two characters in striking antithesis. Far more interesting, because less natural, is the distinction between Rosalind and Jaques. Each represents an aspect of wit: only Jaques' is the wit of the scoffer. He is intellectual and endowed with a keen capacity to feel; but he lacks moral soundness, and sensibility minus morality too often ends in cynicism. The cynicism of Jaques, partly conscious and exaggerated, partly unconscious and quasi-constitutional, is the cynicism of men like Heine. The duke, indeed, charges Jaques with having been a mere libertine, and Gervinus dismisses him as "a *blasé* man, an epicurean." But the duke was not a great judge of character—he was not great at anything except mild moralities—and perhaps the Heidelberg philosopher-critic went equally stray. I think we shall be much nearer the truth if we regard Jaques as typical of the emotional man who is offended by the incongruities and injustices of life, by the sight of evils which he cannot explain, and who, for lack of faith and firmness, takes refuge in what is the last resource of the witty and unwise, indiscriminate mocking. Rosalind has all the wit of Jaques, but she has something more, a something that keeps her intellect clear and trustful. Rosalind and Jaques—these are the central figures of the play, or rather those on which the poet has mainly expended the resources of his art. But throughout the characterization is fine. Orlando is simply the ideal lover; the dainty, delicate, imperious Phebe we have often met, now on a piece of Dresden china, now in a *fête champêtre* by Watteau; Touchstone is an elder brother of the clown in the Comedy of Errors and The Two Gentlemen, only his fooling has an uncomfortable amount of wisdom about it; and Audrey, Adam, William—these may have lived, and their counterparts be still living, not a hundred miles from Stratford.

It is a just criticism that Shakespeare is

always "at the height of the particular situation;" that whatever he writes he writes, not merely well, but perfectly; that every dramatic style comes naturally to him. As You Like It admirably illustrates this maxim: from the first page to the last there is nothing, nothing at any rate of significance, to which we can point and say: "Were not this best away?"

THE SEVEN AGES.

AS YOU LIKE IT.

ACT I.

SCENE I. *Oliver's orchard.*

Enter ORLANDO *and* ADAM.

Orl. As I remember, Adam, it was upon this fashion,—he bequeathed me by will but poor a thousand crowns; and, as thou say'st, charged my brother, on his blessing, to breed me well: and there begins my sadness. My brother Jaques he keeps at school, and report speaks goldenly of his profit: for my part, he keeps me rustically at home, or, to speak more properly, stays me here at home unkept; for call you that keeping for a gentleman of my birth, that differs not from the stalling of an ox? His horses are bred better; for, besides that they are fair with their feeding, they are taught their manage, and to that end riders dearly hired: but I, his brother, gain nothing under him but growth; for the which his animals on his dunghills are as much bound to him as I. Besides this nothing that he so plentifully gives me, the something that nature gave me his countenance seems to take from me: he lets me feed with his hinds, bars me the place of a brother, and, as much as in him lies, mines[1] my gentility with my education. This is it, Adam, that grieves me; and the spirit of my father, which I think is within me, begins to mutiny against this servitude: I will no longer endure it, though yet I know no wise remedy how to avoid it.

Adam. Yonder comes my master, your brother.

Orl. Go apart, Adam, and thou shalt hear how he will shake me up. [*Adam retires.*

Enter OLIVER.

Oli. Now, sir! what make you here?

Orl. Nothing: I am not taught to make any thing.

Oli. What mar you then, sir?

Orl. Marry, sir, I am helping you to mar that which God made, a poor unworthy brother of yours, with idleness.

Oli. Marry, sir, be better employed, and be naught awhile![2]

Orl. Shall I keep your hogs, and eat husks

[1] *Mines, i.e.* undermines.

[2] *Be naught awhile*, a north-country expression = "a mischief on you."

with them? What prodigal portion have I spent, that I should come to such penury?

Oli. Know you where you are, sir? 43

Orl. O, sir, very well: here in your orchard.

Oli. Know you before whom, sir?

Orl. Ay, better than him I am before knows me. I know you are my eldest brother; and, in the gentle condition of blood, you should so know me. The courtesy of nations allows you my better, in that you are the first-born; but the same tradition takes not away my blood, were there twenty brothers betwixt us: I have as much of my father in me as you; albeit, I confess, your coming before me is nearer to his reverence.

Oli. What, boy!

Orl. Come, come, elder brother, you are too young in this.

Oli. Wilt thou lay hands on me, villain?

Orl. I am no villain: I am the youngest son of Sir Roland de Bois; he was my father; and he is thrice a villain that says such a father begot villains. Wert thou not my brother, I would not take this hand from thy throat till this other had pulled out thy tongue for saying so: thou hast railed on thyself.

Adam. [*Coming forward*] Sweet masters, be patient: for your father's remembrance,[1] be at accord. 67

Oli. Let me go, I say.

Orl. I will not, till I please: you shall hear me. My father charg'd you in his will to give me good education: you have train'd me like a peasant, obscuring and hiding from me all gentleman-like qualities. The spirit of my father grows strong in me, and I will no longer endure it: therefore allow me such exercises as may become a gentleman, or give me the poor allottery[2] my father left me by testament; with that I will go buy my fortunes.

Oli. And what wilt thou do—beg?—when that is spent? Well, sir, get you in: I will not long be troubled with you; you shall have some part of your will: I pray you, leave me.

Orl. I will no further offend you than becomes me for my good.

Oli. Get you with him, you old dog!

Adam. Is "old dog" my reward? Most true, I have lost my teeth in your service.—God be with my old master! he would not have spoke such a word.

[*Exeunt Orlando and Adam.*

Oli. Is it even so? begin you to grow upon me? I will physic your rankness,[3] and yet give no thousand crowns neither.—Holla, Denis! 93

Enter Denis.

Den. Calls your worship?

Oli. Was not Charles the duke's wrestler here to speak with me?

Den. So please you, he is here at the door, and importunes access to you.

Oli. Call him in. [*Exit Denis.*]—'T will be a good way; and to-morrow the wrestling is.

Enter Charles.

Cha. Good morrow to your worship. 100

Oli. Good morrow, Monsieur Charles.—What's the new news at the new court?

Cha. There's no news at the court, sir, but the old news: that is, the old duke is banished by his younger brother the new duke; and three or four loving lords have put themselves into voluntary exile with him, whose lands and revenues enrich the new duke; therefore he gives them good leave to wander.

Oli. Can you tell if Rosalind, the duke's daughter, be banished with her father? 111

Cha. O, no; for the duke's daughter, her cousin, so loves her,—being ever from their cradles bred together,—that she would have followed her exile, or have died to stay behind her. She is at the court, and no less beloved of her uncle than his own daughter; and never two ladies lov'd as they do.

Oli. Where will the old duke live?

Cha. They say, he is already in the forest of Arden, and a many merry men with him; and there they live like the old Robin Hood of England: they say, many young gentlemen flock to him every day, and fleet[4] the time carelessly, as they did in the golden world.

Oli. What, you wrestle to-morrow before the new duke? 127

[1] *For your father's remembrance*, i.e. for sake of your father's memory.

[2] *Allottery*, portion.

[3] *Rankness*, insolence.

[4] *Fleet*, make it pass quickly.

Cha. Marry, do I, sir; and I came to acquaint you with a matter. I am given, sir, secretly to understand that your younger brother, Orlando, hath a disposition to come in disguis'd against me to try a fall. To-morrow, sir, I wrestle for my credit; and he that escapes me without some broken limb shall acquit him well. Your brother is but young and tender; and, for your love, I would be loth to foil him, as I must, for my own honour, if he come in: therefore, out of my love to you, I came hither to acquaint you withal; that either you might stay him from his intendment,[1] or brook such disgrace well as he shall run into, in that it is a thing of his own search, and altogether against my will.

Adam. [*Coming forward*] Sweet masters, be patient: for your father's remembrance, be at accord.—(Act i. 1. 65-67.)

Oli. Charles, I thank thee for thy love to me, which thou shalt find I will most kindly requite. I had myself notice of my brother's purpose herein, and have by underhand means labour'd to dissuade him from it; but he is resolute. I'll tell thee, Charles, it is the stubbornest young fellow of France; full of ambition, an envious emulator of every man's good parts, a secret and villanous contriver against me his natural brother: therefore use thy discretion; I had as lief thou didst break his neck as his finger. And thou wert best look to't; for if thou dost him any slight disgrace, or if he do not mightily grace himself on thee, he will practise against thee by poison, entrap thee by some treacherous device, and never leave thee till he hath ta'en thy life by some indirect means or other; for, I assure thee, and almost with tears I speak it, there is not one so young and so villanous this day living. I speak but brotherly of him; but should I anatomize[2] him to thee as he is, I must blush and weep, and thou must look pale and wonder.

Cha. I am heartily glad I came hither to you. If he come to-morrow, I'll give him his payment: if ever he go alone again, I'll never wrestle for prize more: and so, God keep your worship!

Oli. Farewell, good Charles. [*Exit Charles.*] Now will I stir this gamester: I hope I shall

[1] *Intendment*, purpose.

[2] *Anatomize*, i.e. expose his faults.

see an end of him; for my soul, yet I know not why, hates nothing more than he. Yet he's gentle; never school'd, and yet learned; full of noble device; of all sorts enchantingly beloved; and, indeed, so much in the heart of the world, and especially of my own people, who best know him, that I am altogether misprised:[1] but it shall not be so long; this wrestler shall clear all: nothing remains but that I kindle the boy thither; which now I'll go about. [*Exit.*

SCENE II. *A lawn before the Duke's palace.*

Enter ROSALIND *and* CELIA.

Cel. I pray thee, Rosalind, sweet my coz, be merry.

Ros. Dear Celia, I show more mirth than I am mistress of; and would you yet I were merrier? Unless you could teach me to forget a banish'd father, you must not learn me how to remember any extraordinary pleasure.

Cel. Herein I see thou lov'st me not with the full weight that I love thee. If my uncle, thy banish'd father, had banished thy uncle, the duke my father, so thou hadst been still with me, I could have taught my love to take thy father for mine: so wouldst thou, if the truth of thy love to me were so righteously temper'd as mine is to thee.

Ros. Well, I will forget the condition of my estate, to rejoice in yours.

Cel. You know my father hath no child but I, nor none is like to have: and, truly, when he dies, thou shalt be his heir; for what he hath taken away from thy father perforce, I will render thee again in affection; by mine honour, I will; and when I break that oath, let me turn monster: therefore, my sweet Rose, my dear Rose, be merry.

Ros. From henceforth I will, coz, and devise sports. Let me see; what think you of falling in love?

Cel. Marry, I prithee, do, to make sport withal: but love no man in good earnest; nor no further in sport neither than with safety of a pure blush thou mayst in honour come off again.

Ros. What shall be our sport, then?

Cel. Let us sit and mock the good housewife Fortune from her wheel, that her gifts may henceforth be bestowed equally.

Ros. I would we could do so; for her benefits are mightily misplaced; and the bountiful blind woman doth most mistake in her gifts to women.

Cel. 'T is true; for those that she makes fair, she scarce makes honest; and those that she makes honest, she makes very ill-favouredly.

Ros. Nay, now thou goest from Fortune's office to Nature's: Fortune reigns in gifts of the world, not in the lineaments of Nature.

Cel. No? when Nature hath made a fair creature, may she not by Fortune fall into the fire? Though Nature hath given us wit to flout at[2] Fortune, hath not Fortune sent in this fool to cut off the argument?

Enter TOUCHSTONE.

[*Ros.* Indeed, then is Fortune too hard for Nature, when Fortune makes Nature's natural the cutter-off of Nature's wit.

Cel. Peradventure this is not Fortune's work neither, but Nature's; who, perceiving our natural wits too dull to reason of[3] such goddesses, hath sent this natural for our whetstone; for always the dulness of the fool is the whetstone of the wits.]—How now, wit! whither wander you?

Touch. Mistress, you must come away to your father.

Cel. Were you made the messenger?

Touch. No, by mine honour; but I was bid to come for you.

Ros. Where learned you that oath, fool?

Touch. Of a certain knight that swore by his honour they were good pancakes, and swore by his honour the mustard was naught: now I'll stand to it, the pancakes were naught, and the mustard was good; and yet was not the knight forsworn.

Cel. How prove you that, in the great heap of your knowledge?

Ros. Ay, marry, now unmuzzle your wisdom.

Touch. Stand you both forth now: stroke

[1] *Misprised*, despised; Fr. *méprisé*.

[2] *Flout at*, jeer, scoff at.

[3] *Reason of*, talk about.

your chins, and swear by your beards that I am a knave.

Cel. By our beards, if we had them, thou art.

Touch. By my knavery, if I had it, then I were; but if you swear by that that is not, you are not forsworn: no more was this knight, swearing by his honour, for he never had any; or if he had, he had sworn it away before ever he saw those pancakes or that mustard.

Cel. Prithee, who is 't that thou meanest?

Touch. One that old Frederick, your father, loves.

Cel. My father's love is enough to honour him enough: speak no more of him; you 'll be whipp'd for taxation[1] one of these days.

Touch. Stand you both forth now: stroke your chins, and swear by your beards that I am a knave.—(Act i. 2. 76-78.)

Touch. The more pity, that fools may not speak wisely what wise men do foolishly.

Cel. By my troth, thou sayest true; for since the little wit that fools have was silenc'd, the little foolery that wise men have makes a great show.—Here comes Monsieur Le Beau.

Ros. With his mouth full of news.

Cel. Which he will put on us,[2] as pigeons feed their young.

Ros. Then shall we be news-cramm'd.

Cel. All the better; we shall be the more marketable.

Enter Le Beau.

Bon jour, Monsieur Le Beau: what's the news?

Le Beau. Fair princess, you have lost much good sport.

Cel. Sport! of what colour?[3]

Le Beau. What colour, madam! how shall I answer you?

Ros. As wit and fortune will.

Touch. Or as the Destinies decree.

Cel. Well said: that was laid on with a trowel.[4]

[*Touch.* Nay, if I keep not my rank,—

[1] *Taxation*, censoriousness, talking satirically.
[2] *Put on us*, pawn off on us.
[3] *Colour*, description.
[4] *With a trowel* = in clumsy fashion.

Ros. Thou losest thy old smell.]

Le Beau. You amaze me, ladies: I would have told you of good wrestling, which you have lost the sight of.

Ros. Yet tell us the manner of the wrestling.

Le Beau. I will tell you the beginning; and, if it please your ladyships, you may see the end; for the best is yet to do; and here, where you are, they are coming to perform it.

Cel. Well,—the beginning, that is dead and buried.

Le Beau. There comes an old man and his three sons,—

Cel. I could match this beginning with an old tale.

Le Beau. Three proper young men, of excellent growth and presence.

Ros. With bills on their necks, "Be it known unto all men by these presents,"—

Le Beau. The eldest of the three wrestled with Charles, the duke's wrestler; which Charles in a moment threw him, and broke three of his ribs, that there is little hope of life in him: so he serv'd the second, and so the third. Yonder they lie; the poor old man, their father, making such pitiful dole over them, that all the beholders take his part with weeping.

Ros. Alas!

Touch. But what is the sport, monsieur, that the ladies have lost?

Le Beau. Why, this that I speak of.

Touch. Thus men may grow wiser every day! it is the first time that ever I heard breaking of ribs was sport for ladies.

Cel. Or I, I promise thee.

Ros. But is there any else longs to feel this broken music in his sides? is there yet another dotes upon rib-breaking?—Shall we see this wrestling, cousin?

Le Beau. You must, if you stay here; for here is the place appointed for the wrestling, and they are ready to perform it.

Cel. Yonder, sure, they are coming: let us now stay and see it. [*They retire.*

Flourish. Enter DUKE FREDERICK, *Lords,* ORLANDO, CHARLES, *and Attendants.*

Duke F. Come on: since the youth will not be entreated, his own peril on his forwardness.

Ros. Is yonder the man?

Le Beau. Even he, madam.

Cel. Alas, he is too young! yet he looks successfully.

Duke F. How now, daughter, and cousin! are you crept hither to see the wrestling?

Ros. Ay, my liege, so please you give us leave.

Duke F. You will take little delight in it, I can tell you, there is such odds in the man. In pity of the challenger's youth, I would fain dissuade him, but he will not be entreated. Speak to him, ladies; see if you can move him.

Cel. Call him hither, good Monsieur Le Beau.

Duke F. Do so: I'll not be by. [*Duke goes apart.*

Le Beau. Monsieur the challenger, the princess calls for you.

Orl. I attend them with all respect and duty.

Ros. Young man, have you challeng'd Charles the wrestler.

Orl. No, fair princess; he is the general challenger: I come but in, as others do, to try with him the strength of my youth.

Cel. Young gentleman, your spirits are too bold for your years. You have seen cruel proof of this man's strength: if you saw yourself with your eyes, or knew yourself with your judgment,[1] the fear of your adventure would counsel you to a more equal enterprise. We pray you, for your own sake, to embrace your own safety, and give over this attempt.

Ros. Do, young sir; your reputation shall not therefore be misprised: we will make it our suit to the duke that the wrestling might not go forward.

Orl. I beseech you, punish me not with your hard thoughts: herein I confess me much guilty, to deny so fair and excellent ladies any thing. But let your fair eyes and gentle wishes go with me to my trial; wherein if I be foil'd, there is but one sham'd that was never gracious; if kill'd, but one dead that is willing to be so: I shall do my friends no wrong, for I have none to lament me; the world no injury, for in it I have nothing;

[1] *Knew yourself, &c., i.e.* if you used your senses

only in the world I fill up a place, which may be better supplied when I have made it empty.

Ros. The little strength that I have, I would it were with you.

Cel. And mine, to eke out hers.

Ros. Fare you well: pray heaven I be deceiv'd in you!

Cel. Your heart's desires be with you!

Cha. Come, where is this young gallant [that is so desirous to lie with his mother earth?

Orl. Ready, sir; but his will hath in it a more modest working.]

Duke F. You shall try but one fall.

Cha. No, I warrant your grace, you shall not entreat him to a second, that have so mightily persuaded him from a first.

Orl. You mean to mock me after; you should not have mock'd me before: but come your ways.

Ros. Now Hercules be thy speed, young man!

Cel. I would I were invisible, to catch the strong fellow by the leg.

[*Charles and Orlando wrestle.*

Ros. O excellent young man!

Cel. If I had a thunderbolt in mine eye, I can tell who should down.

[*Charles is thrown. Shout.*

Duke F. [*Advancing*] No more, no more.

Orl. Yes, I beseech your grace: I am not yet well breath'd.[1]

Duke F. How dost thou, Charles?

Le Beau. He cannot speak, my lord.

Duke F. Bear him away.

[*Charles is borne out.*

What is thy name, young man?

Orl. Orlando, my liege; the youngest son of Sir Roland de Bois.

Duke F. I would thou hadst been son to some man else:
The world esteem'd thy father honourable,
But I did find him still[2] mine enemy:
Thou shouldst have better pleas'd me with this deed,
Hadst thou descended from another house.
But fare thee well; thou art a gallant youth:
I would thou hadst told me of another father.

[*Exeunt Duke Frederick, Train, and Le Beau.*

Cel. [*To Rosalind apart*] Were I my father, coz, would I do this?

Orl. I am more proud to be Sir Roland's son,
His youngest son;—and would not change that calling,
To be adopted heir to Frederick. [*Retires back.*

Ros. My father lov'd Sir Roland as his soul,
And all the world was of my father's mind:
Had I before known this young man his son,
I should have given him tears unto entreaties,
Ere he should thus have ventur'd.

Cel. Gentle cousin,
Let us go thank him and encourage him:
My father's rough and envious disposition
Sticks me at heart.—Sir, [*Orlando advances*] you have well deserv'd:
If you do keep your promises in love
But justly, as you have exceeded promise,
Your mistress shall be happy.

Ros. Gentleman,

[*Giving him a chain from her neck.*

Wear this for me, one out of suits with[3] fortune,
That would give more, but that her hand lacks means.—
Shall we go, coz?

Cel. Ay.—Fare you well, fair gentleman.

[*Going.*

Orl. Can I not say, I thank you? My better parts
Are all thrown down; and that which here stands up
Is but a quintain, a mere lifeless block.

Ros. [*Going*] He calls us back: [*Stops*] my pride fell with my fortunes;
I'll ask him what he would. [*Returns*]—Did you call, sir?—
Sir, you have wrestled well, and overthrown
More than your enemies.

Cel. Will you go, coz?

Ros. Have with you.[4]—Fare you well.

[*Exeunt Rosalind and Celia.*

Orl. What passion hangs these weights upon my tongue?
I cannot speak to her, yet she urg'd conference.
O poor Orlando, thou art overthrown!
Or Charles or something weaker masters thee.

---

[1] *I am not yet well breath'd*, i.e. I am not yet warmed to my work.

[2] *Still*, always.

[3] *Out of suits with*, not favoured by.

[4] *Have with you*, come away.

Re-enter LE BEAU.

Le Beau. Good sir, I do in friendship counsel you
To leave this place. Albeit you have deserv'd
High commendation, true applause, and love,

Le Beau. Good sir, I do in friendship counsel you
To leave this place.—(Act i. 2. 273, 274.)

Yet such is now the duke's condition,
That he misconstrues all that you have done.
The duke is humorous: what he is, indeed,
More suits you to conceive than I to speak of.

Orl. I thank you, sir: and, pray you, tell me this,—
Which of the two was daughter of the duke,
That here were at the wrestling?

Le Beau. Neither his daughter, if we judge by manners;
But yet, indeed, the lesser is his daughter:
Th' other is daughter to the banish'd duke,
And here detain'd by her usurping uncle,
To keep his daughter company; whose loves
Are dearer than the natural bond of sisters.
But I can tell you, that of late this duke
Hath ta'en displeasure 'gainst his gentle niece,
Grounded upon no other argument[3]
But that the people praise her for her virtues,
And pity her for her good father's sake;
And, on my life, his malice 'gainst the lady
Will suddenly break forth.—Sir, fare you well:
Hereafter, in a better world than this,
I shall desire more love and knowledge of you.

Orl. I rest much bounden to you: fare you well. [*Exit Le Beau.*
Thus must I from the smoke into the smother;
From tyrant duke unto a tyrant brother:—
But heavenly Rosalind! [*Exit.*

SCENE III. *A room in the palace.*

Enter CELIA *and* ROSALIND.

Cel. Why, cousin; why, Rosalind;—Cupid have mercy!—not a word?

Ros. Not one to throw at a dog.

Cel. No, thy words are too precious to be cast away upon curs; throw some of them at me; come, lame me with reasons.

Ros. Then there were two cousins laid up; when the one should be lam'd with reasons, and the other mad without any.

Cel. But is all this for your father?

Ros. No, some of it is for my child's father. O, how full of briers is this working-day world!

Cel. They are but burs, cousin, thrown upon thee in holiday foolery: if we walk not in the trodden paths, our very petticoats will catch them.

Ros. I could shake them off my coat: these burs are in my heart.

Cel. Hem them away.

Ros. I would try, if I could cry "hem," and have him.

---

[3] *Argument*, reason, occasion.

Cel. Come, come, wrestle with thy affections.

Ros. O, they take the part of a better wrestler than myself!

Cel. [O, a good wish upon you! you will try in time, in despite of a fall.]—But, turning these jests out of service, let us talk in good earnest: is it possible, on such a sudden, you should fall into so strong a liking with old Sir Roland's youngest son?

Ros. The duke my father lov'd his father dearly.

Cel. Doth it therefore ensue that you should love his son dearly? By this kind of chase, I should hate him, for my father hated his father dearly;[1] yet I hate not Orlando.

Ros. No, faith, hate him not, for my sake.

Cel. Why should I? doth he not deserve well?

Ros. Let me love him for that; and do you love him because I do.—Look, here comes the duke.

Cel. With his eyes full of anger.

Enter DUKE FREDERICK, *with Lords.*

Duke F. Mistress, dispatch you with your safest haste,
And get you from our court.

Ros. Me, uncle?

Duke F. You, cousin:[2]
Within these ten days if that thou be'st found
So near our public court as twenty miles,
Thou diest for it.

Ros. I do beseech your grace,
Let me the knowledge of my fault bear with me:
If with myself I hold intelligence,
Or have acquaintance with mine own desires;
If that I do not dream, or be not frantic,
As I do trust I am not,—then, dear uncle,
Never so much as in a thought unborn
Did I offend your highness.

Duke F. Thus do all traitors:
If their purgation did consist in words,
They are as innocent as grace itself:—
Let it suffice thee, that I trust thee not.

Ros. Yet your mistrust cannot make me a traitor:
Tell me whereon the likelihood depends.

Duke F. Thou art thy father's daughter; there's enough.

Ros. So was I when your highness took his dukedom;
So was I when your highness banish'd him:
Treason is not inherited, my lord;
Or, if we did derive it from our friends,
What's that to me? my father was no traitor:
Then, good my liege, mistake me not so much
To[3] think my poverty is treacherous.

Cel. Dear sovereign, hear me speak.

Duke F. Ay, Celia; we stay'd her for your sake,
Else had she with her father rang'd along.

Cel. I did not then entreat to have her stay;
It was your pleasure and your own remorse:[4]
I was too young that time to value her;
But now I know her: if she be a traitor,
Why, so am I; we still have slept together,
Rose at an instant, learn'd, play'd, eat together;
And wheresoe'er we went, like Juno's swans,
Still we went coupled and inseparable.

Duke F. She is too subtle for thee; and her smoothness,
Her very silence, and her patience,
Speak to the people, and they pity her.
Thou art a fool: she robs thee of thy name;
And thou wilt show more bright and seem more virtuous
When she is gone. Then open not thy lips:
Firm and irrevocable is my doom
Which I have pass'd upon her;—she is banish'd.

Cel. Pronounce that sentence, then, on me, my liege:
I cannot live out of her company.

Duke F. You are a fool.—You, niece, provide yourself:
If you outstay the time, upon mine honour,
And in the greatness of my word, you die.
[*Exeunt Duke Frederick and Lords.*

Cel. O my poor Rosalind! whither wilt thou go?
Wilt thou change fathers? I will give thee mine.
I charge thee, be not thou more griev'd than I am.

[1] *Dearly*, extremely.
[2] *Cousin*, here = niece.
[3] *To* = as to.
[4] *Remorse*, clemency.

Ros. I have more cause.
Cel. Thou hast not, cousin;
Prithee, be cheerful: know'st thou not, the duke
Hath banish'd me, his daughter?
Ros. That he hath not.
Cel. No, hath not? Rosalind lacks, then, the love
Which teacheth thee that thou and I am one:
Shall we be sunder'd? shall we part, sweet girl?
No: let my father seek another heir.
Therefore devise with me how we may fly,
Whither to go, and what to bear with us:
And do not seek to take your change upon you,
To bear your griefs yourself, and leave me out;
For, by this heaven, now at our sorrows pale,
Say what thou canst, I 'll go along with thee.
Ros. Why, whither shall we go?
Cel. To seek my uncle in the forest of Arden.
Ros. Alas, what danger will it be to us,
Maids as we are, to travel forth so far!
Beauty provoketh thieves sooner than gold.
Cel. I 'll put myself in poor and mean attire,
And with a kind of umber smirch my face;
The like do you: so shall we pass along,
And never stir assailants.
Ros. Were 't not better,
Because that I am more than common tall,
That I did suit me all points like a man?
A gallant curtle-axe upon my thigh,
A boar-spear in my hand; and—in my heart
Lie there what hidden woman's fear there will—
We 'll have a swashing and a martial outside;
As many other mannish cowards have
That do outface it with their semblances.[1]
Cel. What shall I call thee when thou art a man?
Ros. I 'll have no worse a name than Jove's own page;
And therefore look you call me Ganymede.
But what will you be call'd?
Cel. Something that hath a reference to my state;
No longer Celia, but Aliena.
Ros. But, cousin, what if we assay'd to steal
The clownish fool out of your father's court?
Would he not be a comfort to our travel?
Cel. He 'll go along o'er the wide world with me;
Leave me alone to woo him. Let 's away,
And get our jewels and our wealth together;
Devise the fittest time and safest way
To hide us from pursuit that will be made
After my flight. Now go we in content,
To liberty, and not to banishment. [*Exeunt.*

ACT II.

SCENE I. *The Forest of Arden.*

Enter DUKE SENIOR, AMIENS, *and other Lords, in the dress of foresters.*

Duke S. Now, my co-mates and brothers in exile,
Hath not old custom made this life more sweet
Than that of painted pomp? Are not these woods
More free from peril than the envious court?
Here feel we but[2] the penalty of Adam,
The seasons' difference; as, the icy fang
And churlish chiding of the winter's wind,
Which, when it bites and blows upon my body,
Even till I shrink with cold, I smile, and say,
This is no flattery; these are counsellors
That feelingly persuade me what I am.
Sweet are the uses of adversity;
Which, like the toad, ugly and venomous,
Wears yet a precious jewel in his head:
And this our life, exempt[3] from public haunt,
Finds tongues in trees, books in the running brooks,
Sermons in stones, and good in every thing:
I would not change it.
Ami. Happy is your grace,
That can translate the stubbornness of fortune
Into so quiet and so sweet a style.
Duke S. Come, shall we go and kill us venison?
And yet it irks me, the poor dappled fools,

[1] *Semblances, i.e.* their appearance of being brave.
[2] *But*, the Folios read "not."
[3] *Exempt* = far from.

Being native burghers of this desert city,
Should, in their own confines with forked heads,
Have their round haunches gor'd.
First Lord. Indeed, my lord,
The melancholy Jaques grieves at that;
And, in that kind, swears you do more usurp
Than doth your brother that hath banish'd you.
To-day my Lord of Amiens and myself
Did steal behind him, as he lay along
Under an oak, whose antique root peeps out
Upon the brook that brawls along this wood:
To the which place a poor sequester'd stag,
That from the hunter's aim had ta'en a hurt,
Did come to languish; and, indeed, my lord,
The wretched animal heav'd forth such groans,
That their discharge did stretch his leathern coat
Almost to bursting; and the big round tears
Cours'd one another down his innocent nose
In piteous chase: and thus the hairy fool,
Much marked of the melancholy Jaques,
Stood on th' extremest verge of the swift brook,
Augmenting it with tears.
Duke S. But what said Jaques?
Did he not moralize[1] this spectacle?
First Lord. O, yes, into a thousand similes.
First, for his weeping in the needless stream;
"Poor deer," quoth he, "thou mak'st a testament
As worldlings do, giving thy sum of more
To that which had too much:" then, being alone,
Left and abandon'd of his velvet friends;
"'T is right," quoth he; "thus misery doth part
The flux of company:" anon, a careless herd,
Full of the pasture, jumps along by him,
And never stays to greet him; "Ay," quoth Jaques,
"Sweep on, you fat and greasy citizens;
'T is just the fashion: wherefore do you look
Upon that poor and broken bankrupt there?"
Thus most invectively he pierceth through
The body of the country, city, court,
Yea, and of this our life: swearing that we
Are mere usurpers, tyrants, and what 's worse,
To fright the animals, and to kill them up,[2]
In their assign'd and native dwelling-place.
Duke S. And did you leave him in this contemplation?

Sec. Lord. We did, my lord, weeping and commenting
Upon the sobbing deer.
Duke S. Show me the place:
I love to cope[3] him in these sullen fits,
For then he 's full of matter.
First Lord. I 'll bring you to him straight.
[*Exeunt.*

Scene II. *A room in the palace.*

Enter Duke Frederick, *Lords, and Attendants.*

Duke F. Can it be possible that no man saw them?
It cannot be: some villains of my court
Are of consent and sufferance in this.
First Lord. I cannot hear of any that did see her.
The ladies, her attendants of her chamber,
Saw her a-bed; and, in the morning early,
They found the bed untreasur'd of their mistress.
Sec. Lord. My lord, the roynish[4] clown, at whom so oft
Your grace was wont to laugh, is also missing.
Hesperia, the princess' gentlewoman,
Confesses that she secretly o'erheard
Your daughter and her cousin much commend
The parts and graces of the wrestler[5]
That did but lately foil the sinewy Charles;
And she believes, wherever they are gone,
That youth is surely in their company.
Duke F. Send to his brother's; fetch that gallant hither:
If he be absent, bring his brother to me;
I 'll make him find him: do this suddenly;
And let not search and inquisition quail
To bring again these foolish runaways.
[*Exeunt.*

Scene III. *Before Oliver's house.*

Enter Orlando *and* Adam, *meeting.*

Orl. Who 's there?
Adam. What, my young master?—O my gentle master!

[1] *Moralize*, draw a meaning from, interpret.
[2] *Up*, i.e. completely.
[3] *Cope*, encounter.
[4] *Roynish*, a term of contempt = mangy.
[5] *Wrestler*, pronounced as a trisyllable.

O my sweet master! O you memory
Of old Sir Roland! why, what make you here?
Why are you virtuous? why do people love you?
And wherefore are you gentle, strong, and valiant?

Adam. O unhappy youth,
Come not within these doors! within this roof
The enemy of all your graces lives.—(Act ii. 3. 16-18.)

Why would you be so fond to overcome
The bonny priser of the humorous duke?
Your praise is come too swiftly home before you.
Know you not, master, to some kind of men
Their graces serve them but as enemies?
No more do yours: your virtues, gentle master,
Are sanctified and holy traitors to you.
O, what a world is this, when what is comely
Envenoms him that bears it![1]

Orl. Why, what's the matter?

Adam. O unhappy youth,
Come not within these doors! within this roof
The enemy of all your graces lives:
Your brother—(no, no brother; yet the son—
Yet not the son—I will not call him son
Of him I was about to call his father)—
Hath heard your praises; and this night he means
To burn the lodging where you use to lie,
And you within it: if he fail of that,
He will have other means to cut you off:
I overheard him and his practices.
This is no place; this house is but a butchery:
Abhor it, fear it, do not enter it.

Orl. Why, whither, Adam, wouldst thou have me go?

Adam. No matter whither, so you come not here.

Orl. What, wouldst thou have me go and beg my food?
Or with a base and boisterous sword enforce
A thievish living on the common road?
This I must do, or know not what to do:
Yet this I will not do, do how I can;
I rather will subject me to the malice
Of a diverted[2] blood and bloody brother.

Adam. But do not so. I have five hundred crowns,
The thrifty hire I sav'd under your father,
Which I did store, to be my foster-nurse

[1] An allusion to the poisoned shirt of Nessus by which Hercules was killed.

[2] *Diverted*, i.e. unnatural, that has been turned from its proper course.

When service should in my old limbs lie lame,
And unregarded age in corners thrown:
Take that; and He that doth the ravens feed,
Yea, providently caters for the sparrow,
Be comfort to my age! Here is the gold;
All this I give you. Let me be your servant:
Though I look old, yet I am strong and lusty;
For in my youth I never did apply
Hot and rebellious liquors in my blood;
Nor did not with unbashful forehead woo
The means of weakness and debility;
Therefore my age is as a lusty winter,
Frosty, but kindly: let me go with you;
I'll do the service of a younger man
In all your business and necessities.

Orl. O good old man, how well in thee appears
The constant service of the antique world,
When service swet for duty, not for meed!
Thou art not for the fashion of these times,
Where none will sweat but for promotion;
And having that, do choke their service up
Even with the having: 'tis not so with thee.
But, poor old man, thou prun'st a rotten tree,
That cannot so much as a blossom yield
In lieu of[1] all thy pains and husbandry.
But come thy ways; we'll go along together;
And ere we have thy youthful wages spent,
We'll light upon some settled low content.

Adam. Master, go on, and I will follow thee,
To the last gasp, with truth and loyalty.—

[*Exit Orlando. Adam goes into the house, and immediately returns with pouch, staff, and hat.*

From seventeen years till now almost fourscore
Here lived I, but now live here no more.
At seventeen years many their fortunes seek;
But at fourscore it is too late a week:
Yet fortune cannot recompense me better
Than to die well, and not my master's debtor.

[*Exit.*

SCENE IV. *The Forest of Arden.*

Enter ROSALIND *in boy's clothes, as Ganymede,* CELIA *drest like a shepherdess, and* TOUCHSTONE.

Ros. O Jupiter, how weary are my spirits!

Touch. I care not for my spirits, if my legs were not weary.

Ros. I could find in my heart to disgrace my man's apparel, and to cry like a woman; but I must comfort the weaker vessel, as doublet and hose ought to show itself courageous to petticoat: therefore, courage, good Aliena.

Cel. I pray you, bear with me; I cannot go no further.

Touch. For my part, I had rather bear with you than bear you: yet I should bear no cross,[2] if I did bear you; for I think you have no money in your purse.

Ros. Well, this is the forest of Arden.

Touch. Ay, now am I in Arden; the more fool I; when I was at home, I was in a better place: but travellers must be content.

Ros. Ay, be so, good Touchstone.—Look you, who comes here;
A young man and an old in solemn talk.

Enter CORIN *and* SILVIUS.

Cor. That is the way to make her scorn you still.

Sil. O Corin, that thou knew'st how I do love her!

Cor. I partly guess; for I have lov'd ere now.

Sil. No, Corin, being old, thou canst not guess;
Though in thy youth thou wast as true a lover
As ever sigh'd upon a midnight pillow
But if thy love were ever like to mine,—
As sure I think did never man love so,—
How many actions most ridiculous
Hast thou been drawn to by thy fantasy?[3]

Cor. Into a thousand that I have forgotten.

Sil. O, thou didst then ne'er love so heartily:
If thou remember'st not the slightest folly
That ever love did make thee run into,
Thou hast not lov'd:
Or if thou hast not sat as I do now,
Wearing thy hearer in thy mistress' praise,
Thou hast not lov'd:
Or if thou hast not broke from company
Abruptly, as my passion now makes me,
Thou hast not lov'd.—O Phebe, Phebe, Phebe!

[*Exit.*

[1] *In lieu of* = in reward of.

[2] See note 45.

[3] *Fantasy,* fancy = love.

Ros. Alas, poor shepherd! searching of thy wound,
I have by hard adventure found mine own.

Touch. And I mine. I remember, when I was in love I broke my sword upon a stone, and bid him take that for coming a-night to Jane Smile: and I remember the kissing of her batlet, and the cow's dugs that her pretty chapp'd hands had milk'd: [and I remember the wooing of a peascod instead of her; from whom I took two cods, and, giving her them again, said with weeping tears,[1] "Wear these for my sake."] We that are true lovers run into strange capers; but as all is mortal in nature, so is all nature in love mortal in folly.

Ros. Thou speakest wiser than thou art ware of.

Touch. Nay, I shall ne'er be ware of mine own wit till I break my shins against it.

Ros. Jove, Jove! this shepherd's passion
Is much upon my fashion.

Touch. And mine; but it grows something stale with me.

Cel. I pray you, one of you question yond man,
If he for gold will give us any food:
I faint almost to death.

Touch. Holla, you clown!

Ros. Peace, fool: he's not thy kinsman.

Cor. Who calls?

Touch. Your betters, sir.

Cor. Else are they very wretched.

Ros. Peace, I say. [*Touchstone retires to back of stage with Celia*]—Good even to you, friend.

Cor. And to you, gentle sir, and to you all.

Ros. I prithee, shepherd, if that love or gold
Can in this desert place buy entertainment,
Bring us where we may rest ourselves and feed:
Here's a young maid with travel much oppress'd,
And faints for succour.

Cor. Fair sir, I pity her,
And wish, for her sake more than for mine own,
My fortunes were more able to relieve her;
But I am shepherd to another man,
And do not shear the fleeces that I graze:
My master is of churlish disposition,
And little recks to find the way to heaven
By doing deeds of hospitality:
Besides, his cote,[2] his flocks, and bounds of feed,
Are now on sale; and at our sheepcote now,
By reason of his absence, there is nothing
That you will feed on; but what is, come see,
And in my voice most welcome shall you be.

Ros. What is he that shall buy his flock and pasture?

Cor. That young swain that you saw here but erewhile,
That little cares for buying any thing.

Ros. I pray thee, if it stand with[3] honesty,
Buy thou the cottage, pasture, and the flock,
And thou shalt have to pay for it of us.

Cel. [*Coming forward*] And we will mend thy wages. I like this place,
And willingly could waste my time in it.

Cor. Assuredly the thing is to be sold:
Go with me: if you like, upon report,
The soil, the profit, and this kind of life,
I will your very faithful feeder be,
And buy it with your gold right suddenly.

[*Exeunt Corin, followed by Rosalind and Touchstone supporting Celia.*

Scene V. *Another part of the forest.*

Enter Amiens, Jaques, *and others.*

Song.

Ami.
Under the greenwood tree
Who loves to lie with me,
And turn his merry note
Unto the sweet bird's throat,
Come hither, come hither, come hither:
Here shall he see
No enemy
But winter and rough weather.

Jaq. More, more, I prithee, more.

Ami. It will make you melancholy, Monsieur Jaques.

Jaq. I thank it. More, I prithee, more. I can suck melancholy out of a song, as a weasel sucks eggs. More, I prithee, more.

Ami. My voice is ragged:[4] I know I cannot please you.

Jaq. I do not desire you to please me; I

---

[1] *Weeping tears*, an intentionally affected phrase.

[2] *Cote*, hut.

[3] *Stand with* = be not inconsistent with.

[4] *Ragged*, rough.

do desire you to sing. Come, more; another stanza:—call you 'em stanzas?

Ami. What you will, Monsieur Jaques.

Jaq. Nay, I care not for their names; they owe me nothing. Will you sing?

Ami. More at your request than to please myself.

Jaq. Well, then, if ever I thank any man, I'll thank you: but that they call compliment is like the encounter of two dog-apes; and when a man thanks me heartily, methinks I have given him a penny, and he renders me the beggarly thanks. Come, sing; and you that will not, hold your tongues.

Ami. Under the greenwood tree
Who loves to lie with me,
And turn his merry note
Unto the sweet bird's throat,
Come hither, come hither, come hither.
—(Act ii. 5. 1-5.)

Ami. Well, I'll end the song.—Sirs, cover the while; the duke will drink under this tree.—He hath been all this day to look you.

Jaq. And I have been all this day to avoid him. He is too disputable[1] for my company: I think of as many matters as he; but I give heaven thanks, and make no boast of them. Come, warble, come.

Song.

Who doth ambition shun,
[*All together here.*
And loves to live i' the sun,
Seeking the food he eats,
And pleas'd with what he gets,
Come hither, come hither, come hither:
Here shall he see
No enemy
But winter and rough weather.

Jaq. [I'll give you a verse to this note, that I made yesterday in despite of my invention.

Ami. And I'll sing it.

Jaq. Thus it goes;

If it do come to pass
That any man turn ass,
Leaving his wealth and ease
A stubborn will to please,
Ducdame, ducdame, ducdame:
Here shall he see
Gross fools as he,
An if he will come to me.

[1] *Disputable*, fond of disputing.

Ami. What's that "ducdame"?

Jaq. 'T is a Greek invocation, to call fools into a circle.] I'll go sleep, if I can; if I cannot, I'll rail against all the first-born of Egypt.

Adam. Dear master, I can go no further: O, I die for food! Here lie I down, and measure out my grave. Farewell, kind master.—(Act ii. 6. 1-3.)

Ami. And I'll go seek the duke: his banquet is prepar'd. [*Exeunt severally.*

SCENE VI. *Another part of the forest.*

Enter ORLANDO *and* ADAM.

Adam. Dear master, I can go no further: O, I die for food! Here lie I down, and measure out my grave. Farewell, kind master.

Orl. Why, how now, Adam! no greater heart in thee? Live a little; comfort a little; cheer thyself a little. If this uncouth forest yield any thing savage, I will either be food for it, or bring it for food to thee. Thy conceit[1] is nearer death than thy powers. For my sake be comfortable; hold death awhile at the arm's end: I will be here with thee presently; and if I bring thee not something to eat, I will give thee leave to die: but if thou diest before I come, thou art a mocker of my labour. Well said! thou look'st cheerly; and I'll be with thee quickly.—Yet thou liest in the bleak air: come, I will bear thee to some shelter; and thou shalt not die for lack of a dinner, if there live any thing in this desert. Cheerly, good Adam! [*Exeunt.*

SCENE VII. *Another part of the forest (the same as in* Scene V.). *A table set out.*

Enter DUKE SENIOR, AMIENS, *and others.*

Duke S. I think he be transform'd into a beast;
For I can no where find him like a man.

First Lord. My lord, he is but even now gone hence:
Here was he merry, hearing of a song.

Duke S. If he, compact of jars, grow musical,
We shall have shortly discord in the spheres.[2]
Go, seek him: tell him I would speak with him.

First Lord. He saves my labour by his own approach.

Enter JAQUES.

Duke S. Why, how now, monsieur! what a life is this,
That your poor friends must woo your company!
What, you look merrily!

Jaq. A fool, a fool!—I met a fool i' the forest,
A motley fool;—a miserable world!—
As I do live by food, I met a fool;
Who laid him down and bask'd him in the sun,
And rail'd on Lady Fortune in good terms,
In good set terms,—and yet a motley fool.
"Good morrow, fool," quoth I. "No, sir," quoth he,

[1] *Conceit*, fancy.
[2] *Discord in the spheres*, referring to the old idea of the music of the spheres.

"Call me not fool till heaven hath sent me fortune:"
And then he drew a dial from his poke,[1]
And, looking on it with lack-lustre eye,
Says very wisely, "It is ten o'clock:
Thus we may see," quoth he, "how the world wags:
'T is but an hour ago since it was nine;
And after one hour more 't will be eleven;
And so, from hour to hour, we ripe and ripe,
And then, from hour to hour, we rot and rot;
And thereby hangs a tale." When I did hear
The motley fool thus moral[2] on the time,
My lungs began to crow like chanticleer,
That fools should be so deep-contemplative;
And I did laugh sans intermission
An hour by his dial.—O noble fool!
A worthy fool!—Motley 's the only wear.

Duke S. What fool is this?

Jaq. O worthy fool!—One that hath been a courtier;
And says, if ladies be but young and fair,
They have the gift to know 't: and in his brain,—
Which is as dry as the remainder[3] biscuit
After a voyage,—he hath strange places cramm'd
With observation, the which he vents
In mangled forms.—O that I were a fool!
I am ambitious for a motley coat.

Duke S. Thou shalt have one.

Jaq. It is my only suit;
Provided that you weed your better judgments
Of all opinion that grows rank in them
That I am wise. I must have liberty
Withal, as large a charter as the wind,
To blow on whom I please; for so fools have:
And they that are most galled with my folly,
They most must laugh. And why, sir, must they so?
The "why" is plain as way to parish church:
He that a fool doth very wisely hit
Doth very foolishly, although he smart,
Not to seem senseless of the bob: if not,
The wise man's folly is anatomiz'd
Even by the squandering[4] glances of the fool.
Invest me in my motley; give me leave
To speak my mind, and I will through and through
Cleanse the foul body of th' infected world,
If they will patiently receive my medicine.

Duke S. Fie on thee! I can tell what thou wouldst do.

Jaq. What, for a counter, would I do but good?

Duke S. Most mischievous foul sin, in chiding sin:
For thou thyself hast been a libertine,
As sensual as the brutish sting[5] itself;
And all th' embossed sores and headed evils,
That thou with license of free foot hast caught,
Wouldst thou disgorge into the general world.

Jaq. Why, who cries out on pride,
That can therein tax any private party?
Doth it not flow as hugely as the sea,
Till that the wearer's very means do ebb?
What woman in the city do I name,
When that I say, the city-woman bears
The cost of princes on unworthy shoulders?
Who can come in, and say that I mean her,
When such a one as she, such is her neighbour?
Or what is he of basest function,
That says his bravery[6] is not on my cost—
Thinking that I mean him—but therein suits
His folly to the mettle of my speech?
There then; how then? what then? Let me see wherein
My tongue hath wrong'd him: if it do him right,
Then he hath wrong'd himself; if he be free,
Why, then my taxing like a wild-goose flies,
Unclaim'd of any man.—But who comes here?

Enter ORLANDO *with his sword drawn.*

Orl. Forbear, and eat no more!

Jaq. Why, I have eat none yet.

Orl. Nor shalt not, till necessity be serv'd.

Jaq. Of what kind should this cock come of?

Duke S. Art thou thus bolden'd, man, by thy distress,
Or else a rude despiser of good manners,
That in civility thou seem'st so empty?

---

[1] *Poke*, pocket. [2] *Moral*, i.e. moralize.
[3] *Remainder*, used adjectively = that is, left over.
[4] *Squandering*, aimless.
[5] *Sting*, instinct. [6] *Bravery*, finery.

Orl. You touch'd my vein at first: the thorny point
Of bare distress hath ta'en from me the show
Of smooth civility: yet am I inland bred,
And know some nurture. But forbear, I say:
He dies that touches any of this fruit
Till I and my affairs are answered.
Jaq. An you will not be answered with reason, I must die.
Duke S. What would you have? Your gentleness shall force,
More than your force move us to gentleness.
Orl. I almost die for food; and let me have it.
Duke S. Sit down and feed, and welcome to our table.
Orl. Speak you so gently? Pardon me, I pray you:
I thought that all things had been savage here;
And therefore put I on the countenance
Of stern commandment. But whate'er you are,
That in this desert inaccessible,
Under the shade of melancholy boughs,
Lose and neglect the creeping hours of time;
If ever you have look'd on better days,
If ever been where bells have knoll'd to church,
If ever sat at any good man's feast,
If ever from your eyelids wip'd a tear,
And know what 't is to pity and be pitied,—
Let gentleness my strong enforcement be:
In the which hope I blush, and hide my sword.
Duke S. True is it that we have seen better days,
And have with holy bell been knoll'd to church,
And sat at good men's feasts, and wip'd our eyes
Of drops that sacred pity hath engender'd:
And therefore sit you down in gentleness,
And take upon command[1] what help we have,
That to your wanting may be minister'd.
Orl. Then but forbear your food a little while,
Whiles, like a doe, I go to find my fawn,
And give it food. There is an old poor man,
Who after me hath many a weary step
Limp'd in pure love: till he be first suffic'd,—
Oppress'd with two weak evils, age and hunger,—
I will not touch a bit.
Duke S. Go find him out,
And we will nothing waste till you return.
Orl. I thank you; and be bless'd for your good comfort! [*Exit.*
Duke S. Thou seest we are not all alone unhappy:
This wide and universal theatre
Presents more woeful pageants than the scene
Wherein we play in.
Jaq. All the world 's a stage,
And all the men and women merely players:
They have their exits and their entrances;
And one man in his time plays many parts,
His acts being seven ages. At first the infant,
Mewling and puking in the nurse's arms.
And then the whining schoolboy, with his satchel
And shining morning face, creeping like snail
Unwillingly to school. And then the lover,
Sighing like furnace, with a woeful ballad
Made to his mistress' eyebrow. Then a soldier,
Full of strange oaths, and bearded like the pard,
Jealous in honour, sudden and quick in quarrel,
Seeking the bubble reputation
Even in the cannon's mouth. And then the justice,
In fair round belly with good capon lin'd,
With eyes severe and beard of formal cut,
Full of wise saws and modern[2] instances;
And so he plays his part. The sixth age shifts
Into the lean and slipper'd pantaloon,
With spectacles on nose and pouch on side;
His youthful hose, well sav'd, a world too wide
For his shrunk shank; and his big manly voice,
Turning again toward childish treble, pipes
And whistles in his[3] sound. Last scene of all,
That ends this strange eventful history,
Is second childishness and mere oblivion,
Sans teeth, sans eyes, sans taste, sans everything.

Re-enter ORLANDO *with* ADAM.

Duke S. Welcome. Set down your venerable burden,
And let him feed.
Orl. I thank you most for him.
Adam. So had you need—
I scarce can speak to thank you for myself.

[1] *Upon command* = as you may be pleased to command.

[2] *Modern*, hackneyed.

[3] *His* = Its.

Duke S. Welcome; fall to: I will not trouble you
As yet, to question you about your fortunes.—
Give us some music; and, good cousin, sing.

Song.

Ami. Blow, blow, thou winter wind,
Thou art not so unkind
As man's ingratitude;
Thy tooth is not so keen,
Because thou art not seen,
Although thy breath be rude.
Heigh-ho! sing, heigh-ho! unto the green holly:
Most friendship is feigning, most loving mere folly:
Then, heigh-ho, the holly!
This life is most jolly.

Freeze, freeze, thou bitter sky,
That dost not bite so nigh
As benefits forgot:
Though thou the waters warp,
Thy sting is not so sharp
As friend remember'd not.
Heigh-ho! sing, heigh-ho! &c.

Duke S. If that you were the good Sir Roland's son,—
As you have whisper'd faithfully you were,
And as mine eye doth his effigies[1] witness
Most truly limn'd and living in your face,—
Be truly welcome hither: I'm the duke,
That lov'd your father: the residue of your fortune,
Go to my cave and tell me.—Good old man,
Thou art right welcome as thy master is.—
Support him by the arm.—Give me your hand,
And let me all your fortunes understand.
[*Exeunt*

ACT III.

Scene I. *A room in the palace.*

Enter Duke Frederick, Oliver, *Lords, and Attendants.*

Duke F. Not see him since? Sir, sir, that cannot be:
But were I not the better part made mercy,
I should not seek an absent argument
Of my revenge, thou present. But look to it:
Find out thy brother, wheresoe'er he is;
Seek him with candle; bring him dead or living
Within this twelvemonth, or turn thou no more
To seek a living in our territory.
Thy lands, and all things that thou dost call thine
Worth seizure, do we seize into our hands,
Till thou canst quit thee by thy brother's mouth
Of what we think against thee.

Oli. O, that your highness knew my heart in this!
I never lov'd my brother in my life.

Duke F. More villain thou.—Well, push him out of doors;
And let my officers of such a nature
Make an extent upon his house and lands:
Do this expediently,[2] and turn him going.
[*Exeunt.*

[1] *Effigies*, representation or likeness.
[2] *Expediently*, at once.

Scene II. *The Forest of Arden.*

Enter Orlando, *in a forester's dress, with a paper, which he hangs on a tree.*

Orl. Hang there, my verse, in witness of my love:
And thou, thrice-crowned queen of night, survey
With thy chaste eye, from thy pale sphere above,
Thy huntress' name, that my full life doth sway.
O Rosalind! these trees shall be my books,
And in their barks my thoughts I'll character;[3]
That every eye, which in this forest looks,
Shall see thy virtue witness'd every where.
Run, run, Orlando; carve on every tree
The fair, the chaste, and unexpressive she.
[*Exit.*

Enter Corin *and* Touchstone.

Cor. And how like you this shepherd's life, Master Touchstone?

Touch. Truly, shepherd, in respect of itself,

[3] *Character*, engrave.

it is a good life; but in respect that it is a shepherd's life, it is naught. In respect that it is solitary, I like it very well; but in respect that it is private, it is a very vile life. Now, in respect it is in the fields, it pleaseth me well; but in respect it is not in the court, it is tedious. As it is a spare life, look you, it fits my humour well; but as there is no more plenty in it, it goes much against my stomach. Hast any philosophy in thee, shepherd?

Cor. No more but that I know, the more one sickens, the worse at ease he is; and that he that wants money, means, and content, is without three good friends; that the property of rain is to wet, and fire to burn; that good pasture makes fat sheep; and that a great

Touch. Truly, thou art damn'd; like an ill-roasted egg, all on one side.—(Act iii. 2. 38, 39.)

cause of the night is lack of the sun; that he that hath learned no wit by nature nor art may complain of good breeding, or comes of a very dull kindred.

Touch. Such a one is a natural philosopher. Wast ever in court, shepherd?

Cor. No, truly.

Touch. Then thou art damn'd.

Cor. Nay, I hope,—

Touch. Truly, thou art damn'd; like an ill-roasted egg, all on one side.

Cor. For not being at court? Your reason.

Touch. Why, if thou never wast at court, thou never saw'st good manners; if thou never saw'st good manners, then thy manners must be wicked; and wickedness is sin, and sin is damnation. Thou art in a parlous[1] state, shepherd.

Cor. Not a whit, Master Touchstone: those that are good manners at the court, are as ridiculous in the country as the behaviour of the country is most mockable at the court. [You told me you salute not at the court, but you kiss your hands: that courtesy would be uncleanly, if courtiers were shepherds.

Touch. Instance, briefly; come, instance.

Cor. Why, we are still handling our ewes; and their fells,[2] you know, are greasy.

Touch. Why, do not your courtier's hands sweat? and is not the grease of a mutton as

[1] *Parlous*, dangerous. [2] *Fells*, skins

wholesome as the sweat of a man? Shallow, shallow. A better instance, I say; come.

Cor. Besides, our hands are hard.

Touch. Your lips will feel them the sooner. Shallow again. A more sounder instance, come.

Cor. And they are often tarr'd over with the surgery of our sheep; and would you have us kiss tar? The courtier's hands are perfum'd with civet.

Touch. Most shallow man! thou worms-meat, in respect of a good piece of flesh, indeed!—Learn of the wise, and perpend:[1] civet is of a baser birth than tar,—the very uncleanly flux of a cat. Mend the instance, shepherd.

Cor. You have too courtly a wit for me: I 'll rest.

Touch. Wilt thou rest damn'd? God help thee, shallow man! God make incision in thee! thou art raw.

Cor. Sir,] I am a true labourer: I earn that I eat, get that I wear; owe no man hate, envy no man's happiness; glad of other men's good, content with my harm; and the greatest of my pride is, to see my ewes graze and my lambs suck.

Touch. That is another simple sin in you; to [bring the ewes and the rams together, and to offer to get your living by the copulation of cattle; to be bawd to a bell-wether; and to betray a she-lamb of a twelvemonth to a crooked-pated, old, cuckoldy ram, out of all reasonable match.] If thou beest not damn'd for this, the devil himself will have no shepherds; I cannot see else how thou shouldst scape.

Cor. Here comes young Master Ganymede, my new mistress's brother.

Enter Rosalind; *she takes Orlando's paper from the tree: reading.*

Ros. "From the east to western Ind
No jewel is like Rosalind.
Her worth, being mounted on the wind,
Through all the world bears Rosalind.
All the pictures fairest lin'd
Are but black to Rosalind.
Let no face be kept in mind
But the fair of Rosalind."

Touch. I 'll rhyme you so eight years together, dinners and suppers and sleeping-hours excepted: it is the right butter-women's rank to market.

Ros. Out, fool!

Touch. For a taste;

If a hart do lack a hind,
Let him seek out Rosalind.
If the cat will after kind,
So be sure will Rosalind.
[Winter garments must be lin'd,
So must slender Rosalind.]
They that reap must sheaf[2] and bind;
Then to cart with Rosalind.
Sweetest nut hath sourest rind,
Such a nut is Rosalind.
[He that sweetest rose will find,
Must find love's prick and Rosalind.]

This is the very false gallop of verses: why do you infect yourself with them?

Ros. Peace, you dull fool! I found them on a tree.

Touch. Truly, the tree yields bad fruit.

[*Ros.* I 'll graff it with you, and then I shall graff it with a medlar: then it will be the earliest fruit i' the country; for you 'll be rotten ere you be half ripe, and that 's the right virtue of the medlar.

Touch. You have said; but whether wisely or no, let the forest judge.]

Ros. Peace!
Here comes my sister, reading: stand aside.
[*They retire.*

Enter Celia, *reading a paper.*

Cel. "Why should this a desert be?
For it is unpeopled? No;
Tongues I 'll hang on every tree,
That shall civil sayings show:
Some, how brief the life of man
Runs his erring[3] pilgrimage,
That the stretching of a span
Buckles in his sum of age;
Some, of violated vows
'Twixt the souls of friend and friend:
But upon the fairest boughs,
Or at every sentence' end,
Will I Rosalinda write;
Teaching all that read to know
The quintessence of every sprite
Heaven would in little show.

[1] *Perpend*, ponder.

[2] *Sheaf* = make into sheaves.

[3] *Erring*, in its literal sense, wandering.

Therefore Heaven Nature charg'd
That one body should be fill'd
With all graces wide-enlarg'd:
Nature presently distill'd
Helen's cheek, but not her heart;
Cleopatra's majesty;
Atalanta's better part;
Sad Lucretia's modesty.
Thus Rosalind of many parts
By heavenly synod was devis'd;
Of many faces, eyes, and hearts,
To have the touches dearest priz'd.
Heaven would that she these gifts should have,
And I to live and die her slave."

Ros. O most gentle pulpiter!—what tedious homily of love have you wearied your parishioners withal, and never cried, "Have patience, good people!"

Cel. How now! [*To Touchstone and Corin*] back, friends:—shepherd, go off a little:—go with him, sirrah.

Touch. Come, shepherd, let us make an honourable retreat; though not with bag and baggage, yet with scrip and scrippage.

[*Exeunt Corin and Touchstone.*

Cel. Didst thou hear these verses?

Ros. O, yes, I heard them all, and more too; for some of them had in them more feet than the verses would bear.

Cel. That 's no matter: the feet might bear the verses.

Ros. Ay, but the feet were lame, and could not bear themselves without the verse, and therefore stood lamely in the verse.

Cel. But didst thou hear without wondering how thy name should be hang'd and carved upon these trees?

Ros. I was seven of the nine days out of the wonder before you came; for look here what I found on a palm-tree:—[I was never so be-rhym'd since Pythagoras' time, that I was an Irish rat, which I can hardly remember.]

Cel. Trow you who hath done this?

Ros. Is it a man?

Cel. And a chain, that you once wore, about his neck. Change you colour?

Ros. I prithee, who?

Cel. O Lord, Lord! it is a hard matter for friends to meet; but mountains may be remov'd with earthquakes, and so encounter.

Ros. Nay, but who is it?

Cel. Is it possible?

Ros. Nay, I prithee now with most petitionary vehemence, tell me who it is.

Cel. O wonderful, wonderful, and most wonderful wonderful! and yet again wonderful, and after that, out of all hooping!

Ros. Good my complexion! dost thou think, though I am caparison'd like a man, I have a doublet and hose in my disposition? One inch of delay more is a South-sea of discovery; I prithee, tell me who is it quickly, and speak apace. [I would thou couldst stammer, that thou mightst pour this conceal'd man out of thy mouth, as wine comes out of a narrow-mouth'd bottle,—either too much at once, or none at all. I prithee, take the cork out of thy mouth, that I may drink thy tidings.

Cel. So you may put a man in your belly.

Ros.] Is he of God's making? What manner of man? Is his head worth a hat, or his chin worth a beard?

Cel. Nay, he hath but a little beard.

Ros. Why, God will send more, if the man will be thankful; let me stay the growth of his beard, if thou delay me not the knowledge of his chin.

Cel. It is young Orlando, that tripp'd up the wrestler's heels and your heart both in an instant.

Ros. Nay, but the devil take mocking: speak, sad brow and true maid.

Cel. I' faith, coz, 't is he.

Ros. Orlando?

Cel. Orlando.

Ros. Alas the day! what shall I do with my doublet and hose?—What did he when thou saw'st him? What said he? How look'd he? Wherein[1] went he? What makes he here? Did he ask for me? Where remains he? How parted he with thee? and when shalt thou see him again? Answer me in one word.

Cel. You must borrow me Gargantua's mouth first: 't is a word too great for any mouth of this age's size. To say ay and no to these particulars is more than to answer in a catechism.

Ros. But doth he know that I am in this

[1] *Wherein*, *i.e.* in what dress.

forest, and in man's apparel? Looks he as freshly as he did the day he wrestled?

Cel. It is as easy to count atomies as to resolve the propositions of a lover:—but take a taste of my finding him, and relish it with good observance. I found him under a tree, like a dropp'd acorn.

Ros. It may well be called Jove's tree, when it drops forth such fruit.

[*Cel.* Give me audience, good madam.

Ros. Proceed.]

Cel. There lay he, stretch'd along, like a wounded knight.

Ros. Though it be pity to see such a sight, it well becomes the ground.

Cel. Cry holla! to thy tongue, I prithee; it curvets unseasonably. He was furnish'd like a hunter.

Jaq. God b'wi' you! let 's meet as little as we can.
Orl. I do desire we may be better strangers.—(Act iii. 2. 273, 274.)

Ros. O, ominous! he comes to kill my heart.

Cel. I would sing my song without a burden: thou bring'st me out of tune.

Ros. Do you not know I am a woman? when I think, I must speak. Sweet, say on.

Cel. You bring me out.—Soft! comes he not here?

Ros. 'T is he: slink by, and note him.

[*Celia and Rosalind retire.*

Enter Orlando *and* Jaques.

Jaq. I thank you for your company; but, good faith,
I had as lief have been myself alone.

Orl. And so had I; but yet, for fashion's sake,
I thank you too for your society.

Jaq. God b'wi' you! let's meet as little as we can.

Orl. I do desire we may be better strangers.

Jaq. I pray you, mar no more trees with writing love-songs in their barks.

Orl. I pray you, mar no more of my verses with reading them ill-favouredly.

Jaq. Rosalind is your love's name?

Orl. Yes, just.

Jaq. I do not like her name.

Orl. There was no thought of pleasing you when she was christen'd.

Jaq. What stature is she of?

Orl. Just as high as my heart.

Jaq. You are full of pretty answers. Have you not been acquainted with goldsmiths' wives, and conn'd them out of rings?

Orl. Not so; [but I answer you right painted cloth, from whence you have studied your questions.]

Jaq. [You have a nimble wit: I think 't was made of Atalanta's heels.] Will you sit down with me? and we two will rail against our mistress the world and all our misery.

Orl. I will chide no breather[1] in the world but myself, against whom I know most faults.

Jaq. The worst fault you have is to be in love.

Orl. 'T is a fault I will not change for your best virtue. I am weary of you.

Jaq. By my troth, I was seeking for a fool when I found you.

Orl. He is drown'd in the brook: look but in, and you shall see him.

Jaq. There I shall see mine own figure.

Orl. Which I take to be either a fool or a cipher.

Jaq. I'll tarry no longer with you: farewell, good Signior Love.

Orl. I am glad of your departure: adieu, good Monsieur Melancholy. [*Exit Jaques.*

[*Celia and Rosalind come forward.*

Ros. [*Aside to Celia*] I will speak to him like a saucy lackey, and under that habit play the knave with him.—Do you hear, forester?

Orl. Very well: what would you?

Ros. I pray you, what is 't o'clock?

Orl. You should ask me, what time o' day: there 's no clock in the forest.

Ros. Then there is no true lover in the forest; else sighing every minute, and groaning every hour, would detect the lazy foot of Time as well as a clock.

Orl. And why not the swift foot of Time? had not that been as proper?

Ros. By no means, sir. Time travels in divers paces with divers persons: I'll tell you who Time ambles withal, who Time trots withal, who Time gallops withal, and who he stands still withal.

Orl. I prithee, who doth he trot withal?

Ros. Marry, he trots hard with a young maid between the contract of her marriage and the day it is solemniz'd: if the interim be but a se'nnight, Time's pace is so hard that it seems the length of seven year.

Orl. Who ambles Time withal?

Ros. With a priest that lacks Latin, and a rich man that hath not the gout; for the one sleeps easily, because he cannot study; and the other lives merrily, because he feels no pain: [the one lacking the burden of lean and wasteful learning; the other knowing no burden of heavy tedious penury:] these Time ambles withal.

Orl. Who doth he gallop withal?

Ros. With a thief to the gallows; for though he go as softly as foot can fall, he thinks himself too soon there.

Orl. Who stays it still withal?

Ros. With lawyers in the vacation; for they sleep between term and term, and then they perceive not how Time moves.

Orl. Where dwell you, pretty youth?

Ros. With this shepherdess, my sister; here in the skirts of the forest, like fringe upon a petticoat.

[*Orl.* Are you native of this place?

Ros. As the cony, that you see dwell where she is kindled.[2]]

Orl. Your accent is something finer than you could purchase in so removed a dwelling.

Ros. I have been told so of many: but indeed an old religious uncle of mine taught me to speak, who was in his youth an inland man; one that knew courtship too well, for there he fell in love. I have heard him read many lectures against it; and I thank God I am not a woman, to be touch'd with so many giddy offences as he hath generally tax'd their whole sex withal.

Orl. Can you remember any of the principal evils that he laid to the charge of women?

Ros. There were none principal: they were all like one another as half-pence are; every one fault seeming monstrous till his fellow-fault came to match it.

Orl. I prithee, recount some of them.

---

[1] *No breather*, i.e. no one, no human being.

[2] *Kindled*, littered; a technical term.

Ros. No, I will not cast away my physic but on those that are sick. There is a man haunts the forest, that abuses our young plants with carving Rosalind on their barks; hangs odes upon hawthorns, and elegies on brambles; all, forsooth, deifying the name of Rosalind: if I could meet that fancy-monger, I would give him some good counsel, for he seems to have the quotidian of love upon him.

Orl. I am he that is so love-shak'd: I pray you, tell me your remedy.

Ros. There is none of my uncle's marks upon you: he taught me how to know a man in love; in which cage of rushes I am sure you are not prisoner.

Orl. What were his marks?

Ros. A lean cheek,—which you have not; a blue[1] eye and sunken,—which you have not; an unquestionable[2] spirit,—which you have not; a beard neglected,—which you have not;—but I pardon you for that; for simply your having in beard is a younger brother's revenue:—then your hose should be ungarter'd, your bonnet unbanded, your sleeve unbutton'd, your shoe untied, and every thing about you demonstrating a careless desolation;—but you are no such man,—you are rather point-devise in your accoutrements, as loving yourself than seeming the lover of any other.

Orl. Fair youth, I would I could make thee believe I love.

Ros. Me believe it! you may as soon make her that you love believe it; which, I warrant, she is apter to do than to confess she does: that is one of the points in the which women still give the lie to their consciences. But, in good sooth, are you he that hangs the verses on the trees, wherein Rosalind is so admired?

Orl. I swear to thee, youth, by the white hand of Rosalind, I am that he, that unfortunate he.

Ros. But are you so much in love as your rhymes speak?

Orl. Neither rhyme nor reason can express how much.

Ros. Love is merely a madness; and, I tell you, deserves as well a dark house and a whip as madmen do: and the reason why they are not so punish'd and cured is, that the lunacy is so ordinary, that the whippers are in love too. Yet I profess curing it by counsel.

Orl. Did you ever cure any so?

Ros. Yes, one; and in this manner. He was to imagine me his love, his mistress; and I set him every day to woo me: at which time would I, being but a moonish[3] youth, grieve, be effeminate, changeable, longing, and liking; proud, fantastical, apish, shallow, inconstant, full of tears, full of smiles; for every passion something, and for no passion truly any thing, as boys and women are for the most part cattle of this colour: would now like him, now loathe him; then entertain him, then forswear him; now weep for him, then spit at him; that I drave my suitor from his mad humour of love to a living humour of madness; which was, to forswear the full stream of the world, and to live in a nook merely monastic. And thus I cur'd him; and this way will I take upon me to wash your liver as clean as a sound sheep's heart, that there shall not be one spot of love in 't.

Orl. I would not be cured, youth.

Ros. I would cure you, if you would but call me Rosalind, and come every day to my cote and woo me.

Orl. Now, by the faith of my love, I will: tell me where it is.

Ros. Go with me to it, and I'll show it you: and, by the way, you shall tell me where in the forest you live. Will you go?

Orl. With all my heart, good youth.

Ros. Nay, you must call me Rosalind.—Come, sister, will you go? [*Exeunt.*

SCENE III. *Another part of the forest.*

Enter TOUCHSTONE *and* AUDREY; [JAQUES *behind.*]

Touch. Come apace, good Audrey: I will fetch up your goats, Audrey. And how, Audrey? am I the man yet? doth my simple feature content you?

---

[1] *Blue*, that is, with blue lines under it.

[2] *Unquestionable*, unwilling to be questioned.

[3] *Moonish*, wayward.

Aud. Your features! Lord warrant us! what features?

Touch. I am here with thee and thy goats, as the most capricious poet, honest Ovid, was among the Goths.

[*Jaq.* [*Aside*] O knowledge ill-inhabited,—worse than Jove in a thatch'd house!]

Touch. When a man's verses cannot be understood, nor a man's good wit seconded with the forward child, understanding, it strikes a man more dead than a great reckoning in a little room.—Truly, I would the gods had made thee poetical.

Aud. I do not know what poetical is: is it honest in deed and word? is it a true thing?

Touch. Truly, I would the gods had made thee poetical.—(Act iii. 3. 16, 17.)

Touch. No, truly; for the truest poetry is the most feigning; and lovers are given to poetry; and what they swear in poetry, may be said, as lovers, they do feign.

Aud. Do you wish, then, that the gods had made me poetical?

Touch. I do, truly; for thou swear'st to me thou art honest: now, if thou wert a poet, I might have some hope thou didst feign.

Aud. Would you not have me honest?

Touch. No, truly, unless thou wert hard-favoured; for honesty coupled to beauty is to have honey a sauce to sugar.

[*Jaq.* [*Aside*] A material fool!]

Aud. Well, I am not fair; and therefore I pray the gods make me honest.

Touch. Truly, and to cast away honesty upon a foul[1] slut, were to put good meat into an unclean dish.

Aud. I am not a slut, though I thank the gods I am foul.

Touch. Well, praised be the gods for thy foulness! sluttishness may come hereafter.

[1] *Foul*, ugly.

But be it as it may be, I will marry thee: and to that end I have been with Sir Oliver Martext, the vicar of the next village; who hath promised to meet me in this place of the forest, and to couple us.

[*Jaq.* [*Aside*] I would fain see this meeting.]

Aud. Well, the gods give us joy!

Touch. Amen. A man may, if he were of a fearful heart, stagger in this attempt; for here we have no temple but the wood, no assembly but horn-beasts. But what though? Courage! As horns[1] are odious, they are necessary. It is said, "Many a many knows no end of his goods:" right; many a man has good horns, and knows no end of them. Well, that is the dowry of his wife; 't is none of his own getting. Horns? Even so. Poor men alone? No, no; the noblest deer hath them as huge as the rascal.[2] Is the single man therefore blessed? No: as a walled town is more worthier than a village, so is the forehead of a married man more honourable than the bare brow of a bachelor; [and by how much defence is better than no skill, by so much is a horn more precious than to want.—Here comes Sir Oliver.

Enter Sir OLIVER MARTEXT.

Sir Oliver Martext, you are well met: will you dispatch us here under this tree, or shall we go with you to your chapel?

Sir Oli. Is there none here to give the woman?

Touch. I will not take her on gift of any man.

Sir Oli. Truly, she must be given, or the marriage is not lawful.

Jaq. [*Coming forward*] Proceed, proceed: I 'll give her.

Touch. Good even, good Master What-ye-call 't: how do you, sir? You are very well met: God ild you for your last company: I am very glad to see you:—even a toy in hand here, sir:—nay, pray be cover'd.

Jaq. Will you be married, motley?

Touch. As the ox hath his bow, sir, the horse his curb, and the falcon her bells, so man hath his desires; and as pigeons bill, so wedlock would be nibbling.

Jaq. And will you, being a man of your breeding, be married under a bush, like a beggar? Get you to church, and have a good priest that can tell you what marriage is: this fellow will but join you together as they join wainscot; then one of you will prove a shrunk panel, and like green timber warp, warp.

Touch. [*Aside*] I am not in the mind[3] but I were better to be married of him than of another: for he is not like to marry me well; and not being well married, it will be a good excuse for me hereafter to leave my wife.

Jaq. Go thou with me, and let me counsel thee.

Touch.] Come, sweet Audrey:
We must be married, [or we must live in bawdry.—
Farewell, good Master Oliver:—not,
O sweet Oliver,
O brave Oliver,
Leave me not behind thee;—
but,
Wind away,
Begone, I say,
I will not to wedding with thee.]

[*Exeunt* [*Jaques, Touchstone, and Audrey.*

Sir Oli. 'T is no matter: ne'er a fantastical knave of them all shall flout me out of my calling. [*Exit.*]

SCENE IV. *Another part of the forest. Before a cottage.*

Enter ROSALIND *and* CELIA.

Ros. Never talk to me; I will weep.

Cel. Do, I prithee; but yet have the grace to consider that tears do not become a man.

Ros. But have I not cause to weep?

Cel. As good cause as one would desire; therefore weep.

[*Ros.* His very hair is of the dissembling colour.

Cel. Something browner than Judas's: marry, his kisses are Judas's own children.

Ros. I' faith, his hair is of a good colour.

Cel. An excellent colour: your chestnut was ever the only colour.

[1] *Horns, i.e.* the horns of a cuckold.

[2] *Rascal,* the technical term for deer not in good condition.

[3] *Not in the mind,* not certain whether.

Ros. And his kissing is as full of sanctity as the touch of holy bread.

Cel. He hath bought a pair of cast[1] lips of Diana: a nun of winter's sisterhood kisses not more religiously; the very ice of chastity is in them.]

Ros. But why did he swear he would come this morning, and comes not?

Cel. Nay, certainly, there is no truth in him.

Ros. Do you think so?

[*Cel.* Yes; I think he is not a pick-purse nor a horse-stealer; but for his verity in love, I do think him as concave as a cover'd goblet or a worm-eaten nut.

Ros.] Not true in love?

Cel. Yes, when he is in; but I think he is not in.

Ros. You have heard him swear downright he was.

Cel. "Was" is not "is:" besides, the oath of a lover is no stronger than the word of a tapster; they are both the confirmers of false reckonings. He attends here in the forest on the duke your father.

Ros. I met the duke yesterday, and had much question[2] with him: he ask'd me of what parentage I was; I told him, of as good as he; so he laugh'd, and let me go. But what talk we of fathers, when there is such a man as Orlando?

Cel. O, that 's a brave man! he writes brave verses, speaks brave words, swears brave oaths, and breaks them bravely, quite traverse, athwart the heart of his lover; as a puisny[3] tilter, that spurns his horse but on one side, breaks his staff like a noble goose: but all's brave that youth mounts and folly guides. —Who comes here?

Enter CORIN.

Cor. Mistress and master, you have oft inquired
After the shepherd that complain'd of love,
Who you saw sitting by me on the turf,
Praising the proud disdainful shepherdess
That was his mistress.

Cel. Well, and what of him?

Cor. If you will see a pageant truly play'd,
Between the pale complexion of true love
And the red glow of scorn and proud disdain,
Go hence a little, and I shall conduct you,
If you will mark it.

Ros. O, come, let us remove:
The sight of lovers feedeth those in love.—
Bring us to see this sight, and you shall say
I 'll prove a busy actor in their play.
[*Exeunt.*

SCENE V. *Another part of the forest.*

Enter SILVIUS *and* PHEBE.

Sil. Sweet Phebe, do not scorn me; do not, Phebe:
Say that you love me not; but say not so
In bitterness. The common executioner,
Whose heart th' accustom'd sight of death makes hard,
Falls not the axe upon the humbled neck
But[4] first begs pardon: will you sterner be
Than he that dies and lives by bloody drops?

Enter ROSALIND, CELIA, *and* CORIN, *behind.*

Phe. I would not be thy executioner:
I fly thee, for I would not injure thee.
Thou tell'st me there is murder in mine eye:
'T is pretty, sure, and very probable,
That eyes—that are the frail'st and softest things,
Who shut their coward gates on atomies—
Should be call'd tyrants, butchers, murderers!
Now I do frown on thee with all my heart;
And, if mine eyes can wound, now let them kill thee:
Now counterfeit to swoon; why, now fall down;
Or, if thou canst not, O, for shame, for shame,
Lie not, to say mine eyes are murderers!
Now show the wound mine eye hath made in thee:
Scratch thee but with a pin, and there remains
Some scar of it; lean but upon a rush,
The cicatrice and capable impressure[5]
Thy palm some moment keeps: but now mine eyes,
Which I have darted at thee, hurt thee not;
Nor, I am sure, there is no force in eyes
That can do hurt.

[1] *Cast*=cast-off. [2] *Question*, talk. [3] *Puisny*, feeble.

[4] *But*=without. [5] *Impressure*, for *impression*.

Sil. O dear Phebe,
If ever—as that ever may be near—
You meet in some fresh cheek the power of fancy,
Then shall you know the wounds invisible
That love's keen arrows make.

Phe. But, till that time,
Come not thou near me: and, when that time comes,
Afflict me with thy mocks, pity me not;
As, till that time, I shall not pity thee.

Ros. [*Coming forward*] And why, I pray you? Who might be your mother,
That you insult, exult, and all at once,
Over the wretched? What—though you have no beauty,—
As, by my faith, I see no more in you
Than without candle may go dark to bed,—
Must you be therefore proud and pitiless?
Why, what means this? Why do you look on me?
I see no more in you than in the ordinary
Of nature's sale-work:[1]—'Od 's my little life,
I think she means to tangle my eyes too!—
No, faith, proud mistress, hope not after it:
'T is not your inky brows, your black-silk hair,
Your bugle eyeballs, nor your cheek of cream,
That can entame my spirits to your worship.—
You foolish shepherd, wherefore do you follow her,
Like foggy south, puffing with wind and rain?
You are a thousand times a properer[2] man
Than she a woman: 't is such fools as you
That make the world full of ill-favour'd children:
'T is not her glass, but you, that flatters her;
And out of you she sees herself more proper
Than any of her lineaments can show her.—
But, mistress, know yourself: down on your knees,
And thank heaven, fasting, for a good man's love:
For I must tell you friendly in your ear,—
Sell when you can: you are not for all markets:
Cry the man mercy; love him; take his offer:
Foul is most foul, being foul to be a scoffer.—
So, take her to thee, shepherd:—fare you well.

Phe. Sweet youth, I pray you, chide a year together:
I had rather hear you chide than this man woo.

[*Ros.* He 's fallen in love with your foulness, and she 'll fall in love with my anger:—if it be so, as fast as she answers thee with frowning looks, I 'll sauce her with bitter words.—Why look you so upon me?

Phe. For no ill will I bear you.]

Ros. I pray you, do not fall in love with me,
For I am falser than vows made in wine:
Besides, I like you not.—If you will know my house,
'T is at the tuft of olives here hard by.—
Will you go, sister?—Shepherd, ply her hard.—
Come, sister.—Shepherdess, look on him better,
And be not proud: though all the world could see,
None could be so abus'd[3] in sight as he.—
[Come, to our flock.
[*Exeunt Rosalind, Celia, and Corin.*

Phe. Dead shepherd, now I find thy saw of might,—
"Whoever lov'd that lov'd not at first sight?"].

Sil. Sweet Phebe,—

Phe. Ha, what say'st thou, Silvius?

Sil. Sweet Phebe, pity me.

Phe. Why, I am sorry for thee, gentle Silvius.

Sil. Wherever sorrow is, relief would be:
If you do sorrow at my grief in love,
By giving love, your sorrow and my grief
Were both extermin'd.

[*Phe.* Thou hast my love: is not that neighbourly?

Sil. I would have you.]

Phe. [Why, that were covetousness.]
Silvius, the time was, that I hated thee;
And yet it is not that I bear thee love:
But since that thou canst talk of love so well,
Thy company, which erst was irksome to me,
I will endure; and I 'll employ thee too:
But do not look for further recompense
Than thine own gladness that thou art employ'd.

Sil. So holy and so perfect is my love,
And I in such a poverty of grace,

[1] *Nature's sale-work*, i.e. the goods (in modern phrase) which nature sells every day.
[2] *Properer*, finer
[3] *Abus'd*, mistaken.

That I shall think it a most plenteous crop
To glean the broken ears after the man
That the main harvest reaps: loose now and then
A scatter'd smile, and that I 'll live upon.

Phe. Know'st thou the youth that spoke to me erewhile?

Sil. Not very well, but I have met him oft;
And he hath bought the cottage and the bounds
That the old carlot once was master of.

Phe. Think not I love him, though I ask for him;
'T is but a peevish boy:—yet he talks well;—
[But what care I for words? yet words do well,
When he that speaks them pleases those that hear.
It is a pretty youth:—not very pretty:—
But, sure, he 's proud; and yet his pride becomes him:
He 'll make a proper man: the best thing in him
Is his complexion; and faster than his tongue
Did make offence, his eye did heal it up.
He is not very tall; yet for his years he 's tall:]
His leg is but so-so; and yet 't is well:
There was a pretty redness in his lip,
[A little riper and more lusty red
Than that mix'd in his cheek; 't was just the difference
Betwixt the constant red and mingled[1] damask.]
There be some women, Silvius, had they mark'd him
In parcels as I did, would have gone near
To fall in love with him: but, for my part,
I love him not, nor hate him not; and yet
I have more cause to hate him than to love him:
For what had he to do to chide at me?
He said mine eyes were black, and my hair black;
And, now I am remember'd, scorn'd at me:
I marvel why I answer'd not again:
But that 's all one; omittance is no quittance.
I 'll write to him a very taunting letter,
And thou shalt bear it; wilt thou, Silvius?

Sil. Phebe, with all my heart.

Phe. I 'll write it straight;[2]
The matter 's in my head and in my heart:
I will be bitter with him and passing short.
Go with me, Silvius. [*Exeunt.*

ACT IV.

SCENE I. *The Forest of Arden.*

Enter ROSALIND, CELIA, *and* JAQUES.

Jaq. I prithee, pretty youth, let me be better acquainted with thee.

Ros. They say you are a melancholy fellow.

Jaq. I am so; I do love it better than laughing.

[*Ros.* Those that are in extremity of either are abominable fellows, and betray themselves to every modern censure worse than drunkards.

Jaq. Why, 't is good to be sad and say nothing.

Ros. Why, then 't is good to be a post.

Jaq. I have neither the scholar's melancholy, which is emulation; nor the musician's, which is fantastical; nor the courtier's, which is proud; nor the soldier's, which is ambitious; nor the lawyer's, which is politic; nor the lady's, which is nice; nor the lover's, which is all these;—but] it is a melancholy of mine own, compounded of many simples, extracted from many objects, and, indeed, the sundry contemplation of my travels, which, by often rumination, wraps me in a most humorous sadness.

Ros. A traveller! By my faith, you have great reason to be sad: I fear you have sold your own lands, to see other men's; [then, to have seen much, and to have nothing, is to have rich eyes and poor hands.]

Jaq. Yes, I have gain'd my experience.

Ros. And your experience makes you sad: I had rather have a fool to make me merry than experience to make me sad; and to travel for it too!

Enter ORLANDO.

Orl. Good day and happiness, dear Rosalind!

[1] *Mingled*, i.e. red and white. [2] *Straight*, at once.

Jaq. Nay, then, God b' wi' you, an' you talk in blank verse! 32

Ros. Farewell, Monsieur Traveller: look, you lisp, and wear strange suits; disable[1] all the benefits of your own country; be out of love with your nativity, and almost chide God for making you that countenance you are; or I will scarce think you have swam in a gondola. [*Exit Jaques.*] Why, how now, Orlando! where have you been all this while? You a lover!—An you serve me such another trick, never come in my sight more.

Orl. My fair Rosalind, I come within an hour of my promise.

Ros. Break an hour's promise in love! He that will divide a minute into a thousand

Ros. And your experience makes you sad: I had rather have a fool to make me merry than experience to make me sad; and to travel for it too!—(Act iv. 1. 26-29.)

parts, and break but a part of the thousandth part of a minute in the affairs of love, it may be said of him that Cupid hath clapp'd[2] him o' the shoulder, but I'll warrant him heart-whole.

Orl. Pardon me, dear Rosalind. 50

Ros. Nay, an you be so tardy, come no more in my sight: I had as lief be woo'd of a snail.

Orl. Of a snail!

Ros. Ay, of a snail; for though he comes slowly, he carries his house on his head,—a better jointure, I think, than you can make a woman: [besides, he brings his destiny with him.

Orl. What's that?

Ros. Why, horns; which such as you are fain to be beholding to your wives for: but he comes armed in his fortune, and prevents the slander of his wife.

Orl. Virtue is no horn-maker; and my Rosalind is virtuous.

Ros. And I am your Rosalind.

Cel. It pleases him to call you so; but he hath a Rosalind of a better leer than you.

Ros.] Come, woo me, woo me; for now I am in a holiday humour, and like enough to consent.—What would you say to me now, an I were your very very Rosalind? 71

Orl. I would kiss before I spoke.

1 *Disable*, disparage. 2 *Clapp'd*, lightly touched.

Ros. Nay, you were better speak first; and when you were gravell'd[1] for lack of matter, you might take occasion to kiss. Very good orators, when they are out, they will spit; and for lovers, lacking (God warn us!) matter, the cleanliest shift is to kiss.

Orl. How if the kiss be denied?

Ros. Then she puts you to entreaty, and there begins new matter.

Orl. Who could be out, being before his beloved mistress?

Ros. [Marry, that should you, if I were your mistress; or I should think my honesty ranker than my wit.

Orl. What, of my suit?

Ros. Not out of your apparel, and yet out of your suit.] Am not I your Rosalind?

Orl. I take some joy to say you are, because I would be talking of her.

Ros. Well, in her person, I say,—I will not have you.

Orl. Then, in mine own person, I die.

Ros. No, faith, die by attorney. The poor world is almost six thousand years old, and in all this time there was not any man died in his own person, *videlicet*, in a love-cause. Troilus had his brains dash'd out with a Grecian club; yet he did what he could to die before; and he is one of the patterns of love. Leander, he would have liv'd many a fair year, though Hero had turn'd nun, if it had not been for a hot midsummer night; for, good youth, he went but forth to wash him in the Hellespont, and, being taken with the cramp, was drown'd: and the foolish chroniclers of that age found it was—Hero of Sestos. But these are all lies: men have died from time to time, and worms have eaten them, but not for love.

Orl. I would not have my right Rosalind of this mind; for, I protest, her frown might kill me.

Ros. By this hand, it will not kill a fly. But come, now I will be your Rosalind in a more coming-on[2] disposition; and ask me what you will, I will grant it.

Orl. Then love me, Rosalind.

Ros. Yes, faith, will I, Fridays and Saturdays and all.

Orl. And wilt thou have me?

Ros. Ay, and twenty such.

Orl. What sayest thou?

Ros. Are you not good?

Orl. I hope so.

Ros. Why, then, can one desire too much of a good thing?—Come, sister, you shall be the priest, and marry us.—Give me your hand, Orlando.—What do you say, sister?

Orl. Pray thee, marry us.

Cel. I cannot say the words.

Ros. You must begin,—"Will you, Orlando,"—

Cel. Go to.—Will you, Orlando, have to wife this Rosalind?

Orl. I will.

Ros. Ay, but when?

Orl. Why now; as fast as she can marry us.

Ros. Then you must say,—"I take thee, Rosalind, for wife."

Orl. I take thee, Rosalind, for wife.

Ros. I might ask you for your commission; but,—I do take thee, Orlando, for my husband:—there's a girl goes before the priest; and, certainly, a woman's thought runs before her actions.

Orl. So do all thoughts,—they are wing'd.

Ros. Now tell me how long you would have her, after you have possess'd her.

Orl. For ever and a day.

Ros. Say a day, without the ever. No, no, Orlando; men are April when they woo, December when they wed: maids are May when they are maids, but the sky changes when they are wives. I will be more jealous of thee than a Barbary cock-pigeon over his hen; more clamorous than a parrot against rain; more new-fangled than an ape; more giddy in my desires than a monkey: I will weep for nothing, like Diana in the fountain, and I will do that when you are dispos'd to be merry; I will laugh like a hyen,[3] and that when thou art inclin'd to sleep.

Orl. But will my Rosalind do so?

Ros. By my life, she will do as I do.

Orl. O, but she is wise.

Ros. Or else she could not have the wit to

[1] *Gravell'd*, at a loss. [2] *Coming-on*, complaisant.

[3] *Hyen*, the old form of *hyena*.

do this: the wiser, the waywarder: make the doors upon a woman's wit, and it will out at the casement; shut that, and 't will out at the key-hole; stop that, 't will fly with the smoke out at the chimney.

[*Orl.* A man that had a wife with such a wit, he might say,—"Wit, whither wilt?"

Ros. Nay, you might keep that check for it till you met your wife's wit going to your neighbour's bed.

Orl. And what wit could wit have to excuse that?

Ros. Marry, to say,—she came to seek you there. You shall never take her without her

Jaq. Which is he that kill'd the deer?
First Lord. Sir, it was I.—(Act iv. 2. 1, 2.)

answer, unless you take her without her tongue. O, that woman that cannot make her fault her husband's occasion,[1] let her never nurse her child herself, for she will breed it like a fool!]

Orl. For these two hours, Rosalind, I will leave thee.

Ros. Alas, dear love, I cannot lack thee two hours!

Orl. I must attend the duke at dinner: by two o'clock I will be with thee again.

Ros. Ay, go your ways, go your ways;—I knew what you would prove: my friends told me as much, and I thought no less:—that flattering tongue of yours won me:—'t is but one cast away, and so,—come, death!—Two o'clock is your hour?

Orl. Ay, sweet Rosalind.

Ros. By my troth, and in good earnest, and so God mend me, and by all pretty oaths that are not dangerous, if you break one jot of your promise, or come one minute behind your hour, I will think thee the most pathetical break-promise, and the most hollow lover, and the most unworthy of her you call Rosalind, that may be chosen out of the gross band of the unfaithful: therefore beware my censure, and keep your promise.

Orl. With no less religion than if thou wert indeed my Rosalind: so, adieu.

[1] *Occasion* = as occasioned by.

Ros. Well, Time is the old justice that examines all such offenders, and let Time try: adieu. [*Exit Orlando.*

Cel. You have simply misus'd[1] our sex in your love-prate: [we must have your doublet and hose pluck'd over your head, and show the world what the bird hath done to her own nest.]

Ros. O coz, coz, coz, my pretty little coz, that thou didst know how many fathom deep I am in love! But it cannot be sounded: my affection hath an unknown bottom, like the bay of Portugal.

Cel. Or rather, bottomless; that as fast as you pour affection in, it runs out.

[*Ros.* No, that same wicked bastard of Venus, that was begot of thought, conceiv'd of spleen, and born of madness; that blind rascally boy, that abuses every one's eyes, because his own are out, let him be judge how deep I am in love:—I 'll tell thee, Aliena, I cannot be out of the sight of Orlando; I 'll go find a shadow, and sigh till he come.

Cel. And I 'll sleep.] [*Exeunt.*

[Scene II. *Another part of the forest.*

Enter Jaques *and Lords in the habit of foresters, with a dead deer.*

Jaq. Which is he that kill'd the deer?

First Lord. Sir, it was I.

Jaq. Let 's present him to the duke, like a Roman conqueror; and it would do well to set the deer's horns upon his head, for a branch of victory.—Have you no song, forester, for this purpose?

Sec. Lord. Yes, sir.

Jaq. Sing it: 't is no matter how it be in tune, so it make noise enough.

Song.

What shall he have that kill'd the deer?
His leather skin, and horns to wear.
Then sing him home.
[*The rest shall bear this burden.*
Take thou no scorn to wear the horn:
It was a crest ere thou wast born;
Thy father's father wore it,
And thy father bore it:
The horn, the horn, the lusty horn,
Is not a thing to laugh to scorn. [*Exeunt.*]

[1] *Misus'd*, covered with abuse.

Scene III. *Another part of the forest.*

Enter Rosalind *and* Celia.

Ros. How say you now? Is it not past two o'clock? and here much Orlando!

Cel. I warrant you, with pure love and troubled brain, he hath ta'en his bow and arrows, and is gone forth—to sleep. Look, who comes here.

Enter Silvius.

Sil. My errand is to you, fair youth;—
My gentle Phebe bid me give you this:
[*Giving a letter.*
[I know not the contents; but, as I guess
By the stern brow and waspish action
Which she did use as she was writing of it,
It bears an angry tenour: pardon me,
I am but as a guiltless messenger.]

Ros. Patience herself would startle at this letter,
And play the swaggerer; bear this, bear all:
She says I am not fair; that I lack manners;
She calls me proud; and that she could not love me,
Were man as rare as phœnix. 'Od 's my will!
Her love is not the hare that I do hunt:
Why writes she so to me?—Well, shepherd, well,
This is a letter of your own device.

Sil. No, I protest I know not the contents:
Phebe did write it.

[*Ros.* Come, come, you 're a fool,
And turn'd into th' extremity of love.
I saw her hand: she has a leathern hand,
A freestone-colour'd hand; I verily did think
That her old gloves were on, but 't was her hands:
She has a housewife's hand; but that 's no matter:
I say, she never did invent this letter;
This is a man's invention, and his hand.

Sil. Sure, it is hers.]

Ros. Why, 't is a boisterous and a cruel style,
A style for challengers; why, she defies me,
Like Turk to Christian: woman's gentle brain
Could not drop forth such giant-rude invention,
Such Ethiop words, blacker in their effect
Than in their countenance.—Will you hear the letter?

Sil. So please you, for I never heard it yet;
Yet heard too much of Phebe's cruelty.
Ros. She Phebes me: mark how the tyrant writes. [*Reads.*

"Art thou god to shepherd turn'd,
That a maiden's heart hath burn'd?"—

Can a woman rail thus?
Sil. Call you this railing?
Ros. [*Reads*]

"Why, thy godhead laid apart,
Warr'st thou with a woman's heart?"

Did you ever hear such railing? [*Reads.*

"Whiles the eye of man did woo me,
That could do no vengeance to me."—

Meaning me a beast.— [*Reads.*

"If the scorn of your bright eyne
Have power to raise such love in mine,
Alack, in me what strange effect
Would they work in mild aspéct!
Whiles you chid me, I did love;
How, then, might your prayers move!
He that brings this love to thee
Little knows this love in me:
And by him seal up thy mind;
Whether that thy youth and kind
Will the faithful offer take
Of me, and all that I can make;
Or else by him my love deny,
And then I 'll study how to die."

Sil. Call you this chiding?
Cel. Alas, poor shepherd!
Ros. Do you pity him? no, he deserves no pity.—Wilt thou love such a woman?—What, to make thee an instrument, and play false strains upon thee! not to be endur'd!—Well, go your way to her,—for I see love hath made thee a tame snake,—and say this to her:—that if she love me, I charge her to love thee; if she will not, I will never have her, unless thou entreat for her.—If you be a true lover, hence, and not a word; for here comes more company. [*Exit Silvius.*

Enter OLIVER.

Oli. Good morrow, fair ones: pray you, if you know,
Where in the purlieus of this forest stands
A sheep-cote fenc'd about with olive trees?
Cel. West of this place, down in the neighbour bottom:
The rank of osiers, by the murmuring stream,
Left on your right hand, brings you to the place.
But at this hour the house doth keep itself;
There 's none within.
Oli. If that an eye may profit by a tongue,
Then should I know you by description;
Such garments and such years:—"The boy is fair,
Of female favour, and bestows himself
Like a ripe sister: the woman low,
And browner than her brother." Are not you
The owner of the house I did inquire for?
Cel. It is no boast, being ask'd, to say we are.
Oli. Orlando doth commend him to you both;
And to that youth he calls his Rosalind
He sends this bloody napkin;—are you he?
Ros. I am: what must we understand by this?
Oli. Some of my shame; if you will know of me
What man I am, and how, and why, and where
This handkercher was stained.
Cel. I pray you, tell it.
Oli. When last the young Orlando parted from you,
He left a promise to return again
Within an hour; and, pacing through the forest,
Chewing the cud of sweet and bitter fancy,
Lo, what befell! he threw his eye aside,
And, mark, what object did present itself:
Under an oak, whose boughs were moss'd with age,
And high top bald with dry antiquity,
A wretched ragged man, o'ergrown with hair,
Lay sleeping on his back: about his neck
A green and gilded snake had wreath'd itself,
Who with her head, nimble in threats, approach'd
The opening of his mouth; but suddenly,
Seeing Orlando, it unlink'd itself,
And with indented glides did slip away
Into a bush: under which bush's shade
A lioness, with udders all drawn dry,
Lay crouching, head on ground, with catlike watch,
When that the sleeping man should stir; for 't is
The royal disposition of that beast
To prey on nothing that doth seem as dead:

This seen, Orlando did approach the man,
And found it was his brother, his elder brother.
Cel. O, I have heard him speak of that same brother;
And he did render[1] him the most unnatural
That liv'd 'mongst men.
Oli. And well he might so do,
For well I know he was unnatural.
Ros. But, to Orlando:—did he leave him there,
Food to the suck'd and hungry lioness?
Oli. Twice did he turn his back, and purpos'd so;

Cel. Why, how now, Ganymede! sweet Ganymede! [*Rosalind faints.*]—(Act iv. 3. 158.)

But kindness, nobler ever than revenge,
And nature, stronger than his just occasion,
Made him give battle to the lioness,
Who quickly fell before him: in which hurtling[2]
From miserable slumber I awak'd.
Cel. Are you his brother?
Ros. Was it you he rescu'd?
Cel. Was 't you that did so oft contrive to kill him?
Oli. 'T was I; but 't is not I: I do not shame
To tell you what I was, since my conversion
So sweetly tastes, being the thing I am.
Ros. But, for the bloody napkin?—
Oli. By and by.
When from the first to last, betwixt us two,
Tears our recountments had most kindly bath'd,
As, how I came into that desert place;—
In brief,[3] he led me to the gentle duke,
Who gave me fresh array and entertainment,
Committing me unto my brother's love;
Who led me instantly unto his cave,
There stripp'd himself, and here upon his arm
The lioness had torn some flesh away,
Which all this while had bled; and now he fainted,
And cried, in fainting, upon Rosalind.
Brief, I recover'd him, bound up his wound;
And, after some small space, being strong at heart,

---

[1] *Render*, describe.
[2] *Hurtling*, din of conflict.
[3] *In brief*, to be brief.

He sent me hither, stranger as I am,
To tell this story, that you might excuse
His broken promise, and to give this napkin,
Dy'd in his blood, unto the shepherd youth
That he in sport doth call his Rosalind.

Cel. Why, how now, Ganymede! sweet Ganymede! [*Rosalind faints.*

Oli. Many will swoon when they do look on blood.

Cel. There is more in it.—Cousin Ganymede!

Oli. Look, he recovers.

Ros. I would I were at home.

Cel. We'll lead you thither.—
I pray you, will you take him by the arm?

Oli. Be of good cheer, youth:—you a man? you lack a man's heart.

Ros. I do so, I confess it. Ah, sirrah, a body would think this was well counterfeited! I pray you, tell your brother how well I counterfeited.—Heigh-ho!

Oli. This was not counterfeit: there is too great testimony in your complexion, that it was a passion of earnest.[1]

Ros. Counterfeit, I assure you.

Oli. Well, then, take a good heart, and counterfeit to be a man.

Ros. So I do: but, i' faith, I should have been a woman by right.

[*Cel.* Come, you look paler and paler: pray you, draw homewards.—Good sir, go with us.

Oli. That will I, for I must bear answer back
How you excuse my brother, Rosalind.

Ros. I shall devise something: but, I pray you, commend my counterfeiting to him:—will you go?] [*Exeunt.*

ACT V.

Scene I. *The Forest of Arden.*

Enter Touchstone *and* Audrey.

Touch. We shall find a time, Audrey; patience, gentle Audrey.

Aud. Faith, the priest was good enough, for all the old gentleman's saying.

Touch. A most wicked Sir Oliver, Audrey, a most vile Martext. But, Audrey, there is a youth here in the forest lays claim to you.

Aud. Ay, I know who 't is: he hath no interest in me in the world: here comes the man you mean.

Touch. It is meat and drink to me to see a clown: by my troth, we that have good wits have much to answer for; we shall be flouting; we cannot hold.

Enter William.

Will. Good even, Audrey.

Aud. God ye good even, William.

Will. And good even to you, sir.

Touch. Good even, gentle friend. Cover thy head, cover thy head; nay, prithee, be cover'd. How old are you, friend?

Will. Five and twenty, sir.

Touch. A ripe age. Is thy name William?

Will. William, sir.

Touch. A fair name. Wast born i' the forest here?

Will. Ay, sir, I thank God.

Touch. Thank God;—a good answer. Art rich?

Will. Faith, sir, so-so.

Touch. So-so is good, very good, very excellent good:—and yet it is not; it is but so-so. Art thou wise?

Will. Ay, sir, I have a pretty wit.

Touch. Why, thou say'st well. I do now remember a saying, "The fool doth think he is wise; but the wise man knows himself to be a fool." The heathen philosopher, when he had a desire to eat a grape, would open his lips when he put it into his mouth; meaning thereby, that grapes were made to eat, and lips to open. You do love this maid?

Will. I do, sir.

Touch. Give me your hand. Art thou learned?

Will. No, sir.

Touch. Then learn this of me:—to have, is to have; for it is a figure in rhetoric, that

[1] *Of earnest*, i.e. genuine.

drink, being poured out of a cup into a glass, by filling the one doth empty the other; for all your writers do consent that *ipse* is he: now, you are not *ipse*, for I am he.

Will. Which he, sir?

Touch. He, sir, that must marry this woman. Therefore, you clown, abandon,—which

Ros. O, my dear Orlando, how it grieves me to see thee wear thy heart in a scarf!—(Act v. 2. 22, 23.)

is in the vulgar leave,—the society,—which in the boorish is company,—of this female,—which in the common is woman; which together is, abandon the society of this female, or, clown, thou perishest; or, to thy better understanding, diest; or to wit, I kill thee, make thee away, translate thy life into death, thy liberty into bondage: I will deal in poison with thee, or in bastinado, or in steel; I will bandy with thee in faction; I will o'er-run thee with policy; I will kill thee a hundred and fifty ways: therefore tremble, and depart.

Aud. Do, good William.

Will. God rest you merry, sir. [*Exit.*

Enter Corin.

Cor. Our master and mistress seek you; come, away, away!

Touch. Trip, Audrey, trip, Audrey.—I attend, I attend. [*Exeunt.*

Scene II. *Another part of the forest.*

Enter Orlando *and* Oliver.

Orl. Is't possible that, on so little acquaintance, you should like her? that, but seeing, you should love her? and, loving, woo? and, wooing, she should grant? and will you persever to enjoy her?

Oli. Neither call the giddiness of it in question, the poverty of her, the small acquaintance, my sudden wooing, nor her sudden consenting; but say with me, I love Aliena; say with her, that she loves me; consent with both that we may enjoy each other: it shall be to your good; for my father's house, and all the revenue that was old Sir Roland's, will I estate[1] upon you, and here live and die a shepherd.

Orl. You have my consent. Let your wedding be to-morrow: thither will I invite the duke, and all 's contented followers. Go you and prepare Aliena; for, look you, here comes my Rosalind.

Enter Rosalind.

Ros. God save you, brother.

Oli. And you, fair sister. [*Exit.*

Ros. O, my dear Orlando, how it grieves me to see thee wear thy heart in a scarf!

Orl. It is my arm.

Ros. I thought thy heart had been wounded with the claws of a lion.

Orl. Wounded it is, but with the eyes of a lady.

Ros. Did your brother tell you how I counterfeited to swoon when he show'd me your handkercher?

Orl. Ay, and greater wonders than that.

Ros. O, I know where you are:—nay, 't is true: there was never any thing so sudden, but the fight of two rams, and Cæsar's thra-

[1] *Estate*, settle.

sonical brag of—"I came, saw, and overcame:"[1] for your brother and my sister no sooner met, but they look'd; no sooner look'd, but they lov'd; no sooner lov'd, but they sigh'd; no sooner sigh'd, but they ask'd one another the reason; no sooner knew the reason, but they sought the remedy: [and in these degrees have they made a pair of stairs to marriage, which they will climb incontinent, or else be incontinent[2] before marriage:] they are in the very wrath of love, and they will together; clubs cannot part them.

Orl. They shall be married to-morrow; and I will bid the duke to the nuptial. But, O, how bitter a thing it is to look into happiness through another man's eyes! By so much the more shall I to-morrow be at the height of heart-heaviness, by how much I shall think my brother happy in having what he wishes for.

Ros. Why, then, to-morrow I cannot serve your turn for Rosalind?

Orl. I can live no longer by thinking.

Ros. I will weary you, then, no longer with idle talking. Know of me, then,—for now I speak to some purpose, [—that I know you are a gentleman of good conceit:[3] I speak not this that you should bear a good opinion of my knowledge, insomuch I say I know you are; neither do I labour for a greater esteem than may in some little measure draw a belief from you, to do yourself good, and not to grace me. Believe, then, if you please,] that I can do strange things: I have, since I was three year old, convers'd with a magician, most profound in his art, and yet not damnable. If you do love Rosalind so near the heart as your gesture cries it out, when your brother marries Aliena, shall you marry her: [I know into what straits of fortune she is driven; and it is not impossible to me, if it appear not inconvenient to you, to set her before your eyes to-morrow human as she is, and without any danger.]

Orl. Speak'st thou in sober meaning?

Ros. By my life, I do; which I tender dearly, though I say I am a magician. Therefore, put you in your best array, bid your friends; for if you will be married to-morrow, you shall; and to Rosalind, if you will.—Look, here comes a lover of mine, and a lover of hers.

Enter SILVIUS *and* PHEBE.

Phe. Youth, you have done me much ungentleness,
To show the letter that I writ to you.

Ros. I care not, if I have: it is my study
To seem despiteful and ungentle to you:
You are there follow'd by a faithful shepherd;
Look upon him, love him; he worships you.

Phe. Good shepherd, tell this youth what 't is to love.

Sil. It is to be all made of sighs and tears;
And so am I for Phebe.

Phe. And I for Ganymede.

Orl. And I for Rosalind.

Ros. And I for no woman.

Sil. It is to be all made of faith and service;—
And so am I for Phebe.

Phe. And I for Ganymede.

Orl. And I for Rosalind.

Ros. And I for no woman.

[*Sil.* It is to be all made of fantasy,
All made of passion, and all made of wishes;
All adoration, duty, and observance,
All humbleness, all patience, and impatience,
All purity, all trial, all obedience;—
And so am I for Phebe.

Phe. And so am I for Ganymede.

Orl. And so am I for Rosalind.

Ros. And so am I for no woman.

Phe. If this be so, why blame you me to love you? [*To Rosalind.*

Sil. If this be so, why blame you me to love you? [*To Phebe.*

Orl. If this be so, why blame you me to love you?

Ros. Why do you speak too,—"Why blame you me to love you?"

Orl. To her that is not here, nor doth not hear.

Ros.] Pray you, no more of this; 't is like the howling of Irish wolves against the moon.—I will help you [*to Silvius*], if I can:—I would love you [*to Phebe*], if I could.—To-morrow

[1] *Veni, vidi, vici:* Cæsar's despatch to the senate after the battle of Zela, B.C. 47.

[2] *Incontinent*, an obvious quibble.

[3] *Conceit* = intelligence.

meet me all together.—I will marry you [*to Phebe*], if ever I marry woman, and I'll be married to-morrow:—I will satisfy you [*to Orlando*], if ever I satisfied man, and you shall be married to-morrow:—I will content you [*to Silvius*], if what pleases you contents you, and you shall be married to-morrow.—As you [*to Orlando*] love Rosalind, meet:—as you [*to Silvius*] love Phebe, meet: and as I love no woman, I'll meet.—So, fare you well: I have left you commands. 131

Sil. I'll not fail, if I live.

Phe. Nor I.

Orl. Nor I. [*Exeunt.*

Song. It was a lover and his lass,
With a hey, and a ho, and a hey nonino.—(Act v. 3. 17, 18.)

[SCENE III. *Another part of the forest.*

Enter TOUCHSTONE *and* AUDREY.

Touch. To-morrow is the joyful day, Audrey; to-morrow will we be married.

Aud. I do desire it with all my heart; and I hope it is no dishonest[1] desire, to desire to be a woman of the world.[2] Here come two of the banished duke's pages.

Enter two Pages.

First Page. Well met, honest gentleman.

Touch. By my troth, well met. Come, sit, sit, and a song. 9

Sec. Page. We are for you: sit i' the middle.

First Page. Shall we clap into 't[3] roundly, without hawking, or spitting, or saying we are hoarse, which are the only prologues to a bad voice?

Sec. Page. I' faith, i' faith; and both in a tune, like two gipsies on a horse.

Song.

It was a lover and his lass,
  With a hey, and a ho, and a hey nonino,
That o'er the green corn-fields did pass
  In spring-time, the only pretty ring-time,
When birds do sing, hey ding a ding, ding:
Sweet lovers love the spring. 22

Between the acres of the rye,
  With a hey, and a ho, and a hey nonino,
These pretty country-folks would lie
  In spring-time, &c.

This carol they began that hour,
  With a hey, and a ho, and a hey nonino,
How that a life was but a flower
  In spring-time, &c. 30

[1] *Dishonest*, unchaste. [2] *To be a woman, &c.* = to marry.
[3] *Clap into 't* = begin it at once.

And therefore take the present time,
With a hey, and a ho, and a hey nonino;
For love is crowned with the prime
In spring-time, &c.

Touch. Truly, young gentlemen, though there was no great matter in the ditty, yet the note was very untuneable.

First Page. You are deceived, sir: we kept time, we lost not our time.

Touch. By my troth, yes; I count it but time lost to hear such a foolish song. God b' wi' you; and God mend your voices!—Come, Audrey.] [*Exeunt.*

SCENE IV. *Another part of the forest.*

Enter DUKE SENIOR, AMIENS, JAQUES, ORLANDO, OLIVER, *and* CELIA.

Duke S. Dost thou believe, Orlando, that the boy
Can do all this that he hath promised?

Orl. I sometimes do believe, and sometimes do not;
As those that fear they hope, and know they fear.

[*Enter* ROSALIND, SILVIUS, *and* PHEBE.

Ros. Patience once more, whiles our compáct is urg'd:—
You say, if I bring in your Rosalind, [*To the Duke.*
You will bestow her on Orlando here?

Duke S. That would I, had I kingdoms to give with her.

Ros. And you say, you will have her, when I bring her? [*To Orlando.*

Orl. That would I, were I of all kingdoms king.

Ros. You say, you'll marry me, if I be willing? [*To Phebe.*

Phe. That will I, should I die the hour after.

Ros. But if you do refuse to marry me,
You'll give yourself to this most faithful shepherd?

Phe. So is the bargain.

Ros. You say, that you'll have Phebe, if she will? [*To Silvius.*

Sil. Though to have her and death were both one thing.

Ros. I've promis'd to make all this matter even.
Keep you your word, O duke, to give your daughter;—
You yours, Orlando, to receive his daughter:—
Keep your word, Phebe, that you'll marry me,
Or else, refusing me, to wed this shepherd:—
Keep your word, Silvius, that you'll marry her,
If she refuse me:—and from hence I go,
To make these doubts all even.
[*Exeunt Rosalind and Celia.*]

Duke S. I do remember in this shepherd boy
Some lively touches of my daughter's favour.

Orl. My lord, the first time that I ever saw him
Methought he was a brother to your daughter:
But, my good lord, this boy is forest-born,
And hath been tutor'd in the rudiments
Of many desperate studies by his uncle,
Whom he reports to be a great magician,
Obscured in the circle of this forest.

Jaq. There is, sure, another flood toward, and these couples are coming to the ark. Here comes a pair of very strange beasts, which in all tongues are called fools.

Enter TOUCHSTONE *and* AUDREY.

Touch. Salutation and greeting to you all!

Jaq. Good my lord, bid him welcome: this is the motley-minded gentleman that I have so often met in the forest: he hath been a courtier, he swears.

Touch. If any man doubt that, let him put me to my purgation.[1] I have trod a measure; I have flattered a lady; I have been politic with my friend, smooth with mine enemy; I have undone three tailors; I have had four quarrels, and like to have fought one.

Jaq. And how was that ta'en up?[2]

Touch. Faith, we met, and found the quarrel was upon the seventh cause.

Jaq. How seventh cause?—Good my lord, like this fellow.

Duke S. I like him very well.

Touch. God ild you, sir; I desire you of the like. I press in here, sir, amongst the rest

[1] *Let him put me to my purgation*, let him put my statements to the proof. [2] *Ta'en up* = settled.

of the country copulatives, to swear and to forswear; according as marriage binds and blood breaks:—a poor virgin, sir, an ill-favour'd thing, sir, but mine own; a poor humour of mine, sir, to take that that no man else will: rich honesty dwells like a miser, sir, in a poor house; as your pearl in your foul oyster.

Duke S. By my faith, he is very swift and sententious.[1]

Touch. According to the fool's bolt, sir, and such dulcet diseases.

Jaq. But, for the seventh cause; how did you find the quarrel on the seventh cause?

Touch. Upon a lie seven times removed:—bear your body more seeming, Audrey:—as thus, sir. I did dislike the cut of a certain courtier's beard: he sent me word, if I said his beard was not cut well, he was in the mind it was: this is called the Retort Courteous. If I sent him word again, it was not well cut, he would send me word, he cut it to please himself: this is called the Quip Modest. If again, it was not well cut, he disabled[2] my judgment: this is called the Reply Churlish. If again, it was not well cut, he would answer, I spake not true: this is called the Reproof Valiant. If again, it was not well cut, he would say, I lied: this is called the Countercheck Quarrelsome: and so to the Lie Circumstantial and the Lie Direct.

Jaq. And how oft did you say, his beard was not well cut?

Touch. I durst go no further than the Lie Circumstantial, nor he durst not give me the Lie Direct; and so we measured swords, and parted.

Jaq. Can you nominate in order now the degrees of the lie?

Touch. O sir, we quarrel in print, by the book; as you have books for good manners: I will name you the degrees. The first, the Retort Courteous; the second, the Quip Modest; the third, the Reply Churlish; the fourth, the Reproof Valiant; the fifth, the Countercheck Quarrelsome; the sixth, the Lie with Circumstance; the seventh, the Lie Direct. All these you may avoid, but the Lie Direct; and you may avoid that too with an "if." I knew when seven justices could not take up a quarrel; but when the parties were met themselves, one of them thought but of an "if," as, "If you said so, then I said so;" and they shook hands, and swore[3] brothers. Your "if" is the only peace-maker; much virtue in "if."

Jaq. Is not this a rare fellow, my lord? he's as good at any thing, and yet a fool.

Duke S. He uses his folly like a stalking-horse, and under the presentation of that, he shoots his wit.

[*Still music.*] *Enter* [*a person representing*, HYMEN, *leading*] ROSALIND *in woman's clothes; and* CELIA.

[*Hym.* Then is there mirth in heaven,
When earthly things made even
Atone[4] together.
Good duke, receive thy daughter:
Hymen from heaven brought her,
Yea, brought her hither,
That thou mightst join her hand with his
Whose heart within his bosom is.]

Ros. To you I give myself, for I am yours. [*To Duke Senior*
To you I give myself, for I am yours. [*To Orlando.*

Duke S. If there be truth in sight, you are my daughter.

Orl. If there be truth in shape, you are my Rosalind.

Phe. If sight and shape be true,
Why, then,—my love adieu!

Ros. I'll have no father, if you be not he:— [*To Duke Senior.*
I'll have no husband, if you be not he:— [*To Orlando.*
Nor ne'er wed woman, if you be not she. [*To Phebe.*

[*Hym.* Peace, ho! I bar[5] confusion:
'T is I must make conclusion
Of these most strange events:
Here's eight that must take hands
To join in Hymen's bands,
If truth holds true contents.
You and you no cross shall part:— [*To Orlando and Rosalind.*

[1] *Sententious*, i.e. full of *sententiæ* or maxims.
[2] *Disabled*, denied the ability of.

[3] *Swore*, swore to be.
[4] *Atone*, are made one, reconciled.
[5] *Bar*, forbid.

You and you are heart in heart:—
[*To Oliver and Celia.*
You to his love must accord, [*To Phebe.*
Or have a woman to your lord:—
You and you are sure together,
[*To Touchstone and Audrey.*
As the winter to foul weather.
Whiles a wedlock-hymn we sing,
Feed yourselves with questioning;
That reason wonder may diminish,
How thus we met, and these things finish.

Song.

Wedding is great Juno's crown:
O blessed bond of board and bed!
'T is Hymen peoples every town;
High wedlock, then, be honoured:
Honour, high honour, and renown,
To Hymen, god of every town!]

Duke S. O my dear niece, welcome thou art to me!
Even daughter, welcome, in no less degree.

Phe. I will not eat my word, now thou art mine;
Thy faith my fancy to thee doth combine.
[*To Silvius.*

Enter Jaques de Bois.

Jaq. de B. Let me have audience for a word or two:
I am the second son of old Sir Roland,
That bring these tidings to this fair assembly.—
Duke Frederick, hearing how that every day
Men of great worth resorted to this forest,
Address'd a mighty power;[1] which were on foot,
In his own conduct, purposely to take
His brother here, and put him to the sword;
And to the skirts of this wild wood he came;
Where meeting with an old religious man,
After some question with him, was converted
Both from his enterprise and from the world;
His crown bequeathing to his banish'd brother,
And all their lands restor'd to them again
That were with him exiled. This to be true,
I do engage my life.

Duke S. Welcome, young man;
Thou offer'st fairly[2] to thy brothers' wedding:
[To one, his lands withheld; and to the other,
A land itself at large, a potent dukedom.]
First, in this forest, let us do those ends
That here were well begun and well begot:
And after, every of this happy number,

Jaq. de B. Where meeting with an old religious man,
After some question with him, was converted
Both from his enterprise and from the world.
—(Act v. 4. 166-168.)

That have endur'd shrewd[3] days and nights with us,
Shall share the good of our returned fortune,
According to the measure of their states.
Meantime forget this new-fall'n dignity,
And fall into our rustic revelry.—
Play, music!—and you, brides and bride-grooms all,
With measure heap'd in joy, to the measures fall.

Jaq. Sir, by your patience.—If I heard you rightly,

[1] *Power*, army.
[2] *Offer'st fairly*, i.e. dost make a fair offering.
[3] *Shrewd*, hard, disagreeable.

The duke hath put on a religious life,
And thrown into neglect the pompous[1] court?
Jaq. de B. He hath.
Jaq. To him will I: out of these convertites
There is much matter to be heard and learn'd.—
You [*to Duke S.*] to your former honour I bequeath;
Your patience and your virtue well deserve it:—
You [*to Orlando*] to a love that your true faith doth merit:—
You [*to Oliver*] to your land, and love, and great allies:—
You [*to Silvius*] to a long and well-deserved bed:—
And you [*to Touchstone*] to wrangling; for thy loving voyage
Is but for two months victuall'd.—So, to your pleasures:
I am for other than for dancing measures.
Duke S. Stay, Jaques, stay.
Jaq. To see no pastime I:—what you would have
I'll stay to know at your abandon'd cave.
[*Exit.*
Duke S. Proceed, proceed: we will begin these rites,
As we do trust they'll end, in true delights.
[*A dance.*

EPILOGUE.

Ros. [It is not the fashion to see the lady the epilogue; but it is no more unhandsome than to see the lord the prologue.] If it be true that good wine needs no bush, 't is true that a good play needs no epilogue: yet to good wine they do use good bushes; and good plays prove the better by the help of good epilogues. What a case am I in, then, that am neither a good epilogue, nor cannot insinuate with you in the behalf of a good play! I am not furnished like a beggar, therefore to beg will not become me: my way is, to conjure you; and I'll begin with the women. I charge you, O women, for the love you bear to men, to like as much of this play as please you: and I charge you, O men, for the love you bear to women (as I perceive by your simpering, none of you hates them), that between you and the women the play may please. If I were a woman, I would kiss as many of you as had beards that pleased me, complexions that liked me, [and breaths that I defied not:] and, I am sure, as many as have good beards, or good faces, [or sweet breaths,] will, for my kind offer, when I make curtsy, bid me farewell.
[*Exeunt.*

[1] *Pompous*, ceremonious.

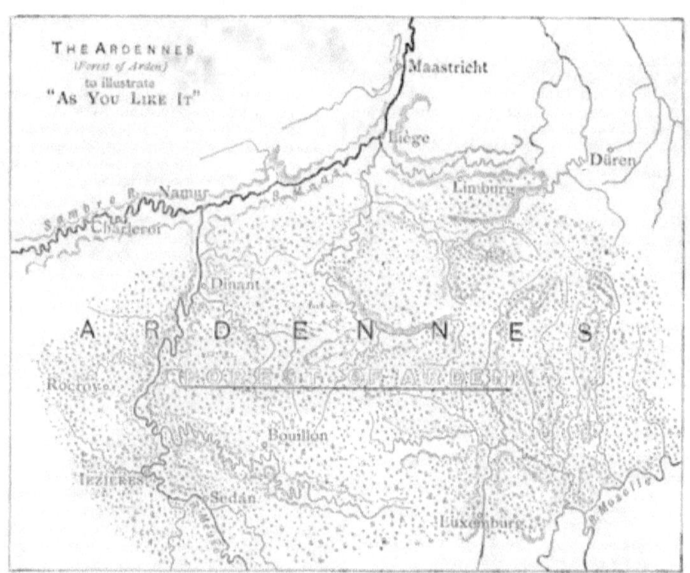

NOTES TO AS YOU LIKE IT.

ACT I. Scene 1.

1. Line 1.—It may be convenient to give the commencement of Lodge's Rosalynde: "There dwelled adjoyning to the cittie of Bordeaux a knight of most honourable parentage, whome Fortune had graced with many favors, and Nature honoured with sundry exquisite qualities, so beautified with the excellence of both, as it was a question whether Fortune or Nature were more prodigall in deciphering the riches of their bounties. Wise he was, as holding in his head, a supreme conceipt of pollicie, reaching with Nestor into the depth of all civil governement; and to make his wisedome more gratious, he had that *salem ingenii*, and pleasant eloquence that was so highly commended in Ulisses: his valour was no lesse than his witte, and the stroke of his launce no lesse forcible than the sweetnesse of his tongue was perswasive; for he was for his courage chosen the principall of all the Knights of Malta. This hardy knight thus enricht with Vertue and honour, surnamed Sir John of Burdeux, having the prime of his youth in sundry battailes against the Turkes, at last (as the date of time hath his course) grewe aged. His haires were silver hued, and the map of his age was figured on his forehead: honour sate in the furrowes of his face, and many yeares were pourtrayed in his wrinckled lineaments, that all men might perceive his glasse was runne, and that nature of necessitie chalenged her due. Sir John (that with the phenix knewe the tearme of his life was now expired, and could. with the swan, discover his end by her songs) having three sons by his wife Lynida, the very pride of all his forepassed yeares, thought now (seeing death by constraint would compel him to leave them) to bestow upon them such a legacie as might bewray his love, and increase their insuing amitie. Calling therefore these yong gentlemen before him, in the presence of his fellow Knights of Malta, he resolved to leave them a memorial of all his fatherly care in setting downe a methode of their brotherly duties. Having therefore death in his lookes to moove them to pittie, and teares in his eyes to paint out the depth of his passions, taking his eldest sonne by the hand, he began thus. . . . First, therefore, unto thee Saladyne, the eldest, and therefore the chiefest piller of my house, wherein should bee ingraved as wel the excellency of thy fathers qualities, as the essentiall fortune of his proportion, to thee I give foureteene ploughlands, with all my manor and richest

plate. Next, unto Fernandine I bequeath twelve ploughlands. But, unto Rosader, the youngest, I give my horse, my armour, and my launce with sixteene ploughlands; for if the inwarde thoughts be discovered by outward shadows, Rosader will exceed you all in bountie and honour" (Collier, Shakespeare's Library, i. pp. 7, 8).

2. Line 2: HE *bequeathed*.—Ff. read: "upon this fashion bequeathed me by will," &c., leaving the verbs *bequeathed* and *charged* below without any apparent nominative. Warburton, Hanmer, and Heath inserted the words *my father* before *bequeathed*. The very simple emendation in the text is Blackstone's conjecture, adopted by Malone and followed by Dyce. The *he* would easily drop out before the *be* of the *bequeathed*. As the sentence stands in Ff. it certainly does not seem to make much sense unless we suppose that both verbs *bequeathed* and *charged* are impersonal.

3. Line 5: *My brother Jaques he keeps at school*.—So in Lodge's romance Saladin (the eldest son) says: "My brother Fernandine, hee is at Paris, poring on a fewe papers, having more insight into sophistrie and principles of philosophie, than anie warlyke indeveurs" (Collier, i. p. 17).

4. Line 6: *school*.—For *school*="university," we may compare Hamlet, i. 2. 112-114:

For your intent
In going back to *school* in Wittenberg,
It is most retrograde to our desire.

That the distinction between the school and the university was very slight many facts would show. Thus Lord Herbert of Cherbury tells us in his delightful autobiography that he entered at Queen's College, Oxford, in his thirteenth year; Sir Thomas More was a Master of Arts at sixteen; while various quaint enactments that survive in the statutes of the two universities, Oxford and Cambridge, point very decidedly the same way. For instance, at Cambridge it is expressly required that no undergraduate should play marbles on the steps of the senate-house; likewise no undergraduate is allowed to bowl his hoop down the Petty Cury, a crowded thoroughfare; and at Oxford, if I am not mistaken, the whipping of students is a contingency for which the statutes still provide. At any rate, in the seventeenth century the birching of undergraduates was by no means unusual. Milton, if we may credit Aubrey, experienced the indignity; and à propos of a line in Middleton's Chaste Maid in Cheapside, iii. 2. 131, "you'll ne'er lin (*i.e.* cease) till I make your tutor *whip you*," Mr. Bullen quotes a curious passage from a letter written by Chamberlain in 1612: "I know not," (it runs) "whether you have heard that a son of the Bishop of Bristol killed himself with a knife to avoid the disgrace of *breeching*" (Middleton's Works, Bullen's ed. v. 60).

From these references it will be seen that *school* and *university* were almost synonymous terms.

5. Line 13: *taught their* MANAGE.—A word specially used of the training of horses. So Todd (Johnson's Dictionary, *sub voce*) quotes from Peacham: "The horse you must draw in his career with his *manage* and turn, doing the curvetto." Compare, too, for a good instance in point, Richard II. iii. 3. 178, 179:

Down, down I come; like glist'ring Phaethon,
Wanting the *manage* of unruly jades.

6. Line 44: *here in your* ORCHARD.—*Orchard* and *garden* were almost interchangeable terms (see Much Ado, note 62); though Harrison in his Description of England (New Shakspere Society Publications, p. 323) only includes under the latter "such grounds as are wrought with the spade by man's hand, for so the case requireth."

7. Line 46.—A curious commentary on the first two scenes in this play is furnished in Earle's Characters. Earle describes in his own delightful way a variety of people, amongst them the "Younger Brother," and really in some of his remarks he might be directly alluding to As You Like It. It may be worth while to quote a few of these pithy sentences: "The pride of his house has vndone him (*i.e.* the younger brother, the Orlando of Earle's sketch), which the elder Knighthood must sustaine, and his beggery that Knighthood. His birth and bringing vp will not suffer him to descend to the meanes to get wealth: but hee stands at the mercy of the World, and which is worse of his brother. He is something better than the Seruing-men; yet they more saucy with him, then hee bold with the master, who beholds him with a countenance of sterne awe, and checks him oftner then his Liueries. His brothers old suites and hee are much alike in request, and cast off now and then one to the other. . . . If his Annuity stretch so farre he is sent to the Vniuersity, and with great heart burning takes vpon him the Ministry. . . . Hee is commonly discontented, and desperate, and the forme of his exclamation is, that Churle my brother" (John Earle's Micro-cosmographie, Arber's Reprint, pp. 29, 30).

8. Line 121: *in the forest of* ARDEN.—The scene, of course, is borrowed from Lodge. Malone quotes from Spenser, Astrophel (1595):

Into a forest wide and waste he came,
Where store he heard to be of salvage pray;
So wide a forest and so waste as this,
Nor famous *Ardeyn*, nor fowle Arlo, is.

9. Line 150: *an envious* EMULATOR.—*Emulate*, with its cognates, always has a bad sense in Shakespeare. Compare Troilus and Cressida, ii. 3. 242:

He is not *emulous*, as Achilles is;

Julius Cæsar, ii. 3. 13, 14:

My heart laments that virtue cannot live
Out of the teeth of *emulation*.

10. Line 170: *Now will I stir this* GAMESTER.—Here, as elsewhere, *gamester* has the general sense of "a merry fellow." Compare Taming of the Shrew, ii. 402, 403:

Sirrah young *gamester*, your father were a fool
To give thee all.

So Henry VIII. i. 4. 45.

ACT I. Scene 2.

11. Line 35: *Fortune from her* WHEEL.—We have a dissertation on "giddy *fortune's* furious fickle *wheel*" in Henry V. iii. 6. 31-41.

12. Line 52: *Nature's* NATURAL; *i.e.* fool, as in Romeo and Juliet, ii. 4. 96: "like a great *natural*, that runs loll-

ing up and down." Scotch people are fond of using the word in this sense.

13. Line 95: *since the little wit that fools have was silenc'd.*—It has been plausibly suggested that this line refers to some inhibition of the players. Compare the vexed passage in Hamlet, ii. 2. 340–360, with the discussion of the subject in the Introduction to the Clarendon Press Ed. The relations between the civic authorities and the theatrical companies were very strained, and the intolerance of the former seems to have come in for a plentiful supply of satire. Compare the Induction to Beaumont and Fletcher's Knight of the Burning Pestle:

> *Citizen.* Hold your peace, goodman boy!
> *Speaker of Prologue.* What do you mean, sir?
> *Cit.* That you have no good meaning. This seven years there hath been plays at this house, I have observed it, you have still girds at citizens.
> *S. of Prol.* Are you a member of the noble city?
> *Cit.* I am.
> *S. of Prol.* And a freeman?
> *Cit.* Yea, and a grocer.
> *S. of Prol.* So, grocer; then by your sweet favour, we intend no abuse to the city.
> *Cit.* No, sir? Yes, sir; if you were not resolved to play the jacks, what need you study for new subjects, purposely to abuse your betters?

14. Line 131: *With bills on their necks.*—Farmer thought that these words should form the conclusion of Le Beau's speech, and Dyce printed the passage so. Without venturing to adopt the proposal, I think a good deal may be said in its favour. For the expression we may compare Lodge's romance: "on a day, sitting with Aliena in a great dumpe, she cast up her eye, and saw where Rosader came pacing towardes them with *his forrest bill on his necke.*" So a page or two further on: "seeing not only a shepheardesse and her boy forced, but his brother wounded, he heaved up a forrest *bill* he had *on his neck*" (Collier, i. p. 85). Steevens refers (rather vaguely, *more suo*) to Sidney's Arcadia, bk. i.: "with a sword by his side, a forest *bille on his necke.*" For a similar word-play, compare Much Ado, iii. 3. 191, and see note 231 of that play. But the *bill* on which the *équivoque* turns was not a commercial *bill*, but such *bills* as were posted up as advertisements (see Much Ado, note 8), or perhaps such a *bill* or "paper" as was hung round the necks of condemned perjurers (see Love's Labour's Lost, note 110). The "forest *bill*" of Lodge's story was probably a *bill-hook*, and not a watchman's or soldier's *bill*.

15. Line 132: "*Be it known unto all men by these presents;*" i.e. the formal phrase with which all deeds-poll commenced, the Latin running *Noverint universi per presentes.* "This," says Lord Campbell, "is the technical phraseology referred to by Thomas Nash in his Epistle to the Gentlemen Students of the two Universities, in the year 1589, when he is supposed to have denounced the author of Hamlet as one of those who had 'left the trade of *Noverint*, whereto they were born, for handfuls of tragical speeches'—that is, an attorney's clerk become a poet, and penning a stanza when he should engross" (Shakespeare's Legal Acquirements, pp. 40, 41).

16. Line 133.—This incident, it will be seen, is taken directly from Lodge. "At last when the tournament ceased, the wrastling beganne, and the Norman presented himselfe as a chalenger against all commers, but hee looked lyke Hercules when he advaunst himselfe agaynst Achelolis, so that the furie of his countenance amazed all that durst attempte to incounter with him in any deed of activitie: til at last a lustie Francklin of the country came with two tall men, that were his sonnes, of good lyniaments and comely personage: the eldest of these dooing his obeysance to the king entered the lyst, and presented himselfe to the Norman, who straight coapt with him, and as a man that would triumph in the glorie of his strength, roused himselfe with such furie, that not onely hee gave him the fall, but killed him with the weight of his corpulent personage; which the yoonger brother seeing, lepte presently into the place, and thirstie after the revenge, assayled the Norman with such valour, that at the first incounter hee brought him to his knees: which repulst so the Norman, that recovering himselfe, feare of disgrace doubling his strength, hee stept so stearnely to the yoong Francklin, that taking him up in his armes hee threw him against the grounde so violently, that hee broake his necke, and so ended his dayes with his brother. At this unlookt for massacre the people murmured, and were all in a deepe passion of pittie; but the Franklin, father unto these, never chaunged his countenance, but as a man of a courageous resolution tooke up the bodies of his sonnes without shewe of outward discontent" (Collier, i. pp. 19, 20).

17. Line 150: *to feel this* BROKEN MUSIC.—For some explanation of this phrase we must turn to Chappell's Popular Music of the Olden Time. In volume i. p. 246, Mr. Chappell has the following passage:—"Richard Braithwait, a writer of this reign (James I.'s), has 'set down *some Rules for the Government of the House of an Earl,*' in which the Earl was to keep 'five musitions skillfull in that commendable sweete science,' and they were required to teach the Earl's children to sing, and to play upon the base-viol, the virginals, the lute, and the bandora, or cittern. When he gave 'great feasts,' the musicians were to play, whilst the service was going to the table, upon sackbuts, cornets, shawms, and 'such other *instruments going with wind,*' and upon '*viols, violins, or other broken musicke,*' during the repast." Thus far Mr. Chappell, who in a note adds this comment, "'Broken Music,' as is evident from this and other passages, means what we now term 'a string band.' . . . The term originated probably from harps, lutes, and such other stringed instruments as were played without a bow, not having the capability to sustain a long note to its full duration of time." This account has been generally accepted; it will be found in the note on Troilus and Cressida, iii. 1. 52–54. Apparently, however, Mr. Chappell has now changed his opinion in favour of the following view:—"Some instruments, such as viols, violins, flutes, etc., were formerly made in sets of fours, which when played together formed a 'consort.' If one or more of the instruments of one set were substituted for the corresponding ones of another set, the result was no longer a 'consort,' but '*broken music.*'" This explanation, privately communicated to Mr. Aldis Wright, will be found in the latter's note on the present passage; as Mr. Chappell's authority on

musical points is final, it must be agreed to. For the same quibbling use of the phrase, cf. Henry V. v. 2. 261:

> Come, your answer in *broken music*; for thy voice is *music* and thy English *broken*.

18. Line 169: *such* ODDS *in the* MAN.—So the Folios: "*Men*" is an obvious, but unnecessary, correction. The sense is, "such advantage, superiority on the side of the *man*," *i.e.* Charles. Compare Richard II. iii. 4. 89: "And with that *odds* he weighs King Richard down."

19. Lines 211-232.—This is the wrestling scene in Lodge's romance. "On the contrary part, Rosader while he breathed was not idle, but stil cast his eye upon Rosalynde, who to incourage him with a favour lent him such an amorous looke, as might have made the most coward desperate: which glance of Rosalynd so fiered the passionate desires of Rosader, that turning to the Norman hee ranne upon him and braved him with a strong encounter. The Norman received him as valiantly, that there was a sore combat, hard to judge on whose side fortune would be prodigal. At last Rosader, calling to minde the beautie of his new mistresse, the fame of his fathers honours, and the disgrace that should fal to his house by his misfortune, rowsed himselfe and threw the Norman against the ground, falling uppon his chest with so willing a weight, that the Norman yelded nature her due, and Rosader the victorie" (Collier, i. p. 21).

20. Line 230: *I am not yet well* BREATH'D.—As we should say, "I have not yet got my wind." Compare Love's Labour 's Lost, note 212.

21. Line 254: STICKS *me at heart*.—We have *stick* = "stab" in Troilus and Cressida, iii. 2. 202: "to *stick* the heart of falsehood."

22. Line 258: *Wear this for me*.—Lady Martin (Helen Faucit) says "She has taken a chain from her neck, and stealthily kissing it—at least I always used to do so—she gives it to Orlando. . . ." (Some of Shakespeare's Female Characters, p. 306).

It may be worth while to note that with Elizabethan ladies the wearing of jewelry was a universal habit, against which indeed satirists raised an occasional protest. So Stubbes says: "their fingers (*i.e.* women's) are decked with gold, silver and precious stones, their wrists with bracelets and armlets of gold, and other precious jewels: their hands are covered with their sweet washed gloves, embroidered with gold, silver and what not" (Anatomy of Abuses, New Shaks. Soc. Reprint, part i. p. 79).

23. Line 263: *Is but a* QUINTAIN, *a mere lifeless block*.—"*Quintine*" in the Folios. Riding at the *quintain* was a popular sport of which Strutt gives the following description: "Tilting or combating at the *quintain* is a military exercise of high antiquity, and antecedent, I doubt not, to the jousts and tournaments. The *quintain* originally was nothing more than the trunk of a tree, a post set up for the practice of the tyros in chivalry. Afterwards a staff or spear was fixed in the earth, and a shield being hung upon it, was the mark to strike at. The dexterity of the performer consisted in smiting the shield in such a manner as to break the ligatures and bear it to the ground. In process of time this diversion was improved, and instead of a staff and the shield, the resemblance of a human figure carved in wood was introduced. To render the appearance of this figure more formidable, it was generally made in the likeness of a Turk or a Saracen, armed at all points, bearing a shield upon his left arm, and brandishing a club or a sabre with his right. The *quintain* thus fashioned was placed upon a pivot, and so contrived as to move round with facility. In running at this figure, it was necessary for the horseman to direct his lance with great adroitness, and make his stroke upon the forehead between the eyes or upon the nose; for if he struck wide of these parts, especially upon the shield, the *quintain* turned about with much velocity, and, in case he was not exceeding careful, would give him a severe blow upon the back with the wooden sabre held in the right hand, which was considered as highly disgraceful to the performer, while it excited the laughter and ridicule of the spectators" (Sports and Pastimes, bk. iii. ch. 1. ed. 1801, p. 89).

Compare too Stow: "I have seen a *quinten* set up on Cornehill, by the Leaden Hall, where the attendants on the lords of merry disports have run and made great pastime; for he that hit not the broad end of the quinten was of all men laughed to scorn; and he that hit it full if he rid not the faster, had a sound blow in his neck with a bag full of sand hanged on the other end" (quoted in Brand, Popular Antiquities, vol. i. p. 302, where Ellis gives other interesting references). Illustrations of the *quintain* in its various forms will be found in the Var. Ed. vi. p. 517. At the village of Offham in Kent there still stands an old *quintain*, which was repaired in 1834, and which is said to be the only one now remaining in England. (See the Antiquary, vol. xvi. p. 101.)

24. Line 278: *The duke is* HUMOROUS.—For *humorous* = "capricious," cf. King John, iii. 1. 119, 120:

> Thou Fortune's champion that dost never fight
> But when her *humorous* ladyship is by.

So Henry V. ii. 4. 28:

> a vain, giddy, shallow, *humorous* youth.

Ben Jonson applies the epithet, in the same sense, to the moon.

> O, you awake them: Come away,
> Times be short, are made for play;
> The *humorous* moon too will not stay:
> What doth make you thus delay.

See Todd's Johnson, *sub voce* "humorous," where the lines are quoted, without reference.

25. Line 284: *But yet, indeed, the* LESSER *is his daughter*.—Ff. have *taller*, an obvious slip (cf. next scene, 117) on the part of Shakespeare or of the printer. Mr. Spedding proposed *lesser*, which, following the Globe ed., I have printed. We have here an instance of the fact, which has been pointed out by more than one writer, that there evidently were two youths who took the women's parts, in the company of which Shakespeare was part manager, one tall and the other short. Compare Midsummer Night's Dream, iii. 2. 289-292, 303-335, and other passages in that scene, whence it is clear that Hermia was played by the short actor, and Helena by the tall one.

26. Line 299: *from the smoke into the* SMOTHER.—*Smother* does not occur elsewhere in Shakespeare as a

substantive. Todd—Johnson's Dictionary, *s.v.*—quotes from Bacon's Essays: "A man were better relate himself to a statue than suffer his thoughts to pass in *smother*."

ACT I. Scene 3.

27. *Lines* 1-140.—How far this scene is founded on Lodge's narrative some extracts from the latter will show. "Scarce had Rosalynde ended her madrigale, before Torismond (*i.e.* the usurping duke) came in with his daughter Alinda and many of the peers of France, who were enamoured of her beauty; which Torismond perceiving, fearing lest her perfection might be the beginning of his prejudice, and the hope of his fruit ende in the beginning of her blossomes, he thought to banish her from the court; for, quoth he to himselfe, her face is so ful of favour, that it pleads pittie in the eye of every man: her beautie is so heavenly and devine, that she wil prove to me as Helen did to Priam: some of the Peeres will ayme at her love, end the marriage, and then, in his wives right attempt the kingdome. To prevent therefore had I wist in all these actions, shee tarryes not about the court, but shall (as an exile) eyther wander to her father, or else seeke other fortunes. In this humour, with a sterne countenance, ful of wrath, he breathed out this censure unto her before the peers, that charged that that night shee were not seene about the court: for (quoth he) I have heard of thy aspiring speeches and intended treasons. This doome was strange unto Rosalynde, and presently covred with the shield of her innocence, she boldly brake out in reverent tearmes to have cleared herself; but Torismond would admit of no reason, nor durst his lords plead for Rosalynde" (Collier, i. pp. 27, 28).

Rosalind is thus banished, and Alinda resolves to follow her, and they concert measures for flight: "At this Rosalynd began to comfort her (*i.e.* Alinda), and after shee had wept a fewe kinde teares in the bosome of her Alinda, shee gave her heartie thankes, and then they sat them downe to consult how they should travel. Alinda grieved at nothing but that they might have no man in their company, saying, it would bee their greatest prejudice in that two women went wandring without either guide or attendant. Tush (quoth Rosalynd) art thou a woman, and hast not a sodeine shift to prevent a misfortune? I (thou seest) am of a tall stature, and would very wel become the person and apparel of a page: thou shalt bee my mistresse, and I wil play the man so properly, that (trust me) in what company so ever I come I wil not be discovered. I will buy me a suite, and have my rapier very handsomly at my side, and if any knave offer wrong, your page wil show him the poynt of his weapon. At this Alinda smiled, and upon this they agreed, and presently gathered up al their jewels, which they trussed up in a casket, and Rosalynd in all hast provided her of robes; and Alinda being called Aliena, and Rosalynd Ganimede, they travelled along the vineyardes, and by many bywaies, at last got to the forrest side, where they travelled by the space of two or three dayes without seeing anye creature, being often in danger of wilde beasts, and payned with many passionate sorrowes" (Collier, i. pp. 31, 32).

28. Line 11: *No, some of it is for my* CHILD'S FATHER.—So the Folio. Rowe (sec. ed.) changed the words to *my father's child*, a reading also given by Collier's MS. Corrector; it was approved by Coleridge and printed by Dyce, and is always adopted on the stage. Personally I think there is not a little to be said in its favour, though we should remember that throughout the play there are similar free touches to which modern taste may take exception. Rosalind may only mean to say "for the father of my child if ever I have one;" *i.e.* "for him whom I love." [There can be no doubt that, for the purposes of the theatre, Pope's emendation is preferable to the reading of the F.; but it is a most puzzling point to decide whether or not the emendation is justifiable. This is precisely one of those cases in which the poet does not make one of his characters say what we expect him to say; but something quite the contrary. Rosalind is in such a mischievous humour just now, and so excited by the sudden passion she has conceived for Orlando, that she can think of nothing else but of him; and it is quite natural that she should use such a singular expression, however indelicate it may seem, as she is speaking in confidence to Celia Such a violent feat of anticipation as picturing herself the wife of the man she has just fallen in love with at first sight, and already a mother, would have a certain fascination for her from its very audacity; and she might use this expression, under such circumstances, with far less indelicacy than she could had they been long acquainted, or lovers, in the ordinary sense of the term. But all this is too subtle to be made clear by the actress in speaking; and therefore no one can quarrel with the Rosalind who does not speak the exact text here.—F. A. M.]

29. Line 114: *And with a kind of* UMBER SMIRCH *my face.*—*Umber*, according to Nares, is a species of ochre, so called because originally brought from *Umbria*. Ben Jonson has the verb "to *umber*," *i.e.* to stain a dark, dull colour, in the Alchemist, v. 3:

> You had taken the pains
> To dye your beard, and *umbre o'er your face*.
> —Gifford's Ben Jonson, vol. iv. p. 184.

Compare also Henry V. act iv. Chorus, 8, 9:

> Fire answers fire, and through their paly flames,
> Each battle sees the other's *umber'd face*.

In Johnson's Dict. (Todd's ed.) I find the following from Dryden: "*Umbre* is very sensible and earthy; there is nothing but pure black which can dispute with it" (reference not given).

30. Line 119: *a gallant* CURTLE-AXE *upon my thigh.*—For the form compare Henry V. iv. 2. 21:

> To give each naked *curtle-axe* a stain.

In Cotgrave the word appears as "*cuttelas*, or *courtelas*;" "perhaps," says Skeat, "borrowed from Ital. *Coltellaccio*, which is at any rate the same word."

31. Line 122: *a* SWASHING *and a martial outside*; *i.e.* a swaggering, blustering air; cf. *swash-buckler*. The word, according to Skeat, is partly imitative, and was defined by the old lexicographers as meaning "to make a noise with swords against targets" (see Johnson's Dict. Todd's ed. *s.v.*). For its use compare Romeo and Juliet, i. 1. 70:

> Draw, if you be men.—Gregory, remember thy *swashing* blow;

and Ben Jonson, Staple of News, v. 2:

> I do confess a *swashing* blow.
> —Ben Jonson, Works, vol. v. 305.

For *swashers* = "bullies," "braggarts," see Henry V. iii. 2. 30; and the substantive *swash* (= bluster) occurs in The Three Ladies of London:

> I will flaunt and brave it after the lusty *swash*.

32.—In the acting edition act I. ends with the scene between Orlando and Adam, which is the third scene of the present act in the Folio. This arrangement is, perhaps, an improvement; as we may suppose the flight of Orlando and that of Rosalind and Celia to have taken place about the same time; but another change made in the acting version is almost indefensible, and that is the transference of the speeches of the First Lord in the present scene to Jaques, a transference made, of course, with the object of giving more importance to that part, which, demanding great elocutionary skill, is generally assigned to a leading actor. This change involves a most ridiculous alteration of the text, by which the Duke is made to address all his speeches *to* Jaques personally, instead of speaking *of* him in his absence. It is to be hoped that when next this play is revived in any one of our first class theatres this unjustifiable tampering with the text may be omitted, and the speeches of the First Lord restored to the proper speaker. If the actor of Jaques likes to double the parts of the First Lord and Jaques there cannot be much objection to that arrangement.—F. A. M.

ACT II. Scene 1.

33. Lines 13, 14:

> *Which, like the toad, ugly and venomous,*
> *Wears yet a precious jewel in his head.*

"Among the vulgar errors of Shakespeare's day was the belief that the head of the toad contained a stone possessing great medicinal virtues" (Thiselton Dyer's Folklore of Shakespeare, pp. 245, 246). This superstition is perpetually alluded to: *e.g.* in The Woman's Prize, v. 1:

> And as we say verbatim,
> Fell to the bottom, broke his casting-bottle,
> Lost a fair *toadstone* of some eighteen shillings.
> —Beaumont & Fletcher, Works, vol. vii. p. 199;

and in Monsieur Thomas, iii. 1:

> In most physicians heads
> There is a kind of *toadstone* bred, whose virtue . . .
> —Vol. vii. (Dyce), p. 356.

So Ben Jonson (quoted by Nares), The Fox, ii. 3:

> His saffron jewel with the *toadstone* in 't.

Steevens gives an extract from Lupton's Book of Notable Things: "You shall knowe whether the *Tode-stone* be the ryght and perfect stone or not. Holde the stone before a Tode, so that he may see it; and if it be a ryght and true stone the Tode will leape towarde it, and make as though he would snatch it. He envieth so much that man should have that stone." Elsewhere Lupton says that the *toadstone, or crepaudina,* "touching any part envenomed by the bite of a rat, wasp, spider, or any other venomous beast, ceases the pain and swelling thereof" (Var. Ed. vi. p. 381).

34. Line 23: *Being native* BURGHERS *of this desert* CITY.—Steevens aptly refers to Drayton's Polyolbion, song 13, l. 60:

> Where, fearless of the hunt, the hart securely stood,
> And everywhere walk'd free, a *burgess* of the wood.

Perhaps Shakespeare remembered a couplet in Lodge's romance:

> About her wondering stood
> *The citizens of wood.*

Compare line 55.

35. Line 24: *with* FORKED HEADS.—That is, arrow heads. Compare Middleton's A Mad World My Masters:

> While the broad arrow with the *forked head*
> Misses.

So Lear, i. 1. 145–147:

> *Lear.* The *bow is bent and drawn;* make from the shaft.
> *Kent.* Let it fall rather, though the *fork* invade
> The region of my heart;

where the Clarendon Press editor shows that a *forked* arrow was *not* (as Steevens asserted) a barbed arrow.

36. Line 33: *a poor* SEQUESTER'D *stag.*—"Retired," "withdrawn," the verb being usually transitive; for the other use cf. Milton: "To *sequester* out of the world into Atlantick and Eutopian polities, which can never be drawn into use, will not mend our condition" (Areopagitica, Hales, p. 25). Every one will remember Gray's "adown the cool *sequestered* vale of life" (Elegy, l. 75).

37. Lines 38–40:

> *the big round tears*
> *Cours'd one another down his innocent nose*
> *In piteous chase.*

We have repeated allusions to the idea that the hunted deer *shed tears* at the approach of death. Thus Dyer (Folklore of Shakespeare, p. 171) quotes Bartholomæus (De Proprietate Rerum): "When the hart is arered, he fleethe to a ryver or ponde, and roreth cryeth and *wepeth* when he is take." Again, Steevens refers (Malone, Var. Ed. vi. p. 382) to Drayton's Polyolbion, xiii. 160–161, where, upon the lines:

> He who the Mourner is to his owne dying Corse.
> Upon the ruthlesse earthe his *precious teares lets fall,*

the marginal note runs: "the harte *weepeth* at his dying; his tears are held to be precious in medicine." Classical scholars will remember the beautiful verses in the seventh book of the Æneid, 500–502:

> Saucius at quadrupes nota intra tecta refugit,
> Successitque gemens stabulis, questuque cruentus
> Atque *imploranti similis* tectum omne replebat;

which Conington (iii. p. 40) aptly parallels by an expression in Dryden's Annus Mirabilis:

> She (the hare) trembling creeps upon the ground away
> And looks back to him (the hound) *with beseeching eyes;*
> —Stanza 132.

a humanizing touch that recalls many of Landseer's pictures. Every one will recollect Hamlet's

> Why, let the *stricken deer* go *weep.*
> —iii. 2. 282.

38. Line 57: *that poor and broken bankrupt.*—The Rugby editor suggests that Shakespeare may have been thinking of the experiences of his own father. In line 50 I have followed Dyce and others in reading "*the* coun-

try;" F. 1 has *country* alone, which would then be pronounced as a trisyllable.

ACT II. Scene 2.

39. Line 3: *Are of consent and sufferance.*—Explained as being a quasi-legal term, "applied to a landlord who takes no steps to eject a tenant whose time is expired."

40. Line 8: *My lord, the* ROYNISH *clown, at whom so oft . . .*—"*Roynish.* Mangy, or scabbed; from *rogneux*, Fr. A Chaucerian word," says Nares (Halliwell's Ed. *sub voce*), who quotes from Gabriel Harvey's Pierce's Supererogat:

> Although she were a lusty rampe, somewhat like Gallemetta or Maid-Marian, yet she was not such a *roinish* rannel.

Compare, too, Romaunt of the Rose, 988:

> The foule crooked bowe hidous,
> That Knottie was, and all *roinous*.
> —Bell's Ed. of Chaucer's Works, vol. vii. p. 43.

It is of the same derivation as *ronyon;* compare Macbeth, i. 3. 6:

> "Aroint thee, witch!" the rump-fed *ronyon* cries;

and Merry Wives, iv. 2. 195.

ACT II. Scene 3.

41. Line 8: *The* BONNY PRISER *of the humorous duke.*—So F. 2, F. 3, F. 4. F. 1 has *bonnie.* What exception can be taken *to bonny* I am at a loss to understand; it makes excellent sense here, and it occurs elsewhere in Shakespeare, *e.g.* II. Henry VI. v. 2. 11, 12:

> And made a prey for carrion kites and crows
> Even of the *bonny* beast he lov'd so well.

Warburton conjectured *boney*, which Dyce accepted—"as Charles is here called '*bony*,' so in the preceding scene he is called '*sinewy*.'" The change seems to me to be at once unnecessary and undesirable. *Priser* may, as Singer thinks, have been the technical title of a wrestler, a *prise* (French, *prendre, pris*) being the ordinary wrestling term for grappling with the adversary. Probably, however, Mr. Aldis Wright is correct in his explanation: "prize-fighter, champion; properly one who contends for a prize." He quotes two passages from Ben Jonson's Cynthia's Revels—iv. 1: "Well, I have a plot upon these *prizers;*" and v. 2: "Appeareth no man yet to answer the *prizer?*"

42. Lines 59, 60:

> *Thou art not for the fashion of these times,*
> *Where none will sweat but for promotion.*

Possibly in these verses the poet himself is speaking.

43. Line 74: *it is too late* A WEEK.—Perhaps "*in the* week" is the meaning; or, which seems to me more probable, "*by* a week."

ACT II. Scene 4.

44. Line 1: *O Jupiter, how* WEARY *are my spirits!*—Theobald's correction of the Folios, which give *merry.* The change seems to me absolutely necessary. Retaining *merry* we might argue (1) that the words are spoken ironically; or (2) that Rosalind feigns cheerfulness to keep up the courage of her friend. The context, however, is, I think, decisive in favour of *weary.*

45. Line 12: *yet I should bear no* CROSS.—Alluding, of course, to the *cross* stamped on the reverse of silver coins. For the quibble compare Love's Labour 's Lost, i. 2. 34–36; and see note 20 on that play:

> *Arm.* I love not to be cross'd.
> *Moth.* [*Aside*] He speaks the mere contrary; *crosses* love not him.

So II. Henry IV. i. 2. 253: "you are too impatient to bear *crosses.*"

46. Line 49: *the kissing of her* BATLET.—So F. 2; F. 1 has *batter.* It was an instrument used by washers in beating out clothes, and according to Halliwell (Dictionary of Archaic Works, *sub voce*) was variously called *batler, batlet, batling-staff, batstaff*, and in Cotgrave (under *bacule*) *batting-staff.* Nares suggests a possible connection with *beetle*, and compares Beaumont and Fletcher's The Tamer Tamed, ii. 5:

> Have I lived thus long to be knocked o' the head
> With half a *washing-beetle!*

The latter occurs in II. Henry IV. i. 2. 255: "fillip me with a three-man *beetle.*" The New English Dictionary is not particularly instructive on the subject.

47. Line 52: *the wooing of a* PEASCOD.—Properly *peascod* is the husk containing the peas; so Lear, i. 4. 210: "That's a shealed *peascod.*" Here it would seem from what follows that the word must signify the whole plant. Lower down *weeping tears* is an obvious touch of burlesque.

48. Line 61: *Jove, Jove! this shepherd's passion.*—There is, perhaps, something to be said for the reading of Collier's MS. Corrector: *Love, love.*

49. Lines 83–100.—A detail taken from Lodge. Cf. the following. Montanus, the shepherd, is the speaker:—"'My landlord intends to sell both the farme I tyll, and the flocke I keepe, and cheape you may have them for ready money: and for a shepheards life (oh mistres) did you but live awhile in their content, you would say the court were rather a place of sorrow then of solace. Here, mistresse, shal not fortune thwart you, but in mean misfortunes, as the losse of a few sheepe, which, as it breedes no beggery, so it can bee no extreame prejudice: the next yeare may mend all with a fresh increase. Envy stirres not us, we covet not to climbe, our desires mount not above our degrees, nor our thoughts above our fortunes. Care cannot harbour in our cottages, nor doe our homely couches know broken slumbers: as wee exceed not in dyet, so we have inough to satisfie: and, mistresse, I have so much Latin, *satis est quod sufficit.*'

"'By my trueth, shepheard (quoth Aliena) thou makest mee in love with your countrey life, and therfore send for thy landlord, and I will buy thy farme and thy flocks, and thou shalt still under me bee overseer of them both: onely for pleasure sake I and my page will serve you, lead the flocks to the field, and folde them. Thus will I live quiet, unknowne, and contented'" (Collier, i. p. 42).

ACT II. Scene 5.

50. Line 3: *And* TURN *his merry note.*—Rowe, followed by Pope, changed to *tune*, and Dyce adopted the correction, comparing Two Gentlemen of Verona, v. 4. 5, 6:

> And to the nightingale's complaining notes
> *Tune* my distresses and record my woes.

But to *turn a note* is a perfectly feasible expression, and Singer's quotation from Hall's Satires, vi. 1. 105:

> While threadbare Martial *turns his merry note*—

practically settles the question. Dyce indeed gives the latter, and then boldly remarks that "*turns* is manifestly an error;" the dictum is rather autocratic. Compare Love's Labour 's Lost, note 20.

51. Line 13: *as a* WEASEL SUCKS EGGS.—Compare Henry V. i. 2. 169–171:

> For once the eagle England being in prey,
> To her unguarded nest the *weasel* Scot
> Comes sneaking and so *sucks* her princely *eggs*.

52. Line 33: *Sirs,* COVER *the while; i.e.* set the places for the feast.—Compare Merchant of Venice, iii. 5. 67.

53. Line 56: *Ducdame.*—It is useless to attempt to explain this. The word is an obvious and intentional piece of nonsense, of which the point lies in its very meaningless absurdity. To secure a double rhyme Farmer, rather ingeniously, suggested the following arrangement of the lines:

> *Ducdàme, ducdàme, ducdàme*
> Here shall he see
> Gross fools as he,
> An if he will come to *Ami;*

i.e. to Amiens. Hanmer read ("very acutely and judiciously," says Johnson) *duc ad me*="bring him to me." Of course line 56 is intended to reproduce the rhythm of line 44.

54. Line 63: *all the* FIRST-BORN *of* EGYPT.—A proverbial expression, says Johnson, for "high-born persons." I do not see the point of the phrase.

ACT II. Scene 6.

55. Lines 1–14.—For this and the next scene compare the following extracts from Lodge: "At these wordes Rosader lifted up his eye, and looking on Adam Spencer, began to weep. Ah, Adam, quoth he, I sorrow not to dye, but I grieve at the maner of my death. Might I with my launce encounter the enemy, and so die in the field, it were honour, and content: might I (Adam) combate with some wilde beast, and perish as his praie, I were satisfied; but to die with hunger, O, Adam, it is the extreamest of all extreames! Maister (quoth he) you see we are both in one predicament, and long I cannot live without meate; seeing therefore we can finde no foode, let the death of the one preserve the life of the other. I am old, and overworne with age, you are yoong, and are the hope of many honours: let me then dye, I will presently cut my veynes, and, maister, with the warme blood relieve your fainting spirites: sucke on that till I ende, and you be comforted. With that Adam Spencer was ready to pull out his knife, when Rosader full of courage (though verie faint) rose up, and wisht A. Spencer to sit there til his returne" (Collier, i. p. 51).

Rosader goes off, as in the play, to seek for food, and soon falls in with the duke and his companions; and the narrative continues thus: "Hee stept boldly to the boords end, and saluted the company thus:—'Whatsoever thou be that art maister of these lustie squiers, I salute thee as graciously as a man in extreame distresse may: know, that I and a fellow friend of mine are here famished in the forrest for want of food: perish wee must, unlesse relieved by thy favours. Therefore, if thou be a gentleman, give meate to men, and to such as are everie way worthie of life. Let the proudest squire that sits at thy table rise and incounter with mee in any honorable point of activitie whatsoever, and if hee and thou proove me not a man, send me away comfortlesse. If thou refuse this, as a niggard of thy cates, I will have amongst you with my sword; for rather wil I dye valiantly, then perish with so cowardly an extreame'" (Collier, i. p. 52).

56. Line 3: *and* MEASURE *out my* GRAVE.—We are reminded of Romeo and Juliet, iii. 3. 69, 70:

> And fall upon the ground, as I do now,
> Taking the *measure* of an unmade *grave*.

ACT II. Scene 7.

57. Line 5: *If he,* COMPACT *of* JARS, *grow musical; i.e.* made up of discords. For much the same quibble upon *jar* in its double sense of ordinary discord and discord in music, compare Taming of the Shrew, v. 2. 1:

> At last, though long, our *jarring* notes agree.

Compact="composed of:" as in Midsummer Night's Dream, v. 8:

> Are of imagination all *compact*.

See note 248 of that play.

58. Line 13: *A* MOTLEY *fool.*—Alluding, one need hardly remark, to the traditional dress of *court fools.* Beaumont and Fletcher have *men of motley* in Wit Without Money, iii. 4, end (Dyce, iv. 15), and in Bonduca, ii. 2, early:

> *Motley* on thee,
> Thou art an arrant ass.

59. Line 19: "*Call me not fool till heaven hath sent me fortune.*"—Alluding to the proverb, *fortuna favet fatuis.* Reed quotes (Var. Ed. vi. p. 401) from the prologue to the Alchemist:

> *Fortune, that favours fools,* these two short hours
> We wish away

60. Line 39: *Which is as dry as the remainder* BISCUIT.—Cf. Troilus and Cressida, ii. 1. 42, 43: "He would pun thee into shivers with his fist, as a sailor breaks a *biscuit;*" and still more to the point is Boswell's quotation from Every Man Out of His Humour: "And now and then breaks a dry *biscuit* jest." A *dry* brain in Shakespeare's time seems to have been synonymous with dulness. For the use of *remainder* here, adjectively, compare Richard II. note 155.

61. Line 48: *as large a* CHARTER *as the* WIND.—We may remember Henry V. i. 1. 48:

> The air, a *charter'd* libertine, is still.

62. Line 55: NOT TO *seem senseless of the* BOB.—Without the first two words the line has neither meaning nor metre. The correction (made by Theobald) seems to me quite right, the explanation being in effect that which Whiter gave, though Whiter adopted a different reading: "A wise man whose feeling should chance to be well rallied by a simple unmeaning jester, even though he should be weak enough to be hurt by so foolish an attack, appears always insensible of the stroke." Or taking the

present text the exact sense will be: "A wise man whose folly . . . will be foolish *if he does not seem senseless*." Dr. Ingleby's defence of the Folios I have not been able to master. The Cambridge editors print *not to;* Dyce, *but to*. For *bob* cf. Ascham's School-Master: "cruellie threatened, yea presentlie some tymes, with pinches, nippes, and *bobbes*" (Arber's Reprint, p. 47). Compare also Richard III. v. 3. 333, 334:

> whom our fathers
> Have in their own land beaten, *bobb'd*, and thump'd;

and compare note 651 of that play.

63. Line 63: *What, for a* COUNTER, *would I do but good?*—See note on Troilus and Cressida, ii. 2. 28.

64. Line 73: *Till that the* WEARER'S *very means do ebb.*—F. 1 gives "the *wearie* very," an obvious piece of nonsense. Pope suggested *very very*, and was followed by Malone and others (see Var. Ed. vol. vi. p. 405); but such emphasis is quite pointless. Mr. Kinnear in his Cruces Shakesperianæ proposes "the *wasted* very," comparing Othello, iv. 2. 187, 188: "I have *wasted* myself out of my *means*." But there is an obvious objection to this: an adjective before *very* is extremely awkward and unrhythmical. The difficulty is solved by Singer's convincing emendation, *wearer's*, which has been adopted in the Clarendon Press ed., though not in the Globe, which, following the reading of F. 1, marks the passage as corrupt.

65. Lines 75, 76:

> *When that I say, the city-woman* BEARS
> *The cost of princes on unworthy shoulders.*

We are reminded at once of II. Henry VI. i. 3. 83:

> She *bears a duke's revenues on her back.*

See note 74 of that play. The commentators do not seem to have noticed that Shakespeare (?) was giving a terse version of what must, I think, have been a proverbial saying. Compare, at any rate, the following from Gascoigne's Steel Glass—Epilogue:

> The elder sorte, go stately stalking on,
> *And on their backs, they beare* both land and see,
> *Castles and Towres, revenewes and receits,*
> Lordships and manours, fines, yea fermes and al.
> —Arber's Reprint, p. 82.

See also King John, note 72.

66. Line 139: *All the world 's a stage.*—This is one of those natural conceptions which occur in widely different literatures, and to which no writer can lay claim. Thus in the old play of Damon and Pythias (a masterpiece, by the way, of unreadableness) we have:

> Pythagoras said that this *world was like a stage*
> Where *many play their parts*. —Dodsley, iv. 31.

Again, Malone refers to the Legend of Orpheus and Euridice, 1597:

> Unhappy man . . .
> Whose life a sad continual tragedy,
> Himself the actor, in *the world, the stage*,
> While as the acts are measured by his age.

And Mr. Aldis Wright reminds us that, according to tradition, the motto of the Globe Theatre was Petronius' saying—Totus mundus agit histrionem, the sign of the house being a globe representing the world, supported by Hercules. (See Collier, History of the Stage, iii. 238.)

Compare, for the same idea, though not developed, Merchant of Venice, i. 1. 78, 79.

67. Line 143: *His acts being* SEVEN AGES.—Here, again, Shakespeare is reproducing a time-honoured idea. For the division of a man's life into seven stages the editors refer us to various authors. Hippocrates is rather vaguely appealed to. Malone reminds us of Sir Thomas Browne's chapter on the subject in his Vulgar Errors (iv. 2); and Staunton gives the following from Arnold's Chronicle:

> The vij Ages of Mā liuing I the World.

"The first age"—I modify the spelling—"is infancy and lasteth from the birth unto VIIth year of age. The IInd is childhood and endureth unto XV year age. The IIIrd age is adolescence and endureth unto XXV year age. The IVth age is youth and endureth unto XXXV year age. The Vth age is manhood and endureth unto L year age. The VIth is elde and lasteth unto LXX year age. The VIIth age of man is crepil and endureth unto death." Henley says: "I have seen more than once an old print, The Stage of Man's Life, divided into seven ages. As emblematical representations of this sort were formerly stuck up, both for ornament and instruction, in the generality of houses, it is probable that Shakespeare took his hint from thence" (See Var. Ed. vi. pp. 520, 521, and the Introduction to Clarendon Press ed.) It is pretty clear that the conception was as familiar to Shakespeare's contemporaries as it is now to us through the poet's own lines, and it is quite immaterial when exactly he first came across the thought. Such ideas belong to every man; the use made of them is everything—originality counts for little.

68. Line 143: *with a woeful* BALLAD.—"*Ballat* or *ballad*, says Professor Hales, in a note on the Areopagitica ("composing in a higher straine than their owne souldierly ballats and roundels"), "is by no means confined in older usage to its present meaning of a certain kind of popular narrative poem. It came to be so confined, I think, only in the last century on the revival of mediæval literature. In the older writers it means a song of any sort. . . . No doubt it originally denoted a dance-song, and is cognate with our *ball* (a dance-party), *ballet*, etc., from Low Lat. *ballare*, Ital. *ballare*, to dance." For the less limited use of the word compare Midsummer Night's Dream, iv. 1. 221: "I will get Peter Quince to write a *ballad* of this dream." The first half of the present line we may illustrate by Cymbeline, i. 6. 66, 67:

> he *furnaces*
> The thick *sighs* from him.

69. Line 158: *Into the lean and slipper'd* PANTALOON.—The allusion here is to the contemporary Italian stage, where "Don Pantaleone" (the old man deceived by his young wife) was one of the four stock characters, the other three being the *Doctor*, *Harlequin*, and *Coviello*, the Sharper. "There is," says Warburton (Var. Ed. vi. 410), "a greater beauty than appears at first sight in this image. He is here comparing human life to *a stage play* of seven acts. The sixth he calls the *lean and slippered pantaloon*, alluding to that general character in Italian comedy, called *Il* Pantalóne; one who is a thin emaciated old man in *slippers;* and well designed, in that epithet, because Pan-

talóne is the only character that acts in *slippers*." Warburton's philology I do not guarantee. According to the editors *Pantalone* was properly applied to a Venetian, and St. Pantaleon was the patron saint of Venice. As to parallel allusions, Capell quotes from a play entitled The Travels of Three English Brothers, first printed in 1607, where, in a dialogue between an Italian Harlequin and Kemp (the actor) we have:

> *Harl.* Marry sir, first we will have an old *Pantaloune.*
> *Kemp.* Some jealous coxcombe.
> *Harl.* Right.

A less recondite reference, which seems to have escaped the commentators, occurs in Middleton's The Spanish Gipsy, iv. 2. 65, 66:

> Play him up high; *not like a pantaloon,*
> *But hotly, nobly.* —Works (Bullen's ed.), vi. 196.

70. Lines 177, 178:

> *Thy tooth is not so keen,*
> *Because thou art not seen.*

Why *because?* Is the second line as the text stands a logical explanation of the preceding one? I confess I cannot help suspecting some corruption. Accepting the Folio reading we must interpret with Johnson: "thy rudeness gives the less pain, as thou art not seen, as thou art an enemy that dost not brave us with thy presence, and whose unkindness is therefore not aggravated by insult." But this, to my mind, is very forced and feeble. On the other hand, none of the emendations can be regarded as at all satisfactory. They are: "Thou causest not that teen" (Hanmer); "because thou art foreseen" (Staunton); "As griefs that are not seen" (Cruces Shakesperianæ, p. 113); with others, amongst which we may pick out Warburton's, "because thou art not *sheen*," *i.e.* smiling, shining. Warburton's sense of the ridiculous was not abnormally acute. He prefaced his proposal with the remark: "Without doubt, Shakspeare wrote the line thus." But critics still have their doubts on the subject.

71. Line 187: *Though thou the waters* WARP.—Etymologically *warp* contains two ideas: "to throw, cast," and "to twist out of shape" (Skeat). The former has survived in German *werfen;* the latter—Johnson's sonorous definition is worth giving: "to change from the true situation by intestine motion"—underlies most passages where the English verb occurs. Take, for instance, Shakespeare's use of the word, in The Winter's Tale, i. 2. 364, 365:

> This is strange: methinks
> My favour here begins *to warp;*

i.e. is going amiss, is losing its true nature.

Again, Lear, iii. 6. 56, 57:

> And here 's another, whose *warp'd* looks proclaim
> What store her heart is made on;

so Measure for Measure, iii. 1. 140–143:

> What should I think?
> Heaven shield my mother play'd my father fair!
> For such a *warped* slip of wilderness
> Ne'er issued from his blood;

where *warped* obviously = "contrary to his father's nature;" "twisted out of all likeness to." Later on in this play, iii. 3. 89, 90, the word is applied to wood that shrinks: "then one of you will prove a shrunk panel, and like green timber *warp, warp;*" that is, get out of place, become awry. The word having this sense, it is perfectly appropriate in the present passage, whether it was intended to suggest the action of frost upon the water, or the ruffling effect of wind passing over the surface, and, as it were, twisting the broad expanse from its natural calm.

ACT III. Scene 1.

72. Lines 1-12.—The idea of banishing the elder brother in this way is taken from Lodge.

73. Line 6: *Seek him with candle.*—Alluding presumably to Luke xv. ver. 8: "if she lose one piece doth (she) not light a candle . . . and seek diligently till she find it?"

74. Line 17: MAKE AN EXTENT *upon his house and lands.*—Referring to this passage, Lord Campbell remarks (Shakespeare's Legal Acquirements, p. 42) that here "a deep technical knowledge of law is displayed, however it may have been acquired. The usurping Duke, Frederick, wishing all the real property of Oliver to be seized, awards a writ of *extent* against him, in the language which would be used by the Lord Chief Baron of the Court of Exchequer. An *extendi facias* applying to house and lands, as a *fieri facias* would apply to goods and chattels, or a *capias ad satisfaciendum* to the person." For a similar use of the expression in literature cf. Wit Without Money, iii. 2:

> Mark me; widows
> Are long *extents in law* upon men's livings.
> —Beaumont and Fletcher, Works, vol. i. p. 182.

The verb *extend*, in same sense, occurs in A New Way to Pay Old Debts, v. 1:

> but when
> This manor is *extended* to my use,
> You 'll speak in an humbler key.
> —Works, p. 418.

ACT III. Scene 2.

75. Line 1.—We come now to what is in some respects the crown of Shakespeare's lighter lyric comedy, the forest love-scenes of this perfect play. How should these scenes be conceived and played? Are we to regard them as simple comedy, or as comedy touched by something deeper? Fortunately, the question has been asked and answered by one of our greatest dramatic artists: "It was surely a strange perversion which assigned Rosalind, as at one time it had assigned Portia, to actresses whose strength lay only in comedy. Even the joyous buoyant side of her nature could hardly have justice done to it in their hands; for that is so inextricably mixed with deep womanly tenderness, with an active intellect disciplined by fine culture, as well as tempered by a certain native distinction, that a mere comedian could not give the true tone and colouring even to her playfulness and her wit. *Those forest scenes between Orlando and herself are not, as a comedy actress would be apt to make them, merely pleasant fooling.* At the core of all that Rosalind says and does, lies a passionate love as pure and all-absorbing as ever swayed a woman's heart. Surely it was the finest and boldest of all devices, one on which only a Shakespeare could have ventured, to put his heroine into such a position that she could, without revealing her own secret, probe the heart of her lover to the very bottom,

and so assure herself that the love which possessed her own being was as completely the master of his. Neither could any but Shakespeare have so carried out this daring design, that the woman, thus rarely placed for gratifying the impulses of her own heart, and testing the sincerity of her lover's, should come triumphantly out of the ordeal, charming us, during the time of probation, by wit, by fancy, by her pretty womanly waywardnesses playing like summer lightning over her throbbing tenderness of heart, and never in the gayest sallies of her happiest moods losing one grain of our respect. No one can study this play without seeing that, through the guise of the brilliant-witted boy, Shakespeare meant the charm of the high-hearted woman, strong, tender, delicate, to make itself felt. Hence it is that Orlando finds the spell which 'heavenly Rosalind' had thrown around him, drawn hourly closer and closer, he knows not how, while at the same time he has himself been winning his way more and more into his mistress' heart. Thus, when at last Rosalind doffs her doublet and hose, and appears arrayed for her bridal, there seems nothing strange or unmeet in this somewhat sudden consummation of what has been in truth a lengthened wooing. The actress will, in my opinion, fail signally in her task, who shall not suggest all this, who shall not leave upon her audience the impression that, when Rosalind resumes her state at her father's court, she will bring into it as much grace and dignity, as by her bright spirits she had brought of sunshine and cheerfulness into the shades of the forest of Arden" (Some of Shakespeare's Female Characters, pp. 295, 296).

76. Line 2: THRICE *crowned queen of night; i.e.* as Luna, Diana, and Hecate. Cf. Horace's "diva *triformis*," Odes, bk. I. xxii. 4.

77. Line 10: *The fair, the chaste, and* UNEXPRESSIVE *she; i.e.* "inexpressible;" only here in Shakespeare. The editors naturally refer to Milton's Hymn on the Nativity:

> Harping with loud and solemn quire,
> With *unexpressive* notes to heaven's new born heir

So also Lycidas, 176: "and hears the *unexpressive* nuptial song;" where Warton suggests that the adjective was coined by Shakespeare. Cf. Todd's Milton, vol. vi. p. 13.

78. Line 31: *may* COMPLAIN OF GOOD *breeding; i.e.* of not having had, of the want of, *good breeding*. Hanmer printed "*bad* breeding," Warburton "*gross* breeding;" but no change is necessary.

79. Line 55: *and their* FELLS . . . *are greasy.*—*Fell* is here used correctly for the hide or skin with the hair still on. Cotgrave gives "skin; *fell*, hide, or pelt" as an equivalent for "peau." Compare Lear, v. 3. 24:

> The good-years shall devour them, flesh and *fell*.

So, too, Macbeth, v. 5. 11-13:

> and my *fell* of hair
> Would at a dismal treatise rouse and stir
> As life were in't.

80. Line 66: *perfum'd with* CIVET.—Compare the following passage from Stubbes, Anatomy of Abuses: "Is not this a certen sweete Pride to have *civet*, muske, sweete powders, fragrant Pomanders, odorous perfumes, and such like, whereof the smel may be felt and perceived, not only all over the house or place, where they be present (he is speaking of women's extravagant use of scents), but also a stone's cast of almost, yea, the bed wherin they have laid their delicate bodies, the places where they have sate, the clothes, and thinges which they have touched, shall smell a weeke, a moneth, and more, after they begon. But the prophet *Esaias* telleth them, instead of their Pomanders, musks, *civets*, balmes, sweet odours and perfumes, they shall have stench and horrour in the nethermost hel" (New Shak. Soc. Reprint, part I. p. 77). Compare Much Ado, note 196.

81. Line 100: *But the* FAIR *of Rosalind.*—For *fair*= fairness cf. Venus and Adonis, 1085, 1086:

> But when Adonis lived, sun and sharp air
> Lurk'd like two thieves, to rob him of his *fair*.

Again, Comedy of Errors, ii. 1. 98, 99:

> My decayed *fair*
> A sunny look of his would soon repair.

But the use of the word is common. Compare Love's Labour's Lost, note 81.

82. Line 103: *butter-women's* RANK *to market; i.e.* the verses follow one upon another, as regular and monotonous as a cavalcade of butterwomen trotting along to market. This seems to me quite satisfactory, and I do not understand why the passage should have raised so much discussion. Of the proposed emendations Mr. Aldis Wright's *rack* is tempting. He quotes from Cotgrave: "*Amble:* an amble, pace, *racke;* an ambling, or racking pace; a smooth, or easie gate;" and *ambler* (the verb): "to amble, pace, *racke*." The objection, perhaps, to *rack* is that the word appears to have implied smooth, easy motion, which would be complimentary, and consequently in the present case somewhat inappropriate. Hanmer suggested *rate*.

83. Line 110: *This is the very* FALSE GALLOP.—Evidently a proverbial expression. Malone quotes (Var. Ed. vi. p. 423) from Nash's Apologie of Pierce Pennilesse (1593): "I would trot a *false gallop* through the rest of his ragged verses, but that if I should retort the rime doggrell aright, I must make my verses (as he does his) run hobbling, like a brewer's cart upon the stones, and observe no measure in their feet." Compare, too, Much Ado, iii. 4. 93, 94:

> *Beat.* What pace is this that thy tongue keeps?
> *Marg.* Not a *false gallop*.

The idea, no doubt, is that of a horse thrown out of its paces (détraqué), and moving with a jerky, irregular amble. Shakespeare is thinking of the same thing when he writes, I. Henry IV. iii. 1. 133-135:

> And that would set my teeth nothing on edge,
> Nothing so much *as mincing poetry*.
> *'Tis like the forc'd gait of a shuffling nag.*

84. Line 120.—For the same piece of word-play compare Timon of Athens, iv. 3. 307-310:

> *Apem.* Dost hate a *medlar?*
> *Tim.* Ay, though it look like thee.
> *Apem.* An thou hadst hated *meddlers* sooner, thou shouldst have loved thyself better now.

85. Line 140: BUCKLES *in his sum of age; i.e.* "confines," "encompasses." We have a similar use of the word in Troilus and Cressida, ii. 2. 28-31:

will you with counters sum
The past-proportion of his infinite?
And *buckle-in* a waist most fathomless
With spans and inches?

86. Line 155: ***Atalanta's better part.***—This is rather perplexing. What was *Atalanta's better part?* Obviously her swiftness of foot. So classical tradition, and so Shakespeare himself, line 294: "You have a nimble wit: I think 't was made of *Atalanta's heels.*" Either the poet was simply careless, or else *Atalanta* stood for him as a type not merely of nimbleness, but also of ease and grace of form. So Malone explains, aptly suggesting that Shakespeare may have remembered some lines in Golding's translation of Ovid, Metamorphoses, x.:

He was amazed . . . . .
and thought that she
Did flie as swift as arrow from a Turkish bow, yet hee
More wondred at her beautie than at swiftness of her pace;
Her running greatly did augment her beautie and her grace.

87. Line 163: ***O most gentle*** PULPITER!—The Folios read *Jupiter*, which seems to me sheer nonsense; the correction, *pulpiter*, was made by Mr. Spedding; it has been adopted in the Globe edition, and I think deservedly. Many editors print the Folio reading.

88. Line 184: *seven of the* NINE DAYS.—Alluding obviously to the proverb. So III. Henry VI. iii. 2. 113, 114:

Glo. That would be *ten days'* wonder at the least.
Clar. That's a day longer than a wonder lasts.

89. Lines 187, 188: ***I was never so be-rhym'd since Pythagoras' time, &c.***—"Rosalind," says Johnson, "is a very learned lady. She alludes to the Pythagorean doctrine, which teaches that souls transmigrate from one animal to another, and relates that in his time she was an *Irish* rat, and by some metrical charm was rhymed to death." The susceptibility of Irish rats, in the sixteenth and seventeenth centuries, to the influence of verse is repeatedly alluded to. The editors have brought together various references to this interesting fact in natural history. Thus Grey (Notes, vol. i.) quotes from Randolph, The Jealous Lovers, v. 2:

my poets
Shall with a satire, steep'd in gall and vinegar,
Rhyme 'em to death, as they do *rats in Ireland*.
—Works (edn. 1875), vol. i. p. 156.

Compare again (with Steevens) Ben Jonson's Poetaster, Address to the Reader:

Rhime them to death, as they do *Irish rats*
In drumming tunes;

and Sidney's Apologie for Poetry (Arber's Reprint, p. 72): "nor to bee driuen by a Poets verses to hang himselfe, nor to be *rimed to death*, as is sayd to be doone in Ireland."

90. Line 203: ***out of all*** HOOPING; *i.e.* beyond all measure or reckoning. We have the word in Henry V. ii. 2. 108: "That admiration did not *hoop* at them," where, as here, Theobald changed to the form *whoop*. Nares compares an old expression, "There 's no ho," quoting from Nash's Lenten Stuffe: "*There's no ho with him;* but once hartned thus, he will needes be a man of warre." So, too, with an obviously playful air of antiquarianism, Swift writes to Stella: "When your tongue runs *there 's no ho with you*" (Letter 20). Halliwell (Dictionary of Archaic Words, *s.v.*) mentions an old game *Hoop and Hide*, and the editors parallel the phrase in our text by the not unfamiliar, and, in sense, identical, expressions—"out of all cry," "without all cry." With the form *hoop* cf. French *houper*, *hooping*-cough, &c.

91. Line 207: ***a South-sea of discovery.***—That is, "Delay another minute and I shall have a thousand questions to ask you, shall, in fact, be embarking upon a perfect ocean of discovery." There is no need to admit into the text any change, though Warburton's "*of* discovery" is rather ingenious, the sense then being, "if you delay me one inch of time longer, I shall think this secret as far from *discovery* as the *South-sea* is."

92. Line 238: GARGANTUA'S *mouth.*—It is superfluous, perhaps, to note that *Gargantua* was the giant in Rabelais who swallowed five pilgrims in a single mouthful. Mr. Aldis Wright appositely quotes from Cotgrave: "*Gargantua*. Great throat. Rab;" while to Steevens we owe two entries that occur in the registers of the Stationers' Company. From the first we find that "*Gargantua* his prophesie" was entered on April 6th, 1592, and "A booke entituled, the historie of *Gargantua*," on Dec. 4th, 1594. For a similar allusion compare Ben Jonson, Every Man in His Humour, ii. 2: "I'll go near to fill that huge tumbrel-slop of yours with somewhat, an I have good luck; your *Garagantua* breech cannot carry it away so." In connection with the present line readers of Boswell will remember an anecdote which it may not be amiss to give. "This season," says the incomparable biographer, under date of the year 1778, "there was a whimsical fashion in the newspapers of applying Shakespeare's words to describe living persons well known in the world; which was done under the title of *Modern Characters from Shakespeare*, many of which were admirably adapted. The fancy took so much, that they were afterwards collected into a pamphlet. Somebody said to Johnson, across the table, that he had not been in those characters. 'Yes (said he), I have. I should have been sorry to be left out.' He then repeated what had been applied to him—*I must borrow Garagantua's mouth.* Miss Reynolds not perceiving at once the meaning of this, he was obliged to explain it to her, which had something of an awkward and ludicrous effect. 'Why, madam, it has a reference to me, as using big words, which require the mouth of a giant to pronounce them. *Garagantua* is the name of a giant in *Rabelais*.' Boswell. 'But, sir, there is another amongst them for you' (Boswell then quotes a couplet from Coriolanus, iii. 1. 256, 257). Johnson. 'There is nothing marked in that. No, Sir, *Garagantua* is the best.' Notwithstanding this ease and good-humour, when I, a little afterwards, repeated his sarcasm on Kenrick, which was received with applause, he asked, 'Who said that?' and on my suddenly answering *Garagantua*, he looked serious, which was a sufficient indication that he did not wish it to be kept up'" (Boswell, ed. Birbeck Hill, Oxford, 1887, vol. iii. pp. 256, 257). Those who have seen Opie's portrait of Johnson will appreciate the literal applicability of *Gargantua* (not *Garagantua*) as descriptive of his remarkable face.

93. Line 257: ***Cry holla! to thy tongue;*** *i.e.* hold in,

restrain; a term borrowed from riding. Compare Venus and Adonis, 283, 284:

> What recketh he his rider's angry stir,
> His flattering "*Holla*," or his "Stand, I say"?

It seems to have been used also in calling up a pack of hounds; cf. Thierry and Theodoret, ii. 2:

> Not to-day; the weather
> Is grown too warm; besides, the dogs are spent:
> We'll take a cooler morning. Let's to horse,
> And *halloo* in the troop. —Works, vol. ii. p. 411.

Perhaps, however, "troop" is equivalent, in modern phrase, to "the hunt."

94. Lines 261: *I would sing my song without a* BURDEN.—Commenting on a passage of considerable musical interest that occurs in the Two Gentlemen of Verona (i. 2. 79-96), Mr. Chappell (Popular Music of the Olden Time, p. 222) remarks that "the *burden* of a song, in the old acceptation of the word, was the base, foot, or undersong. It was sung throughout, and not merely at the end of the verse." Eventually *burden* came to have the general sense of "ditty." For its original and correct use cf. Chaucer:

> This Sompnour bar to him a stif *burdoun*,
> Was never trompe of half so gret a soun.

So in Much Ado, iii. 4. 43, 44: "Clap's into *Light o' love;* that goes without a *burden:* do you sing it, and I'll dance it." As to derivation, from French *bourdon*, a drone-bee, humming of bees, drone of a bagpipe; probably, says Skeat, of imitative origin. Also spelt *burthen*.

95. Line 289: *rings; i.e.* the so-called "posy rings;" to inscribe a motto or "posy" within the hoop of the betrothal ring was not an unusual thing. See Merchant of Venice, v. 1. 147-150, and compare note 355 of that play. So Hamlet, iii. 2. 162: "Is this a prologue, or the *posy of a ring?*" Allusions outside Shakespeare are common enough; *e.g.* Herrick, in the Hesperides, has:

> What *posies for our wedding rings*,
> What gloves we'll give and ribbonings.

And Euphues (quoted by Mr. Aldis Wright): "Writing your judgments as you do the *posies in your rings*, which are alwayes next to the finger" (Arber's ed. p. 221).

96. Line 290: *I answer you* RIGHT PAINTED CLOTH.—As to these *painted cloths*, a full explanation will be found in my note on Troilus and Cressida, v. 10. 47. Compare also I. Henry IV. note 200. To the passages there given add Lucrece, 244, 245:

> Who fears a sentence or an old man's saw
> Shall by a *painted cloth* be kept in awe.

For the form of the expression, cf. Twelfth Night, i. 5. 115:

> he speaks nothing but madman: fie on him!

and Henry V. v. 2. 156:

> I speak to thee plain soldier.

For *right* in this sense compare line 103 above: "it is the *right* butter-women's rank to market."

97. Line 315: *Do you hear, forester?*—"Not for the world would she have Orlando recognise her in her unmaidenly guise; but now a sudden impulse determines her to risk all, and even to turn it to account as the means of testing his love. Boldness must be her friend, and to avert his suspicion, her only course is to put on a 'swashing and a martial outside,' and to speak to him 'like a saucy lackey and under that habit play the knave with him.' He must not be allowed for an instant to surmise the hidden woman's fear that lies in her heart. Besides, it is only by resort to a rough and saucy greeting and manner that she could master and keep under the trembling of her voice, and the womanly tremor of her limbs. I always gave her 'Do you hear, forester?' with a defiant air" (Some of Shakespeare's Female Characters, pp. 322, 323).

98. Line 380: *in which* CAGE *of* RUSHES.—In the Transactions of the New Shakspere Society, 1877-1879, p. 463, it is ingeniously suggested that Rosalind is laughingly alluding to the custom of marrying with a *rush-ring*, a custom to which Shakespeare refers in All's Well That Ends Well, ii. 2. 24: "as Tib's *rush* for Tom's fore-finger." That rings were often made of *rushes* the poets perpetually remind us; *e.g.* Chapman in The Gentleman Usher, iv.:

> Rushes make true-love knots, *rushes make rings;*

and Fletcher (?) in the Two Noble Kinsmen, iv. 1. 88, 89:

> *Rings* she made
> Of *rushes* that grew by.

99. Line 398: *your hose should be* UNGARTER'D.—So Ophelia describes Hamlet, ii. 1. 78-80:

> Lord Hamlet, with his doublet all unbraced;
> No hat upon his head; his stockings foul'd,
> *Ungarter'd*—

Malvolio, on the other hand, would be "strange, stout, in yellow stockings and *cross-gartered*" (Twelfth Night, ii. 5. 180).

100. Line 399: *your shoe untied.*—For a *résumé* of the appropriate love-symptoms, Steevens refers us to Heywood's Fair Maid of The Exchange:

> No, by my troth, if every tale of love,
> Or love itself, or fool-bewitching beauty,
> Make me cross-arm myself; study *ay-mes;*
> Defy my hatband; *tread beneath my feet*
> *Shoe-strings* and garters; practise in my glass
> Distressed looks— —Vol. ii. (ed. 1874), p. 16.

Compare also p. 20 of the same volume.

101. Line 401: *you are rather* POINT-DEVISE.—Compare Love's Labour's Lost, v. 1. 21:

> Such insociable and *point-devise* companions:

and Twelfth Night, ii. 5. 176:

> I will be *point-devise* the very man.

The derivation is obvious—*point de vice:* hence meaning "precise." See, also, Love's Labour's Lost, note 146.

02. Line 421: *a* DARK HOUSE *and a* WHIP *as* MADMEN *do.*—Everybody will recollect Malvolio's epistle: "By the Lord, madam, you wrong me, and the world shall know it: though you have *put me into darkness*" (Twelfth Night, v. 1. 312); and same play, same scene, 349, 350:

> Why have you suffer'd me to be imprison'd,
> *Kept in a dark house*, visited by the priest.

So Comedy of Errors, v. 1. 246-248:

> They fell upon me, bound me, bore me thence,
> And in a *dark* and dankish *vault* at home
> They left me.

103. Lines 427-445.—A passage which the ordinary reader might pass by without observing in it anything very

noticeable: but which is rich in opportunities and consequently in difficulties. Compare the following criticism: "In the range of Shakespearian comedy there is probably no passage that demands more subtle treatment in the actress than this. Rosalind's every faculty is quickened by delight, and this delight breaks out into a bitter picture of all the wayward coquettishness that has ever been imputed to her sex. She rushes into this vein of humorous detraction, in order to keep up the show of curing Orlando of his passion by a picture of some of their 'giddy offences.' Note the aptness, the exquisite suggestiveness and variety of every epithet, which, woman as she is, she is irresistibly moved to illustrate and enforce by suitable changes of intonation and expression. But note also, so ready is her intelligence, that she does not forget to keep up the illusion about herself, by throwing in the phrase, that 'boys as well as women are for the most part cattle of this colour.' All the wit, the sarcasm, bubble up, sparkle after sparkle, with bewildering rapidity. Can we wonder that they should work a charm upon Orlando? . . . I need scarcely say how necessary it is for the actress in this scene, while carrying it through with a vivacity and dash that shall avert from Orlando's mind every suspicion of her sex, to preserve a refinement of tone and manner suitable to a woman of Rosalind's high station and cultured intellect; and by occasional tenderness of accent and sweet persuasiveness of look to indicate how it is that, even at the outset, she establishes a hold upon Orlando's feelings, which in their future intercourse in the forest deepens, without his being sensibly conscious of it, his love for the Rosalind of his dreams. I never approached this scene without a sort of pleasing dread, so strongly did I feel the difficulty and the importance of striking the true note in it. Yet when once engaged in this scene, I was borne along I knew not how. The situation, in its very strangeness, was so delightful to my imagination, that from the moment when I took the assurance from Orlando's words to Jaques, that his love was as absolute as woman could desire, I seemed to lose myself in a sense of exquisite enjoyment. A thrill passed through me; I felt my pulse beat quicker; my very feet seemed to dance under me. . . . Of all the scenes in this exquisite play, while this is the most wonderful, it is for the actress certainly the most difficult" (Some of Shakespeare's Female Characters, pp. 327-329).

104. Line 430: *to a* LIVING *humour of madness*.—So the Folio, and I hardly think we are justified in changing to the more obvious "*loving* humour." "Living" (=actual) gives good sense: the "mad humour of love" ended in *real* madness.

105. Line 443: *take upon me to wash your* LIVER.—See Love's Labour's Lost, note 113.

106. Line 455: *Nay, you must call me Rosalind.*—The idea that Orlando should regard the pseudo Rosalind, *i.e.* Ganymede, as the real Rosalind, is "conveyed" from Lodge. Compare the following:—"Assoone as they had taken their repast, Rosader, giving them thankes for his good cheeare, would have been gone; but Ganimede, that was loath to let him passe out of her presence, began thus: Nay, forrester, quoth she, if thy busines be not the greater, seeing thou saist thou art so deeply in love, let me see how thou canst wooe; I will represent Rosalynde, and thou shalt bee as thou art, Rosader; see in some amorous eglogue, how, if Rosalynd were present, how thou couldst court her; and while we sing of love, Aliena shall tune her pipe, and plaie us melodie. Content, (quoth Rosader.)" Then follows a "wooing eglogue betwixt Rosalynde and Rosader," after which the narrative is resumed. "Truth, gentle swaine, Rosader hath his Rosalynde; but as Ixion had Juno, who, thinking to possesse a goddesse, only imbraced a clowd: in these imaginary fruitions of fancie I resemble the birds that fed themselves with Zeuxis painted grapes . . . so fareth it with me, who to feed my self with the hope of my mistres favors, soothe my selfe in thy sutes, and onely in conceipt reape a wished for content; but if my foode bee no better than such amorous dreames, Venus at the yeares end, shal find me but a leane lover. Yet do I take these follyes for high fortunes, and hope these fained affections do devine some unfained ende of ensuing fancies. And thereupon (quoth Aliena) Ile play the priest: from this daye forth Ganimede shall call thee husband, and thou shalt cal Ganimede wife, and so weele have a marriage. Content (quoth Rosader) and laught. Content (quoth Ganimede) and chaunged as red as a rose: and so with a smile and a blush, they made up this jesting match, that after proved to be a marriage in earnest, Rosader full little thinking hee had wooed and woonne his Rosalynde" (Collier, vol. i. pp. 70-75).

ACT III. SCENE 3.

107. Line 3: *doth my simple* FEATURE *content you?*—I think the correct explanation of these words is that given in the Transactions of the New Shakspere Society—for 1877-9, pp. 101-103—viz. that *feature* is used in the not uncommon sense "composition," "writing;" this agrees fairly well with what follows.

108. Line 8: *among the* GOTHS.—Shakespeare is guilty of what Malone deplores as "a poor quibble" on *goats* and *Goths;* also, as the editors observe, *capricious* is a *double entendre*. For the story of Ovid's banishment the Tristia may, or may not, be consulted.

109. Line 10: *O knowledge* ILL-INHABITED.—Apparently the sense is "ill-lodged," but no satisfactory instance of a parallel use of "inhabited" is given. The reference, of course, is to the familiar story of Baucis and Philemon. See Much Ado, note 92.

110. Line 22: *the truest poetry is the most feigning.*—We are reminded of Sidney's Apologie for Poetrie, where, as Professor Arber puts it, the poet man-of-letters "is really defending the whole art and craft of Feigning." See Arber's Reprint of the Apologie, with his Introduction.

111. Line 58: *Horns! Even so.*—I have retained here the ordinarily-received reading, though at least one of the suggested alternatives, that of Spedding, is worth mentioning—*Horns* are not for *poor men alone.*

112. Line 64: *Here comes* SIR *Oliver.*—The title *sir* was given to those who were Bachelors of Arts of any university; it was meant, no doubt, as an equivalent for

the "Dominus" which still partially survives at Cambridge. For its use compare Fletcher's Monsieur Thomas, v. 3. late:

> Get you afore, and stay me at the Chapel
> Close by the Nunnery; there you shall find a night-priest,
> Little *Sir* Hugh.
> —Dyce's Beaumont and Fletcher, vii. 398.

So again in the same writer's The Pilgrim, iv. 2. middle:

> Oh, that *Sir* Nicholas now, our priest were here.
> —*Ut supra*, viii. p. 68.

In Shakespeare, of course, we have *Sir* Hugh Evans (Merry Wives of Windsor), and in Love's Labour's Lost, "*Sir* Nathaniel, a Curate."

113. Line 81: *and the* FALCON HER BELLS.—Compare III. Henry VI. i. 1. 47, 48, and note 46 of that play. And Lucrece, 509-511, where the idea is brought out more clearly:

> So under his insulting falchion lies
> Harmless Lucretia, marking what he tells
> With trembling fear, *as fowl hears falcon's bells.*

Strictly the *falcon* was the female hawk, the "tercel" the male bird; the distinction is seen in a passage in Troilus and Cressida, iii. 2. 57, 58: "The *falcon* as the tercel, for all the ducks i' the river." Compare the note on that passage.

114. Line 101: *O sweet Oliver.*—In the books, says Steevens, of the Stationers' Company, August 6, 1584, was entered, by Richard Jones, the ballad of

> "*O Swete Olyver*
> Leave me not behinde thee."

Again, "The answere of *O Sweete Olyver.*" Again, in 1586: "*O Sweete Olyver* altered to ye Scriptures." The same old ballad is alluded to in Ben Jonson's Underwoods, lxii. 70:

> All the mad Rolands, and *sweet Olivers.*
> —*An Execration upon Vulcan.*

Compare, too, Gifford's note on Every Man in His Humour, iii. 3:

> "*Sweet Oliver,*" would I could do thee any good.
> —Ben Jonson's Works, vol. i. pp. 98, 99.

115. Lines 104-106: *Wind away.*—This fragment has been needlessly changed about in various ways. Farmer proposed "Leave me not *behi thee*,"="behind," and, to complete the rhyme, abbreviated "with thee" to "wi thee." Collier's MS. Corrector gave:

> But *wend* away,
> Begone, I say,
> I will not to wedding *bind* thee.

The alterations are not happy. Touchstone, as Johnson pointed out, is in all probability quoting different parts of the old song: why then make the end-lines of the two pieces correspond? As to *wind*, there is no difficulty; *wind* and "wend" are cognate in meaning and origin, and the use of the former="depart," is sufficiently attested by the line which Steevens cites from Cæsar and Pompey, 1607:

> *Winde* we then, Antony, with this royal queen.

Dyce, too, compares The History of Pyramus and Thisbie:

> That doone, away hee *winder*, as fier of hell or Vulcan's thunder.

ACT III. SCENE 4.

116. Line 9: *Something browner than* JUDAS'S.—In old tapestries Judas was always represented with a *red beard* and hair. For similar references compare Middleton's A Chaste Maid in Cheapside, iii. 2. 43-47:

> *First Puritan.* Sure that was Judas then with the *red beard.*
> *Second Puritan.* —*red hair.*
> The brethren like it not, it consumes them much:
> 'T is not the sisters' colour.
> —Bullen's Ed. v. 5.

Again, in Bonduca (by Fletcher alone?) we have a corporal with the grotesque name, Judas, who is spoken of (ii. 3) as:

> That hungry fellow
> With the *red beard* there.
> —Dyce's Beaumont and Fletcher, vol. v. p. 41.

117. Line 17: *a nun of* WINTER'S *sisterhood.*—We must not pass over Theobald's amazing suggestion: "a nun of *Winifred's* sisterhood," the very last word, surely, in bathos. For *sisterhood*, cf. Measure for Measure, i. 4. 5:

> Upon the *sisterhood*, the votarists of Saint Claire.

So Romeo and Juliet, v. 3. 157.

118. Line 33: *no stronger than the word of a* TAPSTER.—The next words may be compared with Troilus and Cressida, i. 2. 124, where scorn is thrown upon "a *tapster's* arithmetic;" and the same play, iii. 3. 252, 253: "like an *hostess* that hath no arithmetic but her brain to set down her reckoning." So, too, Love's Labour's Lost, i. 2. 42, in rather the opposite sense: "I am ill at reckoning; it fitteth the spirit of a *tapster.*"

119. Line 46: *as a* PUISNY *tilter; i.e.* "petty, having but the skill of a novice" (Schmidt, Shakespeare Lexicon). *Puisny* is the spelling of the Folios and it is unnecessary to change, with Malone, to the more usual *puny*. Derivation: *Puny = puiné = puisné, i.e. post natus,* "younger, born after" (Cotgrave). The etymological sense of the word is well brought out in Milton's expression "must appear . . . *like a punie with his guardian.*" Richardson, *sub voce*, quotes from Bishop Hall: "If still this priviledge were ordinary left in the church, it were not a work for *punieness, and novices,* but for the greatest master and most learned, and eminently holy doctors."

ACT III. SCENE 5.

120. Line 5: FALLS *not the axe upon the humbled neck.*—For *fall*=let fall, cf. Two Noble Kinsmen, i. 1:

> oh, when
> Her twinning cherries shall their sweetness *fall*
> Upon thy tasteful lips.

So Lucrece, 1551:

> For every tear he *falls* a Trojan bleeds.

121. Line 7: *Than he that* DIES *and* LIVES *by bloody drops; i.e.* his whole life long, from the cradle to the grave, is an executioner. The reversal of the natural order is not very uncommon; *e.g.* Dyce quotes from Barclay's Ship of Fooles, fol. 67, 1570:

> He is a foole, and so shall he *dye and live*,
> That thinketh him wise, and yet can be nothing.

Steevens, of course, is afraid that "our bard is at his quibbles again."

122. Line 13: *Who shut their coward gates on* ATOMIES; *i.e.* motes in the sunbeams, says Mr. Aldis Wright, who quotes the following definition of the word in Cockeram's Dictionarie: "A mote flying in the sunne-beames:

anything so small that it cannot be made lesse." In the Faithful Friend, iv. 4, we have:

> *Tulius.* To tell thee truth, not wonders, for no eye
> Sees thee but stands amazed, and would turn
> His crystal humour into *atomies*.
> —Beaumont and Fletcher, vol. iv. p. 263.

Everyone will remember Mercutio's:

> O, then, I see Queen Mab hath been with you.
> She is the fairies' midwife, and she comes
> . . . .
> Drawn with a team of little *atomies*.

Compare, too, iii. 2. 245 of this play.

123. Line 37: *What—though you have* NO *beauty.*—So the Folios; the sense is not very good. On the other hand, the corrections "*some* beauty," "*mo* beauty," are equally unsatisfactory.

124. Lines 82, 83: *Dead shepherd, &c.*—The reference is to Marlowe's Hero and Leander, 1598; there, in the first sestiad, we have:

> Where both deliberate, the love is slight:
> Who ever loved that loved not at first sight.

For Shakespeare's allusions to his great predecessor, see note on Troilus and Cressida, ii. 2. 81, 82. Marlowe died in 1593, slain in a tavern-brawl.

125. Line 108: *That the old* CARLOT *once was master of.*—Properly a diminutive form of *Carle*=*Ceorl* (A. S.), *Churl*; cf. German *Karl*. Here, as Douce says, the meaning is "rustic," "peasant." For *Carl* cf. Cymbeline, v. 2. 4, 5:

> or could this *carl*,
> A very drudge of nature's, have subdued me?

So The Maid in the Mill, iii. 1. early:

> Obstreperous *carl*,
> If thy throat's tempest could o'erturn my house,
> What satisfaction were it for thy child?
> —Beaumont and Fletcher, vol. ix. p. 240.

ACT IV. Scene 1.

126. Lines 10-20.—Shakespeare seems to be satirizing in this speech a contemporary affectation to which he alludes elsewhere, the pretence, namely, of melancholy "only for wantonness." Compare King John, iv. i. 12-15, and see note 180 of that play.

In the Queen of Corinth a character abruptly remarks (iv. i. end):

> I ne'er repented anything yet in my life,
> And scorn to begin now. Come, let 's be *melancholy*.
> —Beaumont & Fletcher, v. 460.

Earle in his Micro-cosmographie, or, A Peece of the World Discovered; in Essayes and Characters, has an amusing "study" of the "Discontented Man:" He is "vain glorious in the ostentation of his melancholy. His composure of himselfe is a studied carelessnesse with his armes a crosse, and a neglected hanging of his head and cloake, and he is as great an enemie to an hatband, as Fortune. . . . If he turne any thing, it is commonly one of these, either Friar, traitor, or mad-man" (Arber's Reprint, pp. 27, 28).

127. Line 14: *nor the lady's, which is* NICE.—*Nice* often bears the general sense of "squeamish," "super-subtle," "finicking." Compare note on Troilus and Cressida, iv. 5. 250. Milton has: "But then all human learning and controversie in religious points must remove out of the world, yea, the Bible itself: for that of times relates blasphemy not *nicely*," *i.e.* in a straightforward, unsqueamish manner (Areopagitica, Hale's Ed. p. 19). A late use of the word in this sense occurs in Cowper's Task, ii. 256:

> That no rude savour maritime invade
> The nose of *nice* nobility.

We may remember, too, Swift's definition of a "*nice* man."

128. Lines 33-41.—With the general drift of Rosalind's satirical sketch we may compare the following from Ascham, whom we shall have occasion to quote lower down: "An other propertie of this our English *Italians* is to be mervelous singular in all their matters: singular in knowledge, ignorant of nothyng: so singular in wisedom (in their owne opinion) as scarse they counte the best counsellor the Prince hath comparable with them: Common discoursers of all matters: busie searchers of most secret affaires" (Scholemaster, Mayor's ed. pp. 89, 90). And a closer parallel is given by Mr. Aldis Wright, who refers to Overbury's Characters (Works, Ed. Fairholt, p. 58), where the "Affectate Traveller" is thus described: "He censures all things by countenances, and shrugs, and speakes his own language with shame and lisping."

129. Line 38: *scarce think you have swam in a* GONDOLA.—The Folios have "Gundello." Johnson's comment is, "*i.e.* been at Venice, the seat at that time of all licentiousness, where the young English gentlemen wasted their fortunes, debased their morals, and sometimes lost their religion." Many are the references in Elizabethan literature to the prevailing practice of travelling in Italy, a point upon which contemporary moralists are very eloquent. "I was once," says Ascham, "in Italie my selfe: but I thanke God, my abode there was but ix days: and yet I sawe in that little tyme, in one citie, more libertie to sinne, than ever I hard tell of in our noble citie of London in ix yeare. I sawe, it was there as free to sinne, not onelie without all punishment, but also without any mans marking, as it is free in the citie of London to chose without all blame, whether a man lust to wear shoo or pantocle." The "citie" in question was Venice, concerning which Mayor in his masterly edition of the Scholemaster, p. 227, reminds us that there was a common proverb, quoted in one of Howell's Familiar Letters, to the effect that, "*the first handsome woman that ever was made was made of Venice Glass*; which implies Beauty, but Brittleness withal." The "Italianated Englishman" passed into a household word, and a very uncomplimentary one too:

> An Englishman Italianate
> Is a Devil incarnate.

For the other side of the question, the less moral aspect, we may turn to Beaumont and Fletcher's Wildgoose Chase, i. 2, where Italy and things Italian come in for a good deal of eulogy:

> *Mirabel.* Ha! Roma la Santa, Italy for my money!
> Their policies, their customs, their frugalities,
> Their courtesies so open, yet so reserv'd too.
> *Pinac.* 'T is a brave country:
> Not pester'd with your stubborn precise puppies,

> That turn all useful and allowed contentments
> To scabs and scruples—hang 'em, capon-worshippers.
> *Belim.* I like that freedom well.
>
> —The Wildgoose Chase.

130. Line 67: *of a better* LEER; *i.e.* complexion. *Leer* is merely the A. S. *hleór*, the cheek; hence, the face, look, mien. The middle English *lere*, says Skeat, was generally used in a good sense, as *leer* itself in the present passage.

For much the same use of the word, cf. Titus Andronicus, iv. 2. 119:

> Here's a young lad fram'd of another *leer*.

In Merry Wives of Windsor, i. 3. 50, the noun occurs in what is now its invariable signification: "she discourses, she carves, she gives the *leer* of invitation." For its original sense, compare Skelton's Phyllyp Sparowe:

> The orient perle so clere
> The whytenesse of her *lere*.
>
> —Dyce's Skelton, vol. i. p. 82.

And again:

> Her lothely *lere*
> Is nothynge clere,
> But ugly of chere. —i. p. 95.

131. Line 75: *you might take occasion to kiss.*—Steevens quotes aptly enough Burton's Anatomy of Melancholy—"and when he hath pumped his wits dry, and can say no more, *kissing* and colling are never out of season" (Ed. 1632, p. 511).

132. Line 94: *die* BY ATTORNEY.—"Shakespeare," says Lord Campbell, "gives us the true legal meaning of the word 'attorney,' viz. *representative* or deputy—celui qui vient à tour d'autrui; qui alterius Vices subit; legatus" (Shakespeare's Legal Acquirements, p. 43). For a similar use compare Richard III. v. 3. 83, 84:

> I, *by attorney*, bless thee from thy mother,
> Who prays continually for Richmond's good;

and see note 516 on that play. So in Holinshed (iii. 510) we have: "John lord Latimer, although he was under age, for himselfe and the duke of Norfolke, notwithstanding that his possessions were in the king's hands, *by his atturnie* claimed and had the office of almoner for that day." A good instance, too, occurs in the Alchemist, ii. 1:

> *Face.* Sir, shall I say
> You 'll meet the captains worship?
> *Sur.* Sir, I will—
> But, *by attorney* (*aside*).
>
> —Ben Jonson, Gifford's ed. vol. iv. p. 76.

133. Line 98: *Troilus had his brains dash'd out.*—Not so in Shakespeare's own play; see the note on Troilus and Cressida, v. 30. 31.

134. Line 105: *and the foolish* CHRONICLERS *of that age* FOUND.—The Folio has "chronoclers," which Hanmer changed to "coroners," arguing that "found" would be technically said of a coroner's verdict. This, of course, is correct enough, and every one will remember the clown's statement in Hamlet: "the crowner hath sat on her, and *finds* it Christian burial" (v. 1. 5). But surely *found* in the present passage would, by a metaphor, be perfectly appropriate as applied to *chroniclers*. They are the recording angels, so to speak, of history: they bring in their verdicts and pass sentence like any other judge; and so in this case they summed up the facts and *found*—"Hero of Sestos." Unfortunately their "finding" was wrong. The emendation is needless and intrinsically prosaic.

135. Line 100: *Hero of Sestos.*—Shakespeare is fond of alluding to the Hero and Leander story, which to an Elizabethan audience would be familiar enough from Marlowe's great poem. Compare, for similar references, Two Gentlemen of Verona, i. 1. 20-22:

> *Pro.* Upon some book I love I 'll pray for thee.
> *Val.* That 's on some shallow story of deep love:
> How young Leander cross'd the Hellespont.

And Much Ado, v. 2. 30: "Leander the good swimmer."

136. Line 126: *I take thee, Rosalind.*—"It is not merely in pastime, I feel assured, that Rosalind has been made by Shakespeare to put these words into Orlando's mouth. This is for her a marriage, though no priestly formality goes with it; and it seems to me that the actress must show this by a certain tender earnestness of look and voice as she replies: 'I do take thee, Orlando, for my husband.' I could never speak these words without a trembling of the voice, and the involuntary rushing of happy tears to the eyes, which made it necessary for me to turn my head away from Orlando" (Some of Shakespeare's Female Characters, p. 340).

137. Line 152: *more* NEW-FANGLED *than an ape.*—The history of this word is not without interest. First as to etymology. "The *d*," says Skeat, "has been added. M.E. *newe fangel*, *i.e.* fond of what is new. Compounded of *newe*, new, and *fangel*, ready to catch, from A. S. *fangen*, pp. (past part.) of *fôn*, to catch."

Fangle, the substantive, is defined by Johnson: "silly attempt: trifling scheme;" and he remarks that "it is never used, or rarely, but in contempt and with the epithet *new*." Todd, however, in his edition of Johnson quotes two passages where *fangle* is used alone, and substantivally. (i) Greene's Mamillia, 1583:

> There was no feather, no *fangle*, gem, nor jewel—left behind.

(ii) Antony à Wood, Athenæ Oxonienses, ii. col. 450:

> A hatred to *fangles* and the French fooleries of his time.

The adjective occurs not infrequently. So Ascham has: "Also, for maners and life, quicke wittes commonlie be, in desire *new fangle*, in purpose, unconstant" (Scholemaster, Mayor's ed. p. 12).

Compare, too, in the same work *new fanglenesse*: "painefull without werinesse, heedful without wavering, constant without *new fanglenesse*" (p. 16); and again, p. 19: "desirous of good thinges without *new fanglenesse*." The following couplet occurs in Milton's Vacation Exercise, 19, 20:

> Not those *new-fangled* toys, and trimming slight,
> That takes our late fantasticks with delight;

and note Spenser, Faerie Queene, bk. i. c. iv. xxv:

> full of vaine follies and *new-fanglenesse*.

Compare Love's Labour's Lost, note 6.

138. Line 154: *like* DIANA *in the fountain.*—"The allusion," says Malone, "is to the cross in Cheapside;" and he quotes the following passage from Stow:—"There was then set up (1596) a curious wrought tabernacle of grey marble, and in the same an alabaster image of *Diana*, and water conveyed from the Thames, prilling from her

naked breast." The reference is not impossible, but it seems to me rather far-fetched; as the editors show, the figure of Diana in a fountain was no novelty. Compare Drayton's Epistle of Rosamond to Henry II.:

> Here in the garden, wrought by various hands,
> Naked *Diana in the fountain* stands.

See Var. Ed. vol. vi. pp. 470, 471.

139. Line 162: MAKE *the doors upon a woman's wit.*—For *make*="close," see Comedy of Errors, iii. 1. 93: "Why at this time the doors are *made* against you."

[At the end of this speech it is the custom of nearly all actresses who play Rosalind to introduce the "Cuckoo" song from Love's Labour's Lost. Such a custom is most deplorable. The song is quite out of place; if Shakespeare had intended Rosalind to sing a song he would have written one for her.—F. A. M.]

140. Line 196: *most* PATHETICAL *break-promise.*—Apparently *pathetical* bears much the same sense as "pitiful." So Love's Labour's Lost, iv. 1. 149, 150:

> And his page at other side, that handful of wit!
> Ah, heavens, it is a most *pathetical* nit!

141. Line 213: *like the* BAY *of* PORTUGAL.—The reference is satisfactorily explained by the Clarendon Press editor, whose note I venture to transcribe. "In a letter to the Lord Treasurer and Lord High Admiral, Ralegh gives an account of the capture of a ship of Bayonne by his man Captain Floyer in 'the Bay of Portugal' (Edwards, Life of Ralegh, ii. 56). This is the only instance in which I have met with the phrase, which is not recognised, so far as I am aware, in maps and treatises on geography. It is, however, I am informed, still used by sailors to denote that portion of the coast of Portugal from Oporto to the headland of Cintra. The water there is excessively deep, and within a distance of forty miles from the shore it attains a depth of upwards of 1400 fathoms, which in Shakespeare's time would be practically unfathomable." It may be remembered that at a time when expeditions to Spain and Portugal were of periodical occurrence the allusion would be sufficiently understood, and therefore sufficiently pointed.

ACT IV. Scene 2.

142. Lines 1-19.—This is a thoroughly artificial scene, introduced, as Johnson notes, for the sole purpose of filling up the interval of two hours. Should it find a place in an acting edition of the play? [It is included in Macready's arrangement, as played at Drury Lane in 1842, which is the stage version generally accepted. It is, however, omitted altogether in the acting version of this play, prepared for Miss Ada Cavendish in America, the song only being given at the beginning of act v.—F. A. M.]

143. Line 12: *Then sing, &c.*—In the Folios the line stands thus: "Then sing him home, the rest shall beare this burthen;" i.e. the words, "the rest shall bear this burthen," were regarded as forming part of the song. Pope, following Rowe, retained this arrangement; and Theobald was the first to suggest that the words here printed as a stage-direction had been wrongly incorporated in the song. Dyce and other writers (Collier, Grant White) take the whole line as given in the Folios to be a stage-direction; and other suggestions have been made. I have followed the Cambridge editors (see their note, vol. ii. pp. 463, 464) in adopting Theobald's proposal. Knight gives Hilton's setting of the words, published in 1652, and reprinted, according to Boswell, in Playford's Musical Companion, 1673.

ACT IV. Scene 3.

144. Line 9: *By the stern brow and* WASPISH *action.*—So Julius Cæsar, iv. 3. 49, 50:

> I'll use you for my mirth, yea, for my laughter,
> When you are *waspish*.

The epithet is appropriately applied to Katharina in The Taming of the Shrew, ii. 1. 211:

> If I be *waspish*, best beware my sting.

145. Line 17: *Were man as rare as* PHŒNIX.—The fabulous phœnix has always been a prolific source of variously diverting and impossible legends. The favourite classical theory was, that only one specimen could be alive at any date; the solitary bird lived for an almost indefinite period, eventually seated itself on a burning heap of aromatic wood, and managed as the result of this fiery self-immolation to give birth to a fresh phœnix. Ovid refers to it—Amores, ii. 6. 54—as *Vivax Phœnix, unica semper avis;* Claudian devotes the first of his *Idyllia* to a description of its mythic capacities; while Pliny (10. 2. 2) frankly tells us that he does not know what to make of the immortal fowl—"whether it be a tale or no, that there is never but one of them in the whole world, and that not commonly seen." Turning to English literature, Mr. Aldis Wright (see his note to The Tempest, iii. 3. 23) gives a passage from Sir Thomas Browne's Vulgar Errors, bk. 3. ch. 12: "That there is but one Phœnix in the world, which after many hundred years burneth itself, and from the ashes thereof ariseth up another, is a conceit not new or altogether popular, but of great Antiquity." Various countries were assigned as the home of the phœnix—Ethiopia, Egypt, India (Claudian hazards nothing more definite than "trans Indos Eurumque"), and Arabia; for the last on the list we may compare the first stanza of the "Phœnix and the Turtle":

> Let the bird of loudest lay,
> On the sole *Arabian* tree,
> Herald sad and trumpet be,
> To whose sound chaste wings obey.

So too Lyly's Euphues (quoted by Malone): "For as there is but one *Phœnix* in the world, so is there but one tree in *Arabia*, where-in she buyldeth" (Arber's Reprint, p. 312). The Tempest passage (iii. 3. 22-24) should be referred to.

146. Line 35: *Such* ETHIOP *words; i.e.* swarthy, dark; the adjective here is ἅπαξ λεγόμενον. For substantive, cf. Romeo and Juliet, i. 5. 48:

> Like a rich jewel in an *Ethiope's* ear.

So Two Gentlemen of Verona, ii. 6. 25, 26:

> And Silvia . . .
> Shows Julia but a swarthy *Ethiope*.

Compare also Love's Labour's Lost, note 132, and Mids. Night's Dream, note 197.

147. Line 53: *Would they work in mild* ASPÉCT!—An

astrological term. Compare (amongst other passages) The Winter's Tale, ii. 1. 105-107:

> There 's some ill planet reigns:
> I must be patient till the heavens look
> With an *aspect* more favourable.

And Lear, ii. 2. 112:

> Under the allowance of your great *aspect*.

148. Line 68: *What, to* MAKE THEE AN INSTRUMENT.—We are reminded of Hamlet's "You would play upon me; you would seem to know my stops" (iii. 2. 380).

149. Line 71: *love hath made thee a tame* SNAKE.—*Snake* was frequently used as a term of contempt. So in Fletcher's The Spanish Curate, iii. 1:

> That makes you feared, forces the *snake* to kneel to you.
> —Beaumont and Fletcher, Dyce's ed. viii. 431.

Malone too (Var. Ed. vi. p. 479) refers to Lord Cromwell:

> The poorest *snake*,
> That feeds on lemons, pilchards.

150. Line 87: *and* BESTOWS *himself*.—That is, "behaves," "acquits himself," as in II. Henry IV. ii. 2. 186: "How might we see Falstaff *bestow* himself to-night in his true colours?" And King John, iii. 1. 225:

> And tell me how you would *bestow* yourself.

151. Line 115: *A lioness, with udders all* DRAWN DRY.—Steevens refers to Arden of Feversham:

> The starven lioness,
> When she is *dry-suckt* of her eager young.

152. Line 118: *The* ROYAL DISPOSITION *of that beast*.—Dyer remarks (Folklore, p. 182) that the traditions and romances of the dark ages are full of references to the supposed generosity of the lion. So (following Douce) he quotes Bartholomæus: "also their mercie (*i.e.* of lions) is known by many and oft ensamples: for they spare them that lie on the ground." Compare, for the general idea, Troilus and Cressida, v. 3. 37, 38:

> Brother, you have a vice of mercy in you,
> Which better fits a *lion* than a man.

There was a curious superstition that a *lion* would not harm any one of royal blood; see 1. Henry IV. ii. 4. 330: "you are *lions* too, you ran away upon instinct, you will not touch the true prince; no, fie!" a passage that may be paralleled by Beaumont and Fletcher's Mad Lover, iv. 5:

> Fetch the Numidian lion I brought over;
> If she be sprung from royal blood, *the lion*
> *He'll do you reverence, else* . . .
> . . . .
> *He'll tear her all to pieces.*

153. Lines 132, 133:

> *in which* HURTLING
> *From miserable slumber I awak'd.*

Compare *heurter*—and *hurler* (?). The word suggests crashing, dinning noise. Only here in Shakespeare and Julius Cæsar, ii. 2. 22:

> The noise of battle *hurtled* in the air.

Steevens quotes Nashe's Lenten Stuffe (1591): "hearing of the gangs of good fellows that *hurtled* and bustled hither."

154. Line 133.—Shakespeare, it will be seen, follows in this scene the line of Lodge's narrative: "All this while did poore Saladyne (banished from Bourdeux and the court of France by Torismond) wander up and downe in the forrest of Arden, thinking to get to Lyons, and so travail through Germany into Italie: but the forrest beeing full of by pathes, and he unskilfull of the country coast, slipt out of the way, and chaunced up into the desart, not farre from the place where Gerismond was, and his brother Rosader. Saladyne, wearie with wandring up and downe, and hungry with long fasting, finding a little cave by the side of a thicket, eating such fruite as the forest did affoord, and contenting himselfe with such drinke as nature had provided and thirst made delicate, after his repast he fell in a dead sleepe. As thus he lay, a hungry lyon came hunting downe the edge of the grove for pray, and espying Saladyne began to ceaze upon him: but seeing he lay still without any motion, he left to touch him, for that lyons hate to pray on dead carkasses; and yet desirous to have some foode, the lyon lay downe and watcht to see if he would stirre. While thus Saladyne slept secure, fortune that was careful of her champion began to smile, and brought it so to passe, that Rosader (having stricken a deere that but slightly hurt fled through the thicket) came pacing downe by the grove with a boare-speare in his hande in great haste. He spyed where a man lay a sleepe, and a lyon fast by him: amazed at this sight, as he stoode gazing, his nose on the sodaine bledde, which made him conjecture it was some friend of his. Whereuppon drawing more nigh, he might easily discerne his visage, perceived by his phisnomie that it was his brother Saladyne. . . . With that his brother began to stirre, and the lyon to rowse himselfe, whereupon Rosader sodainly charged him with the boare speare, and wounded the lion very sore at the first stroke. The beast feeling himselfe to have a mortall hurt, leapt at Rosader, and with his pawes gave him a sore pinch on the brest, that he had almost faln; yet as a man most valiant, in whom the sparks of Sir John Bourdeaux remained, he recovered himselfe, and in short combat slew the lion, who at his death roared so lowd that Saladyne awaked, and starting up, was amazed at the sudden sight of so monstrous a beast lying slaine by him, and so sweet a gentleman wounded" (Collier, i. pp. 76-79).

155. Line 139: *But, for the bloody* NAPKIN? *i.e.* handkerchief. So Emilia in Othello, iii. 3. 290, speaking of the handkerchief upon which so much is destined to turn, says:

> I am glad I have found this *napkin*.

156. Line 160: *There is more in it.*—So F. 1 and F. 2; one is tempted, I think, to read with F. 3 "there is no more in it."

157. Lines 163-183.—"The rest of the scene, with the struggle between actual physical faintness and the effort to make light of it, touched in by the poet with exquisite skill, calls for the most delicate and discriminating treatment in the actress. The audience, who are in her secret, must be made to feel the tender loving nature of the woman through the simulated gaiety by which it is veiled; and yet the character of the boy Ganymede must be sustained. This is another of the many passages to which the actress of comedy only will never give adequate expression" (Helena Faucit Martin).

158. Line 106: *a* BODY *would think, &c.*—For *body* in this sense, cf. the following from the New English Dictionary, *s.v.*: "A human *body* of either sex, an individual. Formerly, as still dialectically, and in the combinations Any-, Every-, No-, Some-*Body*, etc., exactly equivalent to the current 'person;' but now only as a term of familiarity, with a tinge of compassion, and generally with adjectives implying this." The same authority quotes a variety of instances of the occurrence of the word: *e.g.* Coverdale, Psalm xiv. 1: "The foolish *bodyes* saye in their hertes;" and Walton, Complete Angler, p. 56: "It shall be given away to some poor *body;*" with other passages, amongst which Carlyle's graphic "a puir *body*" might have been recorded. For Shakespeare, compare Merry Wives, i. 4. 105.

ACT V. Scene 1.

159. Line 11: *It is* MEAT AND DRINK.—The same phrase occurs in Merry Wives, i. 1. 306.

160. Line 14: *we cannot* HOLD; *i.e.* "refrain." Cf. Henry VIII. Epilogue, 13, 14:

> All the best men are ours; for 't is ill hap,
> If they *hold* when their ladies bid 'em clap.

161. Line 16: *God ye good even;* that is, "give ye good even." So Romeo and Juliet, ii. 4. 114, 115:

> *Nurse.* God ye good morrow, gentlemen.
> *Mer.* God ye good den, fair gentlewoman.

162. Line 58: TRANSLATE *thy life into death; i.e.* transform, as in the immortal "Bless thee, Bottom! bless thee! thou art *translated*" (Mid. Night's Dream, iii. 1. 121).

163. Line 60: *or in* BASTINADO.—So King John, ii. 463:

> He gives the *bastinado* with his tongue.

The word is Spanish—*bastonada*, a beating. Mr. Aldis Wright quotes Cotgrave: "Bastonnade: A bastonadoe; a banging, or beating with a cudgell."

164. Line 61: *I will* BANDY *with thee.*—A term used in tennis—meaning "to strike the ball to and fro over the net," and so the word came to be used of a rapid interchange of jests. Compare Love's Labour's Lost, v. 2. 29: "Well *bandied* both; a set of wit well play'd."

The noun *bandy* is used by Drayton in the Battaile of Agincourt (1627):

> He send him Balls and Rackets if I live
> That they such Rackets shall in Paris see
> When over lyne with *Bandies* I shall drive. —p. 7.

"*Bandy* seems to have been used sometimes in much the same sense as a *rest* is now used in Tennis and 'a knock up' in Rackets; that is, to signify the continual return of the ball from one player to another, keeping the park alive" (see Julian Marshall's Annals of Tennis, pp. 57, 95, 179).

ACT V. Scene 2.

165. Lines 20, 21:

> *God save you, brother.*
> *And you, fair* SISTER.

Why *sister?* Does Oliver know the secret of Rosalind's disguise? Yes, says Grant White; Celia, of course, has told him. No, reply other editors: but he enters into Orlando's joke of treating Rosalind as a woman. I don't think either explanation is very satisfactory; it seems to me possible that the commentators have tried to get too much out of the words. Rosalind addresses him as *brother*, and he laughingly retorts *sister*, intending, perhaps, to remind her of the last occasion when they met (iv. 3). Had he not then said to her—"you a man? you lack a man's heart."? Of course various emendations have been proposed. Johnson's "and you, and your fair *sister*" is fairly ingenious; better, however, to my mind, is "And you, *forester*" (Cruces Shakesperianæ, p. 123).

166. Line 23: *thy heart in a* SCARF.—As we should say, in a sling. We have *scarf'd* in Hamlet: "my sea-gown *scarf'd* about me," where the idea is "loosely thrown on" (v. 2. 13).

167. Line 34: *Cæsar's* THRASONICAL *brag.*—See Love's Labour's Lost, note 144. So in the curious tract *Tell-Trothies Message and his Pens Complaint*, edited by Dr. Furnivall for the New Shakspere Society, we have (p. 127):

> Wrath puffes men up with mindes *Thrasonicall*,
> And makes them brave it braggadoccio-like:
> Wrath maketh men triumph tyrannicall,
> With sword, with shield, with gunne, with bill and pike.

168. Line 44: CLUBS *cannot part them.*—Alluding, as the editors explain, to the cry raised when any street affray occurred. So Romeo and Juliet, i. 1. 80:

> *Clubs*, bills, and partisans; strike: beat them down!

And Titus Andronicus, ii. 1. 37—a very clear instance:

> *Clubs, clubs!* these lovers will not keep the peace.

Schmidt (Shakespeare Lexicon) also refers to I. Henry VI. i. 3. 84 (not so obvious), and Henry VIII. v. 4. 53. I need scarcely say that the *locus classicus* on "London Cries" is *The Spectator*, No. 251.

169. Line 78: *though I say I am a* MAGICIAN.—It has been suggested that this line refers to the statute against Witchcraft passed in 1604, a point which affects the date of the play. There had, however, been legislation on the subject in Elizabeth's reign, and trials for witchcraft were of not uncommon occurrence. Compare, for instance, the famous trials that took place in Scotland in 1590, when certain people were accused, and convicted, of having raised the storms that nearly shipwrecked James on his return from Denmark (Spalding's Elizabethan Demonology, pp. 110–115). In view of these persecutions men may well have been slow to proclaim themselves the possessors of occult powers; hence Rosalind's remark.

170. Line 90.—In the parallel scene in Lodge's novel Montanus apostrophizes love in a charming French lyric, which it may be worth while to disinter from its quaint but little-known surroundings:

> Hélas, tyran, plein de rigueur,
> Modère un peu ta violence:
> Que te sert si grande dispense?
> C'est trop de flammes pour un cœur.
> Épargnez en une étincelle,
> Puis fais ton effort d'émouvoir
> La fière qui ne veut point voir
> En quel feu je brûle pour elle.
> Exécute, Amour, ce dessein,
> Et rabaisse un peu son audace,
> Son cœur ne doit être de glace,
> Bien qu'elle ait de neige le sien.

171. Line 119: *like the howling of* IRISH WOLVES *against the moon.*—A touch partially taken from Lodge's romance, where we have: "I tell thee, Montanus, in courting Phœbe, thou barkest with the *wolves of Syria against the moone.*" For *wolves in Ireland*, compare the following from Mr. Gomme's Gentleman's Magazine Library, Archæology Section, pt. i. pp. 7, 8: "In a work entitled 'De Regno Hiberniæ, &c.,' written about the beginning of the seventeenth century, by Dr. Peter Lombard, titular primate of Armagh, he notices wild boars as then in Ireland. He also mentions several kinds of hounds now extinct, then kept for the chase, amongst which were those for hunting otters, deer, *wolves*, and the boar. . . . In the same work Dr. Lombard states that *wolves* were so numerous, that the cattle had to be secured at night from their ravages. Fynes Morison in his Itinerary, likewise mentions the depredations committed on cattle in Ireland by the wolves, the destruction of which, he says, is neglected by the inhabitants; and adds, that these animals were 'so much grown in numbers as sometimes in winter nights they will enter into villages and the suburbs of cities.' This statement of their numbers and boldness is also corroborated by accounts of a later date, particularly by Blennerhassett, in his Directions for the Plantation of Ulster, printed in 1610. In 1662 we find Sir John Ponsonby in the Irish House of Commons, reporting from the Committee of Grievances, the 'great increase of *wolves*,' and that the same was a grievance, and requesting that the House would be pleased to take the same 'into their consideration.' These notices of their numbers and boldness are still further confirmed by later accounts. In a dialogue entitled Some Things of Importance to Ireland, published in Dublin in 1751, the author states that an old man, near Lurgan, informed him, that when he was a boy, *wolves* during winter used to come within two miles of that town and destroy cattle. *This must have been about the beginning of the last century.*" According to tradition the last *wolf* observed in Ireland was killed in 1710, in County Kerry; a wolf was shot in Scotland as late as 1680.

ACT V. Scene 3.

172. Line 2: TO-MORROW *will we be married.*—There is nothing to fix the day on which the weddings take place, but in Lodge's romance we are expressly told, "in these humours the week went away, that at last *Sunday* came;" *à propos* of which I may quote a few lines from Jeaffreson's Brides and Bridals. "A fashionable wedding," he says, "celebrated on the *Lord's Day* in London, or any part of England, would nowadays be denounced by religious people of all Christian parties. But in our feudal times, and long after the Reformation, *Sunday* was of all days of the week the favourite one for marriage. Long after the theatres had been closed on *Sundays*, the day of rest was the chief day for weddings with Londoners of every social class." Shakespeare refers to the custom (which is still prevalent on the Continent) in the Taming of the Shrew, ii. 1. 324-326:

> I will to Venice; *Sunday* comes apace:
> We will have rings, and things, and fine array;
> And kiss me, Kate, we will be married o' *Sunday*.

See note 92 on that play.

173. Lines 17-34: Song.—Two points must be noted in connection with this song as given in the Folios; the order of stanzas 2 and 4 is reversed—an obvious blunder—and in line 20 *rang* (for which Johnson proposed *rank*, and Pope *spring*) was substituted for *ring*. The corrections were made by Mr. Chappell from a MS. of the song now in the Advocate's Library at Edinburgh.

174. Line 18: *With a hey, and a ho, and a hey nonino.*—A favourite burden. So Mr. Chappell quotes from Coverdale's preface to his Goastly Psalmes and Spirituall Songs (1538): "Wolde God that our Mynstrels had none other thynge to play upon, neither our carters and plowmen other thynge to whistle upon, save psalmes, hymns, and such like godly songes. . . . And if women at the rockes (distaffs), and spinnynge at the wheles, had none other songes to pass their tyme withall, than such as Moses' sister, . . . have sung before them, they should be better occupied than with *Hey, nonny nonny*—and such like fantasies" (see Popular Music, pp. 53, 54). Compare also Much Ado, note 150.

ACT V. Scene 4.

175. Lines 12-14.—Compare the following from Lodge's story: "Truth, q. Phœbe, and so deeply I repent me of my frowardnesse toward the shepheard, that could I cease to love Ganimede, I would resolve to like Montanus. What if I can with reason perswade Phœbe to mislike of Ganimede, wil she then favour Montanus? When reason (quoth she) doth quench that love I owe to thee, then will I fancie him; conditionally, that if my love can bee suppreat with no reason, as being without reason, Ganimede will onely wed himselfe to Phœbe. I graunt it, faire shepheardesse, quoth he; and to feed thee with the sweetnesse of hope, this resolve on: I wil never marry my selfe to woman but unto thy selfe" (Collier, vol. i. pp. 114, 115).

176. Line 27: *Some lively touches of my daughter's* FAVOUR.—As often, *favour* = "face," "looks;" cf. Troilus and Cressida, i. 2. 102: "Helen herself swore th' other day, that Troilus, for a brown *favour*;" and Measure for Measure, iv. 2. 32, 33: "Pray, sir, by your good *favour*—for surely, sir, a good *favour* you have, but that you have a hanging *look*." So Bacon's Essays (43): "In beauty, that of *favour* is more than that of colour, and that of decent and gracious motion more than that of *favour*." But the use of the word is too common to require illustration.

177. Line 48: *I have undone three* TAILORS.—The world seems to have gone but poorly with tailors some three hundred years ago; they had an evil reputation. Compare The Changeling, i. 2. 160, 161: "I must ask him easy questions at first—Tony, how many true fingers has a *tailor* on his right hand?" (Middleton's Works, vi. p. 23).

178. Line 73: *a certain courtier's* BEARD.—The cut of the beard was a very important matter; it served, indeed, to distinguish the profession of its wearer. There was the *bishop's beard*, and the *citizen's beard*, and the *judge's beard*, and the *soldier's beard*, and the *clown's beard* (which had to be very bushy), and other varieties might be men-

tioned. For a reference to the *beard military*, see Henry V. iii. 6. 80, 81; for the *beard* of civil life note Mrs. Quickly's description, Merry Wives, i. 4. 21: "like a glover's paring-knife." Much hair about the face was to be deprecated, "more hair than head," or, as we have it in Two Gentlemen of Verona, iii. 1. 361: "more hair than wit," being a very common expression, *e.g.* cf. A Mad World, My Masters, ii. 1. 137. For a contemporary criticism on the *beard* question we may turn to Harrison's Description of England, edited for the New Shakspere Society by Dr. Furnivall. "Neither," says Harrison (pt. i. pp. 169, 170), "will I meddle with our varietie of *beards*, of which some are shaven from the chin like those of Turks, not a few cut short like to the *beard* of Marquess Otto, some made round (*vide supra*, Merry Wives passage) like a rubbing brush, others with a *pique de vaut* (O fine fashion!) or now and then suffered to grow long, the barbers being growen to be so cunning in this behalfe as the tailors. And therefore if a man have a leane and streight face, a Marquesse Ottons cut will make it broad and large; if it be platter-like, a long, slender *beard* will make it seem narrow; if he be wesell (*i.e.* weasel) becked, then much heare left on the cheekes will make the owner look big like a boudled hen, and so grim as a goose: many old men do weare no beards at all." So in Stubbes' Anatomy of the Abuses (1583), we are told that barbers ("there are no finer fellows under the sun," says Amphilogus) have "the French cut, another the Spanish cut, one the Dutch cut, another the Italian, one the newe cut, another the old, one of the bravado fashion, another of the meane fashion." For a general and diverting dissertation upon the Elizabethan *coiffure*, the reader must be referred to Stubbes, edited for New Shakspere Society by Dr. Furnivall, pt. ii. pp. 50–52.

179. Line 80: *he* DISABLED *my judgment; i.e.* disparaged. So act iv. 1. 34: "*Disable* all the benefits of your own country."

180. Lines 94–108.—Shakespeare is alluding to a treatise by Vincentio Saviolo, printed in 1594 (or 1595?). This volume, of which some account is given in the Variorum Ed. vi. 503, 504, was described by its author as: "A Discourse most necessary for all gentlemen that have in regard their honours, touching the giving and receiving the Lie, whereupon the Duello and the Combat in divers forms doth ensue; and many other inconveniences, for lack only of the true knowledge of honour, and the right understanding of words, which here is set down." Proceeding in the orthodox manner of moralists, the essayist discusses his weighty subject under various "heads," differentiating the diverse forms of the Lie. So we have "Lies certain," "Foolish Lies," "The Lie in General," "The Lie in Particular," and the "Conditional Lie," which perhaps was the special *genre* that Touchstone had in mind. Apparently the great merit of the "Lie Conditional" is, that it must inevitably lead to "words upon words, whereof no sure conclusion can arise." In reading the description of this treatise we are reminded of some of the more humorous aspects of modern duelling.

181. Line 94: *we quarrel in print,* BY THE BOOK.—Compare Fletcher's The Elder Brother, v. 1:

> Come not between us. I'll not know, nor spare you—
> Do you *fight by the book?*
>
> —Beaumont and Fletcher, vol. x. p. 284.

182. Line 95: *as you have* BOOKS FOR GOOD MANNERS.—Steevens says: "One of these books I have. It is entitled, 'The Boke of Nurture, or Schole of good Manners, for Men, Servants, and Children, with *stans puer ad mensam*,' black letter, without date. It was written by Hugh Rhodes, a gentleman, or musician, of the Chapel Royal; and was first published in the reign of King Edward VI." Mr. Aldis Wright suggests that we have a similar allusion in Hamlet, v. 2. 114: "he is the card or calendar of gentry."

183. Line 111: *He uses his folly like* A STALKING-HORSE.—See Much Ado About Nothing, note 152.

184. Line 114: *Hymen.*—The God of Marriage was a familiar and imposing figure at these quasi-pagan celebrations, and the stage-directions are very minute always as to his robes. Compare, for instance, Women Beware Women, v. 1. 90, where the stage-direction runs: "Enter *Hymen* in a yellow robe" (Bullen's Middleton, vi. 363). Still more to the point is Ben Jonson's *Masque of Hymen:* "On the other hand entered *Hymen*, in a saffron-coloured robe, his under vestures white, his socks yellow, a yellow veil of silk on his right arm." Gifford's Ben Jonson, vol. vii. 51. Every one will remember Milton's—

> There let *Hymen* oft appear
> In Saffron robe, —L'Allegro.

So Beaumont and Fletcher, Dyce's ed. vol. i. p. 259.

185. Line 114: *Then is there.*—A point in connection with the stage representation of the drama. Should this masque be omitted? "Mr. Macready" (says the writer whom we have quoted so frequently, and, let us add, so gladly) "in his revival of the play at Drury Lane, with Mrs. Nesbit as Rosalind, restored it to the stage; but beautiful as it is in itself, and bringing this charming love-romance most appropriately to a close, yet it delays the action too much for scenic purposes" (Shakespeare's Female Characters, p. 352). And yet I think we should be slow to dispense with this stately, impressive pageant; accompanied by music, it should shed upon the close of the comedy the halo of dignity and peace that makes the final scene in Midsummer Night's Dream so wonderfully effective and touching.

186. Line 143: *Whiles a* WEDLOCK-HYMN *we sing.*—"Music," says Mr. Thiselton Dyer, "was the universal accompaniment of weddings in olden times. The allusions to wedding music that may be found in the works of Shakespeare, Ben Jonson, and other Elizabethan dramatists, testify that, in the opinion of their contemporaries, a wedding without the braying of trumpets, and beating of drums, and clashing of cymbals was a poor affair" (Folklore of Shakespeare, p. 330). It would be easy to multiply quotations in support of this remark; enough, perhaps, if we refer to Romeo and Juliet, iv. 5. 87, 88:

> Our wedding cheer to a sad burial feast;
> Our solemn hymns to sullen dirges change.

Curiously enough, it was to illustrate Shakespeare's genius that the most popular, if not musically the finest, of wedding marches was written; I refer, of course, to the march in Mendelssohn's incidental music to A Midsummer Night's Dream, a play that, by some cruel freak of fate, is seldom seen off the German stage.

187. Lines 147-152.—There is a classical ring in these lines that reminds us somewhat of Catullus' "Hymen O Hymenæe, Hymen ades O Hymenæe."

188. Line 157.—So in the romance the third brother arrives on the scene, bringing the news that the twelve Peers of France have taken up arms on the side of the exiled Duke and that the usurper is ready to give them battle. The Duke and his companions ride off, discover "where in a valley both the battailes were joyned," and "to be short, the peeres were conquerors, Torismonds army put to flight, and himselfe slain in battaile. The peeres then gathered themselves together and saluted their king, conducted him royally into Paris, where he was received with great joy of all the cittizens" (Collier, vol. i. p. 125). And thus "all's well that ends well."

189. Line 179: *That have endur'd* SHREWD *days and nights with us.*—*Shrewd* here, as so often in Shakespeare, has its original sense of "bad," "evil;" cf. Merry Wives, ii. 2. 232:

> There is *shrewd* construction made of her.

See Richard II. note 208. Wicliffe translates *καὶ πᾶν φαῦλον πρᾶγμα* (James, ch. iii. v. 16) by "and al *schrewed* werk," *i.e.* "and every *evil* work"—quoted in Todd's Johnson; and Schmidt (Shakespeare Lexicon) gives *böse, arg*, as its German equivalents.

190. Lines 192-199: *You to your, &c.*—It is worth noticing that old Adam does not come in for any mention. Lodge is more generous, since "that fortune might every way seeme frolicke," he makes Montanus "Lord over all the Forrest of Arden, Adam Spencer Captaine of the Kings Gard, and Coridon maister of Alindas flocks;" than which what more satisfactory?

191. Line 199: *I am for other than for dancing* MEASURES.—*Measure* generally implies a stately, dignified dance: cf. Much Ado, ii. 1. 80: "the wedding, mannerly-modest, *as a measure*, full of state and ancientry." The word, however, is used more widely to signify any kind of dance; *e.g.* Love's Labour 's Lost, v. 2. 209:

> Then, in our *measure* but vouchsafe one change.

EPILOGUE.

192. Lines 1-23.—"One word about the Epilogue before I conclude. This, as it is written, was fit enough for the mouth of a boy-actor of women's parts in Shakespeare's time, but it is altogether out of tone with the Lady Rosalind. It is the stage-tradition to speak it, and I, of course, followed the tradition—never, however, without a kind of shrinking distaste for my task. Some of the words I omitted, and some I altered, and I did my best, in giving it, to make it serve to show how the high toned winning woman reasserted herself in Rosalind, when she laid aside her doublet and hose. I have been told that I succeeded in this. Still, speaking the Epilogue remained the one drawback to my pleasure. In it one addresses the audience neither as Ganymede nor as Rosalind, but as one's own very self. Anything of this kind was repugnant to me, my desire always being to lose myself in the character I was representing. When taken thus perforce out of my ideal, I felt stranded and altogether unhappy. Except when obliged, as in this instance, I never addressed an audience, having neither the wish nor the courage to do so. Therefore, as I advanced to speak the Epilogue, a painful shyness came over me, a kind of nervous fear, too, lest I should forget what I had to say—a fear I never had at other times—and thus the closing words always brought to me a sense of inexpressible relief" (Helena Faucit Martin).

193. Line 4: *good wine needs no bush.*—It seems to have been usual for tavern keepers to hang a *bunch* or garland of ivy over their doors as a sign. Ivy, no doubt, was chosen from its traditional association with Bacchus. Steevens supplies us with several passages where the custom is alluded to; *e.g.* in Gascoigne's Glass of Government, 1575, we have:

> Now a days the good wyne needeth none *ivye-garland*.

So, too, in The Rival Friends, 1632:

> 'T is like the *ivy-bush* unto a tavern.

Compare also the following from Middleton's Anything for a Quiet Life:

> *Cawn.* He 's at the tavern, you say?
> *Sweet.* At the Man in the Moon, above stairs; so soon as he comes down, and the *bush* left at his back, Ralph is the dog behind him.
> —Middleton's Works, Bullen's ed. v. 272.

In Mr. Gomme's delightful antiquarian collection, The Gentleman's Magazine Library (Dialect, Proverbs, Word-Lore Section), I find the following curious contribution —"*The Bush*, the principal tavern at Bristol, and the *Ivy Bush*, the head inn at Carmarthen, originated in the ancient practice of hanging a *bush* at the door of those houses that sold wine, whence the proverb 'good wine, etc. An inn-keeper in Aldersgate Street, London, when Charles I. was beheaded, had the carved representation of a *bush* at his house painted black, and the tavern was long afterwards known by the name of the 'Mourning *Bush* in Aldersgate'" (p. 264). Again, in that very curious volume Earle's Micro-cosmographie (1628) we have amongst the "Characters" a description of the "Tauerne," in which the writer remarks: "If the Vintners nose be at the doore, it is a signe sufficient, but the absence of this is supplyed by the Iuie *bush*" (Arber's Reprint, p. 33). Lastly, cf. Wit Without Money, ii. 3:

> He 's a beggar,
> Only the sign of a man; the *bush* pulled down,
> Which shews the house stands empty.
> —Dyce, iv. p. 123;

and The Fair Maid of the West, i. 1:

> She 's the flower
> Of Plymouth held: the Castle needs no *bush*,
> Her beauty draws to them more gallant customers
> Than all the signs i' the town else.
> —Heywood's Plays, Ed. for Old Shakespeare Society by Collier, vol. i. p. 8.

194. Line 19: *If I were a* WOMAN.—Alluding obviously to the fact that women's parts were not played by women. So Coriolanus, ii. 2. 100:

> When he might act the *woman* in the scene.

When the innovation of allowing women to appear on

the stage was first made is a much-debated question. Upon the prejudice which required that female parts should be taken by boys Professor Ward has the following remarks: "The Puritans objected to the acting of female characters by male performers on grounds all their own; they deemed it a plain offence against Scripture for one sex to put on the apparel of the other. This of course by no means implied any approval of the performance of female characters by women. When, in 1629, actresses made their first public appearance in England in the persons of Frenchwomen belonging to the company which visited London in that year, Prynne saluted them as 'monsters' rather than women; and in this instance the opinion of the theatrical audience coincided with that of the outside censor, for the strangers were 'hissed, hooted and pippin-pelted from the stage' (Collier, Hist. of Dramatic Poetry, ii. 23). The next French company appears to have comprised no actresses; and the innovation was probably but little imitated on the English stage before the Restoration. It is clear that it was considered open to grave doubts even by persons who were warm friends of the theatre. At the same time it should be remembered—and the circumstance increases our surprise at the tardiness with which the practice was domesticated on the public stage in England—that in the masks at Court ladies constantly took part as performers; so that when in Christmas 1632-3 the Queen with her ladies acted in a Pastoral at Somerset House, there was no real novelty in the proceeding" (Ward, Dramatic Literature, ii. p. 422). Professor Ward shows that in all probability isolated cases of women appearing on the stage occurred during the reign of Charles I., and up to the time of the closing of the theatres. Such performances, however, would be irregular, a fact which, to some extent, explains the curiously conflicting contemporary accounts that we have. For instance, Colley Cibber declares that *no* actress had ever been seen on the English stage prior to the Restoration; yet there is a theatrical tradition that a woman played the part of Ianthe in Davenant's Siege of Rhodes in 1656; and again, there is the contradictory statement that absolutely the first occasion when an actress publicly came upon the boards was in Dec. 1660, the play being Othello. However, this last account must be incorrect. Compare Pepys under date of Jan. 3, 1660: "To the Theatre, where was acted 'Beggars Bush,' it being very well done; and here the first time that I ever saw women upon the stage." Perhaps we shall not be far wrong if we suppose that the innovation had been made tentatively and possibly with some secrecy, and that at the Restoration the practice was formally legalized, the following Royal Patent being issued in 1662:—"Whereas the women's parts in plays have hitherto been acted by men in habits of women, at which some have taken offence, we do permit and give leave from this time to come that all women's parts be acted by women" (see Fitzgerald's New History of the English Stage, i. p. 61). Evidently the advantages of the change were quickly appreciated; cf. Pepys, Feb. 12, 1661: "By water to Salsbury Court Play-house, where not liking to sit, we went out again, and by coach to the Theatre, and there saw 'The Scornful Lady,' now done by a woman, which makes the play appear much better than ever it did to me." A famous actor of women's parts was Alexander Goffe, at Blackfriars; and the last, and perhaps best, of the boy-actors was the Edward Kynaston who kept Charles II. waiting while he finished his shaving operations. Of Kynaston the great Betterton said "it has been disputed among the judicious, whether any *woman* could have more sensibly touched the passions;" I owe this reference to Ashton's Social Life in the reign of Queen Anne, ii. p. 23. And one more quotation from Pepys, apropos of the same actor. "Tom and I and my wife to the Theatre, and there saw 'The Silent Woman.' Among other things here, Kinaston, the boy, had the good turn to appear in three shapes: first, as a poor woman in ordinary clothes; then in fine clothes, as a gallant; and in them was clearly the prettiest woman in the whole house; and lastly, as a man, and then likewise did appear the handsomest man in the house" (Jan. 7, 1661).

WORDS OCCURRING ONLY IN AS YOU LIKE IT.

NOTE.—The addition of sub., adj., verb, adv. in brackets immediately after a word indicates that the word is used as a substantive, adjective, verb, or adverb only in the passage or passages cited.
The compound words marked with an asterisk (*) are printed as two separate words in F. 1.

	Act	Sc.	Line
Abruptly	ii.	4	41
Allottery	i.	1	77
A-night	ii.	4	48
Ark	v.	4	36
Basked	ii.	7	15
Batlet	ii.	4	50
Bob (sub.)	ii.	7	55
Boorish	v.	1	54
Bottomless[1]	iv.	1	214

1 = without a bottom; it occurs = fathomless, Lucrece, 701; Titus Andronicus, iii. 1. 218.

	Act	Sc.	Line
Bow[2]	iii.	3	80
Brambles[3]	iii.	2	381
Break-promise	iv.	1	196
Butchery[4]	ii.	3	27
Calling[5] (sub.)	i.	2	246

2 = a yoke.

3 Venus and Adonis, 629.

4 = slaughter-house; used four times in ordinary sense of slaughter.

5 = appellation; used frequently = trade, profession.

	Act	Sc.	Line
Capricious	iii.	3	8
Cariot	iii.	5	108
Caters	ii.	3	44
Catlike	iv.	3	116
Chestnut (adj.)	iii.	4	12
Circumstantial[6]	v.	4	87, 91
*City-woman	ii.	7	75

6 This word occurs also in Cymbeline, v. 5. 383; Schmidt distinguishes between the meanings of the word in the two passages; but there is little if any real distinction.

	Act	Sc.	Line
Clownish	i.	3	132
Cock-pigeon	iv.	1	150
Co-mates	ii.	1	1
Coming-on (adj.)	iv.	1	113
Copulatives (sub.)	v.	4	58
*Corn-fields	v.	3	19
Cote (sub.)	ii.	4	83
	iii.	2	448
Crooked-pated	iii.	2	86
Curvets[7] (verb)	iii.	2	258
*Cutter-off	i.	2	53

7 Venus and Adonis, 279.

WORDS PECULIAR TO AS YOU LIKE IT.

Word	Act	Sc.	Line
Debility	ii.	3	51
*Deep-contemplative	ii.	7	31
Deify[1]	iii.	2	381
Despiser	ii.	7	92
Disputable	ii.	5	36
Dog-apes	ii.	5	27
Effigies[2]	ii.	7	193
Emulator	i.	1	151
Enchantingly	i.	1	173
Entame	iii.	5	48
Eventful	ii.	7	164
Expediently	iii.	1	18
Extent[3]	iii.	1	17
Extermined	iii.	5	89
Fancy-monger	iii.	2	382
Fawn[4] (sub.)	ii.	7	128
Fenced[5]	iv.	3	78
Fleet (verb tr.)	i.	1	124
Flux	ii.	1	52
	iii.	2	72
*Forest-born	v.	4	30
Foulness[6]	iii.	3	41
	iii.	5	66
*Freestone-coloured	iv.	3	25
Gentility[7]	i.	1	23
*Giant-rude	iv.	3	34
Giddiness	v.	2	6
Glances[8] (sub.)	ii.	7	57
Glides (sub.)	iv.	3	113
Glow (sub.)	iii.	4	57
Goldenly	i.	1	7
Gravelled	iv.	1	74
Greenwood	ii.	5	1
Hawking[9]	v.	3	12
Headed	ii.	7	67
*Heart-heaviness	v.	2	50
*Heart-whole	iv.	1	48
Holly	ii.	7	180, 182
Homewards	iv.	3	179
Homily	iii.	2	164
*Horn-beasts	iii.	3	52
*Horn-maker	iv.	1	63
Horse-stealer	iii.	4	25
Hospitality[10]	ii.	4	82
Hugely[11]	ii.	7	72
Huntress	iii.	2	4
Hyen[12]	iv.	1	156
*Ill-inhabited	iii.	3	10
*Ill-roasted	iii.	2	38
Inconvenient	v.	2	72
Indented[13]	iv.	3	113
Injure[14]	iii.	5	9
Insomuch	v.	2	61
Invectively	ii.	1	58
Keeping[15]	i.	1	10
Key-hole	iv.	1	165
Kindled[16]	iii.	2	358
Lack-lustre	ii.	7	21
Limned[17]	ii.	7	194
Lined[18]	iii.	2	97
*Love-cause	iv.	1	98
Love-prate	iv.	1	205
Love-shaked	iii.	2	385
Material[19]	iii.	3	32
Mewling	ii.	7	144
Mockable	iii.	2	50
Monastic	iii.	2	441
Moonish	iii.	2	439
Moral[20] (verb)	ii.	7	29
Motley[21]	iii.	3	79
Motley-minded	v.	4	41
Narrow-mouthed	iii.	2	211
News-crammed	i.	2	101
Often (as adj.)	iv.	1	19
Omittance	iii.	5	133
Ordinary[22]	iii.	5	42
Outstay	i.	3	90
*Palm-tree	iii.	2	186
Panel	iii.	3	90
Poke (sub.)	ii.	7	20
Priser[23]	ii.	3	8
Private[24] (adj.)	ii.	7	71
Propositions[25]	iii.	2	245
Providently	ii.	3	44
Pulsny	iii.	4	46
Puking	ii.	7	144
Pulpiter	iii.	2	163
Purlieus	iv.	3	77
Quintain	i.	2	263
Recountments	iv.	3	141
Redness	iii.	5	120
Reference[26]	i.	3	129
Residue	ii.	7	196
Retort (sub.)	v.	4	76, 90
Revelry	v.	4	183
Rib-breaking	i.	2	151
Righteously	i.	2	14
*Ring-time	v.	3	20
Roynish	ii.	2	8
Rumination	iv.	1	19
Rustically	i.	1	8
Sale-work	iii.	5	43
Satchel	ii.	7	145
Scoffer	iii.	5	62
Scrip[27]	iii.	2	171
Scrippage	iii.	2	171
Seizure[28]	iii.	1	10
Sheaf (verb)	iii.	2	113
She-lamb	iii.	2	85
Slippered	ii.	7	158
Sluttishness	iii.	3	41
Smother (sub.)	i.	2	299
Sprite[29]	iii.	2	147
Squandering (intr.)	ii.	7	57
Stalking-horse	v.	4	112
Stammer	iii.	2	200
Straits[30]	v.	2	71
Subject[31] (verb)	ii.	3	30
Tarred	iii.	2	63
Taxation[32]	i.	2	91
Traverse (adv.)	iii.	4	44
Trowel	i.	2	112
Udders	iv.	3	115
Umber	i.	3	114
Unbanded	iii.	2	390
Unbashful	ii.	3	50
Unbuttoned	iii.	2	399
Unclaimed	ii.	7	87
Unexpressive	iii.	2	10
Unfaithful	iv.	1	199
Ungentleness	v.	2	83
Unkept	i.	1	9
Unlinked	iv.	3	112
Unquestionable	iii.	2	394
Unregarded	ii.	3	42
Unseasonably	iii.	2	258
Untreasured	ii.	2	7
Vacation	iii.	2	349
Vehemence[33]	iii.	2	200
Wainscot	iii.	3	80
*Wedlock-hymn	v.	4	143
Whippers	iii.	2	424
Wiser[34]	ii.	4	58
*Working-day[35]	i.	3	12

[1] Lover's Complaint, 84.

[2] A Latin word (=likeness) used as an English one.

[3] Used in legal sense (=seizure of goods). In other senses the word occurs four times.

[4] Venus and Adonis, 876.

[5] =inclosed; used in other senses frequently.

[6] =ugliness.

[7] =good extraction.

[8] Here=oblique censures; occurs in its ordinary sense several times.

[9] =clearing the throat.

[10] Lucrece, 575.

[11] Sonn. cxxiv. 11.

[12] =hyena.

[13] =zig-zag. Compare *indenting*, Venus and Adonis, 704. The verb *indent* occurs in 1. Henry IV. i. 3. 87, where it means "to covenant."

[14] =to hurt bodily; several times used=to wrong.

[15] =maintenance.

[16] =delivered of a litter.

[17] Venus and Adonis, 290.

[18] =delineated.

[19] =full of matter. Occurs three times in ordinary sense.

[20] Some commentators take the word to be an adjective=moralizing, in which sense it occurs in Much Ado, v. 1. 30 and Lear, iv. 2. 58.

[21] =a fool. Sonn. cx. 2.

[22] In the phrase *in the ordinary* =in the mass; *ordinary*=a repast, is used twice, in All's Well, ii. 3. 211, and Ant. and Cleo. ii. 2. 230.

[23] =a prize-fighter. *Prizer*, in its ordinary sense, occurs in Troilus, ii. 2. 56.

[24] Also in Sonn. ix. 7, =" particular," opposed to "general;" in other senses it occurs frequently.

[25] =questions asked. *Proposition* occurs in Troilus and Cressida, i. 3. 3=promise.

[26] =relation, respect.

[27] =a wallet; occurs also in Mids. Night's Dream, i. 2. 3=a written list.

[28] In legal sense. Occurs three times elsewhere in ordinary sense.

[29] =soul; Lucrece, 1728. Occurs frequently in other senses.

[30] =difficulties.

[31] =to expose. Occurs once elsewhere, Tempest, i. 2. 114=to make subject.

[32] =censure.

[33] Shakespeare uses *vehemency* frequently in same sense.

[34] Used adverbially.

[35] Used adjectively.

TWELFTH NIGHT;

OR, WHAT YOU WILL.

NOTES AND INTRODUCTION BY

ARTHUR SYMONS.

DRAMATIS PERSONÆ.

ORSINO, Duke of Illyria.
SEBASTIAN, a young gentleman, brother to Viola.
ANTONIO, a sea captain, friend to Sebastian.
A Sea Captain, friend to Viola.
VALENTINE, } gentlemen attending on the Duke.
CURIO, }
SIR TOBY BELCH, uncle to Olivia.
SIR ANDREW AGUECHEEK.
MALVOLIO, steward to Olivia.
FABIAN, } servants to Olivia.
Clown, }

OLIVIA, a rich Countess.
VIOLA, sister to Sebastian, in love with the Duke.
MARIA, Olivia's woman.

Lords, a Priest, Sailors, Officers, Musicians, and Attendants.

SCENE—A city in Illyria, and the sea-coast near it.

HISTORIC PERIOD: The historic period is absolutely indefinite.

TIME OF ACTION.

The time of action (according to Daniel) comprises three days, with an interval of three days between the first and second days.

Day 1: Act I. Scenes 1-3.—Interval.
Day 2: Act I. Scenes 4 and 5; Act II. Scenes 1-5.
Day 3: Act II. Scene 4 and 5; Acts III., IV., and V.

TWELFTH NIGHT;

OR, WHAT YOU WILL.

INTRODUCTION.

LITERARY HISTORY

Twelfth Night was first printed in the Folio of 1623, where it occupies pp. 255–275 of the Comedies. Its date is fixed, within certain limits, by a reference discovered by Mr. Hunter in 1828. It is found in a MS. volume in the British Museum (MSS. Harl. 5353) containing the diary of John Manningham, a member of the Middle Temple, from January 1601–2 to April 1603. The entry for February 2, 1601–2, is as follows:—

"At our feast[1] wee had a play called Twelue night or what you will. much like the commedy of errores or Menechmi in Plautus, but most like and neere to that in Italian called Inganni a good practice in it to make the steward beleeue his Lady widdowe was in Loue with him by counterfayting a letter, as from his Lady, in generall termes, telling him what she liked best in him, & prescribing his gesture in smiling his apparaile &c. And then when he came to practise making him beleeue they tooke him to be mad."

This entry proves that Shakespeare's play must have been written before February 1601–2; its absence from the list in Meres' Palladis Tamia shows that it could not have been known before September 1598. The introduction in the play of some fragments from the song, "Farewell, dear heart, since I must needs be gone," further narrows the limits of conjecture; for this song first appeared in 1601 in the Booke of Ayres composed by Robert Jones. The play is therefore assigned with great probability to 1601–2; and it has been conjectured by Mr. Halliwell-Phillipps that it was one of four plays acted in the Christmas of that year before the Court at Whitehall by the Lord Chamberlain's company, to which Shakespeare belonged, and that it was probably acted on Twelfth Night, and derived its name from that circumstance.

[1] *i.e.* the Candlemas feast at the Middle Temple Hall.

Manningham, as we have seen, remarks on the likeness of the play to the Menæchmi of Plautus and an Italian play named Gl' Inganni. There were three plays of this name, one by Nicolo Secchi (Florence, 1562), another by Curzio Gonzaga (Venice, 1592), both containing incidents of a certain resemblance to some of Shakespeare's, and the latter of them a sister who assumes male attire and the name Cesare (which might have suggested Cesario); the third play, by Cornaccini (Venice, 1604), has less resemblance. But there is yet another Italian play, named Gl' Ingannati (Venice, 1537), which really does bear some likeness to Twelfth Night, the whole outline of the primary plot of the English play being found in the Italian one, and the name Malevolti (which might have suggested Malvolio—the name only) occurring in the induction. Gl' Ingannati was translated by Peacock in 1862; it is given in the the 3rd volume of his collected works (Bentley, 1885). The story on which it was founded is told by Bandello (Novelle, ii. 36), and in Belleforest's translation (Histoires Tragiques, tom. iv., hist. vii.). There is what may be called another version of the same story (though whether or not directly copied, it is hard to say) in Barnabe Riche's Historie of Apolonius and Silla, the second story in his Farewell to Militarie Profession (1581), reprinted in Malone's Variorum, and in Hazlitt's Shakespeare Library (pt. I. vol. i. p. 387). This at least it seems almost certain that Shakespeare must have seen and made use of as the framework of his comedy; all the underplot, if we may so call what is virtually the mainstay of the play, is so far as we know entirely of his own invention. Grant White, speaking of certain coincidences, remarks on the "reminiscence" which appears in Sir Andrew's complaint to Sir Toby, "Marry, I saw your niece do more favours to the count's serving-man," &c., of a passage in Apolonius and Silla, where the servants "debating betweene them, of the likelihood of the marriage, betweene the duke & the ladie, one of them said: that he neuer saw his lady & mistresse, vse so good countenance to the duke himself, as she had done to Siluo his man." Shakespeare has condensed and simplified the entanglements, and he has purified them from certain grossnesses which found place in the plain-speaking pages of his originals.

STAGE HISTORY.

The earliest mention of the performance of this comedy seems to be in a passage in the diary of John Manningham of The Middle Temple, under date February 2nd, 1601–2, already quoted above. The next reference to this play, at least as far as regards its Stage History, is in the verses of Leonard Digges prefixed to Shakespeare's Poems, 1640. After alluding to Henry IV. and Much Ado, the author says:

let but Falstaffe come:
Hall, Poines, the rest you scarce shall have a roome
All is so pester'd; let but Beatrice
And Benedicke be seene, loe in a trice
The Cockpit Galleries, Boxes, all are full
To hear *Malvoglio, that cross-garter'd Gull.*

—Ingleby's Shakespeare's Centurie of Prayse, p. 233.

This seems to show that Twelfth Night rivalled Much Ado and the Two Parts of Henry IV. in popularity. It is curious that Digges refers to no other comedy of Shakespeare's except Much Ado about Nothing. Pepys, under date September 11th, 1661, says: "Walking through Lincoln's Inn Fields observed at the Opera a new play 'Twelfth Night,' was acted there, and the King there; so I, against my own mind and resolution, could not forbear to go in, which did make the play seem a burthen to me, and I took no pleasure at all in it." On January 6th, 1622–23, he again saw Twelfth Night; on which occasion we learn from Downes that "it was got up on purpose to be acted on Twelfth Night" (Roscius Anglicanus, p. 32), and appears to have been revived with very great success. Pepys does not seem to have formed any more favourable opinion of its merits; for though he confesses it was acted well, he says that it was "but a silly play, and not related at all to the name or day." He saw the piece again on January 20th, 1669, when it was revived at the Duke of York's play-house in Lincoln's Inn Fields. He adds: "I think one of the weakest plays that I ever saw on the stage." This comedy seems, like most of Shakespeare's plays, to have been suffered to lie on the shelf for a long time. On January 15th, 1741, Genest records that it was revived at Drury Lane, and acted about eight times during that season. The cast was a strong one. It included Macklin as Malvolio, Woodward as Sir Andrew Aguecheek, Milward as Sebastian, with Mrs. Pritchard as Viola, and Mrs. Clive as Olivia. Twelfth Night does not seem to have been again represented till 1746, when on April 15th it was revived "for the benefit of Raftor and Miss Edwards," on which occasion Neal was Sir Andrew Aguecheek, and Yates the Clown, Mrs. Woffington appearing for the first time as Viola. On the 18th of the same month the play was again represented for Neal's benefit. We may presume the cast was the same. Genest only gives the names of Mills as playing Orsino, and Sparks as Sir Toby Belch, with Mrs. Macklin as Maria. On January 6th and 7th, 1748, at Drury Lane, Twelfth Night was again revived with much the same cast, except that Berry played Sir Toby Belch, and Mrs. Pritchard resumed the part of Viola. On November 9th, 1748, at the same theatre, Woodward played Sir Andrew Aguecheek, a performance which he repeated on January 7th, 1751; on which occasion the part of Malvolio, which hitherto belonged to Macklin, was taken by Yates, Shuter playing the Clown, and Palmer the small part of Sebastian; Mrs.

Pritchard and Mrs. Clive retaining their original parts of Viola and Olivia respectively. The next performance of this comedy, which is worth recording, was at Drury Lane on January 6th, 1755, when Viola was represented by Mrs. Davies, the pretty wife of Tom Davies, the gossiping biographer of Garrick, and author of the Dramatic Miscellanies; to which latter work, in spite of many inaccuracies, the historians of the English stage are so much indebted. Genest, quoting the State of the Stage, says of her: "she gave infinite pleasure by her figure, and prejudiced the audience in her favour as soon as she was seen—she was likewise mistress of extreme justice in her enunciation" (vol. iv. p. 406). The next representation of this comedy appears to have been on October 19th, 1763: "not acted five years." This is probably a mistake; at least there is no performance recorded since the one last mentioned in 1755. On this occasion O'Brien was Sir Andrew Aguecheek, and Love Sir Toby Belch, Yates being again Malvolio. Miss Plym made her first appearance as Viola; Miss Haughton was the Olivia, and Mrs. Lee the Maria. About Miss Plym little seems to be known. She continued in the Drury Lane company, playing mostly small parts, till the season 1766–77, when she retired from the stage.[1]

For eight years this play seems to have been neglected. It was revived at Drury Lane on December 10th, 1771 with a very strong cast, including King as Malvolio, Dodd as Sir Andrew Aguecheek, Love as Sir Toby Belch, with Miss Young as Viola, and Mrs Abington as Olivia (with a song). What this song was we are not told. This revival was successful, and the piece was performed fourteen times. During this season, on April 1st, 1773, at the same theatre, Palmer played Sir Toby Belch, for the first time, for Dodd's benefit.

Up to this period Twelfth Night had never been performed at Covent Garden. It was produced there, for the first time, on March 31st, 1772, with Yates as Malvolio, Woodward as Sir Andrew Aguecheek, Dunstall as Sir Toby Belch, Mrs. Yates as Viola, Mrs. Mattocks as Olivia, and Mrs. Green as Maria. It was acted again on May 5th. This comedy does not seem to have been revived at this theatre till March 17th, 1777, when the playbill announces it for Mrs. Barry's benefit "not acted 6 years," with the following cast: Wilson as Malvolio; Quick, Sir Andrew Aguecheek; Dunstall, Sir Toby Belch; Lee Lewes, the Clown; and Mrs. Barry for the first time as Viola. We pass over several performances at Drury Lane, Bath, Liverpool, Dublin. On October 23rd, 1779, at Drury Lane, the beautiful Mrs. Robinson, known as Perdita, appeared for the first time as Viola—she had made her debut as an actress there on December 10th, 1776—and at the end of this season she, unhappily, left the stage, of which she promised to be a most distinguished ornament, for the sake of the most contemptible prince that ever appeared in the rôle of Florizel. On May 20th, 1780, at the same theatre, Miss Farren appeared for the first time (with a song) as Olivia.

At the Haymarket Theatre, on August 15th, 1782, Twelfth Night was presented for the first time at that house, for Mrs. Bulkley's benefit; on which occasion Bensley played Malvolio; Edwin, Sir Andrew Aguecheek; Palmer, Sir Toby Belch; and Parsons appeared as the Clown; the *bénéficiaire* herself taking the part of Viola, and Miss Harper that of Olivia. On September 21st of the same year Mrs. Bulkley made her first appearance at Drury Lane in the character of Viola, the only other member of the cast mentioned being Bannister, jun., who played Sebastian. On May 7th, 1782, Twelfth Night was revived at Covent Garden for the benefit of Edwin, who played Sir Andrew Aguecheek. On this occasion Henderson appeared as Malvolio for the first time; and a Mrs. Robinson[2] is announced as Viola "for the first time" (Genest, vol. vi. p.

[1] Genest says that in "A Dialogue in the Shades between the celebrated Mrs. Cibber and the no less celebrated Mrs. Woffington, both of amorous memory," published not long after Mrs. Cibber's death in 1766 (Genest, vol. v. p. 102)—"Miss Plym is said to have withstood a regular siege from an experienced and popular general" (*ut supra*, p. 127).

[2] It does not appear who this Mrs. Robinson was; she played one or two leading characters during this season; but I can find no subsequent mention of her. She appears to have been the original Victoria in Mrs. Centlivre's "Bold Stroke for a Husband."

274). The comedy was repeated twice in the same month. On May 3rd, 1784, at Drury Lane, for the benefit of Suett and Palmer, Miss Phillips made her first appearance as Olivia. The rest of the cast is not given; probably Suett played the Clown, and Palmer Sir Toby Belch; for their names appear in the cast of this comedy at the same theatre on November 11th, 1785, when Dodd played Sir Andrew Aguecheek; Bensley, Malvolio; and Mrs. Jordan made her first appearance as Viola. This was one of her favourite parts, as it gave her the opportunity of showing her figure. On this occasion Mrs. Crouch, that charming actress and beautiful woman, played Olivia; we suppose, "with a song," though Genest does not mention it. With the exception of Moody appearing as Sir Toby Belch in 1788, there was no performance of this comedy worthy of notice till on May 13th, 1789, when—for Mrs. Goodall's benefit, who appeared as Viola—John Kemble played Malvolio, apparently for this occasion only, as I can find no record of his having repeated this impersonation, which must have been a very interesting one. In Boaden's Life of John Kemble no mention is made of his Malvolio. On February 10th, 1790, apparently for the first time, the device of making a brother and sister impersonate Sebastian and Viola respectively was attempted; Bland, the brother of Mrs. Jordan, being selected for the former character. Whether he resembled his sister much or not we are not told; but the same device was employed, with great success, at the Theatre Royal, Edinburgh, February 4th, 1815, when W. Murray, the brother of Mrs. H. Siddons, played Sebastian to his sister's Viola. The resemblance was so close that the mistakes incidental to the plot appeared quite natural. On May 17th, 1797, at Drury Lane, Suett, for his benefit, essayed the part of Sir Andrew Aguecheek, in which no doubt his inimitable power of assuming stolid simplicity, which Charles Lamb so much praises, would stand him in good stead. Young Bannister on this occasion played Malvolio for the first time, Mrs. Jordan was still the Viola, and Mrs. Crouch the Olivia, while Miss Mellon appeared as Maria. Suett repeated this performance on May 26th, 1801, at Drury Lane, when Dowton, who had succeeded to the part, played Malvolio, and R. Palmer appeared, for the first time, as Sir Toby Belch; and Miss Biggs, for whose benefit the performance was, played Olivia. In this same year, on June 9th, Twelfth Night, after a long interval, was revived at Covent Garden. The bill says "not acted 25 years," but it had been played three times in May, 1783. On this occasion Munden was Malvolio, and Knight Sir Andrew Aguecheek; Emery played Sir Toby Belch, and Bland the Clown.

Passing over some occasional performances of this comedy at Drury Lane in the next six seasons, during which it appears to have been revived now and then for the purpose of Mrs. Jordan appearing in her favourite part of Viola, we find on May 31st, 1808, the elder Mathews played the part of Sir Andrew Aguecheek in a scene in this play, the Viola being Mrs. Jordan. Twelfth Night was revived on January 5th, 1811, at Covent Garden, under Kemble's management, with the following cast:—Liston as Malvolio, Blanchard as Sir Andrew Aguecheek, Emery as Sir Toby Belch, Fawcett as the Clown, with Mrs. S. Booth as Viola and Mrs. Charles Kemble as Olivia. Genest says: "Liston was truly comic in the scene when he read the letter, and in that when he entered cross-gartered, but on the whole Malvolio was a part out of his line" (Genest, vol. viii. p. 228). In the next season it seems to have been revived once; and on January 6th, 1813, after an interval of nine years, it was again produced at Drury Lane Theatre with Dowton as Malvolio, Mrs. Davison as Viola, Mrs. Glover as Olivia, and Miss Millar as Maria; but it was only acted once. In the next season, on April 29th, 1814, for the purpose of a young actress, Miss Stanley, making her appearance as Viola, Twelfth Night was performed once; and then, for some time, it seems entirely to have dropped out of the *répertoire* of this theatre. At Covent Garden it was equally neglected; there being only one or two isolated performances in the various seasons until November 8th, 1820, when the relentless Reynolds laid hands upon this charming comedy, and turned it into an opera. Genest, in his energetic language, says: "In the Devil's name, why does not Reynolds turn his own plays into Operas?—does he think them so bad, that even with such music as he has put into Twelfth Night, they would not prove successful!—or has he such a fatherly affection for his own offspring, that he cannot find in his heart to mangle them?" (vol. ix. p. 100). On this occasion the cast was a strong one; William Farren was Malvolio and Liston was seen to great advantage as Sir Andrew Aguecheek, while Emery retained his part of Sir Toby Belch, and Fawcett that of the Clown; Miss M. Tree was the Viola, Miss Greene Olivia and Mrs. Gibbs Maria. The addition of music seems to have rendered the play more attractive to the audiences of that time, for it was acted seventeen times. It was revived again on June 13th, 1825, for Blanchard's benefit, who played Sir Andrew Aguecheek.

It will be seen, from the above record, that this comedy was never, up to the end of the period of which Genest treats, a popular one; nor has it ever, in more recent times, enjoyed a very lengthened run. It is difficult to explain the causes of this comparative unpopularity; for Twelfth Night contains so many admirable characters, so much amusing dialogue interspersed with occasional gems of poetry, that it would seem to be, of all Shakespeare's comedies, one of the most likely to be popular on the stage. Although the female parts are not to be compared with those in Much Ado and As You Like It, still Viola must always prove an atractive impersonation to any young actress with an elegant figure, and Maria is a good soubrette's part. The male characters are nearly all such as find favour with actors. Malvolio, Sir Toby, Sir Andrew, the Clown, are each of them rôles which give great opportunities to those actors who shine in high, or low, or eccentric comedy. Malvolio, which may be considered the chief male character in the comedy, is a very difficult part to act. It reads most amusingly; but the difficulty on the stage is to avoid making the part too serious or too comic. If the actor attempts to render Malvolio's self-conceit at all genial or unctuous in the great letter scene, he finds that this is completely at variance with other parts of the character. On the other hand, if he takes what is generally considered the right view of the character; if he makes him grave, austere, and almost Puritanical, with something of the sombre dignity of a Spaniard, and with a vanity so supreme in its perfection as almost to take rank with pride; if, in fact, he invests Olivia's steward with sufficient dignity to gain the respect of the audience, the scene in the dark chamber becomes almost a painful one. Many a great actor has been disappointed in the effect he produced by his Malvolio. Very often the disappointment has been exactly in proportion to the care and finish bestowed on the impersonation. Some very good actors have declared that, after all, Sir Toby is the best part in the piece. But the great defect of Twelfth Night as an acting comedy lies, no doubt, in the fact that the love interest never takes very much hold on our sympathies. Viola is a charming young woman, and makes a very pretty boy; but who can possibly sympathize with her in her ardent pursuit of such a lover as the Duke, a man whose elaborate sentimentality reminds one of those delicacies which cloy rather than delight the palate, and whose plastic readiness to transfer his affections makes one suspect they were, after all, scarcely worth so much trouble to win? Again, who can be moved by Olivia's spasmodic and almost mechanical passion? However charming the actress may be, she can never, in this part, touch our hearts; and it is probably on this account—that is, owing to the weakness of its love interest—that Twelfth Night, as an acting play, never can hold its own with Much Ado or As You Like It.

Coming to our own times, Twelfth Night has been frequently acted, but never for any long run. Malvolio was one of Phelps's great parts; but in spite of this he does not seem to have reproduced the play—after its first production in his fourth season on January 26th, 1848,—till 1857, when it was played for some nights with considerable success. Meanwhile The Princess's Theatre was opened in 1850 under the management of Charles Kean and Robert Keeley, the first piece produced being Twelfth Night with Mrs. Charles Kean as Viola, Mr. J. F. Cathcart as Sebastian, Mrs. Keeley as Maria, Meadows as Malvolio and Harley as the Clown. It would be difficult to find so perfect a representative of Malvolio's lively persecutrix as the bright-faced actress who is still, happily, left amongst us, a picture of sunny old age. On June 7th, 1865, this comedy was produced at the Olympic Theatre, when Miss Kate Terry doubled the parts of Viola and Sebastian, a bold device for getting rid of the difficulty caused by the supposed likeness between brother and sister. Another novelty on this occasion was the appearance, in the part of the Clown, of an actress, Miss E. Farren, whose undoubted talents have, unfortunately, been lost to the higher form of comedy in which she promised to excel. Viola was one of the favourite parts of Miss Kate Terry, an actress who retired too soon from the stage. Many theatre-goers now alive declare that she has never been equalled in this part even by her own sister. This comedy was always a favourite one in the *répertoire* of the old Haymarket Company; Mr. Howe's Malvolio, and Mr. Buckstone's Sir Andrew, being both very successful performances. Nothing could be more irresistibly comic than the fatuous expression of Buckstone's face in this latter character. At the same theatre on February 2nd, 1878, Miss Adelaide Neilson appeared as Viola with considerable success. The latest important revival of this comedy was at the Lyceum Theatre on the 8th July, 1884. This revival was put on the stage with the same care and good taste which are generally admitted to distinguish the productions at that theatre; and, on the whole, the cast was an admirable one. But, though received with considerable favour, it did not obtain that hold on the public which Much Ado About Nothing did, and it has not been revived since.—F. A. M.

CRITICAL REMARKS.

The play of Twelfth Night, coming midway in the career of Shakespeare, perhaps just between As You Like It, the Arcadian comedy, and All's Well That Ends Well, a comedy in name, but kept throughout on the very edge of tragedy, draws up into itself the separate threads of wit and humour from the various plays which had preceded it, weaving them all into a single texture. It is in some sort a farewell to mirth, and the mirth is of the finest quality, an incomparable ending. Shakespeare has done greater things, but he has never done anything more delightful. One might fancy that the play had been composed in a time of special comfort and security, when soul and body were in perfect equipoise, and the dice of circumstance had fallen happily. A golden mean, a sweet moderation, reigns throughout. Here and there, in the more serious parts of the dialogue, we have one of Shakespeare's most beautiful touches, as in the divine opening lines, in Viola's story of the sister who "never told her love," and in much of that scene; but in general the fancy is moderated to accord with the mirth, and refrains from sounding a very deep or a very high note. Every element of the play has the subtlest links and connections with its fellow. Tenderness melts into a smile, and the smile broadens imperceptibly into laughter. Without ever absolutely mingling, the two streams of the plot flow side by side, following the same windings, and connected by tributary currents. Was ever anything more transparently self-contradictory than the theory which removes a minute textual difficulty or two by the tremendous impossibility of a double date? No characteristic of the play is more patent and unmistakable than its perfect unity and sure swiftness of composition, the absolute rondure of the O of Giotto, done at a single sweep of the practised arm. It is such a triumph of construction that it is hard, in reading it, to get rid of the feeling that it has been written at one sitting.

The protagonist of the play, the centre of our amused interest, is certainly Malvolio, but it is on the fortunes of Viola, in her relations with the Duke and Olivia, that the action really depends. The Duke, the first speaker on the stage, is an egoist, a gentle and refined specimen of the class which has been summed up finally in the monumental character of Sir Willoughby Patterne. He is painted without satire, with the gentle forbearance of the profound and indifferent literary artist; shown, indeed, almost exclusively on his best side; yet, though sadly used as a lover, he awakes no pity, calls up no champion in our bosoms. There is nothing base in his nature; he is incapable of any meanness, never harsh or unjust, gracefully prone to the virtues which do not take root in self-denial—to facile kindness, generosity, sympathy; he can inspire a tender love; he can love, though but with a desire of the secondary emotions; but he is self-contemplative, in another sense from Malvolio, one of those who play delicately upon life, whose very sorrows have an elegant melancholy, the sting of a sharp sauce which refreshes the palate cloyed by an insipid dish: a sentimental egoist. See, for a revealing touch of Shakespeare's judgment on him, his shallow words on woman's incapacity for love (ii. 4), so contradictory with what he has said the moment before, an inconsistency so exquisitely characteristic; both said with the same lack of vital sincerity, the same experimental and argumentative touch upon life. See how once only, in the fifth act, he blows out a little frothy bluster, a show of manliness, harsh words but used as goblin-tales to frighten children; words whose vacillation in the very act comes out in the "What shall I do?" in the pompous declaration, "My thoughts are ripe in mischief," in the side-touches, like an admiring glance cast aside in the glass at his own most effective attitude,—"a savage jealousy that sometime savours nobly," and the like. When he coolly gives up the finally-lost Olivia, and turns to the love and sympathy he knows he shall find in Viola (as, in after days, Sir Willoughby will turn to his Lætitia), the shallowness of his nature reveals itself in broad daylight.

Olivia is the complement to Orsino, a tragic sentimentalist, with emotions which it pleases her to play on a little consciously, yet capable of feeling of a pitch beyond the duke's too loudly-speaking passion. Her cloistral mourning for her brother's death has in it something theatrical, not quite honest—a playing with the emotions. She makes a luxury of her grief, and no doubt it loses its sting. Then when a new face excites her fancy, the artificial condition into which she has brought herself leaves her an easy prey, by the natural rebound, to a possessing imagination. She becomes violently enamoured, yet honestly enough, of the disguised Viola, and her passion survives the inevitable substitution. Shakespeare has cleansed her from the stains of the old story, as he cleansed the heroine of Measure for Measure: the note of wantonness is never struck. She is too like the duke ever to care for him. She has and she fills her place in the play, but the place is a secondary one, and she is without power over our hearts.

We turn to Viola with relief. She is a true woman, exquisitely beautiful in her mute service of a seeming-hopeless love; yet all the same I cannot give her a place in the incomparable company of Shakespeare's very noblest women. She has a touch of the sentimental, and will make a good wife for the duke; she is without the compelling strength of nature or dignity of intellect which would scorn a delicately sentimental egoist. She is incapable of the heroism of Helena, of Isabella; she is of softer nature, of slighter build and lowlier spirit than they, while she has none of the overbrimming life, the intense and dazzling vitality of Rosalind. Her male disguise is almost unapparent; she is covered by it as by a veil; it neither spurs her lips to sauciness, as with Rosalind, nor frightens her with a shrinking shame and dread, as with Imogen; she is here, as she would be always, quiet, secure, retiring yet scarcely timid, with a pleasant playfulness breaking out now and then—the effect, not of high spirits, but of a whimsical sense of her secret when she feels safe in it, coming among women. Without any of the more heroic lineaments of her sex, she has the delicacy and tender truth that we all find so charming—an egoist supremely, when the qualities are his for possessing. She represents the typical female heart offering itself to the man—an ingenuous spectacle, with the dew upon it of youth and early morn and May. She is permitted to speak the tenderest words in which pathos crowns and suffuses love; and once, under the spell of music, her small voice of low and tender changes rings out with immortal clearness, and for the moment, like the words she says,

It gives a very echo to the seat
Where Love is thron'd."

Of Malvolio it is hopeless hoping to say anything new, and but little shall be said of him here. He is a Don Quixote in the colossal enlargement of his delusions, in the cruel irony of Fate, which twists topsy-turvy, making a mere straw in the wind of him, an eminently sober and serious man of the clearest uprightness, unvisited by a stray glimpse of saving humour. He is a man of self-sufficiency, a noble quality perilously near to self-complacency, and he has passed the bounds without knowing it. His unbending solemnity is his ruin. Nothing presents so fair a butt for the attack of a guerrilla-fighting wit. It is indeed the most generally obnoxious of all tolerable qualities; for it is a living rebuke of our petty levities, and it hints to us of a conscious superior. Even a soldier is not required to be always on drill. A lofty moralist, a starched formalist, like Malvolio is salt and wormwood in the cakes and ale of gourmand humanity. It is with the nicest art that he is kept from rising sheer out of comedy into a tragic isolation of attitude. He *is* restrained, and we have no heart-ache in the laughter that seconds the most sprightly of clowns, the sharpest of serving-maids, and the incomparable pair of roysterers, Sir Toby and Sir Andrew.

Shakespeare, like Nature, has a tenderness for man in his cups, and will not let him come to grief. Sir Toby's wit bubbles up from no fountain of wisdom; it is shallow, radically bibulous, a brain-fume blown from a mere ferment of wits. His effect is truly and purely comic; but it is rather from the way in which the playwright points and places him than from his own comic genius—in this how unlike Falstaff, who appears to owe nothing to circumstances, but to escape from and dominate his creator. Sir Toby is the immortal type of the average "funny fellow" and boon-companion of the clubs or the public-houses: you may meet him any day in the street, with his portly build, red plump cheeks, and merry eyes twinkling at the incessant joke of life. His mirth is facile, contagious, continual; it would become wearisome perhaps at too long a dose, but through a single comic scene it is tickling, pervasive, delightful. Sir Andrew is the grindstone on which Sir Toby sharpens his wit. He is an instance of a natural fool becoming truly comic by the subtle handling in which he is not allowed to awaken too keenly either pity or contempt. In life he would awaken both. He is a harmless simpleton, an innocent and unobtrusive bore, "a Slender grown adult in brainlessness;" and he is shown up in all his fatuity without a note or touch of really ill-natured sarcasm. Shakespeare's humour plays round him, enveloping him softly; his self-esteem has no shock; unlike Malvolio he is permitted to remain undeceived to the end. It is to his credit that he is not without glimmerings that he is a fool. The kindness is, that the conviction is not forced upon him from without.

Duke. If music be the food of love, play on.—(Act i. 1. 1.)

TWELFTH NIGHT;

OR, WHAT YOU WILL.

ACT I.

SCENE I. *An apartment in the Duke's palace.*

Enter DUKE, CURIO, *and other Lords; Musicians attending.*

Duke. If music be the food of love, play on;
Give me excess of it, that, surfeiting,
The appetite may sicken, and so die.
That strain again! it had a dying fall:
O, it came o'er my ear like the sweet sound
That breathes upon a bank of violets,
Stealing and giving odour! Enough; no more:
'Tis not so sweet now as it was before.
[O spirit of love, how quick and fresh art thou,
That, notwithstanding thy capacity
Receiveth as the sea, nought enters there,
Of what validity[1] and pitch soe'er,
But falls into abatement and low price,
Even in a minute! so full of shapes is fancy,[2]
That it alone[3] is high-fantastical.]

Cur. Will you go hunt, my lord?

Duke. What, Curio?

Cur. The hart.

Duke. Why, so I do, the noblest that I have:
O, when mine eyes did see Olivia first,
Methought she purg'd the air of pestilence!
That instant was I turn'd into a hart;
And my desires, like fell and cruel hounds,
E'er since pursue me.

Enter VALENTINE.

How now! what news from her?

Val. So please my lord, I might not be admitted;
But from her handmaid do return this answer:
The element[4] itself, till seven years' heat,[5]
Shall not behold her face at ample view;
But, like a cloistress,[6] she will veiled walk,
And water once a day her chamber round
With eye-offending brine: all this to season
A brother's dead love, which she would keep fresh
And lasting in her sad remembrance.[7]

Duke. O, she that hath a heart of that fine frame

[1] *Validity*, i.e. value. [2] *Fancy*, love.
[3] *Alone*, i.e. without a parallel.

[4] *Element*, sky.
[5] *Till seven years' heat*, i.e. till seven years' heat have passed. [6] *Cloistress*, nun.
[7] *Remembrance*, pronounced *rememberance*, in four syllables.

To pay this debt of love but to a brother,
How will she love, when the rich golden shaft
Hath kill'd the flock of all affections else
That live in her; when liver, brain, and heart,
These sovereign thrones, are all supplied, and fill'd
Her sweet perfections,[1] with one self king!
Away before me to sweet beds of flowers!
Love-thoughts lie rich when canopied with bowers. [*Exeunt.*

Scene II. *The sea-coast.*

Enter Viola, *a Captain, and Sailors.*

Vio. What country, friends, is this?
Cap. This is Illyria, lady.
Vio. And what should I do in Illyria?
My brother he is in Elysium.
Perchance he is not drown'd: what think you, sailors?
Cap. It is "perchance" that you yourself were saved.
Vio. O my poor brother! and so perchance may he be.
Cap. True, madam: and, to comfort you with chance,
Assure yourself, after our ship did split,
When you, and those poor number sav'd with you,
Hung on our driving boat, I saw your brother,
Most provident in peril, bind himself,
Courage and hope both teaching him the practice,
To a strong mast that liv'd upon the sea;
Where, like Arion on the dolphin's back,
I saw him hold acquaintance with the waves
So long as I could see.
Vio. For saying so, there's gold:
Mine own escape unfoldeth to my hope,
Whereto thy speech serves for authority,
The like of him. Know'st thou this country[2]?
Cap. Ay, madam, well; for I was bred and born
Not three hours' travel from this very place.
Vio. Who governs here?
Cap. A noble duke, in nature as in name.
Vio. What is his name?
Cap. Orsino.
Vio. Orsino! I have heard my father name him:
He was a bachelor then.
Cap. And so is now, or was so very late;
For but a month ago I went from hence,
And then 't was fresh in murmur,—as, you know,
What great ones do, the less will prattle of,—
That he did seek the love of fair Olivia.
Vio. What's she?
Cap. A virtuous maid, the daughter of a count
That died some twelvemonth since; then leaving her
In the protection of his son, her brother,
Who shortly also died: for whose dear love,
They say, she hath abjur'd the company
And sight of men.
Vio. O that I serv'd that lady,
And might not be delivered[3] to the world,
Till I had made mine own occasion mellow
What my estate is!
Cap. That were hard to compass;
Because she will admit no kind of suit,
No, not the duke's.
Vio. There is a fair behaviour in thee, captain;
And though that nature with a beauteous wall
Doth oft close in pollution, yet of thee
I will believe thou hast a mind that suits
With this thy fair and outward character.
I prithee,—and I'll pay thee bounteously,—
Conceal me what I am; and be my aid
For such disguise as haply shall become
The form of my intent. I'll serve this duke:
Thou shalt present me as an eunuch to him:
It may be worth thy pains; for I can sing
And speak to him in many sorts of music
That will allow me[4] very worth his service.
What else may hap, to time I will commit;
Only shape thou thy silence to my wit.
[*Cap.* Be you his eunuch, and your mute I'll be:
When my tongue blabs, then let mine eyes not see.
Vio. I thank thee: lead me on.] [*Exeunt.*

[1] *Perfections*, pronounced as a quadrisyllable.
[2] *Country*, pronounced as a trisyllable.
[3] *Delivered*, i.e. discovered.
[4] *Allow me*, approve me, make me acknowledged.

SCENE III. *A court-yard in Olivia's house.*

Enter SIR TOBY BELCH *and* MARIA.

Sir To. What a plague means my niece, to take the death of her brother thus? I am sure care 's an enemy to life.

Mar. By my troth, Sir Toby, you must come in earlier o' nights: your cousin, my lady, takes great exceptions to your ill hours.

Sir To. Why, let her except before excepted.

Mar. Ay, but you must confine yourself within the modest limits of order.

Sir To. Confine! I 'll confine myself no finer than I am: these clothes are good enough to drink in; and so be these boots too: an they be not, let them hang themselves in their own straps.

Mar. That quaffing and drinking will undo you: I heard my lady talk of it yesterday; and of a foolish knight that you brought in one night here to be her wooer.

Sir To. Who, Sir Andrew Aguecheek?

Mar. Ay, he.

Sir To. He 's as tall[1] a man as any 's in Illyria.

Mar. What 's that to the purpose?

Sir. To. Why, he has three thousand ducats a year.

Mar. Ay, but he 'll have but a year in all these ducats: he 's a very fool and a prodigal.

Sir To. Fie, that you 'll say so! he plays o' the viol-de-gamboys,[2] and speaks three or four languages word for word without book, and hath all the good gifts of nature.

Mar. He hath, indeed, almost natural: for besides that he 's a fool, he 's a great quarreller; and but that he hath the gift of a coward to allay the gust[3] he hath in quarrelling, 't is thought among the prudent he would quickly have the gift of a grave.

Sir To. By this hand, they are scoundrels and substractors[4] that say so of him. Who are they?

Mar. They that add, moreover, he 's drunk nightly in your company.

Sir To. With drinking healths to my niece: I 'll drink to her as long as there is a passage in my throat and drink in Illyria: he 's a coward and a coystril[5] that will not drink to my niece till his brains turn o' the toe like a parish-top. What, wench! *Castiliano vulgo!* for here comes Sir Andrew Agueface.

Sir And. [*Without*] Sir Toby Belch,—

Enter SIR ANDREW AGUECHEEK.

How now, Sir Toby Belch!

Sir To. Sweet Sir Andrew!

Sir And. [*To Maria*] Bless you, fair shrew.

Mar. And you too, sir.

Sir To. Accost, Sir Andrew, accost.

Sir And. What 's that?

Sir To. My niece's chambermaid.

Sir And. Good Mistress Accost, I desire better acquaintance.

Mar. My name is Mary, sir.

Sir And. Good Mistress Mary Accost,—

Sir To. You mistake, knight: "accost" is front her, [board her,] woo her, assail her.

Sir And. [By my troth, I would not undertake her in this company.] Is that the meaning of "accost"?

Mar. Fare you well, gentlemen.

Sir To. An thou let part so, Sir Andrew, would thou mightst never draw sword again.

Sir And. An you part so, mistress, I would I might never draw sword again. Fair lady, do you think you have fools in hand?

Mar. Sir, I have not you by the hand.

[*Sir And.* Marry, but you shall have: and here 's my hand.

Mar. Now sir, "thought is free": I pray you, bring your hand to the buttery-bar and let it drink.

Sir And. Wherefore, sweet-heart? what 's your metaphor?

Mar. It 's dry, sir.

Sir And. Why, I think so: I am not such an ass but I can keep my hand dry. But what 's your jest?

Mar. A dry jest, sir.

Sir And. Are you full of them?

Mar. Ay, sir, I have them at my fingers' ends: marry, now I let go your hand, I am barren.] [*Exit.*

[1] *Tall*, stout, valiant.

[2] *Viol-de-gamboys*, i.e. *viol da gamba*, the precursor of the violoncello.

[3] *Gust*, relish.

[4] *Substractors*: he means of course to say *detractors*.

[5] *Coystril*, a low fellow.

Sir To. O knight, thou lack'st a cup of canary:[1] when did I see thee so put down?

Sir And. Never in your life, I think; unless you see canary put me down. Methinks sometimes I have no more wit than a Christian or an ordinary man has: but I am a great eater of beef, and I believe that does harm to my wit.

Sir To. No question.

Sir And. An I thought that, I'd forswear it. I'll ride home to-morrow, Sir Toby.

Sir To. *Pourquoi*, my dear knight?

Sir And. What is "*pourquoi?*" do or not do? I would I had bestowed that time in the tongues that I have in fencing, dancing and bear-baiting: O, had I but followed the arts!

Sir To. Then hadst thou had an excellent head of hair.

Sir And. Why, would that have mended my hair?

Sir To. Past question; for thou seest it will not curl by nature.

Sir And. But it becomes me well enough, does't not?

Sir To. Excellent; it hangs like flax on a distaff; [and I hope to see a housewife take thee between her legs and spin it off.]

Sir And. Faith, I'll home to-morrow, Sir Toby: your niece will not be seen; or if she be, it's four to one she'll none of me: the count himself here hard by woos her.

Sir To. She'll none o' the count: she'll not match above her degree, neither in estate, years nor wit; I have heard her swear't. Tut, there's life in't, man.

Sir And. I'll stay a month longer. I am a fellow o' the strangest mind i' the world; I delight in masques and revels sometimes altogether.

Sir To. Art thou good at these kickshawses,[2] knight?

Sir And. As any man in Illyria, whatsoever he be, under the degree of my betters; and yet I will not compare with an old man.

Sir To. What is thy excellence in a galliard,[3] knight?

Sir And. Faith, I can cut a caper.

Sir To. And I can cut the mutton to't.

Sir And. And I think I have the back-trick simply as strong as any man in Illyria. [*Dances fantastically.*

Sir To. Wherefore are these things hid? wherefore have these gifts a curtain before 'em? are they like to take dust, like Mistress Mall's picture? why dost thou not go to church in a galliard[3] and come home in a coranto?[4] My very walk should be a jig; [I would not so much as make water but in a sink-a-pace.[5]] What dost thou mean? is it a world to hide virtues in? [I did think, by the excellent constitution of thy leg, it was form'd under the star of a galliard.]

Sir And. Ay, 't is strong, and it does indifferent well in a dam'd-colour'd stock.[6] Shall we set about some revels?

Sir To. What shall we do else? were we not born under Taurus?

Sir And. Taurus! that's sides and heart.

Sir To. No, sir; it is legs and thighs. Let me see thee caper: [*Sir Andrew dances again*] ha! higher: ha, ha!—excellent! [*Exeunt.*

SCENE IV. *Orsino's palace.*

Enter VALENTINE, *and* VIOLA (*as* CESARIO), *in man's attire.*

Val. If the duke continue these favours towards you, Cesario, you are like to be much advanced: he hath known you but three days, and already you are no stranger.

Vio. You either fear his humour or my negligence, that you call in question the continuance of his love: is he inconstant, sir, in his favours?

Val. No, believe me.

Vio. I thank you. Here comes the count.

Enter DUKE ORSINO, CURIO, *and Attendants.*

Duke. Who saw Cesario, ho?

Vio. On your attendance, my lord; here.

Duke. Stand you awhile aloof.—Cesario,
Thou know'st no less but all; I have unclasp'd

---

1 *Canary*, sweet sack, from the Canary Islands.

2 *Kickshawses*, a corruption of French *quelque-chose*.

3 *Galliard*, a lively dance.

4 *Coranto*, another brisk dance.

5 *Sink-a-pace*, *i.e.* *cinque-pace*, a French dance, the steps of which were regulated by the number five.

6 *Stock*, stocking.

To thee the book even of my secret soul:
Therefore, good youth, address thy gait unto her;
Be not deni'd access, stand at her doors
And tell them, there thy fixed foot shall grow
Till thou have audience.
Vio. Sure, my noble lord,
If she be so abandon'd to her sorrow
As it is spoke, she never will admit me.
Duke. Be clamorous, and leap all civil bounds,
Rather than make unprofited return.
Vio. Say I do speak with her, my lord, what then?

Sir To. Let me see thee caper: [*Sir Andrew dances again* ha! higher: ha, ha!—excellent!—(Act i. 3. 149-151.)

Duke. O, then unfold the passion of my love,
Surprise her with discourse of my dear faith!
It shall become thee well to act my woes;
She will attend it better in thy youth
Than in a nuncio's[1] of more grave aspect.
Vio. I think not so, my lord.
Duke. Dear lad, believe it;
For they shall yet belie thy happy years,
That say thou art a man: Diana's lip
Is not more smooth and rubious;[2] thy small pipe
Is as the maiden's organ, shrill and sound,[3]
And all is semblative[4] a woman's part.
I know thy constellation[5] is right apt
For this affair.—Some four or five attend him;
All, if you will; for I myself am best
When least in company.—Prosper well in this,
And thou shalt live as freely as thy lord,
To call his fortunes thine.
Vio. I'll do my best
To woo your lady—[*Aside*] Yet, a barful[6] strife!
Whoe'er I woo, myself would be his wife.
[*Exeunt.*

SCENE V. *Terrace of Olivia's house.*

Enter MARIA *and* CLOWN.

Mar. Nay, either tell me where thou hast been, or I will not open my lips so wide as a

[1] *Nuncio's*, messenger's.
[2] *Rubious*, ruddy.
[3] *Sound*, pure in tone.
[4] *Semblative*, suited to.
[5] *Constellation*, figuratively used = a number of good qualities.
[6] *Barful*, full of impediments.

bristle may enter in way of thy excuse: my lady will hang thee for thy absence.

Clo. Let her hang me: he that is well hang'd in this world needs to fear no colours.[1]

Mar. Make that good.

Clo. He shall see none to fear.

Mar. A good lenten answer: I can tell thee where that saying was born, of "I fear no colours."

Clo. Where, good Mistress Mary?

Mar. In the wars; and that may you be bold to say in your foolery.

Clo. Well, God give them wisdom that have it; and those that are fools, let them use their talents.

Mar. Yet you will be hang'd for being so long absent; or, to be turn'd away, is not that as good as a hanging to you?

Clo. Many a good hanging prevents a bad marriage; and, for turning away let summer bear it out.

Mar. You are resolute, then?

Clo. Not so, neither; but I am resolv'd on two points.

Mar. That if one break, the other will hold; or, if both break, your gaskins[2] fall.

Clo. Apt, in good faith; very apt. Well, go thy way; if Sir Toby would leave drinking, thou wert as witty a piece of Eve's flesh as any in Illyria.

Mar. Peace, you rogue, no more o' that. Here comes my lady: make your excuse wisely, you were best. [*Exit.*

Clo. Wit, an't be thy will, put me into good fooling! Those wits, that think they have thee, do very oft prove fools; and I, that am sure I lack thee, may pass for a wise man. For what says Quinapalus? "Better a witty fool than a foolish wit."

Enter OLIVIA, MALVOLIO, *and Ladies attending Olivia.*

God bless thee, lady!

Oli. Take the fool away.

Clo. Do you not hear, fellows? Take away the lady.

[*Oli.* Go to, you're a dry[3] fool; I'll no more of you: besides, you grow dishonest.

Clo. Two faults, madonna,[4] that drink and good counsel will amend: for give the dry fool drink, then is the fool not dry: bid the dishonest man mend himself; if he mend, he is no longer dishonest; if he cannot, let the botcher mend him. Any thing that's mended is but patch'd: virtue that transgresses is but patch'd with sin; and sin that amends is but patch'd with virtue. If that this simple syllogism will serve, so: if it will not, what remedy? As there is no true cuckold but calamity, so beauty's a flower. The lady bade take away the fool; therefore, I say again, take her away.]

Oli. Sir, I bade them take away you.

Clo. Misprision in the highest degree! Lady, *cucullus non facit monachum;*[5] that's as much to say as, I wear not motley in my brain. Good madonna, give me leave to prove you a fool.

Oli. Can you do it?

Clo. Dexteriously, good madonna.

Oli. Make your proof.

Clo. I must catechize you for it, madonna: good my mouse of virtue, answer me.

Oli. Well, sir, for want of other idleness, I'll bide your proof.

Clo. Good madonna, why mournst thou?

Oli. Good fool, for my brother's death.

Clo. I think his soul is in hell, madonna.

Oli. I know his soul is in heaven, fool.

Clo. The more fool, madonna, to mourn for your brother's soul being in heaven.—Take away the fool, gentlemen.

Oli. What think you of this fool, Malvolio? doth he not mend?

Mal. Yes, and shall do till the pangs of death shake him: infirmity, that decays the wise, doth ever make the better fool.

Clo. God send you, sir, a speedy infirmity, for the better increasing your folly! Sir Toby will be sworn that I am no fox; but he will not pass his word for twopence that you are no fool.

Oli. How say you to that, Malvolio?

Mal. I marvel your ladyship takes delight in such a barren rascal: I saw him put down

[1] *Fear no colours, i.e.* fear nothing.

[2] *Gaskins*, breeches.

[3] *Dry*, insipid.

[4] *Madonna* = my lady.

[5] *Cucullus non facit monachum*, the cowl does not make the monk.

the other day with an ordinary fool, that has no more brain than a stone. Look you now, he's out of his guard already; unless you laugh and minister occasion to him, he is gagg'd. I protest, I take these wise men, that crow so at these set kind of fools,[1] no better than the fools' zanies.[2]

Oli. O, you are sick of self-love, Malvolio, and taste with a distemper'd appetite. To be generous, guiltless and of free disposition, is to take those things for bird-bolts[3] that you deem cannon-bullets: there is no slander in an allow'd[4] fool, though he do nothing but rail; nor no railing in a known discreet man, though he do nothing but reprove.

Clo. Now Mercury endue thee with leasing,[5] for thou speak'st well of fools!

Re-enter MARIA.

Mar. Madam, there is at the gate a young gentleman much desires to speak with you.

Oli. From the Count Orsino, is it?

Mar. I know not, madam: 't is a fair young man, and well attended.

Oli. Who of my people hold him in delay?

Mar. Sir Toby, madam, your kinsman.

Oli. Fetch him off, I pray you; he speaks nothing but madman: fie on him! [*Exit Maria.*] Go you, Malvolio: if it be a suit from the count, I am sick, or not at home; what you will, to dismiss it. [*Exit Malvolio.*] Now you see, sir, how your fooling grows old, and people dislike it.

Clo. Thou hast spoke for us, madonna, as if thy eldest son should be a fool,—whose skull Jove cram with brains! for here he comes, one of thy kin, has[6] a most weak *pia mater.*[7]

Enter SIR TOBY BELCH.

Oli. By mine honour, half drunk. What is he at the gate, cousin?

Sir To. A gentleman.

Oli. A gentleman! what gentleman?

Sir To. 'T is a gentleman here . . . A plague o' these pickle-herring!—How now, sot!

Clo. Good Sir Toby!

Oli. Cousin, cousin, how have you come so early by this lethargy?

Sir To. Lechery! I defy lechery. There 's one at the gate.

Oli. Ay, marry, what is he?

Sir To. Let him be the devil, an he will; I care not! give me faith, say I! Well, it 's all one. [*Exit.*

Oli. What 's a drunken man like, fool?

Clo. Like a drown'd man, a fool, and a madman: one draught above heat makes him a fool; the second mads him; and a third drowns him.

Oli. Go thou and seek the crowner,[8] and let him sit o' my coz; for he 's in the third degree of drink, he 's drown'd: go, look after him.

Clo. He is but mad yet, madonna; and the fool shall look to the madman. [*Exit.*

Re-enter MALVOLIO.

Mal. Madam, yond young fellow swears he will speak with you. I told him you were sick; he takes on him to understand so much, and therefore comes to speak with you. I told him you were asleep; he seems to have a foreknowledge of that too, and therefore comes to speak with you. What is to be said to him, lady? he 's fortified against any denial.

Oli. Tell him he shall not speak with me.

Mal. Has been told so; and he says, he 'll stand at your door like a sheriff's post, and be the supporter to a bench, but he 'll speak with you.

Oli. What kind o' man is he?

Mal. Why, of mankind.

Oli. What manner of man?

Mal. Of very ill manner; he 'll speak with you, will you or no.

Oli. Of what personage and years is he?

Mal. Not yet old enough for a man, nor young enough for a boy; as a squash[9] is before 't is a peascod, or a codling[10] when 't is almost

[1] *These set kind of fools*, i.e. the professional jesters.

[2] *Fools' zanies*, subordinate buffoons, who mimicked the tricks of the chief clown.

[3] *Bird-bolts*, blunt-headed arrows.

[4] *Allow'd*, licensed.

[5] *Leasing*, lying.

[6] *Has*, i.e. who has.

[7] *Pia mater*, the membrane that covers the brain.

[8] *Crowner*, coroner.

[9] *Squash*, unripe peascod.

[10] *Codling*, young raw apple.

an apple: 't is with him in standing water, between boy and man. He is very well-favour'd, and he speaks very shrewishly;[1] one would think his mother's milk were scarce out of him.

Oli. Let him approach: call in my gentlewoman.

Mal. Gentlewoman, my lady calls. [*Exit.*

Re-enter MARIA.

Oli. Give me my veil: come, throw it o'er my face.
We'll once more hear Orsino's embassy.

Enter VIOLA.

Vio. The honourable lady of the house, which is she?

Oli. Speak to me; I shall answer for her. Your will?

Vio. Most radiant, exquisite and unmatchable beauty, . . . [*To Maria*] I pray you tell me if this be the lady of the house, for I never saw her: I would be loth to cast away my speech; for, besides that it is excellently well penn'd, I have taken great pains to con it. [[*To Olivia and Maria*] Good beauties, let me sustain no scorn; I am very comptible,[2] even to the least sinister usage.]

Oli. Whence came you, sir?

Vio. I can say little more than I have studied, and that question's out of my part. Good gentle one, give me modest assurance if you be the lady of the house, [that I may proceed in my speech.

Oli. Are you a comedian?

Vio. No, my profound heart: and yet, by the very fangs of malice I swear, I am not that I play. Are you the lady of the house?]

Oli. If I do not usurp myself, I am.

Vio. Most certain, if you are she, you do usurp yourself; for what is yours to bestow is not yours to reserve. But this is from[3] my commission: I will on with my speech in your praise, and then show you the heart of my message.

Oli. Come to what is important in 't: I forgive you the praise.

Vio. Alas, I took great pains to study it, and 't is poetical.

Oli. It is the more like to be feigned: I pray you, keep it in. I heard you were saucy at my gates, and allow'd your approach rather to wonder at you than to hear you. If you be not mad, be gone; if you have reason, be brief: 't is not that time of moon with me to make one in so skipping[4] a dialogue.

Mar. Will you hoist sail, sir? here lies your way.

Vio. No, good swabber;[5] I am to hull[6] here a little longer.—Some mollification for your giant, sweet lady. Tell me your mind: I am a messenger.

Oli. Sure, you have some hideous matter to deliver, when the courtesy of it is so fearful. Speak your office.

Vio. It alone concerns your ear. [I bring no overture of war, no taxation[7] of homage: I hold the olive in my hands;] my words are as full of peace as matter.

Oli. Yet you began rudely. What are you? what would you?

Vio. The rudeness that hath appear'd in me have I learn'd from my entertainment.[8] What I am, and what I would, are [as secret as maidenhead:] to your ears, divinity; [to any other's, profanation.]

Oli. Give us the place alone: we will hear this divinity. [*Exeunt Maria and Attendants.*] Now, sir, what is your text?

Vio. Most sweet lady,—

Oli. A comfortable doctrine, and much may be said of it. Where lies your text?

Vio. In Orsino's bosom.

Oli. In his bosom! In what chapter of his bosom?

Vio. To answer by the method, in the first of his heart.

Oli. O, I have read it: it is heresy. Have you no more to say?

Vio. Good madam, let me see your face.

Oli. Have you any commission from your lord to negotiate with my face? You are now out of your text: but we will draw the cur-

[1] *Shrewishly*, tartly. [2] *Comptible*, sensitive. [3] *From*, i.e. apart from.

[4] *Skipping*, brisk, flighty.
[5] *Swabber*, one who scrubs the deck of a ship.
[6] *Hull*, to drive to and fro without sails or rudder.
[7] *Taxation*, demand. [8] *Entertainment*, treatment.

tain, and show you the picture. [*Unveils.*] Look you, sir, such a one I was this present: is't not well done?

Vio. Excellently done, if God did all.

Oli. 'T is in grain,[1] sir; 't will endure wind and weather.

Vio. 'T is beauty truly blent, whose red and white
Nature's own sweet and cunning[2] hand laid on:
Lady, you are the cruell'st she alive
If you will lead these graces to the grave
And leave the world no copy.

Oli. [*Unveils.*] Look you, sir, such a one I was this present: is't not well done?—(Act i. 5. 252, 253.)

Oli. O, sir, I will not be so hard-hearted; I will give out divers schedules of my beauty: it shall be inventoried, and every particle and utensil labell'd to my will: as, item, two lips, indifferent red; item, two grey eyes, with lids to them; item, one neck, one chin, and so forth. Were you sent hither to praise[3] me?

Vio. I see you what you are, you are too proud;
But, if you were the devil, you are fair.
My lord and master loves you: O, such love
Could be but recompens'd, though you were crown'd
The nonpareil[4] of beauty!

Oli. How does he love me?

Vio. With adorations, fertile tears,
With groans that thunder love, with sighs of fire.

Oli. Your lord does know my mind; I cannot love him:
Yet I suppose him virtuous, know him noble,
[Of great estate, of fresh and stainless youth;

[1] *In grain*, innate, natural.
[2] *Cunning*, i.e. skilful.
[3] *Praise*, used in the double sense of "to praise," and "to appraise."
[4] *Nonpareil*, paragon.

In voices well divulg'd,[1] free, learn'd, and valiant;
And in dimension and the shape of nature]
A gracious person: but yet I cannot love him;
He might have took his answer long ago.

Vio. If I did love you in my master's flame,
With such a suffering, such a deadly life,
In your denial I would find no sense;
I would not understand it.

Oli. Why, what would you?

Vio. Make me a willow cabin at your gate,
And call upon my soul within the house;
Write loyal cantons[2] of contemned love
And sing them loud even in the dead of night;
Halloo your name to the reverberate[3] hills
And make the babbling gossip of the air
Cry out "Olivia!" O, you should not rest
Between the elements of air and earth,
But you should pity me!

Oli. You might do much.
What is your parentage?

Vio. Above my fortunes, yet my state is well:
I am a gentleman.

Oli. Get you to your lord;
I cannot love him: let him send no more;
Unless, perchance, you come to me again,
To tell me how he takes it. Fare you well:
I thank you for your pains: spend this for me.

Vio. I am no fee'd post, lady; keep your purse:
My master, not myself, lacks recompense.
Love make his heart of flint that you shall love,
And let your fervour, like my master's, be
Plac'd in contempt! Farewell, fair cruelty. [*Exit.*

Oli. "What is your parentage?"
"Above my fortunes, yet my state is well:
I am a gentleman." I'll be sworn thou art;
Thy tongue, thy face, thy limbs, actions and spirit,
Do give thee fivefold blazon: not too fast: soft, soft! . . .
Unless the master were the man. How now!
Even so quickly may one catch the plague?
Methinks I feel this youth's perfections[4]
With an invisible and subtle stealth
To creep in at mine eyes. Well, let it be.
What ho, Malvolio!

Re-enter MALVOLIO.

Mal. Here, madam, at your service.

Oli. Run after that same peevish[5] messenger,
The county's[6] man: he left this ring behind him,
Would I or not: tell him I'll none of it.
Desire him not to flatter with his lord,
Nor hold him up with hopes; I am not for him:
If that the youth will come this way to-morrow,
I'll give him reasons for 't. Hie thee, Malvolio.

Mal. Madam, I will. [*Exit.*

Oli. I do I know not what; and fear to find
Mine eye too great a flatterer for my mind.
Fate, show thy force: ourselves we do not owe;[7]
What is decreed must be: and be this so! [*Exit.*

ACT II.

SCENE I. *The sea-coast.*

Enter ANTONIO *and* SEBASTIAN.

Ant. Will you stay no longer? nor will you not that I go with you?

Seb. By your patience, no. My stars shine darkly over me: the malignancy of my fate might perhaps distemper yours; therefore I shall crave of you your leave that I may bear my evils alone: it were a bad recompense for your love, to lay any of them on you.

Ant. Let me yet know of you whither you are bound.

Seb. No, sooth, sir: my determinate[8] voyage is mere extravagancy.[9] But I perceive in you so excellent a touch of modesty, that you will not extort from me what I am willing to keep in; therefore it charges me in manners the

[1] *In voices well divulg'd*, i.e. well spoken of.
[2] *Cantons*, songs or verses. [3] *Reverberate*, echoing.
[4] *Perfections*, pronounced as a quadrisyllable.
[5] *Peevish*, testy. [6] *County's*, count's. [7] *Owe*, own.

[8] *Determinate*, fixed. [9] *Extravagancy*, vagrancy.

rather to express myself.[1] You must know of me then, Antonio, my name is Sebastian, which I called Roderigo; my father was that Sebastian of Messaline, whom I know you have heard of. He left behind him myself and a sister, both born in an hour: if the heavens had been pleas'd, would we had so ended! but you, sir, alter'd that; for some hour before you took me from the breach[2] of the sea was my sister drown'd.

Ant. Alas the day!

Seb. A lady, sir, though it was said she much resembled me, was yet of many accounted beautiful; but, though I could not, with such estimable wonder, overfar believe that, yet thus far I will boldly publish her: she bore a mind that envy could not but call fair. She is drown'd already, sir, with salt water, though I seem to drown her remembrance again with more.

Ant. Pardon me, sir, your bad entertainment.

Seb. O good Antonio, forgive me your trouble!

Ant. If you will not murder me for my love, let me be your servant.

Seb. If you will not undo what you have done, that is, kill him whom you have recover'd, desire it not. Fare ye well at once: my bosom is full of kindness; and I am yet so near the manners of my mother, that upon the least occasion more mine eyes will tell tales of me. I am bound to the Count Orsino's court: farewell. [*Exit.*

Ant. The gentleness of all the gods go with thee!
I have many enemies in Orsino's court,
Else would I very shortly see thee there.
But, come what may, I do adore thee so,
That danger shall seem sport, and I will go.
[*Exit.*

[1] *Express myself*, make myself known.
[2] *Breach*, surf, breaking of the waves.

SCENE II. *Near Olivia's house.*

Enter VIOLA, MALVOLIO *following.*

Mal. Were not you even now with the Countess Olivia?

Seb. Fare ye well at once: my bosom is full of kindness; and I am yet so near the manners of my mother, that upon the least occasion more mine eyes will tell tales of me.—(Act ii. 1. 40-43.)

Vio. Even now, sir; on a moderate pace I have since arriv'd but hither.

Mal. She returns this ring to you, sir: you might have sav'd me my pains, to have taken it away yourself. She adds, moreover, that you should put your lord into a desperate assurance she will none of him: and one thing more, that you be never so hardy to come again in his affairs, unless it be to report your lord's taking of this. Receive it so.

Vio. She took the ring of me: I 'll none of it.

Mal. Come, sir, you peevishly threw it to her; and her will is, it should be so return'd: if it be worth stooping for, there it lies in your eye; if not, be it his that finds it. [*Exit.*

Vio. I left no ring with her: what means this lady?
Fortune forbid my outside have not charm'd her!
She made good view of me; indeed, so much,
That methought her eyes had lost her tongue,
For she did speak in starts distractedly.
She loves me, sure; the cunning of her passion
Invites me in this churlish messenger.
None of my lord's ring! why, he sent her none.
I am the man: if it be so, as 't is,
Poor lady, she were better love a dream.
Disguise, I see, thou art a wickedness
Wherein the pregnant[1] enemy does much.
How easy is it for the proper-false[2]
In women's waxen hearts to set their forms!
Alas, our frailty is the cause, not we!
For such as we are made of, such we be.
How will this fadge?[3] my master loves her dearly;
And I, poor monster, fond[4] as much on him;
And she, mistaken, seems to dote on me.
What will become of this? As I am man,
My state is desperate for my master's love;
As I am woman,—now alas the day!—
What thriftless sighs shall poor Olivia breathe!
O Time, thou must untangle this, not I;
It is too hard a knot for me to untie! [*Exit.*

SCENE III. *Olivia's house. The Servants' hall.*

SIR TOBY *and* SIR ANDREW *discovered.*

Sir To. [Approach, Sir Andrew:] not to be a-bed after midnight is to be up betimes; and "*diluculo surgere*,"[5] thou knowst,—

[1] *Pregnant*, dexterous, expert.
[2] *The proper-false*, i.e. the good-looking but false [men].
[3] *Fadge*, prosper.
[4] *Fond*, dote.
[5] *Diluculo surgere* [*saluberrimum*], to rise early is most healthful (Lilly's Grammar).

Sir And. Nay, by my troth, I know not: but I know, to be up late is to be up late.

Sir To. A false conclusion: I hate it as an unfill'd can. To be up after midnight, and to go to bed then, is early: so that to go to bed after midnight is to go to bed betimes. Does not our life consist of the four elements?

Sir And. Faith, so they say; but I think it rather consists of eating and drinking.

Sir To. Thou 'rt a scholar; let us therefore eat and drink. Marian, I say! a stoup[6] of wine!

Enter CLOWN.

Sir And. Here comes the fool, i' faith.

Clo. How now, my hearts! did you never see the picture of "We three"?

Sir To. Welcome, ass. Now let 's have a catch.[7]

Sir And. By my troth, the fool has an excellent breast.[8] I had rather than forty shillings I had such a leg, and so sweet a breath to sing, as the fool has. In sooth, thou wast in very gracious fooling last night, when thou spok'st of Pigrogromitus, of the Vapians passing the equinoctial of Queubus: 't was very good, i' faith. [I sent thee sixpence for thy leman:[9] hadst it?

Clo. I did impeticos thy gratillity; for Malvolio's nose is no whipstock, my lady has a white hand, and the Myrmidons are no bottle-ale houses.

Sir And. Excellent! why, this is the best fooling, when all is done. Now, a song.

Sir To. Come on; there is sixpence for you: let 's have a song.

Sir And. There 's a testril[10] of me too: if one knight give a—

Clo. Would you have a love-song, or a song of good life?

Sir To. A love-song, a love-song.

Sir And. Ay, ay: I care not for good life.

Clo. [*Sings*]

O mistress mine, where are you roaming?
O, stay and hear; your true love 's coming,
That can sing both high and low:

[6] *Stoup*, a drinking-vessel.
[7] *Catch*, a song in which the parts follow one another.
[8] *Breast*, voice.
[9] *Leman*, sweetheart.
[10] *Testril*, tester or sixpence.

Trip no further, pretty sweeting;[1]
Journeys end in lovers meeting,
Every wise man's son doth know.

Sir And. Excellent good, i' faith.

Sir To. Good, good.

Clo. [*Sings*]

What is love? 't is not hereafter;
Present mirth hath present laughter;
What 's to come is still unsure:
In delay there lies no plenty;
Then come kiss me, sweet and twenty,
Youth 's a stuff will not endure.

Sir And. A mellifluous voice, as I am true knight.

Sir To. A contagious breath.

Sir And. Very sweet and contagious, i' faith.

Sir To. To hear by the nose, it is dulcet in contagion.] But shall we make the welkin dance indeed? shall we rouse the night-owl in a catch that will draw three souls out of one weaver? shall we do that?

Sir And. An you love me, let 's do 't: I am dog at a catch.

Clo. By 'r lady, sir, and some dogs will catch well.

Sir And. Most certain. Let our catch be, *Thou knave.*

Clo. *Hold thy peace, thou knave*, knight? I shall be constrain'd in 't to call thee knave, knight.

Sir And. 'T is not the first time I have constrained one to call me knave. Begin, fool: it begins, *Hold thy peace.*

Clo. I shall never begin if I hold my peace.

Sir And. Good, i' faith. Come, begin.

[*They sing the catch, "Hold thy peace."*

Enter MARIA.

Mar. What a caterwauling do you keep here! If my lady have not call'd up her steward Malvolio and bid him turn you out of doors, never trust me.

Sir To. My lady 's a Cataian,[2] we are politicians, Malvolio's a Peg-a-Ramsey, and [*Sings*] Three merry men be we. Am not I consanguineous? am I not of her blood? Tillyvally,[3] lady! [*Sings*] There dwelt a man in Babylon, lady, lady!

[1] *Sweeting*, a term of endearment.
[2] *Cataian*, term of reproach.
[3] *Tillyvally*, an expression of contempt and impatience.

Clo. Beshrew me, the knight 's in admirable fooling.

Sir And. Ay, he does well enough if he be dispos'd, and so do I too: he does it with a better grace, but I do it more natural.

Sir To. [*Singing uproariously*] O, the twelfth day of December,—

Mar. For the love o' God, peace!

Enter MALVOLIO.

Mal. My masters, are you mad? or what are you? Have you no wit, manners nor honesty,[4] but to gabble like tinkers at this time of night? Do ye make an alehouse of my lady's house, that ye squeak out your coziers'[5] catches without any mitigation or remorse of voice? Is there no respect of place, persons nor time, in you?

Sir To. We did keep time, sir, in our catches. Sneck up![6]

Mal. Sir Toby, I must be round[7] with you. My lady bade me tell you, that, though she harbours you as her kinsman, she 's nothing allied to your disorders. If you can separate yourself and your misdemeanours, you are welcome to the house; if not, an it would please you to take leave of her, she is very willing to bid you farewell.

Sir To. [*Sings*] Farewell, dear heart, since I must needs be gone.

Mar. Nay, good Sir Toby.

Clo. [*Sings*] His eyes do show his days are almost done.

Mal. Is 't even so?

Sir To. But I will never die.

Clo. Sir Toby, there you lie.

Mal. This is much credit to you.

Sir To. Shall I bid him go?

Clo. What an if you do?

Sir To. Shall I bid him go, and spare not?

Clo. O, no, no, no, no, you dare not.

Sir To. [*To Malvolio*] Out o' tune, sir? ye lie. Art any more than a steward? Dost thou think, because thou art virtuous, there shall be no more cakes and ale?

Clo. Yes, by Saint Anne, and ginger shall be hot i' the mouth too.

Sir To. Thou 'rt i' the right. Go, sir, rub

[4] *Honesty*, propriety.
[5] *Coziers'*, cobblers'.
[6] *Sneck up!* go hang!
[7] *Round*, plain.

your chain with crumbs. A stoup of wine, Maria!

Mal. Mistress Mary, if you priz'd my lady's favour at any thing more than contempt, you would not give means for this uncivil rule:[1] she shall know of it, by this hand. [*Exit.*

Mar. Go shake your ears.[2]

Sir And. 'T were as good a deed as to drink when a man 's a-hungry, to challenge him the field, and then to break promise with him, and make a fool of him.

Sir To. Do 't, knight: I 'll write thee a challenge; or I 'll deliver thy indignation to him by word of mouth.

Mar. Sweet Sir Toby, be patient for to-night: since the youth of the count's was to-

Mar. If I do not gull him into a nayword, and make him a common recreation, do not think I have wit enough to lie straight in my bed!—(Act ii. 3. 145-148.)

day with my lady, she is much out of quiet. For Monsieur Malvolio, let me alone with him: if I do not gull him into a nayword,[3] and make him a common recreation, do not think I have wit enough to lie straight in my bed! I know I can do it.

Sir To. Possess[4] us, possess us; tell us something of him.

Mar. Marry, sir, sometimes he is a kind of puritan.

Sir And. O, if I thought that, I 'd beat him like a dog!

Sir To. What, for being a puritan? thy exquisite reason, dear knight?

Sir And. I have no exquisite reason for 't, but I have reason good enough.

Mar. The devil a puritan that he is, or any thing constantly, but a time-pleaser; an affection'd[5] ass, that cons state without book, and utters it by great swarths:[6] the best persuaded of himself, so cramm'd, as he thinks with excellencies, that it is his grounds of faith that all that look on him love him; and on that vice in him will my revenge find notable cause to work.

Sir To. What wilt thou do?

[1] *Rule*, behaviour.

[2] *Go shake your ears*, a common expression of contempt.

[3] *Nayword*, byword.

[4] *Possess*, inform.

[5] *Affection'd*, affected.

[6] *Swarths*, swaths.

Mar. I will drop in his way some obscure epistles of love; wherein, by the colour of his beard, the shape of his leg, the manner of his gait, the expressure[1] of his eye, forehead and complexion, he shall find himself most feelingly[2] personated. I can write very like my lady your niece: on a forgotten matter we can hardly make distinction of our hands.

Sir To. Excellent! I smell a device.

Sir And. I have 't in my nose too.

Sir To. He shall think, by the letters that thou wilt drop, that they come from my niece, and that she 's in love with him.

Mar. My purpose is, indeed, a horse of that colour.

Sir And. And your horse now would make him an ass.

Mar. Ass, I doubt not.

Sir And. O, 't will be admirable!

Mar. Sport royal, I warrant you: I know my physic will work with him. I will plant you two, and let the fool make a third, where he shall find the letter: observe his construction of it. For this night, to bed, and dream on the event. Farewell. [*Exit.*

Sir To. Good night, Penthesilea.[3]

Sir And. Before me, she 's a good wench.

Sir To. She 's a beagle, true-bred, and one that adores me: what o' that?

Sir And. I was ador'd once too.

Sir To. Let 's to bed, knight. Thou hadst need send for more money.

Sir And. If I cannot recover[4] your niece, I am a foul way out.

Sir To. Send for money, knight: if thou hast her not i' the end, call me cut.[5]

Sir And. If I do not, never trust me, take it how you will.

Sir To. Come, come, I 'll go burn some sack; 't is too late to go to bed now: come, knight; come, knight. [*Exeunt.*

SCENE IV. *The Duke's palace.*

Enter DUKE, VIOLA, CURIO, *and others, with music.*

Duke. Give me some music. Now, good morrow, friends.
Now, good Cesario, but that piece of song,
That old and antique[6] song we heard last night:
Methought it did relieve my passion much,
More than light airs and recollected terms
Of these most brisk and giddy-paced times.
Come, but one verse.

Cur. He is not here, so please your lordship, that should sing it.

Duke. Who was it?

Cur. Feste the jester, my lord; a fool that the Lady Olivia's father took much delight in. He is about the house.

Duke. Seek him out: and play the tune the while. [*Exit Curio. Music plays.*
[*To Viola*] Come hither, boy. If ever thou shalt love,
In the sweet pangs of it remember me;
For such as I am all true lovers are,
Unstaid and skittish in all motions else,
Save in the constant image of the creature
That is belov'd. How dost thou like this tune?

Vio. It gives a very echo to the seat
Where Love is thron'd.

Duke. Thou dost speak masterly:
My life upon 't, young though thou art, thine eye
Hath stay'd upon some favour that it loves!
Hath it not, boy?

Vio. A little, by your favour.

Duke. What kind of woman is 't?

Vio. Of your complexion.[7]

Duke. She is not worth thee, then. What years, i' faith?

Vio. About your years, my lord.

Duke. Too old, by heaven! Let still the woman take
An elder than herself; so wears she to him,
So sways she level in her husband's heart:
For, boy, however we do praise ourselves,
Our fancies are more giddy and unfirm,
More longing, wavering, sooner lost and worn,[8]
Than women's are.

Vio. I think it well, my lord.

Duke. Then let thy love be younger than thyself,

---

1 *Expressure*, expression. 2 *Feelingly*, exactly.
3 *Penthesilea*, the queen of the Amazons. 4 *Recover*, win.
5 *Call me cut*, a term of abuse; a *cut* was a docked horse.

6 *Antique*, *i.e.* old-fashioned and quaint.
7 *Complexion*, personal appearance.
8 *Worn*, *i.e.* worn out.

Or thy affection cannot hold the bent;[1]
For women are as roses, whose fair flower,
Being once display'd, doth fall that very hour.
Vio. And so they are: alas, that they are so;
To die, even when they to perfection grow!

[*Re-enter* CURIO *and* CLOWN.

Duke. O, fellow, come, the song we had last night!
Mark it, Cesario, it is old and plain;
The spinsters[2] and the knitters in the sun
And the free maids that weave their thread with bones,[3]
Do use to chant it: it is silly sooth,[4]
And dallies with the innocence of love,
Like the old age.[5]
Clo. Are you ready, sir?
Duke. Ay; prithee, sing. [*Music.*

Song.

Clo. Come away, come away, death,
And in sad cypress let me be laid;
Fly away, fly away, breath;
I am slain by a fair cruel maid.
My shroud of white, stuck all with yew,
O, prepare it!
My part of death, no one so true
Did share it.

Not a flower, not a flower sweet,
On my black coffin let there be strown;
Not a friend, not a friend greet
My poor corpse, where my bones shall be thrown:
A thousand thousand sighs to save,
Lay me, O, where
Sad true lover never find my grave,
To weep there!

Duke. There 's for thy pains.
Clo. No pains, sir; I take pleasure in singing, sir.
Duke. I 'll pay thy pleasure, then.
Clo. Truly, sir, and pleasure will be paid, one time or another.
Duke. Give me now leave to leave thee.
Clo. Now, the melancholy god protect thee; and the tailor make thy doublet of changeable taffeta,[6] for thy mind is a very opal! I would have men of such constancy put to sea, that their business might be every thing, and their intent every where; for that 's it that always makes a good voyage of nothing. Farewell. [*Exit.*]

Duke. Let all the rest give place.
[*Exeunt all but Duke and Viola.*
Once more, Cesario,
Get thee to yond same sovereign cruelty:
Tell her, my love, more noble than the world,
Prizes not quantity of dirty lands;
The parts that fortune hath bestow'd upon her,
Tell her, I hold as giddily[7] as fortune;
But 't is that miracle and queen of gems
That nature pranks[8] her in attracts my soul.
Vio. But if she cannot love you, sir?
Duke. I cannot be so answer'd.
Vio. Sooth, but you must.
Say that some lady, as perhaps there is,
Hath for your love as great a pang of heart
As you have for Olivia: you cannot love her;
You tell her so; must she not then be answer'd?
Duke. There is no woman's sides
Can bide the beating of so strong a passion
As love doth give my heart; no woman's heart
So big, to hold so much; they lack retention.
Alas, their love may be call'd appetite,—
No motion of the liver,[9] but the palate,—
That suffer surfeit, cloyment and revolt;
But mine is all as hungry as the sea,
And can digest as much: make no compare
Between that love a woman can bear me
And that I owe Olivia.
Vio. Ay, but I know . . .
Duke. What dost thou know?
Vio. Too well what love women to men may owe:
In faith, they are as true of heart as we.
My father had a daughter lov'd a man,
As it might be, perhaps, were I a woman,
I should your lordship.
Duke. And what 's her history?
Vio. A blank, my lord. She never told her love,
But let concealment, like a worm i' the bud,
Feed on her damask cheek: she pin'd in thought,

[1] *Bent*, tension.
[2] *Spinsters*, i.e. female spinners.
[3] *Bones*, i.e. bobbins of bone or ivory.
[4] *Silly sooth*, simple truth.
[5] *The old age*, i.e. the primitive age.
[6] *Taffeta*, a silken fabric.
[7] *Giddily*, negligently.
[8] *Pranks*, decks.
[9] *Liver*, formerly held to be the seat of love.

And, with a green and yellow melancholy,
She sat like Patience on a monument,
Smiling at grief. Was not this love indeed?
[We men may say more, swear more, but indeed
Our shows are more than will; for still we prove
Much in our vows, but little in our love.]

Duke. But died thy sister of her love, my boy?

Vio. I am all the daughters of my father's house,
And all the brothers too: [*aside*] and yet I know not.
Sir, shall I to this lady?

Duke. Ay, that 's the theme.
To her in haste; give her this jewel; say,
My love can give no place, bide no denay.[1]

[*Exeunt.*

Scene V. *Olivia's garden.*

Enter Sir Toby Belch, Sir Andrew Aguecheek, *and* Fabian.

Sir To. Come thy ways, Signior Fabian.

Fab. Nay, I'll come: if I lose a scruple of this sport, let me be boil'd to death with melancholy.

Sir To. Wouldst thou not be glad to have the niggardly rascally sheep-biter come by some notable shame?

Fab. I would exult, man: you know he brought me out o' favour with my lady about a bear-baiting here.

Sir To. To anger him, we'll have the bear again; and we will fool him black and blue: shall we not, Sir Andrew?

Sir And. An we do not, it is pity of our lives.

Sir To. Here comes the little villain.

Enter Maria.

How now, my metal of India![2]

Mar. Get ye all three into the box-tree: Malvolio 's coming down this walk: he has been yonder i' the sun practising behaviour to his own shadow this half hour: observe him, for the love of mockery; for I know this letter will make a contemplative idiot of him. Close, in the name of jesting! [*The others hide themselves.*] Lie thou there [*throws down a letter*]; for here comes the trout that must be caught with tickling. [*Exit.*

Enter Malvolio.

Mal. 'T is but fortune; all is fortune. Maria once told me she did affect me: and I have

Duke. Get thee to yond same sovereign cruelty:
Tell her, my love, more noble than the world,
Prizes not quantity of dirty lands.—(Act ii. 4. 83-85.)

heard herself come thus near, that, should she fancy, it should be one of my complexion. Besides, she uses me with a more exalted respect than any one else that follows her. What should I think on 't?

Sir To. Here 's an overweening rogue!

Fab. O, peace! Contemplation makes a rare turkey-cock of him: how he jets[3] under his advanced plumes!

[1] *Denay*, denial.

[2] *Metal of India*, i.e. girl of gold.

[3] *Jets*, struts.

Sir And. 'S light,[1] I could so beat the rogue!

Sir To. Peace, I say.

Mal. To be Count Malvolio!

Sir To. Ah, rogue!

Sir And. Pistol him, pistol him.

Sir To. Peace, peace!

Mal. There is example for 't; the lady of the Strachy married the yeoman of the wardrobe.

Sir And. Fie on him, Jezebel!

Fab. O, peace! now he 's deeply in: look how imagination blows[2] him.

Mal. Having been three months married to her, sitting in my state,[3]—

Sir To. O for a stone-bow,[4] to hit him in the eye!

Mal. Calling my officers about me, in my branch'd[5] velvet gown; having come from a day-bed,[6] where I have left Olivia sleeping,—

Sir To. Fire and brimstone!

Fab. O, peace, peace!

Mal. And then to have the humour of state; and after a demure travel of regard, telling them I know my place as I would they should do theirs, to ask for my kinsman Toby,—

Sir To. Bolts and shackles!

Fab. O, peace, peace, peace! now, now!

Mal. Seven of my people, with an obedient start, make out for him: I frown the while; and perchance wind up my watch, or play with my—some rich jewel. Toby approaches; court'sies there to me,—

Sir To. Shall this fellow live?

Fab. Though our silence be drawn from us with cars, yet peace.

Mal. I extend my hand to him thus, quenching my familiar smile with an austere regard of control,—

Sir To. And does not Toby take you a blow o' the lips, then?

Mal. Saying, "Cousin Toby, my fortunes having cast me on your niece, give me this prerogative of speech;"—

Sir To. What, what?

Mal. "You must amend your drunkenness."

Sir To. Out, scab!

Fab. Nay, patience, or we break the sinews of our plot.

Mal. "Besides, you waste the treasure of your time with a foolish knight,"—

Sir And. That 's me, I warrant you.

Mal. "One Sir Andrew,"—

Sir And. I knew 't was I; for many do call me fool.

Mal. What employment have we here?[7]

[*Taking up the letter.*

Fab. Now is the woodcock[8] near the gin.

Sir To. O, peace! and the spirit of humours intimate reading aloud to him!

Mal. By my life, this is my lady's hand: these be her very C's, her U's, and her T's; and thus makes she her great P's. It is, in contempt of question,[9] her hand.

Sir And. Her C's, her U's, and her T's: why that?

Mal. [*Reads*] "To the unknown beloved, this, and my good wishes:" her very phrases! By your leave, wax. Soft! and the impressure[10] her Lucrece, with which she uses to seal: 't is my lady. To whom should this be?

Fab. This wins him, liver and all.

Mal. [*Reads*]

"Jove knows I love:
But who?
Lips, do not move;
No man must know."

"No man must know." What follows? the numbers alter'd! "No man must know;" if this should be thee, Malvolio?

Sir To. Marry, hang thee, brock![11]

Mal. [*Reads*]

"I may command where I adore;
But silence, like a Lucrece' knife,
With bloodless stroke my heart doth gore:
M, O, A, I, doth sway my life."

Fab. A fustian riddle!

Sir To. Excellent wench, say I.

Mal. "*M, O, A, I*, doth sway my life." Nay, but first, let me see, let me see, let me see.

---

1 *'Slight*, a corruption of God's light. 2 *Blows*, puffs up.
3 *My state*, i.e. my chair of state.
4 *Stone-bow*, a cross-bow for throwing stones (Lat. *balista*). 5 *Branch'd*, ornamented with leafy patterns.
6 *Day-bed*, couch or sofa.
7 *i.e.* What 's to do here?
8 *Woodcock*, a common metaphor for fool, the bird being supposed to have no brains.
9 *In contempt of question*, past question.
10 *Impressure*, impression.
11 *Brock*, badger, a term of contempt.

Fab. What dish o' poison has she dress'd him!

Sir To. And with what wing the staniel[1] checks at it!

Mal. "I may command where I adore." Why, she may command me: I serve her; she is my lady. Why, this is evident to any formal capacity; there is no obstruction in this: and the end,—what should that alphabetical position portend? If I could make that resemble something in me, . . . Softly! *M, O, A, I.*

Sir To. O, ay, make up that: he is now at a cold scent.

Fab. Sowter[2] will cry upon 't, for all this, though it be as rank as a fox.

Mal. M,—Malvolio; *M,*—why, that begins my name.

Fab. Did not I say he would work it out? the cur is excellent at faults.[3]

Mal. M,—but then there is no consonancy in the sequel; that suffers under probation: *A* should follow, but *O* does.

Fab. And *O* shall end, I hope.

Sir To. Ay, or I'll cudgel him, and make him cry O!

Mal. And then *I* comes behind.

Fab. Ay, an you had any eye behind you, you might see more detraction at your heels than fortunes before you.

Mal. M, O, A, I: this simulation is not as the former; and yet, to crush this a little, it would bow to me, for every one of these letters are in my name. Soft! here follows prose.

[*Reads*] "If this fall into thy hand, revolve. In my stars I am above thee; but be not afraid of greatness: some are born great, some achieve greatness, and some have greatness thrust upon 'em. Thy Fates open their hands; let thy blood and spirit embrace them: and, to inure thyself to what thou art like to be, cast thy humble slough, and appear fresh. Be opposite[4] with a kinsman, surly with servants; let thy tongue tang[5] arguments of state; put thyself into the trick of singularity: she thus advises thee that sighs for thee. Remember who commended thy yellow stockings, and wished to see thee ever cross-garter'd: I say, remember. Go to, thou art made, if thou desirest to be so; if not, let me see thee a steward still, the fellow of servants, and not worthy to touch Fortune's fingers. Farewell. She that would alter services with thee,

THE FORTUNATE-UNHAPPY."

Daylight and champaign discover not more: this is open. I will be proud, I will read politic authors, I will baffle Sir Toby, I will wash off gross acquaintance, I will be point-devise[6] the very man. I do not now fool myself, to let imagination jade[7] me; for every reason excites to this, that my lady loves me. She did commend my yellow stockings of late, she did praise my leg being cross-garter'd; and in this she manifests herself to my love, and with a kind of injunction drives me to these habits of her liking. I thank my stars, I am happy. I will be strange, stout,[8] in yellow stockings, and cross-garter'd, even with the swiftness of putting on. Jove and my stars be praised! Here is yet a postscript.

[*Reads*] "Thou canst not choose but know who I am. If thou entertain'st my love, let it appear in thy smiling: thy smiles become thee well; therefore in my presence still smile, dear my sweet, I prithee."

Jove, I thank thee! I will smile; I will do everything that thou wilt have me. [*Exit.*

Fab. I will not give my part of this sport for a pension of thousands to be paid from the Sophy.[9]

Sir To. I could marry this wench for this device.

Sir And. So could I too.

Sir To. And ask no other dowry with her but such another jest.

Sir And. Nor I neither.

Fab. Here comes my noble gull-catcher.

Re-enter MARIA.

Sir To. Wilt thou set thy foot o' my neck?

Sir And. Or o' mine either?

Sir To. Shall I play my freedom at tray-trip,[10] and become thy bond-slave?

Sir And. I' faith, or I either?

Sir To. Why, thou hast put him in such a dream, that when the image of it leaves him he must run mad.

---

1 *Staniel,* kestrel.

2 *Sowter,* term contemptuously applied to a hound; a *sowter* was a cobbler or botcher.

3 *At faults,* where the scent is lost.

4 *Opposite,* contrary.

5 *Tang,* ring with.

6 *Point-devise,* precisely.

7 *Jade, i.e.* make me appear like a jade, ridiculous.

8 *Strange, stout,* distant and proud.

9 *Sophy, i.e. Sufi,* Shah of Persia.

10 *Tray-trip,* a game at dice.

Mar. Nay, but say true; does it work upon him.

Sir To. Like aqua-vitæ with a midwife.

Mar. If you will then see the fruits of the sport, mark his first approach before my lady. He will come to her in yellow stockings, and 't is a colour she abhors, and cross-garter'd, a fashion she detests; and he will smile upon her, which will now be so unsuitable to her disposition, being addicted to a melancholy as she is, that it cannot but turn him into a notable contempt. If you will see it, follow me.

Sir To. To the gates of Tartar,[1] thou most excellent devil of wit!

Sir And. I 'll make one too. [*Exeunt.*

ACT III.

Scene I. *Olivia's garden.*

Enter Viola, *and* Clown *with a tabor.*

Vio. Save thee, friend, and thy music! Dost thou live by thy tabor?

Clo. No, sir, I live by the church.

Vio. Art thou a churchman?

Clo. No such matter, sir: I do live by the church; for I do live at my house, and my house doth stand by the church.

[*Vio.* So thou mayst say, the king lies by a beggar, if a beggar dwell near him; or, the church stands by thy tabor, if thy tabor stand by the church.

Clo. You have said, sir. To see this age! A sentence is but a cheveril[2] glove to a good wit: how quickly the wrong side may be turned outward!

Vio. Nay, that 's certain; they that dally nicely with words may quickly make them wanton.

Clo. I would, therefore, my sister had had no name, sir.

Vio. Why, man?

Clo. Why, sir, her name 's a word; and to dally with that word might make my sister wanton. But indeed words are very rascals, since bonds disgrac'd them.

Vio. Thy reason, man?

Clo. Troth, sir, I can yield you none without words; and words are grown so false, I am loth to prove reason with them.

Vio. I warrant thou art a merry fellow, and car'st for nothing.

Clo. Not so, sir, I do care for something; but in my conscience, sir, I do not care for you: if that be to care for nothing, sir, I would it would make you invisible.]

Vio. Art not thou the Lady Olivia's fool?

Clo. No, indeed, sir; the Lady Olivia has no folly: she will keep no fool, sir, till she be married; and fools are as like husbands as pilchards are to herrings,—the husband's the bigger: I am, indeed, not her fool, but her corrupter of words.

Vio. I saw thee late at the Count Orsino's.

Clo. Foolery, sir, does walk about the orb like the sun, it shines everywhere. I would be sorry, sir, but the fool should be as oft with your master as with my mistress: I think I saw your wisdom there.

Vio. Nay, an thou pass upon[3] me, I 'll no more with thee. Hold, there 's expenses for thee. [*Gives him a piece of money.*

Clo. Now Jove, in his next commodity of hair, send thee a beard!

Vio. By my troth, I 'll tell thee, I am almost sick for one; [*aside*] though I would not have it grow on my chin. Is thy lady within?

Clo. [Would not a pair of these have bred, sir? [*Showing the piece of money.*

Vio. Yes, being kept together and put to use.

Clo. I would play Lord Pandarus of Phrygia, sir, to bring a Cressida to this Troilus.

Vio. I understand you, sir; 't is well begg'd.

Clo. The matter, I hope, is not great, sir, begging but a beggar: Cressida was a beggar.] My lady is within, sir. I will construe to them whence you come; who you are and

---

[1] *Tartar, i.e.* Tartarus.

[2] *Cheveril*, kid.

[3] *Pass upon, i.e.* make a thrust at.

what you would are out of my welkin; I might say element, but the word is over-worn. [*Exit.*

Vio. This fellow's wise enough to play the fool,
And to do that well craves a kind of wit:
He must observe their mood on whom he jests,
The quality of persons, and the time,
Not, like the haggard, check at every feather
That comes before his eye. This is a practice
As full of labour as a wise man's art:
For folly, that he wisely shows, is fit,
But wise men, folly-fall'n, quite taint their wit.

Enter SIR TOBY BELCH *and* SIR ANDREW AGUECHEEK.

Sir To. Save you, gentleman.

Vio. And you, sir.

Sir And. *Dieu vous garde, monsieur.*[1]

Vio. *Et vous aussi; votre serviteur.*[2]

Sir And. I hope, sir, you are; and I am yours.

Sir To. Will you encounter the house? my niece is desirous you should enter, if your trade[3] be to her.

Vio. I am bound to your niece, sir; I mean, she is the list[4] of my voyage.

Sir To. Taste your legs, sir; put them to motion.

Vio. My legs do better under-stand me, sir, than I understand what you mean by bidding me taste my legs.

Sir To. I mean, to go, sir, to enter.

Vio. I will answer you with gait and entrance:—but we are prevented.[5]

Enter OLIVIA *and* MARIA.

Most excellent accomplished lady, the heavens rain odours on you!

Sir And. [*Aside*] That youth's a rare courtier: "Rain odours;" well.

Vio. My matter hath no voice, lady, but to your own most pregnant[6] and vouchsafed ear.

Sir And. [*Aside*] "Odours," "pregnant" and "vouchsafed:" I'll get 'em all three all ready.

Oli. Let the garden door be shut, and leave me to my hearing. [*Exeunt Sir Toby, Sir Andrew, and Maria.*] Give me your hand, sir.

Vio. My duty, madam, and most humble service.

Oli. What is your name?

Vio. Cesario is your servant's name, fair princess.

Oli. My servant, sir! 'T was never merry world
Since lowly feigning[7] was call'd compliment:
You're servant to the Count Orsino, youth.

Vio. And he is yours, and his must needs be yours:
Your servant's servant is your servant, madam.

Oli. For him, I think not on him: for his thoughts,
Would they were blanks, rather than fill'd with me!

Vio. Madam, I come to whet your gentle thoughts
On his behalf:—

Oli. O, by your leave, I pray you,
I bade you never speak again of him:
But, would you undertake another suit,
I had rather hear you to solicit that
Than music from the spheres.

Vio. Dear lady,—

Oli. Give me leave, beseech you. I did send,
After the last enchantment you did here,
A ring in chase of you: so did I abuse[8]
Myself, my servant and, I fear me, you:
Under your hard construction must I sit,
To force that on you, in a shameful cunning,
Which you knew none of yours: what might you think?
Have you not set mine honour at the stake
And baited it with all the unmuzzled thoughts
That tyrannous heart can think? To one of your receiving[9]
Enough is shown: a cyprus,[10] not a bosom,
Hides my heart. So, let me hear you speak.

Vio. I pity you.

Oli. That's a degree to love.

Vio. No, not a grise;[11] for 't is a vulgar proof
That very oft we pity enemies.

Oli. Why, then, methinks 't is time to smile again.

---

1 "God keep you, sir."
2 "And you too; your servant."
3 *Trade*, business.
4 *List*, limit.
5 *Prevented*, anticipated.
6 *Pregnant*, ready.
7 *Lowly feigning*, affected humility.
8 *Abuse*, deceive.
9 *Receiving*, i.e. ready apprehension.
10 *Cyprus*, transparent stuff.
11 *Grise*, step.

O world, how apt the poor are to be proud!
If one should be a prey, how much the better
To fall before the lion than the wolf!
[*Clock strikes.*
The clock upbraids me with the waste of time.
Be not afraid, good youth, I will not have you:
And yet, when wit and youth is come to harvest,
Your wife is like to reap a proper man.
There lies your way, due west.

Vio. Then westward-ho!
Grace and good disposition attend your ladyship!
You'll nothing, madam, to my lord by me?

Oli. Stay!
I prithee, tell me what thou think'st of me.

Oli. Stay!
I prithee, tell me what thou think'st of me.—(Act iii. 1. 149, 150.)

Vio. That you do think you are not what you are.

Oli. If I think so, I think the same of you.

Vio. Then think you right: I am not what I am.

Oli. I would you were as I would have you be!

Vio. Would it be better, madam, than I am?
I wish it might, for now I am your fool.

Oli. O what a deal of scorn looks beautiful
In the contempt and anger of his lip!
A murderous guilt shows not itself more soon
Than love that would seem hid: love's night is noon.
Cesario, by the roses of the spring,
By maidhood, honour, truth and every thing,
I love thee so, that, maugre[1] all thy pride,
Nor wit nor reason can my passion hide.
Do not extort thy reasons from this clause,
For that I woo, thou therefore hast no cause;
But rather reason thus with reason fetter:
Love sought is good, but given unsought is better.

Vio. By innocence I swear, and by my youth,
I have one heart, one bosom and one truth,
And that no woman has; nor never none
Shall mistress be of it, save I alone.

[1] *Maugre*, in spite of.

And so adieu, good madam: never more
Will I my master's tears to you deplore.

Oli. Yet come again; for thou perhaps mayst move
That heart, which now abhors, to like his love.
[*Exeunt.*

SCENE II. *The court-yard of Olivia's house.*

Enter SIR TOBY, SIR ANDREW, *and* FABIAN.

Sir And. No, faith, I 'll not stay a jot longer.

Sir To. Thy reason, dear venom, give thy reason.

Fab. You must needs yield your reason, Sir Andrew.

Sir And. Marry, I saw your niece do more favours to the count's serving-man than ever she bestow'd upon me; I saw 't i' the orchard.

Sir To. Did she see thee the while, old boy? tell me that.

Sir And. As plain as I see you now.

Fab. This was a great argument of love in her toward you.

Sir And. 'S light, will you make an ass o' me?

Fab. I will prove it legitimate, sir, upon the oaths of judgment and reason.

Sir To. And they have been grand-jury-men since before Noah was a sailor.

Fab. She did show favour to the youth in your sight only to exasperate you, to awake your dormouse valour, to put fire in your heart and brimstone in your liver. You should then have accosted her; and with some excellent jests, fire-new from the mint, you should have bang'd the youth into dumbness. This was look'd for at your hand, and this was balk'd: the double gilt of this opportunity you let time wash off, and you are now sail'd into the north of my lady's opinion; where you will hang like an icicle on a Dutchman's beard, unless you do redeem it by some laudable attempt either of valour or policy.

Sir And. An 't be any way, it must be with valour; for policy I hate: I had as lief be a Brownist as a politician.

Sir To. Why, then, build me thy fortunes upon the basis of valour. Challenge me the count's youth to fight with him; hurt him in eleven places: my niece shall take note of it; and assure thyself, there is no love-broker in the world can more prevail in man's commendation with woman than report of valour.

Fab. There is no way but this, Sir Andrew.

Sir And. Will either of you bear me a challenge to him?

Sir To. Go, write it in a martial hand; be curst[1] and brief; it is no matter how witty, so it be eloquent and full of invention: taunt him with the license of ink: if thou "thou'st" him some thrice, it shall not be amiss; and as many lies as will lie in thy sheet of paper, although the sheet were big enough for the bed of Ware in England, set 'em down: go, about it. Let there be gall enough in thy ink; though thou write with a goose-pen, no matter: about it.

Sir And. Where shall I find you?

Sir To. We 'll call thee at the *cubiculo:*[2] go.
[*Exit Sir Andrew.*

Fab. This is a dear manakin to you, Sir Toby.

Sir Toby. I have been dear to him, lad, some two thousand strong, or so.

Fab. We shall have a rare letter from him: but you 'll not deliver 't?

Sir To. Never trust me, then; and by all means stir on the youth to an answer. I think oxen and wainropes[3] cannot hale[4] them together. For Andrew, if he were open'd, and you find so much blood in his liver as will clog the foot of a flea, I 'll eat the rest of the anatomy.

Fab. And his opposite,[5] the youth, bears in his visage no great presage of cruelty.

Sir To. Look, where the youngest wren of nine comes.

Enter MARIA.

Mar. If you desire the spleen, and will laugh yourselves into stitches, follow me. Yond gull Malvolio is turn'd heathen, a very renegado; for there is no Christian, that means to be sav'd by believing rightly, can ever believe such impossible passages[6] of grossness. He 's in yellow stockings.

Sir To. And cross-garter'd?

[1] *Curst*, sharp, petulant.
[2] *Cubiculo* (i.e. *cubiculum*), chamber.
[3] *Wainropes*, cart-ropes.
[4] *Hale*, draw.
[5] *Opposite*, opponent.
[6] *Passages*, acts.

Mar. Most villanously; like a pedant[1] that keeps a school i' the church. I have dogg'd him, like his murderer. He does obey every point of the letter that I dropp'd to betray him: he does smile his face into more lines than is in the new map with the augmentation of the Indies: you have not seen such a thing as 't is; I can hardly forbear hurling things at him. I know my lady will strike him: if she do, he 'll smile, and take 't for a great favour.

Sir To. Come, bring us, bring us where he is. [*Exeunt.*

SCENE III. *The Market Place.*

Enter SEBASTIAN *and* ANTONIO.

Seb. I would not by my will have troubled you,
But, since you make your pleasure of your pains,
I will no further chide you.

Ant. I could not stay behind you: my desire,
More sharp than filed steel, did spur me forth;
And not all love to see you, though so much
As might have drawn one to a longer voyage,
But jealousy[2] what might befall your travel,
Being skilless in these parts, which, to a stranger,
Unguided and unfriended, often prove
Rough and unhospitable. My willing love,
The rather by these arguments of fear,
Set forth in your pursuit.

Seb. My kind Antonio,
I can no other answer make, but thanks,
And thanks: and, ever oft,[3] good turns
Are shuffled off with such uncurrent pay:
But, were my worth[4] as is my conscience firm,
You should find better dealing. What's to do?
Shall we go see the reliques[5] of this town?

Ant. To-morrow, sir; best first go see your lodging.

Seb. I am not weary, and 't is long to night:
I pray you, let us satisfy our eyes
With the memorials and the things of fame
That do renown this city.

Ant. Would you'd pardon me!
I do not without danger walk these streets:
Once, in a sea-fight, 'gainst the count his galleys
I did some service; of such note, indeed,
That were I ta'en here it would scarce be answer'd.

[*Seb.* Belike you slew great number of his people?

Ant. The offence is not of such a bloody nature,
Albeit the quality of the time and quarrel
Might well have given us bloody argument.
It might have since been answer'd in repaying
What we took from them; which, for traffic's sake,
Most of our city did: only myself stood out;
For which, if I be lapsed[6] in this place,
I shall pay dear.]

Seb. Do not then walk too open.

Ant. It doth not fit me. Hold, sir, here 's my purse.
In the south suburbs, at the Elephant,
Is best to lodge: I will bespeak our diet,
Whiles you beguile the time and feed your knowledge
With viewing of the town: there shall you have me.

Seb. Why I your purse?

Ant. Haply your eye shall light upon some toy
You have desire to purchase; and your store,
I think, is not for idle markets, sir.

Seb. I 'll be your purse-bearer, and leave you for
An hour.

Ant. To the Elephant.

Seb. I do remember. [*Exeunt.*

SCENE IV. *Olivia's garden.*

Enter OLIVIA *and Ladies.*

Oli. [*Aside*] I have sent after him: he says he 'll come;
How shall I feast him? what bestow of[7] him?
For youth is bought more oft than begg'd or borrow'd.
I speak too loud.
Where is Malvolio? he is sad[8] and civil,[9]
And suits well for a servant with my fortunes:

[1] *Pedant*, *i.e.* pedagogue. [2] *Jealousy*, apprehension.
[3] *Ever oft*, *i.e.* with perpetual frequency.
[4] *Worth*, wealth. [5] *Reliques* = monuments.

[6] *Lapsed*, perhaps = "caught" "taken by surprise" (see note 108). [7] *Of*, on.
[8] *Sad*, grave. [9] *Civil*, well-mannered.

Enter MARIA.

Where is Malvolio?

Mar. He's coming, madam; but in very strange manner. He is, sure, possess'd, madam. [*Exeunt Ladies.*

Oli. Why, what's the matter? does he rave?

Mar. No, madam, he does nothing but smile: your ladyship were best to have some guard about you, if he come; for, sure, the man is tainted in's wits.

Oli. Go call him hither. [*Exit Maria.*] I'm as mad as he,
If sad and merry madness equal be.

Mal. Not black in my mind, though yellow in my legs. It did come to his hands, and commands shall be executed: I think we do know the sweet Roman hand.—(Act iii. 4. 28-31.)

Re-enter MARIA, *with* MALVOLIO.

How now, Malvolio!

Mal. Sweet lady, ho, ho!

Oli. Smil'st thou?
I sent for thee upon a sad occasion.

Mal. Sad, lady! I could be sad: this does make some obstruction in the blood, this cross-gartering; but what of that? if it please the eye of one, it is with me as the very true sonnet is, "Please one, and please all."

Oli. Why, how dost thou, man? what is the matter with thee?

Mal. Not black in my mind, though yellow in my legs. It did come to his hands, and commands shall be executed: I think we do know the sweet Roman hand.

[*Oli.* Wilt thou go to bed, Malvolio?

Mal. To bed! ay, sweet-heart; and I'll come to thee.]

Oli. God comfort thee! Why dost thou smile so, and kiss thy hand so oft?

Mar. How do you, Malvolio?

Mal. At your request! yes; nightingales answer daws.

Mar. Why appear you with this ridiculous boldness before my lady?

Mal. "Be not afraid of greatness:" 't was well writ.

Oli. What mean'st thou by that, Malvolio?

Mal. "Some are born great,"—

Oli. Ha?

Mal. "Some achieve greatness,"—

Oli. What say'st thou?

Mal. "And some have greatness thrust upon them."

Oli. Heaven restore thee!

Mal. "Remember who commended thy yellow stockings,"—

Oli. Thy yellow stockings?

Mal. "And wish'd to see thee cross-garter'd."

Oli. Cross-garter'd?

Mal. "Go to, thou art made, if thou desir'st to be so;"—

Oli. Am I made?

Mal. "If not, let me see thee a servant still."

Oli. Why, this is very midsummer madness.

Enter Servant.

Ser. Madam, the young gentleman of the Count Orsino's is returned: I could hardly entreat him back: he attends your ladyship's pleasure.

Oli. I'll come to him. [*Exit Servant.*] Good Maria, let this fellow be look'd to. Where's my cousin Toby? Let some of my people have a special care of him: I would not have him miscarry for the half of my dowry.

[*Exeunt Olivia and Maria.*

Mal. O, ho! do you come near me now? no worse man than Sir Toby to look to me! This concurs directly with the letter: she sends him on purpose, that I may appear stubborn to him; [for she incites me to that in the letter. "Cast thy humble slough," says she; "be opposite with a kinsman, surly with servants; let thy tongue tang with arguments of state; put thyself into the trick of singularity;" and consequently sets down the manner how: as, a sad face, a reverent carriage, a slow tongue, in the habit of some sir of note, and so forth.] I have lim'd her; but it is Jove's doing, and Jove make me thankful! [And when she went away now, "Let this fellow be look'd to:" fellow! not Malvolio, nor after my degree, but fellow.[1] Why, every thing adheres together, that no dram of a scruple, no scruple of a scruple, no obstacle, no incredulous[2] or unsafe circumstance . . . What can be said? Nothing that can be can come between me and the full prospect of my hopes. Well, Jove, not I, is the doer of this, and he is to be thanked.]

Sir To. [*Without*] Which way is he, in the name of sanctity? If all the devils of hell be drawn in little, and Legion himself possess'd him, yet I'll speak to him.

Re-enter MARIA *with* SIR TOBY BELCH *and* FABIAN.

Fab. Here he is, here he is. How is't with you, sir? how is't with you, man?

Mal. Go off; I discard you: let me enjoy my private:[3] go off.

Mar. Lo, how hollow the fiend speaks within him! did not I tell you? Sir Toby, my lady prays you to have a care of him.

Mal. Ah, ha! does she so?

Sir To. Go to, go to; peace, peace; we must deal gently with him: let me alone. How do you, Malvolio? how is't with you? What, man! defy the devil: consider, he's an enemy to mankind.

Mal. Do you know what you say?

Mar. La you, an you speak ill of the devil, how he takes it at heart! Pray God, he be not bewitch'd!

[*Fab.* Carry his water to the wise woman.

Mar. Marry, and it shall be done to-morrow morning, if I live. My lady would not lose him for more than I'll say.]

Mal. How now, mistress!

Mar. O Lord!

Sir To. Prithee, hold thy peace; this is not the way: do you not see you move him? let me alone with him.

Fab. No way but gentleness; gently, gently: the fiend is rough, and will not be roughly us'd.

Sir To. Why, how now, my bawcock![4] how dost thou, chuck?

Mal. Sir!

[*Sir To.* Ay, Biddy, come with me. What,

---

[1] *Fellow*, i.e. companion.

[2] *Incredulous*, incredible.

[3] *Private*, privacy.

[4] *My bawcock*, my fine fellow

man! 't is not for gravity to play at cherry-pit with Satan: hang him, foul collier!]

Mar. Get him to say his prayers, good Sir Toby, get him to pray.

Mal. My prayers, minx!

Mar. No, I warrant you, he will not hear of godliness.

Mal. Go, hang yourselves all! you are idle shallow things. I am not of your element: you shall know more hereafter. [*Exit.*

Sir To. Is't possible?

Fab. If this were play'd upon a stage now, I could condemn it as an improbable fiction.

Mal. How now, mistress!
Mar. O Lord!—(Act iii. 4. 118, 119.)

Sir To. His very genius hath taken the infection of the device, man.

Mar. Nay, pursue him now, lest the device take air and taint.

Fab. Why, we shall make him mad indeed.

Mar. The house will be the quieter.

Sir To. Come, we'll have him in a dark room and bound. My niece is already in the belief that he's mad: we may carry it thus, for our pleasure and his penance, till our very pastime, tired out of breath, prompt us to have mercy on him: at which time we will bring the device to the bar, and crown thee for a finder of madmen. But see, but see.

Enter Sir Andrew.

Fab. More matter for a May morning.

Sir And. Here's the challenge, read it: I warrant there's vinegar and pepper in 't.

Fab. Is't so saucy?

Sir And. Ay, is't, I warrant him: do but read.

Sir To. Give me. [*Reads*] "Youth, whatsoever thou art, thou art but a scurvy fellow."

Fab. Good, and valiant.

Sir To. "Wonder not, nor admire not in thy mind, why I do call thee so, for I will show thee no reason for 't."

Fab. A good note, that; keeps you from the blow of the law.

Sir To. "Thou com'st to the Lady Olivia, and in my sight she uses thee kindly: but thou liest in thy throat; that is not the matter I challenge thee for."

Fab. Very brief, and to exceeding good sense—less.

Sir To. "I will waylay thee going home; where if it be thy chance to kill me,"—

Fab. Good.

Sir To. "Thou kill'st me like a rogue and a villain."

Fab. Still you keep o' the windy side of the law: good.

Sir To. "Fare thee well; and God have mercy upon one of our souls! He may have mercy upon mine, but my hope is better; and so look to thyself. Thy friend, as thou usest him, and thy sworn enemy,

ANDREW AGUECHEEK."

If this letter move him not, his legs cannot: I'll give 't him.

Mar. You may have very fit occasion for 't: he is now in some commerce with my lady, and will by and by depart.

Sir. To. Go, Sir Andrew, scout me for him at the corner of the orchard, like a bum-baily: so soon as ever thou seest him, draw; and, as thou draw'st, swear horrible; for it comes to pass oft that a terrible oath, with a swaggering accent sharply twang'd off, gives manhood more approbation than ever proof itself would have earn'd him. Away!

Sir And. Nay, let me alone for swearing.

[*Exit.*

Sir To. Now will not I deliver his letter: for the behaviour of the young gentleman gives him out to be of good capacity and breeding; his employment between his lord and my niece confirms no less: therefore this letter, being so excellently ignorant, will breed no terror in the youth: he will find it comes from a clodpole. But, sir, I will deliver his challenge by word of mouth; set upon Aguecheek a notable report of valour; and drive the gentleman, as I know his youth will aptly receive it, into a most hideous opinion of his rage, skill, fury and impetuosity. This will so fright them both, that they will kill one another by the look, like cockatrices.

Fab. Here he comes with your niece: give them way till he take leave, and presently after him.

Sir To. I will meditate the while upon some horrid message for a challenge.

[*Exeunt Sir Toby, Fabian, and Maria.*

Re-enter OLIVIA, *with* VIOLA.

[*Oli.* I have said too much unto a heart of stone,
And laid mine honour too unchary[1] on 't:
There's something in me that reproves my fault;
But such a headstrong potent fault it is,
That it but mocks reproof.

Vio. With the same 'haviour that your passion bears
Goes on my master's grief.]

Oli. Here, wear this jewel[2] for me, 't is my picture:
Refuse it not, it hath no tongue to vex you!
And, I beseech you, come again to-morrow.
What shall you ask of me that I 'll deny,
That honour sav'd may upon asking give?

Vio. Nothing but this: your true love for my master.

Oli. How with mine honour may I give him that
Which I have given to you?

Vio. I will acquit you.

Oli. Well, come again to-morrow: fare thee well:
A fiend like thee might bear my soul to hell.

[*Exit.*

Re-enter SIR TOBY *and* FABIAN.

Sir To. Gentleman, God save thee!

Vio. And you, sir.

Sir To. That defence thou hast, betake thee to 't: of what nature the wrongs are thou hast done him, I know not; but thy intercepter, full of despite, bloody as the hunter, attends thee at the orchard-end: dismount thy tuck,[3] be yare[4] in thy preparation, for thy assailant is quick, skilful and deadly.

Vio. You mistake, sir; I am sure no man hath any quarrel to me: my remembrance is very free and clear from any image of offence done to any man.

Sir To. You'll find it otherwise, I assure you: therefore, if you hold your life at any price, betake you to your guard; for your opposite hath in him what youth, strength, skill and wrath can furnish man withal.

Vio. I pray you, sir, what is he?

Sir To. He is knight, dubb'd with unhatch'd[5] rapier and on carpet consideration; but he is a devil in private brawl: souls and

[1] *Unchary*, recklessly. [2] *Jewel*, any trinket.
[3] *Dismount thy tuck*, draw thy sword. [4] *Yare*, nimble.
[5] *Unhatch'd*, unhacked.

bodies hath he divorc'd three; and his incensement at this moment is so implacable, that satisfaction can be none but by pangs of death and sepulchre. Hob nob is his word; give't or take't.

Vio. I will return again into the house, and desire some conduct[1] of the lady. I am no fighter. I have heard of some kind of men that put quarrels purposely on others, to taste their valour: belike this is a man of that quirk.[2]

Sir To. Sir, no; his indignation derives itself out of a very competent injury: therefore, get you on, and give him his desire.

Fab. He is, indeed, sir, the most skilful, bloody and fatal opposite that you could possibly have found in any part of Illyria.—(Act iii. 4. 292-295.)

Back you shall not to the house, unless you undertake that with me which with as much safety you might answer him: therefore, on, or strip your sword stark naked; for meddle you must, that's certain, or forswear to wear iron about you.

Vio. This is as uncivil as strange. I beseech you, do me this courteous office, as to know of the knight what my offence to him is: it is something of my negligence, nothing of my purpose.

Sir To. I will do so. Signior Fabian, stay you by this gentleman till my return. [*Exit.*

Vio. Pray you, sir, do you know of this matter?

Fab. I know the knight is incens'd against you, even to a mortal arbitrement; but nothing of the circumstance more.

Vio. I beseech you, what manner of man is he?

Fab. Nothing of that wonderful promise, to read him by his form, as you are like to find

[1] *Conduct*, escort.

[2] *Quirk*, whim.

him in the proof of his valour. He is, indeed, sir, the most skilful, bloody and fatal opposite that you could possibly have found in any part of Illyria. Will you walk towards him? I will make your peace with him, if I can.

Vio. I shall be much bound to you for 't: I am one that had rather go with sir priest than sir knight: I care not who knows so much of my mettle. [*Exeunt.*

Re-enter SIR TOBY *with* SIR ANDREW.

Sir To. Why, man, he 's a very devil; I have not seen such a firago.[1] I had a pass with him, rapier, scabbard and all, and he gives me the stuck[2] in with such a mortal motion, that it is inevitable; and on the answer, he pays you as surely as your feet hit the ground they step on. They say he has been fencer to the Sophy.

Sir And. Pox on 't, I'll not meddle with him.

Sir To. Ay, but he will not now be pacified. Fabian can scarce hold him yonder.

Sir And. Plague on 't, an I thought he had been valiant and so cunning in fence, I 'd have seen him damn'd ere I 'd have challeng'd him. Let him let the matter slip, and I 'll give him my horse, gray Capilet.

Sir To. I 'll make the motion: stand here, make a good show on 't: this shall end without the perdition of souls. [*Aside*] Marry, I 'll ride your horse as well as I ride you.

Enter FABIAN *and* VIOLA.

[*Aside to Fabian*] I have his horse to take up the quarrel: I have persuaded him the youth 's a devil.

Fab. [*Aside to Sir Toby*] He is as horribly conceited of him; and pants and looks pale, as if a bear were at his heels.

Sir To. [*Aside to Viola*] There 's no remedy, sir; he will fight with you for 's oath sake: marry, he hath better bethought him of his quarrel, and he finds that now scarce to be worth talking of: therefore draw, for the supportance of his vow; he protests he will not hurt you.

Vio. [*Aside*] Pray God defend me! A little thing would make me tell them how much I lack of a man.

Fab. [*Aside to Viola*] Give ground, if you see him furious.

Sir To. [*Aside to Sir Andrew*] Come, Sir Andrew, there 's no remedy; the gentleman will, for his honour's sake, have one bout with you; he cannot by the duello[3] avoid it: but he has promised me, as he is a gentleman and a soldier, he will not hurt you. Come on; to 't.

Sir And. [*Aside to Sir Toby*] Pray God he keep his oath! [*Draws.*

Vio. [*To Fabian*] I do assure you, 'tis against my will. [*Draws.*

Enter ANTONIO.

Ant. [*To Sir Andrew*] Put up your sword. If this young gentleman
Have done offence, I take the fault on me:
If you offend him, I for him defy you.

Sir To. You, sir! why, what are you?

Ant. One, sir, that for his love dares yet do more
Than you have heard him brag to you he will.

Sir To. Nay, if you be an undertaker,[4] I am for you. [*They draw.*

Fab. O good Sir Toby, hold! here come the officers.

Sir To. [*To Antonio*] I 'll be with you anon.

Vio. [*To Sir Andrew*] Pray, sir, put your sword up, if you please.

Sir And. Marry, will I, sir; and, for that I promis'd you, I 'll be as good as my word: he will bear you easily, and reins well.

Enter Officers.

First Off. [*Points to Antonio*] This is the man; do thy office.

Sec. Off. Antonio, I arrest thee at the suit of Count Orsino.

Ant. You do mistake me, sir.

First Off. No, sir, no jot; I know your favour[5] well,
Though now you have no sea-cap on your head.
Take him away: he knows I know him well.

Ant. I must obey.—[*To Viola*] This comes with seeking you:

[1] *Firago*, corruption of *virago*.
[2] *Stuck*, corruption of *stoccado*, a thrust in fencing.
[3] *Duello*, the laws of the duel.
[4] *Undertaker*, intermeddler.
[5] *Favour*, face.

But there's no remedy; I shall answer it.
What will you do, now my necessity
Makes me to ask you for my purse? It grieves me
Much more for what I cannot do for you
Than what befalls myself. You stand amaz'd;
But be of comfort.

Sec Off. Come, sir, away.

Ant. I must entreat of you some of that money.

Vio. What money, sir?
For the fair kindness you have show'd me here,
And, part, being prompted by your present trouble,
Out of my lean and low ability
I'll lend you something: my having[1] is not much;
I'll make division of my present[2] with you:
Hold, there's half my coffer.

Ant. Will you deny me now?
Is't possible that my deserts to you
Can lack persuasion? Do not tempt my misery,
Lest that it makes me so unsound a man
As to upbraid you with those kindnesses
That I have done for you.

Vio. I know of none;
Nor know I you by voice or any feature:
I hate ingratitude more in a man
Than lying, vainness, babbling, drunkenness,
Or any taint of vice whose strong corruption
Inhabits our frail blood.

Ant. O heavens themselves!

Sec. Off. Come, sir, I pray you, go.

Ant. Let me speak a little. This youth that you see here
I snatch'd one half out of the jaws of death,
Reliev'd him with such sanctity of love,
And to his image, which methought did promise
Most venerable worth, did I devotion.

First Off. What's that to us? The time goes by: away!

Ant. But O how vile an idol proves this god!
Thou hast, Sebastian, done good feature shame.
In nature there's no blemish but the mind;
None can be call'd deform'd but the unkind:
Virtue is beauty; but the beauteous evil[3]
Are empty trunks o'erflourish'd by the devil.

First Off. The man grows mad: away with him!—Come, come, sir.

Ant. Lead me on. [*Exit with Officers.*

Vio. Methinks his words do from such passion fly,
That he believes himself: so do not I.
Prove true, imagination, O prove true,
That I, dear brother, be now ta'en for you!

Sir To. Come hither, knight; come hither, Fabian: we'll whisper o'er a couplet[4] or two of most sage saws. [*They go apart.*

Vio. He nam'd Sebastian: I my brother know
Yet living in my glass; even such and so
In favour was my brother; and he went
Still in this fashion, colour, ornament,
For him I imitate. O, if it prove,
Tempests are kind, and salt waves fresh in love!
[*Exit. Sir Toby, Fabian, and Sir Andrew come forward.*

Sir To. A very dishonest paltry boy, and more a coward than a hare: his dishonesty appears in leaving his friend here in necessity and denying him; and for his cowardship, ask Fabian.

Fab. A coward, a most devout coward, religious in it.

Sir And. 'Slid, I'll after him again, and beat him.

Sir To. Do; cuff him soundly, but never draw thy sword.

Sir And. An I do not,— [*Exit.*

Fab. Come, let's see the event.

Sir To. I dare lay any money 't will be nothing yet. [*Exeunt.*

ACT IV.

Scene I. *Before Olivia's house.*

Enter Sebastian *and* Clown.

Clo. Will you make me believe that I am not sent for you?

Seb. Go to, go to, thou art a foolish fellow: Let me be clear of thee.

Clo. Well held out, i' faith! No, I do not know you; nor I am not sent to you by my lady, to bid you come speak with her; nor

[1] *Having*, property. [2] *Present*, i.e. my *present* having.

[3] *Evil*, i.e. persons of evil nature. [4] *Couplet*, couple.

your name is not Master Cesario; nor is this not my nose neither. Nothing that is so is so.

Seb. I prithee, vent thy folly somewhere else:
Thou know'st not me.

Clo. Vent my folly! he has heard that word of some great man, and now applies it to a fool. Vent my folly! I am afraid this great lubber, the world, will prove a cockney. I prithee, now, ungird thy strangeness, and tell me what I shall vent to my lady: shall I vent to her that thou art coming?

Seb. I prithee, foolish Greek, depart from me:
There's money for thee: if you tarry longer,
I shall give worse payment.

Seb. [*Beating Sir Andrew*] Why, there's for thee, and there, and there!—(Act iv. 1. 28.)

Clo. By my troth, thou hast an open hand. These wise men that give fools money get themselves a good report—after fourteen years' purchase.

Enter Sir Andrew, Sir Toby, *and* Fabian.

Sir And. Now, sir, have I met you again? there's for you. [*Striking Sebastian.*

Seb. [*Beating Sir Andrew*] Why, there's for thee, and there, and there!
Are all the people mad? [*Draws his dagger.*

Sir To. [*Holding Sebastian*] Hold, sir, or I'll throw your dagger o'er the house.

Clo. This will I tell my lady straight: I would not be in some of your coats for two-pence. [*Exit.*

Sir To. Come on, sir; hold.

Sir And. Nay, let him alone: I'll go another way to work with him; I'll have an action of battery against him, if there be any law in Illyria: though I struck him first, yet it's no matter for that.

Seb. Let go thy hand.

Sir To. Come, sir, I will not let you go. Come, my young soldier, put up your iron: you are well flesh'd; come on.

Seb. I will be free from thee. [*Frees himself.*] What wouldst thou now?

If thou dar'st tempt me further, draw thy
sword. [*Draws.*

Sir To. What, what? Nay, then I must have an ounce or two of this malapert blood from you. [*Draws.*

Enter OLIVIA.

Oli. Hold, Toby; on thy life, I charge thee, hold!

Sir To. Madam!

Oli. Will it be ever thus? Ungracious wretch,
Fit for the mountains and the barbarous caves,
Where manners ne'er were preach'd! out of my sight!
Be not offended, dear Cesario.
Rudesby,[1] be gone! [*Exeunt Sir Toby, Sir Andrew, and Fabian.*
I prithee, gentle friend,
Let thy fair wisdom, not thy passion, sway
In this uncivil and unjust extent[2]
Against thy peace. Go with me to my house,
And hear thou there how many fruitless pranks
This ruffian hath botch'd up, that thou thereby
Mayst smile at this: thou shalt not choose but go:
Do not deny. Beshrew his soul for me,
He started one poor heart of mine in thee.

Seb. [*Aside*] What relish is in this? how runs the stream?
Or I am mad, or else this is a dream:
Let fancy still my sense in Lethe steep;
If it be thus to dream, still let me sleep!

Oli. Nay, come, I prithee: would thou'dst be rul'd by me!

Seb. Madam, I will.

Oli. O, say so, and so be! [*Exeunt.*

SCENE II. *Olivia's house. On one side the dark room, in which* MALVOLIO *is seen, bound: on the other side another room, into which enter* MARIA *and* CLOWN.

Mar. Nay, I prithee, put on this gown and this beard; make him believe thou art Sir Topas the curate: do it quickly; I'll call Sir Toby the whilst. [*Exit.*

Clo. Well, I'll put it on, and I will dissemble myself in't; and I would I were the first that ever dissembled in such a gown. [*Putting on gown and beard*] I am not tall enough to become the function well, nor lean enough to be thought a good student: [but to be said an honest man and a good housekeeper goes as fairly as to say a careful man and a great scholar. The competitors[3] enter.]

Re-enter MARIA *with* SIR TOBY.

Sir To. Jove bless thee, master Parson.

Clo. *Bonos dies,*[4] Sir Toby: [for, as the old hermit of Prague, that never saw pen and ink, very wittily said to a niece of King Gorboduc, "That that is is;" so I, being master Parson, am master Parson; for, what is "that" but "that," and "is" but "is"?]

Sir To. To him, Sir Topas.

Clo. [*In a feigned voice to Malvolio*] What, ho, I say! peace in this prison! [*Opening door between rooms.*

Sir To. [*Aside to Maria*] The knave counterfeits well; a good knave.

Mal. [*Within the dark room*] Who calls there?[5]

Clo. Sir Topas the curate, who comes to visit Malvolio the lunatic.

Mal. Sir Topas, Sir Topas, good Sir Topas, go to my lady.

Clo. Out, hyperbolical fiend! how vexest thou this man! talkest thou nothing but of ladies?

Sir To. Well said, master Parson.

Mal. Sir Topas, never was man thus wronged. good Sir Topas, do not think I am mad: they have laid me here in hideous darkness.

Clo. Fie, thou dishonest Satan! I call thee by the most modest terms; for I am one of those gentle ones that will use the devil himself with courtesy: say'st thou that house is dark?

Mal. As hell, Sir Topas.

Clo. Why, it hath bay-windows transparent as barricadoes, and the clear-stories toward the south-north are as lustrous as ebony; and yet complainest thou of obstruction?

Mal. I am not mad, Sir Topas: I say to you, this house is dark.

---

1 *Rudesby,* blusterer.

2 *Extent,* legal seizure; hence, attack.

3 *Competitors,* confederates.

4 *Bonos dies,* good day.

5 Malvolio speaks from the inner or dark room all through this scene.

Clo. Madman, thou errest: I say, there is no darkness but ignorance; in which thou art more puzzled than the Egyptians in their fog.

Mal. I say, this house is as dark as ignorance, though ignorance were as dark as hell; and I say, there was never man thus abus'd. I am no more mad than you are: make the trial of it in any constant[1] question.

Clo. What is the opinion of Pythagoras concerning wildfowl?

Mal. That the soul of our grandam might haply inhabit a bird.

Clo. What think'st thou of his opinion?

Mal. I think nobly of the soul, and no way approve his opinion.

Clo. Fare thee well. Remain thou still in darkness: thou shalt hold the opinion of Pythagoras ere I will allow of thy wits; and fear to kill a woodcock, lest thou dispossess the soul of thy grandam. Fare thee well.

Mal. Sir Topas, Sir Topas!

Sir To. My most exquisite Sir Topas!

Clo. Nay, I am for all waters.

Mar. Thou might'st have done this without thy beard and gown: he sees thee not.

Sir To. To him in thine own voice, and bring me word how thou find'st him: I would we were well rid of this knavery. If he may be conveniently deliver'd, I would he were; for I am now so far in offence with my niece, that I cannot pursue with any safety this sport to the upshot. Come by and by to my chamber. [*Exit with Maria.*

Clo. [*Advances and sings*]

"Hey, Robin, jolly Robin,
Tell me how thy lady does."

Mal. Fool!

Clo. "My lady is unkind, perdy."[2]

Mal. Fool!

Clo. "Alas, why is she so?"

Mal. Fool, I say!

Clo. "She loves another"—Who calls, ha?

Mal. Good fool, as ever thou wilt deserve well at my hand, help me to a candle, and pen, ink and paper: as I am a gentleman, I will live to be thankful to thee for 't.

Clo. Master Malvolio?

Mal. Ay, good fool.

Clo. Alas, sir, how fell you besides your five wits?

Mal. Fool, there was never man so notoriously abus'd: I am as well in my wits, fool, as thou art.

Clo. But as well? then you are mad indeed, if you be no better in your wits than a fool.

Mal. They have here propertied[3] me; keep me in darkness, send ministers to me, asses, and do all they can to face me out of my wits.

Clo. Advise you what you say; the minister is here. [*As Sir Topas*] Malvolio, Malvolio, thy wits the heavens restore! endeavour thyself to sleep, and leave thy vain bibble-babble.

Mal. Sir Topas!

Clo. Maintain no words with him, good fellow. [*As Clown*] Who, I, sir? not I, sir. God be wi' you, good Sir Topas! [*As Sir Topas*] Marry, amen. [*As Clown*] I will, sir, I will.

Mal. Fool, fool, fool, I say!

Clo. Alas, sir, be patient. What say you, sir? I am shent[4] for speaking to you.

Mal. Good fool, help me to some light and some paper: I tell thee, I am as well in my wits as any man in Illyria.

Clo. Well-a-day, that you were, sir!

Mal. By this hand, I am. Good fool, some ink, paper and light; and convey what I will set down to my lady: it shall advantage thee more than ever the bearing of letter did.

Clo. I will help you to 't. But tell me true, are you not mad indeed? or do you but counterfeit?

Mal. Believe me, I am not; I tell thee true.

Clo. Nay, I 'll ne'er believe a madman till I see his brains. I will fetch you light and paper and ink.

Mal. Fool, I 'll requite it in the highest degree: I prithee, be gone.

Clo. [*Sings*]

I am gone, sir,
And anon, sir,
I 'll be with you again,

[1] *Constant*, consistent, logical.

[2] *Perdy*, a corruption of *pardieu*, a common French oath.

[3] *Propertied*, made a property of, as a thing having no will of its own.

[4] *Shent*, reproved.

In a trice,
Like to the old Vice,
Your need to sustain;
[Who, with dagger of lath,
In his rage and his wrath,
Cries, ah, ha! to the devil:
Like a mad lad,
Pare thy nails, dad;
Adieu, goodman devil.] [*Exit.*

Scene III. *Olivia's garden.*

Enter Sebastian.

Seb. This is the air; that is the glorious sun;
This pearl she gave me, I do feel 't and see 't:
And though 't is wonder that enwraps me thus,
Yet 't is not madness. Where 's Antonio, then?

Seb. I 'll follow this good man, and go with you;
And, having sworn truth, ever will be true.—(Act iv. 3. 32, 33.)

I could not find him at the Elephant:
Yet there he was; and there I found this credit,[1]
That he did range the town to seek me out.
His counsel now might do me golden service,
For though my soul disputes well with my sense
That this may be some error, but no madness,
Yet doth this accident and flood of fortune
So far exceed all instance,[2] all discourse,[3]
That I am ready to distrust mine eyes,
And wrangle with my reason, that persuades me
To any other trust but that I am mad,—
Or else the lady 's mad; yet, if 't were so,
She could not sway her house, command her followers,
Take and give back affairs and their dispatch
With such a smooth, discreet and stable bearing,
As I perceive she does: there 's something in 't
That is deceivable.[4] But here the lady comes.

[1] *Credit*, intelligence. [2] *Instance*, precedent. [3] *Discourse*, reason.

[4] *Deceivable*, deceptive.

Enter Olivia and Priest.

Oli. Blame not this haste of mine. If you mean well,
Now go with me and with this holy man
Into the chantry by: there, before him,
And underneath that consecrated roof,
Plight me the full assurance of your faith;
That my most jealous and too doubtful soul
May live at peace. He shall conceal it
Whiles[1] you are willing it shall come to note,
What time we will our celebration keep
According to my birth. What do you say?

Seb. I'll follow this good man, and go with you;
And, having sworn truth, ever will be true.

Oli. Then lead the way, good father: and heavens so shine,
That they may fairly note this act of mine!
[*Exeunt.*

ACT V.

Scene 1. *Before Olivia's house.*

Enter Clown *and* Fabian.

Fab. Now, as thou lov'st me, let me see his letter.

Clo. Good Master Fabian, grant me another request.

Fab. Any thing.

Clo. Do not desire to see this letter.

Fab. This is, to give a dog, and, in recompense, desire my dog again.

Enter Duke, Viola, Curio, *and Lords.*

Duke. Belong you to the Lady Olivia, friends?

Clo. Ay, sir, we are some of her trappings.

Duke. I know thee well: how doest thou, my good fellow?

Clo. Truly, sir, the better for my foes, and the worse for my friends.

Duke. Just the contrary; the better for thy friends.

Clo. No, sir, the worse.

Duke. How can that be?

Clo. Marry, sir, they praise me, and make an ass of me; now my foes tell me plainly I am an ass: so that by my foes, sir, I profit in the knowledge of myself; and by my friends I am abused: [so that, conclusions to be as kisses, if your four negatives make your two affirmatives, why, then, the worse for my friends, and the better for my foes.]

Duke. Why, this is excellent.

Clo. By my troth, sir, no; though it please you to be one of my friends.

Duke. Thou shalt not be the worse for me: there's gold.

[*Clo.* But that it would be double-dealing, sir, I would you could make it another.

Duke. O, you give me ill counsel.

Clo. Put your grace,[2] in your pocket, sir, for this once, and let your flesh and blood obey it.

Duke. Well, I will be so much a sinner to be a double-dealer: there's another.

Clo. *Primo, secundo, tertio,* is a good play; and the old saying is, the third pays for all: the triplex, sir, is a good tripping measure; or the bells of Saint Bennet, sir, may put you in mind: one, two, three.

Duke. You can fool no more money out of me at this throw:] if you will let your lady know I am here to speak with her, and bring her along with you, it may awake my bounty further.

Clo. Marry, sir, lullaby to your bounty till I come again. [I go, sir; but I would not have you to think that my desire of having is the sin of covetousness: but,] as you say, sir, let your bounty take a nap, I will awake it anon. [*Exit.*

Vio. Here comes the man, sir, that did rescue me.

Enter Antonio *and Officers.*

Duke. That face of his I do remember well;
Yet, when I saw it last, it was besmear'd
As black as Vulcan in the smoke of war.

1 *Whiles*, until. 2 *Grace*, virtue.

[A bawbling[1] vessel was he captain of,
For shallow draught and bulk unprizable;[2]
With which such scathful[3] grapple did he make
With the most noble bottom of our fleet,
That very envy and the tongue of loss
Cried fame and honour on him. What 's the matter?]

First Off. Orsino, this is that Antonio
That took the Phœnix and her fraught from Candy;
And this is he that did the Tiger board,
When your young nephew Titus lost his leg.
[Here in the streets, desperate of shame and state,
In private brabble[4] did we apprehend him.]

Vio. He did me kindness, sir; drew on my side;
But in conclusion put strange speech upon me,—
I know not what 't was but distraction.[5]

Duke. Notable pirate! thou salt-water thief!
What foolish boldness brought thee to their mercies,
Whom thou, in terms so bloody and so dear,[6]
Hast made thine enemies?

Ant. Orsino, noble sir,
Be pleas'd that I shake off these names you give me:
Antonio never yet was thief or pirate,
Though, I confess, on base and ground enough,
Orsino's enemy. A witchcraft drew me hither:
That most ingrateful boy there by your side
From the rude sea's enrag'd and foamy mouth
Did I redeem; a wreck past hope he was:
His life I gave him, and [did thereto add
My love, without retention or restraint,
All his in dedication;] for his sake
Did I expose myself, pure[7] for his love,
Into the danger of this adverse town;
Drew to defend him when he was beset:
Where being apprehended, his false cunning,
Not meaning to partake with me in danger,
Taught him to face me out of his acquaintance,
And grew a twenty-years-removed thing
While one would wink; denied me mine own purse,
Which I had recommended to his use
Not half an hour before.

Vio. How can this be?

Duke. When came he to this town?

Ant. To-day, my lord: and for three months before,
No interim, not a minute's vacancy,
Both day and night did we keep company.

Duke. Here comes the countess: now heaven walks on earth.
But for thee, fellow,—fellow, thy words are madness:
[Three months this youth hath tended upon me;
But more of that anon. Take him aside.]

Enter OLIVIA *and Attendants.*

Oli. What would my lord, but that he may not have,
Wherein Olivia may seem serviceable?
Cesario, you do not keep promise with me.

Vio. Madam!

Duke. Gracious Olivia,—

Oli. What do you say, Cesario?—Good my lord,—

Vio. My lord would speak; my duty hushes me.

Oli. If it be aught to the old tune, my lord,
It is as fat[8] and fulsome to mine ear
As howling after music.

Duke. Still so cruel?

Oli. Still so constant, lord.

Duke. What, to perverseness? you uncivil lady,
To whose ingrate and unauspicious altars
My soul the faithfull'st offerings hath breath'd out
That e'er devotion tender'd! What shall I do?

Oli. Even what it please my lord, that shall become him.

Duke. Why should I not, had I the heart to do it,
Like to the Egyptian thief at point of death,
Kill what I love? a savage jealousy
That sometime savours nobly. But hear me this:

---

[1] *Bawbling*, like a bauble, insignificant.
[2] *Unprizable*, invaluable.
[3] *Scathful*, harmful.
[4] *Brabble*, brawl.
[5] *Distraction*, madness; pronounced as a quadrisyllable.
[6] *Dear*, heart-felt.
[7] *Pure* = purely.
[8] *Fat*, dull, cloying.

Since you to non-regardance cast my faith,
And that I partly know the instrument
That screws me from my true place in your favour,
Live you, the marble-breasted tyrant, still;
But this your minion,[1] whom I know you love,
And whom, by heaven I swear, I tender[2] dearly,
Him will I tear out of that cruel eye,
Where he sits crowned in his master's spite.
Come, boy, with me; my thoughts are ripe in mischief:
I'll sacrifice the lamb that I do love,
To spite a raven's heart within a dove. [*Going.*

Vio. And I, most jocund, apt, and willingly,
To do you rest, a thousand deaths would die. [*Following.*

Oli. [*Staying Viola*] Where goes Cesario?

Vio. After him I love
More than I love these eyes, more than my life,
More, by all mores, than e'er I shall love wife.
If I do feign, you witnesses above
Punish my life for tainting of my love!

Oli. Ay me, detested! how am I beguil'd!

Vio. Who does beguile you? who does do you wrong?

Oli. Hast thou forgot thyself? is it so long?
Call forth the holy father. [*Exit an Attendant.*

Duke. [*To Viola*] Come away!

Oli. Whither, my lord? Cesario, husband, stay.

Duke. Husband!

Oli. Ay, husband: can he that deny?

Duke. Her husband, sirrah!

Vio. No, my lord, not I.

Oli. [Alas, it is the baseness of thy fear
That makes thee strangle thy propriety:[3]]
Fear not, Cesario; take thy fortunes up;
Be that thou know'st thou art, and then thou art
As great as that thou fear'st.

Enter Priest.

O, welcome, father!
Father, I charge thee, by thy reverence,
Here to unfold, though lately we intended
To keep in darkness what occasion now
Reveals before 't is ripe, what thou dost know
Hath newly pass'd between this youth and me.

Priest. A contract of eternal bond of love,
Confirm'd by mutual joinder of your hands,
Attested by the holy close of lips,
Strengthen'd by interchangement of your rings,
And all the ceremony of this compáct
Seal'd in my function, by my testimony;
[Since when, my watch hath told me, toward my grave
I have travell'd but two hours.]

Duke. O thou dissembling cub! what wilt thou be
When time hath sow'd a grizzle on thy case?[4]
[Or will not else thy craft so quickly grow
That thine own trip shall be thine overthrow?]
Farewell, and take her; but direct thy feet
Where thou and I henceforth may never meet.

Vio. My lord, I do protest—

Oli. O, do not swear!
Hold little[5] faith, though thou hast too much fear.

Enter Sir Andrew *with his head broken.*

Sir And. For the love of God, a surgeon! Send one presently to Sir Toby.

Oli. What's the matter?

Sir And. He has broke my head across, and has given Sir Toby a bloody coxcomb too: for the love of God, your help! I had rather than forty pound I were at home.

Oli. Who has done this, Sir Andrew?

Sir And. The count's gentleman, one Cesario: we took him for a coward, but he's the very devil incardinate.

Duke. My gentleman Cesario?

Sir And. 'Od's lifelings,[6] here he is! [*To Viola*] You broke my head for nothing; and that that I did, I was set on to do't by Sir Toby.

Vio. Why do you speak to me? I never hurt you:
You drew your sword upon me without cause,
But I bespake you fair, and hurt you not.

Sir And. If a bloody coxcomb be a hurt, you have hurt me: I think you set nothing by a bloody coxcomb. Here comes Sir Toby

[1] *Minion* (Fr. *mignon*), darling, favourite.
[2] *Tender*, cherish.
[3] *Strangle thy propriety*, i.e. disown what thou really art.
[4] *Case*, skin.
[5] *Little*, i.e. a little.
[6] *'Od's lifelings*, corruption and diminutive of *God's life*.

halting; you shall hear more: but if he had not been in drink, he would have tickled you othergates[1] than he did.

Enter SIR TOBY *with his head broke, and* CLOWN.

Duke. How now gentleman! how is't with you?

Sir To. That's all one: 'has hurt me, and there's the end on't. Sot, didst see Dick surgeon, sot?

Clo. O, he's drunk, Sir Toby, an hour agone: his eyes were set at eight i' the morning.

Sir To. Then he's a rogue and a passy measures pavin: I hate a drunken rogue.

Oli. Away with him! Who hath made this havoc with them?

Sir And. I'll help you, Sir Toby, because we'll be dress'd together.

Sir To. Will you help? an ass-head and a coxcomb and a knave! a thin-faced knave, a gull!

Oli. Get him to bed, and let his hurt be look'd to.

[*Exeunt Clown, Fabian, Sir Toby, and Sir Andrew.*

Enter SEBASTIAN.

[*All start at sight of Sebastian.*

Seb. I am sorry, madam, I have hurt your kinsman;
But, had it been the brother of my blood,
I must have done no less with wit and safety.
[You throw a strange regard upon me, and by that
I do perceive it hath offended you:
Pardon me, sweet one, even for the vows
We made each other but so late ago.]

Duke. [*Points to Sebastian and Viola*] One face, one voice, one habit, and two persons!
A natural perspective, that is and is not!

Seb. Antonio, O my dear Antonio!
How have the hours rack'd and tortur'd me,
Since I have lost thee!

Ant. Sebastian are you?

Seb. Fear'st thou that, Antonio?

Ant. How have you made division of yourself? [*Points to Viola.*

[1] *Othergates*, otherwise.

An apple, cleft in two, is not more twin
Than these two creatures. Which is Sebastian?

Oli. Most wonderful!

Seb. Do I stand there? I never had a brother;
Nor can there be that deity in my nature,

Enter SIR TOBY *with his head broke, and* CLOWN.—(Act v. 1. 199.)

Of here and every where. I had a sister,
Whom the blind waves and surges have devour'd.
[*To Viola*] Of charity, what kin are you to me?
What countryman? what name? what parentage?

Vio. Of Messaline: Sebastian was my father;
Such a Sebastian was my brother too;

So went he suited[1] to his watery tomb:
[If spirits can assume both form and suit,
You come to fright us.]

Seb. [A spirit I am indeed,
But am in that dimension grossly clad
Which from the womb I did participate.]
Were you a woman, as the rest goes even,
I should my tears let fall upon your cheek,
And say, "Thrice-welcome, drowned Viola!"

[*Vio.* My father had a mole upon his brow.

Seb. And so had mine.

Vio. And died that day when Viola from her birth
Had number'd thirteen years.

Seb. O, that record[2] is lively in my soul!
He finished, indeed, his mortal act
That day that made my sister thirteen years.]

Vio. If nothing lets[3] to make us happy both
But this my masculine usurp'd attire,
Do not embrace me till each circumstance
Of place, time, fortune, do cohere and jump[4]
That I am Viola: [which to confirm,
I'll bring you to a captain in this town,
Where lie my maiden weeds;[5] by whose gentle help
I was preserv'd to serve this noble count.
All the occurrence of my fortune since
Hath been between this lady and this lord.

Seb. [*To Olivia*] So comes it, lady, you have been mistook:
But nature to her bias drew in that.
You would have been contracted to a maid;
Now are you therein, by my life, deceiv'd,
You are betroth'd both to a maid and man.]

Duke. [Be not amaz'd; right noble is his blood.]
If this be so, as yet the glass seems true,
I shall have share in this most happy wreck.
[*To Viola*] Boy, thou hast said to me a thousand times
Thou never shouldst love woman like to me.

Vio. And all those sayings will I over-swear,
And all those swearings keep as true in soul
As doth that orbed continent[6] the fire
That severs day from night.

Duke. Give me thy hand;
And let me see thee in thy woman's weeds.

Vio. The captain that did bring me first on shore
Hath my maid's garments: he upon some action
Is now in durance, at Malvolio's suit,
A gentleman and follower of my lady's.

Oli. He shall enlarge him: fetch Malvolio hither:
And yet, alas, now I remember me,
They say, poor gentleman, he's much distract.
[A most extracting frenzy of mine own
From my remembrance clearly banish'd his.]

Re-enter CLOWN *with a letter, and* FABIAN.

[*To Clown*] How does he, sirrah?

Clo. Truly, madam, he holds Beelzebub at the stave's end as well as a man in his case may do: 'has here writ a letter to you; [I should have given't you to-day morning, but as a madman's epistles are no gospels, so it skills[7] not much when they are deliver'd.]

Oli. Open't, and read it.

Clo. Look, then, to be well edified when the fool delivers the madman. [*Shouting*] "By the Lord, madam!"...

Oli. How now! art thou mad?

Clo. No, madam, I do but read madness: [an your ladyship will have it as it ought to be, you must allow *Vox*.[8]

Oli. Prithee, read i' thy right wits.

Clo. So I do, madonna; but to read his right wits is to read thus: therefore perpend,[9] my princess, and give ear.]

Oli. [*To Fabian*] Read it you, sirrah.

Fab. [*Reads*] "By the Lord, madam, you wrong me, and the world shall know it. Though you have put me into darkness and given your drunken cousin rule over me, yet have I the benefit of my senses as well as your ladyship. I have your own letter that induced me to the semblance I put on; with the which I doubt not but to do myself much right, or you much shame. Think of me as you please. I leave my duty a little unthought of, and speak out of my injury. THE MADLY-US'D MALVOLIO."

Oli. Did he write this?

Clo. Ay, madam.

Duke. This savours not much of distraction.

Oli. See him deliver'd, Fabian; bring him hither. [*Exit Fabian.*

[1] *Suited*, dressed.
[2] *Record*, remembrance.
[3] *Lets*, hinders.
[4] *Jump*, agree.
[5] *Weeds*, garments.
[6] *That orbed continent*, i.e. the sun.
[7] *Skills*, matters.
[8] *Vox*, i.e. a voice in keeping; a loud and frantic tone.
[9] *Perpend*, consider.

My lord, so please you, these things further thought on,
To think me as well a sister as a wife,
One day shall crown the alliance on 't, so please you,
Here at my house, and at my proper cost.[1]

Duke. Madam, I am most apt to embrace your offer.
[*To Viola*] Your master quits you; and, for your service done him,
[So much against the mettle of your sex,
So far beneath your soft and tender breeding,
And since you call'd me master for so long,]
Here is my hand: you shall from this time be
Your master's mistress.

Oli. A sister! you are she.

Cl. [*Sings*] When that I was and a little tiny boy,
With hey, ho, the wind and the rain.—(Act v. 1. 398, 399.)

Re-enter FABIAN, *with* MALVOLIO.

Duke. Is this the madman?

Oli. Ay, my lord, this same.
How now, Malvolio!

Mal. Madam, you have done me wrong,
Notorious wrong.

Oli. Have I, Malvolio? no.

Mal. Lady, you have. Pray you, peruse that letter:
You must not now deny it is your hand:
Write from it if you can, in hand or phrase;
Or say 't is not your seal, not your invention:
You can say none of this. Well, grant it then,
And tell me, in the modesty of honour,
Why you have given me such clear lights of favour,
Bade me come smiling and cross-garter'd to you,
To put on yellow stockings and to frown
Upon Sir Toby and the lighter people;
And, acting this in an obedient hope,
Why have you suffer'd me to be imprison'd,
Kept in a dark house, visited by the priest,
And made the most notorious geck[2] and gull
That e'er invention play'd on? Tell me why.

Oli. Alas, Malvolio, this is not my writing,
Though, I confess, much like the character:
But out of question 't is Maria's hand.
And now I do bethink me, it was she
First told me thou wast mad: then cam'st[3] in smiling,
And in such forms which here were presuppos'd
Upon thee in the letter. Prithee, be content:
This practice[4] hath most shrewdly pass'd upon thee;
But, when we know the grounds and authors of it,
Thou shalt be both the plaintiff and the judge
Of thine own cause.

[1] *My proper cost*, my own expense.

[2] *Geck*, dupe. [3] *Cam'st* = thou cam'st. [4] *Practice*, trick.

Fab. Good madam, hear me speak;
And let no quarrel nor no brawl to come
Taint the condition of this present hour,
Which I have wonder'd at. In hope it shall not,
Most freely I confess, myself and Toby
Set this device against Malvolio here,
Upon[1] some stubborn and uncourteous parts
We had conceiv'd against him: Maria writ
The letter at Sir Toby's great importance;[2]
In recompense whereof he hath married her.
How with a sportful malice it was follow'd,
May rather pluck on[3] laughter than revenge,
If that the injuries be justly weigh'd
That have on both sides pass'd.

Oli. Alas, poor fool, how have they baffled[4] thee!

Clo. Why, "some are born great, some achieve greatness, and some have greatness thrown upon them." I was one, sir, in this interlude; one Sir Topas, sir; but that's all one. "By the Lord, fool, I am not mad!" But do you remember? "Madam, why laugh you at such a barren rascal? an you smile not, he's gagg'd." And thus the whirligig of time brings in his revenges.

Mal. I'll be reveng'd on the whole pack of you. [*Exit.*

Oli. He hath been most notoriously abus'd.

[1] *Upon*, in consequence of.
[2] *Importance*, importunity.
[3] *Pluck on*, excite.
[4] *Baffled*, treated contemptuously.

Duke. Pursue him, and entreat him to a peace.
He hath not told us of the captain yet:
When that is known, and golden time convents,[5]
A solemn combination shall be made
Of our dear souls. Meantime, sweet sister,
We will not part from hence. Cesario, come;
For so you shall be, while you are a man;
But when in other habits you are seen,
Orsino's mistress and his fancy's[6] queen.
[*Exeunt all, except Clown.*

Cl. [*Sings*]
When that I was and a little tiny boy,
With hey, ho, the wind and the rain,
A foolish thing was but a toy,
For the rain it raineth every day.

But when I came to man's estate,
With hey, ho, the wind and the rain,
'Gainst knaves and thieves men shut their gate,
For the rain it raineth every day.

But when I came, alas, to wive,
With hey, ho, the wind and the rain,
By swaggering could I never thrive,
For the rain it raineth every day.

But when I came unto my beds,
With hey, ho, the wind and the rain,
With toss-pots still had drunken heads,
For the rain it raineth every day.

A great while ago the world begun,
With hey, ho, the wind and the rain,
But that's all one, our play is done,
And we'll strive to please you every day.
[*Exit.*

[5] *Convents*, suits (or invites).
[6] *Fancy's*, love's.

NOTES TO TWELFTH NIGHT.

ACT I. Scene 1.

1. Line 5: *O, it came o'er my ear like the sweet* SOUND.—So in Ff. Pope substituted *south*, and has been followed by Dyce, Cowden Clarke, Singer, and many editors. Surely this is a very unnecessary emendation. "*Sound*," as Grant White remarks, "appears in the authentic text, and, to say the least, is comprehensible and appropriate, and is therefore not to be disturbed, except by those who think that Shakespeare must have written that which they think best." But we may go further than this, and contend that *sound* is decidedly superior to *south*. The allusion to the *sound* or murmur of the breeze as it passes over the flowers is dexterously combined with a reference to the odours caught and carried from the flowers by the breeze: the metonymy by which it is apparently the *sound* that "steals and gives" the "odours" is thoroughly Shakespearean.

2. Line 21: *That instant was I turn'd into a* HART.—The play on sound is sufficiently obvious; it may be compared with the melancholy punning of the dying Gaunt on his own name (Rich. II. ii. 1. 73-87)—both little flights of fancy by which a sad man strives to blunt the edge of his sorrow. The allusion in the next two lines is of course to the story of Diana and Actaeon; suggested, possibly, as Malone thinks, by a sonnet of Daniel's (Sonnets to Delia, 1594, No. v.: "My thoughts, like hounds, pursue me to my death"), who in turn may have derived his comparison from Whitney's Emblems, 1586, and Whitney his from

the dedication of Adlington's Translation of the Golden Ass of Apuleius, 1566.

3. Line 20: *The element itself, till seven years'* HEAT.—Rowe altered *heat* into *hence*, and his reading is adopted and defended by Dyce. Schmidt explains the word as a substantive meaning a course at a race; *i.e.* "till seven years have run their course." Johnson would understand *heat* as a participle, signifying "heated" (compare King John, iv. 1. 61: "though *heat* red-hot"), which gives but indifferent sense. It is best to take it in its simplest sense—"till seven years' heat have passed."

4. Line 27: *Shall not behold her face at* AMPLE VIEW.—Compare Troilus and Cressida, iii. 3. 89, where "at ample point" is used for "in full measure."

5. Lines 35, 36:

How will she love, when the rich golden shaft
Hath kill'd the flock of all affections else.

Compare Midsummer Night's Dream, i. 1. 169, 170:

I swear to thee, by Cupid's strongest bow,
By his best *arrow with the golden head.*

See note 30 on that play. The allusion to the gold and leaden tipped arrows of Cupid is a common one, particularly in Massinger.

6. Line 36: *the flock of all affections.*—Cf. Sidney's Arcadia, book first: "*the flocke of vnspeakable vertues* laid up delightfully in that best builded folde" (ed. 1590, leaf 2, verso).

7. Lines 37–39:

when liver, brain, and heart,
These sovereign thrones, are all supplied, and fill'd
Her sweet perfections, with one self king!

F. reads:

When Liuer, Braine, and Heart,
These soueraigne thrones, are all supply'd and fill'd
Her sweet perfections with one selfe king.

The words, *her sweet perfections*, are usually taken as an exclamatory parenthesis, referring to *thrones*. Capell substituted *perfection*, taking the word to mean her husband (compare King John, ii. 1. 440, and the passages quoted from Froissart, Overbury, and Donne in Rolfe). The Cambridge edd. insert a comma after *supplied*, which is a step in the right direction. Furnivall and Stone, in their Old-Spelling Shakespeare, add another comma after *perfections*, which may be accepted as the simplest, clearest, and most probable conjecture yet made. Pointed in this way, the sense of the passage is, "when these sovereign thrones are supplied, and her sweet perfections filled, with one self king." For *self* compare Lear, iv. 3. 36, 37:

Else one *self* mate and mate could not beget
Such different issues.

ACT I. Scene 2.

8. Line 2: *This is* ILLYRIA, *lady.*—Peter Heylyn gives a detailed account of *Illyria* in his Cosmographie, 1652, bk. ii. p. 92. I extract a few sentences: "Contado di Zara, or the Countrie of Zara, called anciently Liburnia, and *Illyris* specially so named, is bounded on the East with Dalmatia, on the West with Histria, on the North with Croatia, and on the South with the Adriatick Sea, or Golfe of Venice. It took this latter name (the former being long discontinued) from Zara, the chief town thereof, the Jadera of Ptolemie and the Ancients; a Roman Colonie at that time, now an Archbishops See; enjoying a safe and large Port, situate on a low Chersonese thrusting out like a Promontorie into the Adriatick; belonging to the State of Venice, by whom well fenced and fortified against forein invasions. . . . The ancient name of this Country was Liburnia, as before is said, but extending more Northwards beyond the mountains of Ardium or Scardonici; this and Dalmatia being then the Membra dividentia of the whole Illyricum."

9. Line 6: *It is* "PERCHANCE" *that you yourself were saved.*—Following the Old-Spelling Shakespeare I have put *perchance* in inverted commas, to show better the play upon words—*perchance* here meaning "by chance."

10. Line 10: THOSE *poor number.*—Changed by Capell to *this.* The alteration is unnecessary. Shakespeare evidently regarded *number* as plural.

11. Line 14: *a strong mast that* LIV'D *upon the sea.*—Compare the phrase still used of a vessel: "No boat could *live* in such a sea." Aldis Wright quotes Admiral Smyth, The Sailor's Wordbook: "To *Live.* To be able to withstand the fury of the elements; said of a boat or ship," &c. (Clarendon Press ed. p. 81).

12. Line 15: *like Arion on the dolphin's back.*—Ff., by an obvious misprint, read *Orion.* The allusion is to the story of the poet and musician Arion, who, having gained much treasure in a musical contest in Sicily, was in fear of death from the sailors as he returned on board ship to Corinth; but obtaining leave for one last song, he, as soon as it was finished, threw himself into the sea, and was borne to land on the back of one of the dolphins who had gathered round for delight in his music.

13. Line 30: *for whose dear* LOVE.—Walker unnecessarily altered *love* to *loss*, and Dyce unreasonably declared, in adopting the emendation, that it was "*made certain* by other passages of Shakespeare," which he gives.

14. Lines 40, 41:

she hath abjur'd the COMPANY
AND SIGHT *of men.*

Hanmer's emendation, adopted by most editors. The Ff. read:

she hath abiur'd the *sight*
And company of men.

15. Lines 43, 44:

Till I had made mine own occasion mellow
What my estate is!

So Ff. Most editors introduce a comma after *mellow*, and understand, with Johnson, "I wish I might not be made public to the world, with regard to the state of my birth and fortune, till I have gained a ripe opportunity for my design;" or, with Clarke, "till I have myself prepared the occasion for declaring what my condition really is." The Old-Spelling editors retain the reading of the Ff., taking *mellow* as a verb, and understanding, "till I had made my service improve my present bad condition."

16. Line 56: *Thou shalt present me as an* EUNUCH *to him.*—As Malone notes, "Viola was presented to the

duke as a *page*, not as a *eunuch*, which would have been inconsistent with the course of the play."

17. Line 50: *That will* ALLOW *me very worth his service.* --Shakespeare often uses *allow* in the sense of "acknowledge," but only here with the meaning, "cause to be acknowledged," or approve.

ACT I. Scene 3.

18. Line 5: *your* COUSIN, *my lady.*—*Cousin* was frequently used in the general sense of relation (see the list of Shakespeare references in Schmidt). Coles, in his Latin Dictionary, renders *cousin* by *consanguineus*.

19. Line 7: *except before excepted.*—This is a legal phrase (*exceptis excipiendis*), which Halliwell illustrates from West's Symboleography, 1594 (part 1. book 2, sect. 444): "and the said R. . . . shall and may peaceably & quietly haue, hold, occupie, and inioy all the said Church, Rectorie, and Parsonage, mansion house, cottage, glebe landes, tithes, and all other the demised tenementes and premisses with the appurtenances (*except before excepted*) according to the true meaning of these presentes" (edn. 1594, vol. i. leaf E E, 4).

20. Line 30: *almost natural.*—Dyce reads *all most natural*, and gives as authorities Upton and Collier's MS. Corrector. It is a needless change, and a change for the worse. The meaning is "almost naturally," in its double sense of by nature and like a natural, or idiot.

21. Line 43: *coystril.*—"Properly, an inferior groom, or a lad employed by the esquire to carry the knight's arms and other necessaries. Probably from *coustillier*, Old French, of the same signification. See Cotgrave. It is surely not a corruption of *kestrel*, as Mr. Todd and others have supposed."—Nares' Glossary, 1867, *s.v.* "*Coistril*, or *Coystril*." Cotgrave has: "*Coustillier*: M. An Esquire of the bodie; an Armourbearer vnto a Knight; the seruant of a man at Armes; also, a groome of a stable, a horse-keeper." Above he has: "*Coustille*: f. A kind of long Pouniard, vsed heretofore by Esquires." A *Coustillier* is perhaps one who bears a *coustille*. See the note in the Clarendon Press edition of Twelfth Night, pp. 84, 85.

22. Line 44: *like a parish-top.*—"A large top was formerly kept in every village, to be whipped in frosty weather, that the peasants might be kept warm by exercise, and out of mischief, when they could not work" (Steevens).

23. Line 45: Castiliano vulgo!—"Spanish of Sir Toby's own making, good enough to impose on Maria and Sir Andrew, and very unnecessarily changed to *Castiliano volto* by some modern editors" (Schmidt). Warburton, who proposed the reading *volto*, took the phrase to mean: "Put on your Castilian countenance, *i.e.* grave serious looks;" the Spaniards being famed for a solemnity which was thought to carry craftiness enough beneath it. Aldis Wright compares, "for a similar bacchanalian shout, Marlowe, Jew of Malta, iv. 5: 'Hey, *Rivo Castiliano!* a man's a man' (Works, ed. Dyce, 1862, p. 172); and I. Henry IV. ii. 4. 124: '*Rivo!* says the drunkard" (Clarendon Press ed. p. 85).

24. Line 52: *Accost.*—Cotgrave has: "*Accoster.* To accoast, or ioine side to side; to approach or draw neere vnto; also, to wax acquainted, or grow familiar with."

25. Line 73: "*thought is free.*"—An allusion to Lyly's Euphues, 1581: "A noble man in Sienna, disposed to iest with a gentlewoman of meane birth, yet excellent qualities, between game and earnest gan thus to salute hir. 'I know not how I shold commend your beautie, because it is somewhat too brown, nor your stature being somewhat to low, and of your wit I can not iudge.' 'no,' quoth she, 'I beleeue you, for none can iudge of wit, but they that haue it,' 'why then,' quoth he, 'doest thou thinke me a foole,' '*thought is free* my Lord,' quoth she, 'I wil not take you at your word'" (Arber's Reprint, p. 281). The phrase is found in Gower. See Confessio Amantis, book v.:

> I haue heard said, that *thought is free.*
>
> —Ed. Pauli, ii. 277.

26. Line 74: *bring your hand to the buttery-bar and let it drink.*—"A proverbial phrase among forward Abigails, to ask at once for a kiss and a present" (Dr. Kenrick).

27. Line 77: *It's dry, sir.*—A dry hand was formerly considered a sign of bodily weakness, or of a disposition not prone to love. Compare Othello, iii. 4. 36–38:

> *Oth.* Give me your hand: this hand is moist, my lady.
> *Des.* It yet hath felt no age nor known no sorrow.
> *Oth.* This argues fruitfulness and liberal heart.

28. Line 90: *I am a great* EATER OF BEEF.—Compare Troilus and Cressida, ii. 1. 14: "thou mongrel *beef-witted* lord!" It seems, from the passages cited by Halliwell and Aldis Wright, that beef was considered both a "grosse diot," and one tending to melancholy. See the latter part of note 160 to the Taming of the Shrew.

29. Line 100: *Then hadst thou had an excellent head of hair.*—The joke is an allusion to Sir Andrew's previous remark, "I would that I had bestowed that time in the *tongues* that I have in fencing," &c. Sir Toby's imagination "seizes upon Sir Andrew's *tongues* and converts them into *tongs*—curling-tongs—the very article required in Sir Andrew's toilet to 'mend' his hair withal, which, without their assistance, hung 'like flax on a distaff,' and most persistently and stubbornly refused to 'curl by *nature*'" (Joseph Crosby, article on Shakespeare's Puns in the American Bibliopolist, June 1875).

30. Line 105: *curl by nature.*—This is Theobald's emendation. The Ff. read *coole my nature.*

31. Line 122: *Art thou good at these* KICKSHAWSES, *knight?*—Some editors read *kickshaws*; but the plural seems to add a point to the fooling. It is used again in the Ff. of II. Henry IV. v. 1. 29. The word is a corruption of *quelque chose*, and it is spelt by Cotgrave, *s.v.* "Fricandeaux," *Quelkchoses*. In F. 1 it is printed *kickechawses*.

32. Line 126: *and yet I will not compare with* AN OLD MAN.—Theobald proposed to read *a nobleman*, understanding the allusion to be to Orsino ("it's four to one she'll none of me: the count himself here hard by woos her," lines 112–114, above). The change is quite unjustifiable. Of the phrase as it stands, Clarke's is perhaps the

best attempt at explanation: "We take its signification to be, that the knight by the term '*an old man*' means 'a man of experience,' just as he has before deferred to 'his betters;' while the use of the word 'old' gives precisely that absurd effect of refraining from competing in dancing, fencing, etc., with exactly the antagonist incapacitated by age, over whom even Sir Andrew might hope to prove his superiority" (Cassell's Illustrated Shakespeare, *ad loc.*).

33. Line 128: *What is thy excellence in a* GALLIARD, *knight?*—Aldis Wright (Clarendon Press ed. p. 87) quotes Barnaby Riche his Farewell to Militarie profession (p. 4, Shakespeare Soc. ed.): "Our galliardes are so curious, that thei are not for my daunsyng, for thei are so full of trickes and tournes, that he which hath no more but the plaine sinquepace, is no better accompted of them then a verie bungler."

34. Line 131: *back-trick.*—A caper backwards in dancing; perhaps a quibble; the trick of going back in a fight (Schmidt).

35. Line 135: *Mistress Mall's picture.*—"No doubt a mere impersonation, like 'my lady's eldest son' in Much Ado About Nothing, ii. 1. 10. She is merely a type of any lady solicitous for the preservation of her charms even when transferred to canvas" (Singer). Schmidt gives the rather far-fetched suggestion that "perhaps Sir Toby means only to say: like a picture intended for a beauty but in fact representing Mall the kitchen-wench." That no allusion can be intended to Mall Cutpurse (Mary Frith, born 1589), the notorious heroine of Day's lost comedy of 1610, and Middleton and Dekker's Roaring Girl, 1611, is evident from the date of the play (1601 probably).

36. Line 145: *a* DAM'D-COLOUR'D *stock.*—So Ff. Rowe suggested *flame-coloured* (cf. "*flame-coloured* taffeta," I. Henry IV. i. 2. 11), and his reading has been generally adopted; Knight reads *damask-coloured*, and is followed by Delius. The Old-Spelling Shakespeare preserves the reading of the F., from which I see no reason to deviate. Sir Andrew is a little peculiar in his phrases, and it would be a pity to reduce him to a mere respectable level of verbal propriety. Probably he got his word, more or less consciously, from the French. Cotgrave has "*couleur d'enfer*, a darke and smoakie browne."

37. Line 146: *Taurus.*—"In that classic annual, The Old Farmer's Almanac, may still be seen the ancient astronomical figure of the human body with lines radiating from its various parts to the symbols of the zodiacal signs; and in the column devoted to the 'moon's place' in the calendar pages the names of the parts of the body are given instead of the corresponding signs. It is to be noted that Sir Andrew and Sir Toby are both wrong in the parts they assign to *Taurus*. The latter either burlesques the other's ignorance, or takes advantage of it for the sake of argument. *Taurus* was supposed to govern the neck and throat" (Rolfe). Compare Chaucer, Astrolabe: "and euerich of thise 12 signes hath respecte to a certein parcelle of the body of a man and hath it in gouernance; as aries hath thin head, and *taurus* thy nekke and thy throte | gemyni thyn armholes and thin armes, and so forth" (Early English Text Society ed. p. 13).

ACT I. Scene 4.

38. Line 9: *Here comes the* COUNT.—Shakespeare seems to have forgotten that in i. 2. 25 he has called Orsino a *duke;* and as *count* he appears in the rest of the play.

39. Lines 13, 14:

> *I have unclasp'd*
> *To thee the book even of my secret soul.*

This metaphor, which is pretty obvious, is found several times in Shakespeare. Browning uses a very similar expression in The Inn Album, p. 93:

> I'll so far open you *the locked and shelved*
> *Volume, my soul*, that you desire to see.

40. Line 28: *Than in a* NUNCIO'S *of more grave aspect.*—Theobald, with needless grammatical precision, reads *nuntio.*

41. Lines 32, 33:

> *thy small* PIPE
> *Is as the maiden's organ, shrill and sound.*

Compare Coriolanus, iii. 2. 112-115:

> my throat of war be turn'd,
> Which quired with my drum, into a *pipe*,
> Small as an eunuch, or the virgin voice
> That babies lulls asleep!

Coles (Latin Dictionary) has "Puellatorius, a, um, *childishly, maidenly.* Tibia puellatoria, *a shrill pipe.*"

ACT I. Scene 5.

[This scene is scene 1 of act ii. in the acting-version.—F. A. M.]

42. Line 6: *fear no colours.*—Probably a military term meaning to fear no enemy. Cotgrave has: "*Adventureux*, hazardous, adventurous, that *feares no colours.*" The phrase is often used by the Elizabethan dramatists.

43. Line 9: *A good* LENTEN *answer.*—That is, dry and scanty, like lenten fare. Compare "*lenten* entertainment," Hamlet, ii. 2. 329.

44. Line 24: *on two* POINTS, &c.—*Points* were tagged laces, used to tie the breeches (*gaskins*, or galligaskins) to the doublet. The play on words is very obvious. It is used again in I. Henry IV. ii. 4. 238.

45. Line 34: *you were best.*—Compare Julius Cæsar, iii. 3. 13: "Ay and truly, *you were best.*" The construction (like that in "if you please") was very common; compare Whetstone, Promos and Cassandra, iv. 1. 9: "Be packing both, and that betymes, *you are best.*"

46. Line 39: *Quinapalus.*—The clown is not the only humorist who, for variety, will father his wit or his wisdom upon an apocryphal philosopher—Quinapalus or Sauerteig.

47. Line 62: *that's as much to say as.*—So Ff. Many editors read "that's as much as to say," unnecessarily, as both forms were used in Shakespeare's time, and by Shakespeare (*e.g.* II. Henry VI. iv. 2. 18: "which is *as much to say as*," &c.).

48. Line 66: *Dexteriously.*—So in F. 1. The mispronunciation is no doubt intentional, though some editors have been careful to smoothen it over, after the fashion of

F. 4, which reads *dexterously*. Aldis Wright (Clarendon Press ed. p. 93) quotes two examples (one from Bacon) of the word actually being printed *dexteriously*.

49. Line 69: *good my* MOUSE *of virtue.*—*Mouse* was used as a term of endearment. Compare Hamlet, iii. 4. 183: "call you his *mouse*." The French colloquial use of *mon chat* is very similar. Compare Guy de Maupassant, La Maison Tellier, p. 288: "Il lui demanda d'une voix très douce . . . Elle repondit:—'Oui, *mon chat*.'"

50. Lines 94-96: *I protest, I take these wise men, that crow so at these set kind of fools, no better than the fools' zanies.*—Capell, preferring grammar to Shakespeare, would read (for *no better*) *to be no better*. *Zany* is derived from the Italian *zane*, which Florio renders: "Zane, the name of Iohn [*i.e.* in the Venetian dialect]. Also a sillie Iohn, a gull, a noddie. Vsed also for a simple vice, clowne, foole, or simple fellowe in a plaie or comedie." Cotgrave has: "*Zanit:* m. *A Vice to a Tumbler, &c, or in a Play.*" The Clarendon Press editor quotes Ben Jonson, Every Man Out of His Humour, iv. 1:

> He's like a tumbler,
> That tries tricks after him, to make men laugh;

and Cynthia's Revels, ii. 1: "The other gallant is his *zany*, and doth most of these tricks after him." Shakespeare uses the word only here and in Love's Labour's Lost, v. 2. 463: "some please-man, some slight *zany*."

51. Line 96: *no better.*—Capell, preferring grammar to Shakespeare, would read *to be no better.*

52. Lines 105, 106: *Mercury endue thee with leasing;* *i.e.* give thee the gift of lying. Compare Chaucer, Knightes Tale, 1069:

> Charmes and force, *lesynges* and flaterye.

Aldis Wright remarks with dry humour: "Warburton, who was afterwards a bishop, read '*pleasing*.' But Mercury, as the patron of thieves and cheating, may be supposed to have had the power of endowing his devotees with a faculty which was of the first importance to them" (Clarendon Press ed. p. 95).

53. Line 115: *he speaks nothing but madman.*—Compare Henry V. v. 2. 156: "I speak to thee plain soldier."

54. Lines 122, 123: *for here he comes, one of thy kin, has a most weak* pia mater.—The Ff. read: "for here he comes. One of thy kin has a most weak *Pia-mater*." The reading in the text is that of the Old-Spelling editors; *has* of course=*who* has; as *desires* in line 108 above. The Cambridge edd. read: "For,—here he comes,—one of thy kin has," &c. Rolfe adopts the emendation; Dyce, who omits *he*, observes that the reading "would have surprised Shakespeare." *Pia mater* is referred to again in Troilus and Cressida, ii. 1. 77; also, probably, in Love's Labour's Lost, iv. 2. 71. Aldis Wright quotes from Burton, Anatomy of Melancholy, part i. sec. i. mem. 2, subs. 5: "Nature hath covered it [the brain] with a skull of hard bone, and two skins or membranes, whereof the one is called *dura mater*, or *meninx*, the other *pia mater*. The *dura mater* is next to the skull, above the other, which includes and protects the brain. When this is taken away, the *pia mater* is to be seen, a thin membrane, the next and immediate cover of the brain, and not covering only, but entering into it."

55. Line 129: *these pickle-herring.*—This is an example of the singular form used in the plural, as in *trout, deer*, &c.

56. Line 140: *above* HEAT.—That is, says Schmidt, *thirst*. Compare King John, iii. 1. 341, 342:

> A rage whose *heat* hath this condition,
> That nothing can allay, nothing but blood.

Steevens understands it as the proper degree of warmth.

57. Line 142: *Go thou and seek the* CROWNER.—*Crowner* for *coroner* is employed again in the churchyard scene in Hamlet, v. 1. 4; and, below, line 24, "*crowner's* quest law." "*Crowner's* quest" is still used in the country for coroner's inquest.

58. Line 157: *sheriff's post.*—This was the name given to painted posts set up at the sheriffs' doors, to which notices and proclamations were affixed. Warburton quotes Ben Jonson, Every Man Out of His Humour, iii. 3:

> How long should I be ere I should put off
> To the lord chancellor's tomb, or the *shrives' posts*?

59. Line 168: IN *standing water.*—Capell, followed by Dyce, &c., reads *e'en*. The meaning is, between ebb and flow.

60. Line 211: *If you be* NOT *mad.*—So Ff. Mason proposed to omit *not*, and is followed by many editors. In defence of the F. reading Clarke says: "We believe Shakespeare means Olivia to say, 'If you are not quite without reason, begone; if you have some reason, be brief, that you may soon be gone;' giving the effect of antithetical construction without actually being so."

61. Line 218: *Some mollification for your* GIANT, *sweet lady.*—Maria was a little person, as pert waiting-maids usually are. See below, ii. 5. 16: "Here comes the little villain;" and iii. 2. 70: "Look, where the youngest wren of nine comes." The transposition of sense is quite enough for the purpose (as Falstaff, II. Henry IV. i. 2. 1, addresses his page, "Sirrah, you *giant*"); but, perhaps, as some have thought, there is a further allusion to the household giants in old romances, who acted as guardians of the heroines.

62. Lines 219, 220: Vio. . . . *Tell me your mind: I am a messenger.*—So Ff. Warburton, followed by many editors, gives the earlier clause to Olivia, and prints thus:

> *Ol.* . . . Tell me your mind.
> *Vio.* I am a messenger.

"Viola, I think," Mr. W. G. Stone writes me, "speaks impatiently, eager to hear Olivia's mind, and discharge the irksome part of messenger; a duty which is retarded by Maria's resolve to be pleasant. The connection in Viola's mind between Maria's obstruction and the wished-for answer from Olivia is, I fancy, so close as to warrant us in following the F.'s arrangement of the sentence."

63. Line 252: *such a one I was* THIS PRESENT.—So Ff.; and to be understood, "*this* (*sc.* woman) *present*, *i.e.* before you" (Old-Spelling Shakespeare). Many emendations have been proposed.

64. Line 261: *And leave the world no copy.*—This thought is developed in the 3rd, 9th, and 13th of Shakespeare's sonnets.

65. Line 274: *With adorations, fertile tears.*—So Ff.

Pope reads: "With adorations, *with* fertile tears;" and his reading is accepted by most editors, though not by the Cambridge or the Old-Spelling. Possibly, as the former suggest, something is lost before *adorations; with*, if admitted, would force us to say *adoratiöns*.

66. Line 289: *Write loyal* CANTONS *of contemned love.*—*Cantons* has been needlessly altered by Capell to *canzons*, by Rowe to *cantos*. Heywood describes his Troia Britannica: or, Great Britaines Troy, 1609, as "a Poem deuided into xvii seuerall *cantons*;" and on the second page of the address "to the two-fold Readers" he says: "I haue taskt my selfe to such succinctnesse and breuity, that in the iudiciall perusall of these fewe *Cantons* (with the Scolies annexed) as little time shall bee hazzarded, as profite from them be any way expected." Compare The London Prodigal, 1605, iii. 2: "What-do-you-call-him hath it there in his third *canton*" (Tauchnitz ed. p. 247).

67. Line 291: *Halloo your name to the* REVERBERATE *hills.*—*Reverberate* is here obviously used in the sense of "reverberant." For an instance of a participle similarly formed compare Coriolanus, i. 1. 106: "mutually *participate* [= participant]." Steevens cites a precisely similar use of *reverberate* from Ben Jonson, The Masque of Blackness:

> which skill Pythagoras
> First taught to men by a *reverberate* glass.

68. Line 313: *Unless the master were the man.*—A vague and unfinished phrase, meaning, "If only the master were the man!" or something to that effect.

69. Line 320: *The* COUNTY'S *man.*—This is Capell's emendation. F. 1 has *countes*, the other Ff. *counts*.

ACT II. Scene 1.

[This scene, in the acting-version, becomes scene 2 of act iii.; thus the action of the play is rendered more consecutive.—F. A. M.]

70. Line 12: *my determinate voyage is mere* EXTRAVAGANCY.—This is the only instance of the word *extravagancy* (that is, vagrancy) in Shakespeare; but he uses *extravagant*, in the same sense, in Othello, i. 1. 136-138:

> Tying her duty, beauty, wit and fortunes
> In an *extravagant* and wheeling stranger
> Of here and every where;

in Hamlet, i. 1. 154:

> The *extravagant* and erring spirit;

and, probably in the same sense, in Love's Labour's Lost, iv. 2. 68: "a foolish *extravagant* spirit."

71. Line 18: *Messaline.*—A place unknown in prose geography, possibly intended for *Mitylene*, as Capell conjectured.

72. Lines 28, 29: *but, though I could not, with such* ESTIMABLE WONDER, *overfar believe that.*—"I suppose," Mr. Stone writes me, "that Sebastian, modestly depreciating his good looks, means that he could not regard himself with *wonder* (cf. [illegible]—Odyssey, xi. 286—said of a beautiful woman) of such high estimation as beauty deserves.

73. Line 36: *If you will not murder me for my love.*—"Knight," says Aldis Wright, "suggests that Shakespeare in this may have referred to a superstition of which Scott makes use in The Pirate, that any one who was saved from drowning would do his preserver a capital injury. But Antonio seems only to appeal to Sebastian not to kill him as a reward for his love by abandoning him" (Clarendon Press ed. 104).

74. Line 41: *the manners of my mother.*—Compare Henry V. iv. 6. 31, 32:

> And *all my mother* came into mine eyes,
> And gave me up to tears.

ACT II. Scene 2.

75. Line 13: *She took* THE *ring of me.*—Malone substituted *no*, and is followed by Dyce and other editors. Such a substitution quite spoils the idea. Viola, with quick-witted consideration, accepts the fiction of the ring, and so avoids exposing Olivia's fond deception to her steward.

76. Line 16: *there it lies* IN YOUR EYE; *i.e.* "in your sight." Compare Hamlet, iv. 4. 5, 6:

> If that his majesty would aught with us,
> We shall express our duty *in his eye*;

and Antony and Cleopatra, ii. 2. 211, 212:

> Her gentlewomen, like the Nereides,
> So many mermaids, tended her i' *the eyes*.

77. Line 21: *That methought her eyes had lost her tongue.*—So Ff. Most editors follow the reading of F. 2: "that *sure* methought." Dyce would read "that *as* methought." No alteration is necessary, for the line as it stands is quite rhythmical, like Chaucer's "In a gowne of faldyng to the kne" (Canterbury Tales, Prologue, 391). Such lines not unfrequently occur in Shakespeare (cf. *inf.* iii. 1. 122 and 133).

78. Lines 30, 31:

> *How easy is it for the proper-false*
> *In women's waxen hearts to set their forms!*

Had not Johnson thought well to misunderstand this passage, it would scarcely have seemed necessary to say that its meaning is, "How easy is it for handsome and deceitful persons to make an impression, or to fix their image, in the yielding hearts of women!"

79. Line 32: OUR *frailty.*—So F. 2, and all modern editors. F. 1 reads *O*.

80. Line 33: *For such as we are made* OF, *such we be.*—Ff.: "For such as we are made, *if* such we bee." The reading in the text is Tyrwhitt's conjecture, universally received.

81. Line 34: *How will this* FADGE?—Boswell quotes Florio: "*Andar' a vango*, to *fadge*, to prosper with, to go as one would have it." Skeat derives the word from A.S. *fégan*, to fit (see Love's Labour's Lost, note 102).

82. Line 36: AND *she, &c.*—Dyce would read, "*as* she," with only a comma after *him*. This would make excellent sense, but so does the reading of the Folio; and why change?

ACT II. Scene 3.

83. Line 10: *Does not our* LIFE *consist of the four* ELEMENTS?—Ff. print *lives*. The reading in the text is the emendation of Rowe, justified by *it* in Sir Andrew's an-

swer; it is followed by most modern editors. The allusion is to the absurd medical theory of the four elements in the human frame, choler being ascribed to fire, blood to air, phlegm to water, and melancholy to earth. "And there is none, let him have the humors never so well balanced within him, but is subject unto anxiety of mind somtimes, for while we are composed of *foure differing Elements*, wherewith the humours within us symbolise we must have perpetuall ebbings and flowings of mirth and melancholy, which have their alternatif turnes in us, as naturally as it is for the night to succeed the day" (Howell, Instructions for Forraine Travell, 1642, Arber's Reprint, p. 24). Compare Antony and Cleopatra, v. 292, 293:

> I am fire and air; my other *elements*
> I give to baser life.

84. Line 14: MARIAN, *I say!*—Some editors, with over precision, read *Maria*. Marian is only another form of Mary or Maria.

85. Line 17: *did you never see* THE PICTURE OF "WE THREE"?—An allusion to a common old sign representing two fools or loggerheads, under which was inscribed "*We three* Loggerheads be," the spectator being the third. There is at the present day a public-house in Upper Red-Cross Street, Leicester, which has the same figure and device on its sign-board. Dekker (The Gull's Hornbook, ch. vi.: "How a Gallant should behave himself in a Playhouse") says, speaking of the fops whose fancy it was to sit on the stage: "Assure yourself by continual residence, you are the first and principal man in election to begin the number of *We three*."

86. Line 19: *the fool has an excellent* BREAST.—*Breast*, for voice, is often met with in early literature. Warburton cites the statutes of Stoke College: "which said queristers, after their *breasts* [*i.e.* voices] are broken;" and Fiddes, Life of Wolsey: "singing-men well-*breasted*."

87. Line 20: *I had rather than forty shillings.*—Compare Merry Wives, i. 1. 205: "*I had rather than forty shillings* I had my Book of Songs and Sonnets here;" and Henry VIII. ii. 3. 89: "*forty pence*, no!"

88. Lines 23-25: *Pigrogromitus, . . . the Vapians passing the equinoctial of Queubus.*—These Rabelaisian-sounding freaks of nomenclature are attributed by Mr. Swinburne to the direct influence of Rabelais. "We cannot but recognize on what far travels, in what good company, Feste the jester had but lately been on that night of 'very gracious fooling,' when he was pleased to enlighten the unforgetful mind of Sir Andrew as to the history of Pigrogromitus, and of the Vapians passing the equinoctial of Queubus" (A Study of Shakespeare, pp. 155, 156).

89. Lines 27-29: *I did impeticos thy gratillity*, &c.—Intentional nonsense, upon which it is amusing to see grave commentators bending their spectacles. *Impeticos thy gratillity* very likely means, so far as it means anything, "impeticoat (or impocket) thy gratuity," as Johnson suggested.

90. Line 34: *There's a* TESTRIL *of me too.*—A *testril*, or *tester* (which is used in II. Henry IV. iii. 2. 296), was the name of a coin worth at different times from twelve pence to 2½d. The word is a corruption of the French *teston*, which Cotgrave defines as "a piece of siluer coyne worth xviijd. sterling."

91. Line 35: *if one knight give a—.*—F. 1 has no stop after *a*, which comes at the end of a line; the later Ff. add a dash. The hiatus may or may not be intentional, but the sense may very likely be (as Singer proposes): "if one knight give another should." Mr. Marshall writes me: "I think it is quite clear that a portion of a line (*—nother knight should*) has been left out here in printing. There is no sign of Sir Andrew being interrupted by the clown. Dramatically speaking an interruption here would be out of place. Sir Andrew would take a little time to get the coin out of his pocket; the completion of the sentence would give him that time. I should certainly myself not scruple to print *a-nother* [*knight*] *should*, according to Singer's suggestion."

92. Line 40: *O mistress mine*, &c.—"'This tune is contained in both the editions of Morley's *Consort Lessons*, 1599 and 1611. It is also in Queen Elizabeth's Virginal Book, arranged by Boyd. As it is to be found in print in 1599, it proves either that Shakespeare's *Twelfth-Night* was written in or before that year, or that, in accordance with the then prevailing custom, *O mistress mine* was an old song, introduced into the play.' [The latter supposition is doubtless the true one.] Chappell's *Popular Music of the Olden Time*, vol. i. p. 209, sec. ed." (Dyce's note).

93. Line 44: *Journeys end in* LOVERS *meeting.*—Warburton, followed by Dyce, &c., reads *lovers' meeting*.

94. Line 61: *a catch that will draw three souls out of one weaver.*—Compare Much Ado, ii. 3. 60-62: "Is it not strange that sheeps' guts should *hale souls* out of men's bodies?" Weavers were supposed to be good singers: compare I. Henry IV. ii. 4. 147: "I would I were *a weaver*; I could sing psalms or any thing." Many of them were Calvinistic refugees from the Netherlands: hence their predilection for psalm-singing. The whole phrase is no doubt a picturesque equivalent of "thrice delightful."

95. Line 64: *I am* DOG *at a catch.*—A familiar phrase of the time, meaning to be apt at anything. Some editors unnecessarily alter, with Ff. 2 and 3, to *a dog*; which is used in Two Gent. of Verona, iv. 4. 14: "to be, as it were, *a dog* at all things." Compare Middleton, Women beware Women, i. 2: "I'm *dog* at a hole."

96. Line 65: *By'r lady.*—With reference to this corruption of "By our Lady," so frequently met with in the dramatists, I can corroborate the statement given in note 145 to A Midsummer Night's Dream, that the oath is still occasionally (not, I think, commonly) used by the lower classes at Atherstone, in Warwickshire. The word is pronounced more like *be-lady* than *birleddy*.

97. Line 68: *Let our catch be, Thou knave.*—This catch is to be found in "Pammelia, Musickes Miscellanie, or mixed Varietie of pleasant Roundelays and delightful Catches of 3, 4, 5, 6, 7, 8, 9, 10 Parts in one," 2nd ed. 1618. It is extant, says Dyce, in Ravencroft's Deuteromelia, 1609. The words are:

> Hold thy peace, and I prithee hold thy peace,
> Thou knave, thou knave! hold thy peace, thou knave!

"It appears to be so contrived," says Sir John Hawkins, "as that each of the singers calls the other *knave* in turn."

98. Line 80: *Cataian*.—A native of Cathay, or China; that is, as we should say now, "a heathen Chinee." Nares says the word "was used to signify a sharper, from the dexterous thieving of those people; which quality is ascribed to them in many old books of travel." Shakespeare uses it again in Merry Wives, ii. 1. 148: "I will not believe such a *Cataian*, though the priest o' th' town commended him for a true man." Compare Dekker, Honest Whore, Part II. iv. 1: "I'll make a wild *Cataian* of forty such."

99. Line 81: *Peg-a-Ramsey*.—There are two tunes that go under the name of *Peg-a-Ramsey*, both as old as the time of Shakespeare. The oldest is found in William Ballet's Lute Book, and this, according to Sir John Hawkins, is the one referred to here. The words of the original ballad have not come down to us; but in Durfey's Wit and Mirth, or Pills to Purge Melancholy (1719, vol. v. p. 139), there is a song called "Bonnie Peggie Ramsey."

"*Three merry men be we*."—"The tune [by W. Lawes] is contained in a MS. commonplace book, in the handwriting of John Playford, the publisher of The Dancing Master" (Chappell's Popular Music, p. 216). See Playford's Musical Companion, 1673. The words are quoted as follows in Peele, Old Wives' Tale, 1595:

> Three merrie men and three merrie men,
> And *three merrie men be wee*,
> I in the wood, and thou on the ground,
> And Jacke sleepes in the tree.
>
> —Works, ed. Dyce, 1861, p. 445.

The song is found again in Dekker and Webster's Westward Ho, v. 4; in Beaumont and Fletcher's Knight of the Burning Pestle, ii. 5; and The Bloody Brother, iii. 2; and in Ram Alley, ii. 1 (Hazlitt's Dodsley's Old Plays, vol. x. p. 298).

100. Line 83: *Tillyvally*.—"Is not this house, quoth he, as nigh heaven as my own? To whom she after her accustomed homely fashion, not liking such talk, answered, Tylle-valle, Tylle-valle" (Roper's Life of Sir Thomas Moore, p. 79, ed. 1822, cited by Nares). Compare II. Henry IV. ii. 4. 90: "*Tilly-fally*, Sir John."

101. Line 84: *There dwelt a man in Babylon, lady, lady!*—From the old ballad of Susanna, licensed by T. Colwell in 1562, under the title of The Goodly and Constant Wyfe Susanna. Probably quoted again in Romeo and Juliet, ii. 4. 151, where Mercutio mocks the nurse with, "*lady, lady, lady*."

102. Line 90: *O, the twelfth day of December*.—Probably the opening of a ballad now lost to us. Aldis Wright (Clarendon Press ed. p. 111) compares the beginning of the ballad of Brave Lord Willoughby: "The fifteenth day of July."

103. Line 94: *to gabble like* TINKERS.—"Proverbial tipplers and would-be politicians" (Schmidt). Compare I. Henry IV. ii. 4. 19–21: "I am so good a proficient in one quarter of an hour, that I can drink with any *tinker* in his own language during my life." I should like to add, in reference to the latter passage, the very curious fact that Shakespeare seems to have been aware of the language peculiar to the tinkers, and known as Shelta, or, as the Gipsies call it, "Mumper's talk." This is a language perfectly distinct from Romany, or from common slang. Mr. Leland was the first to give some account of it, with a partial vocabulary, in his book The Gypsies (Trübner, 1882), where he notes the remarkable fact that the single reference to this language found in print during three centuries is to be found in the pages of Shakespeare.

104. Line 96: COZIERS' *catches*.—Minsheu has, "A Cosier or sowter, from the Spanish word *coser*, *i.e.* to sew. Vide Botcher, Souter, or Cobler."

105. Line 101: *Sneck up!*—"This was a scoffing interjection, tantamount to 'Go hang!' and here has the added humorous effect of a hiccup" (Clarke). Compare Beaumont and Fletcher, The Knight of the Burning Pestle, iii. 2: "Give him his money, George, and let him go *snick up*" (Works, vol. ii. p. 86, col. 1); and see the quotations given in the Variorum Shakspere, *ad loc.*

106. Line 110: *Farewell, dear heart, since I must needs be gone*.—This line, and those which follow, are taken, with a good many alterations, from Corydon's Farewell to Phillis, in The Golden Garland of Princely Delights, reprinted in Percy's Reliques (1857, vol. i. p. 222). Halliwell-Phillipps (Outlines of the Life of Shakespeare, 5th edn. pp. 520, 521) says: "The song 'Farewell, dear love' first appeared in the Booke of Ayres composed by Robert Jones, fol., London, 1601. Jones does not profess to be the author of the words of this song. . . . As the tune and ballad were evidently familiar to Shakespeare, the original of the portion to which he refers in the comedy is here given,—

> Farewel, dear love, since thou wilt needs be gon,
> Mine eies do show my life is almost done;
> Nay, I will never die,
> so long as I can spie;
> There be many mo,
> though that she do go.
> There be many mo, I feare not;
> Why, then, let her goe, I care not.
>
> Farewell, farewell, since this I find is true,
> I will not spend more time in wooing you;
> But I will seeke elswhere,
> if I may find her there.
> Shall I bid her goe?
> what and if I doe?
> Shall I bid her go and spare not?
> Oh, no, no, no, no, I dare not.

107. Line 122: *Out o' tune, sir?*—So the Cambridge edd. Ff. have *Out o' tune, sir, ye lie*. Many editors read *Out o' time, sir* (Theobald's emendation). Various explanations have been suggested; and some have supposed the words are addressed to the clown. It seems to me that the whole speech is addressed to Malvolio, and that Sir Toby is still harping on Malvolio's offensive remark about "squeaking out your coziers' catches without any mitigation or remorse of voice." He has already replied, playing on Malvolio's "Is there no respect of place, persons nor *time*, in you?"—"We did keep *time*, sir, in our catches;" and now, after his parenthesis in song, he returns, still profoundly aggrieved, and with the drunkard's recurrent memory, to the injurious insinuation.

108. Line 129: *rub your chain with crumbs.*—Stewards formerly wore *chains* of silver or gold as a badge of office. Crumbs were much used for cleaning them. See the passage quoted by Steevens from Webster's Duchess of Malfy, iii. 2:

> 4th Off. Well, let him go.
> 1st Off. Yes, and the chippings of the buttery fly after him, to *scour his gold chain*.

Aldis Wright (Clarendon Press ed. p. 113) gives references to six other parallel passages from dramatists of the period.

109. Line 131: *this uncivil* RULE; *i.e.* "behaviour." See A Midsummer Night's Dream, note 170.

110. Line 134: *'T were as good a deed as to drink.*—Compare I. Henry IV. ii. 1. 32, 33: "An 't were not *as good deed as drink*, to break the pate on thee, I am a very villain."

111. Line 130: *challenge him* THE FIELD.—So Ff. Rowe would read *to the field;* Schmidt, *to field*.

112. Line 140: *a nayword.*—Ff. *an ayword*. Rowe's emendation is almost universally adopted. *Nayword* is used in Merry Wives, ii. 2. 131 and v. 2. 5 for a password; here it evidently means a byword.

113. Line 149: SIR TO. *Possess us, &c.*—Dyce would give this speech to *Sir Andrew,* quoting Walker: "Surely Sir Toby needed no information respecting Malvolio." But there is nothing unnatural in the remark coming from Sir Toby. It was not so much that he "wanted information" as that he wanted to hear what the sharp-tongued Maria had to say of Malvolio, and what handle she could find against him.

114. Line 164: *his* GROUNDS *of faith.*—So F. 1. Later Ff. read *ground*, and are followed by some editors.

115. Line 183: SIR AND. *And your horse, &c.*—Dyce, following Tyrwhitt's conjecture, gives this to *Sir Toby*. The change is worse than unnecessary; the infinitesimal witticism is not a hair's-breadth above Sir Andrew's capacity.

116. Line 184: ASS, *I doubt not.*—Walker would see a pun here; "*As* I doubt not;" compare Hamlet, v. 2. 43: "And many suchlike '*As*'es of great charge."

117. Line 195: *She's a beagle, true-bred.*—A kennel metaphor, quite in the style of the Sir Tobys of to-day.

118. Line 203: *call me* CUT.—Steevens suggests that *cut* is used here for gelding; but it is probably no more than an abbreviation of *curtal*, a docked horse. *Cut* or *curtal* was often used as a term of abuse. Compare The London Prodigal, ii. 4: "An I do not meet him, chill give you leave to call me cut" (Tauchnitz ed. p. 238).

119. Line 206: *I'll go burn some sack.*—See I. Henry IV. note 41, for a long note on *sack*.

ACT II. SCENE 4.

[With this scene, in the acting-edition, act iii. commences.—F. A. M.]

120. Line 5: *recollected terms.*—"Studied" (Warburton), "repeated" (Johnson), "refined" or "trivial" (Schmidt). "I incline," Mr. W. G. Stone tells me, "to accept Warburton's explanation, that *recollected* = studied. The old simple language (terms), which pleased Orsino, is opposed to a highly artificial composition, in which invention and memory are strained to gather together new and uncommon phrases."

121. Line 22: *Thou dost speak masterly.*—Clarke observes that this is "one of the few instances in which Shakespeare indirectly (and of course unconsciously) comments upon himself. Certainly there never was more masterly speaking on the effect produced by music upon a nature sensitively alive to its finest influences than Viola's few but intensely expressive words."

122. Line 35: *sooner lost and* WORN.—So Ff. Hanmer proposed to read *won*, and the reading has been adopted by Johnson and others. But *worn* in the sense of *worn out* is supported by II. Henry VI. ii. 4. 69: "These few days' wonder will be quickly *worn*."

123. Line 53: *in sad* CYPRESS *let me be laid.*—By *cypress* Warton understood a shroud of the crape known as *cypress*, Malone a coffin of *cypress*-wood. The words *let me be laid* seem to confirm Malone's explanation, as does also the epithet *sad*. Although *cyprus* was, like modern crape, made both black and white, the black seems to have been always used as an emblem of mourning. (See Nares *sub Cyprus*.) Douce (Illustrations of Shakespeare, p. 50) says, on the authority of Gough's Introduction to Sepulchral Monuments, p. lxvi., that *cyprus*-wood was used for *coffins*. Note also that the *shroud* is expressly mentioned in line 56 below.

124. Line 54: *Fly away, fly away, breath.*—Ff. print *Fye away, fie away breath*. The reading in the text is Rowe's obvious emendation.

125. Line 66: *Sad* TRUE LOVER.—So Ff. Some editors read *true-love*, which certainly makes a smoother line, but there is no authority for the change.

126. Line 74: *Give me now leave to leave thee.*—A courteous form of dismissal, as Dyce notes. Compare I. Henry IV. i. 3. 20: "You have good leave to leave us."

127. Line 76: *changeable taffeta.*—*Taffeta* denoted a sort of thin silk. Compare Chaucer, Prologue, line 440:

> In sangwin and in pers he clad was al,
> Lined with *taffata* and with sendal.

Changeable taffeta apparently means some sort of shot-silk. Compare Taylor the Water-Poet: "No *taffaty* more *changeable* than they" (Works, 1630, ii. 40, quoted by Halliwell).

128. Line 77: *a very* OPAL.—Compare Drayton, The Muses Elizium, 1630, 9th Nimphall (p. 79):

> With *Opalls*, more then any one,
> We 'll deck thine Altar fuller,
> For that of euery precious stone,
> It doth reteine some colour.

129. Line 89: *pranks.*—Compare Winter's Tale, iv. 4. 10: "Most goddess-like *prank'd* up."

130. Line 91: *I cannot be so answer'd.*—Hanmer's emendation. Ff. read: "*It* cannot."

131. Lines 117, 118:

> *She sat like Patience on a monument,*
> *Smiling at grief.*

Compare Pericles, v. 1. 138-140:

> yet thou dost look
> Like *Patience* gazing on kings' graves, and *smiling*
> Extremity out of act.

132. Line 127: *denay*.—Compare II. Henry VI. i. 3. 107:

> Then let him be *denay'd* the regentship.

ACT II. Scene 5.

133. Line 6: *sheep-biter*.—Originally a cant term for a thief, as in Taylor the Water-Poet:

> And in some places I have heard and seene
> That currish *sheep-biters* have hanged beene.

It came to mean, as Schmidt understands it, a surly malicious fellow. Compare Scot, Discoverie of Witchcraft, p. 215: "They comfort in vain, and therefore they went awale like sheepe, &c. If anie *sheepebiter* or witchmonger will follow them, they shall go alone for me." Shakespeare has *sheep-biting* in Measure for Measure, v. 1. 360: "your *sheep-biting* face."

134. Line 17: *How now, my* METAL *of India!*—F. 1 reads *mettle*; F. 2 *nettle*. Many editors follow the Second Folio, supposing that by *nettle of India* is meant the *Urtica marina*, a plant of itching properties; but the reading of F. 1 is at least as good, and quite as likely to come from Sir Toby.

135. Line 25: *here comes the trout that must be caught with tickling*.—"This fish of nature loveth flatterie: for, being in the water, it will suffer itselfe to be rubbed and clawed, and so to be taken" (Cogan, Haven of Health, 1595, cited by Steevens). [This mode of taking fish is still practised with great success in mountain streams, especially when the water is low, and the fish are compelled to take refuge in the "dubs" or deep holes. Last year (1887) two youths in Westmoreland, in one day, took 75 trout out of one stream by *tickling*.—F. A. M.]

136. Line 36: *jets*.—Compare Cymbeline, iii. 3. 5: "arch'd so high that giants may *jet* through;" Pericles, i. 4. 26:

> Whose men and dames so *jetted* and adorned;

and see Richard III. note 287.

137. Line 45: *the lady of the* STRACHY *married the yeoman of the wardrobe*.—This is one of the insoluble puzzles in Shakespeare. Payne Knight conjectured that *Strachy* is a corruption of *Stratici*, a title anciently given to governors of Messina; and that the phrase therefore means, "the governor's lady." Halliwell derives it from a Russian word (which he supposes Shakespeare to have met with in some novel or play) meaning judge or lawyer. Such names as *Strozzi*, *Stracci*, *Stratarch*, &c., have been suggested. Prof. Dowden, in his Shakspere Primer, pp. 116, 117, observes: "It has been suggested (see Hunter, New Illustrations of Shakespeare, vol. i. p. 380) that Shakspere ridicules, in the scene between the clown, as Sir Topas, and Malvolio, the exorcisms by Puritan ministers, in the case of a family named *Starchy* (1596-99), and that the difficult word *Strachy* was a hint to the audience to expect subsequent allusion to the Starchy affair. But all this is highly doubtful." "The solution of the mystery contained in this name probably lies hid," says the Clarendon Press ed. (p. 123), "in some forgotten novel or play. The incident of a lady of high rank marrying a servant is the subject of Webster's Dutchess of Malfi, who married the steward of her household, and would thus have supplied Malvolio with the exact parallel to his own case of which he was in search."

[The story on which the Dutchess of Malfi is founded was published in Painter's Palace of Pleasure, and in Beard's Theatre of God's Judgments, both of which books were printed before this comedy was written. If in any story or play relating to this subject of a lady marrying her servant, such a title as *the yeoman of the wardrobe* were given to the latter, it would afford a strong clue to the source of Malvolio's allusion.—F. A. M.]

138. Line 51: *O for a* STONE-BOW, *to hit him in the eye!*—Cotgrave has "Arbaleste à boulet. *A Stone-bow*." Coles, in his Latin Dictionary, gives it as the equivalent of *balista*. The Clarendon Press ed. (p. 123) compares Wisdom, v. 22: "And hailstones full of wrath shall be cast as out of a *stone bow* (ἐκ πετροβόλου)."

139. Line 54: *my* BRANCH'D *velvet gown*.—Boyer, French Dictionary, has "Branched velvet, *Veleurs à ramage*, *Veleurs figuré*, ou *en feuillage*." Cotgrave renders *Velours figuré*, "branched velvet."

140. Line 55: *a day-bed*.—Compare the Qq. of Richard III. iii. 7. 72, where the Ff. read *love-bed*. A *day-bed* was an old and excellent name for a couch or sofa. Compare Richard III. note 423.

141. Line 66: *play with* MY—SOME RICH JEWEL.—F. 1 reads *my some rich jewel*. F. 3 and F. 4 omit *my*. The dash was inserted by Collier. The meaning is no doubt what Dr. Brinsley Nicholson has suggested, that Malvolio was about to say "my chain," but remembering that he would no longer be a steward, nor wearing the chain of office, he changes his phrase, in his own lofty way, into *some rich jewel*.

142. Line 71: *with cars*.—So F. 1; later Folios, *with cares*. *Carts*, *cords*, &c., have been suggested. Hanmer would read *by th' ears* (pronounced "*bith ears*," easily corrupted into *with cars*), and is followed by Dyce and others. Whether or not it is true, as Steevens asserted, that *cars* and *carts* have the same meaning (compare Two Gent. of Verona, iii. 1. 265: "a team of horses shall not pluck that from me"), I see no reason why the F. reading should be changed. I fancy it should be taken as a mere piece of impromptu extravagance, Fabian of course having in mind such a phrase as I have just quoted.

143. Line 72, &c.—Singer remarks on the resemblance of this situation to that of Alnaschar in the Arabian Nights. He adds: "Some of the expressions too are very similar. Many Arabian fictions had found their way into obscure Latin and French books, and from thence into English ones, long before any version of the Arabian Nights had appeared. In the Dialogues of Creatures Moralized, black letter, printed early in the sixteenth century, a story similar to that of Alnaschar is related."

144. Line 96: *these be her very C's, her U's, and her T's*.—Ritson suggests that the full direction of the letter may have been "*To the Unknown Beloved, this, and my good wishes, with Care Present.*"

145. Line 114: *Marry, hang thee, brock!*—Boyer, French Dictionary, has "Brock (or Badger), *Blereau*, *Taisson*." The term was frequently used in contempt. Compare Day's Ile of Guls, v. 1. (p. 101, ed. Bullen): "I faith, olde *brocke*, haue I tane you in the maner?"

146. Line 123: *What dish o' poison*, &c.—This and the following speech are followed in Ff. by a note of interrogation. The meaning obviously is, "What *a* dish," &c.

147. Line 124: *staniel.*—The Ff. by an obvious misprint read *stallion*. The correction, which is generally adopted, is Hanmer's. *Check* is defined by Dyce as "a term in falconry applied to a hawk when she forsakes her proper game, and follows some other of inferior kind that crosses her in her flight."

148. Line 135: *Sowter.*—Boyer, French Dictionary, ed. 1702, has "Sowter (an obsolete Word for a Shoo-maker or Cobler) *V.* Shoo-maker, &c."

149. Line 154: *every one of these letters* ARE *in my name.*—Compare Julius Cæsar, v. 1. 33:

> The posture of your blows are yet unknown.

150. Line 157: *some are* BORN *great.*—Ff. print *become*. The correction, which is Rowe's, is confirmed by the recurrence of the same phrase in iii. 4. 45, where the Ff. properly read *born*.

151. Line 166: *yellow stockings.*—These were much in use at the time, and the fashion still survives in the saffron-coloured stockings of the Blue-Coat boys, who preserve unchanged the costume worn at the time of the foundation of Christ's Hospital in the reign of Edward VI. "They appear," says the Clarendon Press ed. (p. 128), "to have been specially worn by the young, if any importance is to be attached to the burden of a song set to the tune of Peg a Ramsey (Chappell, Popular Music of the Olden Time, p. 218), in which a married man laments the freedom of his bachelor days:

> Give me my yellow hose again,
> Give me my yellow hose!"

The passage quoted by Steevens from Dekker's Honest Whore, Part ii. 1. 1, is scarcely to the point, I think, in proving the fashionableness of yellow stockings, for we see by the context that there is a special allusion to yellow as the colour of jealousy. Lodovico says to Infelice: "What *stockings* have you put on this morning, madam? if they be not *yellow*, change them; that paper is a letter from some wench to your husband." And Infelice replies: "O sir, you cannot make me jealous."

152. Line 167: *cross-garter'd.*—This was another fashion of the time. Steevens cites Ford, The Lover's Melancholy, 1629: "As rare a youth as ever walk'd *cross-gartered*." Singer suggests that Olivia's dislike of these fashions arose from thinking them coxcombical. Rather the reverse, one would think, from the allusion in iii. 2. 80 to a *pedant*.

153. Line 176: *point-devise.*—See Love's Labour's Lost, note 140.

154. Line 185: *I will be* STRANGE, STOUT.—That is, distant and proud. Compare Comedy of Errors, ii. 2. 112: "look *strange* and frown;" and II. Henry VI. i. 1. 187:

> As *stout* and proud as he were lord of all.

155. Line 192: *dear my sweet.*—So all editors, I believe, but the Old-Spelling, who, following Mr. P. A. Daniel's conjecture, read "Therefore in my presence still smile, *deer! O my sweete, I prethee!*" This seems to me very far-fetched. The F. reads *deero my sweete*. Surely the *o* is an obvious misprint for *e*, and could never have been intended for an exclamatory *O*. *Deer my sweet* is just such a phrase as "good my mouse," i. 5. 69 above.

156. Line 198: *a pension of thousands to be paid from the Sophy.*—For the word *Sophy* compare Merchant of Venice, ii. 1. 25: "the *Sophy*, and a Persian prince;" and see note 114 of that play. There is probably some allusion to Sir Robert Shirley, who had just returned from an embassage to Persia, greatly enriched by the liberality of the Shah. See Day, Rowley and Wilkins' indifferent play, The Travels of the Three English Brothers, a *rifacimento* of scenes developed from the apocryphal accounts of the Shirley brothers' biographer.

157. Line 208: *tray-trip.*—A game at dice, which depended upon throwing a *tray* or trois. Tyrwhitt thinks it was something in the nature of draughts. See the long quotation from Machiavel's Dogge, 1617, in Malone's Var. Ed. vol. xi. p. 428.

ACT III. Scene 1.

[In the acting-edition, this scene forms a continuation of the previous one, and concludes act iii. The arrangement is perfectly justifiable, as the events of act ii. scenes 4 and 5, and of acts iii. iv. and v. all take place on the same day. For stage purposes such a division of the acts is preferable, as, with Olivia's declaration of love to the supposed Cesario, an important step in the more serious interest of the play is reached.—F. A. M.]

158. Line 2: *tabor.*—An instrument much used by professional fools, perhaps in imitation of Tarleton, the celebrated jester, who appears with one in his hands in a print prefixed to his Jests, 1611.

159. Line 8: *lies.*—So Ff. Some editors have altered *lies* into *lives*. But the word was often used in the sense of "dwells" or "lodges."

160. Line 13: *cheveril.*—Compare Romeo and Juliet, ii. 4. 87: "O, here's a wit of *cheveril*, that stretches from an inch narrow to an ell broad." Steevens cites a proverb in Ray's Collection: "He hath a conscience like a *cheverel's* skin." Boyer, in his French dictionary, has "Cheveril Conscience, (made of stretching Leather) *Une Conscience large, une Conscience qui prête.*"

161. Line 39: *fools are as like husbands as* PILCHARDS *are to* HERRINGS.—Pilchards are often sold as small herrings, and many people are unable to distinguish between them. Ff. spell *pilchers*, which in Shakespeare's time was an alternative spelling of the word.

162. Line 43: *Foolery, sir, does walk about the orb like the sun, it shines everywhere.*—Dyce prefers to insert a semicolon after *orb*, thus re-writing Shakespeare's sentence for him.

163. Line 49: *there's* EXPENSES.—No doubt a *pour-boire*, or drinking-money. Dr. Badam (cited in Dyce) would read *sixpence!*

164. Line 55: *have bred.*—Malone believes that Shakespeare wrote *have breed*, but does not introduce it into his text.

165. Line 62: *Cressida was a beggar.*—Malone cites Henryson, Testament of Creseid (ed. Laing, p. 86):

> And greit penuritie
> Thow suffer sall, and as ane beggar die.

166. Line 63: *I will* CONSTRUE *to them.*—Ff. spell *conster*, which was simply a variant of *construe*.

167. Line 71: NOT, *like the haggard.*—Ff. have *and;* the reading in the text was suggested by Johnson. "The wise clown is discriminative in his jests: he does not play the fool with everybody and on all occasions, like a hawk which (I quote Bailey's Dictionary, 1753, *s.v.* 'Chick') 'forsakes her natural flight to follow Rooks, or other Birds, when they come in view.' If we read *and*, where is the contrast?" (W. G. Stone). For *haggard*, see Much Ado, note 170.

168. Line 75: *But wise men,* FOLLY-FALL'N, *quite taint their wit.*—So Capell, after Theobald and Tyrwhitt's conjecture. F. 1 reads *wisemens* [F. 2 *wise mens*] *folly falne, quite taint their wit.* Hanmer and Warburton would read *wise men's folly shown.* Rolfe adopts this reading. The reading in the text is that most generally adopted, and seems the nearest to the Ff. It means, of course, "wise men, fallen into folly." The Clarendon Press editor quotes, very appositely, Love's Labour's Lost, v. 2. 75–78:

> Folly in fools bears not so strong a note
> As foolery in the wise, when wit doth dote;
> Since all the power thereof it doth apply
> To prove, by wit, worth in simplicity.

169. Line 78: SIR AND. Dieu vous garde, &c.—Theobald gives the French to Sir Toby, and the *Save you, gentleman*, to Sir Andrew, because in i. 3. 96 the latter did not know the meaning of *pourquoi*. But as Malone remarks: "The words, *Save you, gentleman*, which [Theobald] has taken from Sir Toby, and given to Sir Andrew, are again used by Sir Toby in a subsequent scene; a circumstance which renders it the more probable that they were intended to be attributed to him here also. With respect to the improbability that Sir Andrew should understand French here, after having betrayed his ignorance in a former scene, it appears from a subsequent passage that he was a picker-up of phrases, and might have learned by rote from Sir Toby the few French words here spoken. If we are to believe Sir Toby, Sir Andrew 'could speak three or four languages word for word without book.'"

170. Line 83: *if your* TRADE *be to her.*—Compare Hamlet, iii. 2. 346: "Have you any further *trade* with us?"

171. Line 86: *she is the* LIST OF *my voyage.*—Compare I. Henry IV. iv. 1. 51, 52:

> The very *list*, the very utmost bound
> Of all our fortunes;

and Hamlet, iv. 5. 99:

> The ocean, overpeering of his *list*.

172. Line 87: TASTE *your legs.*—Steevens cites Aristophanes, Frogs, 462: *γεῦσαι τῆς θύρας*, *taste* the door, *i.e.* knock gently at it; but I suppose he did not attribute to Shakespeare a familiarity with the Greek of Aristophanes?

173. Line 89: *My legs do better* UNDER-STAND *me.*—I have printed this word as a compound, to show the pun at a glance.

174. Line 94: *but we are* PREVENTED.—*Prevented*, in the sense of "anticipated," is familiar to all from its use in the Bible, *e.g.* "Mine eyes *prevent* the night-watches" (Psalm cxix. 148).

175. Line 102: *I'll get 'em all three* ALL READY.—F. 1 has *already*. The reading in the text is Malone's, who says: "The editor of the 3rd Folio reformed the passage by reading only *ready*. But omissions ought always to be avoided if possible. The repetition of the word *all* is not improper in the mouth of Sir Andrew."

176. Line 122: *beseech you.*—So F. 1; F. 3 and F. 4 insert *I*, and Steevens, Dyce, &c., follow them. But *I* is frequently omitted in Shakespeare, and the line certainly reads better without it.

177. Line 123: *After the last enchantment you* DID HERE.—Ff. *did heare;* and some editors would read, with no small violence to the sense, *did hear*. The emendation is Warburton's. Malone cites instances of *here* being spelt *heare* from the Qq. and Ff. of Shakespeare, and adds: "Throughout the first edition of our author's Rape of Lucrece, 1594, which was probably printed under his own inspection, the word we now spell *here*, is constantly written *heare*."

178. Lines 132, 133:

> *a* CYPRUS, *not a bosom,*
> *Hides my heart.*

Compare ii. 4. 53 above (and note 123), and Winter's Tale, iv. 4. 221:

> *Cyprus* black as e'er was crow.

The *cyprus* or *cypress* here is of course the crape. Halliwell quotes the Ballad of Robin Hood, Will Scadlock, and Little John:

> Her riding-suit was of sable-hew black,
> *Cypress* over her face
> Through which her rose-like cheeks did blush
> All with a comely grace.

Aldis Wright (Clarendon Press Ed. pp. 135–137) gives an exhaustive note on the subject, chiefly on the etymology of the word.

179. Line 133: *Hides my heart.*—So F. 1. F. 2: *hides my poor heart.* Many editors follow this reading. The line is perfectly good without the interpolation. It must be read with a heavy accent on the first syllable, as in line 122: "Give me leave, beseech you. I did send."

180. Line 135: *No, not a* GRISE.—*Grise* is from the Latin *gressus*, through Old French *grés*, a step. It is used again in Othello, i. 3. 200: "Which, as a *grise* or step;" and in Timon of Athens, iv. 3. 16, 17:

> every *grise* of fortune
> Is smooth'd by that below.

181. Line 146: *westward-ho!*—A cry of the watermen on the Thames. Used by Webster and Dekker as the name of a comedy (1607). It is referred to in Peele's Edward 1st (first printed in 1593), in a stage-direction [*Make a noise*, WESTWARD HO! (Dyce's Peele, 2nd edn. vol. i. p. 132). The village of that name, and Kingsley's novel, render *Westward-ho* very familiar to our ears.

182. Line 147: *Grace and good disposition* ATTEND *your ladyship!*—Many editors adopt Steevens' reading of '*tend*, and the Cambridge edd. alter (and spoil) the arrangement of the lines. The line as it stands is perfectly rhythmical.

183. Line 162: *maidhood.*—This form of "maidenhood" occurs again in Othello, i. 1. 172-174:

> Is there not charms
> By which the property of youth and *maidhood*
> May be abused?

ACT III. Scene 2.

[In the acting-edition this and the following scene are transposed, forming scenes 1 and 2 respectively of act iv. —F. A. M.]

184. Line 9: *Did she see* THEE *the while?*—F. 1 and F. 2 omit *thee*, which was added in F. 3.

185. Line 23: FIRE-NEW *from the mint.*—Brand-new. Cf. Richard III. i. 3. 256:

> Your *fire-new* stamp of honour is scarce current;

and see Love's Labour 's Lost, note 12.

186. Line 34: *Brownist.*—A Puritan sect, the frequent butt of dramatic ridicule. They obtained their name from Robert Browne, a noted separatist of the time. Steevens cites mocking references to the sect from L. Barry's Ram-Alley, 1611, and Sir W. D'Avenant's Love and Honour, 1649. Aldis Wright (Clarendon Press ed. p. 139) quotes Earle's Micro-cosmographia (ed. Arber, p. 64), where, speaking of "A shee precise Hypocrite," the author says: "No thing angers her so much as that Woemen cannot Preach, and in this point onely thinkes the *Brownist* erroneous."

187. Line 40: *curst.*—Generally used of women, in the sense of shrewish (compare Taming of Shrew, *passim*).

188. Line 48: *if thou* "THOU'ST" *him some thrice.*—To *thou* anyone was a mark of disrespect. Compare the French *tutoyer*, which Cotgrave renders "to *thou* one."

189. Line 51: *the bed of Ware.*—This hugest of beds (capable of holding twelve persons) was ten feet nine inches square and seven feet and a half high. It was formerly at the Saracen's Head Inn at Ware, and is now, says the Clarendon Press editor, to be seen at the Rye-House. A cut of it is given in Halliwell's folio ed. and Knight's Pictorial, as well as in Chambers's Book of Days, vol. i. p. 229.

190. Line 70: *the youngest wren of* NINE.—So Theobald. Ff. read *mine*. "The wren generally lays *nine* or ten eggs at a time, and the last hatched of all birds are usually the smallest and weakest of the whole brood" (Steevens).

191. Line 72: *If you desire the* SPLEEN, *and will laugh yourselves into stitches, follow me.*—See note 174 to Love's Labour 's Lost. Aldis Wright (Clarendon Press ed. p. 140) quotes Holland's Pliny, xi. 37 (vol. i. p. 343d): "For sure it is, that intemperate laughers have alwaies great *Splenes*."

192. Line 81: *that keeps a school i' the church.*—This appears to have been no very unusual custom. The Clarendon Press editor (p. 141) refers to Fosbroke, Encyclopædia of Antiquities (ed. 1825), pp. 395 and 452. It is there mentioned that in 1447 several clergymen in London petitioned Parliament for leave to open school in their parish churches. Halliwell states that the grammar-school at Stratford was kept in the adjacent chapel of the Guild, at intervals, during the time of Shakespeare.

193. Lines 84, 85: *he does smile his face into more lines than is in the new map.*—Compare Love's Labour 's Lost, v. 2. 465: "*That smiles his cheek in years*," and see note 197 to that play. I have come across a curious parallel passage, or confirmation of Shakespeare's observation, in Stendhal, La Chartreuse de Parme (ed. Michel Lévy, 1869, pp. 103, 104): "La marquise Balbi, jeune femme de vingt-cinq ans . . . vue de près, sa peau était parsemée d'un nombre infini de petites rides fines, qui faisaient de la marquise comme une jeune vieille . . . Elle prétendait à une finesse sans bornes, et toujours souriait avec malice . . . Le comte Mosca disait que *c'étaient ces sourires continuels*, tandis qu'elle bâillait intérieurement, *qui lui donnaient tant de rides*."

194. Line 85: *the new map with the augmentation of the Indies.*—"The editors have generally followed Steevens in seeing here an allusion to a map engraved for Linschoten's Voyages, an English translation of which was published in 1598. Knight has a cut (not perfectly accurate in its details) showing the multilineal character of the map. But, as Mr. [C. H.] Coote has proved [in a paper read before the New Shakspere Society, June 14, 1878], this map was not a *new* one, but 'a feebly reduced copy of an old one, the latest geographical information to be found on it when T. N. appeared being at least thirty years old,' and 'it showed no portion of the great Indian peninsula.' The true *new map* was pretty certainly one which Hallam in his Literature of Europe calls 'the best map of the 16th century,' and which he says is 'found in a few copies of the *first* edition of Hakluyt's Voyages.' This edition, however, was published in 1589, while the map records discoveries made at least seven years later. 'The truth,' as Mr. Coote remarks, 'seems to be that it was a separate map well known at the time, made in all probability for the convenience of the purchasers of either one or the other of the two editions of Hakluyt' [the 2nd was published in 1598-1600]. The author of the map was probably Mr. Emmeric Mollineux of Lambeth, who was also the first Englishman to make a terrestrial globe.

"The *augmentation of the Indies* on this map consists in 'a marked development of the geography of India proper, then known as the land of the Mogores or Mogol, the island of Ceylon, and the two peninsulas of Cochin-China and the Corea.' . . . It may be added that this map has *more lines* than the one in Linschoten's Voyages, there being *sixteen* sets of rhumb-lines on the former to *twelve* in the latter" (Rolfe).

ACT III. Scene 3.

195. Line 15: *And thanks: and, ever oft, good turns.*—F. 1 reads, *and thankes: and euer oft good turnes.* Theobald's emendation is followed by some edd.: *and thanks, and ever thanks; and oft good turns.* The reading in the text is that of the Old-Spelling Shakespeare, and the explanation given in the foot-note is due to Furni-

vall and Stone. The Camb. edd. treat the line as hopelessly corrupt and print *and thanks; and ever . . . oft good turns.*

196. Line 17: *worth.*—For *worth* in the sense of wealth or fortune, see Romeo and Juliet, ii. 6. 32:

> They are but beggars that can count their *worth*, &c.

M. Mason quotes Ben Jonson, Cynthia's Revels, iii. 2:

> Such as the satirist paints truly forth,
> That only to his crimes owes all his *worth*.
> —Works, vol. ii. p. 283.

197. Line 20: *the count his galleys.*—This was frequently the form of the genitive in Shakespeare's time, owing to a mistaken notion that the "'s" of the genitive was merely a contraction of the possessive pronoun *his*. Malone, however, thinks the right reading may have been *the county's* [= count's] *galleys*. See Love's Labour's Lost, note 101.

198. Line 30: *lapsed.*—Schmidt explains as "surprised, taken in the action," and refers to a passage in Hamlet, iii. 4. 107, of doubtful interpretation. *Straying* has also been suggested by Clarke, and *transgressing* by Singer.

199. Lines 47, 48:

> *I 'll be your purse-bearer, and leave you for*
> *An hour.*

F. 1 reads:

> Ile be your purse-bearer, and leave you
> For an houre.

Most editors print as in text; the Cambridge edd. follow the F. precisely; some print as prose.

ACT III. Scene 4.

200. Line 1: *he says he'll come.*—This is of course hypothetical: "suppose him to say . . ."

201. Line 2: *what bestow* OF *him?*—Compare All's Well, iii. 5. 103:

> I will bestow some precepts *of* [F. 1 *on*] this virgin.

202. Line 5: *Where is Malvolio? he is* SAD *and civil.*—*Sad* means here grave, serious; there is a play upon the two meanings of the word in lines 20, 21 below. A good instance of *sad* in the sense of grave is found in Whetstone's Promos and Cassandra, part ii. i. 9 (stage-direction after line 30): "During the first parte of the song, the King faineth to talke *sadlie* with some of his Counsell."

203. Lines 24, 25: *it is with me as the very true sonnet is, "Please one, and please all."*—A ballad of this name was entered on the Stationers' Registers in January 18, 1591-92. It is entitled "A prettie newe Ballad, intytuled: The Crowe sits vpon the wall, Please one and please all. To the tune of, Please one and please all." The initials at the end, "R. T.," are perhaps those of Richard Tarleton, the actor. The ballad is printed in Staunton's edition of Shakespeare. *Sonnet*, in Shakespeare's time, was often used loosely for a short song or poem. Compare the second title of The Passionate Pilgrim, "*Sonnets* to Sundry Notes of Musicke"—not one *sonnet*, in the proper sense of the word, being contained in that part of the book. Cotgrave gives: "Sonnet: m. *A sonnet, or canzonet, a song (most commonly) of 14 verses.*"

204. Line 26.—Ff. have *Mal.* for *Oli.*

205. Line 46: *Ha?*—So Ff. Most editors change the note of interrogation into a note of exclamation; but the word is probably, as the Old-Spelling edd. suggest = "eh?"

206. Line 50: *Am I* MADE?—Some, who believe Manningham's hasty and preposterous conjecture that Olivia was a widow, would read *maid*. Clarke explains the sentence as an expression of surprise on the part of the wealthy Olivia that she should be supposed to have a chance of making her fortune, of becoming a *made* woman. Compare Winter's Tale, iii. 3. 124: "You're a *made* old man."

207. Line 61: *midsummer madness.*—Steevens cites from Ray's Proverbs: "'Tis *midsummer* moon with you," *i.e.* you are mad; and Halliwell refers to Poor Richard's Almanack: "Some people about *midsummer* moon are affected in their brain."

208. Lines 67-70.—"Good Maria, let this *fellow* be look'd to" refers to Malvolio; the latter part of the speech to Viola. "I would not have him miscarry" is explained by the Old-Spelling edd. "*him* (Viola) *miscarry*, &c. through Toby's violence." Malvolio understands it all as applying to him, and is mightily gratified.

209. Line 78: *tang with.*—F. 1 has *langer with*. Some editors omit *with* in order to make the phrase precisely uniform with the first version of it; but these little variations are very natural.

210. Line 82: *but it is* JOVE'S *doing, and* JOVE *make me thankful.*—Here, and in one or two other places, it is probable that Shakespeare wrote *God's* and *God*, and that in printing it was changed on account of the act of James I. against the stage use of the name of God. Halliwell reads *God's* and *God* in his edition.

211. Line 86: *no dram of a scruple.*—Compare a similar pun in II. Henry IV. i. 2. 146: "but how I should be your patient to follow your prescriptions, the wise may make some *dram of a scruple*, or indeed a scruple itself."

212. Line 114: *Carry his water to the wise woman.*—Compare II. Henry IV. i. 2. 2, and Macbeth, v. 3. 51. See note 61 to the former play. Douce says, speaking of the present passage: "Here may be a direct allusion to one of the two old ladies of this description mentioned in the following passage from Heywood's play of The Wise Woman of Hogsdon, ii. 1: "You have heard of Mother Notingham, who for her time, was prettily well skill'd in *casting of Waters*; and after her, Mother Bombye" (Works, vol. v. p. 292).

213. Line 128: *Ay,* BIDDY, *come with me.*—Malone says that "Come, *Bid*, come, are words of endearment used by children to chickens." In Cornwall, and perhaps in other parts of the country, children will speak of or to a chicken as *ticky-biddy*.

214. Line 129: *to play at* CHERRY-PIT.—This was a game in which cherry-stones were pitched into a small hole. Steevens cites Day, Isle of Gulls, 1606: "if she were here, I would have a bout at cobnut or *cherry-pit*."

215. Line 130: *collier.*—The devil was called so for his

traditional attribute of blackness: "Like will to like, quoth the Devil to the *Collier*" (proverb cited by Johnson). *Collier* was a frequent and most obnoxious term of reproach in Shakespeare's time. See Romeo and Juliet, note 4.

216. Line 154: *a finder of madmen.*—"*Finders of madmen* must have been those who acted under the writ 'De lunatico inquirendo;' in virtue whereof they *found* the man *mad*" (Ritson).

217. Line 156: *More matter for a* MAY MORNING.—This is an allusion to the festive celebration of *May-day*, when it was customary to have the morris-dance, comic interludes, &c. The Clarendon Press editor quotes from Stow's Survey of London, 1603, p. 9: "I find also that in the moneth of May, the Citizens of London of all estates, lightly in euery Parish, or sometimes two or three parishes ioyning togither, had their seuerall mayings, and did fetch in Maypoles, with diuerse warlike shewes, with good Archers, Morice dauncers and other deuices for pastime all the day long, and towards the Euening they had stage playes, and Bonefiers in the streetes." "Merry England" is getting too sober for that sort of thing now; but at least the children do not forget to keep up *May-day*. In Shakespeare's county it is customary for them to go round in the morning, carrying sticks wreathed and crowned with flowers, and singing a song or hymn about "the merry month of May" at all the doors where pennies are likely to be forthcoming. Compare Midsummer Night's Dream, note 29.

218. Line 168: *A good note, that; keeps you, &c.*—This is the reading of the Old-Spelling Shakespeare. There is no special authority for the punctuation, but it seems to me vigorous, and I have adopted it. The customary reading is *A good note: that keeps you*. Ff. have simply a comma after note.

219. Line 185: *He may have mercy upon* MINE.—Johnson would read *thine*, but as Mason remarks: "The present reading is more humorous than that suggested by Johnson. The man on whose soul he hopes that God will have mercy, is the one that he supposes will fall in the combat; but Sir Andrew hopes to escape unhurt, and to have no present occasion for that blessing." Compare Henry V. ii. 3. 20-23: "Now I, to comfort him, bid him a' should not think of God; I hop'd there was no need to trouble himself with any such thoughts yet."

220. Lines 215, 216: *they will kill one another by the look, like cockatrices.*—See II. Henry VI. note 185.

221. Line 222: *And* LAID *mine honour too unchary* ON 'T.—So Ff. Theobald's emendation of *out* is very frequently adopted by modern edd. Schmidt takes *laid* in the sense of *staked*. Compare Hamlet, v. 2. 174: "he hath *laid* on twelve for nine."

222. Line 227: GOES *on my master's* GRIEF.—This is Rowe's emendation. Ff. have *greefes*. Some editors read "*Go* on my master's *griefs*."

223. Line 244: DISMOUNT *thy* TUCK.—Cotgrave has "Verdun, m. *The little Rapier, called a Tucke*." Boyer (French Dictionary) gives "Tuck, *subst.* (*or* Rapier) *Estoc, longue Epée*." It is from *estoc* that the word came into English. The Clarendon Press editor very aptly remarks: "The hangers or straps by which the rapier was attached to the sword belt are called in the affected language of Osric the 'carriages' (Hamlet, v. 2. 158, &c.), and Sir Toby's 'dismount' is in keeping with this phraseology" (p. 149).

224. Line 257: *dubb'd with* UNHATCH'D *rapier.*—Some editors (after Pope) read *unhacked*. In either case the sense is the same, and, as Singer remarks, we have still the word *hatch* in the technical term *cross-hatching* used of engravings. Mr. P. A. Daniel has four illustrations of the word *unhatched* in his Notes and Conjectural Emendations of certain Doubtful Passages in Shakespeare's Plays, 1870. One of these illustrations is quite pat:

> Unharden'd with relentless thoughts; *unhatch'd*
> With blood and bloody practice.
> —Fletcher, Knight of Malta, iv. 5.

Another illustration (from Fletcher's Tragedy of Valentinian, ii. 3) refers to "swords, *hatch'd* with the blood of many nations."

225. Line 258: *on carpet consideration* = a *carpet-knight.* There is a long quotation in the Variorum Ed. (vol. xi. pp. 458, 459) concerning carpet-knights from Francis Markham's Booke of Honour, 1625. "*Carpet knights*" are explained as being "men who are by the prince's grace and favour made knights at home and in the time of peace by the imposition or laying on of the king's sword." The word came to have a sense worse than that of mere idleness and absence from active service. Cotgrave gives "Mignon de couchette: *A Carpet-Knight, one that euer loves to be in womens chambers*." Compare the expression *carpet-mongers*, in Much Ado, v. 2. 31, and see note 374 thereon.

226. Line 262: HOB NOB *is his word.*—This is said to be a corruption of *hab or nab*, have or have not, hit or miss. Malone cites Holinshed's History of Ireland: "The Citizens in their rage . . . shot *habbe or nabbe* at randon." Coles (Latin Dictionary) has "Hab-nab, *temerè, sine consilio*," and Cotgrave renders "Conjecturalement. *Coniecturally, by ghesse, or coniecture, habnab, hittie-missie*."

227. Line 268: *quirk.*—Compare All's Well, iii. 2. 51:

> I 've felt so many *quirks* of joy and grief;

and Pericles, iv. 6. 8: "she has me her *quirks*, her reasons."

228. Line 275: MEDDLE *you must.*—Malone compares the common phrase, "I 'll not make nor *meddle* with it." Schmidt explains *meddle* as "have to do."

229. Line 298: *I am one that had rather go with* SIR *priest than sir knight.*—*Sir* (the English equivalent of the Latin *dominus*) was a title customarily given to the clergy as well as to those of the rank of knights. Compare "*Sir* Topas the curate," iv. 2. 2 below. See Richard III. note 345.

230. Line 300: Re-enter *Sir Toby.*—Dyce begins a new scene (5) with this entry. I give his remarks, acknowledging their justice, but not making any change in the text because of the practical inconvenience of doing so. "Higher up in the same page, Sir Toby, before going out, has desired Fabian to 'stay by this gentleman' (Viola) till his return from talking with Sir Andrew: a little while after, Fabian says to Viola, 'Will you *walk towards him*' (Sir Andrew)? and accordingly *makes his exit with her.* Sir Toby now enters accompanied by Sir Andrew; and though the F. does not mark a new scene, it is certain that, previous to the entrance of the two knights, the audience of Shakespeare's days (who had no painted movable scenery before their eyes) were to suppose a change of scene. Presently Antonio enters, draws his sword in defence of Viola (whom he mistakes for Sebastian), and is arrested by the Officers: and from the speech of the First Officer in v. 1. 67, 68, we learn distinctly where his arrest took place:

> Here *in the streets*, desperate of shame and state,
> In private brabble did we apprehend him.

Sir Andrew, then, was waiting for the pretended page 'at the corner of the orchard' (iii. 4. 194), 'at the orchard-end' (iii. 4. 244), that is, in the street at the extremity of Olivia's orchard or garden; there Sir Toby had joined him; and thither Fabian and Viola walk.

[In the acting-edition of this play, as prepared for the Lyceum Theatre, scene 4 of act iv. commences here, the place being *The Orchard End.* There can be no doubt that a change of scene is necessary here.—F. A. M.]

231. Line 302: *firago.*—A corruption of *virago;* "the expression," says Schmidt, "is used at random by Sir Toby to frighten Sir Andrew, who 'has not bestowed his time in the tongues.'"

232. Line 303: *stuck.*—*Stuck* or *stock* is the same thing as *stoccado* or *stoccata*, a thrust in fencing. Compare Hamlet, iv. 7. 162: "your venom'd *stuck;*" Marston, Antonio's Revenge, 1602: "I would pass on him with a mortal *stock.*"

233. Line 322: *He is as* HORRIBLY CONCEITED *of him.*—"That is, he has as horrid an idea or conception of him" (Malone). *To conceit* is used three times in Shakespeare in the sense, "to form an idea" (Julius Cæsar, i. 3. 162; iii. 1. 192; Othello, iii. 3. 149).

234. Line 326: *for's* OATH SAKE.—Compare "for *conscience sake.*" The change made, after Capell, by some modern edd. (*oath's sake*), is quite needless.

235. Line 349: *undertaker.*—The Old-Spelling edd. cite Cotgrave: "Entrepreneur. An . . . *undertaker;* also a Broker, Pettifogger or intermedler in other mens controuersies."

236. Line 389: *Than lying, vainness, babbling, drunkenness.*—Ff. have *Then lying, vainnesse, babling drunkennesse.* Editors are almost equally divided as to whether this line should be read as in the text or connecting *lying vainness* and *babbling drunkenness.*

237. Line 404: *empty trunks o'erflourish'd.*—An allusion to the ornamental chests, richly decorated with carving and scroll work, which in Shakespeare's time were part of the furniture of handsome houses.

238. Line 412: *couplet.*—This word, meaning "couple," is used by Shakespeare only here and in Hamlet, v. 1. 309, 310:

> patient as the female dove,
> When that her golden *couplets* are disclosed.

ACT IV. Scene 1.

[In the acting-edition this scene forms part of the preceding one.—F. A. M.]

239. Lines 14, 15: *I am afraid this great lubber, the world, will prove a cockney.*—"That is, affectation and foppery will overspread the world" (Johnson). Douce would read, "this great lubberly *word*" (*i.e. vent*), and various far-fetched explanations have been put forward by ingenious persons who are not content with a straightforward meaning. Shakespeare has used the word *cockney* again in Lear, ii. 4. 123, 124: "Cry to it, nuncle, as the *cockney* did to the eels when she put 'em i' the paste alive."

240. Line 19: *foolish Greek.*—*Merry Greek* was a sort of slang term for a jolly companion. *Mathewe Merygreeke* is the name of one of the characters in Roister Doister. Coles has "Pergræcor, ari., *to revel, to play the merry* Greek, or *boon companion.*" Compare Troilus and Cressida, i. 2. 118: "Then she's a *merry Greek* indeed;" and iv. 4. 58:

> A woeful Cressid 'mongst the *merry Greeks!*

241. Line 24: *after* FOURTEEN *years' purchase; i.e.* at a high rate, the current price in Shakespeare's time being *twelve* years' purchase.

242. Line 28: *Why, there's for thee, and there, and there!*—So Ff. Capell added, in order to make the line complete, a third *and there.* It does not seem certain, though it is probable enough, that Shakespeare left the line imperfect, as in Ff., so I have not altered the text.

243. Line 43: *you are well* FLESH'D.—Schmidt explains *fleshed* as "made fierce and eager for combat (as a dog fed with flesh only)," and compares Henry V. iii. 3. 11: "the *flesh'd* soldier," &c. See Day, Ile of Gulls, ii. 2 (ed. Bullen, p. 33): "he expects your presence to see the *fleshing* of a couple of Spartane hounds in the wasting blood of the spent Deare."

244. Line 55: RUDESBY, *be gone!*—This word is used again in Taming of the Shrew, iii. 2. 10: "a mad-brain *rudesby* full of spleen." Nares gives no example except these two Shakespearian ones.

245. Line 57: *extent.*—"I conjecture that, by a bold metaphor, Sir Toby is said to make an '*extent*' (the writ so called) upon Viola's peace; depriving her of it wholly or in great measure. In Phillips's New World of Words, ed. Kersey, 1720, *s.v.* '*Extent*,' it is said that in 'Common Law *an Extent* signifies 1. a Writ or Commission to the Sheriff for the valuing of Lands or Tenements; 2. the Sheriff's Act upon that Writ; 3. the Estimate or Valuation of such Lands; which when done to the utmost Value, was said *to be to the full extent.*' Shakspere was fond of legalities" (W. G. Stone).

246. Line 62: BESHREW *his soul for me.*—See note 137 to A Midsummer Night's Dream.

247. Line 64: *What relish is in this!*—"How does this taste? What judgment am I to make of it?" (Johnson).

ACT IV. Scene 2.

248. Line 2: Sir Topas *the curate.*—See note 229 above. The name of *Sir Topas* is a little compliment to Chaucer; see Chaucer's tale of Sir Thopas in the Canterbury Tales.

249. Line 7: *I am not* TALL *enough to become the function well.*—The innocent word *tall* has been a stumbling-block to some editors, whose ideas of the clerical profession are not to be harmonized with *tall.* Farmer would read *fat*, and Tyrwhitt *pale.* Perhaps the Clown plays upon the double sense of the word *tall*, which is commonly used as = bold, sturdy.

250. Line 8: *student.*—Ff. print *studient*, as in Merry Wives, iii. 1. 38. The Clarendon Press editor thinks that perhaps the misspelling is intentional, common as it is to the Clown and to Justice Shallow.

251. Line 15: *the old hermit of Prague.*—Douce says that by this is meant, "not the celebrated heresiarch, Jerome of Prague, but another of that name, born likewise at Prague, and called the *hermit* of Camaldoli in Tuscany."

252. Line 16: *King Gorboduc.*—An ancient British king, the hero of the first English tragedy, Gorboduc, or Ferrex and Porrex, written by Sackville and Norton, and represented in 1562.

253. Line 41: *barricadoes.*—*Barricado* was the unnaturalized form of this word in Shakespeare's time. It is used again in Winter's Tale, i. 2. 204, and as a verb in All's Well, i. 1. 124. Cotgrave has "Barriquade: f. *A barricado; a defence of barrels, timber, pales, &c.*"

254. Line 41: *clear-stories.*—F. 1 has *cleere stores*; F. 2 *cleare stones.* The reading in the text (Blakeway's conjecture in Boswell) is the most generally accepted, and seems to me far the best. *Clear-story* or *clerestory* is the name given to the windows above the arches of the nave of a Gothic church.

255. Lines 54, 55: *What is the opinion of Pythagoras concerning wildfowl?*—Compare Merchant of Venice, iv. 1. 131 and As You Like It, iii. 2. 187, and see note 285 to the former play.

256. Line 68: *I am* FOR ALL WATERS.—Malone interprets: "I can turn my hand to anything; I can assume any character I please; like a fish, I can swim equally well in all waters." He quotes Nash's Lenten Stuffe, 1599, "Not a slop of a rope halter they send forth to the Queenes ships, but hee is first broken to the Sea in the Herring mans Skiffe or Cockboate, where hauing learned to brooke *all waters*, and eate poor Iohn out of swuttie platters, there is no ho with him but once hartned thus, he will needes be a man of warre, or a Tobacco taker, and weare a siluer whistle."

257. Line 78: "*Hey, Robin,*" &c.—This song is printed in Percy's Reliques (ed. 1794, vol. i. p. 194). It begins:

> A Robyn
> Jolly Robyn,
> Tell me how thy leman doeth,
> And thou shalt knowe of myn.
> "My lady is unkind perde."
> Alack! why is she so?
> "She loueth another better than me;
> And yet she will say no."

258. Line 92: *Alas, sir, how fell you* BESIDES *your* FIVE WITS?—The *five wits*, we learn from Stephen Hawes' poem, the Graunde Amoure, ch. xxiv. (cited by Malone), were: "common wit, imagination, fantasy, estimation, and memory."—*Besides* was often used as a preposition. Compare Comedy of Errors, iii. 2. 78–81, where the phrase "*besides* myself or thyself" occurs three times.

259. Line 99: *They have here* PROPERTIED *me.*—Compare King John, v. 2. 79–82:

> I am too high-born to be *propertied*,
> To be a secondary at control,
> Or useful serving-man, and instrument,
> To any sovereign state throughout the world."

260. Line 104: *endeavour thyself.*—Halliwell cites Latimer, Sermons: "The devil, with no less diligence, *endeavoureth himself* to let and stop our prayers;" and Holinshed, Chronicles: "*He endevored himself* to answer the expectation of his people, which hoped for great wealth to ensue by his noble and prudent governaunce."

261. Line 134: *Like to the old* VICE.—The *Vice* was the clown of the old moralities. "He was grotesquely dressed in a cap with ass's ears, a long coat, and a dagger of lath. One of his chief employments was to make sport with the devil, leaping on his back and belabouring him with his dagger till he made him roar. The devil, however, always carried him off in the end" (Singer). Compare Henry V. iv. 4. 74–77: "Bardolph and Nym had ten times more valour than this roaring devil i' the old play, that every one may pare his nails with a wooden dagger." See note 305 to Richard III.

262. Line 141: *goodman devil.*—F. 1 has *good man diuell;* F. 2 *good man Divell;* F. 3 and F. 4 *good man Devil.* Rowe suggested *goodman drivel*, and so many modern edd. read.

ACT IV. Scene 3.

[In the acting-edition this scene is the first scene of act v.—F. A. M.]

263. Line 6: *credit.*—According to some this means merely "current belief," according to others, "oral intelligence." Singer quotes from a letter of Elizabeth to Sir Nicholas Throckmorton among the Conway Papers: "This beror came from you with great spede. . . . We haue heard his *credit* & fynd your carefulness and diligence very great."

264. Line 12: *discourse.*—Singer quotes from Granville: "The act of the mind which connects propositions, and deduceth conclusions from them, the schools call *discourse*, and we shall not miscall it if we name it *reason.*" Compare Hamlet, i. 2. 150: "a beast, that wants *discourse* of reason."

265. Lines 20, 21:

> *there's something* in 't
> *That is* DECEIVABLE.

Deceivable is again used in the sense of deceptive in Richard II. ii. 3. 84, 85:

> Show me thy humble heart, and not thy knee,
> Whose duty is *deceivable* and false.

266. Line 24: *chantry*.—A private chapel endowed with revenues for priests to chant masses for the souls of their donors.

267. Line 26: *Plight me*, &c.—Douce has shown that this was not a marriage, but a betrothal, formerly known as *espousals*, a term which has come to be applied to the marriage ceremony.

268. Line 27: *jealous*.—This is spelt in F. 1 *iealious*. In Arden of Feversham the word is always a trisyllable, and in Q. 1 it is usually spelt "Jelious."

269. Line 28: *May live at peace. He shall conceal it*.—Hanmer reads "*henceforth* live," to fill up the missing foot in the metre. The interpolation does not commend itself to my mind.

270. Line 29: WHILES *you are willing it shall come to note*.—*While* is used again in the sense of "until" in Macbeth, iii. 1. 44. Schmidt compares Euphues' Golden Legacy (ed. Collier), p. 47: "and stood there *while* the next morning;" p. 89: "to pass away the night *while* bedtime."

ACT V. SCENE 1.

271. Line 23: *conclusions to be as kisses, if your four negatives make your two affirmatives*.—Farmer cites Lust's Dominion, i. 1:

> *Queen*. Come, let 's kiss.
> *Moor*. Away, away.
> *Queen*. *No, no, says, ay;* and twice away, says stay.
> —Hazlitt's Dodsley, vol. xiv. p. 98.

272. Line 30: *grace*.—Compare Rape of Lucrece, 712: "Desire doth fight with *Grace*" [*i.e.* virtue].

273. Line 39: PRIMO, SECUNDO, TERTIO, *is a good play*.—See Scot, Discoverie of Witchcraft, p. 198: "I omit to speake anie thing of the lots comprised in verses, concerning the lucke ensuing, either of *Virgil*, *Homer*, or anie other, wherein fortune is gathered by the sudden turning unto them: because it is a childish and ridiculous toie, and like unto children's plaie at *Primus secundus*, or the game called The philosopher's table." On this Dr. Nicholson remarks (p. 549 of his reprint): "This goes far to show—proves, I think—that the Clown's '*Primo, secundo, tertio* is a good *play*' (Twelfth Night, v. 1), a passage on which no commentator known to me has touched, thinking it merely a jocular remark, is, in fact, taken from a well-known *play* or game. What the game was is unknown to me, but children still use various numerals, provincial or otherwise, mingled with rhyme, to settle anything, as, for instance, who shall hide in the game of hide and seek."

274. Line 43: *the bells of* SAINT BENNET.—This church, according to Halliwell, was *St. Bennet's*, Paul's Wharf, London, destroyed in the great fire of 1666.

275. Line 46: *at this throw*.—The allusion is, of course, to a *throw* at dice. Some, however, would take *throw* to be from Anglo-Saxon *thrah*, *thrag*, "a half space of time," "a truce." Compare Chaucer, The Man of Lawes Tale, 5373:

> Now let us stint of Custance but a *throw*.

276. Lines 57, 58:

> *A* BAWBLING *vessel was he captain of,*
> *For shallow draught and bulk* UNPRIZABLE.

Bawbling is used here for insignificant, as *bauble* in Troilus and Cressida, i. 3. 34-37:

> the sea being smooth,
> How many shallow *bauble* boats dare sail
> Upon her patient breast, making their way
> With those of nobler bulk!

Unprizable is used for invaluable, not, as some have taken it, "what is without value." Boyer (French Dictionary) has "Unprisable, *Adj.* (*or* unvaluable) *inestimable, qu'on ne peut assez estimer;* "Coles renders the word by *inestimabilis;* and Cotgrave gives "Inappreciable . . . *unprisable, unvaluable* [*i.e.* invaluable]."

277. Line 68: *In private* BRABBLE *did we apprehend him*.—Compare Titus Andronicus, ii. 1. 62:

> This petty *brabble* will undo us all.

The word occurs four times in Merry Wives as *prabbles*, the Welsh mispronunciation of Evans and Fluellen. Boyer (French Dictionary) has "Brabble, S. *Dispute, querelle, Debat, Chamaillis*."

278. Line 74: *dear*.—Heart-felt, touching the heart, used of disagreeable as well as agreeable affections (Schmidt). Compare Love's Labour 's Lost, v. 2. 874:

> Deaf'd with the clamours of their own *dear* groans;

and see note 223 on that passage, and Richard II. note 78.

279. Line 82: *wreck*.—Ff., here as always, spell *wracke*.

280. Lines 85-87:

> *for his sake*
> *Did I expose myself, pure for his love,*
> INTO *the danger of this adverse town.*

Compare Henry V. i. 2. 102:

> Look back *into* your mighty ancestors;

and All's Well, i. 3. 259, 260:

> I 'll stay at home,
> And pray God's blessing *into* thy attempt.

281. Line 97: *three months*.—Compare i. 4. 3: "he hath known you but *three days*." Shakespeare seems to have overlooked the contradiction: the *three days* were necessary for stage-purposes, the *three months* would be nearer the probabilities of things.

282. Line 117: *My soul the faithfull'st offerings* HATH *breath'd out*.—*Hath* is Capell's emendation; Ff. print *have*, which may have been written by Shakespeare. Similar instances are not uncommon of a plural verb being used by attraction from a substantive in the plural immediately before it.

283. Line 121: *Like to the Egyptian thief at point of death*.—"Theobald pointed out that Shakespeare here refers to the story of Theagenes and Chariclea in the Ethiopica of Heliodorus. The hero and heroine were carried off by Thyamis, an Egyptian pirate, who fell in love with Chariclea, and being pursued by his enemies, shut her up in a cave with his treasure. When escape seemed impossible, he was determined that she should not survive him, and going to the cave, thrust her through, as he thought, with his sword. 'If ye barbarous people,' says the Greek novelist, 'be once in despaire of their owne safetie, they haue a custome to kill all those by whome they set much, and whose companie they desire after death (fol. 20, ed. 1587). There was an English

translation of Heliodorus by Thomas Underdowne, which was licensed to Francis Coldocke in 1568-9, and of which a copy, without date, is in the Bodleian Library. Another edition appeared in 1587, and Shakespeare may very well have read it, as it was a popular book" (Clarendon Press ed. p. 104).

284. Line 129: *tender dearly.*—Schmidt explains the verb *to tender*, as "to regard or treat with kindness: to like; to hold dear; to take care of." Compare Comedy of Errors, v. 132: "so much we *tender* him."

285. Lines 149, 150:

Alas, it is the baseness of thy fear
That makes thee STRANGLE THY PROPRIETY.

Strangle thy propriety is a somewhat forced expression for "disown what thou really art." Compare Henry VIII. v. 1. 157, 158:

He has *strangled*
His language in his tears.

And for *propriety*, in the sense here used, compare Othello, ii. 3. 175, 176:

Silence that dreadful bell; it frights the isle
From her *propriety*.

286. Line 159: *A contract* OF *eternal bond of love.*—So Ff. and most editors. Dyce (following a conjecture of Malone) reads *and*.

287. Line 160: *Confirm'd by mutual* JOINDER *of your hands.*—*Joinder* occurs nowhere else in Shakespeare, but *rejoindure* is used in Troilus and Cressida, iv. 4. 37, 38:

rudely beguiles our lips
Of all *rejoindure*.

288. Line 162: *interchangement of your rings.*—Douce (Illustrations of Shakspeare, 1839, pp. 67-72) held that the ceremony which the priest describes was a betrothal, not a marriage (compare what Olivia says in iv. 3. 23-31). In the note which Douce has written on this subject he does not quote any real authority for the interchange of rings between the parties. He says (pp. 67, 68): "The form of betrothing at church in this country has not been handed down to us in any of its ancient ecclesiastical service books; but it is to be remembered that Shakspeare is here making use of foreign materials, and the ceremony is preserved in a few of the French and Italian rituals."—[Douce's long note on this passage is, in the main, correct; but a great deal of confusion appears to exist in the minds of many persons as to the exact nature of the Betrothal, or Espousal, as it is called in the Catholic Church, and of the relations which it bears to the ceremony of marriage. As has been stated in Much Ado, note 259, many of the ceremonies observed in the Service of Matrimony, as it now exists in the Roman Catholic Church, belonged originally to the Betrothal; and what Douce does not clearly state in his note is that the Church of Rome has always, from the earliest times, held the Betrothal or Espousal of two persons to be as binding as marriage itself. Such a solemn contract, as that described in the text, entered into between two adults, whether in the presence of a priest or not, and whether confirmed by the interchange of rings or not, would be held binding—provided there were no impediment to the marriage of the two persons—till such an engagement had been dissolved by mutual consent. Cohabitation could not lawfully take place without the sacrament of Matrimony; but neither would be free to contract any other marriage as long as such Betrothal or Espousal remained in force. There is at present, as far as I can find out, no extant ritual in the Church of Rome for the ceremony of Espousal. In the Greek Church the ceremony of Espousal always precedes that of marriage, and in this ceremony "two rings, one of gold and another of silver, are placed on the altar and given by the priest to bridegroom and bride respectively" (Addis and Arnold's Catholic Dictionary, *sub voce* Marriage). The giving of "the ring, or *annulus pronubus*, was used to plight troth before Christian time by the Romans" (*ut supra*). The joining of hands accompanied by a kiss is alluded to by Tertullian (De Virg. Veland. 11). Another ceremony, not mentioned here, but still observed in the Order of Matrimony in the Church of Rome, is the giving to the bride by the bridegroom of a gold and a silver coin; and this ceremony, curiously enough, is also of ante-Christian origin; it having existed among the Franks as well as among the Jews. The ceremony of placing the ring on the fourth finger of the left hand of the bride is retained in the order of Matrimony both by the Church of Rome and by the Church of England.—F. A. M.]

289. Line 168: *When time hath sow'd a grizzle on thy* CASE.—Malone cites Cary, Present State of England, 1626: "Queen Elizabeth asked a knight, named Young, how he liked a company of brave ladies? He answered, as I like my silver-haired conies at home: the *cases* are far better than the bodies." The Clarendon Press editor (p. 160) quotes Chapman, Bussy d'Ambois: "And why not? as well as the Asse, stalking in the Lion's *case*, beare himselfe like a Lion, braying all the huger beasts out of the Forrest?" (Works, ii. 10).

290. Line 176: *Send one.*—So F. 1; F. 3 *and one*. Dyce combines both readings, and prints *and send one*.

291. Line 198: *othergates; i.e.* otherwise. The word is still used, provincially, in the North. Nares quotes Hudibras, part I. canto iii. line 42:

When Hudibras, about to enter
Upon an *othergates* adventure.

In Walker's Dictionary (ed. 1837) the word is given, but marked "obsolete."

292. Line 206: *a passy measures* PAVIN.—F. 1 *panyn*, F. 2 *pavin*. Halliwell says that the *passy measures pavin* is described in an early MS. list of dances [printed in the Old Shakespeare Soc.'s Papers, vol. i. p. 24] as "The passing measure *Pavyon*,—2 singles & a double forward, & 2 singles syde,—Reprynce back." *Passy measure* is a corruption of the Italian *passamezzo* ("a *passa-measure* in dancing, a cinque pace," Florio, 1598); "a slow dance, differing little from the action of walking" (Sir John Hawkins). Sir John derives *pavin* (or *pavan*) from *pavo*, a peacock; it was a grave Spanish dance, many allusions to which (*e.g.* "a doleful *pavin*," Davenant) are given in the Variorum Ed. There is a curious allusion to the dance and its Spanish origin in Dekker's Old Fortunatus, iii. 1, where the Spanish lord Insultado says, "Oyerer la a pavan española; sea vuestra musica y gravidad, y ma-

jestad"—*i.e.* "You shall hear the Spanish *pavan;* let your music be grave and majestic." After Insultado has danced, Agripyne says: "The Spaniard's dance is as his deeds are, full of pride." The meaning of the phrase in the text is, according to Malone, "that the surgeon is a rogue, and a *grave solemn coxcomb.*" A metaphor derived from dances comes very characteristically from Sir Toby.

293. Line 212: *Will you help? &c.*—Ff. have *Will you helpe an Asse-head, and a coxcombe, & a knaue: a thin-fac'd knaue, a gull!* The pointing in the text is Malone's, which is generally accepted. Steevens follows the reading of the F., understanding these reproaches to be addressed to Sir Andrew.

294. Line 224: *perspective.*—"A glass cut in such a manner as to produce an optical delusion" (Schmidt). Compare Richard II. ii. 2. 18-20 (and see note 150 on the passage):

> Like *perspectives,* which rightly gaz'd upon
> Show nothing but confusion,—ey'd awry
> Distinguish form.

Tollet quotes from Humane Industry, 1661, pp. 66, 67: "It is a pretty art that in a pleated paper and table furrowed or indented, men make one picture to represent several faces—that being viewed from one place or standing, did show the head of a Spaniard, and from another, the head of an ass. . . . A picture of a chancellor of France presented to the common beholder a multitude of little faces; but if one did look on it through a *perspective,* there appeared only the single pourtraicture of the chancellor himself."

295. Lines 258-260:

> *Do not embrace me till each circumstance*
> *Of place, time, fortune, do cohere and* JUMP
> *That I am Viola.*

Compare Taming of the Shrew, i. 1. 195:

> Both our inventions meet and *jump* in one.

Jump is sometimes used joined to *with* (as in Merchant of Venice, ii. 9. 32), and sometimes as an adverb (as in Hamlet, i. 1. 65), meaning always "to agree precisely with, to be *just* so and so." Coles, in his Latin Dictionary, renders "To jump with" by *cum altero sentire.*

296. Line 262: *Where lie my* MAIDEN WEEDS.—Theobald changed *maiden* to *maid's,* and *preserved* in the next line to *preferred.* Both readings are followed by Dyce. For *weeds* in the sense of garments, compare Lucrece, 196: "love's modest snow-white weed." Milton in his translation of the fifth ode of the first book of Horace renders *uvida vestimenta,* "dank and dropping weeds."

297. Line 267: *But nature to her* BIAS *drew in that.*—A metaphor taken from the game of bowls. Compare Taming of Shrew, iv. 5. 24, 25:

> thus the bowl should run,
> And not unluckily against the *bias.*

298. Line 272: *the glass.*—*The glass* perhaps refers to the *perspective,* line 224 above.

299. Line 288: *extracting.*—So F. 1; F. 2 *exacting.* Schmidt explains *extracting* as "drawing other thoughts from my mind." The metaphor in the word is very forcible, and there is no reason in the world why it should be toned down to the F. 2 *exacting* or Hanmer's *distracting.*

300. Line 290: Re-enter *Clown, &c.*—This entry occurs in Ff. and most editors after line 287. The Old-Spelling edd. make the transposition which I follow in the text. It seems to me very desirable.

301. Line 292: *at the stave's end.*—Halliwell quotes Withals, Dictionary: "To hold off, keepe aloofe, as they say, *at the staves ende.*"

302. Line 308: *therefore* PERPEND, *my princess, and give ear.*—See note to Hamlet, ii. 2. 105.

303. Line 313: *your drunken* COUSIN.—*Cousin* was used for any kinsman (see Richard III. note 242); Rowe's emendation of *uncle* is therefore unnecessary as well as unjustified.

304. Line 326: *the alliance* ON'T.—Dyce reads *on's,* and Heath conjectured *an't so please you.* But compare II. Henry IV. iii. 2. 270: "grow till you come *unto it.*"

305. Line 351: *geck.*—Used by Shakespeare only in one other passage, viz. in Cymbeline, v. 4. 67, 68:

> And to become the *geck* and scorn
> O' th' other's villany.

306. Line 370: *against.*—So Ff. I am tempted to adopt Tyrwhitt's conjecture *in,* which would simplify both metre and sense. But there *is* a meaning in *against.* Mr. Stone writes: "The emendation '*in*' gives a much clearer sense, and '*against*' may have been, as you suggest, caught from line 368. The metre does not seem to me to be affected by the reading '*against.*' If this reading is to stand, we must suppose an ellipsis of 'to be' before '*against;* and may compare As You Like It, iii. 2. 297, 298: 'I will chide no breather in the world but myself, *against* whom I know most faults.'"

307. Lines 370-372:

> *Maria writ*
> *The letter at Sir Toby's great importance;*
> *In recompense whereof he hath married her.*

Importance, meaning "importunity," is used again in King John, ii. 1. 7:

> At our *importance* hither is he come.

Daniel seems to have found it singular that Fabian should here say that Maria writ "the letter at" Sir Toby's "great *importance,*" when it originated entirely with her. But he evidently says it to shield her. Sir Toby, Olivia's kinsman, could bear the blame of the mischief better than a mere serving-maid, who might get her dismissal for it. Not that this would have mattered if it is true that Sir Toby married her. But is this true, or is it another of Fabian's fibs? Daniel, in his "time-analysis" of the play, asks: "When could Sir Toby have found time for the marriage ceremony on this morning, which has been so fully occupied by the plots on Malvolio and Sir Andrew Aguecheek? It could not have been since he last left the stage, for he was then drunk and wounded, and sent off to bed to have his hurts looked to." Were it not for Sir Toby's remark in ii. 5. 200, "I could marry this wench for this device," I should quite suppose the marriage to have been a mere fiction; nor is it very strongly confirmed by even this line, which may seem to point to it. If Sir Toby really is supposed to marry Maria, I fancy the hasty marriage must have been thrown in to end the play merrily and in good humour, without much thought of its likelihood or much care in providing for its possibility. [Neither Sir Toby nor Maria are on the stage in this last scene (at least not after line 214). It may be noted that no *Exit* is marked for the Friar or Priest; if he were to go off with Sir Toby and Fabian after line 214, we might suppose a hasty stage-marriage to take place in the interval before Fabian's re-entrance at line 335.—F. A. M.]

308. Line 374: *pluck on.*—Compare Richard III. iv. 2. 63: "sin will *pluck on* sin."

309. Line 377: *poor fool.*—The term is often used by Shakespeare as a term of endearment and pity. Compare Much Ado, ii. 1. 326; "Yea, my lord; I thank it [my heart], *poor fool*, it keeps on the windy side of care;" As You Like It, ii. 1. 22: "the *poor* dappled *fools;*" and, most prominently of all, Lear's allusion to Cordelia (Lear, v. 3. 305): "And my *poor fool* is hang'd!"

310. Line 380: *thrown.*—Theobald reads *thrust*, and is followed by Dyce, who takes *thrown* to have been either an oversight of the author or a printer's error. Staunton very properly replied: "We believe it to be neither one nor the other, but a purposed variation common to Shakespeare in cases of repetition, possibly from his knowing, by professional experience, the difficulty of quoting with perfect accuracy."

311. Line 393: *Of our dear souls. Meantime, sweet sister.*—Hanmer reads, for the metre, *in the meantime.* Walker indulges in the delightful supposition that Shakespeare may have written *sister-in-law*—by anticipation!

312. Line 398: *When that I was* AND *a little tiny boy.*—*And* is often used redundantly in old ballads. Compare the fragment of much the same song in Lear, iii. 2. 74–77:

> He that has *and a* little tiny wit,—
> With hey, ho, the wind and the rain,—
> Must make content with his fortunes fit,
> For the rain it raineth every day.

The words and the music are given by Chappell, Popular Music of the Olden Time, p. 225.

313. Lines 404, 410, 412: *knaves and thieves*, and *beds* and *heads* (the readings of Ff.), have been changed by many modern editors to *knave and thief*, *bed* and *head.* I take them to have been intentional doggerel.

Very different opinions are held as to the merit of this song by way of epilogue. Knight holds it to be the most philosophical clown's song upon record, and is of opinion that "a treatise" (of which he supplies the heads) "might be written upon its wisdom." Staunton describes this "philosophical song" as "evidently one of those jigs with which it was the rude custom of the clown to gratify the groundlings upon the conclusion of a play." It is doubtless an old song altered.

WORDS OCCURRING ONLY IN TWELFTH NIGHT.

NOTE.—The addition of sub., adj., verb, adv. in brackets immediately after a word indicates that the word is used as a substantive, adjective, verb, or adverb only in the passage or passages cited.

The compound words marked with an asterisk (*) are printed as two separate words in F. 1.

Word	Act	Sc.	Line
Accost	i.	3	52
	iii.	2	23
Affectioned	ii.	3	159
Affirmatives	v.	1	25
Alphabetical	ii.	5	130
Alter[1]	ii.	5	171
Augmentation	iii.	2	85
Back-trick	i.	3	131
Barful	i.	4	41
Bawbling	v.	1	57
*Bay-windows	iv.	2	40
Biddy	iii.	4	128
Blank[2] (sub.)	ii.	4	113
	iii.	1	115
Bounteously	i.	2	52
*Box-tree	ii.	5	18
Branched	ii.	5	54
Breach[3]	ii.	1	23
Breast[4]	ii.	3	22
Bristle[5] (sub.)	i.	5	3
Brock	ii.	5	114
Bum-baily	iii.	4	194
*Buttery-bar	i.	3	74
Can (sub.)	ii.	3	7
*Cannon-bullets	i.	5	101
Cantons	i.	5	289
Caper[6] (sub.)	i.	3	129
Changeable[7]	ii.	4	76
Chapter	i.	5	242
Cherry-pit	iii.	4	129
Clause	iii.	1	165
*Clear-stories	iv.	2	41
Clodpole	iii.	4	209
Cloistress	i.	1	28
Cloyment	ii.	4	102
Codling	i.	5	167
Coffer[8]	iii.	4	381
Comptible	i.	5	187
Consanguineous	ii.	3	82
Constant[9]	iv.	2	53
Convents (verb)[10]	v.	1	391
Cowardship	iii.	4	423
Coziers	ii.	3	97
*Cross-gartered	ii.	5	167, 181, 180, 220
	iii.	4	55
Cross-gartering (sub.)	iii.	4	22
Cubiculo[11]	iii.	2	55
Curl (verb intr.)	i.	3	105
Dam'd-coloured	i.	3	145
Decay[12] (verb tr.)	i.	5	82
Dedication[13]	v.	1	85
Denay (sub.)	ii.	4	127
Determinate[14] (adj.)	ii.	1	11
Dexteriously	i.	5	67
Dissemble[15]	iv.	2	5

[1] = to exchange.

[2] = a blank sheet of paper. Sonn. lxxvii. 10.

[3] = the breaking of waves, surf.

[4] = voice.

[5] Venus and Adonis, 625.

[6] *i.e.* a pickled *caper*; used in a punning sense; *caper* = a leap (in dancing) occurs in As You Like It, ii. 4. 56, and Pericles, iv. 2. 116.

[7] = varying in colour; used elsewhere in sense of *inconstant*.

[8] Used figuratively for money, *i.e.* the contents of a *coffer*.

[9] = consistent, logical.

[10] here = suits; or, perhaps, invites. Used three times elsewhere = to summon.

[11] Used by Sir Toby as = apartment: really the ablative of Latin *cubiculum*, a bedroom.

[12] Sonn. lxv. 8; and compare Cymb. i. 5. 56, where it means "to destroy."

[13] = devotedness. Used absolutely here; the word occurs in different senses; Timon, i. 1. 19; Winter's Tale, iv. 4. 577.

[14] Sonn. lxxxvii. 4.

[15] = to disguise. Used by the Clown in this scene; it is used transitively also (in a figurative sense) several times.

WORDS PECULIAR TO TWELFTH NIGHT.

	Act	Sc.	Line
Distractedly[1]	ii.	2	22
Dormouse (adj.)	iii.	2	21
*Double-dealing	v.	1	32
Draught[2]	v.	1	58
Endure[3]	ii.	3	53
Enwraps	iv.	3	3
Epistles	ii.	3	160
	v.	1	295
Equinoctial	ii.	3	27
Expressure[4]	ii.	3	171
Extravagancy	ii.	1	12
Eye-offending	i.	1	30
Fall[5] (sub.)	i.	1	4
Firago[6]	iii.	4	302
Fivefold	i.	5	312
Foamy	v.	1	81
*Folly-fallen	iii.	1	75
Fond (verb)	ii.	2	35
Foreknowledge	i.	5	150
*Fortunate-unhappy	ii.	5	172
Gagged	i.	5	94
	v.	1	384
Gaskins	i.	5	27
Giddy-paced	ii.	4	6
Goose-pen	iii.	2	52
Gospels	v.	1	295
*Grand-jurymen	iii.	2	17
Gratillity[7]	ii.	3	26
Grizzle	v.	1	168
Grossness[8]	iii.	2	77
*Gull-catcher	ii.	5	205
Gust[9] (sub.)	i.	3	33
Halloo (verb tr.)	i.	5	291
High-fantastical	i.	1	15
Hob[10]	iii.	4	262
Impeticos[11]	ii.	3	26
Impetuosity	iii.	4	214
Implacable	iii.	4	260
Improbable	iii.	4	140
Incardinate[12]	v.	1	185
Incensement	iii.	4	250
Intercepter	iii.	4	242
Interchangement	v.	1	162
Inure[13]	ii.	5	160
Inventoried	i.	5	264
Joinder	v.	1	160
Knitters	ii.	4	45
Labelled	i.	5	265
Legitimate[14]	iii.	2	15
Lifelings	v.	1	187
Lived[15]	i.	2	14
Love-broker	iii.	2	39
Love-thoughts	i.	1	41
Maid[16]	v.	1	270
Malignancy	ii.	1	4
Manakin	iii.	2	56
Marble-breasted	v.	1	127
Mellifluous	ii.	3	54
Misdemeanours	ii.	3	106
Mollification	i.	5	218
Murmur[17]	i.	2	32
Natural[18]	i.	3	30
Natural[19]	ii.	3	89
Nayword	ii.	3	146
Negatives (sub.)	v.	1	24
Nob[20]	iii.	4	262
Non-regardance	v.	1	124
Notoriously	iv.	2	94
	v.	1	388
Nuncio	i.	4	28
O'erflourished	iii.	4	404
Opal[21]	ii.	4	77
Othergates	v.	1	198
Overfar	ii.	1	29
*Over-swear	v.	1	276
*Parish-top	i.	3	45
Participate (verb)	v.	1	245
Passy (measures)	v.	1	206
Peevishly	ii.	2	14
Pepper (sub.)	iii.	4	158
Perverseness	v.	1	115
*Pickle-herring	i.	5	129
Pilchards	iii.	1	39
Pistol (verb)	ii.	5	42
*Point-devise[22]	ii.	5	176
Position[23]	ii.	5	130
Presupposed	v.	1	358
*Proper-false	ii.	2	30
Purse-bearer	iii.	3	47
Quarreller	i.	3	31
Rank[24] (adj.)	ii.	5	130
Relus (verb intr.)	iii.	4	357
Renegado	iii.	2	75
Reverberate (adj.)	i.	5	291
Rubious	i.	4	32
Saucy[25]	iii.	4	159
Scathful	v.	1	59
Scoundrels	i.	3	36
Scout[26] (verb)	iii.	4	193
Sea-cap	iii.	4	364
Semblative	i.	4	34
Shackles	ii.	5	62
Sheep-biter	ii.	5	6
Shrewishly	i.	5	160
Simulation	ii.	5	151
Sink-a-pace[27]	i.	3	140
'Slight	ii.	5	38
	iii.	2	14
Sneck[28]	ii.	3	101
Stable (adj.)	iv.	3	19
Staniel	ii.	5	125
Stitches	iii.	2	73
Stone-bow	ii.	5	51
Straps	i.	3	14
Substractors	i.	3	37
Supportance[29]	iii.	4	328
Swarths	ii.	3	161
Swearings	v.	1	277
Syllogism	i.	5	55
Tang (verb)	ii.	5	163
	iii.	4	78
Taxation[30]	i.	5	225
Testril	ii.	3	34
*Thin-faced	v.	1	213
Thonest (verb)	iii.	2	43
Thriftless[31]	ii.	2	40
Toss-pots	v.	1	412
Tray-trip	ii.	5	208
Trip (sub.)	v.	1	170
Triplex	v.	1	41
Twanged	iii.	4	198
Twin (adj.)	v.	1	230
Unauspicious	v.	1	116
Unchary	iii.	4	222
Uncourteous	v.	1	369
Ungird	iv.	1	16
Unhatched[32]	iii.	4	257
Unhospitable	iii.	3	11
Unprizable[33]	v.	1	58
Unprofited	i.	4	22
Unsound	iii.	4	384
Viol-de-gamboys	i.	3	27
Vox	v.	1	304
Wainropes	iii.	2	64
Wears[34] (intr.)	ii.	4	31
*Westward-ho	iii.	1	146
Whirligig	v.	1	384
Wittily[35]	iv.	2	16

1 Lover's Complaint, 28.

2 Of a ship.

3 = to last. Venus and Adonis, 507; Sonn. cliii. 6.

4 = accurate description; occurs in other senses twice; in Troilus, iii. 3. 204, and Merry Wives, v. 5. 71.

5 = a cadence.

6 Sir Toby's form of virago.

7 A coined word, used by the Clown.

8 Used figuratively = stupidity; used five times in other senses.

9 = taste, relish. Sonn. cxiv. 11.

10 In the phrase hob nob. See note 726.

11 A word coined by the Clown.

12 Sir Andrew's blunder for *incarnate*.

13 Lucrece, 321.

14 = logical.

15 = floated.

16 Used of a man.

17 Figuratively = a rumour.

18 = idiotic.

19 Used adverbially.

20 In the phrase *hob nob*. See note 726.

21 Lover's Complaint, 215.

22 Used adverbially.

23 = place; used three times = assertion.

24 = strong-scented; and used figuratively in the same sense, Hamlet, iii. 3. 36.

25 = pungent; frequently used by Shakespeare in other senses.

26 = to keep a look-out; = to sneer at, Tempest, iii. 2. 130.

27 This is merely the anglicized form of *cinque-pace*, which occurs twice in Much Ado.

28 In the exclamation *sneck up!* See note 105.

29 Used figuratively; occurs in its literal sense of "support" in Rich. II. iii. 4. 32.

30 = demand, claim. Used several times in its fiscal sense, and once = censure, As You Like It, i. 2. 91.

31 = unprofitable. Sonn. ii. 8.

32 = not blunted by blows.

33 = valueless.

34 Used with *to* = "becomes gradually fitted."

35 Venus and Adonis, 471.

www.ingramcontent.com/pod-product-compliance
Lightning Source LLC
Chambersburg PA
CBHW031052110726
47900CB00003B/894